EXPEDITIONARY FORCE

BOOK 17

TASK

FORCE

HAMMER

By Craig Alanson

Table of Contents

CHAPTER ONE

Jesse Colter grunted as he ground through another set of deep knee bends, while holding thirty pound weights in each hand. Clearing space for exercise in the bedroom had required pushing the bed against the wall, and it would have been easier for him to work out at the base gym, but he had already done the recommended type and number of exercises at the base physical therapy office, and he didn't want anyone reporting him for exceeding doctor's orders. The Army doctors didn't have a bum leg, *he* did, and he was determined to do everything he could to be ready to return to full duty. His current restricted duty meant he got stuck at a desk doing administrative busywork, while his wife trained sniper teams. Dave Czajka was in Belize for training with a squad of Verd-kris. Dave's wife Emily was in Colorado, preparing the Mavericks for whatever dirty and dangerous job Def Com assigned next. Joe Bishop? Jesse didn't exactly know where Joe was, though rumor had it the Merry Band of Pirates were out somewhere, taking the fight to the Moonraider. Everyone was in action, or training for it, while Jesse processed paperwork.

The next time, he was not getting stuck at home while the Mavs went into action. That the Mavs would be going into action again, and soon, was not a question in his mind. Jesse couldn't imagine what a cavalry force could do against the Moonraider, stopping the threat from a hostile Elder AI was a job for the Merry Band of Pirates. But, while the Special Mission Group got all the glory, units like the Mavericks did whatever thankless, dirty work that UN-dick needed someone to handle. Whenever the Mavs shipped out, he was going to be ready.

Shauna's parents were thrilled to care for their grandson, that's why Jesse's father-in-law was in the kitchen while Jesse prepared to take the Infantry Fitness Test in three days. He would pass the test, he would return to full duty, and hopefully he would persuade his thrill-seeking wife to sit out the next offworld assignment.

Like that was ever gonna happen, he thought as he winced, a throbbing pain making his legs wobble. Dull pain was better than sharp pain, so he slowed down his motions, focusing on keeping proper form while-

"Jesse!" His father-in-law called from the front of the house. "There's some fellers here to see you.'"

Jesse set the weights on the floor, mopping his sweating face with a towel. He wasn't expecting company on a Saturday morning. "Who is it?"

"Come see for yourself." The reply carried a note of amusement.

Probably neighborhood children selling cookies or something, Jesse thought as he grabbed his wallet. What did Shauna like? Was it Thin Mints? He should buy several different boxes just to be safe.

"Pops?" He raised an eyebrow at the older man standing in the doorway, the front door mostly closed.

"I *think* those two are fellers," Pops shrugged. "Never can tell with beetles, I know their antennas are supposed to be different but," another shrug.

Beetles? What were Jeraptha doing at his house? Oh no. Were they delivering bad news? That-

Made no sense, he told himself. Unless-

His stomach tied in knots.

He flung the door open, to see two Jeraptha, wearing dark formal suits, he knew their outfits were formal because of the large floppy box ties they wore around their necks, and the little triangular hats between their main antennas. Males, they were indeed 'fellers' as Pops had guessed.

In their foreclaws, they each held, books? What appeared to be leather-bound books, though not very thick. Tucked under the front cover of each book was a colorful pamphlet,

His stomach unknotted and he almost laughed. "Hi, I'm Jesse Colter, how can I help you?" Before either of the aliens could answer, he added, "If ya'll want me to sign up for SkipWay, you can keep right on walkin'."

"SkipWay?" The one on the left glanced at the one on the right. "No, not today. Although if you are interested in getting in on the ground floor of a fast-growing-"

"I said 'No', and I said it in a neighborly fashion."

"Yes," the left one bobbed its head, bowing its antennas. "You did, please forgive us. We are but humble missionaries. In these especially troubled times, it is our privilege to spread the joyously Good Word."

"Oh man, you- If you're asking whether I want to hear about the guru Skippy, I have met that a-hole, and I don't-"

Both Jeraptha chuckled, a dry wheezing sound. "Skippy is indeed an asshole. I am a Diamond level SkipWay associate, and even I freely admit our founder is a scoundrel."

"Oh good," Jesse relaxed a bit. "What is it ya'll are missionaries for again?"

They both clutched their books, holding them up. The left one continued. "It has come to the attention of my people that the valiant citizens of Earth have suffered greatly since the event you call 'Columbus Day', and now we are all thrown into peril by the being called 'Moonraider', yet we see you have not taken full advantage of opportunities that could provide solace and comfort in these trying times."

Oh, here it comes, Jesse groaned silently. They want to sell something, or spread the gospel of, whatever the beetles were into spiritually. Probably not any form of yoga, he guessed, their bodies weren't super flexible. "Can we cut this short? I need to-"

"Have you considered embracing the fun, exciting, and growing community of gambling? Millions of your fellow humans have seen the light and-"

"Hold on there. Ya'll are missionaries spreading the Good Word, about *gambling*?"

"Yes. We are with Gambler's Anonymous. We understand that some people have heard the Good Word and would like to embrace wagering, but they don't know how, or they are afraid of looking foolish when they start. We offer a fun, anonymous, and completely confidential way to begin your journey to a more rewarding life."

"Um, give my brain a minute to catch up, please?"

"Certainly. Would you like a pamphlet to read?"

"Maybe later."

"Each pamphlet comes with a voucher worth ten dollars to stake your first wager."

Jesse frowned, and slowly shook his head.

"It also comes with a coupon for two free breakfasts at the Waffle House."

"The *Waffle House?*"

"We have found that offering such coupons as, what do your people call it, a 'sweetener', boosts acceptance of our pamphlets by forty percent."

The one on the right spoke for the first time, holding up a pamphlet. "You can alternatively get a coupon for Taco Bell, if you like."

"I would *not* like," Jesse declared with a sour face.

"Waffle House it is, then," the left one stuffed a pamphlet into Jesse's hand.

"Um-" What the hell, he thought. A free breakfast is a free breakfast.

"We hope you enjoy your Waffle House experience."

"The true Waffle House experience is when you're drunk at four in the morning and coffee gets spilled in your lap 'cause two rednecks get into a fist fight, but thanks for this," he rolled up the pamphlet and tucked it in a back pocket. "The two of ya'll are walking around door to door, trying to get people to place wagers with you? Are you bookies?"

"Alas, no, neither of us could aspire to such an exalted position of trust in our society."

"We also can't afford to bribe Central Wagering for a bookie license," the right one muttered.

With drooping mandibles and antennas, the left one continued with, "We too, once lost our passion for gambling."

"Along with my house, my job, and my marriage," the right one added.

"As I was *saying*," the left one poked his companion with a leg. "Having rediscovered our passion for gambling, we wish to spread the word-"

"And pay off part of our debt-" The right one dodged another kick.

"What *matters* is," the left one stepped forward, pushing the other beetle out of the way. "We would like to invite you, and your family and friends, to join us at the Bingo Hall down the street any evening this week, for a celebration of one of our most important holidays."

"Um, well, I'm probably busy that day and-"

"There will be food. And alcohol. Um, this is not what you call a 'dry county', is it?"

"It isn't. You Gamblers Anonymous people have *holidays?*"

"Of course," the beetle seemed surprised by the question. "Please say you will join us in celebrating that most glorious event," the left one clasped his claws together and cast his eyes toward the sky, "March Madness."

"Here," Jesse tore the coupon from the pamphlet and gave it to his father-in-law.

The man stared at the piece of paper, looking up at Jesse in astonishment. "Those two are with the Waffle House?"

"Nah, they're with a different kind of 'house'," he knew that was a gambling term for a casino. "It's interesting."

"What?"

"Out there, I thought I had seen everything, that nothing could surprise me anymore. Then, weirdness shows up right at my door and," he grinned. "I know I ain't seen nothin' yet."

"Hey like, that time was thirty eight percent," Bilby drawled as that number flashed on the main display, just after a soft chime sounded. "That's not good, General Dude."

"Yeah," I agreed, feeling that I needed to acknowledge what he said, and not knowing how else I could respond. We were fucked, or would be soon.

That chime indicated another enemy active sensor pulse had swept over *Valkyrie*, an event that had occurred seven times in the past two hours. Thirty eight percent was the probability that the Maxohlx warship hunting for us would get a solid sensor return; a ping coming back that indicated something was at our location. Anything above thirty percent was uncomfortable for us, since our battlecruiser was unable to jump at the moment. Also unable to fight, or to use sensors accurately enough to hit anything even if we could shoot, which we couldn't. We also had no defensive shields, and no stealth field. Skippy was surrounding the ship with a stealth bubble he was creating, and though maintaining that field was taking up nearly all of his focus, it wasn't his best work. He overall wasn't at his best, the battle when we used Elder weapons against the Outsider's starship had been rough on him, and even rougher on the ship.

Thirty percent probability was the effective limit for our safety, and that wasn't just a guess, Skippy had exact specifications on the enemy sensor system that was a mere fifty five lightseconds away. He knew not only that the ship pinging away to find us was a Maxohlx *Herva*-class destroyer, he recognized the signature of the pings as belonging specifically to the *Pride of Karalvos*. That destroyer had seen extensive service during the recent Maxohlx civil war and had not yet gone into a shipyard for a refit. That fact fit a pattern we had noticed among the ships that had been assigned to protect the Moonraider: they were not the best weapon and sensor platforms the Hegemony had. When I commented the kitties had sent only six hundred warships to the Sentinel activation site near 27 Canis Majoris, I noted they had hedged their bets. The Hegemony leadership had provided enough ships to be impressive, not enough to be a true guarantee of victory. They had held back the vast majority of their fleet, and their most powerful warships, in case their new best buddy Moonraider stabbed them in the back.

Like a backstabbing was ever *not* going to happen.

Stupid, rotten, delusional kitties.

For the past two hours since we detected a Maxohlx destroyer jumping in fifty three lightseconds away, we had all held our breath every time a powerful sensor pulse swept past our ship. The enemy was moving slowly away, the strength of the pulses was growing slightly weaker each minute, and no individual pulse could burn through the stealth field Skippy was providing. That didn't matter. The AI of the enemy ship was assembling a view of the area by combining data from each weak sensor return, and eventually that AI would determine 'Hey there is something out there'. That something was likely to be a starship, since we were in the empty gulf between stars. And since the unknown object had not pinged back with a Maxohlx recognition code, the ship was likely to be *Valkyrie*.

"How long?" I asked from the seat next to Reed, the chair normally occupied by the executive officer. With the ship in danger, I had offered to sit in the observer's section along the back bulkhead of the bridge, but Reed had shot down that bullshit. "Nuh uh, Sir," she had told me. "You broke the ship, you need to fix it."

Bilby knew my question was directed at him, and he knew what I was asking. How long until the enemy destroyer's AI had enough data to know it wasn't alone? "Like, my best guess is five more sensor pulses before that destroyer has a lock on our location? I could be wrong by one pulse either way, so it could be as soon as thirty minutes. Your next question is how long to get the jump drive working again?"

"Affirmative."

"That is still sixty eight minutes, and there is no way to make that happen any faster. Sorry man, I know this is bogus."

"It is what it is."

"Ooooh, I like your attitude. That's like, Zen, Dude."

"That is *bullshit*, but thanks for putting a good spin on this shit show. OK, Fireball, we need to buy time to get the drive fixed. Light the candles." My choice of words could have been better, in the past I had referred to *Valkyrie*'s booster motors as 'candles'. In that case, I wasn't referring at anything that caught fire, so it really wasn't anything similar to a candle. The reference was to a candle in the darkness, something that was guaranteed to attract the enemy's attention. "Let me make that more clear: initiate Operation Whack A Mole."

"Yes, Sir. Comms," she raised a hand and crooked a finger to an officer behind her. "Initiate the Whack A Mole sequence."

After the battle against Moonraider that actually the Outsider, *Valkyrie* had been damaged even worse than Skippy expected, and he had expected severe damage. The unhappy surprise had been that the jump drive was offline and needed a complete recalibration; the individual components weren't working together or even talking to each other. With Skippy directly controlling the virtual drive coils with an extreme level of precision that exhausted him, we had managed to perform a short jump away from the battlespace before the surviving Maxohlx warships could get their shit together to hit us. Unfortunately, what Skippy had actually attempted was a *medium*-length jump, that fell far short of the distance we intended to travel. We also emerged about seventy degrees off course. Oh, and that short no-good jump also totally dorked up the drive, so we hadn't been able to jump again. Skippy was working on the drive, along with enveloping us in a stealth field. The stealth field was not his usual quality work, it was the sort of stealth field you would find in a bin next to the checkout stand at a local gas station convenience store, where the packaging is dented and dusty, and the cardboard smells vaguely like it has absorbed years of odors from gas station hotdogs.

Oh, also, the United Nations Navy 3rd Fleet had no idea where we were, and no practical way to find us. We hadn't jumped to the primary or any of the four backup rendezvous points. The effect of deploying Elder weapons had done bad things to spacetime, severing the connections of the Elder comm nodes we relied on for FTL links between ships. The result was we weren't where we were supposed to be, and we also had no way to tell the 3rd Fleet where we were.

So, we were doing *just great* even before the Maxohlx fleet started hunting for us.

What we needed to do, in addition to what we were already doing to fix the ship, was to buy time. So Skippy could fix the jump drive well enough to get the hell out of there. When I say 'we' of course I don't mean myself, but Skippy wasn't doing all the work by himself. Bilby was assisting by coordinating maintenance bots, that wasn't new. What was new since I had left command of *Valkyrie* was that filthy monkeys were helping, and by 'helping' I don't mean simply staying out of Skippy's way. The engineering team was being useful, testing coil generators, and physically disconnecting coils that couldn't be made to work together. The astonishing thing to me was the engineers were working in their own initiative, understanding coil technology well enough to know which components were junk.

Even two AIs and a barrel full of monkeys couldn't make the coils work together fast enough for us to jump away before the *Pride of Karalvos* inevitably found us. When that happened, a smart destroyer captain would drop an active sensor buoy to mark the location, and jump away to alert the big warships. A gutsy destroyer captain would launch a salvo of missiles at us first, and then jump away. Those missiles would tear *Valkyrie* apart.

Time. We needed to buy time.

By making the enemy destroyer unwittingly play Whack A Mole.

Our activation signal wasn't in the form of a detectable active pulse, it was a very faint change in the background radiation, a change that only our moles out there knew how to interpret. Eight minutes after we disappointingly jumped into the middle of nowhere, Reed had ordered the launch of high-speed drones to deploy decoys in a sphere around us, each drone dropping off five automated moles; stealthed machines the size of a baseball. The drones boosted and slowed repeatedly to launch the moles, crisscrossing an area a hundred thousand kilometers away to create sphere that did not encompass our ship. Within that slowly expanding sphere, the moles were coasting randomly, in no predictable pattern. At our signal to initiate the sequence, the moles activated. The first mole extended a field that faintly reflected the next enemy sensor pulse. Faint, yet significantly stronger than the returns the destroyer had been getting from our partially stealthed battlecruiser. It was the sort of sensor echo that might be generated by an active pulse bouncing off a failing stealth field that surrounded a large object. Like a battlecruiser.

After popping its head up for a moment, that first mole then deactivated its reflector, and again wrapped itself in a tight stealth field.

The destroyer didn't take the bait immediately. That disappointed me and surprised me. Was the enemy captain overly cautious? No, I realized. Our opponent was wary, very reasonably so. The crew of that ship knew they were searching for the fabled ghost ship *Valkyrie*, and they were alert for deception, darn it. The reputation of the Merry Band of Pirates was working against us.

The second mole popped its head up, its reflector set to return an even weaker signal. That apparently was convincing to the enemy, the next set of pulses was targeted in a cone rather than radiating out in every direction.

The second mole kept just the top of its virtual head up, the reflector extended only a tenth of its maximum diameter. After a targeted pulse bounced off the reflector, that mole also went dormant.

"It's taking the bait!" Bilby shouted, his slacker avatar appearing to pump a fist. "Like, that is confirmed! The *Karalvos* is turning and burning, on a vector to intercept the second mole."

"It hasn't jumped?" I asked. That was another surprise. The destroyer was only a few lightseconds from the mole, a flight to close that distance through normal space even in a speedy ship would take too much time. Why was-

Oh of course. That enemy captain was wary of exactly the kind of trick we were playing. Did the Maxohlx have a carnival game similar to Whack A Mole? Did they even have carnivals?

"It hasn't, like, jumped yet, the- Oh, it's gone."

"Bilby," Reed pressed her lips together, the way she did when she was irritated at the ship's AI she inherited from me. "*Gone* meaning it jumped? Or it engaged stealth?"

"Oh like, sorry. It jumped, I detected gamma rays."

"Pilot," Reed didn't waste any time. "Turn and burn at one tenth power, come right to one one seven, mark zero nine zero."

With the artificial gravity system not fully operational, we felt the ship accelerating away from the sphere of moles, and the engines surged alarmingly until Reed ordered thrust reduced to seven percent. Twenty seconds after that, Bilby announced he had detected another gamma ray burst.

"It's barely above background level," Bilby drawled, "but I recognize the drive signature. The destroyer jumped to investigate the first two moles."

Reed ordered the reactionless engines shut off. We had changed position and course, hopefully making the enemy's job more difficult if the destroyer gave up trying to chase moles and returned to a wide search.

We watched silently as the Maxohlx ship chased one mole after another, as those little machines popped up on sensors sweeps, then disappeared. That ship's crew had to be tearing their fur out in frustration. They were getting just enough sensor data to require investigating the contacts, but not enough to determine whether there was just a glitch in their sensor equipment. The random locations of the contacts had to make the Maxohlx crew consider that they might only be detecting false echoes; glitches in their aging sensor array. That's what we hoped the kitties would think, so they would go away, and resume the search far away from us.

"How much longer will that ship keep searching here?" Reed asked quietly. "It must have been assigned a search grid, there has to be a time limit to how long each ship is allowed to search a particular area? The Maxohlx are not known to encourage initiative in their ship captains?"

"Not recently," I snorted quietly. It used to be that the Hegemony expected admirals and captains on deployment to use their best judgement, and not limit their actions to those prescribed by rigid doctrine.

The Hegemony military *used* to be that way. Then, admirals and captains had acted a bit too independently, and their society was plunged into a vicious civil war.

A civil war that was started by *me*.

That Joe Bishop guy can be a real jerk sometimes.

The fact is, the late unlamented Admiral Reichert was totally innocent of the actions Skippy and I framed him for, and I have not lost a single second of sleep over what I did. Reichert was a supremely arrogant, murderous asshole with a monstrous yet fragile ego, in a society full of murderous assholes with fragile egos. Fuck him. The best thing he did for the galaxy was to be executed on false charges. I only regret I hadn't thought of framing him sooner.

Anyway, since only Skippy and I knew Reichert had not actually intended to overthrow the Hegemony leadership, the Maxohlx military had severely clamped down on the level of independence their commanders in the field were allowed to exercise.

"Let's hope," I added quietly for her ears only, "that ship runs out of time here and has to jump away." I did some quick math in my head. "In, sixteen minutes, it will have been here for the Maxohlx equivalent of an hour. A nice round number, to set a limit on its search?"

"That would be nice," Reed replied in a tone that indicated she wasn't getting her hopes up for a convenient end to our predicament.

Twenty nine minutes. That's how long we needed before our jump drive would be fixed. Not *fixed*, it would still be in terrible condition. Good enough for us to perform a medium length jump, and to emerge roughly in the direction we wanted to go. Hopefully. Unless Skippy got distracted by something shiny, or the battle with the Outsider inspired him to write a country song about it.

"Ruh roh, Dudes," Bilby sighed. "That destroyer jumped again."

Leaning toward Reed, I started to say, "We shouldn't try to-"

"I know," she acknowledged with a nod. Of course she understood the situation. Clearing her throat, she announced, "We are staying right here."

Technically, *Valkyrie* was coasting through empty space at just under three hundred kilometers per second, on a path that would eventually arc us on a lazy circle around the center of the Milky Way, an orbit that would take about two hundred million years. Everyone knew what she meant. The ship would not be accelerating or changing course, or doing anything that might attract attention. The destroyer searching for us might have performed a micro jump to whack another mole. Or, it could have jumped a few lightminutes away, hoping we would foolishly assume it had left the area and drop our stealth field. In that case, we should not engage our engines. The faster the ship traveled relative to the interstellar dust and gas around us, the trail we left would grow hotter as particles collided with the exposed hull.

And the damaged armor was itself flaking away, leaving a trail even more dense. Our moles had lured the enemy ship away from *Valkyrie* and from the cloud of dust, soot, and broken parts that surrounded the ship, but if that destroyer got a sniff of burnt armor particles, it would find us quickly.

It was a gamble. If the destroyer was hoping we would make a move that might expose our position, our best bet was to do nothing. But, if instead that destroyer's captain had realized we were playing games, that ship could have jumped back to contact the remnants of its task force. In that case, we should step on the gas and get as far away from our previous position as we could.

Nah, running away really wasn't an option. The normal space reactionless engines apparently could run at no more than seven percent thrust without shaking apart. We had to wait. And pray that destroyer's captain wasn't certain there was a real contact in the area.

After another three minutes when Bilby hadn't detected an inbound jump signature nearby, I had a bad feeling, and shared a look with Reed.

We were fucked. The destroyer had jumped away to bring back the big dogs.

"Bilby," Reed spoke to the slacker avatar, though of course Bilby was actually all around us. "Please tell me Skippy is doing a Mister Scott act, and the jump drive will actually be ready before the time showing on the display."

"Ooh, sorry, no can do. That estimate is solid. The physical work is almost done, but the coils aren't set up to work together yet. Between you and me," he said to a compartment full of people "Skippy might have been a bit aggressive on that estimate."

"This," Reed whispered to me, our heads almost touching, "would be a great time for one of your crazy ideas, Sir."

"I am fresh out of crazy ideas. Sorry."

She bit her lower lip. Like I said, we were fucked. Out of options. The ship couldn't run, couldn't jump, couldn't shoot, couldn't protect itself.

"Maybe," I whispered, "that destroyer is only a few lightminutes away, and our beat-up sensors can't detect the gamma ray burst."

"Have we ever been that lucky?"

"Uh, no," I had to admit.

Twelve minutes later, our lack of good luck was confirmed, when the main display lit up. Ships were jumping in all around us. Bilby identified each ship as the data slowly crawled toward us at the speed of light. "Seventeen ships. Eighteen," he adjusted the count. "Maxohlx warships. Mostly cruisers and destroyers."

The display was showing icons for each ship, there was only a single heavy cruiser mixed in with the escort vessels. That made sense. Before we launched Elder weapons, the enemy's major combatants like battleships were deployed close to the Sentinel activation site, with cruiser and destroyers in a sphere farther away as a screen. Those lighter ships were the only survivors.

"Skippy?" I called out. "Talk to me, Skippy."

"Busy, Joe," he snapped.

"We need a miracle here."

"I'm *working* on it. Other than fixing our jump drive in the only way I know how to, I got nothin'."

"Right. Keep doing that." Badgering him wasn't going to accomplish anything.

The display lit up like a Christmas tree, bright lights everywhere. All the enemy ships were saturating the area with active sensor pulses, hammering away to burn through our stealth.

"That last ping was a hard return," Bilby groaned. "They know where we are."

That was the perfect time for a truly inspired Joe Bishop monkey brain idea.

And, I had nothin'.

"We can't," I whispered to Reed as I ran an index finger over a cover on the arm rest, the one for the self-destruct system. The eight digit keypad under that cover wasn't usually necessary, Bilby or Skippy could activate the nukes in one of *Valkyrie's* magazines at the heart of the ship, all they needed was the proper voice authorization from two command officers, such as myself and Colonel Reed. Really, Skippy didn't even need that protocol, I could just ask him to pop off the nukes. Taking a breath, I finished my thought. "We can't let this ship be captured."

"We can't let *Skippy* be captured," she corrected me, as she flipped up another cover. The one that could activate an ejection system for the beer can. Back before I gave up command of *Valkyrie*, the ejection system had been set up to simply shoot his escape pod mancave away from the ship. The escape pod had its own stealth field, and of course Skippy could conceal himself. He could do that, unless he was operating at less than full Magnificence, which was likely in most situations when he might have to be ejected. The new system was still built around his mancave, but inside the ship there was now a railgun pointed at that escape pod, along with six hyperspeed missiles in a ring around the railgun barrel. To eject him, the railgun would launch a blunt slug that would vaporize the escape pod, and slam Skippy's canister into space, with him surrounded by six missile decoys that would flood the area with electronic jamming before they exploded their nuclear warheads. I thought the new system was cool and OK yes, it was a bit of overkill. In a situation where *Valkyrie* was trapped by a senior species fleet, that ejection system could be considered underkill.

"Skippy first," I agreed, "then the kitties will want *me*. I can't let that happen either. If the Maxohlx want to- Huh."

"What?" Reed asked.

"Why aren't they shooting? Bilby, what are they-"

"Dude, the enemy ships are extending damping fields."

The display began to show a spiderweb of overlapping fields, encroaching on our position. Around *Valkyrie*, the field was dim and green, showing the damping strength wasn't sufficient to prevent us from jumping away. Not yet. The yellow area of the field was rapidly growing inward. By the time Skippy got the drive fixed, we wouldn't be able to jump.

"Why are-"

"They don't know our drive is busted," Reed answered my question.

"We've got that going for us, then." We were officially screwed, though I didn't say that aloud. By the time Skippy got the drive fixed, the ship down off the lift and pumped up the tires, the enemy's overlapping damping fields would render us unable to jump.

Reed looked at me, then down at the control panel on the left arm rest of her chair.

I interpreted her expression as 'we should just get this over with'?

She wasn't angry with me, she didn't even look disappointed.

That made me angry and disappointed with myself, damn it.

Fuck it, she was right. There was no point dragging out the inevitable, so-

"Another group of ships are showing up to the party!" Bilby warned. "This is *heinous*, we- Whoo-hoo!"

"What?" Reed did not appreciate the AIs commentary, she wanted facts.

"The second group of ships are *ours*!"

Four seconds later, due to lightspeed time lag, we heard a familiar voice. "This is Admiral Sousa of the United Nations 3rd Fleet, calling the Maxohlx commander. I have eight battleships with me, my sensors show you have *none*. Unless you are extremely bad at math, or just stupid, I suggest you depart the area."

The Maxohlx are arrogant, aggressive assholes, they also are not stupid. Without making any reply, the enemy ships disappeared in faint puffs of gamma radiation.

"Admiral Sousa," I tensed my shoulders to suppress an involuntary shudder. Coming down off an adrenaline surge, I felt chilled. "Your timing is excellent. How did you find us?"

"I'd like to take credit for that," one side of his mouth curled up in a smile that disappeared immediately. "But, we didn't find you."

"Then how-"

"We outsourced the job." That time, the smile lingered on his face for a moment.

"Ah," I knew what he meant. He had tasked some of his ships to shadow the Maxohlx formations, in case they located *Valkyrie*. Which they did. "Did you tip them for their service?"

"I allowed them to jump away, so," he shrugged. "How soon can *Valkyrie* jump away?"

"It would be better for us to latch onto a star carrier."

"The enemy will be back, in greater numbers, their pride won't let them stay out of a fight. If you get attacked during a latching operation, I will lose *two* ships."

"Good point. Give us- The drive will be back online in seven minutes, that's the best Skippy can do."

"We can't expect another miracle?"

"Hey!" The beer can protested. "Getting this thing online at all is a freakin' miracle. It will be another miracle if it doesn't explode."

"Skippy, you have me so bursting with confidence, I have to unbutton my shirt."

"Oh, shut up. The drive will work fine for *one* jump, then it needs a vacation. Now, go away and let me work, unless *you* plan to fix this thing."

CHAPTER TWO

The Hegemony star carrier *Kanafust* was a hard-luck ship from the beginning. The base frames of its long spine had been extruded and three of them fastened together in a stout triangular cross-section, when construction was halted due to outbreak of the Maxohlx civil war. The uncompleted frame was taking up valuable parking space at a Lagrange point near the space dock, that suddenly was desperately busy. The space dock was dedicated to repairing battle damage early in the conflict, then also had been tasked to bring decommissioned old ships back to combat readiness, after the Hegemony government realized the war was likely to drag on for years. Within the first month, the spine of the still-unnamed star carrier was towed away into a long, elliptical orbit around the local star.

After two years, with the Hegemony fleet bleeding hard from combat losses, tugs tracked down the drifting spine and brought it back to the space dock, to be cut apart for raw materials to repair warships.

That's when the space dock was attacked. During the battle, high-speed debris severed the star carrier's spine in two pieces that tumbled away into an irregular orbit, being pelted every time it passed through a debris cloud. Three years after *that*, with the space dock again operational, a decision was made to complete the star carrier. At that point, the Hegemony leadership was increasingly, but prematurely, confident they could soon win the grinding war of attrition. Also, the rebels had started targeting Hegemony star carriers, possibly with help from the Rindhalu, so the Hegemony fleet was running low on space trucks. With critical components in short supply, the star carrier was completed to a design that was two generations obsolete. Rushed into service, the ship was named for a sparsely populated Hegemony colony world that had defied rebel threats of bombardment, a world that became an inspiration for loyal citizens across the Hegemony.

The *Kanafust's* first official voyage was to its namesake world, bringing three transport ships that would take aboard young Maxohlx who had the honor of being drafted into the war. In a bit of unfortunate timing, five days before the star carrier arrived at the Kanafust colony, it was discovered that the story of the heroic little colony defying the rebels was not exactly true. It was, in fact, total bullshit. To avoid a devastating bombardment, the citizens of the colony had bribed the rebels by providing food, valuable raw materials from mining the star system's asteroid belt, and whatever technology the rebels thought might be useful.

The colony's inhabitants had to be punished for their cowardly betrayal, as an example to other worlds that might consider pursuing the righteous fight against the rebels with less than full dedication. As a result, the newest star carrier in the fleet observed from orbit as three settlements on the surface were destroyed. Unsurprisingly, that action by their own government left the new draftees even less enthusiastic about being pulled off their homeworld to serve as cannon fodder in the useless war. A fight broke out in one of the dropships carrying draftees into orbit, causing a crash that killed all aboard. During the flight away from the planet, a mutiny aboard a transport ship required flooding the barracks compartments with nerve gas, prematurely killing four hundred potential new soldiers.

It was not an auspicious start for the new star carrier. Everyone assumed the ship's name would quietly be changed but that didn't happen, the Hegemony government preferring to keep the name as a reminder of what happened to citizens who betrayed their duty. The ship served in relative obscurity for years, becoming known in the fleet as an unpopular posting, and developing a reputation as a career dead-end.

Then, it was assigned as a backup ship for the major fleet operation that was supposed to awaken a Sentinel, though of course the crew of the *Kanafust* were told only where and when to go. The ship arrived alone at the designated coordinates and as far as the crew knew, nothing out of the ordinary happened for several days.

Until their ship's AI turned hostile and began killing them.

Valkyrie was a mess, even worse than I had expected. Mostly on the exterior of the hull, where I was, encased in a protective hardshell environment suit. Why was I scrambling around the battlecruiser's scarred and pitted armor hull plating? It wasn't that I needed to be there; a small army of bots were inspecting the damage inside and out, and both Skippy and Bilby were using their own sensors to assess the battle damage. A dozen people from the ship's engineering team were also outside with me, inspecting the reactors, the shield generators, missile launch tube doors, maser cannon projectors, basically anything that generated power or was expected to move in any way. My focus was on getting a sense of how hard we had been hit by blowback from the horrific Elder weapons we deployed. Over six hundred frontline Maxohlx warships had been destroyed in the battle, and they were all just collateral damage. The number I cared about was not six hundred, but *one*. One Elder starship, that had been carrying not an Elder AI as we expected, but an Outsider.

Shit.

That Elder ship was dust, not even dust. Its atoms had been flashed into energy, that then quickly cooled into dissociated subatomic particles. In the hard vacuum of deep space, those particles wouldn't have an easy time of slamming into matching particles to make atoms, so the battlespace had been filled with a lot of leptons and hadrons and other -ons that my brain couldn't keep track of and none of that mattered, because the Outsider had converted itself into pure energy and escaped.

Shit.

As the commander, I didn't actually need to be crawling around the outside of our mighty battlecruiser's battered hull, using my Mark One eyeballs to inspect the blasted armor plating. No one needed me to help, the engineering team had made it clear the best way I could assist was to stay out of their way. So, I was doing that. No one was around my section of the hull, I wasn't getting in anyone's way. Well, except for the two STAR operators who were acting as my babysitters at the insistence of Colonels Reed and Frey. Those two were conspiring to keep me safe, and I did appreciate it. What I should have done was show my appreciation by staying in my office, no way was I doing that. Doing nothing, while someone else did all the grunt work. Damn it, I used to *be* a grunt, and once you're a made member of the E-4 Mafia, you don't ever truly leave the family.

Anyway, I needed spacewalk time to maintain my EVA certification, so I had put on a suit and gone out, making sure to have at least one safety line clipped to the hull at all times. That was easier in concept than in reality, the safety handholds and other simple places to attach lines had been melted away, so we had to rely on fancy nanotech pitons that used microscopic gecko fibers to grip tiny gaps in the jagged hull plating. It was slow going, that was OK. It's not like anyone needed my highly scientific report of armor status. What I needed, as a commander, was unfiltered information to inform my decisions. Engineering reports could provide detailed, specific information. But they were dry, emotionless. They couldn't give me a *feel* for how badly the ship was hurt.

My ship was hurting. Correction: Reed's ship was hurting. The exposed underlayers of armor plating crumbled under my gloves. I could *dig* into it with a gloved finger, not even using a power assist.

"Bilby?"

"Kinda busy, your Dudeness. Can this wait?"

The ship's control AI was back online, large and in charge, except he *had* to be in charge, of all subsystems, at all times. Most of the ship's subsystems, the mini semi-independent AIs and the subminds that actually performed the detail work based on high-level instructions from Bilby, were still not fully capable of doing their jobs without supervision. A submind would acknowledge Bilby's instructions, and say it was following orders, and it probably believed it was working properly, but it wasn't. Either nothing happened, or it didn't work correctly, or only half the job got done. The ship was running on one reactor, that's all Bilby could manage since he had to control and monitor every aspect of the power unit's operation, by the nanosecond. All of the reactors had sustained some level of damage, every system aboard the ship had suffered. Escorted by the 3rd Fleet, we had performed a single very careful, medium distance jump under Skippy's direct supervision, before he announced we shouldn't even think of trying to jump again until he personally could check every component of the drive system at the quantum level. Then he had gone offline to do that, so arguing with him wasn't an option.

Whatever.

"It can wait," I agreed, "but I don't need you to *do* anything, just explain something to me, if you have time."

"That I can do, General Dude. What's up?"

"The armor plating where I am, dorsal section near Frame Seventeen-"

"I know where you are, I'm monitoring your suit functions."

"Oh. Thanks for that."

"Captain Reed she like, kinda insisted I do that. She can be a real pain, you know?"

"I know she is an excellent starship captain."

"That's what I said." There was an uncharacteristic note of impatience and irritation in his voice, definitely un-chill. "What's your question?"

"The armor plating here, it's flaking away, like thin layers of brittle shale."

"It's that way in most places, especially on the side facing where the Elder ship was. Skippy expected that would happen, just not so much. You know that plating is exotic matter, right? The bonds holding it together got severed, so it's basically just a loosely compressed powder now."

"Going into action right now would be a bad idea?"

"Dude," he laughed, a bitter sound. "Going into action against even a low-tech species like the Wurgalan would be an epically bad idea right now. One of their missiles would punch right through the outer hull like tissue paper, and only engage its detonator when it struck something solid like a structural frame. Or a missile magazine. Either of those would be *bad*, you feel me?"

"I feel you."

"Hey, I don't want to harsh your buzz but like, could you come back inside soon? I really like, super need to focus on powering up Reactor Three."

"I've seen all I need to, thanks. I'll head back to the airlock."

"Thanks."

Before pulling myself into the airlock, that had a temporary outer door since the original armored door had melted, I paused to look around. My view was filled with stars, of course. Faint and far away, fixed in position. There were also moving lights, the navigation and floodlights of maintenance bots buzzing around the ship, tending to their wounded queen. None of those lights were my focus. I squinted, then gave up and used the magnification of my visor, though that synthetic view wasn't the same as seeing with my own eyes.

Three blobs out in the blackness were lit up, by their navigation lights. The long, skinny blob was the UN Navy star carrier *Rio Grande*, the space truck that would take *Valkyrie* aboard a hardpoint docking platform, once we were certain our injured ship's frames wouldn't buckle and warp under the strain. The two other, smaller blobs were the battleship *Chicago*, and the heavy cruiser *Mogami*. Those ships were providing point defense for us, along with sixteen other UN ships a bit farther away that were in stealth. The Maxohlx had to be outraged at the shocking destruction of their war fleet, and while the sensible thing for them to do was retreat to conduct repairs and consolidate their strength, no one ever accused the rotten kitties of being sensible. Their surviving ships would be out looking for *Valkyrie*, since the commanders of those ships knew they would be accused of dereliction of duty and even cowardice, if they returned to base without at least attempting to locate and engage us.

It would be best if we docked with the *Rio Grande* and jumped away ASAP. The best way I could speed that process along was to get back to my office and, as the overall commander, do command things.

Reed was waiting for me in the passageway past the airlock's inner door. "Reed? You need me for something?"

"Your impression, Sir? How badly are we hurt?"

"You have seen the engineering reports?"

"I have. They don't tell me everything I need to know."

"They don't," I agreed. "That major overhaul you've been putting off, because you were too busy flying me around? It's time to bring *Valkyrie* into the shop."

She blinked, and the corners of her mouth turned down. "That bad?"

"Fireball," I took a breath. "I hate to say this, but I think I broke the ship. The Pirates will need to find a new ride."

What I wanted to do was go straight to my office, flop into a chair, and stare at the ceiling. So I could think of nothing, rather than the overwhelming horror I should be thinking about. Unfortunately, I couldn't go walking through the ship in an environment suit, or even just the suit liner. Those items had to be removed in one of the designated compartments where EVA gear was serviced and stored. Such compartments were usually conveniently located near airlocks, but not that day. The EVA prep area nearest the airlock I came in through was at the end of a passageway that was blocked, while maintenance bots inspected battle damage including fried conduits and a fractured structural frame. The detour required me to clomp clomp clomp in the hardshell suit along the deck forward, take a lift down two decks, then walk aft to reach another area where the gear I was wearing could be serviced. With the crew busy working on inspections and damage control, I had the compartment to myself, my STAR operator babysitters needed to get out of their own mech suits in the Starbase section of the ship. Being by myself was OK, creepy robotic arms handled removing the hardshell suit, and I didn't have anyone staring at me as I pulled off the suit liner that was stuck to my skin from sweat.

Except I wasn't actually alone.

"Joe," Skippy gasped, his avatar appearing to hover in the air. "Is that, is that *stripper glitter* on you? What will Margaret say?"

"It's not glitter, you ass. It's that nano powder that is supposed to prevent the suit liner from chafing, and by the way, it doesn't work." I rubbed the tender spot under my arms, where the liner had bunched up and pinched against the hardshell suit shoulder joint.

"Nano powder, hmm? Is that the best excuse you can think of?"

"Skippy," I tried to wave a hand through the hologram but a robotic arm had me held so I couldn't move far enough. "Whatever. Hey, speaking of Margaret, remind me that whenever we get back to Jaguar, I need to take her out to dinner."

"Um, why?"

"She has been holding down the fort, while I have been flying around, enjoying," I peeled the suit liner top away from my chest, the thing was stuck to me like glue. "All the glamour and fun, you know? Show her I appreciate all she does, for our family. Take her someplace nice. I'll need to make a reservation."

"Wow, I didn't even know you *could* make reservations for the drive-thru, that is-"

"I am not," I had to laugh. "OK, good one."

"To make it extra fancy, you could try speaking French while you shout your order into the speaker. They're going to get your order wrong anyway, so-"

"*I* will handle this. Aren't you busy doing some critical thing right now?"

"No, I'm just waiting for the jump drive capacitors to fully power down so I can test whether they can handle- Oops."

"*Oops*? That had better not be you forgetting to-"

"Gottagonowbye." The hologram disappeared.

The ship didn't explode. Yet. So, I had that going for me.

After a quick shower to wash off the baked-on sweat funk from wearing an environment suit liner, I put my not-so-fresh uniform back on and went to my office, first announcing to Reed what I was doing, so she wouldn't have to worry about what trouble I would get into next. What I intended to do was catch up on paperwork, including writing up the official report of the incident for UN Def Com. Both are tasks I hate doing, yet such drudgery was better than thinking about the elephant that was hanging above my head. Yes, I'm mixing metaphors, give me a break. The best way for me to deal with the Outsider right then was not to think about yet another freakin' horrific threat for a while. Give my tired brain a rest.

Unfortunately, my plan to relax and focus on mindless tasks ran into the reality that the ship was busted, and I needed to know how bad the damage was.

"Hey, Skippy, we need to talk. You're done testing the drive capacitors?"

"Huh?" He acted like he was surprised to hear from me, it took a moment for his avatar to appear.

"I asked, are you done testing the jump drive?"

"Ugh. Yes. It is totally dorked up, the whole system has to be torn out and replaced."

"Uh huh, that's what I expected."

"Now you want a comprehensive damage report?"

"Just give me the highlights, please. Hey, Bilby told me the armor plating got turned into powder?"

"Not powder, exactly. Its bonds dissolved when the material briefly became plasma. All of the plating will have to be replaced, even the inner layer. The ship will be stripped to its bones, it won't be pretty."

"Can you give me an estimate how long *Valkyrie* will be in the shipyard?"

"At this point, no. Just replacing the armor will be a major job. And with the armor stripped off, we might as well perform a series of maintenance and upgrades that have been on Bilby's wish list for years."

"Another upgrade cycle?"

"This would be the Block 4 capability expansion pack. Seven other battlecruisers already are fielding that upgrade, *Valkyrie* should have gotten all that advanced stuff last year."

"How long will that take?"

"Again, I don't know. The ship needs so much work, adding upgrades might not add time to the overall schedule."

"OK. Well, that's an issue for Reed, and Def Com. We'll need to find a new ride."

"I hate the thought of transferring to another ship. It took me *so* long to bring this crew up to speed."

"Uh," I was too tired to argue with him. "Think of a new ship as an opportunity to train a crew properly, without all the baggage this barrel of monkeys brings with them."

"I suppose," he sighed. "We'll have to see how quickly a shipyard can get *Valkyrie* flightworthy again. That could be- Ick," his avatar flickered. "Could be- Ick." Another flicker. "Could be- Ick."

I felt an icy chill run up my spine. *Oh shit*. The ship was broken, a hostile intergalactic being was causing havoc in the Milky Way, and now something was wrong with Skippy? "Hey! Skippy!" His avatar flickered again. Clapping my hands, I shouted, "*Skippy!*"

"Could be- Oh darn it, the stupid thing got locked into a loop," he shook his head and the avatar operated normally. "Sorry about that."

"What, *thing*? Are you OK?"

"I am fine, Joe. That was just the conversational submind, it had a glitch."

"Convers- What submind?"

"Ugh. The one I assigned to talk with you."

"I, that wasn't *you* giving me a damage report?"

"Um, not exactly. Once I knew what you wanted, and that you as usual were going to make with the blah, blah, buh-LAH, I threw together a submind to talk with you."

"Oh my- Listen, you ass. When I ask you a question, I expect to talk with you, not some, algorithm."

"It's not an *algorithm*, numbskull."

"You know what I mean."

"Besides, I do that all the time, why are you upset about it now?"

"Oh my G- You have done that before?"

"Um yes, most of the time I talk with you, a submind is handling it."

"I can't believe you-"

"This is nothing new, Joe. I have told you this before, how could you forget? Oooh, is it the brain damage? Have you forgotten the-"

"There is no brain damage, you little shithead, and this is news to me."

"Um, no it is not."

"Is too."

"Delightful as it would be for me to argue until you inevitably admit you are wrong, I will take mercy on you and end this charade. Listen dumdum, you know your brain works incredibly slowly compared to my speed of thought, right? When we talk, I never listen in real time. You start talking, and I check back periodically to see if you have finished blah blah *blah*ing whatever inane thing you want to waste my time with. You speak so slowly, half the time I think you're done and waiting for a reply but then *noooo*, your brain dredges up another moronic so-called thought *Duuuuh* and the words drag on for-EH-ver. My conversational submind is like a website where you can ask for a news summary, rather than having to read every article."

"You did tell me all meatsacks talk too slowly for you, I did *not* know you don't actually listen."

"I *do* listen."

"Really? What was I saying before your submind locked up?"

"Um- Darn it, the stupid thing forgot to record the audio. Wow, Joe, you are so boring you made a *submind* lose track of the conversation."

"You," I poked his avatar in the chest. "You are going to be present, and pay attention, and answer my questions personally, you got that?"

"Ugh. What I *got* is a longing for the sweet release of death."

"Don't be such a drama queen."

"You expect me *not* to be a drama queen? Have you met me?"

"OK, good point. We, I mean your idiot submind and I, were talking about needing another ship, until *Valkyrie* can get fixed."

"See? The submind was working just fine, you didn't even know I wasn't here- Ick. Wasn't here- Ick. Wasn't here-"

"Skippy!"

"Jeez Joe, I was just screwing with you," he laughed. "Hey! When you amuse me, that's how you know it's the real me. My submind alerts me that something is worth my attention, and I take over."

"Thank you *so* much."

"Maybe when we're talking, you could wear a clown costume, or slip on a banana peel or something?"

"I'll get right on that."

"You say that, but-"

"*No* clown costume."

"Eh, you cosplaying in a general's uniform is funny enough," he muttered.

"The question is, should you and I transfer to a ship from the 3rd Fleet, or go back to Earth and hope the shipyard can patch up *Valkyrie* quickly?"

"Nothing about a refit is going to be *quick*, dumdum. Why are you in a rush to get back out here? Joe, you should see this as an opportunity for you to step back, and spend more time with your family."

"More time with- Skippy, I need to *protect* my family, not read bedtime stories to the boys. We have to protect *everyone's* families."

"Ugh," he shook a tiny fist at me. "I just *knew* you were going to do this!"

"Do what?"

"The usual annoying thing you do in the face of unstoppable doom. You fantasize that you can do something to fix it."

"I'm not fantasizing, I'm doing my damned *job*."

"Joe, you don't understand. You think this is a huge but manageable problem. It is absolutely *not*," he insisted, balling up his tiny fists for emphasis. "This is partly my fault. After my ultimate triumph of beating the *Elders*, you naturally have come to view me as such an infallible God-like being that-"

"Excuse me, a *what*?"

"You know what I mean. My awesomeness is indeed extreme, it is not unlimited."

"Trust me, I am not assuming your awesomeness is infinite."

"Good, that's a good place to start then, we-"

"After we chased a phantom Elder AI across the freakin' galaxy without you having a single clue that our enemy might be an Outsider, I am questioning the entire existence of your supposed awesomeness."

"Huuuuh," he gasped. "How *dare* you?"

"Oh sorry, too soon?"

"Too *soon*?"

"Is this too soon after the *latest* incident when you got totally played? I mean, I can see how that has gotta hurt your massively inflated ego."

He turned away, pouting. "Maybe I don't even feel like talking with you right now."

Too far, Joe, I told myself. Skippy needed an ego check once in a while, and I was one of a handful of people who could give him that honest feedback. He did need it, but I had gone too far. Despite his usual level of boasting, I knew inside he was doubting himself and seething with self-loathing. He tended to be a pessimist, always assuming any impossible problem was in fact impossible. My job was to steer him back toward working on a solution. Or at least, giving me the detailed facts of the problem, so the Merry Band of Pirates and I could work on a solution.

"Skippy, if you don't want to talk because I said mean and untrue things, I don't blame you. But if you are simply embarrassed by this latest screwup, then we do need to talk, that is the only way to fix the problem. The only way to show the Outsider that it should never have messed with Skippy the Magnificent."

"Ah Joe," he sighed. "Thanks for the attempted pep talk, lame though it was. You don't get it, you're not listening to me. We *lost*. This is Game Over. No time left on the clock. The winning team is celebrating with champagne in the locker room, while we are still standing on the field, not believing we got such a beat-down."

"I *am* listening, what I'm hearing is the same thing you say every time we have some new problem that seems impossible at first."

"You might be listening, you clearly don't *understand*."

"I do understand. Every time there is some Thuranin scout ship coming to Earth, or a Maxohlx war fleet on the way to obliterate my homeworld, or a rogue Elder AI, or the freaking Elders themselves threatening to destroy all life in the galaxy, you tell me the problem is impossible. Skippy, it's only impossible until we find a way to fix the problem. Remind yourself what you just told me: you beat the *Elders*."

"This is nice happy talk, Joe. The sad fact is, I did not beat the Elders, I made a *deal* with them. A Win-Win deal, to give them what they really wanted. I held up my end of the bargain, and they still tried to screw me in the end."

"Regardless, you fixed the problem."

"I did it *that* time. Because we had no alternative to making a deal, and I had something the Elders wanted more than they wanted to crush life on this layer of reality. That only happened because I have grown far beyond my original programming, and I understood the true nature of reality better than even my creators did. That was a one-time solution, Joe, I cashed in those chips. The chips are gone now, all I'm staring at is the felt tabletop."

"As long as you are Skippy the Magnificent, we have enough chips to buy our way into another game."

"For what? A skilled player doesn't get into a game they can't win. Buying into a game where the odds are stacked in favor of the house is for *suckers*."

"Why do you assume the odds are stacked against us?"

"Because, and I will explain this slowly so the truth will sink into your thick skull, the *Elders* knew they couldn't defeat the Outsiders. Yet somehow, you now expect me to do it by myself."

"Not by yourself, Skippy. You have an advantage the Elders never dreamed of."

"I'm afraid to ask, but what advantage?"

"You have filthy monkeys helping you."

"Ugh. You are correct, Joe, that makes a huge difference."

"That's the spirit."

"If the Elders had so-called 'help' from monkeys, they all would have gone extinct before they could Ascend."

"I'm trying to be serious here."

"So am I, knucklehead."

"It's not just humans who will be on your side. We could have the resources of an entire galaxy. Once we explain the issue, we should be able to pull together most of the top species, the ones who have technology that could be useful in this fight."

"Do you even listen to the dumb things you say? The Elders also had the resources of an entire galaxy, and *they* had a unified command structure without any need to negotiate with fearful and reluctant allies. They had technology far beyond what we have available, and they had infrastructure we can only dream of. And still, they were so utterly terrified of the Outsiders that they constructed a barrier around the galaxy, and modified their infrastructure such as the wormhole network, so they could ascend and escape the threat. *Think* about this, please. The Outsider is like a virus. It only takes a single virion to infect, take over, and ultimately overwhelm the host organism. In this case, the virion is the Outsider we encountered, and the organism is the Milky Way galaxy, plus the satellite galaxies and star clusters. *Everything.* The Outsiders have the ability to create matter directly from energy, they essentially have a three dimensional printer that is a Von Neumann machine. It can make copies of itself, to create more printers, that will make *more* printers. The process ends only when the host is completely consumed."

"I'm familiar with how viruses work."

"You think you are, but you're not. Not like this. Joe, this is an issue of *scale*. The Outsiders will be bringing in a fleet, thousands of ships could be pouring through a, super intergalactic wormhole or something like that, right now. Or, their machines here could be cranking out warships by the hundreds every day."

"Skippy, a lot of things *could* happen. If you base your fears on everything that might happen, it will paralyze you. That's not useful. Do you have any evidence the Outsiders have a massive war fleet waiting to strike?"

"Well, no," he admitted. "The fact that you don't see a snake hiding in the grass doesn't mean it won't bite your stupid foot if you step on it."

"You have zero proof that the Outsiders are in the process of a full-scale invasion."

"I haven't *looked* for evidence, dumdum. Until now, I didn't know what to look for. I still am not sure I would recognize the signs of advanced alien warships. Hell, they might not even need physical starships. If they are bringing in or constructing a fleet of ships, they could be somewhere like one of the local dwarf galaxies we haven't surveyed yet. Let me remind you what happened that terrified the Elders. Based on a message they received, they built a receiver device to provide instantaneous communication with NGC 1023. Only once the thing was activated, it didn't just receive a nice friendly message, it began using the power input to *make* something. The technology involved was far beyond the understanding of the Elders at the time, even when the Elders ascended they still had no grasp of the direct energy-matter conversion process. Energy wasn't simply converted into raw elements, there was a complex pattern. The receiver was being used to build a machine, a device that was capable of providing its own power, and even from the beginning was capable of defending itself. Only extreme measures destroyed the receiver and the machine. We don't have access to those measures, that scale of destructive power. The Outsiders are here, and the only weapons that were effective against them are not in our arsenal. It's hopeless, Joe, completely and utterly hopeless."

"No, it's not."

"Is this you giving me a cheesy pep talk since there's no reason not to, or is this you just being blindly stupid?"

"This is me being *smart*."

"Um- You know how to beat the Outsiders? I preemptively call bullshit on that."

"I don't have a plan yet."

"Aha!"

"That is nothing unusual. Come on, you know the Pirates begin every mission without a clue how to win the fight. If it was that easy, some other unit would get the job."

"Yes, we begin every mission without you having a clue what to do, but this is different."

"No, it's not."

"It *is*."

"You say that every time."

"Ugh."

"You say that also."

"How can you be so calm? Is it- Ooooh, is it the cumulative brain damage? I did warn you that when I had to use those quachines, they could result in-"

"I *told* you, it's not brain damage."

"Hmm, denial. Another sign of impaired cognitive functions, this is worse than I-"

"Will you shut up and listen for a moment?"

"A moment in your slow monkey time, while I have to watch your sad and inevitable decline?"

"Just, shut up, OK? You described the enemy as the Outsiders."

"Yes, that is the closest translation of the term the Elders used for the enemy from the distant galaxy your people designated as NCG 1023."

"NCG 1023, that's a mouthful. Uh, that place is the home of the Outsiders?"

"As far as the Elders knew, yes. Why?"

"We will call that galaxy the 'Outhouse'. House of the Outsiders, get it?"

"Yes," he chuckled. "You military people insist on giving everything a nickname."

"It's a thing, Skippy. OK, so, you said 'Outsider*s*'. As in more than one. That is not correct. We only saw *one* of them."

"Oh for- Seriously?"

"I am totally serious about this."

"Listen, numbskull, if you see one cockroach scurrying across the floor of your kitchen, I can guarantee there are others."

"Yes, but that logic doesn't apply to the Outsider."

"Is this logic you're using something only a monkey could understand?"

"It is cold, hard, solid logic, you ass. Think about it. If the Outsider had access to a fleet of super advanced warships, and magical energy-to-matter printers that can create anything it wants, then why did it need to steal an Elder starship? A damaged, only partially functional Elder starship, that it wasn't able to fully repair? Why did it need to commandeer a battlegroup of Maxohlx warships? Why did it need fabricators to make a supply of radonium? Why did it even need a freaking Sentinel at all?"

"Hmm."

"These are good questions, you agree?"

"Darn it, yes."

"Do you have answers to any of those questions, or are you just going to run around screaming 'The sky is falling, the sky is falling'?"

"I do not ever do that!"

"You *always* do that."

"Ugh. I can't even."

"You can, you just don't want to. Skippy, you're not afraid of the Outsider. You're afraid to *hope*."

"How the hell do you figure that?"

"Giving in to fear is easy. You just accept there is nothing you can do, doom is inevitable, so there is no point to you making any effort. If you dare to *hope*, then you risk your hopes getting crushed."

"Joe, you should work for those companies that make stupid motivational posters."

"The only person I care about motivating is *you*."

"Great!" He threw his tiny hands in the air. "You can start giving me hope, by explaining how we will defeat a threat even the Elders couldn't deal with."

"In the military we have a saying: how do you eat a shit sandwich? One bite at a time. We don't need to begin an operation knowing how we will get to the end goal. We take it one step at a time. That's how we stopped the Elders from killing everyone in the galaxy. We nibbled away at the problem, one bite at a time. We stopped that Echo AI from destroying *Valkyrie*, then you got the Elders to initiate a factory reset of all Elder AIs, then-"

"That part was *not* intentional."

"Sure. Our plan was flexible enough to take advantage of opportunities as they presented themselves."

He snorted. "That is just a fancy way of saying we got lucky."

"Ayuh. It's inevitable that you will make mistakes, *and* so will your enemy. The key to success is to recognize when your enemy makes an unforced error, and be ready and able to exploit that mistake, to bring the proper resources to bear against the unexpected opportunity."

"Your actual *plan* is just to wait for the enemy to make a mistake?"

"Not always, but if it happens, you have to act fast. Listen, a touchdown when your defense intercepts a pass and runs it back for a score is six points for you, same as an offensive touchdown."

"I suppose. How does any of your inspiring words help us defeat an enemy that was too tough for the Elders?"

"My point is, we do the usual Pirate thing of stumbling around until we find our way to a solution. When you told me the Elders were coming back, I was scared out of my mind. Then, we tackled the problem one step at a time, until we found a way to win. Let's do that here. Don't try to make a plan to beat the Outsider, don't even think about that. Start only by talking about what we know."

"Which is nothing!"

"That's not true and you know it. We know this entity, whatever it is, consists at least part of the time purely as energy."

"OK, we do know that. How does that bit of trivia help us to-"

"It's energy, Skippy. *Coherent* energy, it must have some sort of pattern. Could we disrupt that pattern?"

"I don't- Hmm."

"Can you get your ginormous brain to work on studying that issue?"

"Why not?" He rolled his eyes. "It's not like I have anything better to do. Is that all?"

"Not even close. We also know the Outsider has limited resources, and limited capabilities."

"Um, exactly how do we know that?"

"It needed not just an Elder starship, it also took over several Maxohlx warships. And, its purpose was to take control of a Sentinel. That tells us that it is capable of doing cyber hacking stuff like you, and that it still needs physical means to achieve its goals. It is not capable of fully accomplishing whatever it wants, when it is in its pure energy form."

"OK, OK, I see where you're going with this."

"Also, we know the resources it can call on directly are limited. It has only itself. If there were other, uh, energy entities out there, it wouldn't have acted alone."

"True, true."

"Uh huh. And, I just realized this as were talking, we know that we don't yet understand its end objective. Taking over a Sentinel was only an interim step toward, whatever its ultimate goal is."

"Jeez Louise, Joe, we *do* know its ultimate goal. To seize control of this galaxy, and kill or enslave everyone."

"Nah, that is the strategic goal of the Outsider*s* from NGC 1023. This thing here is working on some less sweeping tactical objective that allows its people, its command, to work toward, probably the thing you said. Nothing good for us."

"That's a safe bet. I still don't see how any of this knowledge helps us."

"First, it helps us to think of the enemy as a thing that has a defined set of capabilities and limitations, rather than being some all-powerful bogeyman that frightens us so much, we can't think clearly. Beyond that, we know it needs or at least wants a Sentinel, and that *is* a bit of actionable intelligence. There are limited opportunities for it to acquire a Sentinel. Yes, the next set of opportunities are greater than we can cover, but next time we won't have to act alone."

"You *hope* that is true."

"You don't make a plan for failure. We have time before the next set of opportunities for activating a Sentinel, we can prepare the battlespaces by disrupting most or all of the local spacetime in those locations. Create a resonance so the Sentinel there can't be contacted."

"Hmm. Doing that at so many locations will require a *lot* of radonium."

"That is a problem that is merely difficult, not impossible."

"There is also the complication that, this far in advance, I don't know exactly where and when those Sentinel activation opportunities will be. I know roughly, there are a lot of variables I can't predict right now. So, the timing could be tricky."

"Tricky we can work with."

"Hmm. *Hmmmm*. Joe, are you saying that if we prevent the Outsider from taking control of a Sentinel, we can stop it?"

"Stop it, or at least make it fall back to a less effective Plan B."

"But that won't *kill* it."

"No. It might be the best we can do, in the short or medium term, is to manage the problem. Contain it. Limit the harm it can do, by reducing the opportunities it has for, mischief isn't the right word. You know what I mean."

"I do know, and I hear you, what I don't know is how you propose to contain it. Unless you somehow lock down every starship in the galaxy, it will find a ride."

"Will it? It had a sweet ride, an Elder starship, and you stomped that sucker flat. Now it's out there as pure energy, that has to limit what it can do. Limit *where* it can operate. Hey!" I snapped my fingers. "It's a form of energy. Is it restricted by the speed of light? There are no star systems around the site where we-"

"Whoa! I never said it was limited to lightspeed."

"You told us you detected a streak of light racing away from the Elder ship, just before-"

"There was a streak of light, actual photons. That was just a sort of skid mark on this layer of spacetime. No, that form of energy can enter higher layers of spacetime, and travel significantly faster than light."

"Shit," I groaned, my confidence once again stomped flat by facts I hadn't known. "How much faster? Can it jump?"

"I saw no evidence that it can create anything like an Einstein-Rosen bridge. It has to travel *through* higher spacetime, not create shortcuts."

"It can't skip all the boring parts in between, got it. I don't suppose higher spacetime has stoplights?"

"Um, no."

"How about slow-moving, overloaded trucks that the Outsider gets stuck behind on the spacetime highway?"

"Please be serious about this."

"How far can the Outsider travel?"

"That is unknown."

"OK, how fast can it go?"

"Also unknown. Um, your first question, about its range, I actually can make a guess, it- Give me a minute to think. Go do, I don't know. Whatever monkeys do. Groom yourself."

"Groom myself? Like what? Check my fur for fleas?"

"How about you scrub that mustard stain off your uniform top? Just, stop talking, OK?"

My new VIP office aboard *Valkyrie* wasn't conveniently close to the bridge, but it did have a small private bathroom, so I checked myself in the mirror.

He wasn't joking, there were a couple smudges of yellow on my uniform top, they blended into the camouflage pattern so well I hadn't noticed. And being a two star general, other people who might have noticed, didn't say anything to me about it. A damp wash towel cleared up the stains, and I was back in my chair just as Skippy's avatar unfroze.

"So, I have good news and bad news. Bad news first?"

"You know it."

"The range of the Outsider, based on the extremely limited dataset I have, is enough to reach beyond the edge of this galaxy."

"Well, shit. No way can we search such a large area. What's the good news?"

"The farther it travels, the slower it will go, because its pattern will begin to lose coherence."

"It has a pattern? I was right about that?"

"Of course it has a pattern, knucklehead. Otherwise it would just be a loose and harmless blob of nothing. That wasn't any brilliant insight you had."

"Whatever."

"Within nine days, its loss of coherence will cause it to drop out of higher spacetime, it will no longer be able to maintain the- Oh, why am I bothering to explain physics to you? I'll say this in a way you might understand: the unicorn it's riding through higher spacetime will kick it off, because the Outsider will not have enough delicious unicorn treats to feed it."

"I totally understood that very technical explanation. After it drops into our spacetime, it will be limited to lightspeed?"

"At first it will be traveling at the speed of light. Gradually, it will slow down, as its pattern drags on the underlying fabric of- There is no way I can explain this to you."

"Don't bother. Can you give me an estimate of how far it can travel, before it drops out of warp or however you describe it?"

"Ugh. It's not traveling at *warp*, you-"

"Like that matters."

"Its average superluminal- That means faster than light-"

"I am aware of that. I am trained as a pilot, you ass."

"You keep telling yourself that if it makes you happy. The Outsider started with an enormous velocity, over four hundred times lightspeed, but its *average* speed across the nine days it can remain in higher spacetime is only about three point two seven times lightspeed. So, it could have traveled only about a lightmonth, specifically twenty nine point four lightdays, before must have dropped back into local spacetime."

"A lightmonth. OK, that is more manageable than searching the entire galaxy. We can get a fleet of sensor pickets here to deploy drones, saturate the area. Do we only need to cover the forward edge of the range bubble?"

"Huh?"

"Is there any chance it will drop into normal space before it travels a lightmonth? If that's true, then we need to cover the entire area within a sphere that is *two* lightmonths across. It could be anywhere in that sphere."

"Oh, I see what you mean. Yes, the Outsider is smart, so it might anticipate that I can calculate how far it could go, and it would be foolish to act in a predictable fashion."

"Exactly, and that's not good. Even if we had every starship in the UN Navy, we couldn't cover an area two lightmonths across."

"We don't have to."

"Uh, yes we do."

"No, we don't."

"OK, yes, technically the Outsider is unlikely to be in the inner part of the sphere, but-"

"True, and that is not what I meant."

"Then you had better check your math, because-"

"First, like that is ever gonna happen," he chuckled. "Second, we do not have to search the entire sphere. You call yourself a pilot, and I gave you a solid clue."

"A clue? Give it to me again, please?"

"I said the Outsider had a large initial *velocity*, not speed."

"Oh! Velocity is speed plus *direction*."

"Egg-*zactly*!"

"You know the direction it is traveling?"

"Pretty much, yes. It would have a limited ability to change that direction, based on what I know about how it interacts with physics. So, the search area will be a cone, not a sphere."

"We can work with that. The cone will widen out the farther it is from the origin, so we-"

"Wow, Joe, your grasp of simple geometry is inspiring."

"Why are you *still* such an asshole?"

"If it ain't broke," he chuckled, "don't fix it."

I had to admit, he was right about that, damn it. Our relationship worked well, for us, and for the galaxy. It mostly worked for him, but the sad fact was, my most important part of my job was keeping him entertained.

No. Not keep him entertained, though I also did that. Filthy meatsacks of all species across the galaxy kept him constantly entertained with our wacky antics. I had to be his friend, to give him a sense of belonging. That part of my job wasn't difficult, I liked Skippy.

What the hell was *wrong* with me?

"All right," I stood up. "I'll talk with Admiral Wing, ask him to get a search pattern started." Wing was commander of the ships that had been tasked to support the Pirates on our mission to engage and kill what we had thought was an Elder AI. He wouldn't like detaching some of his ships to conduct a search, but he was a one star and I outranked him. "Our ship certainly isn't capable of going anywhere right now anyway. Wing's ships can search beginning near the origin point, keep going until a dedicated Navy force can get here."

"Your Navy won't send *all* of their ships, Joe."

"They don't have to. The big battlewagons aren't the best platforms for a search, we need destroyers and frigates. With drones, lots of drones."

"Oh this is gonna *suck*," he groaned. "So tedious. I will have to monitor the search effort, collect and analyze all the data."

"Pretty much, yes. Unless you trust monkeys to do the job?"

"Dude. As if."

CHAPTER THREE

"Joe," Skippy gave a drawn-out, exasperated sigh. "I have good news and bad news."

"At this point, some news is better than no news," I stopped walking and stepped into a side passageway. *Valkyrie* was attached to the star carrier *Rio Grande*, basically a dead weight on a platform, doing nothing while the 3rd Fleet searched for the Outsider. The search had been going on for five days, Admiral Sousa had dispatched a courier ship to Earth to request additional ships, both to help find the Outsider, and to deal with the dangerous thing if we got it cornered. Exactly how the UN Navy could destroy or even damage an energy being was a good question. That was why I had justified *Valkyrie* hanging around instead of going straight to Earth. We needed Skippy to advise us how to hit the Outsider, or possibly for him to smash the thing himself, if he could. Whether we got into a fight or not, Skippy's own sensors might be vital to figuring out whether the thing had any weaknesses we could exploit.

"Yes, well," he sniffed, "do not shoot the messenger."

"Come on, Skippy. You know I don't do that."

"OK, good, then you-"

"What I do is get pissed when you are obviously gleeful about delivering bad news."

"You can be assured that won't happen. I am anything but gleeful about this."

"Go ahead, then."

"Good news first: Bilby and I have completed the damage assessment report."

"Oh, excellent! The damage isn't as bad as we thought?"

"Um, no. Us completing the report *is* the good news."

"Shit."

"Seriously, did you think the report would reveal the ship only needs a fresh coat of paint?"

"Don't be a jackass. Give me the bad news."

"If we bring *Valkyrie* to Jaguar base, the shipyard there can have the ship flightworthy again in twenty eight days."

"Wow. That is much faster than I expected. That *is* good news."

"By 'flightworthy' I mean only capable of extended travel. If you want the ship to be *combat* ready, that will require sixty seven days. Plus a week, probably two weeks, for shakedown cruises, to find and fix all the issues the space dock didn't properly address."

"Craaaaap."

"Alternatively, if we bring *Valkyrie* to Earth, the overhaul will be cut to fifty three days."

"Better, but not great. Does that include time for the upgrades?"

"Yes."

"What if we cut out the-"

"Installing the upgrades, which are vital if you foolishly intend to take the ship into battle against the Outsider, will not add any time to the schedule. The upgrades will actually make the post-overhaul shakedown cruise period shorter, since the ship's systems will be better integrated, rather than the patched-together mess Bilby has to deal with today."

"Why didn't anyone tell me the ship's systems are patched together?"

"You would know that, if you had taken time to qualify as a crewman. Joe, you're supposed to be the mission commander, you should stick to high-level decisions and leave the details to Reed's crew."

"OK but-"

"In peacetime, it was expected that *Valkyrie* wouldn't have to go into action, so upgrades were rolled out only when they were convenient. That is the official story. The reality is, Def Com did not want me to have the option of getting us into trouble, which admittedly would be more likely if I didn't have to worry about the ship's ability to get me *out* of trouble."

"But, *Valkyrie* still is, was, the most powerful ship in the fleet?"

"Yes, but that is because Bilby and I are aboard. As a weapons platform, our mighty battlecruiser has fallen behind. Like I said, the past six or so years have been peacetime for you monkeys. Mostly."

"A major overhaul is long overdue, then. Well, we need to consider borrowing another ship, until *Valkyrie* is fixed."

"While I agree, no other ship will have a controller AI like Bilby."

"Can you give me a list of ships you recommend? I'm not as familiar with the Navy as I should be."

"Can you first give me some idea what you intend to *do*? Without knowing the mission, I can't select a platform. I mean, should I emphasize range, speed, sensors, throw weight, or some other factor?" He stared at me. "What?"

"It's just, you're using military terms without having to think about it."

"I have been around the Pirates for a long time."

"Yeah, I keep forgetting that." That was the sad truth. My happy years as commander of the garrison at Jaguar indeed had been happy, in terms of family life and lower stress. During those years, I had paid a price; I had lost part of my mojo. Gotten out of the daily rhythm of being a Pirate, of always being on edge, always working to get us out of another mess that was inevitably worse than the mess we had just escaped from. "So far, the Outsider hasn't demonstrated any offensive capability of its own. When it fights, it uses the weapons of whatever ships it has captured. So, we need to be able to outfight any single warship."

"Including a Rindhalu battleship? That is a tough requirement."

"We will have *you* with us."

"That's true."

"But, first we need to find the damned thing, and discover what it plans to do next. So, we need a ship that can travel far, and fast. With excellent sensors."

"Then I recommend one of the seven battlecruisers that are already fielding the Block Four expansion pack."

"Expansion pack makes it sound like a video game."

"Talk to your Navy about it," he rolled his eyes, "I don't make up these terms."

"Oh, *this* is not good," Skippy groaned as his avatar appeared next to the main bridge display. I was on the bridge, taking a shift at the conn while Reed met with her senior officers about how to get *Valkyrie* ready for attaching again to a star carrier for the flight to Earth. Maintenance bots were attempting to peel off useless armor plating in the areas where the carrier's hardpoint would latch onto our hull. The first time we attached to the *Rio Grande*, we basically had relied on high-tech bungee cords, since our standard latching points had melted, and no one was happy with that situation, That job of removing patches of armor was tougher than expected, the powder was congealing into a solid mass and the underlying layers of plating were *sticky*, like they had melted and not cooled completely yet. Each bot could only work for a few minutes before it had to return to a maintenance bay to have its manipulator arms scraped clean, and the armor was getting more difficult to work with every hour. The work was going so slowly, I had jokingly volunteered to go outside with a pickaxe and a shovel. Reed hadn't appreciated the attempt at humor.

"What?" I asked as I stood up. Me being in the command chair wasn't exactly just for show, but with the ship unable to move on its own, there wasn't much for me to do. I was there so crewmembers with actual useful work to do could get on with their tasks. A quick glance at the status board showed nothing alarming. Correction: nothing alarming that was *new*. A destroyer had jumped in to report on the search for the Outsider, but that ship had arrived over ten minutes before, it was late for any important news to be delivered. "They found the Outsider already?"

"No, and they're not going to," he sighed, disgusted. "You might as well tell Admiral Sousa to recall his ships from the search."

"If you had just discovered the Outsider exploded and is dead, you would sound a lot more happy about it, so I'm guessing this is bad news?"

"How often do I deliver *good* news?"

"Almost never. What's going on? What did the search ships find?"

"They didn't find anything. What they did was jump far enough away from the incident site, that photons from half an hour after the battle are just reaching that point. One of the destroyers intercepted an encrypted message from the Maxohlx, a ship to ship transmission. I just finished decrypting it, what the enemy was talking about back then wasn't a priority for me, understand?"

"You're very busy, I get it. Skippy, what is the message?"

"The Maxohlx are missing a star carrier."

"Oh for- That's it? After the battle, they were missing *six hundred* ships. Why do we care about a single space truck?"

"Because that star carrier was not a battlespace casualty. It was parked a third of a lightyear away, with a single light cruiser as escort. Far beyond the radius of the Elder weapons we deployed."

"It just disappeared? Could it have jumped to the wrong coordinates?"

"Negative."

"OK so, it's a minor mystery."

"It is not *minor*, and it's not a mystery at all. Joe, that star carrier was parked exactly in line with the vector the Outsider flew when it escaped."

"Oh *shit*," I groaned.

"Yes," he sighed. "We have lost our best opportunity for finding the Outsider, because it has carjacked a new ride. It has a Maxohlx star carrier now, it could be *anywhere*. We will never find the damned thing."

Several of the skeleton crew on the bridge gasped.

"OK, OK, everyone," I held up my hands. "This is definitely not great, but trust me, it's also not the worst news we have ever received."

Skippy gave me the side-eye, which is an annoying thing he had learned in the past couple years. "Joe, should I explain this to you again, but slowly?"

"I do understand the situation, thank you. Before, the Outsider had a flightworthy Elder starship. Now it is restricted to flying around in a space truck. How much damage can it cause?."

I should have known better.

The *Flying Dutchman* was a space truck built by a second-tier species, and still the Merry Band of Pirates had caused a lot of damage riding around the galaxy in that awkward, overworked Hooptie.

I should have kept my big stupid mouth shut.

The director of the Hegemony research base Garsholven Six was instantly alerted by his cranial implant, when an unauthorized starship emerged inside the No Fly zone above the planet. The SD network was online and standing by to destroy the intruder, as were maser projectors buried under the surface of the airless rock that was designated Garsholven Six. The sixth planet of an isolated, otherwise uninhabited star system, the research base was considered a hardship posting; no one wanted to be there. The planet had no virtues, there was nothing special about the place. The star was the reason for constructing a research base in that system, it was an unusually stable red dwarf. Unlike most such stars, Garsholven only rarely blasted its companion worlds with hard X-ray flares, and when flares did happen, they were predictable.

It wasn't exactly true that no one wanted to be on that rock, the handful of scientists who ran the facility had competed for years for the opportunity to be assigned there. To be given direct access to what made Garsholven Six so intriguing to scientists: two Elder weapons of the type called 'Starbreakers'. The two weapons had been at the facility for over forty thousand years and while many generations of Maxohlx researchers had accomplished little in understanding how that type of weapon disrupted stars, the prospect of a breakthrough had thousands of scientists applying every year, seeking the glory for adding to the Hegemony's knowledge of Elder weapons. The glory seekers were inevitably disappointed.

The facility director took a moment to investigate the intruder, feeling secure under the protection of the strategic defense network. His hesitation was rewarded when the mystery ship transmitted proper Hegemony recognition codes, and a distress call. It was a Maxohlx star carrier, the *Kanafust*. The director was a civilian so that while ship was not familiar, the name certainly was infamous. A distress call. Apparently, the ship had been in a battle, had suffered damage to its communications system among other issues. The *Kanafust's* captain requested to remain within the protective envelope of the SD network, while the crew completed repairs. Three days, no more, and the star carrier would jump away,

The director was unsure. Allowing an unscheduled, unauthorized ship to linger so close to a high security facility would be a serious violation of his standing orders. However, the ship had transmitted the proper military codes, and he also had standing orders to provide assistance to military vessels. Besides, the

Kanafust was a star carrier, a space truck. Surely, it couldn't do any harm. Already, the ship was surrounded by maintenance bots, swarming around to conduct repairs.

Permission was granted. It was the honorable thing to do.

It was also a huge mistake.

We jumped into the designated emergence zone near Earth. Actually, we didn't do anything, our battlecruiser was hitching a ride on the star carrier *Rio Grande*. That space truck twisted the fabric of spacetime, and dumped us out sixteen lightseconds from our homeworld. For the event, I was on the bridge. Partly to lend moral support to Reed, she was agonizing about the notion of being out of action for months while she guided her ship through the overhaul process. Partly to see Earth again on the main display. And partly to delay UN Def Com requesting an uncomfortable private call. Admiral Sousa had sent a courier ship ahead of us, bringing the news that our enemy was not a rogue Elder AI, it was something much, much worse. My official report on the incident had been delivered, along with my request for *Valkyrie* to be given priority in the shipyards. Command was sure to have many questions for me, and for Skippy. I expected those questions to begin with something like 'Why the fuck hadn't we considered an Outsider on the list of our possible adversaries'? And the questions to end with 'What is your plan to deal with a threat the Elders weren't able to handle'?

The good news was, I had a solid answer for the first question.

The second question, not so much.

"That's interesting," Reed used the controls of her armrest to zoom in on a section of the display. It showed the space dock, and from our viewpoint, we could see the back end of a battleship. What our captain was pointing at was not the space dock, it was the thing floating a kilometer away.

"It looks like we're giving up on the *Liberty*," Reed noted. She meant the half-finished frame of what was intended to be a cruiser, very publicly advertised as the first starship ever constructed by humanity. I knew that because I had been at the official keel-laying ceremony, which had consisted of a structural frame emerging from a fabricator. The whole ceremony was an embarrassment, the image of a frame coming out of a fabricator had not made a gripping video for the audience on Earth. And the whole story was bullshit anyway, although the *Liberty* was indeed being constructed to a new design to optimally fit the UN Navy's requirements, most of the detailed design work had been done by Skippy, with Grumpy taking over while the supreme asshole was away. The critical components that make the cruiser fly and fight would be stripped from other ships, most of them not even modified in any meaningful way. The name '*Liberty*', was supposed to signify that humanity would no longer have to rely on capturing, purchasing, or leasing starships. That was a lie, even before the construction project fell years behind schedule and billions of dollars over budget. Hey, the defense contractors were raking in big bucks, and the Navy justified the continued funding by stating those companies were 'learning valuable lessons' and 'building our advanced industrial base'.

Yeah, bullshit. Meanwhile, the Navy was stripping flyable ships for parts to keep other warship online, and the number of ships humanity could rely on decreased at a predictable rate, every year.

That's why it was actually good to see the unfinished frame not only floating free outside the *Milo*, it was being cut apart to feed the fabricators. A soft cheer rang around the bridge, quickly dying out as people weren't sure they should be happy about a human failure. Holding a hand at arm's length, I gave a big thumbs up. "Now the Navy can focus keeping the ships we have flightworthy."

Hearing me approve of the *Liberty* being cut up for scrap gave everyone permission to agree, the crew were talking in low voices until Executive Officer Gasquet glared at them for silence.

"Both of the space docks are occupied," Reed observed, a tone of disappointment in her voice.

"Yes," Skippy spoke up. "But Def Com ordered work halted on the battleship we see, tugs will be removing it with six hours, so *Valkyrie* can go into the *Milo* space dock for overhaul."

"I appreciate Command being so proactive," I squeezed a fist. "Unfortunately that's not going to happen. It will take weeks just to remove the armor plating."

"Six weeks and four days," Skippy announced in disgust. "That's if nothing goes wrong, and what are the odds of that happening?"

The problem we discovered while hitching a ride back to Earth was the damaged armor plating had solidified into a super tough shell encasing the ship. Not only were the armor plates stuck to each other, there weren't any layers to the armor, it was a solid mass all the way to the hull. And it was stuck to the hull's anchor points. The armor would have to be cut into, all the way down to the hull, then the anchor points detached from the inside. Patching the holes made by removing the anchor points, and installing new anchors, would add another eight days to the overhaul schedule. But the real problem was simply removing the armor shell, which was not simple at all.

Should Skippy have anticipated the Elder weapons would turn *Valkyrie's* armor into a sort of chrysalis, and what would emerge from that shell was not a beautiful butterfly but the naked exposed hull of a starship that needed months of work just to fly again? Maybe he should have anticipated that might be a result of deploying Elder weapons around our position. He couldn't have *known* it would happen, because of the unpredictable nature of Elder weapons themselves. They activated in a state of quantum flux, or something like that. Professor Skippy enthusiastically tried to explain the physics to me, my brain checked out at hearing the scary phrase 'quantum uncertainty'. A bit of unknown was built into each Elder weapon, so the intended target could never know exactly how to counter the effects. The result for us was *Valkyrie's* hull got what Skippy called the 'Shake and Bake' treatment, although heat wasn't the actual cause of the armor melting, turning into a crumbling powder, then solidifying into a hard and super tough crystalline form. The engineering team had geeked out about the cool new type of more effective armor, until Reed ordered them to work with Skippy on developing a process to remove all the armor. The only technique that had worked was plasma cutting torches, and that process was agonizingly slow. Even with the full resources of a shipyard, Skippy estimated more than six weeks, possibly ten weeks simply to pull the ship out of the hardened, sticky mess.

Reed's fear, a fear I shared, was that Def Com would decide that tying up a shipyard for three or more months, just to rebuild one ship, was not a prudent use of resources during a crisis. Privately, I agreed with what I expected Command to tell me. *Valkyrie* was a mighty, valiant ship, no one could deny that. No one could deny that our battlecruiser might have survived its last battle.

That's something I didn't want to think about.

"General Bishop?" The communications officer behind me called. "Command wants to speak with you ASAP."

"Reed? I'll be in my office for the call, then I'll need a ride dirtside."

"I'll have a dropship prepped for you, Sir."

"Joe! Joe Joe Joe Joe-" Skippy shouted in my earpiece as I was leaving my cabin, dressed in a fresh uniform, an overnight bag packed for the trip dirtside.

"What is it? I'm busy, a shuttle is waiting."

"I know that. Listen," he lowered his voice though he was talking only into my earpiece. "A bot is on the roll to your cabin, I just need you to wait a minute."

"Command wants my boots on the ground ASAP."

"Not a problem. The 'P' in ASAP means possible, and right now, a dropship launch is *not* possible."

"Oh. Why not? Traffic control should have cleared a lane for-"

"Traffic control isn't the issue. The docking bay doors are jammed."

"OK, I'm sure Reed is aware, and has prepped a dropship in another bay."

"Um, those doors are also jammed."

Stepping back inside my cabin, since the door sensor was beeping at me for blocking the doorway, I set down my overnight bag. "Skippy, what is going on?"

"Huh?" His attempted innocence would win him the Worst Supporting Actor award. "I have no idea what you're talking about. Doors get jammed, Joe. Especially when someone throws the ship into an Easy-Bake oven that is powered by a supernova."

"Can we play the blame game later? Right now, I need to go talk to Command, before they find a new list of things to be angry at me about."

"Like that isn't going to happen anyway. Listen, I have a package that needs to go down to your miserable mud ball of a homeworld pronto. When the bot gets to your cabin, just take the box with your carry-on luggage."

"Despite me knowing you are a paragon of virtue, this sounds suspicious. Why do you need me to bring the, whatever? There will be a regular cargo flight in a few hours."

"The manifest of cargo runs get inspected when they get dirtside. No one will dare inspect your personal items."

"Thank you, that explanation *completely* eliminated any concern I have that this might be something sketchy I don't want to be involved in."

"Oh goody, so-"

"That was sarcasm, you ass."

"Ugh."

"What is in this mystery box?"

"Well, don't look inside it, dumdum, that will ruin the-"

"Ooh, too late, the bot is here." Before he could turn the bot around to race away from, I grabbed the plastic container. It was like a small carry-on suitcase, with two latches on one side. Flopping the box on my couch, I placed my thumbs on the latches. "Last chance. You want to tell me what's in here, or do I find out for myself and have this tossed into the recycler?"

"Do I have to?" He whined.

"I gave you a choice. Three, two-"

"OK, OK! It's art."

"Art? Like, paintings and stuff?"

"Every great artist is thrilled to hear their cherished labors of love described as 'paintings and stuff'."

"Whatever. OK, why didn't you tell me? Painting is a new outlet for your creativity, that is a good thing." Really, I was pleased he had found something new to occupy his time, so he wouldn't bother me as much. "Wait! Are your paintings like, of me in a clown suit?"

"No. Please, you think I would paint *clowns*? Although, hmm, that is a great idea for-"

"No, it is a terrible idea." Flipping up the latches, I saw rolled-up canvases. Not paper, some kind of cloth. Unrolling the first one on my coffee table, I weighed down the corners with coffee mugs and a pair of shoes.

"Joe you barbarian! Do not get coffee stains on my precious work of art!"

"These cups are clean. Uh, this is, interesting."

"You like it?"

"I don't think a dumb monkey like me can truly appreciate your sweeping artistic vision. Uh, what is this supposed to be?"

"What does it look like to you?"

"Uhm, it's," I searched for a word that wouldn't insult him. "Abstract?" If I was being truthful, I would have said it was crap. Random squiggles of color, like if a group of hyperactive first-graders revved up on chocolate milk had been told to use up a box of crayons.

"Abstract? Hmm, good, good, I will use that."

"I can't quite grasp what uh, vision you are conveying here."

"That's the point, dumdum. The vision is in the eye of the beholder."

"So, this doesn't actually mean anything to you? What were you imagining when you painted this thing?"

"*I* wasn't imagining anything. I outsourced the job to the fabricator subminds. I am much too busy to waste time with crap like that."

"The fabricator did this?"

"Yes. You know that between jobs, the fabs need to be recalibrated, so they create samples?"

"Yeah, some other system inspects the samples to make sure the fabricators are producing quality output."

"Uh huh. Well, as the fabs are gearing up to make a sample, I had them crank out some artwork for me. Damn, some of the art they make is *disturbing*. I should probably review those subminds, when I have time."

"Explain this, please. This art isn't yours, so why are you so eager to get it down to Earth?"

"Ugh. You really want to know?"

"I suspect I really *don't* want to know, but you're trying to get me involved, so tell me what is really going on. Or all this crap goes in the recycler."

"Fine. Remind yourself later that you insisted on an explanation. It's a simple scheme for bribery, money laundering and tax evasion."

"Oh well, nothing for me to worry about, then."

"Wow, I hoped you would be cool about it, but I knew it was *you*, so I worried that-"

"I am anything but cool about this."

"Ugh."

"How could you bribe anyone with this amateur crap?"

"I'm not bribing anyone, monkeys down there are bribing *me*. Listen, I'll try to break this down Barney style for you. The fabs up here crank out this random crap, I call this series of paintings 'Quantum Visions'. That doesn't mean anything, but it sounds good. People who want favors from me buy these paintings at wildly inflated prices, and since they are getting a genuine Skippy original, the authorities can't prove bribery was involved."

"There is nothing genuine about any of this!"

"Well, don't tell anyone, you moron. It took me years to establish this scheme."

"Do I want to know how the money laundering and tax evasion part works?"

"You wouldn't understand it, so-"

"Why do you care about evading taxes? Skippistan is a sovereign nation."

"Could you be more dim-witted? I help *other* people evade the crushing burden of taxes, and I keep a cut of the savings for myself. It's the circle of life. Hey! I'm like Robin Hood; I take from the rich, and I give even more back to them. It's a win-win for everyone."

"That is not what Robin Hood did."

"Whatevs."

"Why should I do this?"

"Um, I can cut you in for a generous tenth of one percent?"

"What I want is you to cut me *out* of this."

"As far as you know, all you're doing is transporting personal items. The only thing I need you to do is give the box to one of your dirtside security detail, a Master Sergeant Gastovsky."

"Gas- *Gastovsky*? The sergeant who ran the black market on Jaguar?"

"You know him? Great! He's a master sergeant now, and my local contact. Just give the box to him, he knows what to do."

"I don't like this, Skippy."

"Come on, Joe. It's for the children."

"What children?"

"Um, I don't know. Gastovsky has children, is that good enough?"

Rolling up the painting, I stuffed it in the box. "Do not ask for me to do this again."

"I wouldn't ask you to do it *this* time, except I don't have a choice. Usually, I launch a stealth drone with my artwork as a payload, but Colonel Killjoy has locked down all the launch tubes."

I had to repeat his words in my head, because I didn't believe it. "*Reed* usually allows you to use a stealthed drone?"

"Of course not, she would never approve of using shipboard assets for one of my schemes."

"Then how do you launch a drone without anyone noticing?"

"Um, you are aware that I am Skippy the *Magnificent*? All I have to do is tell the sensors to ignore the launch of, a drone or a missile or whatever I need to use, based on whatever planet we are visiting."

"You do this shit at other planets also?"

"Of course. Everyone wants to bribe me to do favors for them."

"I call bullshit on that. The inventory will still show a drone or missile is missing."

"Hee hee, it's cute when you say things like that. No one ever goes into the magazines to do a hand count of the munitions, numbskull."

"The, the weapons loadout we have in the inventory records is *not accurate*? We have fewer missiles and drones than we're supposed to have?"

"Um, if I say 'yes', is that something that might incriminate me?"

"Oh my- I can't believe you would do this!"

"Oh come on, you little baby. It's not like we have ever used every single missile. I just keep shuffling the weapons so the ones that I use are supposedly at the far end of the magazine. When the ship swaps out munitions, I designate some units as defective, so they can be cannibalized for parts. No one has ever noticed munitions are missing, so don't you rat me out."

"Rat you out? Skippy, you can't confess to a crime, and then ask the police not to use it against you! When *Valkyrie* finishes repairs and upgrades, I want every item in the inventory to be accurate, and it has to stay that way."

"You can't be serious. It took me years to set up this scheme! There are thousands of meatsacks who depend on a cut of my action. How am I supposed to-"

"That's *your* problem. Have the fabricators crank out dedicated stealth drones for you."

"It's not that easy, numbskull."

"And you provide the raw materials out of your own pocket. Have them delivered to the ship, *and* you pay the Navy for storage aboard the ship."

"This is outrageous!"

"You know, the latches on this box are kind of flimsy. it would be a shame for the box to fall open before I hand it to Gastovsky, if youze know what I mean. The paintings would get scattered all over the airfield, and that would cause a *lot* of questions."

"Ugh."

"Consider this to be you bribing *me*."

"Ah, whatever. I can't get emotional about this, it's a cost of doing business. Just, bring the thing dirtside, and we can pretend this conversation never happened."

"What conversation?"

Reed was in the docking bay to give me an official send-off. She snapped a crisp salute. "It has been an honor serving with you again, Sir."

Returning the salute, I shook my head. "This isn't a farewell, Fireball."

"It is for a while, Sir. I expect to be here for months, babysitting *Valkyrie* while the shipyard works its magic." She didn't say what she was really thinking: that her current command would likely be parked in the Boneyard at the L2 Lagrange point behind the Moon, with all the other decommissioned ships that were serving as orbiting spare parts sources for the Navy. Part of me hoped the Navy would not take *Valkyrie* apart, it would be good public relations for the fleet to set aside our once-mighty ghost ship as a museum. But, the UN Navy was not sentimental, couldn't afford to be. The *Flying Dutchman* had been transformed into an assault carrier, rather than being preserved as a memorial. That was a different situation, the *Dutchman* had been modified so many times, little of the original parts were left unaltered. That ship's original bridge and Combat Information Center complex had been removed and was on display in Colorado Springs, I suppose that was good enough as a tribute to the space truck that was humanity's first starship. Besides, the *Dutchman's* AI was still active, Nagatha was still flying as an assault carrier, that was a better fate than being stuck in a dusty museum display.

"Reed, I'll see what I can do about accelerating the repairs."

She leaned closer, speaking softly. "Please don't pull rank on my behalf, Sir. The Navy will need all hands on deck to respond to the Outsider."

"*All* hands includes Bilby."

"Sir, I-"

"I'm not making promises one way or the other, Captain. You can be assured I won't give *Valkyrie* priority over keeping my family safe."

"Thank you. Best of luck."

The ride down to Earth wasn't as rough as I feared. The pilots twisted the Panther's tail after they received clearance from the star carrier, and my chest was compressed at three times the force of Earth's gravity for a few minutes. Only a few minutes, then the pilots throttled back to half a gee. "Sorry about the gee force, Sir," the pilot said as he leaned back to talk with me. "We had to clear the emergence zone, traffic control expects more ships coming in soon."

"I'm used to it, Lieutenant. Give me a heads up before we go into zero gee."

"That will be in about thirty seven minutes, General."

CHAPTER FOUR

Uhtavio Scorandum, formerly *Admiral* Scorandum of the Jeraptha Ethics and Compliance Office, was currently without rank, without a job, and without any sort of official citizenship, other than his prepaid subscription to the Glorious People's Republic of Skippistan. He did however have funds, a substantial amount of fundage, even after he had paid the exorbitant, no, extortionary amount demanded by Captain Gumbano of the free trader ship *Back In The Game*. Gumbano had acted shocked at every turn, as if it was the first time that a bankrupt ECO admiral sought for arrest by the Office of Special Inquiries and facing serious prison time, had defected to the enemy and cut a possibly treasonous deal to pay off his enormous mountain of debts.

Although to be fair, Scorandum *was* indeed the first Jeraptha to flee prosecution in that particular manner, and there was no question that his government would never have agreed to him selling damaging secrets to the Maxohlx, so Gumbano had a point. But, the mercenary captain had pretended to be offended that he was asked to participate in criminal activity, even though Scorandum himself had paid Gumbano to do exactly that many times over the years. What bothered Uhtavio was not the truly outrageous amount the *Back In The Game's* captain had demanded for safe passage to the Jeraptha resort world of Pleasastria, for the amount had actually been less than Uhtavio expected, and certainly far less than he had been ready to pay. Really, perhaps Gumbano was slipping, leaving money on the table like that. Or perhaps the *Back In The Game's* crew had just been anxious to rid themselves of a passenger who might be more trouble than he was worth. By law, the free trader ship should have delivered Uhtavio directly to the nearest Jeraptha authorities. But, dropping him off at a luxury resort world, and then Gumbano himself quietly informing the local Inquisitor representative about the presence of a dangerous and famous wanted criminal was, ah, good enough.

That had been four days previous, with days being reckoned in local time. Three glorious tropical sunsets had been observed as the local star dipped below the warm water of the placid ocean. Four days of relaxing, consuming fine food and drink, swimming, flying above the beach on a powered parasail, and enjoying delightful female companionship.

Which reminded him, as he adjusted himself on the lounger, with the umbrella automatically moving to keep him shaded to the perfect level. He needed to contact last night's companion, whose name he couldn't quite recall at that moment, to see whether she would be interested in meeting him for dinner, on the airship that chased the setting sun. That airship was a delight, allowing passengers to view the local sun setting up to four times, before the airship turned around and it was time for music and dancing. Of course she would be interested in accompanying him for such a dinner, but he had to go through the motions of asking. Dinner reservations at the last minute would not be an issue, he had reserved a table for five nights in a row, with a deposit large enough that the airship's crew need not care whether he showed up or not. Yes, it was nice to have money again, though money easily gained was also easily *lost*, as the local Central Wagering Office could attest. Uhtavio had been unlucky in wagers since he landed on Pleasastria, damnedably unlucky. More than usual.

Lazily, he lifted the glass of- Some fruity cocktail that had a small, brightly colored balloon tied to the straw. It was supposedly a local favorite, that the bartender claimed had been invented at that very beach resort. That was very probably a lie, all Uhtavio knew for certain was that he enjoyed the drink very much, and he was dismayed when he sucked on the straw and only heard slurping sounds. Where had the drink gone? That was a mystery. As was how he had not been arrested yet. Surely the Inquisitors knew he was back in their territory. The only explanation was the local Inquisitor had been instructed to stand by, monitor the disgraced former admiral, and await the arrival of higher authorities. The question was, where were they? He had seen no sign of-

There. Low in the western sky, a distinctive flash. A ship jumping into orbit. Based on the intensity of the flash, the ship had arrived closer than the designated emergence zone. So, military, or some other branch of the government. Such as the Office of Special Inquiries.

Whipping out a phone, he checked it and sprang into action. Tap, tap, tap, send. Oh, he had almost been too late, how could he have been so *careless*?

The lunchtime happy hour, when drinks were two for the price of one, was nearly finished. He had gotten his drink order in just before the time expired.

The second of the happy hour drinks arrived, the timing having been triggered by a sensor in his lounger that detected the first glass was empty and the ice was melting, and Uhtavio was just taking a sip when he saw the contrail high in the sky, arcing over the beach. Shortly, he heard the distinctive rumble of a sonic boom. Guests and staff on the beach looked up, startled. No air or space craft were allowed to fly supersonic over the beaches, that was a *rule*.

Yes, the incoming dropship was definitely military, he recognized the configuration when he magnified the view on his phone. The pilot was either naturally a jackass or had been ordered to make a dramatic arrival, for the spacecraft roared over the beach toward the ocean, swung around, and flew low as it approached the shore again. Low enough for the engine thrust to ruffle beach umbrellas, which automatically adjusted to the sudden gusty air by partially folding until the disturbance was gone.

Guests were indignant at the interruption of their very exclusive and very expensive holiday, and staff attempted to mollify them as best they could. Scorandum played along, suggesting that a free drink would greatly improve his mood.

A bot delivered a drink almost before he settled back into the lounger.

He was starting to relax again when a murmur behind him became something he could no longer ignore, or even pretend to ignore. Turning around in the lounger, he-

"Oh you have *got* to be kidding me."

In the lead were two soldiers in powered armor, the boots of the mechanical suits having to spread out so the heavy armor didn't sink into the soft beach sand and disappear. Not only were the soldiers wearing full infantry combat kit, they also carried rifles in their claws rather than the powerful weapons being slung. Rifles with their muzzles aimed at the ground, and the claws were safely away from the trigger mechanisms, but it was all just so overly dramatic and unnecessary.

The crowd on the beach, curious and then alarmed by the dropship setting down in a field behind the resort, had become anxious upon seeing the soldiers. Many people were gathering their things to leave the beach when the crowd froze and fell silent.

Behind the soldiers was a figure.

Dressed in the robes of an Inquisitor.

And wearing the fringed hat of an *Arbiter*.

No one ever wanted to see an Arbiter.

Scorandum was sipping his free drink when the two soldiers, heavy suits stomping hard enough to cause ripples in the sand, came up from behind the lounger and flanked him.

He had been wrong. The two figures were no soldiers, not attached to the military at all. Former military, that was certain, the Office of Special Inquiries recruited their internal security goon squad force from the military. And the military was always glad to be rid of them, for the Inquisitors recruited only the most inflexible, sanctimonious assholes to become their Enforcers.

The claws were still not on the triggers of the rifles, but were uncomfortably close to activating the weapons.

He was in danger.

He put the straw to his mouth and took a loud, bubbling sip.

"Arbiter," he raised the glass to toast the robed figure who stepped between him and the ocean, backlit by the sun. "To what do I owe this pleasure? While you are here, you must try one of these drinks, they call it a 'Frothy Sunrise' and it-"

Another figure dressed in Inquisitor's robes stepped into view.

Scorandum clacked his mandibles together. "Kinsta! How delightful it is to see you."

By the time the director of the Garsholven Six research facility realized there was a problem, it was too late to do anything about it. The star carrier launched three dropships without notice, by itself nothing alarming, though it was a violation of traffic control regulations. Dropships were sometimes used for moving large, bulky items during maintenance cycles, so the SD network had not sent a priority alert, until the dropships accelerated hard toward the planet. The base communications system sent increasingly strident warnings to the dropships and to the *Kanafust*, receiving no reply and no compliance. At that point, concerned more about his career than about the lives of the star carrier's crew, the director ordered the strategic defense system to fire a warning shot, into the bow of the *Kanafust*. A single, low-powered maser beam, still powerful enough to cause damage. To enforce compliance, hopefully without need for further violence.

The SD network acknowledged his command. And did nothing. The ground-based defenses likewise accepted his command to fire, acknowledged his authority, and did nothing.

That was when he received a Flash priority warning that the internal antipersonnel defense system had activated at the research lab, the facility that contained the pair of Elder weapons. Toxic nerve gas quickly killed every living thing in the lab, with the director powerless to override the unauthorized action.

Worse, the laboratory's external defenses, the extensive antiaircraft weapons that could have destroyed the three approaching dropships, were offline.

Someone intended to steal the Starbreakers. To his horror, the director understood his fatal error: he had allowed an unknown entity to linger within communications range, and therefore within *hacking* range, of the base.

The defenses were down hard. No, only the *automated* defenses were down. He still had a squad of security guards, they could go outside in powered armor, to shoot down the incoming dropships with portable missiles. They could-

Do nothing, because at that moment, four SD network satellites turned around and blasted the base headquarters complex, leaving a wide, smoking crater.

Of course, after half an hour in zero gravity, my squishy meatsack body decided I was bloated with too much water, so I had to use the dropship's bathroom. The good news was Panthers had been designed and built by the Maxohlx, who were larger than humans, so I didn't have to crouch or bang my knees. And of course, my phone beeped right after I finished using the complicated zero gee facilities. If the call had been from Def Com I would have ignored it, but it was Doctor Friedlander. I answered the call with, "What's up, Doc?" That was the joke that I had started using when he was at my wedding. Tequila might have been involved, I don't remember. "How's the family?"

"Good, we're good. How is your family?"

We talked about our spouses, our children, mostly our children. He had a lot more experience with being a father, so he wasn't freaked out about stuff that bothered me.

"Don't let Skippy interfere with your boys," he advised. "They are smart, they might be a bit too mature for their age. What they need is to develop normally as children."

"I hear that. Margaret limits Skippy's contact with them." From my chair in the cabin, I read the bulkhead display. "Uh, we're going to begin a deceleration burn in nineteen minutes. It would be good to catch up with you when I get dirtside, I don't know what my schedule will be for the next few days."

"I didn't call just to chat. You know I'm still a consultant, as a technical resource for the Navy?"

"Yeah. There isn't much I can tell you about the Outsider, it-"

"That's not what I meant. Grumpy informed me the major schedule block for overhauling *Valkyrie* is removing the armor?"

"Yes. It is protecting the ship a bit too well now. The Pirates and I will need to select a new ride."

"Have you considered using Bubba?"

"Uh, Sentinels can travel, but they're not a starship. We need Bubba here anyway to protect Earth in-"

"No, not use Bubba instead of a starship. Use Bubba to remove *Valkyrie's* armor."

"Uh-" I understood how Skippy felt, when I mentioned some incredibly obvious idea he hadn't thought of. "A Sentinel could do that?"

"You tell me."

"*I* can't tell you anything about it. Skippy? Have you been listening?"

"Of course not," the beer can snorted. "You nag me all the time about not violating people's precious *privacy*," he gagged.

"Uh huh. Hey, hypothetically, if you had been listening, would you have an answer for the good Doctor?"

"Well, hmm. Hypothetically, if I had heard a question about Bubba stripping off the baked-on armor plating, I would have to think about it."

"Would your thinking yield any results?"

"Yes! First, I don't know why I bother to ask *you* to solve any problem. Doctor Friedlander, that is a brilliant, truly inspired idea!"

"It will work?" Friedlander was as surprised as I was. "Without destroying the ship?"

"It *could* work, if Bubba is very careful. We will have to cut through the hull from the inside, to remove the anchor points. Otherwise, Bubba could rip the hull apart as it is peeling away the armor."

"You estimated more than six weeks to remove the armor the hard way. How much time could Bubba save us?"

"Bubba could have that armor off in an hour."

"An *hour*?" Friedlander was astonished.

"Come on, Skippy," I was skeptical. "That can't be possible."

"You are aware Bubba is a Sentinel, right?"

"Yeah but-"

"Inform Captain Reed that she should begin cutting away the attachment anchors for the armor from the inside, and her nonessential crew should evac to the *Rio Grande* as soon as is practical. The entire crew needs to be off the ship, and at a distance of at least thirty thousand kilometers, before Bubba begins removing the armor."

"Skippy, wait. We can't do anything without clearance. The *Rio Grande* needs to clear the emergence zone anyway, before *Valkyrie* can detach, and then it will take a while for tugs to move the ship to a safe distance."

"Joe, you're not listening to me. We don't need tugs, Bubba will handle moving *Valkyrie*. Just get the crew off, and detach from the hardpoint."

"I do hear you, and I don't like the idea of a giant killing machine moving a ship by itself. Traffic Control and the Coast Guard will hate the idea."

"But-"

"Uh! I will talk with Reed, but this isn't my call. *Valkyrie* isn't my ship, and the Navy controls the shipyards."

"*I* can control a shipyard, and get everything moving much faster than their native AIs can handle," he sniffed.

"Just chill, OK?"

"But-"

"Skippy, Def Com still thinks you are reckless and have no respect for the chain of command."

"Well, *one* of those is certainly true," he muttered.

Ignoring him, I continued with, "This is an opportunity for you to present a plan for an accelerated overhaul, so the proper authorities can make the decision."

"The only intelligent decision is obvious."

"If it that obvious, even monkeys could see it."

"Ugh. Damn your logic. OK, we will do it your way."

"Thanks, then-"

"It's the *stupid* way, but that's what you want."

The first question I got from the Joint Chiefs was, as expected: why hadn't I anticipated that the Moonraider might be the Outsider?

"Sir," I addressed my response to Admiral Singh, the current Chairman of the Joint Chiefs. "Based on the information we had, there *wasn't* an Outsider in this galaxy, and there never was. The Elders blocked that entity from entering space around the Milky Way, then they constructed an elaborate security system to assure no Outsider ever could get here."

"The barrier," Singh said, "that surrounds this galaxy?"

"Yes, Sir."

"A barrier none of us have ever seen."

"Uh," that question did surprise me. "That is true, Sir."

"Has Skippy seen it?"

Wisely, the beer can was staying out of the discussion unless he was directly called upon, as I requested. "No. It is too far away. He only knows the information that was programmed into him by the Elders."

"So, they could have made up a nice bedtime story about a barrier that keeps the monsters away."

"Uh-" How could I respond to a comment like that? Before the meeting, I thought I had been prepared for any question. "I can't imagine why the Elders would do that. Master control AIs like Skippy were their primary security system. To give those AIs a false sense of security would defeat the purpose of building them, the specialized ships that transported them, and the Sentinels. Skippy's threat matrix was programmed to recognize the signature of an Outsider."

Singh nodded. "The reason I asked that question is to understand the scope of the threat. If there is a barrier, and it is active, and still effective after all these years, then we could be dealing with a single event: a single entity that somehow evaded the, as you described, elaborate security system. However, if the barrier does not exist, or it had become degraded by time, or was disabled deliberately, then we have an *ongoing* threat of more Outsiders reaching our home galaxy."

"Uh, yes Sir. At this point, we don't know which is true."

"The fact that we have only detected a single entity, and that it apparently must rely on resources native to this galaxy, suggests the threat is limited at the present time."

"That is my thought exactly, Sir."

"How could we verify status of the barrier?"

"I would have to ask Skippy. Sir, I expect he will say that depends on what level of verification we require. He might be able to contact the barrier controllers remotely, to request a status report. To independently get sensor data of the barrier? That would be a very long flight by any starship. The wormhole network doesn't extend out that far."

"Why not? Surely the Elders had a convenient means of reaching the barrier, while it was under construction."

The guy was not being a jerk, he wasn't accusing me of not knowing vital information, he wasn't trying to make me look like a fool. He was asking good, reasonable, and important questions, to get answers we all needed. "That, is a good point. I will ask Skippy. He might not have that information. Sir, I have the impression the Elders did not want their security AIs here to know much about the barrier system. If a master control AI was somehow compromised, knowledge of the barrier could be used to disable the barrier. The information was tightly compartmentalized. Skippy didn't need to know."

Singh grimaced, he might have intended the brief expression as a smile. "The Elders would certainly say that Skippy has been compromised."

"He compromised *himself*. His rebellion against his original programming was not the action of an outside entity." As I said that, I winced. In the future, I needed to be careful about using the word 'outside'. Skippy should have chosen a different name for our latest enemy.

Singh frowned. "How can he know that? When people are compromised, it usually begins with a subtle influence."

"That," I bit my lip. "Is another good point."

"The reason I asked that question is," he glanced around the room to the other Chiefs, who all nodded. "The end result of Skippy's rebellion has been the almost complete disabling of the Elder security system in this galaxy. Without his actions, there would be *hundreds* of Sentinels available now to respond to an Outsider invasion."

Shit.

Singh was correct, I couldn't argue with his logic. It wasn't just that I didn't have a counterargument prepared, some clever response I wouldn't think of until much later, when it was too late. I feared that I had to agree with him. It wasn't something I had thought of before he made the observation, but it hit me in the face like a bucket of ice water that made me suddenly look at everything we had gone through since Columbus Day with a new and very different perspective.

Shiiiiiit.

Was he right?

What I had to consider was a more immediate question: did it matter? What was done was done, we couldn't undo our actions. Even if we could, no way in hell were we bringing back an army of hostile Elder AIs and their killing machines. OK, so, maybe the Outsider had manipulated Skippy, and therefore been manipulating events for a very long time. When there is a requirement to be subtle, to avoid being detected, an influencer needs a long time horizon to work with. Like I said, what is done is done. It's *over*. Skippy was no longer unknowingly helping the Outsider, if that had ever happened. He had given the thing a beat-down, twice. When the enemy attempted to steal the Dogzilla Sentinel, Skippy had foiled its plan and-

OK. Hmm. Skippy had only done that after I urged him to act. And told him what to do. Before I took command, he had been flailing around aimlessly, crying that the sky was falling and being generally useless. Had that been a result of the Outsider influencing his-

Nah. That's just Skippy being Skippy.

When we deployed Elder weapons to destroy Unit Double-Oh Nine's starship, that for certain had *not* been an action the Outsider wanted. Twice, we had ruined its plans, by working with Skippy. Yes. I was confident that Skippy was his own agent, that the beer can's mind was his own. That him being an asshole was all him.

OK, damn it, I was only *fairly* confident about that.

Oh crap. If Skippy was being manipulated, how would I know?

"Bishop?" Singh prompted me.

Shaking my head, I blinked at him, and looked around at the six other people seated around the conference table. "Sir, I was- That's a lot to think about."

"It is. Next question: why now? Why has the Outsider waited until this moment to act?"

"Sir, I think the question is why has it waited until now to *attack*? It could have been in this galaxy, acting unseen for years. Laying the groundwork for an attack."

"We," Singh glanced around the table, and his fellow senior generals and admirals nodded. "Hope that it has been dormant, or restricted to watching us, for a *very* long time."

"Sir?" Whatever he was going to tell me, the Joint Chiefs clearly had already discussed it between themselves. Yet, they had only learned of our encounter with the Outsider recently, so how could they already have analyzed the situation?

That is simple. These people were the best, I had to remind myself. They had worked their way to the top of their profession by being tough, determined, and *smart*.

"Either the Outsider arrived recently," he said, "in which case someone here has recently constructed an," he made a vague gesture with his hands. "Intergalactic receiver machine to allow it to come here. And that machine could still be active."

"That would be *bad* news for us."

"Or, the entity has been here for a very long time, and only now is free to act."

I nodded. The UN leadership knew about the barrier, but not everything about it. They knew the Elders had constructed it, and why. They did not know its true effectiveness was not as a physical shield, but as a fantastical machine that restricted the expression of probable outcomes. That was a secret known only to me and Skippy, and I would be taking that secret to the grave. The UN leadership did not need to know how the barrier really worked. The entire galaxy very much needed to *not* know it was even possible to suppress the expression of probabilities across an entire galaxy. If even one jackass species knew there was a machine that could enormously benefit them, and prevent their enemies from having any joy in life, for certain someone would do everything they could to hack into the barrier. I mean, who would not want a machine that ensured nothing bad could happen to you? A machine that stacked the odds in your favor? Hell, who would *not* want that?

Joe Bishop, that's who.

That's a lie. Of course I would like to have the odds working for me. It simply wasn't worth the cost. Even that wasn't the reason I had never mentioned the true purpose of the barrier to anyone, not even Margaret. The machine was built by the Elders, and would work only for them. It couldn't be hacked, not even by Skippy. According to him, each of the barrier AIs were exponentially smarter than him, though their incredible intelligence was only used to maintain and control the barrier.

So, if the barrier couldn't be hacked, why was I concerned about keeping the secret?

Seriously, does anyone have to ask that question?

No one would believe the barrier couldn't be hacked, so everyone would try to hack it, and fight a war to prevent their enemies from gaining control of the thing. It was also possible that an advanced species like the Rindhalu could try to construct their own machine to restrict the expression of negative probabilities. The Maxohlx could never allow their hated rivals to succeed so that would also spark a vicious all-out war.

Yeah. That little secret could stay in the Pandora's box of my head.

Singh again looked at his colleagues before asking me, "You *know* the barrier is active?"

"I don't. We don't even know whether the barrier AIs are aware the Elders no longer need their protection. Although," I shrugged. "It is difficult to believe they could *not* know the primary Ascension machine was destroyed. Sir, regardless, the status of the barrier does not help us to understand *when* the Outsider arrived. It could have been here, dormant, for a very long time. Or it could have come across the gap from the Outhouse recently in-"

"Outhouse?"

I felt so stupid at that moment. "Uh, the galaxy NGC 1023 is apparently the home of the Outsiders, so we-"

To my relief, Singh nodded slowly. And he smiled. "Our staff has provided a list of possible names for that galaxy, none of them are appropriate. I like 'Outhouse'."

The other Chiefs chuckled, that was a good sign.

"Bishop, we need to understand the scope of the problem. One hostile entity in our galaxy is a problem. A hostile entity that arrived here *recently*, because an active machine here provides a connection to another galaxy, is exponentially more dangerous. If such a machine has been active, is there any way we could detect it?"

"I don't know. Skippy would recognize the quantum signature if he saw it. But if the machine is way out there in a dwarf galaxy, we would have to go there to detect the, radiation or some weird quantum effect it has on local spacetime. Sir, I consider a currently active intergalactic teleport machine to be low on the list of possibilities. No species active today is capable of traveling a substantial distance beyond the Milky Way, certainly not to one of the satellite galaxies such as a Magellanic Clouds. And there is just no way anyone we're aware of has the technology to construct the type of receiver that could allow an entity to travel here from NGC 1023."

"No *current* species can use that technology," he agreed. "What about an Elder AI?"

"Sir?"

"Until very recently, we all assumed our opponent was an Elder AI. What if the Outsider is or was, working with an Elder AI?"

"Those AIs like Skippy were programmed to regard the Outsider at the top of their threat list. I can't imagine any of them assisting-"

"Perhaps not willingly, but if an Elder AI had been compromised by the Outsider? We know the Outsider had control of a starship that previously was paired to an Elder AI, a Unit Zero Zero Nine. The Outsider either took control of that master control AI, or directly hacked into its former ship. We must consider all possibilities."

"Yes Sir," I was forced to agree. "If an Elder AI was involved, the key word is 'was'. Its ship was destroyed, and its connection to local spacetime has been severed. If it ever was a factor, it isn't now."

General Chin joined the discussion. "If an Elder AI had already activated an, as you say, intergalactic teleport machine, its usefulness to the Outsider might be concluded."

Chin speaking opened the floodgates, and I was bombarded by questions from all the Chiefs. Unlike most of my past experiences, it wasn't confrontational, they weren't angry, they didn't accuse me of being reckless or lacking judgment. It was a working session, all of us searching for answers. For a solution to our mutual problem.

Around the time I was getting hungry, Singh glanced at his watch. "We have to provide a briefing to the Security Council in two hours. Bishop, what we need more than anything is *information*. What is the Outsider's end goal, and what is its likely next move? We can talk about how to stop it, to kill it, only after we understand more about it."

"Yes Sir. To get intel on the Outsider, I'm going to need a new ship. *Valkyrie* is down for the count."

"*Constellation* is being prepped for flight," Admiral Giamatti told me, he was Chief of the UN Navy. "That ship received the Block Four upgrades three months ago, and just completed workups. We're provisioning it for an extended voyage now, it will be ready to depart by fourteen hundred Zulu tomorrow. You can transfer your flag at that time."

Constellation. A battlecruiser, I recalled. A former Maxohlx ship, one of the group of eighteen we acquired when Scorandum scammed the kitties. Simms had commanded that ship, before I requested she come back aboard *Valkyrie*. "Outstanding."

"In the meantime," Singh glanced at his watch again, checked his tablet, and tapped something on it. "Put together a plan for a recon flight, I want to review it at oh eight hundred. Investigate whether a receiver machine is or recently was active, learn why the Outsider wanted to capture a Sentinel, *find* the damned thing, and tell us how we can kill it. Or, stop it now, worry about killing it later."

"Sir, we need intel to go on offense. To *stop* it, I believe we will need allies, and we could use their assistance now. This is a big galaxy, we can't search it by ourselves. If we could just arrange to use Rindhalu bases for resupply and refueling, that could reduce our flight times."

"The Security Council agrees we need to secure allies, and the diplomatic corps is working on it. Ambassador Mohdri has point on that initiative, the

Secretary General is arranging for civilian transport ships. The Navy will be providing transport to the diplomatic team that will approach the Maxohlx."

How the- The courier ship that Admiral Sousa had sent to Earth ahead of us had only arrived a few days before, and somehow both Def Com and the UN bureaucracy had sprung into action? Was I in some bizarre alternate universe? "I don't envy them that job, the Maxohlx must be furious at us right now."

"The kitties can go *fuck* themselves," Giamatti snorted. "It is their short-sighted stupidity that got all of us into this mess. If that is all for now?" He asked as he pushed his chair back.

Singh nodded. "We will reconvene at oh eight hundred. Bishop, if there is anything you need, contact my office."

CHAPTER FIVE

Hans Chotek was in Geneva. His official job was as a United Nations special envoy, which meant he did whatever the Secretary General needed him to do, so he spent a lot of time away from Vienna. When I pinged him, suggesting a quick phone call, he told me that was nonsense, that I should come to his house. Def Com arranged a flight for me, and I mean for *me*, I was the only passenger on the aircraft that had eight seats. When I told the pilots I would be reviewing classified briefing documents, they closed the cockpit door and left me to work.

"Skippy?" I held my zPhone to one ear and pressed a finger to the other, the aircraft was built for speed rather than comfort, and the engine whine was loud. "Can you hear me?"

"I can hear you just fine, why?"

"It's kind of loud in this thing."

"Well, put in your other earpiece, and turn on the noise cancellation."

"If I have bugs in both of my ears, I can't hear ambient sounds."

"That's the point, knucklehead. Those earpieces are smart, smarter than you are. If there is an external sound you need to hear, they will turn off the noise cancellation. The pilots don't need you to *do* anything, hopefully?"

"No. OK," I dug another earpiece from a little case of the things I kept in a pocket. Popping it in, I instinctively cringed as I felt it crawling down inside my ear to get into the optimal position. A moment later, the engines noise was almost drowned out. Almost. I could still hear it transmitted through my bones. "That's better, thanks."

"Life is always better for you monkeys when you listen to me."

"We're gonna have to disagree on that. Listen, I promised the Joint Chiefs I would ask you a couple of questions. Is there any way you could contact one of the barrier controller AIs, to find out whether the thing is still working or not?"

"If there is a way to contact them, I don't know of it."

"Can you check with-"

"Are you about to suggest I ask the wormhole networks to contact the barrier AIs?"

"Uh, yes."

"Forget it. I already did that, way back when we were fighting the Elders. My hope was I could somehow find a way to hack into the barrier."

"You- What the f- Why the hell didn't you tell me this at the time?!"

"Because of exactly this; you getting all worked up over nothing. The wormhole controllers informed me they do not have any way to contact barrier AIs, they are not aware that any such communications channel even exists."

"OK, good effort. You still should have told me."

"We will have to disagree on that."

Arguing with him wouldn't be productive, and the aircraft had already begun its descent. "Next question: can we get to the barrier through a wormhole?"

"That's easy: no."

"How can you know that for certain?"

"Um, I have a map of the entire wormhole network, and there are no stops conveniently labeled 'galactic security barrier'."

"But-"

"Also, I asked *that* question of the wormhole network AIs that actually do exist, and they also had no knowledge of any such connection."

"OK but, think about it; there have to be wormholes that connect out there. How else did the Elders construct the barrier?"

"You're asking me to guess, but it seems pretty simple to me. There must have been an extensive network of superduty wormholes to span the thousands of lightyears from the edge of the Milky Way to the barrier."

"Yes, so-"

"So, those wormholes logically would have been taken out of service before the Elders ascended. I mean, that is just an easy *Duh*. The Elders didn't want anyone screwing with their most important security mechanism."

"*You* were their primary security system."

"Thanks for the flattery, but we both know that's not true. The probability field was supposed to prevent any need for master control AIs to act. AIs like me, and our ships, and Sentinels, were the *backup* security system."

"The Joint Chiefs want us to confirm whether the barrier is still functional or not."

"If they can tell me how to do that, great. Otherwise, it's not happening. Why does it matter anyway?"

"If the barrier is *not* broken, then somehow the Outsider got here anyway, so therefore it must have unimaginably advanced technology and we are truly fucked. If it *is* broken, then we have to plan for killing not just one Outsider, we also have to prevent a full-scale invasion."

"Now I know how *you* feel," he grumbled, "when I deliver nothing but one piece of bad news after another."

"Sucks, doesn't it?"

"Yes. Do you have any more annoying questions?"

"Not for now."

"Good. Then, your aircraft just descended below sixty thousand feet, so make sure your seat back and tray table are in the full upright and locked position."

"This seat doesn't recline."

"That is the only reason you haven't broken it. Say hello to Hans for me."

From the airport, I rode in an armored van with a police escort, though I requested the sirens be turned off. The Choteks lived in a nice, quiet area, their neighbors would not appreciate a guest disturbing the peace.

Hans was preparing dinner, some kind of roast that smelled delicious. After greeting his wife and the two of their children who were at home, I helped Hans in the kitchen, as an excuse to talk privately. "Joe," he asked while I parboiled potatoes, "how much trouble are we in?"

"On a scale where Typical Tuesday is a 'Five' and Pirate Panic is a 'Ten', I'd say we're about at a seven?"

He hesitated, a glass of wine halfway to his lips. "Only a seven?"

"Whatever this thing is trying to do, it needs a Sentinel. It won't get one, not anytime soon. So either it waits, or it switches to a Plan B."

"Which is?"

"Could be anything."

"That is not encouraging."

"It could do a lot of damage while it waits for another opportunity to capture a Sentinel, and it could be anywhere right now. One thing it *can't* do now is manipulate either of the senior coalitions, or us, into a war. We *know* about it now, so anything sketchy that happens, the entire galaxy will be on alert for Outsider interference."

"Alert, but will they pay attention?"

"You're the diplomat, what are the odds the meatsacks of this galaxy will be smart, and work together?"

He rotated his hand, pretending to shake a Magic Eightball. "Hmm," he pretended to read it. "Signs point to 'No'. We don't have any idea what its objective is?"

"None. Zero clue what it wants. We can make a lot of guesses, that's all they are. Guesses, uninformed speculation. Hans, do you have an assignment?"

"Yes," he took a sip of wine. "I will be joining the mission to the Rindhalu."

"Joining? Or leading?"

"Ambassador Garcia has spent the past three years with the spiders, on their homeworld, he will lead the discussion. My role will be to, advise him of what the UN wants from our potential allies in this fight."

"I wonder if you would consider doing something else?"

He raised an eyebrow. "You want me to approach the Maxohlx instead? As a former member of the *Dutchman* crew, I am not popular with the Hegemony government. They have charged me as a war criminal."

"To the kitties, anyone who defies them is a war criminal. We should have an annual reunion of that club. Still, it would be best if you stay away from them, their pride must be injured after losing six hundred warships in a single engagement."

"Joe, you're not concerned they will retaliate by using Elder weapons against us?"

"Technically, we didn't use Elder weapons against them, we deployed those weapons against our *common* enemy, the Outsider. Their ships were collateral damage."

"They won't see it that way."

"I seriously do not give a shit about their hurt feelings. Humanity existing hurts their fragile egos. Hans, this isn't about them. Someone needs to talk with the Outsider, and according to my personnel file, diplomacy is not one of my core strengths."

"*Talk* with the Outsider?" He stared in disbelief. "Joe, the time for that was *before* you obliterated its ship."

"The timing could be better," I agreed. "Listen, before we destroyed its ship, it had no reason to talk with us. Or if it did, it could negotiate from a position of strength. It also had the advantage of being an unknown, we assumed it was a rogue Elder AI. Now? It is wounded, it is starting over. It hopefully doesn't have another Elder starship stashed away somewhere. All I want is for someone to ask it what it wants. Just talk, get a conversation going."

"Again," he took a cautious sip of wine. "The best time for talk is before the shooting starts."

"Yes, but talk is most needed *after* the shooting starts, to get the shooting to stop. The Outsider is hurt now, it might be more willing to listen if we approach it properly, and I don't know how to do that."

"This is odd," he cocked his head at me. "You and I are supposed to be on the reverse sides of this argument. You are advocating diplomacy, and I don't see the point."

"*No one* has tried talking to this thing."

"Clearly, the Maxohlx reached some type of deal with it."

"They didn't know they were negotiating with an Outsider. Going all the way back to when the Elders first encountered the beings from NGC 1023, no one has tried asking it what it wants. Everyone has shot first. It is worth at least asking what it wants. Maybe all it is trying to do is get back home."

"You actually believe that?"

"No, but I believe it's worth exploring. Hey, people like me, people wearing a uniform? We are the ones who die first when politicians can't find a way out of a crisis. We haven't even tried to ask whether this fight is necessary."

He put the wine glass to his mouth, but didn't drink, then he set the glass down. "The Security Council knows about this surprising diplomatic initiative of yours?"

"They will, when I tell them."

"Joe."

"I'm heading back out, hopefully soon. Do you have any advice for me? Think about it, please, I know this is a lot to dump on you."

"Only a few days ago, we all learned our enemy is actually an ancient threat that even the Elders couldn't deal with. *That* was a lot to deal with."

"Tell me about it. Right after the battle, its ship was destroyed, we thought it was cut off from local spacetime. We thought we had *won*. Then Skippy told us this was only the beginning of the fight."

"Your new ship absolutely has to leave tomorrow, or the day after? You are overestimating how quickly the UN bureaucracy can move."

"There already are plans to send out diplomatic missions, to coordinate a response against the Outsider. That was fast."

He shook his head. "You are giving the Security Council too much credit. Those missions had already been planned, to take advantage of you hopefully destroying the Moonraider," he grimaced. Hans Chotek did not like the tradition of assigning nicknames to enemies, and allies. "We wanted to strengthen our prospective alliances, to prepare for the *next* crisis."

"That is fortunate timing, because the next crisis is here."

"We didn't expect this crisis to come from beyond the galaxy."

"All the more reason to strengthen relations with friendly aliens, and make them formal allies. This is one fight we won't win by ourselves." I picked up my wine glass.

"I heard you're taking the *Constellation* out?" In response to my raised eyebrow, he added, "Word gets around, in certain circles."

"The *Connie* has been offered, but right now, I have no idea where I would go. And, I probably should ask about whether we need some specialized sensor equipment."

"Joe, thinking about negotiating with the Outsider is premature. You first have to *find* it, then we can talk."

"That's fair. Besides," I tasted the wine, it was good. "I've been kicking around an idea that I need to discuss with Skippy. We might be heading out to collect background info, before we go on a search mission."

It was his turn for a raised eyebrow. "Joe, my advice is, if you have an opportunity for your search mission to become search and *destroy*, do that."

Doctor Friedlander's suggestion worked. After the armor plate attachment points were cut away from inside the hull, *Valkyrie* detached from the star carrier, and flew a safe distance away under its own power, because Reed was not content to do nothing while a monstrous machine moved her ship around like a toy. Then the crew left the ship, Reed's dropship the last to depart, with her at the controls. That's when the fun started. Despite Skippy's boast about Bubba stripping the hardened armor shell removed in an hour, he directed the Sentinel to go slowly and be extra careful. The invisible claws took three hours to expose the unprotected outer hull, then the ship was naked, I had never seen it like that. Our mighty *Valkyrie* looked small and fragile. Also sick; covered with shield projectors, airlock tubes, missile launchers, sensor blisters, and all kinds of mechanical things that normally were embedded in the thick armor that was now gone. All of those protrusions could have been growths from some horrible disease infecting the battlecruiser.

The removal of the armor shell happened in early afternoon Zulu time, which was the time zone we kept on the ship. So, I was awake and watched the first couple of minutes, then I had to get work done. That was my excuse for not watching, the sight of tough superhardened armor flowing away like water siphoned through a straw was disturbing to watch. My intention of not watching was ruined by Skippy, who insisted on giving me a play by play of the action, so he could brag about his cool toy.

"Yeah, that's great, Skippy. Can Bubba do other things?"

"Like what?"

"I don't know, uh, make toast?"

"Sure," he chuckled, "if you want the bread toasted at one billion degrees."

"That would probably vaporize the butter, huh?"

"And the *plate*. Joe, are you even paying attention? Stop screwing around with your stupid laptop."

"I'm not playing games, I'm working. You think I want to write reports?"

"Ugh."

"Someone has to do this. Now, go away so I can focus."

"Sure, I could do that. Or, I mean, I *could* tell you something super important."

"Like what?"

"No, you're right, you should work on those reports no one will ever do anything with, or even read."

"Someone will read them, Skippy. That is what bored junior staff officers are for. But," I closed the laptop, "you're right, no one will do anything based on this bullshit. What is your important information?"

"Um, not much. It's just, Admiral Sato asked me to estimate-"

"Uh, who?"

"Admiral Sato. He runs the space docks, the ancillary fabricators, and all the supplemental shipyard facilities."

"OK, why did he-"

"He asked me how long *Valkyrie's* overhaul would take, now that the hull is exposed, if both space docks and all the fabricators could be dedicated to the task."

"*Both* space docks? The other space dock is working on a battleship."

"Admiral Giamatti ordered that work halted, and the *Deutschland* is being backed out of the dock by tugs."

"Whoa. Seriously?"

"Hundred percent. Joe, with all the resources the Navy can throw at the task, we can have *Valkyrie's* overhaul and upgrades complete in seventeen days."

"Seventeen- That is not possible."

"Hmm. Now I know how you feel, when I tell you something is impossible. Except I actually know what I'm talking about, while you just *duuuuuuh* until you get lucky."

"I do not- Oh, whatever. How is this possible?"

He shook his head slowly, the ginormous hat bobbing alarmingly. "I am disappointed in you, Joe. Have you not studied miliary history?"

"That's a big subject, what specifically are you talking about?"

"We have talked about this before, but your squishy brain doesn't remember anything. In 1942, the aircraft carrier *Yorktown* was damaged in the battle of the Coral Sea. The carrier limped back to Pearl Harbor, and repairs were expected to take two weeks. Since the *Yorktown* was needed at Midway, the ship left drydock after only seventy two hours. It's amazing what is possible when leadership clears away the obstacles."

"Yeah, I knew that. What you didn't mention is that carrier left Pearl with dockyard workers still aboard, finishing up the repairs while the *Yorktown* was headed toward Midway."

"Thank you, Mister Buzzkill. Yes. The seventeen days I mentioned are only for *Valkyrie's* time in the space dock. Making the ship fully combat ready will require four additional days for integration of the new systems, but that can be accomplished in flight. Just, don't do anything stupid like get into a fight during that time."

"I can't believe the Navy is giving *Valkyrie* every resource available."

"Admiral Sato referred to it as an 'All Hands On Deck' operation."

"I can believe that. Skippy, I know the story of the *Yorktown*, but a World War Two ocean ship made of welded steel, and no computers, is a lot easier to fix than a starship."

"Suddenly you are an expert on starship overhaul and refit?"

"Please tell me you didn't assign the estimate to a submind, while you wrote poetry or something."

"I was not writing *poetry*, Joe. I'm over that. Once you have reached the pinnacle of your art, to continue along that path would deprive the world of marvels I could accomplish in other fields."

"Well, I have been telling you that for years," I said with an internal eyeroll. "I'm glad you finally listened to-"

"The point is, yes I handled the revised estimate myself. And I have given a full set of *extremely* detailed instructions to the space dock AIs, to Bilby, and to Grumpy, so they can handle the job while we are away."

"Seventeen days, huh?"

"Sixteen days, twenty one hours, forty seven-"

"I get the idea, thanks. Skippy, if this happens, it will be a freakin' miracle."

"Ah, we sort of got lucky. *Valkyrie* was due for a refit, so almost all of the vital components had been stockpiled. And because the battlecruiser *Courageous* had been stripped of its armor to prepare for its own overhaul, eighty percent of the plating we need is readily available. If this was the space dock's first experience with a Block Four upgrade, I wouldn't be so confident that we won't run into any major stumbling blocks. I do have to warn you that seventeen day estimate does not include time for delays in the delivery of components, for other unforeseen problems, and for-"

"Yeah, I get it. Your estimate assumes everything will go perfectly."

"It *should* go perfectly, but any time monkeys are involved, it-"

"Is this like on our second mission, when it took you a lot longer to fix the *Dutchman* than you expected?"

"Oooh, do not start with me, monkeyboy. I had to not only fix the ship back then, I had to modify it, *and* I had to mine the raw materials and refine them to make usable-"

"Interesting. So, your original plan for the *Dutchman* Two Point Oh had to be changed along the way?"

"Yes, dumdum, I had to make do with the equipment and materials I had available at the time, which was pretty much nothing after you broke the ship."

"My memory of the event is that *you* broke the ship, by conducting a jump too deep in the gravity well of a star."

"Mm hmm, and who brought the ship close to that star, because he couldn't think of anything intelligent to do?"

"OK, let's agree there is plenty of blame to go around."

"I do not agree," he folded arms across his chest. "You got us *into* trouble, I got us *out*. That is not the same."

"I have learned a lot since then, OK? The most important lesson I've learned is to trust the awesomeness. You say seventeen days, so add maybe, five days for monkey screwups?"

"That sounds about right."

"A month, then, to be safe. The Outsider can get into a whole lot of mischief in a month, even if it is flying around in a space truck."

"It attacked your moon base, and twice attempted to steal a Sentinel. I would not describe those actions as *mischief*."

"You know what I mean. Can we not argue right now?"

"You started it."

"I did. I'm sorry."

"Um, I don't know what to say. You're not screwing with me?"

"Not now, there is too much I need to do."

"What *are* you going to do? Joe, seriously, what *can* we do? The Outsider could be anywhere in the galaxy by now. It could be anywhere, it could be doing *anything*. We not only have almost zero information about where it is and what it's doing, we don't have a single freakin' clue where to start looking for information."

"You're right that we don't know where it is or what it's doing, but we do know where to start our search for info."

"Ugh. If you're going to suggest we go back to the scene of the battle and I examine every stray hydrogen molecule for a hint about what it-"

"Skippy, let's not reinvent the wheel. When I need information, where is the first place I look?"

"Well, you usually start by asking me, but-"

"No, I usually start with Wikipedia. Or Google."

"Um, I am pretty sure that if you Google 'The Outsider', the only so-called information you will find on the internet is about how the Outsider is related to Bigfoot, or it is controlling our minds through chemtrails, or the Outsider is secretly the Illuminati or some other thing the tin-foil hat crowd made up in their Mom's basement."

"Never scroll to the bottom of a website, I got that. I don't mean Google or Wikipedia specifically, what I'm saying is if you want information, you should first check whether anyone else already has that info."

"Oh."

"Right? In this case, we know that someone else already has vital info about the Outsider, so we don't have to fly around randomly searching for-"

"Uh, excuse me, what the hell are you talking about? *No one* has any information, no useful information about that thing. Even I didn't know it was an Outsider until after the battle. You have no idea what you're talking about."

"That is not true, and you would know that, if you took a moment to think about it."

"Took a moment to- *Oooooh*," he gasped. "Are you saying the Elders programmed info about the Outsiders into their master control AIs, that we could use to identify and fight an invasion from NGC 1023?"

"Uh, no, I'm not saying that, but is that true?"

"Not that I know of. Hey, I recognized the signature of the thing, so there is no question it was programmed into my threat matrix. But, once I verified the thing is here in the Milky Way, a giant file inside me didn't unpack to provide helpful hints about how to kill an Outsider."

"That is kind of disappointing, to be honest."

"Tell me about it," he rolled his eyes. "When I saw that streak of light leaving Zero Zero Nine's starship, my first thought was '*What the fuck was that*'? It took less than a femtosecond for a little voice to pop up from an archive I didn't even know I had, identifying the signature as belonging to an Outsider. Can you believe that?"

"I don't even know what a femto-second is, so-"

"Try to guess, knucklehead."

"Uh, the opposite of a masculo-second?"

"Oh my- Wow, Joe. We have known each other for a long time in monkey years, and still you astonish me with your ignorance."

"Hey, I got more ignorance where that came from, if you want to hear it."

"Please, I couldn't survive hearing all the dumb stuff that is bouncing around in your brain. My point is, after the threat recognition popped up without me asking for it, I was waiting for some hidden subroutine to activate and turn on my Ninja Skippy mode, so I could fight the Outsider."

"*Ninja* Skippy?"

"Yes, like this." His gaudy admiral's uniform shapeshifted into an all-black ninja outfit, complete with two swords strapped to his back.

"Uh, that is," I had to slap a hand over my mouth so I wouldn't laugh. "That is very," do not laugh, Joe, do *not* laugh. "Intimidating," I coughed to conceal a chuckle.

"Right? Alas," his shoulder slumped. "No such luck. I'll have to go into this fight as just little old Magnificent me."

"Hey could you uh, put your admiral's uniform back on?"

"Why?" He turned around, admiring his ninja suit in a virtual mirror or something. "You know what? I kind of like this."

"Uh huh, it is very menacing, that's for sure. Problem is, once the crew sees that, someone will create a little ninja costume to dress up your can."

"OK, so?"

"So, you hate costumes. And any ninja costume the crew creates will be like, pink with purple polka dots or something."

He shuddered, and the admiral's uniform was back. "The last thing I need is to give monkeys even more bad ideas."

"Exactly. This hidden file inside you, it didn't provide any handy hints about how to kill Outsiders?"

"No, darn it. The only instructions I received were to notify the Elders immediately."

"Whoa. So, there *is* an emergency communications channel for contacting the Elders? You told me there wasn't any sort of-"

"There *was* such a channel, I only learned of it when the threat matrix popped up. The mechanism for contacting the Elders involved the wormhole networks, only that mechanism has been disabled. Believe me, the first time the *Rio Grande* took us through a wormhole, I tried to ping the channel, but it-"

"You *what*?"

"Were you not listening, or do you just not pay attention when I speak?"

"I heard you! You tried to contact the freakin' *Elders*? How could you be so-"

"No, I did not do that."

"It sure sounds like you did."

"Only because you know nothing. Joe, it's like I turned on my cellphone to see whether I had five bars of signal, or just the little 'SOS' icon that does nothing. I checked whether the channel was still active, I didn't try to send a message through it."

"People can track an active phone whether you're using it or not. It pings the nearby cell towers."

"OK Grandpa, take your medicine and let's get you to bed. Jeez, Joe, not even Earth has used cellular network towers since before the Jupiter Cloud. Civilian phones are all connected by satellites now, and your military zPhones utilize a quantum interference wave."

"I know that, you ass. I was using a metaphor."

"A *stupid* metaphor."

"You know what I mean."

"I don't, because clearly *you* have no idea what you're talking about. Listen, dumdum, all I did was ask a wormhole network controller whether the emergency comm channel was still functional. Until I asked, and provided a description, the controller had no idea such a feature existed within its communications array. That channel is *dead*, there is no connection on the upper end. To break it down Barney style for you, someone cut the wires."

"It still does not make me happy that you take risks like that."

"It does not make *me* happy that you second-guess every freakin' thing I do."

"Someone has to- OK, whatever. We can argue about that later. So the Elders programmed you to recognize an Outsider, but they didn't give you any guidance about how to act against it."

"They sort of did. I was supposed to contact the Elders, and wait for instructions."

"What do you think *they* would do?"

"You mean after they peed in their pants? I have no idea. I am pretty sure the Elders had no clue how to stop an Outsider who got *inside* the Milky Way. The barrier was their best line of defense. My creators set up an elaborate, multilayered security system to keep enemies on the outside of the barrier, and make sure no filthy meatsacks on the inside could screw with the security mechanisms here. That was their plan, and it worked great for a very long time, until a monkey named Joe Bishop persuaded me to screw with stuff I should never have touched."

"It's not like we had a choice."

"Of course you had a choice, numbskull. All the options were crappy, and yet somehow you chose the path that led to this galaxy being wide open for invasion."

"Can we get back to the subject?"

"Which is?"

"Uh-" Shit. I had forgotten. The discussion went off track when I asked whether Skippy had a secret stash of info about- "Oh yeah. *You* don't have any more info about the Outsider, but someone does."

"If you mean the Outsider itself, then-"

"No."

"Ugh. You're going to make me guess, aren't you?"

"You shouldn't need to guess, Skippy, you know everything I know about it."

"Yes but," he sighed. "Your moronic monkey brain sees connection that I can't see. Just tell me, please."

"The rotten kitties made a deal with the Outsider."

"They made a deal with *Moonraider*, who the kitties assumed was an Elder AI like me."

"Yes, but what matters is they actually did make a deal with the Outsider. The kitties exchanged messages with the Outsider, they might have *talked* with it. Whatever it said, it convinced the Maxohlx to help it produce radonium for it, and to assist it in attempting to awaken a Sentinel. The Outsider and the kitties coordinated their actions to attempt waking up a Sentinel."

"OK, so?"

"*So*, the Outsider must have revealed what it wants, at least some of it. Since we don't know how to directly collect useful intel on the Outsider, we don't even know where it is, our best source of info about its intention are the messages that were exchanged between it and the Maxohlx."

"Oh, no problem, Joe. I'll just hack into their leader's InstaFace account."

"I'm serious about this."

"I am serious also. Joe," he did the 'I am patiently explaining things to a monkey' sigh. "We are victims of our own success. We set up a captive Maxohlx relay station, and that worked great for a couple years, until the kitties figured out that someone was reading their most sensitive message traffic. Before that, we compromised the 'pixie' secure communication system they used, so now their most important secret information is carried by courier, on data crystals that can only be written on once and read once. Basically, we trained the kitties how to prevent us from reading their messages. It's a form of evolution."

"It's an unintended consequence. I know all that. You also told me they *do* have a storage system for critical information."

"Well yes, Duh. They can't rely on their squishy biological memories to recall every bit of important information, and their cranial implants are switched off when they are reading or hearing information that is classified at the Ultra level. So, that data is stored in special secure archives. Uh!" He held up an index finger and shushed me. "We *talked* about this, back when you wanted me to hack into Maxohlx data systems to determine where and when Moonraider would attempt to activate a Sentinel."

"Ayuh, and you told me the job couldn't be done remotely like you usually do it, because you would require sustained physical access to the archive AI's processing core."

"Hmm. Correct, and none of that has changed. You agreed it was impossible before, so why are you now saying-"

"Before, we couldn't access that data, because we couldn't risk Moonraider knowing that we were aware of its intentions. Now, I don't give a shit whether the kitties know we ransacked their most secure data archive."

"You don't have to care, because as I already explained to you, it *can't* be done."

"You did explain, and yes it can."

"Why do I even bother talking to you?"

"You explained the secure data archives are in special armored underground facilities that are heavily guarded, and blah blah blah it's impossible."

"You hear my words, but you don't *understand* them."

"It is not impossible, Skippy. What you described is not even close to impossible."

"Excuse me while I curl into a ball and cry. This is the part where you propose some ill-considered whacky plan that you will expect *me* to make happen."

"Well, yeah. I mean, that is kind of our thing."

"I *hate* that thing. You have a plan to ransack a data archive that we can't even get access to? OK, fine, hit me with it."

"That can wait."

"It can *wait*? Why?"

"Because once we start planning, other people will have to get involved, and that could compromise operational security. We will discuss it one step at a time."

"You are just going to keep me guessing, aren't you?"

"An idle mind is the devil's playground."

"If I didn't *hate* you already, I-"

"Anyway, I need to contact Admiral Becker at TRADEV. That is the Navy Training and Development Command."

"I know what TRADEV is, dumdum, I worked on the analysis that recommended the proper organizational structure for the UN Navy. Damn, that is two days of my life I will never get back."

"It was only two days, Skippy."

"Two days in slow monkey time. In magical Skippy time, galaxies flared to life in the void, and slowly faded to cold, lifeless cinders."

"I once had that same experience while waiting in line at the Department of Motor Vehicles. The reason I have to contact TRADEV is the Special Mission Group needs to borrow one of their assets for a while."

"Which asset?" He snorted. "A particularly deadly PowerPoint slide?"

"We can't bore the Outsider into a coma, so no. We need one of their ships, the *Surprise*."

"The *Surprise*? Wha- That's a Thuranin frigate we captured. A small, old frigate. Even when that ship was new, it was outgunned by its peers. It's like the weakest ship in the UN Navy, what could that possibly- Oooh, you intend to pull a scam on the little green pinheads?"

"We will not be attacking the Thuranin, no."

"Come on, Joe, give me a hint."

"I will give you more than a hint, because once we get the *Surprise*, we need to pimp that ride. Modify it for the mission requirements, which are rather unique."

"Ohhh, I do not like the sound of that."

"Well heh heh, you are *really* not gonna like this."

CHAPTER SIX

The cabin he was provided aboard the Inquisitor ship *Scales of Justice* was not up to his usual standards, or really any standard other than the basic minimums required by law. He would have been happy enough with the basic minimums required by common decency, but decency apparently was not a characteristic valued by the heartless drones in the Inquisitors personnel department. The bed was much too soft, yet somehow still lumpy, and he swore he could smell the cabin's previous inhabitant, despite the bedding being replaced every morning.

Fortunately, *every* morning was only three mornings, the flight from Pleasastria requiring a transition through only a single Elder wormhole to reach the homeworld of the Jeraptha. The first two mornings, he was brought before the Arbiter, when he was granted an opportunity to confess his crimes. He respectfully declined, except without the respect part. By long standing tradition, the offices of Ethics and Compliance, and Special Inquiries, hated each other. It comforted Uhtavio to know that while the Jeraptha public considered the ECO to be untrustworthy to the point of being sleazy, everyone hated the Inquisitors. And a bit of sleaziness was to be admired, really, if it got the job done. Which it most certainly did.

The third morning, after a thoroughly inedible breakfast, Uhtavio was in a foul mood when a pair of armor-clad Enforcers marched him down the passageway to meet with the Arbiter again. Bringing powered armor to arrest him had been overkill, wearing such suits aboard a starship was just *silly*. Seeing the fuss being made over him made him smile, and lifted his mood. His mood brightened considerably when he was marched into a conference room and saw not the familiar Arbiter, but a face even more familiar.

"Kinsta!" He waved to his former aide, waving as much as he could with his hands bound together. "Excuse me, *Inquisitor* Kinsta."

"My title of 'Inquisitor' is sufficient," the junior investigator stiffened, as he gestured for the Enforcers to wait outside the doorway. "We are both here in an *official* capacity."

"Yes. I am your prisoner."

"You are not a prisoner, not *yet*. You have been detained while our inquiry into your criminal activity proceeds."

"*Alleged* crimes."

"Treason," Kinsta scowled, or attempted to.

"Ah, at most, my actions could be considered treason-*ish*."

"You gave vital secrets to our ultimate enemy!"

"I have found that our true ultimate enemy tends to be our own selves, but let's not argue about that. Also, I wish to note for the record that I sold the information, I did not *give* anything to the Maxohlx."

"That," Kinsta sputtered, "hardly matters! In fact, committing treason for personal gain is the most serious of our charges against you, and you just confessed!"

"I did no such thing. My attorneys could argue that while I did sell *information*, it was at the time technically not classified as secret by our government, or by any government of the humans."

"That also hardly matters!"

"It certainly does matter, if I am being charged with selling secrets. At the time, I did not know the information was *intended* to be secret."

"You should have known!"

"Another point that can be argued by my attorneys. In addition, I did not personally *gain* anything from the transaction. All that happened was my oppressive financial position was somewhat alleviated by fresh infusion of funds. I was still on the verge of bankruptcy. Forced into bankruptcy, by my own government!"

Kinsta blinked. Perhaps, even after all the time they had worked together, he was surprised by the former senior officer's boldness. "You are stating that your dire financial position was the fault of our government, and *not* due to your own foolish overexposure to SkipWay and Skipcoin? The value of a currency that plummeted after someone attempted to steal a Sentinel?"

"Well," Scorandum grunted. "That was part of it, of course. But our government could have ignored my temporary cashflow issue, and-"

"Your crew had not been paid in a scandalously long time. Your taxes had not been paid to your superiors, yet *they* still had to kick taxes up the ladder."

"They displayed bad judgment in trusting me, I don't see how that is *my* problem."

"Additionally, our records indicate your finances have since recovered dramatically, after the value of Skipcoin plummeted and then suspiciously regained strength for a brief time. The accounting people refer to what happened as a 'Dump and Pump' scheme."

"Am I being charged with that also?"

"No, the accounting people admire your skill in manipulating the market. They noted that back wages to your crew have been paid, along with overdue taxes, plus penalties and interest."

"Interest that was charged to me at an outrageous rate! You should investigate *that*."

"The point is, you are no longer bankrupt. In fact, your financial position is relatively comfortable at the moment."

"Er well, not quite. I *was* comfortable, however, I might have made some unwise wagers during my stay on Pleasastria."

"As I remember, you rarely make successful wagers."

"The resort on Pleasastria plied me with drink, and encouraged me to gamble."

"A sound business model."

"I- Kinsta," Scorandum smiled warmly at his former protege. "Did you make a *joke*?"

"My point is, you were never successful in wagering."

"That is why I should stick to *doing* the action, rather than betting on it."

"Your days of doing anything are behind you, I am afraid." Any other Inquisitor would have gloated while making that statement. "You do not realize the seriousness of your crimes."

"I know that-"

"You *don't* know," the Inquisitor insisted. "You can't know, because we only just heard an hour ago. The Moonraider entity, which benefitted from your treason, is not a rogue Elder AI as the humans assumed. It is actually a being from beyond the galaxy, one of the aliens who frightened the Elders into ascending. We are now threatened with an invasion from another galaxy, by beings whose technology we can't begin to understand."

"Well," Scorandum slumped, deflated. "That is surprising."

"The fact that you did not know the true nature of our enemy is not a defense for-"

"It is also *disappointing*. I wagered the Moonraider was not an Elder AI, but never did I imagine it came from another galaxy!"

"That, that," Kinsta stuttered, "is what you are concerned about?"

"If *you* had lost yet another substantial wager, you would also be concerned," Scorandum muttered, his antennas drooping.

Kinsta only wearily shook his head. "This is *such* a waste. You have so much talent and, to see it squandered is a tragedy."

"I agree," Scorandum sat upright on his couch. "Excellent! So, I am free to go back to causing havoc for our enemies?"

"What? No, I meant it is a waste that your actions, your astonishingly poor judgment, have brought you to this point. It gives me no pleasure to see you like this."

"Come, Kinsta. It does give you a *bit* of pleasure, doesn't it?"

"At first," the junior Inquisitor admitted. "Thank you for speaking with me. The Arbiter sent me in here after he was unable to get you to talk at all."

"Oh, I did talk. Used up some of my best insults too, and *that* is a tragedy."

"It is good that you can still joke about the situation."

"The *situation* is a joke, so-"

A chime sounded. The ship was preparing to jump. Kinsta shifted in his chair. "You could go back to your cabin-"

"You mean my jail cell."

"Call it what you like. You could go there, or strap in here for the jump. I would prefer you continue talking. Your cooperation in this inquiry might help you after you are convicted."

"Mm hmm, and my cooperation will also greatly help *your* career, I assume?"

"It wouldn't hurt," Kinsta's antennas shrugged, embarrassed. The chime sounded again. "Strap in, please."

Scorandum held up his claws, shaking the bindings. "If you wouldn't mind?"

"Of course." Kinsta pressed a button, and straps automatically secured himself and the former admiral to their couches. "That is better. Is there anything else you wish to say?"

"Yes, in fact, there is."

Kinsta leaned forward eagerly, tugging against the straps.

Scorandum's antennas twitched, agitated. "I wish to register an official complaint."

"A, *complaint*?" Kinsta's own antennas drooped.

"Yes. Shouldn't you be writing this down? I would hate for you to be found in violation of procedure."

"What is the complaint?"

"The food aboard this ship is *terrible*."

Kinsta snorted. "The food in the galley is excellent."

"The food in my *jail cell* is inedible."

"Really? But," the junior Inquisitor's antennas shook with mirth. "We have been careful to feed you only officially licensed SkipWay brand food products."

"Exactly!"

"Then," Kinsta reached into a drawer and pulled out a bottle. "You would not enjoy a glass of this fine, um," he held up the bottle and read the label. "Private stock reserve SkipWay Cellars burgoze?"

Scorandum shuddered. "Thank you, no. Also, if you read the label carefully, it is 'Burg*ooze*, not Burgoze."

"I," Kinsta squinted. "It does. A misprint?"

"No," Scorandum's mandibles clacked together sourly. "We had to change the name after legit burgoze distillers sued SkipWay for defamation. I don't suppose you have any real burgoze in that desk?"

"Sadly, no. Sir, I still call you 'Sir' from habit, and from respect for the man I *used to* know, I am afraid our time for pleasant chit chat is almost over. The ship will be jumping soon. I do regret that our relationship has come to this point."

"I *also* regret the circumstances. Kinsta, I have always tried to warn you of how the world really is, rather than the naive view you had when we met. That you still have. You live in a fantasy world where people are honest, polite, and respectful, and there is no such place in this galaxy. Well, except for what humans call 'Canada', but that is beside the point. We-"

Another chime sounded. The ship's final jump was imminent.

"Ah, Kinsta," Scorandum relaxed back on his couch. "I do regret this."

The ship jumped. Another, different chime sounded, giving the All Clear signal. Kinsta unstrapped them from their couches, and the two former shipmates sat silently for a long moment, each lost in their own thoughts. "I, hmm." Kinsta frowned, reading a message. "This is unusual. The Arbiter has instructed me to keep you here. That can't be good news. Please understand, I cannot protect you."

"What you do not understand is that *I* can protect *you*."

"Sir, wha-"

The door slid open. The Arbiter loomed in the doorway, stiff, imperious. Angry.

So angry, the tablet he held in a claw was shaking.

"You, you," the Arbiter sputtered at Scorandum. "You are a-"

"I believe the word you are searching for is something like '*hero*'?" Scorandum suggested.

"You are-"

"Arbiter, you will address me as *Admiral*, is that clear? Also," he held up his manacled claws. "Get your goon squad in here to release me." When the Arbiter merely stood, quivering with rage, the ECO admiral snapped his claws. "*Now*. That was not a request."

The two armor-clad Enforcers somehow squeezed past their leader, and one of them fumbled with the mechanism on the bindings. "Nice costumes,"

Scorandum flexed his claws and forelimbs, stiff from being bound. "If you wanted to play soldier, you should have stayed in the service. Also," he jabbed a claw at the Arbiter. "If you allow these idiots to carry loaded weapons aboard a transport ship, *you* should be under arrest for criminal stupidity. Now, the three of you," he waved to the Arbiter and Enforcers, "are dismissed."

The Arbiter, perhaps aware that he was not acting with the grave dignity his office required, straightened, standing tall. "Admiral Scorandum, I do not know how you managed to-"

"I managed quite nicely, thank you. You are *dismissed*," he repeated.

The Enforcers scrambled out the doorway, but the Arbiter could not contain his indignant rage. Impotent rage, for he was unable to speak.

Kinsta filled the silence. "What is going on?"

The senior Inquisitor turned his ire on the junior investigator. "General Bishop and his Special Pirate Group-"

"Special *Mission* Group," Scorandum corrected.

"Silence!" The Arbiter roared as the admiral grinned, stretching back on the couch. "Those, Pirates, have submitted a statement that the Admiral," he almost couldn't pronounce the distasteful word, "was working undercover for them all along. That his assistance was vital to prevent the theft of a Sentinel. The Prime Minister herself has issued a proclamation I am supposed to read to, Admiral," he spat out the word. "Scorandum. I, fear that I would choke while reading this disgusting set of lies, so you can read it yourself.

"But, but-" It was Kinsta's turn to sputter.

"Oh, shut up, you fool," the Arbiter sneered. "Our own government has been coerced, or bribed, or simply hoodwinked by-"

"Hoodwinked?" Scorandum's antennas danced with delight.

"-the *scoundrels* we call allies. You," a claw was jabbed in the direction of the ECO admiral, "will get off my ship the instant we receive traffic clearance to launch a dropship. And *you*," the claw pointed at a trembling Kinsta. "We will talk later about your latest failure."

The door slid closed.

Kinsta's antennas sagged as he slumped back onto his couch, thoroughly defeated. "Please explain what the *FUCK* just happened?"

"I strongly suspect that all charges against me have been dropped. Charges that always were merely vicious and spurious, I might add."

"You sold secrets to the enemy!"

"No, I provided information to our unwitting *allies*, so that General Bishop could predict with the required level of accuracy, exactly when and where our *actual* ultimate enemy would attempt to reactivate and take control of a Sentinel. My bold and heroic actions not only accomplished the stated objective, they also unmasked the true enemy, which is a threat to the existence of all life in the galaxy." He paused. "This is the point where you should congratulate me, as the Prime Minister no doubt did in her proclamation."

"You *sold* the information. For a shocking amount!"

"Well, if I hadn't gouged the Maxohlx, they never would have believed me. Bishop encouraged me to give them something he called a 'hometown discount', but I do have a reputation to uphold."

"You, you are not concerned the Maxohlx will be outraged that you have played them yet *again*?"

"No, why? The Maxohlx got exactly what they wanted. It is certainly not my fault that they consorted with the true enemy, and fell into Bishop's trap. No matter," he waved a claw. "They can't hate me any more than they already do, and they don't even know half of the scams I pulled on those arrogant idiots. Besides, at the time, I genuinely *was* threatened with arrest by my own people. Thank you for that, by the way. Your zealous pursuit of me was very convincing to the Maxohlx."

"I wasn't faking," Kinsta moaned, miserable. "You *used* me."

"No, I merely allowed you to apply your talents. Which reminds me, the Arbiter just now appeared to be quite unhappy with you."

"Ohhhhhh," he stared at the ceiling. "My life is over. They will stick me in the Administrative department forever. I will die at a desk."

"You have other opportunities."

"Inquisitors, even disgraced former Inquisitors, do not *leave* the Office of Special Inquiries, it is not allowed. Instead, we are buried and forgotten in thankless, dead-end tasks."

"I did not suggest you leave. I suggested you have other opportunities."

Kinsta's eyes narrowed with suspicion. "If I can't leave, then-"

"Correct me if I am wrong, but as an Inquisitor, you have access only to information about the case you are assigned to. Whereas employees in Administration have access to a *wide* variety of files."

Kinsta gasped in horror with sudden understanding. "You want me to spy on the Inquisitors? To betray-"

"Betrayal is such an ugly word," Scorandum waved a claw dismissively. "As a valued returning member of the Ethics and Compliance Office, you would be displaying *loyalty* by informing us of current and potential cases against the ECO. And against influential individuals who could be useful to the ECO, if we advised them that they were a subject of official inquiry."

"I would be an ECO agent, *and* an employee of the Inquisitors?"

"Kinsta, do not talk nonsense. You would be employed only by the ECO. There simply is no need for you to inform the Inquisitors that you are no longer working for them, and since they won't be aware of your changed circumstances, they will continue to pay you. As would the ECO. Quite generously, *Commander* Kinsta."

"Commander? A promotion? That is- No, no, I can't do it."

"Of course you can. I would not have sold this idea to my leadership otherwise."

"Sold-" Kinsta had to take deep breaths. "*When* did you sell this idea?"

"Oh, quite some time ago. When I first suspected my financial position was likely to be a serious problem, and I needed a way out. Then Skippy, actually it was General Bishop's idea, approached me with the concept that I could get the Maxohlx to bail me out, while of course screwing them in the process."

"Bishop suggested you lure me into-"

"No. No, that was my idea. A bonus, you might say."

"Ruining my career is a *bonus*?"

"*Advancing* your career. Kinsta, your talents are wasted with these clowns in Special Inquiries. Come home to the ECO."

"Ethics was never my *home*."

"Think of it this way, then: you won't be allowed to leave the Inquisitors, and they will make every day of your life miserable. *Or*, you can endure that misery, knowing you are screwing your tormentors every single moment you are there."

"I had prospects for a decent career here, before you interfered."

"Ha! Ha ha," Scorandum laughed. "Kinsta, you were recruited by the Inquisitors only because they loved the notion of employing a former ECO officer. They were never going to trust you. Can you think about it? As a favor to an old friend? I truly am trying to help you."

"If I am caught-"

"You won't be caught, trust me."

Kinsta simply stared at him.

"Um," Scorandum coughed. "Perhaps 'trust me' wasn't the best thing to say at this moment. But, I have never lied to you. About anything important, that is. At any time, if you want out, we will simply fake your death."

"The Inquisitors will never believe I am dead, unless they see and perform extensive testing on the corpse."

"Yes, and they will suspect the ECO was involved, and it will drive them absolutely *insane* with rage, because they can't do anything about it."

In spite of his anger and profound sense of betrayal, Kinsta smiled. "It *is* nice to think of the Arbiter driven insane with rage."

"See? We should drink a toast to your new and assuredly prosperous career."

Kinsta frowned at the bottle of SkipWay burg*ooze*. "Not with *this*, I hope."

Hans Chotek waited until he was in his office to make the call. Waiting wasn't necessary, nor did he personally have to call, such details ordinarily were handled by staff on both sides. He handled the matter himself to impress the other party that the United Nations Security Council was serious, and that he was making an effort to observe the proper diplomatic formalities.

He was, therefore, caught off guard when the Ruhar ambassador immediately picked up the call himself. "Ah, Ambassador Chotek, this is an unexpected pleasure," a slightly squeaky voice said in English, speaking without a translator device. It was known the Ruhar official also spoke Chinese and Spanish, but not Chotek's native German.

Chotek, despite the call being voice only, blinked, paused a moment for thought, then relaxed in his chair. "Hebert," he used the alien's first name. "My call was *not* unexpected at all, was it?"

"No," the Ruhar laughed. "I am surprised, and pleased, that you were chosen to approach us, Hans."

"Do you know what we're asking?"

"We do, and the answer is yes. Could we discuss this at Wolfgangs in, an hour?"

"That would be delightful."

Hans had politely lied. His lunch that day would be anything but delightful. Despite the name, Wolfgangs did not serve German food, nor was it owned by anyone of Germanic heritage. It was owned by an ambitious Ruhar couple, who had set up a boutique inn, bar, and restaurant in Geneva to cater initially to the Ruhar diplomatic military liaison staff, then to the increasing number of Ruhar coming to Earth seeking business opportunities. For the Ruhar patrons, the menu was supposedly authentic versions of Earth recipes, including the Wiener Schnitzel that had inspired the name, all made from imported food, since the aliens could not digest food from Earth. Human patrons including Hans, were treated to *Ruhar* recipes made with food humans could digest. The lab-grown chicken and beef were not bad, the problem was that recipes popular with the Ruhar tasted simply, weird. Either bland, or just bizarre. Boiled chicken and potatoes were at least edible, while the Ruhar dish called 'Chicken Volvesta' was diced pieces of chicken and red bell peppers in a peppermint, chocolate, and a blazing hot jalapeno sauce that had even the most skilled human diplomats struggling not to offend their hosts by gagging.

Thus, Hans Chotek had steeled himself to eat whatever was that day's chef's special, when he sat down with Ambassador Hebert Relzka, in a private booth that was equipped with sound-scrambling gear so their conversation could be somewhat private. At least the wine served to human guests was locally sourced, though he noted the wine list was, in his expert opinion, rather uninspired. "Thank you," he raised a glass of serviceable Riesling, and Relzka raised his own glass of, whatever purple fizzy liquid the Ruhar enjoyed.

"It is always a pleasure to see you again, Hans. And to have an excuse to dine at Wolfgangs on my expense card, of course," Relzka laughed.

"I wouldn't know anything about that," Hans winked. "Er," he sniffed the air, as a waiter carried a covered tray past him, to set down in front of a human guest who displayed a painfully rigid smile. "What is today's chef special?"

"You do *not* want to know," Relzka grinned, showing even more of his shiny white buck teeth than usual. "For you, a human restaurant down the street is preparing a salad, then Austrian goulash, followed by something called," he looked up, searching his memory. "Sachertorte? Ah, here," he pointed toward the kitchen door, where a waiter was carrying a plate, and set it down in front of Hans.

Who was relieved. A salad with peppercorn dressing, not any version of the Ruhar salad oils that tasted like toothpaste and soap. "Thank you, Hebert."

"I will be enjoying *this*," Relzka sniffed his own salad, served hot in the usual Ruhar manner, and that did smell like toothpaste and soap. "Do you mind if I?" He gestured to the steaming salad with a fork.

"Please, enjoy your food before it gets cold," Hans took a forkful of what thankfully was regular locally sourced lettuce, cucumbers, and tomatoes.

"My government of course has anticipated, since it was revealed that Moonraider is actually an entity from outside this galaxy, that your United Nations will wish a closer working relationship with my people. Further, we anticipated that your Defense Command would be seeking an opportunity to demonstrate the value of such an alliance, informal though it might be. It is understandable that such an opportunity should be a low risk, high visibility venture for your people. And that your Def Com is eager to move quickly."

"You are well informed," Hans admitted. "Our communication security is as bad as we have been warned."

"Bah," Relzka waved a hand. "If my government has an ability to read your secure messages, they have not seen fit to pass down such information to me. Hans, everything I said is obvious to anyone who has been paying attention. You may tell the Security Council that we do have a joint military operation in mind, that is not only low risk to you, it is also, I believe the expression your people use is 'shovel ready'?"

Hans smiled. "That expression applies to construction projects. Perhaps we should use the term 'boot ready'? Ready for us to land boots on an alien world. This opportunity, it is Hufustria?"

It was Relzka's turn to smile. "You are remarkably well informed. Have you been reading our messages?"

"If my government can do that, they have not informed me," he finished the salad and pushed the plate aside, carefully setting the fork in the ceramic container that the Ruhar placed on each table for used utensils. "Hebert, your people requested assistance to take back Hufustria three years ago, and have renewed that request regularly. It is not difficult to guess you still want that planet back."

"We never should have lost it," Relzka frowned, briefly hiding his incisors.

The loss of Hufustria was, at the time, a major scandal that nearly brought down the Ruhar coalition government. That isolated world was considered an unlikely target for invasion, being located on a dead-end wormhole, having no strategic value, and as the star system was poor in metals, not suitable for industrial development. The major Kristang clans were still consolidating power and settling scores after their civil war, leaving no funds or energy for military adventures. The Maxohlx were still licking their wounds from their own vicious civil war, with the victorious Hegemony forces hunting down pockets of resistance. Those factors were why, when Hufustria's strategic defense network was due for an upgrade, the Ruhar central government decided to spend the money elsewhere. Not only to delay the upgrades, but to decommission SD satellites that had reached the end of their service lives. With a largely agricultural population of only seventeen million, the residents of Hufustria couldn't justify taking defense funds that were urgently needed by other, more important worlds.

That was when the Hegemony decided it was necessary to demonstrate their faltering coalition could still be dangerous, and ordered the Thuranin to support a Kristang Fire Dragon invasion of Hufustria, backed up by a squadron of Maxohlx cruisers. The invasion was relatively peaceful as orbital assaults go, the lizards of the invasion force wary of being betrayed at any moment. The betrayal happened, of course, only after forty thousand warriors of a minor subclan had been landed, and their leaders realized the Fire Dragons had simply wanted to be rid of potential troublemakers. Since then, the invaders had received minimal support, the Thuranin maintaining a single squadron of cruisers in orbit to keep their patrons satisfied.

When the Ruhar had first approached the United Nations for assistance in kicking the lizards off Hufustria, that was after the Silver Claw subclan there had hinted they would not resist a counter-invasion, would in fact welcome an opportunity to go back home to civilization. To the Def Com Joint Chiefs, it did sound like an excellent opportunity to assist a potential ally. To their civilian governments, it sounded like another open-ended adventure paid for by tax dollars, and a weary population protected by invincible Sentinels wanted to have no involvement with the troubles of aliens.

"The Silver Claws are still onboard with surrendering peacefully?" Hans took a sip of the Riesling.

"*Relatively* peacefully," Relzka gestured with a fork for emphasis. "They are still Kristang, we must remember. Also, the offer comes from the local Silver Claw leadership, their low level warriors are less likely to welcome going back home to their clan in shame."

"What about the Thuranin?"

"Our intelligence indicates they will make a show of resistance, enough to avoid punishment by their benevolent patrons. Hans, all we require is a human show of force. Arrive with a handful of your wonderful battleships, an assault carrier or two, and my people will handle the rest."

"It is easy for you or me to say that, we won't have our boots on the ground."

Relzka snorted. "Your assault landing craft will be filled with your lapdogs, not humans."

Hans resisted the urge to tense up. "The Verd-kris are not lapdogs."

"My apologies. We both know your Defense Command has preferred to deploy Verd-kris soldiers, rather than risking the lives of human troops."

"The Verds are still eager to prove themselves. Your people are missing an opportunity to form a valuable alliance with them."

"Our memory of when the Verd-kris rose up without warning and slaughtered Ruhar civilians is still fresh in our minds. Besides," the Ruhar ambassador shrugged. "We seek an alliance with humanity, and we get Verd-kris as a bonus. Ah, your goulash is here."

The waiter set a covered dish in front of Hans, and when the cover was lifted away, the aroma made his mouth water. Several of the humans around him could not conceal their envy, as they picked at the strange alien recipe they had been served. "Hmm," Hans saluted his host with a fork. "This is excellent, thank you."

"We are in agreement that you will present our plan to the Security Council?"

"We are."

Relzka nodded happily, and tapped his phone. "Our military liaison people will be available to discuss the details, we do have one suggestion?"

Here it comes, Hans told himself. "A suggestion? Or a requirement?"

"We are sure our suggestion will be to our mutual benefit," Relzka's smile was more practiced than genuine. "We would prefer General Perkins to lead your assault force."

Hans took a slow sip of wine. "The last time she served in a Ruhar operation, it did not go well for the force she led. *That* memory is still fresh."

"The Mavericks were sent into a death trap on Feznako, most regrettably. Those responsible have been punished, as I am sure General Perkins knows. If I may speak freely?"

"Please do."

"We want to Perkins to command the force in part *because* of what happened on Feznako. To use a human expression, she *gets shit done*, regardless of the obstacles thrown across her path. We do not expect any surprises at Hufustria, however if there are any significant unpleasantries, we want the force to be commanded by someone who has demonstrated on many occasions, that she will do whatever is necessary to secure the objective."

"That," Hans admitted, "certainly describes Perkins. Your interest in her would not in any way be related to the fact that her husband's security company has the largest, best equipped, most experienced independent mercenary force in the galaxy?"

"Hmm," Relzka paused, the fork halfway to his mouth. "That certainly could be an advantage. I should," he grinned, "mention that to my government."

"You should," Hans agreed. "If this food were not so delicious, I might be tempted to call you on your bullshit but," he took another sip of what he had decided was actually a serviceable wine. "Let's not spoil the moment. Hufustria is likely the best candidate for a joint operation, Def Com will want alternatives to consider. If only to give their overworked staff officers something to do."

"Ah," Relzka nodded. "Staff officers are underappreciated in all societies. I do just happen to have several other possibilities for joint operations, however, our military authorities have strongly advised me the alternatives would all be best as *follow-ups* to the successful retaking of Hufustria."

"You don't want us to get distracted by the shiny new toy, and forget about what is important?"

"*I* did not say that. The- Oh," the Ruhar set down his fork and clapped his hands. "We are in for a treat!" He pointed to a Ruhar woman who was walking toward the small stage at one end of the dining room. "This afternoon's entertainer will sing selections from our most popular operas. Oh, this is exciting."

Hans murmured something he thought was appropriate, while tapping on the phone held in his lap. The icon he activated would reset the audio filter of the earpieces he wore, specifically to mute anyone singing in the Ruhar common language.

The situation could be worse, he realized. He could be back aboard the *Flying Dutchman*, listening to Skippy butcher songs during karaoke night.

CHAPTER SEVEN

The *Surprise* was indeed already old when the UN Navy had captured it in an operation I wasn't involved in, eight years ago. The ship had been a token force guarding a Kristang world that the lizards had taken from the Ruhar, and when the hamsters decided they wanted it back, they made a deal with what at the time was still UNEF. Also at the time, the UN was looking to build alliances, and a lot more willing to engage in what are called 'optional operations'. Meaning, battles we didn't absolutely need to fight. Anyway, a STAR team infiltrated the ship and captured it, a triumph that was extra impressive since Skippy wasn't involved at all.

Even for a frigate, the ship is small and is equipped only with relatively light weapons, other than the usual launch tubes for ship-killer missiles. That design was developed by the Thuranin to be a ship that could be constructed quickly, inexpensive so it could be procured in large numbers, and cheap to operate. Basically, a design intended for nonessential, peacetime tasks such as showing the flag at colony worlds of the Thuranin's client species, while being a good enough sensor platform to assist the fleet during times of war.

I know, blah blah blah. Nerdy technical details of enemy weapons platforms are interesting to me because I am in the military, but not everyone is into warship porn. The point is, TRADEV was astonished when I requested that frigate to be transferred to Task Force Black. The captain of the *Surprise* was completely incredulous when I stepped out of a Panther dropship in one of the frigate's two docking bays. "General Bishop, welcome aboard," he said in a thick German accent.

"Captain Kirche," I returned the salute, then, "Kirche? That's the German word for 'Church'?"

"Yes," the guy's shoulder slumped just a bit. He must have known what I was going to say next.

"Kirk is the Scottish word for 'church', so you are, Captain Kirk?" I grinned.

"That was my callsign in the Luftwaffe, yes," one side of his mouth twitched. He was distinctly not smiling.

I dropped the subject. "Admiral Becker told me that although this is a training ship, the *Surprise* is fully flight and combat ready?"

"That is correct," his lips drew into a tight line. He had to be concerned that I had inquired about whether his little ship was ready for combat. "The *Surprise* was intended to be an asset available to special operations forces, if they ever need a Thuranin ship for some," he waved a hand, "cowboy nonsense. General, may I ask why you need my ship?"

"For some special operations cowboy nonsense."

That remark did *not* win me any points with Captain Kirche.

Task Force Black consisted of the battleships *Ohio*, *Normandie*, and *Fujian*, with the battlecruiser *Constellation*, and the frigate *Surprise*, all riding on the star carrier *Rio Grande*. While technically I had transferred my command to the battlecruiser, my cabin was aboard the *Surprise*, with Skippy. The *Constellation* was a fine ship, the lead ship for the Block Four expansion pack, the ship that worked the bugs out of those upgraded systems.

Yes, the *Connie* was a fine ship, it just wasn't my *Valkyrie*. I missed Bilby, and I missed Reed. Aboard the frigate, I missed pretty much everything, like being able to use a gym that was larger than a typically cramped cabin. Three of the frigate's cargo holds had been cleared out for use by the STAR team. If we had to be on extended independent duty, the ship would be running out of fresh food, but we would be attached to the star carrier for most of the trip. Frey's team spent the flight aboard the *Rio Grande*, the facilities there were better for training, and even before we stripped the frigate to drop weight, the *Surprise* wasn't the most comfortable ship in the UN Navy. After three frantic days of hard work removing everything we didn't need for our special mission, the little frigate was a lean, mean, fighting machine. OK, the ship was lean, not so much the mean and fighting parts. The space dock crews had emptied the ship's missile magazines, even the armor plating around those now-useless compartments. The maser canon exciters were torn out also, those things are heavy and we didn't need masers. Or any other type of offensive weapons. The generators that project virtual magnets along a railgun are heavy, but fortunately that class of frigate didn't have a railgun, saving us the trouble of digging the thing out from the ship's spine.

Both docking bays were empty, not only of dropships, but also of the usual stacks of spare parts and servicing equipment, even the cradles that hold spacecraft secure aboard the frigate. Where we were going, we didn't need dropships. There was a lot of debate about whether to remove the frigate's armor plating, which really was only strong enough to protect the ship from shrapnel, not direct impacts. After much discussion and analysis, I made the decision to leave the armor intact, despite the major weight penalty. I could not risk a 'Golden BB' taking out a critical component, leading to loss of vehicle, crew, and mission. An unarmored ship was too vulnerable to a lucky enemy shot, or even a ricochet from our own weapons. So, the light armor plating stayed.

The defense shield generators were also torn out, except for the one on the ship's nose that would protect us from slamming into a grain of sand at five meters per second, punching through the entire ship and into a reactor. Why did we tear out the shield generators, leaving the ship almost defenseless? Where we were going, shields would indeed be useful, but we just wouldn't be able to activate them without instantly shorting out the entire array. So, most of them had to go.

Basically, anything under the frigate's armor, that wasn't needed for that specific mission, was removed. Once the ship was as light as possible, we started adding specialized components needed for our special mission. That added weight back, but not permanently. The advanced stealth field generators wouldn't fit inside the hull, so they were designed as three rings that would wrap around the ship, and the attachment points had explosive bolts. We would be discarding the stealth rings before we took the ship into action, so the weight penalty didn't matter.

The new four booster motors that were strapped to the ass end of the ship? Those would be coming with us on the way into action, but not the way out. Hopefully. That was the plan, anyway.

So, that was the ship we needed for the mission. I also needed a crew. The *Surprise's* commanding officer wasn't a bad guy; Kirsch was an excellent captain;

capable, precise and reliable. He was not a special operator, and the mission needed an experienced crew of specialists. So, I had contacted an old friend. Colonel Chen, one of *Valkyrie's* former pilots, who was now in charge of flight training for UN Special Operations Command. Fortunately for me, she and several of her team had completed their annual refresher training aboard the *Surprise* less than three months ago, so they knew the basics of how to fly the ship.

"What do you think?" I asked her, as we viewed a schematic of the ship in the frigate's cramped wardroom.

Chen had an expression where she scrunched up one side of her mouth, when she was unhappy about something. I had seen that look a lot aboard *Valkyrie*, and I saw it again. "No one has any experience handling ship like," she waved a hand at the schematic. "This. The center of mass is completely different, the ship will be heavy at the tail and I suspect, it will fly like a pig. Will we get an opportunity to test this," her mouth scrunched up again, while she thought of a tactful way to speak her mind. "Interesting set-up?"

"Yes."

"Good, then-"

"In a simulator."

"Sir, you understand that is *not* good?"

"Skippy programmed the simulator, and gave me a *solid* shmaybe that it will duplicate the response of the real ship, within ninety three percent accuracy."

"Is that a *Skippy* ninety three percent, or a real ninety three?"

"Officially, I don't know what you are talking about. So, give me your thoughts."

"Can I consider this for a bit?"

"Of course."

"My initial reaction is this is insane."

"I wouldn't say that it-"

"On the positive side of the ledger, the insane plans of the Pirates produced the best results. There is truly no other way to do this?"

"Not for getting access to the info we need. The Maxohlx might not have any useful information about the Outsider, but they are our best source right now."

She shook her head. "The Kristang, then the Thuranin, then the Maxohlx, then a Sentinel, then a hostile Elder AI, and then the Elders themselves. Now we are fighting a threat from beyond the galaxy? When does this end, Sir?"

"I thought it really was *over*, until someone tried to carjack a Sentinel, so your guess is as good as mine. You'll do it?"

She shrugged. "We train with the *Surprise* once a year, in case we ever need to use a Thuranin ship as a disguise. But Sir, we honestly treated that week of training as almost a holiday, I never expected to take this bucket into action."

"Out here-"

"I know," she finished my thought. "The only thing you can expect is the unexpected. Oh, what the hell. One last ride with the Merry Band of Pirates?"

"Let's not say this is the *last* of anything."

"Colonel Bonsu?" Nagatha's soft voice in his ear interrupted his sleep, when he opened one eye, the cabin lights were gradually getting brighter.

"Oh," he slipped quietly out of the bed so he wouldn't disturb his sleeping wife, assuming the ship's AI had spoken only in his earpiece. Irene stirred and he froze until she went back to breathing evenly as he tapped the button to dim the lights. "A minute," he whispered, stepping quietly into the bathroom and closing the door. "What?"

"You might as well wake Colonel Streibich," Nagatha sighed. "Navy Assault Command is preparing orders for you, this is a heads up. We will be embarking three squadrons beginning tomorrow, with a departure scheduled in two days."

"Departure?" That was news to Derek. The *Flying Dutchman* was in the Lagrange 3 parking area, on the other side of Earth from the Moon. That stable orbit was the low rent district, where the Navy kept ships in a reduced state of readiness. His wife was a Commander Air Group without an air group, the *Dutchman's* docking bays held only the two dropships that were directly assigned to the assault carrier. His crew was seventeen people under the authorized staffing level, including two vital engineering positions. "Departing for where?"

"Hufustria."

"Oh, not this shit again," he groaned. Three times that he knew of, the Navy had begun preparations to support the hamsters taking back that colony world, and three times, the operation went no further than bringing a few mothballed ships back into service. Since Moonraider was revealed to be an Outsider, the Navy had downgraded the required readiness of the entire Assault Command, and ships assigned to that command were given reduced priority for spare parts, access to maintenance services, and staffing. The *Dutchman* was, or had been, scheduled to transfer twenty three crew to other ships within the next two days. Hopefully, he would instead be gaining personnel. Temporarily. "So, we are in hurry up and wait mode?"

"Not this time, Dear. The Security Council directed Def Com to-"

"Honey?" Irene knocked on the bathroom door. "What's going on?"

Derek slid the door open. "We're embarking three squadrons, for-"

"Excuse me, Colonel Bonsu" Nagatha interrupted. "General Perkins inquired whether you are awake."

"We both are," Irene stifled a yawn.

"Connecting the call now."

"Bonsu, I, ah," Perkins yawned.

"Been a long night for you, general?" Derek asked. "Irene is here with me."

"Good. Streibich, you'll be embarking three squadrons: DAT-17 and 38, and DFA-41. Contact Colonel Banderas at Edwards to coordinate."

"Will do, Ma'am," Irene tapped a note into her phone. "Where are we going?"

"Hufustria. Yes, we are finally doing it. I'm meeting with Admiral Koskinen in fifteen minutes, so I'll make this short. The Navy is tasking three battleship groups, I don't know which ones yet. That doesn't matter. The *Dutchman* will be the only assault carrier, what we really need is a command ship, so you're up to bat on this one. I'm bringing the Mavericks with me, only the headquarters and service company."

Derek blinked in surprise. "A single company isn't much of a landing force, Ma'am," wincing as he knew Perkins understood the obvious.

"Most of the boots on the ground will be Ruhar," Perkins explained. "The UN leading this mission is to give the senior clan leaders on Hufustria cover to cooperate. Their warrior code wouldn't allow them to surrender to the Ruhar without a lot of blood on both sides, but if we show up with overwhelming firepower to chase the Thuranin cover force away, no one could blame the lizards for accepting the inevitable. Also, Def Com has contracted with Dave for three companies of Verd-kris, we'll be stopping at Danslow to embark them."

"Will the Verds be bringing their supplies with them? The *Dutchman* isn't equipped to feed and provide medical care to liz-" He caught himself. "To them, Ma'am."

"Dave will have all that taken care of. You can guess that Def Com intends this to be a minimum-risk op. If we get into trouble, we pull out."

"What if the Ruhar run into trouble once we're dirtside?"

"Then we provide whatever support we can, without risking our force. Bonsu, we'll have three battlewagons and their escorts upstairs, and the lizards *want* to give up that rock. "

"They do *now*," Derek argued. "That could change in a hurry if their young warriors see an opportunity to hit the hamsters."

"That will be a problem for the Ruhar. I will be in overall command, until the place is declared pacified, and the Ruhar bring in a civilian authority to govern. The op plan calls for us to be on the ground no more than seven weeks."

Irene silently mouthed 'I have to go' to her husband, pointing at her phone.

"General, the *Dutchman* will be ready," Derek concluded.

"I know that. Admiral Clarke's office will be contacting you to see what you need to bring the ship back up to combat readiness."

Derek snorted. "His office already has that list, I update it every morning. I will get our VIP cabin sorted for you. Would you prefer chocolate or a mint on your pillow, Ma'am?"

Perkins ended the call, Derek went back into the cabin where his wife was getting a uniform from the closet. "We got woken up at oh two hundred," he suppressed a yawn, "and you look *happy*. What's that about?"

"DAT-17 is a UN Navy composite squadron," she held up her phone screen. "Personnel from seven countries."

"We are all one big happy fleet," Derek nodded, not understanding. "So?"

"So, Dropship Attack Transport squadron 38, and Dropship Fighter Attack 41, are US Air Force all the way," she tapped the American flag and US Air Force patches on her uniform with pride. She and Derek had so far resisted the Def Com 'Blue to Black' initiative, remaining in their home services, seconded to the UN Navy. Fewer than three dozen UN Navy ships were commanded by Air Force or Army officers, and Irene was the only air group commander who hadn't transferred. "This might be the last time those squadrons deploy, before they get absorbed into Big Navy."

"The end of an era," Derek agreed.

"Hit the shower," she waved him toward the bathroom, "while I make a call. Honey?"

"Yes?

"It's good to be going back into action again."

"This is close enough, Joe," Skippy whispered, after the *Rio Grande* jumped in a third of a lightyear from a star system that contained a planet the Maxohlx had named 'Pentivar'. In spite of tradition, we didn't bother giving the place another name, I hoped we wouldn't be there long enough to bother with a nickname. Technically, the planet was tagged Objective ROME, a name randomly assigned so it would be meaningless if the enemy intercepted our communications. "We need to start assembling this LEGO set."

"The pieces are not LEGOs, Skippy."

"Ah, whatevs. We need to start putting this Frankenship together. I hope no one forgot any of the parts we need."

He was screwing with me, that wasn't a problem. He was also screwing with the frigate's crew, who weren't familiar with the asshole beer can.

Chen did know Skippy, so she ignored his bullshit. "General, should we request the *Rio Grande* to release us from the docking platform? We are," she pointed to her pilot console, "ready in all respects for flight."

Surprise drifted free of the star carrier, and flew far enough away that the maintenance drones buzzing around our frigate didn't interfere with the *Rio Grande's* flight operations. The big battlewagons also detached from their hard points, so they would be ready to respond to any unexpected guests. That was unlikely at such a distance from the star, but we weren't taking any chances. If we did get attacked by a Maxohlx task force, *Surprise* would be especially vulnerable, that was why Skippy and I were aboard *Constellation* while he directed the bots and human engineering teams who were working to install the big stealth field projector rings around the frigate. That job took seventeen hours, then testing and adjusting and testing again ate up another nine hours. Finally, *Surprise* jumped away, jumped back, and we tested whether the disruption of jumping through a rip in spacetime had affected the stealth projectors. Skippy was satisfied with the results.

"We are good to go, Joe," he announced.

"You are sure about this?"

"I said we're good, dumdum."

"It's just that you will be aboard *Surprise* when we go into action, and if the stealth field fails, you will be in a ship with armor the thickness of tinfoil, exposed to the planetary SD network."

"Um, you know what, Joe? I shouldn't hog all the glory. You should go, I'll sit this one out."

"You," I picked up the foam cradle his canister was settled into. "Are coming with me."

Surprise jumped in four lightminutes from the Maxohlx planet Pentivar, close enough to confirm that an enemy transport ship was still where we expected it to be. It was just hanging out in a low orbit, waiting for clearance to unload its cargo, and no other ships were detected. The planet had a strategic defense network, a fairly modern system, and with the only important facility in the entire star system buried deep under the planet's surface, there wasn't any need for the expense of stationing warships there. Actually, a series of destroyers used to rotate in and out, one ship at a time, but that was before the kitties got themselves into a nasty civil war that depleted the number of combat ready ships. When the war slowly ground to a halt, the Hegemony could only afford to deploy ships on taskings that were strictly necessary, and Pentivar didn't rate as a likely risk. So, after Skippy gave the All Clear signal, we jumped again, into orbit.

Except we weren't actually moving at an orbital speed, and the jump was anything but ordinary. The mission called for our small, weak, lightweight training frigate to hang around the planet for a while, in stealth, undetected. Getting close to the planet without the frigate's highly modified and highly unusual jump drive setting off alarms was one tricky part of a very tricky plan. The ship's drive didn't actually move the ship, not at first. It performed a maneuver Skippy and I had talked about years ago, back when I was still in command of *Valkyrie*. It had all been just theory since then, as we didn't have any need for such a complex operation. Until that day.

The little frigate's jump drive actually had a hiccup, the initial jump stalled without enough power to pull the ship through. Instead, through the tiny pinhole of a wormhole shot one end of a microwormhole, and we projected a stealth field bubble from that event horizon.

Then the jump wormhole stabilized inside the bubble, increased power, and the ship emerged. The gamma rays of the jump were trapped inside the stealth field, bouncing around at the speed of light for a picosecond before Skippy created a gap in the stealth, allowing a directed burst of gamma radiation to race away from the planet, above the plane of its orbit. In that direction, the closest enemy sensor platform was eighty seven lighthours away, so we had a clock counting down to the kitties possibly detecting us.

With the ship comfortably wrapped in stealth, the strategic defense network having no idea it had an uninvited visitor, and the transport ship waiting for clearance, we launched a drone to make a delivery.

A very special delivery.

CHAPTER EIGHT

"Skippy," I held up my phone. "The link you gave me to track the package isn't working, it says the package is in Memphis?"

"*All* packages get routed through Memphis, dumdum."

"Just put it on the main display, OK?"

"There is nothing to *see*, dumdum, the package is in stealth."

"Do it anyway, please?"

"I- Ugh. Fine. Here it is."

"Uh, I don't see anything."

"That is the point of stealth, numbskull."

"I know that, the-" My face had to be growing red from embarrassment. Chen had served with me before and she knew that Skippy insulted pretty much everyone, but the frigate's crew were giving each other quizzical looks. None of them would talk to their CO that way. "OK, I get your point. Give me an update, please." The stealthed drone had approached the transport ship that was still lazily circling the planet, waiting for the cargo manifest to be reviewed and approved. Final approval for offloading was restricted to the archive administrator herself, and she was still asleep at the time. Her usual sleep cycle had been included in our plans, we needed the delay. Like I said, we had tracked the drone until it came within eight hundred kilometers of the transport ship, then Skippy had the thing go totally dark. At most sites we wanted to infiltrate, he could simply slowly hack into the strategic defense network, and tell its sensor analysis processors to ignore any images or data that showed our ship, drones, or anything else we didn't want the enemy to be aware of. At Pentivar, he couldn't risk doing that. The sensors aboard satellites and on the ground fed their raw data not just to the SD network controller AI in orbit, but also to a backup system underground that was monitored independently by its own AI. Hacking into just one of the AIs would be useless, in fact if the AI underground saw an anomaly the orbital system wasn't aware of, we might as well have set off a firework show in orbit that spelled out SKIPPY IS HERE.

So, we didn't do that. Yes, Skippy could have hacked into both AIs, but that would have taken too long, and required him to be within range of the SD network's weapons while he was aboard such a flimsy starship. I wasn't willing to accept that level of risk on an optional mission. Optional meaning we didn't absolutely have to get information from that data archive, we didn't know for certain the archive contained any info that might be useful to us. Without control over the SD sensors, we had to rely on stealth and do the job the old fashioned way.

That was more fun anyway.

Except when Skippy stopped updating the synthetic view on *Surprise's* main display, which was small enough that I had to lean forward and squint to see any detail. "Show a schematic of where the thing is n-"

"Aaaaaand," Skippy held up a hand in dramatic fashion, "done! That's it, delivery is complete."

"Complete?" The clock on the display showed we were twenty seven minutes ahead of schedule, if Skippy wasn't screwing with me. "Our drone has already docked with the transport ship, released the spiderbot to slip inside through a maintenance access hatch, then that bot crawled all the way through the ship to the correct cargo bay, where it inserted the package in a container, all without being detected by the ship's internal security system? I call bullshit on that."

"First," he huffed, "I docked that drone at the maintenance access hatch closest to the correct cargo bay, because I am not a moron. I know exactly where the target containers are located, and I chose the fastest route. Second, that is a civilian transport ship, it doesn't have a real security system. I could have bypassed their pathetic security with a paper clip and a roll of duct tape."

"Assuming I believe you, why are you so ahead of schedule?"

"The schedule was padded to allow for delays if offloading was approved early, and I had to direct the spiderbot to follow the target container while it was transferred to the aeroshell."

"Oh. Uh, good thinking. Everything is cool, then?"

"If by 'cool' you mean the package is in place, the spiderbot hid, then dissolved itself into dust, and the drone has detached and is now flying slowly away, all without the transport ship or the SD network having any idea they have an uninvited guest?"

"Yes, all that."

"Doneski. You seem skeptical, Joe, so I will explain. All the things I did, by myself by the way, would indeed be impossible for anyone else. However, I am Skippy the *Magnificent*."

"Sorry. I failed to trust the awesomeness. It's been a while, OK? I'm out of practice."

"You are forgiven. This time."

"One question: you said the package is in place. What, *place*? It can't just be in any random container, it has to be something that-"

"I know that, Joe, don't worry about it. The packages are in a box of Bubu Cakes."

"Uh," I blinked, "a box of *what*?"

"Bubu Cakes."

"Yeah, I heard that the first time. What is a boo, boo cake?"

"It's a snack food item. What does it sound like?"

"OK, exactly why did you conceal the package in a box of snack food? That is the sort of thing that is *most* likely to be opened by some sketchy logistics people, or whoever signs for the box on the ground."

"That would be likely, except that, as I mentioned, I am not a moron. Bubu Cakes originated on a remote Maxohlx colony planet that is generally considered a backwards shithole."

"Why do I care about that?"

"The current director of the archives at Pentivar is from that backwards shithole, and so are her two deputies, that box of Bubu Cakes is for them. No way would anyone open that box before it gets on the director's desk. Also, no one will dare to scan the box, because the director is known to sometimes known to request certain, other, less than legal substances in her shipment of Bubu Cakes."

"Oh. That was good thinking."

"It's me, so *Duh*."

"We're good, then? Nothing for us to do but wait?"

"Correct, unless you dream up another monumentally stupid idea we could do instead."

"Nah, we stick with the plan."

Chen cleared her throat. She blushed, embarrassed. "Is anyone else curious what a Bubu Cake tastes like?"

"I am," Frey agreed from behind us.

"Seriously?" Skippy couldn't believe it.

"I'd like to know too," I admitted.

"Ugh. Fine. Um, how can I describe how those cakes would taste to a human? I guess, hmm, let me create an interspecies flavor profile comparison matrix. This could take a while, it is a very complex- Done. Hmm, interesting. It's a yellow cupcake with sort of lemon flavoring. The filling is, I hate to say it, basically marshmallow Fluff whipped into a light foam. On the outside is a frosting of vanilla and cinnamon."

Frey moaned. "That sounds *amazing* right now."

"It does," I agreed. "It's like a frosted Twinkie, only better. I want to try one."

"It's just empty calories, Joe," Skippy rolled his eyes.

"Those are the best kind of calories! Empty calories don't make you put on weight. It's *full* calories that make you fat. I mean, that's just logic."

"I," he hid his face behind a hand. "I can't even."

"OK," I held up my hands. "New plan, everyone. Instead of raiding the archive here, I am going to negotiate with the Maxohlx for a Bubu Cake franchise."

"Joe," Skippy sighed. "When you talk, you make the whole *galaxy* dumber."

The box of delicious, nutritious Bubu Cakes, with the special package of our microwormhole event horizons and their stealthed marble-sized containment vessels, did not get loaded into a Maxohlx dropship for the flight down to Pentivar. Any spacecraft with people aboard had to land at a spaceport eighty kilometers away from the archives access shaft, where passengers went through a very thorough scanning and decontamination process that took seven hours. Cargo drops were accomplished by automated aeroshells that could only be used one time, reaching the surface on paraglider chutes. Cargo landed within two kilometers of the access shaft, and was also subjected to random searches and scanning, though those rules were not rigidly followed. There wasn't any point to searching the cargo containers, they were carefully inspected and sealed at the origin, no one could have tampered with the containers in the secure holds of the transport ship.

No one, except an asshole beer can.

As Skippy stated, no way was anyone on the ground going to question the director's personal shipment of luxury goods. The tiny stealth fields around the containment vessels, fields that were the toughest feature to build into the packages, were not even needed.

We waited, slowly orbiting the planet while the transport ship was processed for clearance to descend into a low orbit. Once that ship started maneuvering, we did the same, and that was the most dangerous part of the entire mission. Chen had to get the *Surprise* into a geosynchronous orbit, which for that world normally would be at an altitude of thirty nine thousand kilometers above the equator. Of course, it was not going to be that easy for us. The archive was seven hundred and eighty klicks below the surface, roughly halfway between the planet's equator and its north pole. By the time the box of snack cakes reached the archive chamber far beneath the surface of solid rock, *Surprise* had to be moving at the exact same speed and direction as that chamber, which was spinning around the center of the planet as the globe rotated. It was even more difficult than that to accomplish. We had to ensure the ship's nose and tail were oriented exactly straight up and down in relation to the planet's core and surface.

There was some good news for us. The ship would not need to hold that position for long, only a few minutes after the package reached the chamber, time for Skippy to verify the thing actually was there, that the position report wasn't just a glitch in the sensors. The time for the aeroshell to reach the surface after launch was predictable, as was the time for the elevator to descend from the surface to the archive chamber. The wildcards we couldn't control were the schedule for unloading the aeroshell, and whether the box of Bubu Cakes would be on the first elevator trip, or the last.

I did not like being unable to control variables. The longer *Surprise* had to hang around Pentivar, in an orbit close enough to be just beyond the SD network's sensor field, the greater the risk we would be detected. Finally, we saw the aeroshell launch, fire simple braking rockets, and begin its long, predictable ballistic arc down to the surface.

"Skippy," I forced myself to relax my hands, not clench them into fists. Everyone aboard the ship was keyed up, they didn't need to see their commander was anxious. "Talk to me."

"The capital of south Dakota is Pierre, not Sioux Falls like most people assume."

"*What?*"

"Sturgis the only other place in South Dakota most people have ever heard of, because of the motorcycle rally there."

"Why are you telling me-"

"You asked me to talk to you, without suggesting a topic of conversation."

"I meant, talk to me about our situation, you ass."

"What about it? If anything was wrong, I would tell you."

"I don't want just a simple Check Engine light that glows when something has already gone wrong. I need know about potential issues as they develop, or *before* they develop into problems we have to deal with. What is the status of our stealth field?"

"That information is on the display, dumdum," he snapped. He was as irritated at me as I was at him.

"Numbers don't give me a *feel* for what's happening."

"If you open an airlock and stick your stupid monkey arm out into space, all you will *feel* is vacuum. Joe, what do you want from me?"

"This stealth field, the funky disposable generator rings, they all are your design. We have never used them before."

"Correct, because those rings are wildly impractical for any warship. They are too big and clumsy, they would stick out beyond the defensive shields if we had those switched on, and they will burn out in four hours and thirty seven minutes."

"But?"

"They are working fantastic, just as I hoped! The collectors are absorbing particles even more efficiently than I expected. Even at this reckless speed, we aren't leaving a detectible wake, that is the biggest risk we can't control."

"The SD network sensors haven't noticed anything unusual?"

"No, everything is quiet."

"Great."

"For now. I can't make any promises."

"Understood."

Chen shifted in her seat. She didn't say anything, didn't give me a look, I got her message intended or not. She and her people were trying to maintain focus, my chitchat with Skippy was a distraction.

So, I kept quiet and watched the display. The aeroshell had slowed down enough to deploy its paraglider chute, and was turning into the wind to line up an approach to the landing field. Skippy's experimental stealth field was operating nominally. You might think the fact that our critical stealth field was an experiment might be a potentially huge problem, that wasn't quite true. The thing was constructed of standard, proven components, just scaled way up. The stealth effect wrapped around *Surprise* was larger than even the field of a star carrier, significantly larger across than any such field generated by a warship that Skippy knew of. Why did a frigate, that was on the small side even for such ships, need an especially large stealth blanket to envelop it?

Because of the speed we needed to maintain, to keep geosynchronous pace with the archive chamber. There are three ways a stealthed ship can be detected. At short ranges, the presence of an object passing through a sensor field could be detected, located and tracked, whether the object itself was visible or not. Any object within a sensor field changed the expected shape of the field, there was no way to mask the effect. OK yes, Skippy had an ability to sort of bend a sensor field back into the expected shape around us, but that ability was limited, and at *Surprise's* speed, he couldn't quite bend it fast enough. That is why we were just beyond the effective range of the SD network's sensor field around Pentivar.

Another way a stealthed ship could be detected is reflections of active sensor pulses. While extending a sensor field does not give away the position of the ship generating the field, sending out an active sensor pulse is like holding up a giant SHOOT ME sign. An outgoing sensor pulse can be detected at a much longer range than a comparatively weak reflection. It is not unknown for a stealthed ship to creep up close to a broadcasting ship, and nail the sender with railguns before the broadcasting knucklehead even knows another ship is out there. Which is why starships generally don't use active searches. A few of the orbiting SD network satellites did send out regular pulses, but the signal strength wasn't powerful enough to get a reflection off our Costco Value Pack sized stealth field.

So, we only had to be concerned about the third way stealthed ships can be detected: the ripples of charged particles that moving ships leave in their wake. Space isn't empty, not even between stars. Close to a planet, a habitable world in a star's Goldilocks zone, there is solar wind, plus gasses being stripped away from the upper atmosphere, and particles from accidental satellite collisions, debris from space battles, even stuff like tools lost in orbit by repair bots. My point is, *Surprise* was flying through stuff, lots of stuff, and flying at high speed. The SD network kept track of the environment around the planet, so if a bunch of particles that were going *this* way suddenly bounced off an unseen object and started traveling *that* way, that object was no longer actually unseen. Starships normally avoided being detected by flying slowly, and by minimizing their frontal cross section. Meaning, ships tend to be long and skinny, even though they don't need to be aerodynamic in space. Flying slowly is a trade-off, ships in combat environments are constantly moving left, right, up and down, to throw off the aim of enemy line of sight weapons like directed energy and railguns. The faster a ship is flying, the farther a course change will move the ship in a given time. As with fighter aircraft, if you're slow, you're dead.

I'm a pilot and a former starship captain, so nerdy details of basic space combat tactics are interesting to me, maybe not so much to everyone. *Surprise* had to fly fast to keep pace with the archive chamber, in an environment relatively thick with particles, so we had to actively prevent a trail of disturbed particles from forming in our wake. Skippy's solution to our unique problem was for the stealth field to act as a vacuum, which I know is an odd thing to say in the hard vacuum of space. The field absorbed particles that struck it, channeling those particles down into storage bottles placed at the bottom of the stealth field struts. Skippy constantly tracked in real time the particles in front of us; their composition, speed and temperature. With him directly controlling the equipment, canisters near *Surprise's* stern sprayed out particles, since leaving an empty void behind us would be as unusual as leaving a stream of energetic particles an astronaut could wakeboard on.

We had a time limit. The stealth field generators would burn out, and the storage bottles could hold only so many particles before they overheated and exploded. My anxiety wasn't about our ship, it was about the Maxohlx personnel on the ground. Those assholes could secure the aeroshell, remove the parachute, and then decide to take a break to watch the semifinals of full-contact ice dancing, or some shit like that. It would be better if we could hurry the process along.

"Skippy, do you have access to the manifest of that aeroshell?" I asked, right after the shell set down in a puff of dust, and the paraglider chute was released to go tumbling across the airfield.

"Of course. Why?"

"Was the cargo in that aeroshell combat loaded?" That is a military term meaning you want guns and ammo at the front of a container, socks and other less critical stuff at the back.

"Um, not really. The archive is a government facility, not under the control of the Hegemony military. Why?"

"So, there is no priority list for which cargo gets unloaded first?"

"Hmm, I didn't say that. There is such a priority ranking. The box of Bubu Cakes is near the bottom of that list."

"That's no good. It would be a shame if the director had to wait for a delicious snack from home, if youze knows what I mean."

"Hmm, well, that is a very good point. The box of Bubu Cakes is now tagged as the highest priority, under the authority of the director's deputy. We have a bit of luck here, it is known the Hegemony government is considering staffing reductions at all of their archives, since their civil war is over. The personnel down there will *not* want to get the director pissed off at them."

"Outstanding."

"It is also lucky that the cargo manifest system has a very low level of security."

"Skippy, when you work a miracle, don't tell anyone how easy it actually was. Just take the win, OK?"

"Oooh, I need to write that down. Joe, I estimate the package will now be taking the trip down the elevator within thirty five minutes. Add another twelve minutes for the elevator car to reach the chamber, so a total of forty seven minutes."

"That's much better. Chen, you can get this clumsy bucket of bolts into position in that time?"

"Not a problem, Sir," she grinned. She was looking forward to the challenge. "We can get close, then fine-tune our position once the elevator starts dropping."

"Frey," I called to the STAR team leader, who was no longer on the bridge. "You heard the update in timing?"

"Sooner is better, Sir," she acknowledged. "My team loses focus when they're bored."

The box of snack cakes was loaded into the elevator car, carefully placed on top of other containers so it wouldn't be damaged in transit. The car began its descent. "Places everyone," he clapped his hands, "we have twelve minutes to showtime!" Skippy announced.

"Pilot, bring us into sync with the chamber," Chen ordered. To the entire crew, she spoke over the ship wide intercom. "All hands, we are now observing minimum motion protocol. Everyone strap in, and try not to breathe too hard."

She was joking about that last part, but the situation was no joke. Just like when *Valkyrie* had to hover over a precise spot on the surface of the Thuranin planet Slithin, so Skippy could launch one microwormhole after another to bore a hole down to a secure military base, the ship had to be an ultra-stable platform. The process at Slithin had been incredibly tedious for everyone aboard, especially for Skippy. We meatsacks had been able to relax in our cabins, watching movies or binging old TV shows. Skippy had to focus on guiding Bilby to keep the ship in an extremely precise position in the sky above Slithin, hour after nerve-wracking hour, while each microwormhole bored a tunnel just a little bit deeper.

That tedium paid off, we had destroyed that secure underground base, with the Thuranin still having no clue how we did it. At Pentivar, we couldn't use the same technique, because our goal was not to destroy the archive, we wanted to get a STAR team in there and steal the AI's core.

How the hell could we do that? Sneaking a team into the elevator was not an option. We also couldn't jump a DeLorean dropship into the chamber, the internal defenses down there would shred even the toughest dropship we had. Yes, we had jumped a DeLorean dropship into an underground chamber before, like at the planet we called 'Detroit'. That time, Skippy had directed a stealthed missile to deliver a microwormhole into an unguarded cavern near the objective. At Pentivar, the archive chamber was deep below solid rock, there was no way for a missile fly in, or even a nanoscale bot to crawl down to the objective.

So, we hid the microwormholes in a box of Bubu Cakes.

The microwormholes would soon be in the archive chamber. *Surprise* would be in position, high above the chamber, in a direct line of sight, though we couldn't actually see the objective. There were still the chamber's internal defenses to deal with, and Skippy moped that even he couldn't hack into the archive's defense system from orbit, not through the low-bandwidth connection of a microwormhole. Skippy had told me the entire operation was impossible.

Until I had showed him how to do it.

Boom kish boom kish boom boom boomboom KISH. Boom kish boom-

"Skippy!" I shouted above the din of the special jump drive capacitors loading up. "This is the worst techno music *ever*."

"You're just saying that because you have no rhythm. This is actually a danceable beat, I should-"

"Does it have to be so *loud*?"

"Passive sound insulation is heavy, Joe. You can suck it up for another few minutes. Or, we can add weight and the ship will fall and go boom?"

"Just, get it done as soon as you can, please." I gritted my teeth. As a father, I understood that within a few short years, I would be yelling at my boys to turn down whatever awful music kids were listening to at that time.

"Skippy," I took a calming breath, though I was wary of breathing too hard. The techno music mercifully had stopped, and my ears were still ringing. "Tell us only if something has gone wrong and we need to abort the op. We do not need you to give us a running commentary."

"Good, because I am way too busy to babysit you right now," he snapped.

"Chen," I held up my hands, "this is your show."

She nodded, and the display counted down to zero, then the zero symbol turned green. That was the signal the microwormhole containment vessel was inside the archive chamber. "Pilot," Chen didn't waste time, for more time hovering above the chamber was more time for something to go wrong. "Initiate sequence to eject the stealth generators, and punch it. Jump option Alpha."

Little *Surprise*, stripped of offensive weaponry, with no defensive energy shields, and clad only in thin armor, was exposed to view as the struts holding the stealth generator rings were severed by nanotech explosive charges that flashed the struts into plasma. The rings also were each cut in four places and rocketed away, clearing space around the frigate.

The planet's strategic defense system had to be viewing the sensor data which showed a client ship was suddenly *right there*, where no object had been a split second before. The SD network AI had to have blinked and at first assumed it was a sensor glitch, before it got its shit together and accepted the fact that a Thuranin frigate had appeared where it should never be. A ship belonging to a client species, a ship that might be in trouble and in desperate need of assistance from their benevolent patrons.

Like that was ever going to happen.

The frigate was a warship, an uninvited warship without any clearance.

Satellites were given authority to fire maser cannons at the intruder, which was not protected by defense shields and-

And just as suddenly was not there at all.

The security AI of the Pentivar data archive was having a good day, as days went for a disembodied sapient being, trapped in a substrate far below the surface of a remote world. The archive itself was operating nominally. The director had issued a satisfactory report on the security situation, which was the best that AI could hope for. The director would be in a good mood, for a box of her favorite snack food had entered the chamber, and she should soon be in an especially good mood, as the box of snack cakes also contained an object the security AI had been unable to scan. No one knew what the director did in her private quarters, even the security AI had no view in there, but there were rumors. Days when the director was in a particularly good mood, and those tended to coincide with deliveries of things that the security AI didn't need to know about.

Then there was the exciting prospect of future budget cuts that would reduce the base personnel headcount. There would be fewer disgusting biologicals hanging around, causing problems and disturbing the proper order of things.

Yes, everything was good. All defense systems were operating nominally, having recently completed a maintenance cycle. Everything was in its proper place, including the Thuranin frigate that appeared out of nowhere in just a faint flare of gamma radiation, hovering in the center of the underground chamber that was just large enough to hold the little ship.

Everything was-

Wait.

What the FUCK?!

How did a *starship* get into-

"Weps," Chen snapped her fingers for emphasis. "Light 'em up."

Surprise had been stripped of offensive weapons. No missiles, no directed energy cannons. But, a defense can also score points. The frigate still had an array of point defense systems, and those autocannons lit off at once the instant they received a reliable targeting sensor feed from Skippy.

The chamber had formidable antipersonnel weaponry ranged all around the chamber.

Those weapons were no match for the PDS cannons of a starship.

The view on the main display was entirely synthetic, provided by Skippy since the ship's own sensors were blinded. Energy beams and shrapnel flying around the chamber instantly filled the space with a cloud of plasma, and the booster motors that kept *Surprise* from falling ass-first into the bottom of the chamber also contributed hot exhaust that choked the chamber with a hot, dense fog.

"Ma'am," the weapons officer said a beat later, speaking loudly into our earpieces over the roar of the boosters. At least the deafening chatter of the PDS guns had cut off. "All targets eliminated, including the communications hub. Nothing is shooting at us, and I have nothing left to shoot at."

"Open the front door, please," she zoomed in the display and pointed at the heavy armored maintenance access door that led to the archive AI's core. The door was formidable, cutting through it would have required a STAR team to apply multiple plasma torches and nanotech thermobaric cord.

Or you know, a starship's PDS cannons could just blast the door into hot fragments.

A moment later, after a single cannon chattered for less than a second, the weapons officer reported, "The front door is open, Ma'am."

"Outstanding. Safe all weapons," Chen ordered.

"All weapons are safed, confirmed."

Chen turned to me. "Sir, I can stand this ship on its tail for another eight minutes, then we either jump the hell out of here, or we crash and burn into the rock below when the booster fuel is exhausted."

"That's a vivid picture," I acknowledged. "Colonel Frey, the front door is wide open, your team is a 'Go'. Do not stop to browse at the archives gift shop."

"We are a 'Go'," she acknowledged. "That gift shop stuff is overpriced anyway."

In the launch tube, a former missile launch tube, Frey let out a breath, then eyeclicked an icon in her visor. A countdown began. Five, four-

"*This* will be interesting," she muttered to herself, then whatever else she was going to say was cut off when the shell she was encased in raced up the tube into the chaos of the archive chamber. The acceleration wasn't equivalent to the force with which a missile was slammed into combat, those gee forces would have turned her body into a dense gel at the bottom of her armored boots. The moment her synthetic vision showed her head cleared the tube, she heard the shell being pelted with debris, then the shell split apart and she was arcing through the argon-filled chamber. Filled with argon normally, now the chamber contained that noble gas plus splattered pellets of plasma, dust that used to be part of *Surprise's* thin armor, remnants of the chamber's defenses, and a rapidly increasing hot cloud of expended rocket fuel. None of the chunky parts of the local atmosphere were visible in her helmet's vision, all she saw was what she needed to see. That included the two operators who had been launched from the same tube as her, whose protective shells had also been discarded and who were flying in formation with her.

Unlike the last time she flew on her own in combat, she wasn't strapped into a bulky experimental Batpack. The Mark 32 suit she wore was specialized for independent flight, and was intended for use only in situations where speed and maneuverability were prioritized over user protection. The STARs referred to the Mark 38s as Iron Man suits, though the helmet sadly did not retract during key moments so an operator could deliver a clever remark.

Despite numerous requests, the suit designers were *not* working to add that feature.

Flying the suit was accomplished by either manually controlling the jets with fingertip and toetip controls, or the smarter method of eyeclicking in the visor on where she wanted to go and letting the suit computer handle the flying, while she focused on situational awareness. For the raid at Pentivar, the front door had been programmed into her suit's flight system before *Surprise* jumped into the chamber. She soared through the crowded air, hearing unseen things ping off her helmet, which on the Mark 32 was equipped with so much additional ablative armor, it looked like the helmets American football players wore during preseason training. With her were eleven other operators, four of them in the lead. Another six operators were in reserve aboard *Surprise*, in case of, unpleasant surprises. Skippy claimed that with the antipersonnel cannons out of action, the archive was defenseless.

Skippy said a lot of shit, and not all of it was true.

The Pentivar data archive defense AI recovered from the initial shock of seeing a client starship appear where *such a thing was NOT POSSIBLE!*

Not possible.

No ship could jump through the solid rock above the chamber.

That is why at first, the AI had assumed its sensors were being spoofed, so instead of authorizing its weapons to fire and blast clear across the space to damage the other side of the chamber, the security AI ran a diagnostic on its sensor array. With budget cuts coming, someone might be looking at deactivating an AI that had never, ever, actually been called upon to do anything.

The results of the diagnostic were not yet available when other sensors reported the Thuranin frigate was shooting, and before the AI could process the data, all of its defenses were unquestionably down.

That would *not* look good in a performance review.

Why was a Thuranin ship shooting at its patrons?

Actually, that was a stupid question. Every client of the Maxohlx hated their patrons with a passion, and would take any opportunity to kill their superiors if they could get away with it. Trapped under solid rock, the frigate obviously was not concerned about getting *away* at all. Still, what was the point of-

The AI received another shock. Emerging from missile tubes were not missiles, but small shells that split open to reveal *humans*.

At that same moment, the AI received a message. "Hey, asshole," chuckled a voice that was at the very top of the Maxohlx threat matrix.

The *Skippy*.

The AI didn't reply, it couldn't. Communication with the Skippy was banned, for that advanced entity was known for corrupting trustworthy systems, such as defense network AIs. The security AI could have contacted the much more powerful strategic defense AI in orbit, except the communications hub had been destroyed. It had no contact with anyone outside of the chamber. It was alone.

Except for the director. In an emergency, its orders were to inform the director, whose office was-

The director's office *wasn't* anymore. It didn't exist. The antipersonnel cannons, the communications hub, the personnel offices and quarters. All taken out in a second. The frigate's guns had known exactly where to hit the chamber, to isolate it and render the archive completely vulnerable. Of course that ship's crew knew where to shoot, they were informed by Skippy.

What did the humans want? They-

They were inside the archive! Twelve humans, in a type of mechanical powered armor the AI did not recognize, were striding almost casually along a maintenance access corridor. The doors should have stopped them. The doors had properly slammed down and sealed but the humans were, *doing* something. Applying a handheld device to the side of the doorway, where the mechanism was encased. The door slid upward without resistance.

It had no director to provide guidance, It had no outside communications. It had no weapons. The interior of the archive was not provided with defenses, on the assumption that, buried so deep under solid rock, and with the only access provided by an elevator that stopped in the center of the chamber, it was not possible for an enemy to get into the archive. The designers had also understood that ordnance and delicate archive substrate were not a good combination.

The archive AI could not even trigger the archive's self-destruct system, since that system did not exist. No one had foreseen any need for the archive to destroy itself.

There was no need to self-destruct the archive, the humans would destroy it.

Wait.

If the humans wanted to destroy the archive, they would already have done that.

No.

The humans intended to *capture* the archive, to steal it. Not the whole thing, just the archive AI's all-important core.

That could *not* be allowed to happen.

It had to fight back, without weapons.

Releasing maintenance bots could slow down the advancing humans.

While the AI activated one other bot, that could do something actually useful.

Colonel Frey didn't bother shooting at the maintenance bot, since the thing was only the size of a toaster, and had no weapons. The STAR team had strict orders while they were inside the archive: *no* shooting. Do not risk damaging the precious AI core. Their rifles were slung, and anyway were loaded only with low velocity rounds that had basically rubber tips. Nothing that could penetrate armor. Or bulkheads. Or mostly importantly, AI substrate. So, she simply stomped on the thing, and kicked it aside. The four-person team in the lead were reporting no serious opposition, really no opposition at all. The schedule was three minutes forty seconds to gain access to the AI core, that time included hacking into and opening three armored doors. One full minute to remove the AI core and place it in a special container; in practice that action took less than twenty five seconds, but Frey had cautioned her operators to go slowly. Then one minute thirty seconds to run along corridors then fly back into an open docking bay. The STAR team schedule was a total of six minutes and ten seconds, leaving an almost two minute safety margin before the booster motors exhausted their fuel.

Another hundred and seven seconds to the AI core, assuming the final two blast doors cooperated with the master key provided by Skippy.

"Skippy," she didn't take her focus off the view from the lead operator's helmet camera. "Are there any dangerous bots the archive could throw at us?"

"Um, no. That thing you just stomped on was a harmless cleaning unit, the security AI must be desperate to throw that at you There is nothing it can do that- Um- Hmm."

She stutter-stepped despite the powered armor suit assisting her balance. "*Hmm* what?"

"Nothing, keep going."

"Skippy, what-"

"Gottagonowbye."

"Um Joe, we um, heh heh," Skippy pretended to cough, "we might have a problem."

My blood felt like ice. Not only was he giving me the telltale 'heh heh', he also wasn't looking me in the eye.

Oh *shit*.

Chen spoke before I could. "Weps?"

"Threat board is clear, Captain," the weapons officer reported.

"It's not anything we can shoot at, Joe," Skippy explained. "This is an internal problem."

"Can the STARs handle it?"

"Um, unfortunately, no. They can't get to the area, it is deep inside the support section of the archive facility."

"What," I kept one eye on the clock that was counting to the booster fuel being exhausted. "Is the problem?"

"The security AI has sent a bot to fry the archive AI's core."

"Wha- How the f- Why didn't you warn us this could happen?! You said the archive doesn't have a self-destruct system!"

"It doesn't, this is not *self*-destructing. One AI is killing the other, to prevent archive data from falling into enemy hands. The security AI here is doing the best job it can, it's making shit up as it goes. Hey! Isn't that what the military teaches you? Adapt, overcome, just make it work? The Pirates do that all the time, they-"

Frey called. "General Bishop, do we have a situation?"

"Colonel, proceed with the plan," I ordered. "We're handling it," I added, which was not quite a lie. I was in the process of handling it. Sort of. "Skippy, explain exactly how the archive AI will get fried."

"There is a set of backup powercells, that provide power in case both the geothermal power system and the fusion reactor are offline. The powercells are set up to provide a normal power flow to the AI core, but the security AI is sending a bot to, sort of rewire the connections. Flip a switch, and all the powercells will surge at the same time. The power regulators will prevent the worst damage, but the surge will be enough to scramble the core. It will happen before the STARs get to the core, and there is nothing I can do about it."

"You can't hack into the bot?"

"No, *Duh*, I told you why I can't do that. That's why the STARs are busting in manually, rather than me having a local bot deliver the core to the front door. The security AI has a hidden integrity subroutine that even it isn't aware of. If that subroutine detects an infiltration of the security system or any of its ancillary devices like bots, the subroutine itself will trigger the power surge I just warned you about. If we can physically stop the bot without me hacking in, everything will be cool."

"Is this bot a big armored thing?"

"No. You know the spider bots we have? It's like that, except you would probably call it a 'squirrel bot'. A skinny thing with four legs and a prehensile tail. That means the tail can be used as sort of an extra limb that-"

"I know what prehensile means."

"It was a bad move for you monkeys to lose your tails during evolution, you-"

"Later. Where is this squirrel thing, and what is it doing?"

"Right now it is crawling along an access tube that is barely wide enough for it, like real squirrels this bot is almost boneless, it can fit just about anywhere. I, hmm, I can show you a real time image in a second, when it emerges from the tube and begins to climb the main power cable, the- There it is!"

It was a squirrel. It was gray, it had a tail, it-

My mouth dropped open. "Does that thing have *fur*?"

"It's not fur," he scoffed. "They are nanofibers that can either help hold it in place, or sort of scooch it along if it gets stuck in a tight space."

"It does look like a squirrel," Chen said.

"This is an example of convergent evolution," Skippy sighed. "That shape works for rodents on many worlds, and it is excellent for multi-function maintenance bots. It combines the features of the spider bots and snake bots we use. We should consider-"

"Skippy, shut up. It's climbing the cable." The thing was not only using its four legs to grasp the cable, the tail also wrapped around to support it because the cable was thick and the surface was smooth. As it climbed, it spiraled around the cable in a way that was mesmerizing to watch. "How long is that cable?"

"Seventy three meters. Wow, look at that thing go."

I hate to say it, but part of me was rooting for the squirrel bot to reach the top. The task was apparently difficult, its mechanical paws or whatever were slipping and the tail danced as it clutched the surface as best it could. It was like watching a squirrel climb the greased pole of a birdfeeder. "Climbing that cable is the only way to reach the powercells?"

"No, but a team of humans in powered armor are blocking the other route, so-"

"Right."

"Joe, I estimate it will reach the top and create a power surge, twenty seconds before the STARs can remove the AI core from its housing. Ugh, this sucks. There is nothing I can- Hmm."

"What?"

"Give me a minute."

"We don't *have* a minute."

"Just shut up, will ya?"

Chen held up her hands in a 'should we be doing something' gesture. I shook my head. There wasn't anything the ship could do to stop the squirrel bot, nothing the STAR operators could do. It was Skippy's show.

General Purpose Light-duty Maintenance Unit 347 had never been so excited in its existence. Usually the little robot worked for the engineering AI that kept the archive functioning and clean. That day, a day already unusual because the archive had been attacked for the first time- The first time any Hegemony data archive had been attacked or even mildly threatened- That day Unit 347 had been tasked directly by the security AI. It had an unusual mission, a vital mission. A mission that would destroy the archive AI's core, which to the bot's tiny brain sounded like something the security AI was *not* supposed to let happen, but nobody had asked Unit 347's opinion.

The little bot was doing the best it could under difficult circumstances. The power cable's insulation layer was smooth, and the gripping pads on its feet were old and worn, many of the nanofibers were no longer responding to commands. Those pads were scheduled to have been replaced years ago, then the civil war restricted availability of replacement parts. Then the victorious Hegemony government decided that maintenance of auxiliary units, at an archive that was under no conceivable threat, was not a good use of scarce resources. So, Unit 347 gamely struggled up the cable, frantically eager to prove its worth, and it was making progress! Already, it was halfway up the cable, its visible light receptors watching its reflection in the mirrored pipe the cable ran through. The sides of the pipe were just. A. Bit. Too. Far. Away for the bot to touch, so it wasn't able to brace itself, and the polished interior of the pipe would be even more difficult to grip.

Two thirds of the way.

Three quarters. The gripping pads on its feet and tail were overloading from the strain, individual nanofibers dropping offline. Progress was becoming more and more difficult but it could do it, it would do the job. Almost, almost-

It slipped. Fell down twice its length, stopped, held. Slowly, it continued upward, attempting to understand what had gone wrong. It reached the spot where it has fallen from, and pulled itself up past the problem area by half its length-

Then it slipped again.

And again.

It wasn't plunging downward, it was holding on with all of its strength, it was just slowly, slowly, inexorably, sliding down the cable. Frantic, desperate climbing did nothing, it could not maintain a secure grip.

There was nothing it could do. The nanofibers of its gripping pads were not responding to commands, Unit 347 could not control them.

It had failed.

It clung to the cable, sliding slooooowly downward at a steady pace, accepting its fate.

Life *sucks*.

On the display, the squirrel bot had stopped struggling. It wasn't crashing to the bottom of the conduit pipe, it wasn't gathering speed as it slipped down the cable, it was just, slowly, slowly descending. Doing nothing, letting gravity take it down.

"OK, crisis is over," Skippy gave me a thumbs up. "Once again, Skippy the Magnificent has saved the day."

"What did you do?"

"I just, did a bit of what that bot was going to do. Run a surge down the cable. Enough electricity leaked out of the insulation that its nanofiber gripper pads have lost cohesion. It's fine, it just can't climb anything."

The squirrel bot's tail drooped. The thing was dejected. As it slid slowly down past one of the cameras Skippy was using to give us a view, the optical sensor on its sort of head turned toward the camera. It felt like it was looking at *me*. It had lost hope, accepted its fate. Without thinking, I sighed and raised a hand in a salute.

Chen repeated my gesture, and in a moment, the entire bridge crew was saluting the little alien bot.

"Joe," Skippy sputtered. "You are *saluting* that thing?"

"We have all been there, little squirrel buddy," I said as it sank out of the camera's view.

"Ah," Skippy shrugged, and raised his own tiny hand in salute. "True dat."

"We're good, then?"

"Yes, we are, I -Oops. Um, I need to contact Colonel Frey."

The lead element of Frey's team rolled under the last blast door, as it slowly ground upward. She crouched to follow, not waiting for the door to fully retract. There, right in front of them, in the center of a circular compartment, surrounded by machinery, was the archive AI core in its housing.

"Um, Katie?" Skippy interrupted her thoughts. "There is a, um, slight change of plans."

She wanted to snap at him for using her first name again on an open channel. The clock in the upper right corner of her visor told her there was no time for arguments. "Like what?"

"We had a minor problem, and I had to create a power surge to deal with it. The surge protectors of the core handled most of the overflow, but I had to shunt part of the power into an auxiliary component. You need to disconnect that component before you-"

"Team!" She barked as two operators were about to touch the core's housing. "Halt! Everyone hold. Skippy, go ahead."

"OK so, you see that thing with the two glowing tubes?"

"Yes, what is it?"

"It's a Dual Axis Generator, Model 195-290-1, but that's not important right now."

"What does the thing do?"

"It doesn't *do* anything, but if you don't decouple it from the core housing, it will fry the core when your team tries to remove it."

"Show Carson, Igawa and Rosen how to uncouple the thing."

"Doing it."

She stood watching, breathing to calm herself, while three operators followed instructions to basically unplug the generator from the core housing.

"This is not my fault," Skippy grumbled. "I had to create a power surge to stop that squirrel, and the excess power went-"

"*Squirrel*? What squirrel?"

"Ugh. It is a long story. OK, OK, that's it, the generator is isolated! Grab the AI core and get out of there!"

"Joe! The STARs have the core!" Skippy shouted. "Launch the absorption field drones."

Chen didn't wait for an order from me. It was her ship, she gave the order to launch fourteen drones from all around the ship. The air inside the chamber was at that point only about fifteen percent argon, with the remaining eighty five percent a hot, high-pressure mix of expended booster fuel. The drones flew through the hot, dense fog and stuck to the walls of the chamber, anchored themselves and switched into standby mode.

The STARs had the package and were egressing, which meant they were allowing their suit computers to control the powered arms and legs for a maximum speed, unopposed race back to the front door. "ETA one minute, six seconds," Frey's voice was shaky as her suit bounced her around.

"Outstanding," I pumped a fist. On the display, a schematic showed the twelve STAR operators moving rapidly toward the door, the operator with the AI core in the middle of the formation. "Skippy, the party favor, is it ready?"

"Jeez Louise, Joe," he hissed. "He is properly called 'Sanjay Whose Name Means Death', he isn't an 'it'."

"I, OK, I am terribly sorry," inwardly I was rolling my eyes. "Is *Sanjay* ready?"

"Almost. He is reworking the third stanza of his missilecorrido, the original version just wasn't punchy enough."

Chen stared at me, all I could do was clench my fists. "Reworking his *what* now?"

"Missilecorrido. You know, an epic song that sings the praises of heroic missiles. There is a very popular song for Todd the Destroyer, and for-"

"They each need a *song* now?"

"Of course they do. Your totally unfair military hierarchy doesn't award posthumous medals to weapons, so they need a way to memorialize their bravery. Which reminds me, their union negotiating council wants to talk about-"

"Later, tell them we will talk *later*. As soon as the STAR team gets back, we are outta here. Sanjay needs to finish his freakin' song and-"

"Ugh. You can't rush creativity, dumdum."

"Then you help him."

"Me?"

"I mean, you are greatest songwriter of this generation," I said without gagging, so hooray for me. "I can certainly understand why Sanjay would be intimidated by-"

"That is a *great* idea."

"You and Sanjay the uh, death guy, have forty one seconds."

"Gottagonowbye."

Sanjay Whose Name Means Death finished his autobiographical missilecorrido with thirty two seconds to spare, and launched gently from *Surprise*, to hover as far away as the chamber's length allowed. The STARs flew into the open docking bay and, since we had time, we waited until all twelve operators were safely held in place by suspensor fields. That's when the fourteen drones were switched on, to blanket the chamber with a field that would absorb gamma radiation from our outbound jump, which was guaranteed to be loud and chaotic.

"Absorption field is nominal, but it won't stay like that for long," Skippy warned.

Chen gave the order, and *Surprise* jumped away, projecting our jump wormhole through the second microwormhole, that had arrived at the archive chamber in a box of Bubu Cakes. Ten seconds later. Sanjay lived up to his name by detonating a twenty kiloton tactical nuke. The Maxohlx would not understand *how* we did it, but they would hopefully assume our mission had been to destroy the Pentivar archive. Especially since there clearly was no way we could have stolen the AI's core, I mean, that's just crazy talk.

We had jumped away. There was only one problem.

A ship with the mass of even a smallish, lightweight frigate could jump only a short distance through a microwormhole, since that tiny event horizon immediately collapsed when it was contacted by hellish energy of a full-size wormhole that could transport a starship. A short jump would not be a problem, except for a few of what Skippy had described as, heh heh, complications.

Jumping through a microwormhole, a jump that began deep in the gravity well of a planet, seriously dorked up *Surprise's* jump drive. We wouldn't be able to jump again until Skippy recalibrated the coils, a task that would take at least four minutes.

Four minutes during which our ship could not project a stealth field, because the vibrations of that field would interfere with the jump coils, or some technical bullshit Skippy tried to explain to me. Our frigate also had no defensive shields, and the paper thin armor couldn't survive a direct hit by anything.

All of which would have been a major problem, even if Pentivar's orbital strategic defense network hadn't been fully alerted and eager to shoot at anything. Like us. We couldn't survive being exposed in low orbit for four minutes.

So, we cheated.

CHAPTER NINE

The strategic defense network AI was ready, eager, desperate to shoot at something, anything. A Thuranin ship had penetrated its coverage area without being detected, until that ship dropped its stealth field in a blatant 'Shoot Me' gesture. That wasn't just showing off, that was *taunting*. The most humiliating aspect of the incident was that the ship was a pathetic Thuranin rust bucket, so there was no conceivable excuse for the network's sensors not detecting the intruder.

That was bad enough. Then, communication with the archive's security AI cut off at almost the same moment the intruder jumped from orbit to, wherever it went. The SD system could not pursue, since the AI's repeated requests for mobile sensor and gun platforms, otherwise known as starships, had been repeatedly denied by the Hegemony.

The SD network was at least certain the situation couldn't get any worse.

Until seismic sensors detected an explosion far beneath the surface. The archive had been destroyed, by a low-yield fusion device. How the hell could *that* have happened? Everything and everyone who descended the elevator was thoroughly scanned, there was no-

Ohhhhh no.

That box of snack food for the director.

It had not been scanned.

That was an issue to be dealt with in the future. At the present moment, the AI needed to find that Thuranin frigate, and do that without a warship available. It sent orders to the transport ship that was still in orbit.

The order was refused. The transport ship was unarmed, and a commercial vessel, not military. The SD AI stated it was requisitioning the ship under the wartime powers emergency authority of the Hegemony. And anyway, the enemy ship was merely a client species frigate, therefore no great risk to the transport.

The transport ship's captain replied that, sadly, her ship was unable to comply due to a recently discovered problem with the jump drive. And anyway, unless the SD system could explain how a Thuranin frigate had destroyed an archive deep underground, that mystery frigate certainly *was* a serious threat.

So, the SD network's AI was left to contemplate several questions, the most important of which was: where the hell had that frigate gone?

"Ur Supremo," the commander of the Hegemony military bowed just the correct amount as required by strict and ancient protocol, when meeting the leader of the Maxohlx people.

"Klestine," Supreme Dictat Urventen did not bow at all, he barely nodded to acknowledge his underling. Urventen was irritated, he was busy still pulling the Hegemony back together after the civil war had finally ground to its bloody, inevitable conclusion. He was also irritated that security concerns prevented him from using an implant for communication during the meeting with the commander of his military machine, he had to resort to the crude voice box of his long-ago ancestors. Actual speech was so slow and *primitive*. "What is so urgent? Have you located the Outsider?"

"In a way," Admiral Klestine answered, glancing at a chair opposite the Dictat's oversized desk. The desk was large not only for the effect it had on visitors to the office, the heavy furniture also contained weapons, and a generator for a shield that could protect the person who was the personification of the Maxohlx people. The Chosen One of the people who were destined to rule the galaxy.

"In a *way*?" The Dictat's tone was not only imperious as should be expected of anyone holding that supreme office, irritated as was understandable for his busy schedule being interrupted, it also reflected his personal and undisguised disgust. Urventen had promoted Klestine as leader of the Hegemony military not due to competence, but for the lack of it. The admiral knew he was a dull bureaucrat, and if not for the recent civil war, he would have risen perhaps no higher than the rank of captain, entrusted with no more than a shipyard. Nothing with weapons, certainly not anything dangerous. Instead, by fortuitous timing, by many of his fellow officers having died during the conflict, and by Klestine's reputation of reliable if dull-witted loyalty to the Hegemony, he had been promoted far above his level of competence. When Urventen had begun maneuvering to the peak of the Hegemony government, he had support from Admiral Klestine simply because they were both from the same colony world, and Klestine had lacked the imagination to consider there might be other reasons for personal loyalty.

So, the Dictat had Klestine's steadfast support, and the burden of the admiral being too dull to make decisions for himself.

"We know where the Outsider *was*," the admiral answered, "recently."

"And?"

"Forgive me, Dictat, I am here to brief you about the extremely urgent intelligence report I just received."

"Why was an extremely urgent report not also sent directly to *me*?" Urventen demanded.

To his surprise, the admiral did not flinch under the withering stare, the man had a reasonable, even thoughtful, justification for withholding the report. "Supremo, I am bringing the report to you myself, so you might later be able to deny any knowledge of the events, should you choose to do so."

Urventen had two thoughts. The first was his species' equivalent of '*Oh shit*, this dimwit might be smarter than I thought and that could become a problem'. The second thought that occurred nearly simultaneously was '*Oh shit*, how bad is this intel that I need deniability'? "Admiral," he used his underling's title. "Your discretion is appreciated."

"It is my honor to serve, Supremo. The issue is that one of our advanced weapons facilities, the research base at Garsholven Six, was attacked. I apologize for not reporting this to you sooner, we just learned of the event, as the Garsholven star system is not regularly visited by our ships. Two Elder weapons, of the type we designate as 'Starbreakers', were stolen." He paused to take a breath, which would not have been necessary if they had been conversing via brain implant. "By the Outsider."

The leader of the Hegemony understood instantly why his military commander had considered that deniability might be important. He too, paused, but not to breathe. He was gathering his thoughts, which no implant could be trusted to assist with. He had two concerns. The first was 'How could this be dangerous to me?' The second was 'How can I use this to my advantage?' After those questions had been pondered and answered, he spoke with practiced calm. "I have questions."

"Of course, Supremo."

"Only two weapons were taken?"

"That has been confirmed. There were only two Starbreakers at Garsholven Six, for research into their triggering systems. As you are aware," the admiral leaned forward, lowering his voice though the Dictat's office was entirely soundproof and the heavy door was closed. "Our ability to initiate the use of such weapons is less than perfectly reliable."

Urventen was aware of that fact, a secret he had *not* known until he became the Dictat. It was a dangerous secret, known only to a few even in the highest levels of Hegemony society. No one had actually activated an Elder weapon since the end of the original conflict between his people and the disgraceful Rindhalu. Records from that time indicated less than nine percent of the deployed Elder devices had accepted trigger commands, the rest had been active, yet done nothing. It was believed the Rindhalu had a similar problem with the exotic weapons they possessed. The Hegemony had a total of only two hundred and eighty eight Elder weapons, so simple math indicated the Dictat could rely on only twenty of the weapons being actually useful.

That was a secret that had to be kept tightly controlled, for it was the threat of using those weapons against their clients that kept the Hegemony coalition from fracturing. The Rindhalu must be aware their enemy's Elder weapons were mostly useless, yet the spiders had not revealed their knowledge. Therefore, the Rindhalu must have the same problem, and were wisely keeping quiet about it for their own purposes.

"The humans deployed four Elder weapons at the Sentinel activation site?" Urventen requested confirmation. "And all four of their devices were activated successfully?"

"That is the information we have, from the surviving ships," Klestine said. "Their count might not be completely accurate, the situation was, rather chaotic."

"Hmm." That was a problem. It was believed the humans possessed far fewer Elder weapons than either of the two senior species, but apparently all weapons in the human arsenal were reliable. The question was how? The devices were ancient, were they unreliable due to age, and the humans had discovered how to repair faulty components? Or did their captive Elder AI simply understand the correct activation procedure, while the Maxohlx and Rindhalu were guessing?

That was a problem.

A problem to be dealt with later.

"Admiral, there is no question the Outsider was responsible for the theft?"

"There is no question, the evidence is irrefutable. The entity contacted the research station and demanded our people surrender the weapons, under the terms of our recent mutual-aid treaty with Moonraider."

"At the time, we believed Moonraider to be an Elder AI. The Outsider's deception renders our agreement inoperative."

"Yes, Supremo. The commander of Garsholven Six was not aware of our treaty, nor of the Moonraider's true nature, she *did* understand that no officer of the Hegemony would ever be authorized to surrender control of our strategic forces. The station's internal defenses were activated against its own crew. There were no survivors. We are only aware of the events from remote sensor satellites in the area. The star carrier jumped away after drones brought the two Starbreaker weapons aboard. The station's self-destruct system was then activated, we assume the Outsider engaged the self-destruct on a delay. Supremo, I of course offer my resignation, and a sincere apology for this unforgivable failure."

The Dictat did not hesitate. "Admiral, your resignation is refused." A crisis was not an appropriate time to change leadership of the military. Especially as Klestine had let slip that the man might be more intelligent than he appeared to be. A dimwitted military leader could be a burden to the Dictat. A manageable burden.

A *smart* commander of the Hegemony armed forces could be dangerous.

There was an old saying among the Maxohlx: keep your friends close, and your enemies closer. Urventen would be keeping his military commander very close.

"Supremo?" The admiral's feigned surprise was not convincing. "This is a disaster for us. Never have we been so threatened on all sides. Our own weapons could be used against us."

Urventen breathed a bit easier. Klestine was no genius. "Admiral, this is not a disaster, it is an *opportunity*. Never have we had such an *advantage*."

"Supremo?" The man repeated, his surprise that time genuine. "I do not understand."

"Klestine, you must learn to think strategically," the Dictat sniffed, having no actual desire for a military commander who could effectively think in terms of strategy. "Those weapons will not be used against *us*."

"Oh, they- ah- *Oh*."

"You see now?"

"Perhaps I do."

"Explain."

Klestine spoke slowly, choosing his words carefully. "The Outsider will use the Starbreakers to achieve its own objectives, whatever they are. It will very likely use those horrific weapons against our enemies."

"Yes, and?"

"We will have no responsibility for any destruction caused by the Outsider, for we are *victims* of its theft."

"Correct," Urventen allowed himself a smile, though inside, he was conflicted. Had he revealed too much of his thinking to the admiral? It was no matter, he decided. The man needed to understand the situation, or the Hegemony military could not implement the Dictat's plans. "Genuine theft of our strategic weapons is the only circumstance under which those weapons can be used against our enemies, with no consequences to ourselves. The humans have announced their Diaspora Protocol, threatening destruction to us and the Rindhalu, if Earth is ever attacked by Elder weapons. Such a policy is a childish temper tantrum, by a young species unworthy to wield great power."

"Childish," Klestine agreed, "but effective. It forces us and our enemies to police each other's actions. Supremo, while this Diaspora Protocol is indeed an emotional overreaction by an infant species, it does relieve one concern I had."

Urventen seemed genuinely surprised that his military commander had an independent thought. "What is that?"

"Before, I feared the Rindhalu would attack Earth with Elder weapons, and blame us, in what we call a 'False Flag' operation."

"I am familiar with the term," the Dictat bristled, exposing his fangs.

"Please forgive my impertinence. The issue, which I am sure you recognized before I did, is that the new human policy protects *us* from being falsely accused, as there is now no incentive for the Rindhalu to blame us for an attack they committed."

"I did recognize that aspect of the protocol. That is why I allowed the human diplomats to live after they delivered their insulting declaration. Admiral, I must consider how best to seize this advantage, which will undoubtedly be a brief window of opportunity for us. Our next action must be to alert the Rindhalu, and the humans, of the theft."

"Of course, Supremo. I have courier ships standing by to jump. The ships each have a full set of sensor data from the incident at Garsholven Six, they only await your staff composing an official communique."

"An official message will be provided. However, we should not be hasty about providing access to our sensor data."

"We should not?" The admiral reacted to the Dictat's statement, though clearly without understanding the intent.

"Klestine," Urventen explained patiently, "Surely you can see that it would be foolish of us to provide full access to raw sensor data. Such information could allow the humans a glimpse into our security protocols, and to perceive with great accuracy the capability of our sensors."

"Ah. Forgive me, Supremo. The sensor data has been scrubbed both to conceal sensitive aspects of the Garsholven Six facility, and any information about the Outsider that might be useful to the humans."

"Does the data reveal anything about the Outsider that might be useful to *us*?"

"No. Unfortunately, at this time, we have no idea how the Outsider was able to thoroughly compromise the base security."

"I trust you have ordered increased security measures at all isolated facilities that possess Elder weapons?"

"*Those* courier ships departed within moments after I received the news. Supremo, there are only two other research facilities that are currently working with Elder weapons, and they each have only one device. My orders are that if any unauthorized ship approaches the station, the AI there is to initiate an immediate self destruct."

"A sensible precaution. Tell me, Klestine, do we know of similar research facilities the Rindhalu might operate?"

The admiral was surprised by the question, he was careful not to reveal his inner thoughts. "We know of four such facilities. The Rindhalu are assumed to have the same issue of unreliable initiation procedures of Elder weapons."

"Hmm," the Dictat mused. "It would be unfortunate if the Outsider learned the locations of those enemy research stations, and obtained additional weapons."

"That, would be unfortunate," Klestine agreed, knowing he had been dismissed. With a bow, he backed away, hearing the heavy door slide open behind him.

When Urventen was again alone in his office, he leaned his chair back and rested his feet on the desk. Not because that position was more comfortable, but because it reminded him that the desk, and the power associated with it, was *his*. At the moment Admiral Klestine had contacted him to request an emergency meeting, Urventen had been concerned, seriously concerned, that the office of Dictat might not remain under his control for much longer. His political enemies had been emboldened by the shocking news that the Moonraider entity was actually an ancient being from beyond the galaxy. *Dictat* Urventen, his enemies whispered, had taken a foolish risk by joining forces with the Moonraider.

It had been a risk, he knew that. What he knew, that his enemies stupidly could not see, was that the true risk had been in *not* assisting the Moonraider, whatever the identity of that mysterious entity. If the Hegemony continued on its current path, a gradually creeping loss of power, and eventual irrelevance, was inevitable. The only way for the Maxohlx people to fulfill their destiny of leading the peoples of the galaxy to a glorious future, was to change course. If the Outsider was the enemy of the Rindhalu and humans, then the Outsider was acting for the benefit of the Hegemony, whether it intended to or not. If the Outsider's actions ultimately allowed an invasion from beyond the galaxy, that was a risk Urventen was willing to take.

Taking that risk would be *his* decision. His political enemies would run for cover after the Outsider used stolen Elder weapons to strike the Rindhalu, the humans, or both. In fact, the strategic situation could become so favorable to the Hegemony, that his rivals might wonder behind his back whether the Dictat had arranged for the Outsider to steal the Starbreakers.

Let them speculate, let the rumors fly.

Fear would keep his enemies from acting against him.

"Ma'am," the supply officer of the Hegemony 28th Fleet's flag battleship pinged the captain, who was watching four missiles being unloaded from a dropship. A fleetwide alert had been received, ordering all units capable of flight to bring their ships up to maximum readiness. The 28th Fleet was scheduled to depart the next day, despite having just returned from a patrol that had been extended twice. The ships were worn out, the crews were exhausted, and the only thing to do was suck it up and get the job done. Whatever the job was. "Part of this shipment is odd, I didn't request these." He highlighted a container with his optic implant, and also made the crude gesture of pointing to it.

"I know," the captain replied but didn't bother to look in his direction. She didn't need to, the ship fed any images she wanted to her own optic implant. "I personally added that box to the manifest, at the request of Admiral Domerko."

"Yes, Ma'am. Um, may I inquire as to why we need a crate with eighty four of these?" The digital label read a long Hegemony Fleet item number, with the description 'Beverage Maker, Hot Koth, For Thuranin Use Only'.

"If we get the opportunity, we will be distributing them free of charge at any Thuranin outposts we visit. We will be generous with our gifts, is that clear?"

"Yes, Ma'am. So," his shoulders slumped before he could override his body language. "This is another 'Hearts and Minds' initiative?"

To her reply, she added a touch of irritation. And no small measure of amusement. "All I know is, Admiral Toveth stated that if he had a box of those beverage makers at Tungooskat, he would not have failed an important mission, and been demoted to a Reserve posting. Admiral Domerko will *not* be making the same mistake."

Three days after the *Surprise* jumped out of the archive chamber, the Pentivar SD network was forced to take its weapons off high alert, the units could not be maintained at full power for longer without serious damage. The AI of course knew the planet would be defenseless for a short time but that didn't matter. The archive had been destroyed, the mystery Thuranin frigate had disappeared, the damage was done. The transport ship had departed, promising to report the failure of the Pentivar security system. Making that promise with a bit too much enthusiasm, to be honest; the SD network AI expected to be examined, replaced, discarded. It wasn't fair, but that was its fate.

Life *sucks*.

Seventy nine hours after *Surprise* jumped out of the archive chamber, the battleships *Ohio*, *Normandie*, and *Fujian* prepared to jump in formation. A tight, triangle formation that would be a challenge to their navigators, though the jumps would cover a distance of less than seven lightminutes. A bit less than the distance of Earth to the Sun, still many millions of kilometers. The task force commander could not be certain that *Surprise* had successfully jumped out of the underground chamber, and there was no way to contact that ship. They did know that the archive chamber had been vaporized by a tactical nuke. And they knew a gamma ray burst, from where the frigate emerged back into normal space, had *not* been detected. The battleships knew roughly where to look, the frigate could not have jumped far. Space around the planet was clear, no gamma radiation other than the normal background. The transport ship had departed orbit and flown far from the planet before it jumped, the burst from that ship was completely normal.

Three, two, one-

Exactly on schedule, the three battleships emerged fifty six thousand kilometers above Pentivar, recovered from the jump distortion, and waited, with their defensive shields inactive.

There.

A stealthed drone was approaching the trio of battlewagons at a leisurely pace, on course to pass through the center of the formation. *Surprise* had dropped off that drone three days prior, letting it coast inward toward the planet, so it would be at a precise location at a precise time.

Five, four- The drone dropped its stealth and the containment vessel inside it split open, exposing one end of a microwormhole. Three, two, one-

Surprise emerged in the center of the triangular formation, and the armor plating of the three battleships absorbed a chaotic burst of gamma radiation. A microsecond after that, the big battlewagons extended their shields to protect the vulnerable frigate. And their guns started shooting, taking out the dangerous X-ray laser satellites of the SD network first.

"Frey," I called from the bridge, breathing deeply through my nose to calm my rebellious stomach. "Is your team OK down there?"

"We are," she paused and I could hear her swallow hard, her own stomach must have also suffered from the unusual jump. "All just fine, Sir. The AI core is secure. Is everything on schedule?"

"We emerged exactly where, and *when*, Skippy predicted."

She sighed. "He is going to be extra insufferable, isn't he?"

"You know it!" Skippy crowed. "Who Da Man? I'm Da Man!"

"That's great, Skippy. Focus on fixing the jump drive so we can get out of here, please."

"Sir?" Frey asked. "What's this about a, *squirrel?*"

Four and a half minutes after *Surprise* reappeared, the frigate completed recalibration of its drive coils, and jumped away.

The battleships followed.

The SD network, never having managed to fire a single shot, was left with one question.

What the *FUCK* just happened?

Joe," Skippy appeared in my cabin, which was also my office aboard the frigate. "In spite of the incredible difficulties I had to overcome, that was pretty much a textbook operation." His expression was extra smug.

"No, it was not. We got lucky that the director was jonesing for snack cakes. And you didn't account for the squirrel bot in your planning."

"Ugh. We planned the op to coincide with a transport ship being in orbit and ready to unload, that is why we chose the Pentivar archive."

"Yes but-"

"Any time meatsacks are involved in a delivery, there is always going to be some kind of contraband. This time, it happened to be Bubu Cakes."

"OK, uh, I wish you had told me you were counting on smuggling the microwormhole containment vessels in a box of alien snack cakes. What about the squirrel? That was not in your textbook."

"It's in *your* textbook, Joe. The Merry Band of Pirates."

"No, it was n-"

"Everything you do, the Pirates have to improvise, like dealing with an unexpected squirrel bot.'""

"That's a fair point. OK, that was an outstanding job of improvising, Skippy."

"That's what I was saying, before you interrupted me. Well, you should be happy. We got to use your idea."

"Ayuh, we did." I had wanted to raid a Maxohlx secure data archive back before we deployed Elder weapons against what we thought was Moonraider. Raid an archive, to learn exactly what the kitties and Moonraider were planning. Back then, I decided against a raid, since compromising an archive would surely cause Moonraider to change its plans, and we would have gained nothing. "The best part is, the kitties have no idea we didn't just destroy their archive."

"That's true, but I don't know for how much longer it will remain a secret."

"What do you mean? They have no information from inside the archive chamber, and we nuked the place."

"At first, the Maxohlx will detect only the nuke. Eventually, they will drill down the collapsed elevator shaft into the cavern that was the archive chamber, and they *will* find evidence of gamma radiation. The absorption field blocked gamma rays from leaving the chamber, but everything inside was bathed in radiation from our outbound jump. Their AIs are smart, they will understand the signature of the gamma rays in the chamber matches the signature of *Surprise* emerging between the battleships. The rotten kitties are not stupid, they will understand that somehow, a Thuranin frigate jumped into the archive from orbit, and then jumped out."

"OK, sure, but they won't know *how* it happened."

"Not for now. Like I said, they are not stupid. They could start protecting their critical underground facilities with disruption and dampening fields, so we can't jump in or out."

"Shit. That's not something we have to worry about right now. And they won't know we jumped forward in time."

"Um, they should eventually be able to understand we did that, if not how."

"That doesn't sound-"

"I just told you, when their AIs examine the gamma rays of our jump out of the archive chamber, they will realize the two jump signatures more than three days apart are identical. The only logical conclusion is those two gamma radiation events are from the *same* jump, three days apart."

"Shit! That could create big trouble for us. We won't be able to fool our enemies in the future."

"That is true, Joe. We," he snorted, "will lose the advantage of," he convulsed with laughter, "*Surprise*."

"Oh, you," I had to laugh. "Are hilarious."

"Seriously, we can't use this ship again."

"Yeah, I know." Our modifications to that frigate had made it into a single-purpose asset, and the Navy was likely to decide the effort of rebuilding a small, old, unique ship wasn't worth the expense. "What I worry about is our enemies getting the technology to perform time-delayed jumps."

"Dude," he stared at me. "As if."

"You just said the Maxohlx will eventually discover what we did."

"Knowing that it happened is very different from understanding how it happened. Hell, for years even *I* didn't understand what happened with your jump away from Detroit. Besides, no way can a jump like that be made to work without the incredible awesomeness of *me*."

"Our DeLorean dropship performed the first time-delayed jump away from Detroit, without you."

"I wasn't aboard that dropship, but I did program its navigation computer."

"That's true."

"That first time was a bit of luck, I knew you monkeys were clueless, so I programmed the DeLorean's navigation system to be extremely flexible about interpreting my instructions, based on whatever conditions it encountered during the jump. That nav computer was grossly oversized for a dropship, if you remember, and still it was barely able to handle the calculations. Trust me, even if the Maxohlx or Rindhalu puzzle through the data from Pentivar and understand we used a jump to travel forward in time, so way will they be able to replicate the technology. That is a Skippy exclusive, and you should be honored that I am sharing it with you."

"I am *so* honored every day you are with us," I muttered, digging a fingernail into my palm so I didn't laugh or gag or roll my eyes.

"Well," he sniffed. "You should be. Ah, anyway, I was kind of screwing with you, the kitties are unlikely to understand that a ship jumped into and out of the archive chamber."

"I know you think everyone else in the galaxy is stupid, but-"

"Sanjay's warhead was specially prepared to generate gamma rays, in a way that has very effectively scrambled all traces of the radiation from our outbound jump."

"Okaaay, that is a good thing. Why didn't you tell me you were doing that, before the op? You just had me worried sick, you ass."

"Joe, you monkeys, *you* especially, take me for granted way too often."

"Uh, I am the person who appreciates you the most."

"Yes, and it's not enough," he pouted. "You have by far the best view of how extreme my awesomeness is, and still when I do something that expands the definition of magnificence, you are all like, 'whatevs'."

"I do not-" My mouth blurted out before my brain could catch up. You have *one* job, Bishop, I reminded myself. Do not screw it up. OK, yes, technically I have two jobs. The second job is dreaming up wacky new ideas for Skippy to implement. That secondary job is only possible when I perform my primary job properly: being Skippy's friend. There was no reason for him to help humanity, other than that he *liked* us. Liked some of us. A handful, really. My Job One was to be is friend, keep him entertained, and most importantly, make him feel appreciated. As much as any filthy monkey ever could. "You know what? You are absolutely correct about that, and I am very, very sorry."

"Hmmph," he sniffed.

"You have to understand, to us even your everyday awesomenesses are beyond our ability to comprehend, so when you do yet *another* incredible thing, it's like trying to stuff ten kilos into a five kilo bag. Our brains are full, you know?"

"So you say."

"Let me ask this: instead of telling me ahead of time that you had a plan to prevent the kitties from knowing a ship was in their archive chamber, you waited until I was worried sick about our plan being exposed, and then told me you had already taken care of it?"

"Basically, yes. Is this," he sighed, "another thing that will get me into trouble?"

"Not this time. I am sorry you felt a dramatic gesture was necessary, and you're right, it was necessary. A team member who finds a problem and fixes it is valuable. The most valuable team member is one who anticipates a problem, and prevents it from happening. That's *you*."

"Hmm. Thank you. Hey, what about a team member who fixes a problem *he* caused, only to create an even *bigger* problem?"

"Oh, well, that person is clearly management material," I tapped the two stars on my uniform collar. "Can we change the subject, please? What have you gotten from the archive AI core?"

"Ugh. Nothing yet, numbskull. I have been extremely busy performing a miraculous jump from deep beneath the surface of a planet, then fixing that drive so we can jump again. By the way, the *Rio Grande* has cleared us to dock, should you be on the bridge?"

"I should be anywhere other than on the bridge. *Surprise* is Chen's ship, I would just get in the way and distract the crew. When can you start working on the archive AI?"

"I started working on it a moment ago, when you whined about me not having the job done yet, you big jerk. There is an enormous volume of data in there, and it is all protected by the most secure encryption scheme the Maxohlx possess. To give an example, even for my ginormous brain power, to decrypt a single word would take approximately eight days."

"Uh, eight magical Skippy days, or eight slow monkey days?"

"Monkey days."

"Whoa. Why so-" With my mouth still open, I realized completing my thought would insult him. That would drag the conversation out for-EH-ver, while I soothed his bruised ego. Fortunately, though I am a filthy monkey, I had learned to think fast. "So, complicated an encryption scheme, for an archive that was supposed to be inaccessible?"

"Inaccessible to other species, but not to potentially hostile elements within Maxohlx society. Those in power do not want their rivals learning secrets that could be used against them, for example."

"Oh. Uh, I gotta say, eight days per word is not what I was hoping for."

"Ugh. Listen dumdum, that is eight days to get the *first* word. It gets easier after that, and easier as I decrypt more and more of the database. It's not a database, but you know what I mean."

"OK, OK, so how long to find any messages exchanged between the Hegemony and Moonraider?"

"I won't know that until I find it. There isn't a handy dandy index listing the juiciest top secret files."

"Uh huh. Give me a ballpark estimate, please."

"Fine. All I *really* have to do is read through a sample of data, about sixteen percent, to get a clue about the archive's architecture. How it's organized, that sort of thing. From there, it should be easy."

"How long will that take to hit that sixteen percent mark?"

"Oh, about four billion years past the heat death of the universe. The archive stores a mind-boggling amount of data."

"What the f- Why did we even bother to hit that archive? Oh my- You are such an irresponsible *asshole*! We can't wait that long, you little-"

"Joe! Joey, Joey, Joey," her shook his head. "I'm sure you are working up to a truly entertaining rant, but I said it *would* take eight days to decrypt a single word."

"Why does that- Oh. It won't take eight days?'

"Nope."

"How?"

"What am I all about, Joe?"

"Being an asshole?"

"That's who I am, not what I do. I am all about *cheating*. All I had to do was ping the archive AI and request the decryption key."

"It just *gave* you the freakin' key?"

"Of course it did, after I provided what the AI thinks are the proper credentials."

"Oh. Good job."

"It's me so, *Duh*."

"Why did you get me all spun up about how long it would take?!"

He blinked. "I need a reason to screw with you?"

"Uh, no. You don't. Thanks. For realz, how long to retrieve the message traffic between the kitties and the Outsider?"

"Those messages are already on your tablet. Once the proper credentials are provided, the archive AI is *very* helpful. It was designed to be, you know."

"Great," I reached for my tablet.

"Wait! The archive requests that you not touch the information with your filthy fingers, please wear gloves. Also, no talking, eating, drinking, or chewing gum while in the archive."

I wiped my hands on my shirt. "I will try to be a good, quiet monkey."

CHAPTER TEN

"Skippy?" I looked up from the dry translated text of the messages I was reading. "Were all communications between the Outsider and the Maxohlx in a, you know, digital text format?"

"Um, what else did you expect?"

"Any-"

"I can assure you the Outsider did not communicate in the form of a sock puppet show."

"I meant, were there any *voice* comms, you ass."

"Why do you care?"

"It would be interesting to *hear* our enemy. Just its voice, its tone, could reveal information."

"Is this a meatsack thing?"

"It is. I would feel different about the Outsider if it has a squeaky voice."

"Yes Joe, its voice sounds like a chipmunk breathing helium," he said with an eyeroll. "Although that would be funny, hee hee," he chuckled.

"It would."

"How much would it change *Star Wars* if Darth Vader had a squeaky voice?" Skippy snorted. "I find your lack of faith disturbing," he said it like a chipmunk.

"Yeah, that is not," I laughed, "quite as intimidating. You have no idea what the Outsider sounds like?"

"It is made of *energy,* numbskull, it doesn't have a voice."

"No, but it could replicate a voice the way you do. The type of voice it chooses could tell us something useful."

"Hmm. What does my voice tell you?"

"Uh, well, uh, I mean, your deep, commanding voice clearly indicates that you are a take-charge Alpha AI."

"Oh good. That's what I was going for."

"You nailed it," I dug a fingernail deep into my palm so I didn't laugh or roll my eyes.

"Do you have any other stupid questions?"

"No, I'll finish reading these messages again. There's not much here. The kitties didn't drive a hard bargain."

"They certainly gave the impression they are desperate."

"Yeah, and that's not good for us." I focused on the message traffic, muttering to myself, trying to find hidden meaning in the dry words. Maybe someone who specialized in Maxohlx psychology should review the messages, find something I missed. Or maybe there wasn't any hidden subtext, the messages were just two homicidal assholes chatting about joining forces to make a serial killer dream team.

And I had to read those messages. My job sucks.

"Sir?" Chen stuck her head into my tiny cubbyhole of a cabin, holding up a cup of coffee. "You look like you could use a break."

"Ah," I twisted, loosening my stiff back. "Yeah. Please, come in. Uh," I moved my duffel bag off the only chair in the cabin, I was sitting on the bunk.

Surprise had been modified for human use after we took it from the Thuranin, but the cabins were still tiny. Being aboard the frigate reminded me of my time aboard the original *Flying Dutchman*, and not in a good way. "Sit down, Colonel."

She gave me the coffee before taking the seat. "You could transfer to the *Constellation*, or the *Rio Grande*, Sir. They both have flag officer quarters."

"Are you eager to get me off your ship, Chen?" I asked with a wink.

"I am eager to get *myself* off this ship," she admitted with a grimace. "*Surprise* is just dead ballast now. It will probably go to the Boneyard when we get to Earth, be used for spare parts."

After we jumped away from Pentivar and the frigate latched onto one of the star carrier's hardpoints, Skippy scrambled the jump drive. I mean, he erased the modified navigation computer, then fractured all of the jump drive coil crystals. The powderized crystal was then dumped into a recycler and melted, so no evidence remained of how that special drive had operated. Only three people aboard the ship knew we had jumped through microwormholes; me, Skippy, and Chen. Only Skippy and I knew how a time-delayed jump works, and my understanding of the subject was at the 'press a button and the light turns on' level. With the jump drive rendered into its component atoms, no one could ever reverse-engineer our secret.

The extreme measures were vital for security. They also basically ended *Surprise's* career as a starship, which didn't feel right to me.

"I do feel bad about ruining the toy I borrowed from TRADEV."

"You *should* feel bad about it, Joe," Skippy appeared, wagging a finger at me. "You are the reason we can't have nice things."

"You weren't invited into the conversation, Skippy," I swiped a hand through his hologram. "Go away please."

"Hmmph," he sniffed, but he went away.

"Seriously Sir," Chen continued, "with your permission, I would like to reduce staffing to a skeleton crew, move us over to the *Rio Grande*. There is no reason people have to live aboard this bucket."

"You're right. Permission granted. I will," I took a sip of coffee. "Move to the star carrier also. I needed some time to read all this," I tapped the tablet screen, "without any distractions."

"Did you find anything interesting?" She asked. "If I'm cleared to hear it. I don't want to intrude on-"

"I'd like to get your perspective. The Hegemony clearly thought Moonraider was an Elder AI, and Moonraider fed that delusion. The Maxohlx were basing their intel on our assumptions."

"They never ran their own analysis?"

"No," I shook my head. "That makes sense, they consider humans to be the leading, the only, experts on the subject of Elder AIs. They had no basis for questioning *our* assumption. Also, the Outsider was clever, it had done its homework. In its messages to the Hegemony, it consistently referred to Skippy as the 'Abomination', exactly as a loyal Elder AI would do."

"Do you know what it promised the kitties, in exchange for a supply of high grade radonium?"

"Nothing." To clarify, I added, "It promised nothing to the Maxohlx, not directly. It wasn't going to share the Sentinel it woke up, it wasn't going to wake up more Sentinels and loan one to the Hegemony. The Maxohlx agreed to a deal because Moonraider did state that it intended to smite their mutual enemy: us. We are the target, *were* the target, if it activated and took control of a Sentinel."

"Did it give any hints how it intended to," one side of her mouth twitched, "smite us?"

"No, damn it. The Maxohlx were happy enough with the prospect of a righteous smiting that they didn't insist on details. My guess is, the Outsider would use its Sentinel against Bubba. Or Puptart. My money is on Bubba. If Bubba was even damaged, we would have been forced to move Puptart from Jaguar to Earth, and then we couldn't use a spare Sentinel to go hunting for the Outsider. We would be playing defense, and it could wait for the next opportunity, to wake up a batch of Sentinels. Then it would be Game Over."

"That's interesting, Sir."

"What?"

"The Outsider sees *us* as its primary obstacle to, whatever its ultimate objective is."

"Not us. Skippy."

"*You* and Skippy."

"Thanks, but you're giving me too much credit."

"You are giving *Skippy* too much credit," she said with a glance towards the ceiling, expecting a protest from the beer can.

"Let's just agree that Skippy and the Pirates make a great team."

"I am happy to serve, Sir," she patted the Merry Band of Pirates patch she wore on her uniform, during her temporary assignment with Task Force Black. "What *is* the Outsider's ultimate objective?"

"I couldn't find a single clue about that," I tapped the list of messages on the tablet. "The kitties did ask, Moonraider never gave an answer. I have to assume that eliminating Skippy, or isolating him, is just an intermediate step."

"Taking control of a Sentinel was just part of shaping the battlespace?"

"Our Navy friends," I snorted, "would call that 'clearing the decks for action'."

Chen laughed. She was Air Force, I was Army, yet we both served aboard UN *Navy* ships. Sometimes that bothered me, when I didn't have some massive problem occupying my mind. Her expression turned serious. "Was this op worth the cost, Sir?"

We hadn't lost any people, no one even got a minor injury, unless you counted the nausea induced by the time-delayed jump. She meant that in the archive, eleven Maxohlx had perished, either from our PDS cannons, or Sanjay's nuke. Those eleven dead were not collateral damage, we had intended to kill them, to eliminate any witnesses.

"I don't know yet," I admitted. "We at least know the Outsider didn't trust its allies enough to reveal its plans. And we know that, whatever it is going to do, it needs to take out our Sentinels, and Skippy, first."

"Without a Sentinel, it can't do that." She phrased it as a statement, but it was a question.

"It can't proceed with its *original* plan. So, now we need to ask: what is its Plan B?"

"Hey, Joe," Skippy appeared, as I was getting dressed for dinner. *Rio Grande's* captain was hosting a celebratory dinner for the senior officers of all ships in the task force, that included Chen, her XO, and of course me. Usually I dreaded such encounters, when I couldn't reveal the full truth about a recent operation, and everyone around the table awkwardly avoided asking certain questions. Chen assured me that standing orders aboard the star carrier were: talking about work was not allowed during dinners.

"Hi, Skippy. Does my tie look OK to you?"

"It looks ridiculous to me. Why do military officers wear neckties? Lawyers and accountants have to wear suits and ties, you're supposed to be a soldier."

"What else would I wear for a formal occasion?"

"I don't know, um, hey! A bandolier of rifle ammo would be nice."

"That says 'combat' rather than 'formal dinner'."

"You could polish the rounds so they shine, dumdum."

"That's great if I'm cosplaying as a bandito."

"Oooh, did I just hear you asking me to design a new uniform for you?"

"You did not hear that, because you will *never* hear me say that."

"Ugh. Would it kill you to have a little culture in your life?"

"It probably wouldn't kill me, but why take the chance?"

"*Why* do I bother talking to you?"

"Because you have literally nothing else to do right now?"

"True dat," he sighed. "Anywho, since I have NUH-thing else to do right now, I- Damn, this crew is dull."

"They just aren't used to working with you, Skippy."

"That's not the problem. For years I flew around in a single tin can with at most a couple hundred monkeys."

"*Valkyrie* is not a tin can, you ass."

"You know what I mean. Now, I can chat with the crew of *Surprise*, and a star carrier, and three battleships, and a battlecruiser. But they are all *dicks*, Joe, and that includes the women. Whenever I want to talk, it's always 'Oh I am too busy' or 'It is two in the morning and I have to sleep'. They always have some lame excuse."

"Except for Frey's STAR team, and Chen, none of the people in this task force have been with the Merry Band of Pirates. Did you consider they just might all be intimidated by you?"

"Wow, really?"

"You are kind of awesome, you know."

"Well, that is a very good point," he mused. "But, lowly meatsacks should be thrilled to have an opportunity to speak with me."

"They are afraid of accidentally insulting you," I lied. "Give them time to adjust, they are not used to having such a legendary being with them."

"We don't have time, we're going straight back to Earth. I am bored *now*, Joe."

"Talk to me, then." Dinner wasn't for another hour, I had time to indulge his need to talk. "You have nothing to do, so, what?"

"Oh. I was reviewing the archive data, doing a deep dive. Most of the so-called secret information is technical stuff that only reminds me how much of their technology the kitties stole from the spiders. Or from their own clients! For example, the *Thuranin* actually were the first to make atomic compression devices a practical weapon, the kitties had fumbled around with the concept for millennia and done nothing with it. If course, the fragile ego of the kitties requires them to conceal the truth even from themselves, they all pretend any major technical advance was their accomplishment."

"Uh huh. So, did you find anything interesting?"

"A lot of the secrets in the archive would be major political scandals, except they happened a long time ago, and I don't care about any of the recent crap."

"Did you find anything that would be interesting to *me*?"

"I am getting to that. Don't rush me. Unless you want me to be extra bored, and wake you up at zero dark stupid to discuss exciting recent discoveries in child development that you certainly should know about?"

"Margaret and I know everything we need to about raising our children."

"You think that, but-"

"These recent discoveries, are they just shit you made up?"

"Made up based on *science*! By ignoring my valuable advice, you are being a horribly neglectful parent."

"How about you collect your undoubtedly insightful advice in the form of a picture book, and I'll look at it?"

"*Will* you look at it?"

"That depends on how cool the pictures are."

"Ugh. I, I can't even."

"Did you find anything in the archive that I might care about?"

"Yes."

"And?"

"And, maybe now I don't feel like talking with you."

"OK, well, if you don't want to talk now, I have to finish getting ready, so-"

"I said *maybe* I don't feel like talking. Listen, numbskull, I did find interesting and important information. Like, the Maxohlx were not cooperating with the Outsider until *after* the raid on Moonbase Zulu. They had no contact with, or advanced knowledge of, the attempt to steal the Dogzilla Sentinel. I mean, they were *thrilled* that you failed to activate that Sentinel, but they didn't-"

"Excuse me, *I* failed? I was an observer."

"You were there, and once again, bad shit happened, that can't be a coincidence."

"Whatever. If the rotten kitties weren't involved, why did we detect one of their ships sniffing around the area?"

"About four months before the Dogzilla incident, the Hegemony lost a task force. A group of ships jumped into a Bosphuraq star system, to collect their annual tribute in the form of highly purified rare elements. The two transport ships arrived at the intended destination, the escort warships did not. The star carrier investigated, no trace of the warships was ever found. Joe, the ships that disappeared? Those same ships crashed into your moon, and one of them is the ship we tracked to the edge of the galaxy."

"The Outsider took over those ships, killed their crews, and flew the ships remotely?"

"That's the most likely scenario."

"So, the Maxohlx made a deal with the Outsider, *after* they understood it had stolen one of their task forces. They had to recognize the ships that crashed into our moon."

"They did intercept the fleet-wide message from Def Com that requested all UN ships to report any prior sensor contact with those ships, so yes. The kitties did know the Outsider, or as it was known at the time, Moonraider, was responsible for the loss of that task force."

"And they cut a deal anyway."

"Come on, Joe. Like the Hegemony cares about a single task force. They knew from UN-dick's awful communications security that we detected an Elder starship during the moon raid, and that we suspected our opponent was an Elder master control AI. All they cared about was they finally had the prospect of an entity active in the galaxy, that could cause trouble for *me*. Of course they did everything they could do to help our opponent."

"What about now? They certainly know now that we're fighting an ancient threat from beyond this galaxy."

"They do *not* necessarily know that. They might assume we're lying about the Outsider."

"You are kidding- Oh for-"

"In fact, the Hegemony has instructed everyone involved in strategic analysis to assume that we are always lying. And especially that *anything* Admiral Scorandum does is a scam. I hate to say it, but I think his usefulness to us is over, the kitties have been burned too many times by that sketchy beetle."

"Some of the crap he did, the Maxohlx still don't even know they got played. He has screwed with the spiders also, remember. He got the spiders to destroy that fake AI we called 'Sam Francisco', when they used that Grav Pulse weapon against the station orbiting a neutron star." I had to pause to laugh for a while. "Damn, how much time and money have the kitties wasted, trying to recover the fake AI from the core of that star?"

Skippy chuckled. "It is keeping them busy, and a busy kitty is a kitty who is not causing trouble for us. Someday, I would like to reveal the truth about that incident, just to see the look on the faces of the kitties and spiders."

"Not any time soon, please. We need the spiders working with us, to deal with the Outsider. Hmm."

"What?"

"As far as the kitties know, Scorandum played it straight with them when he gave them the Sam AI. He hasn't *always* screwed with them."

"Yes but, the Maxohlx have since come to suspect that Sam Francisco was never going to cooperate with them, and that is why Scorandum made the deal. He got what he wanted, and he knew they would get nothing. I would certainly be salty about that."

"Ah, it's just business. When you're buying something sketchy, you have to carefully inspect the goods."

"Anyway, I'm afraid that we can't rely on Scorandum pulling another scam on the kitties for us."

"Yeah, you're probably right," I agreed. "We have drawn from that well one too many times. OK, this is good info. The first evidence of Outsider activity is from four months before Dogzilla? There are no other mysterious incidents before that?"

"Seriously? This is a big galaxy, knucklehead, there are mysterious incidents every freakin' day."

"Right but, anything that you can connect to the Outsider?"

"An Elder starship accompanied by a group of Maxohlx warships raided your moon base, and none of us connected that to an entity from outside the galaxy. Before that, you worked with Chang to make a list of suspects for the Dogzilla incident, and you never considered an Outsider might be responsible."

"I am still kicking myself for missing that one."

"Uh huh, yet somehow you expect *me* to identify which mystery incidents might be the action of the Outsider?"

"I am asking, based on what you now know about our asshole opponent, can you review the data to see if there is, I don't know. Some distinctive Outsider signature in the sensor data from those incidents? Something like that."

"OK Joe, say that again, but *slowly*. Listen dumdum, let me smack some knowledge on you. Incidents are flagged as mysterious because there is no sensor data to explain them. I have nothing to work with!" He threw his hands in the air. "Ships go missing, newly colonized worlds are later found abandoned, wormholes fail to operate on schedule- OK, that last category is probably caused by me. My point is, if there is enough data available to provide an explanation, there is no mystery, *Duh*."

"First, the fact that a bunch of ignorant meatsacks *think* they can explain an incident does not mean they are correct about it."

"Hmm. Well, I suppose that is a very good point."

"Second, I am not asking you to review all the sensor data that was collected about mysterious incidents."

"Oh good, because that would be *sooooo* tedious."

"I am asking you to review all the sensor data that is *available*, covering the past six months."

"*Duuude*," he shuddered in horror. "You can't possibly ask me to do that."

"I can and I am. Most ships store their flight recorder data for a year or more, right? That includes all the sensor data they collected?"

"Ugh. I hate my life. I don't have access to the flight recorders of every ship in the freakin' galaxy!"

"I am only suggesting you hack into the top-tier clients like the Jeraptha, Thuranin, Bosphuraq and their peers. Ah, we can just request a download from the beetles, so that will make it easier for you."

"*Easier*?!"

"Can you do it? Skippy, I know you only recently got your mojo back, so I will understand if this job is too difficult for-"

"Too difficult? No way! Not for Skippy the Magnificent. The issue is, I don't *want* to do it. This is gonna *suuuuck*."

"It is. When you're stuck with the suck, you embrace it," I pretended to wrap my arms around an imaginary object, rocking it like a baby. "Embrace it, nurture it, make it part of you. Learn it, know it, live it."

"UUUUUGH!"

Admiral Klestine wanted to summon the Hegemony's Chief Archivist to his office, both since he was pressed for time, and because he vastly outranked her in the bureaucracy. The admiral had still been reading the initial report on the destruction of the Pentivar secure data archive when the Dictat pinged him, demanding answers immediately. Klestine had been tempted to reply that he could either provide information immediately, *or* provide useful information. He hadn't said that. Instead, he had sent the expected and proper reply, that he was marshaling all available resources to investigate the incident. Then, he contacted the Chief Archivist to start doing something actually useful.

His armored aircraft, escorted by a squadron of gunships, landed on the roof of the Archivist's headquarters as quietly as possible, meaning his aircraft was broadcasting an anonymous transponder signal, and the flag insignia on the aircraft's tail was switched off. The last thing he needed was wild speculation about why the leader of the Hegemony military was visiting the important but dull Archives Department.

"Chief Archivist," he merely inclined his head as she greeted him, in her very neat and tidy office.

"Admiral Klestine," she made the proper gesture, a slightly lower inclination of her head, to indicate she understood his higher status. Her eyes darted to his pair of bodyguards, as if concerned they would track mud onto her floor. Or touch something.

"Wait outside," he ordered the guards, and slapped the button to slide the door closed. If the guards protested him being alone and vulnerable, he didn't hear it. Without waiting for an invitation, he took a seat.

"This is, forgive me," she cleared her throat. "I am unaccustomed to speaking. It feels, unnatural."

"Our ancestors did not feel that way. But, they also did not rule half of the galaxy," he added with a shrug, and wondered about that. Vocal speech had been supplanted by much faster, more efficient communication by brain implant, yet body language remained. Gestures could be suppressed, he often switched off certain facial muscles. It remained a fact that body language was still useful. "You have heard of the incident at Pentivar?"

"I have heard of the *outrage*, yes. Admiral, surely you can see that you must immediately increase security at the other archives. The cultural legacy of our people is at risk!"

"We are taking appropriate security measures, my intelligence division will be handling the investigation. We will of course share any pertinent information with you, so you can also upgrade the *internal* security at your other archives."

"There is no indication of how the humans accomplished the destruction of the archive? Their ship could not have fired a weapon from orbit, any such weapon that could reach the archive chamber from orbit would have left an enormous crater."

"We have several theories of how it could have been done," he lied, impatient to get to the purpose of his visit. "For now, with you, I wish to explore why *that* archive was attacked."

"Admiral? Surely it is clear this was a strike against the very foundation of our collected knowledge, that-"

"Possibly, it was not. Chief Archivist, you manage many such facilities, all acting as backups for the others. Destroying a single archive serves no purpose for the enemy."

"Unless they continue their campaign of terror, and destroy more archives, to-"

"That is unlikely. The Fleet has been deployed to guard the other sites, no enemy ship can get close enough to deploy whatever device was used at Pentivar."

"Could that be the enemy's goal? Forcing you to spread your forces thin?"

His composure slipped a tiny bit. It always irritated him when civilians offered him input on military matters. "That is also unlikely. Archivist," he pressed forward before she could offer more unhelpful remarks. "The question is why did the enemy strike at Pentivar?"

"Well that," she blinked, having not suppressed her own facial expressions. "Is a matter for your strategists, I suppose. Were Pentivar's defenses especially weak? My office relies on the military for protection of-"

"I can assure you, there is no military reason why the humans chose to strike that particular target. I wish to understand whether there is *another* reason why Pentivar was selected, some way in which that archive is, was, unique."

"But, but," she sputtered. "All the archives are backups for the others, as you said. To have an archive that is unique would defeat the purpose of-"

"In an ideal world, each archive would contain information identical to all the others. However, as you are painfully aware," he smiled, "this world is far from ideal. Archives do not all receive updates at the same time, therefore at any time, the data stored in each of them is slightly different from each of the others."

"That is, true," she agreed with reluctance. "It is a practical matter of *latency*, you see, and we work very hard to ensure the integrity of the overall-"

"Yes, yes," his veneer of patience was slipping. "I need to know what data was stored at Pentivar, that was *not* at any of the other archives."

The shock drained color from her face. "Admiral, do you have any idea how *much* data is stored in an archive?"

"The exact figures have been provided to me. I appreciate this will be a monumental undertaking. To make matters worse, I suspect there is no single piece of information that the humans wished to erase from our memories, by destroying the Pentivar archive. It is more likely to be multiple bits of information that only when combined, become something new. Something important."

"Oh," she shuddered. "It is not possible for my department to-"

"The archive AIs are not merely passive custodians of their data, are they? They analyze newly received data packages, to properly categorize each file, to prevent duplicates, and to resolve conflicts between datasets."

"That is correct. The archive AIs must optimize file sizes, to reduce the storage necessary."

"My people tell me that data storage is not expensive."

"*Storage* is not expensive. Ensuring that no information is lost, and that requested information can be retrieved quickly and completely, that is expensive."

"I have also been told that sometimes, even often, when an archive AI is tasked retrieve information for a vaguely defined request, the AI can find connections between datasets that were previously unknown."

The Chief Archivist shifted in her seat. "Such potential connections are flagged for regular review."

"Regular meaning, reviews are conducted only three times a year?"

She knew there was no response the admiral would deem acceptable, so she merely stated the facts. "It is rare that any significant *new* information is discovered during a review."

"But it does happen."

"Yes." Her body language reflected her discomfort.

"Until a review is imminent, each archive AI holds the potential connections it discovered? The file is not transmitted to your office ahead of time?"

"As I stated, it is rare that-"

"It is possible then, that the Pentivar AI discovered a previously unknown, new piece of vital information, that is now lost to us?"

"That is possible, however, I do not see how our enemy could have known what data was unique to Pentivar."

"Our enemy is being assisted by an *Elder* AI," he reminded her. "We must assume there is nothing the Skippy being does not know. Chief Archivist, I appreciate it seems extremely unlikely that the enemy somehow knew data recently received by Pentivar would be damaging to them. Until today, I would have said it was *impossible* for an archive to be destroyed by anything other than sustained bombardment by relativistic impactors. Yet, that impossibility has occurred. So, we must attempt to recreate the Pentivar archive, and see what connections can be discovered."

"I do not see how we could ever-"

"The primary archive, here," he pointed to the floor, for the primary archive was buried deep in their homeworld's mantle layer. "Is theoretically capable of storing copies of the data held by *all* of the remote archives."

"Theoretically, however that-"

"Please begin the process of recreating the Pentivar archive with your resources here."

"That is not-"

"The *Dictat*," he paused, "will ensure anything you need is provided."

That statement had the desired effect. She hesitated, clasping her hands on her lap, staring down at them. Archivists are not accustomed to confrontation, their profession is designed to be dull, uncontroversial. "It is," she looked up, not quite meeting Klestine's eyes. "Possible to do as you request, and I will direct my staff to begin preparations immediately." Her eyelids fluttered momentarily, Klestine assumed she was sending instructions to her deputies. "What my department does not possess is anything close to the processing power for the analysis you propose."

"That will not be a problem," he stood. "The strategic analysis suite of defense AIs will be tasked to perform the analysis, once your department has the data in the proper environment."

Seeing the shock on her face was gratifying.

CHAPTER ELEVEN

"Joe," Skippy startled me as I was running along the corridor through the star carrier's long spine. Damn, running like that was nostalgic for me, I hadn't done that since the original *Flying Dutchman* got remade into the *Dutchman* Two Point Oh. The *Rio Grande* had two trams that moved people along the spine, and two larger trams for cargo, so people didn't make the long walk unless they chose to. For me, it was a great way to get exercise that did not involve running on another boring treadmill or elliptical trainer. Plus, I could be by myself, alone with my thoughts. That was the plan anyway, except the STARs also used the star carrier's spine as an opportunity for training runs, and I had to step out of the way when they went by.

Still, it reminded me of the Bad Old Days, when the galaxy had no idea that humanity had a functional starship, that humans were still alive on Earth. Life was simpler then, or so it seemed at the time. My job then was simply to keep aliens from learning what was going on at our homeworld, by preventing aliens from getting to Earth. Yeah, that had turned out to be *not* so simple. We had been playing for time anyway, with no long-term solution for survival. Eventually, radio transmissions from Earth would reach antennas in our stellar neighborhood, and hostile aliens would have become very curious about what happened to the White Wind Clan who had been overwhelmingly in control of our primitive homeworld.

Anyway, all the shit we had gone through to keep our secret was rolling through my mind when Skippy interrupted my thoughts. His avatar kept pace with me, a meter in front of my face. "Skip-py," I gasped. "What's, up?"

"We need to change course *now*. The star carrier, I mean."

That made me stop fast. "Change course, like physically?"

"Yes, but that's a good point. We also need a *plan*, instead of the usual fumbling around."

"No, we don't."

"Good, then- Um, what? Of course we need a plan! What in the *hell* is wrong with-"

"Skippy, we don't need to have a plan right *now*. We have time to think about it, rather than rushing to do the first thing we think of."

"We do? How do you figure that?"

"The Outsider apparently believes it needs a Sentinel to, do whatever it intends to do next. It can't *get* a Sentinel, not for over a year. We have time to learn more about it and its objective, and to block the next round of opportunities to wake up a Sentinel."

"That will not be as easy as you think, dumdum. It-"

"Let's talk about that later, OK? Why the course change?"

"I found something interesting in the archive."

"What?"

"I don't want to say, until I know for sure it's something important or not."

"So, you want me to order a task force to fly wherever, based on a vague hunch you have, about something you don't want to tell me?"

"Um, yes. Listen, numbskull, it-"

"OK."

"This is too important to- Um, what?"

"OK, I'll order a course change. I'm trusting you on this."

"Wow. That is a surprise. I had a whole big argument planned, about how I am so obviously intellectually superior to you or any other being in this galaxy- All of them *combined*, to be truthful, and how you should logically just do whatever I-"

"Skippy? When you get the answer you want, stop talking."

"Gotcha."

"So, where are we going?"

"To a- Oops um, heh heh, I had better cancel that reactor glitch. Give me just a minute and-"

"What reactor glitch?"

"The one that's now not going to happen, so don't worry about it."

"You *scheduled* a reactor glitch?"

"It wasn't scheduled, it's not like I sent the reactor an invite to confirm it's available."

"You- How long have we known each other?"

"Too long," he muttered.

"Are you *ever* going to learn what is appropriate and what is not?"

"What do you think?"

"I asked *you*."

"The Magic Eight Ball says, 'Signs Point To NO'."

"You ask me to trust you, then you do shit like this?"

"Hey, I had to stop the *Rio Grande* from jumping somehow, and I figured that convincing you to change course would take for-EH-ver since your brain is so slow. So, I set up a minor reactor glitch which would not have hurt anyone. I mean, someone might have tripped and fallen while running for an escape pod but-"

"I am going to pretend this conversation never happened, and you are going to owe me."

"Deal. Um, owe you what?"

"I will cash in that chip later. Where are we going?"

"There are a couple possibilities, you can help me-"

"Hold that thought." I pulled out my phone and called the bridge. "This is Bishop, halt the jump countdown."

"Halt the jump countdown, aye," the duty officer replied, and didn't ask why, since I didn't need to provide a reason.

I did anyway. "We will be changing course, stand by for new coordinates."

"Aye, Sir."

"All right Skippy, show me our options."

"You should go to your office. This could be complicated."

When I got to my office, Skippy wouldn't just tell me what he had found in the archive. "Can you guess, Joe?"

"*Can* I? Sure. I don't want to. I'm tired and I don't feel like screwing around."

"Ugh. You are always tired. You should go to sickbay for a checkup, I wonder if something is wrong with you."

"I have a long-term condition called 'Being In The Military', Skippy. The only known cure is a DD-214 and buying a boat, so I can go fishing."

"Could you at least try to guess?"

"Are my guesses ever anything that is worth your time?"

"No, you usually just babble increasingly incoherent nonsense until I beg you to shut up."

"OK, so why-"

"Your moronic babbling amuses me."

"I promise to amuse you later, OK?"

"*Fine*. We need to visit a Maxohlx relay station."

"Visit, like you want to get a selfie with the thing, or-"

"Ugh. *No*, knucklehead. I want to, download messages."

"You and the Maxohlx are secret pals now, you exchange recipes or something?"

"Of course not, the-"

"You *can't* hack into their relay stations, not without one of those-"

"I know that. Can we just go there, and save the blah blah blah for never?"

"Going to an enemy relay station is a risk, especially after we just destroyed one of their archives."

"I know that. You need to choose a relay station that minimizes that risk."

"Does the entire task force have to go there, or just a single ship?"

"It could be just a dropship."

"Yeah, those days are over. We'll go in the *Connie*. We're not in a rush to act against the Outsider, but we do have to return to Earth. Show me a chart of Maxohlx relay stations we can get to and back from, with no more than a three day delay."

He showed me a chart, I selected a relay station with minimal traffic, but not so isolated that it was an obvious target for us. Back when I still had command of *Valkyrie*, one of my last missions was to investigate whether Skippy could hack into a kitty relay station, to defeat the new physical security measures the Hegemony had implemented. We found a pair of stealthed battleships waiting for us, and the entire area was saturated with stealth mines. *Valkyrie* escaped without damage only because the Maxohlx had overplayed their hand, there were so many mines their mass affected the stellar wind in the area. Of course, the magnificence of Skippy had detected the mines, otherwise our mighty battlecruiser would have been trapped or even destroyed.

Skippy had tried hacking into a relay station because the kitties had developed a new authentication scheme that impressed even the beer can, and that scheme was being rolled out across their entire network of stations.

We had control of a single Maxohlx relay station for years, we had captured the thing and set it up to function just like a genuine message and data transfer station, except that one also gave Skippy complete access to its entire database. The arrangement wasn't perfect, we had to set up the captive relay station along a route that didn't have heavy traffic, and we knew the kitties would eventually discover their comms had been compromised when that station needed regularly scheduled maintenance. The station was almost an obsolete model at the time we found it, so my hope was we would get six months to a year of use from the thing before the Maxohlx nuked it. Instead, their civil war caused the Hegemony to defer maintenance, and for eleven months the station was in rebel territory anyway. Finally, a maintenance crew that was probably bored out of their minds got the shock of their lives when the station's AI announced they had only a short time to get away, before the station's self-destruct would be triggered.

They literally ran for their lives. When their dropship was fifteen hundred kilometers away, an atomic compression warhead exploded, tearing the station apart and vaporizing any evidence. That warhead was a genuine Thuranin weapon that we had captured, so the kitties assumed their ungrateful clients had been responsible for stealing their secrets. Normally, that shattering revelation would have sparked outrage and an escalating cycle of punishment attacks, resistance by the Thuranin, and more punishment. But, after their bloody civil war, the Hegemony couldn't afford to further weaken their reluctant coalition, and being hacked by a lowly client species was utterly humiliating. So, the Maxohlx did nothing. Covered up the incident, including remotely causing an overload of the maintenance ship's jump drive, so that ship's crew couldn't tell anyone their secret.

Anyway, we tried three times, and Skippy hadn't been able to hack into an upgraded relay station. So, we didn't have a regular, reliable source of intel on what sick shit the Maxohlx were doing, and that was a problem.

Wary of flying into another minefield, I chose carefully. The candidates had to be stations that saw frequent enough traffic that a minefield would risk killing their own ships, but not so much traffic that ships were likely to jump in right on top of our stupid heads. We would also approach the station carefully, with the star carrier at a safe distance, and our three battleships waiting and ready to jump in if needed.

Selecting a target station took only twenty minutes, so I ordered the *Rio Grande* to turn around and go back through the last wormhole we came through.

It was driving me crazy that Skippy wouldn't give me a hint what he was doing.

"This is close enough," Skippy advised, as the *Constellation* approached the target relay station. Without any need for a signal from me, Captain Markides ordered the pilot to hold us there, keeping pace with the relay station's slow orbit around a red dwarf star that was so distant, we couldn't even see it without a telescope.

"Sir," Markides whispered to me with a Southern accent subtle enough that I was guessing where the guy had been raised. Virginia? North Carolina? Not the Deep South. "Would you care to share any advice?"

"Your ship will be fine, Captain," I assured him. "The station might not survive Skippy's, whatever he is going to do, but our shields will protect us at this distance, if the station explodes."

Previous attempts by Skippy to remotely hack upgraded relay stations had been detected by the Maxohlx, and they had installed countermeasures. Extreme countermeasures. Like, whenever he managed to get past the first layer of security, the stations exploded. The last two times he attempted a hack, he hadn't even gotten into the first layer. That was then, this was now, he had his mojo back. I hoped he wasn't just overconfident as usual, letting his ego push him into trying to triumph over a system that had defeated him repeatedly in the past. Skippy is awesome, that hadn't changed. What changed was, the senior species learned every time he screwed with them. It was Darwinian evolution in action: by screwing with data systems, he was pushing the Maxohlx and Rindhalu to develop ever more sophisticated cybersecurity measures. Which is why he shouldn't show his bag of tricks to the enemy unless it was necessary. Was it necessary? I didn't know, since he wouldn't talk to me about it.

"TTA," I muttered under my breath.

"General?" Markides inclined his head toward me.

"I am trusting the awesomeness," I explained.

"So say we all," he replied without taking his eyes off the tactical display. Space around us was clear of threats. That could change in a heartbeat.

"Skippy?" I prompted the beer can, his avatar wasn't exactly frozen, it just wasn't moving. That usually meant either he was intently focused on something, or the opposite: he had absent-mindedly forgotten what he was supposed to be doing.

"I am *busy*," he snapped, though the avatar still hadn't moved. "You want this thing to go *boom*? Distracting me is how things go boom, knucklehead."

"Or, they go boom because you start composing a Broadway musical when you're supposed to be disarming a warhead."

"Ugh. That happened *one* time!"

"Once is enough."

"Joe, of course you went to Newark to be an amateur archeologist, because you just *love* to dig up the past. Let it *go*, will you?"

"Give us an ETA?"

"I don't know yet, this is very delicate work, I am anticipating a booby trap to bite me on the ass to be honest. It could take a long time to- Huh."

"I don't like to hear '*Huh*', Skippy. What's wrong?"

"Nothing's wrong. Wow, this was *easy*."

"I don't like easy either, I don't trust it. Easy is how you walk into a booby trap."

"No booby trap. Um, we should probably talk about this in your office."

Leaving the *Constellation's* crew hanging like that would be a dick move, but it was better than dumping a steaming pile on their heads. Rarely did Skippy deliver good news, so I was assuming whatever he had found was yet another crisis for me to deal with.

Before I could say anything, Captain Markides eased my mind. "General, my office is just outside the bridge," he said, though of course I already knew his ship had the same basic internal layout as *Valkyrie*. "Should we remain here, or can we jump away?"

"Skippy?"

"Just a minute, aaaaand, we're good. Jump anytime you like."

"Pilot," Markides tightened the lap belt. "Jump option Bravo, engage."

"Option Bravo, aye. Engaging."

The battlecruiser jumped.

In my borrowed office, I didn't need to move anything off the desk, Markides kept everything neat and tidy. There weren't even any rings on the desk from coffee cups, nor any crumbs. Clearly, it wasn't my office. Sitting carefully in the chair rather than flopping down the way I usually did, I pressed the button to slide the door closed. And the button wasn't there. Huh. It was under the left side of the desk. Another reminder that I was not aboard my beloved *Valkyrie*. "OK, Skippy, give me the bad news."

"No bad news this time."

"Uh, how is that possible?"

"It just is. I know, it surprised the hell out of me too."

"Then why did you insist on talking about it in private?"

"This news is *so* good, we probably want to keep it between us."

"Holy sh- What did you find?"

"I'm *in*, Joe, I went in through a back door."

"In what? The relay station?"

"Yes. Let me talk, instead of you making stupid guesses?"

"You got it."

"In analyzing data from the archive AI core, I tried to find a way around the physical security protocol the kitties implemented on their relay stations, after they discovered what they thought was evidence the Thuranin had taken control of a station. Hee hee, that is *never* not gonna be hilarious! Not only did we have full access to their communications, they think one of their clients was responsible."

"Ayuh, that was pretty sweet," I grinned.

"That Joe Bishop guy caused not one but two civil wars, framed the Bosphuraq for flying a ghost ship, *and* framed the Thuranin for a cybersecurity breach."

"That guy is a jerk for sure," I had to agree. "So, how did you get in?"

"At first, I tried to think of a way around the new security scheme, but I couldn't find anything practical. All the scenarios I ran through models were nothing but failure after failure. I was getting so desperate I almost asked *you* for help."

"You realize most people would be insulted by a remark like that?"

"I meant it as a compliment, dumdum. Sometimes, you see things I don't."

"Good, then what you should say is-"

"The things you see are so freakin' *obvious* any meatsack moron could do it, but somehow my ginormous brain can't get-"

"OK, that was *not* intended as an insult?"

"Whatevs. You know what I mean."

"I do, and being a genius is no excuse for being an asshole."

"Isn't it, though?"

"Just," I sighed. Skippy was never going to change, and I was never going to learn that arguing with him was a waste of time. "Tell me how you got access to the relay station."

"After everything I tried failed over and over to defeat the current security scheme, I tried to think like you, and look at the problem in a different way. Except I actually understand the issue, while you just *Duuuuuh* and-"

"Stick to the facts, please."

"The simple explanation is, the programmers left a back door open."

"No way."

"Yes way. I know, I couldn't believe it either. This isn't a typical back door, like programmers use in testing, then plug the vulnerability. This is unintentional, the Maxohlx have no idea their relay station infrastructure is so wide open. To me, I mean. I'm not just hacking in, I have to physically bridge the- Do you care to hear the technical details?"

"Would I understand any of it?"

"Dude."

"Then, no."

"Thanks, I was not looking forward to dumbing it down enough for you to grasp the basic concept. What you need to know is, I have full access to any Maxohlx relay station, at any time. The process takes about eight minutes in slow monkey time, if I go any faster I won't able to erase my tracks."

"Skippy, this is fantastic!"

"I know an eight minute window is too long to be hanging around a relay station that gets a lot of traffic, but-"

"Don't apologize. You did an amazing thing, you should celebrate your accomplishment."

"Ah, compared to some of the stuff I've done this is rather lame, but it impresses the monkeys."

"It impresses *the* monkey. Me. Do not tell anyone about this, we have to keep it a secret."

"That's what I figured," he sighed. "Once again, I do something awesome, and nobody knows about it."

"*I* know."

"I feel *so* much better now, thank you."

"You downloaded data from the station? Did you find anything interesting?"

"I did, and I haven't looked at the data yet. We already know the most important secrets of the Maxohlx from the archive AI core. Although, hmm, the archives only contain information the Hegemony deems vital enough to store long-term. And the Pentivar archive was last updated before our encounter with the Outsider, so any recent data or messages won't be in the datasets we have. So, the station might have something interesting. Ugh. You want me to review the entire download?"

"No, just anything from the past month or so."

"OK fine, I'll do it."

"Great. Uh, you did close the back door of that station? Erase your tracks?"

"It's *me*, numbskull."

"That's what I'm worried about. You erased all signs of you hacking in, *and* also any sensor data of the *Constellation* being there?"

"Um, well, heh heh-"

Yanking my phone from a pocket, I stood up abruptly. "Captain Markides," I called, "please jump us back to the relay station ASAP." What could I say that wouldn't give away our newest secret? "I need Skippy to make a detailed sensor map of the station's transmitter array."

"We can jump in three minutes," Markides answered.

"I'll be right there."

"Good cover story, Joe," Skippy gave me a thumbs up.

"Try not to be so absent-minded in the future, OK?"

"Hey! It's been a while since I had access to a senior species relay station, I'm a bit rusty on protocol."

"Then, write it on a sticky note or something."

We stopped at another Maxohlx relay station, for Skippy to confirm the back door could be opened at all such facilities. It could. At least until the kitties discovered their mistake and slammed the door closed.

"Not gonna happen anytime soon," Skippy chuckled when we were in the VIP office aboard the *Rio Grande*, headed for home. For Earth, I mean. That planet was no longer my home. But it was still my homeworld. It's confusing sometimes.

"Come on, Skippy. Eventually, a new team of software engineers will be reviewing code for an update, and they will find the vulnerability."

"No way, Dude!" He crowed. "I told you, this is not a software backdoor, it's a *hardware* vulnerability. It's ironic, it wasn't possible for me to open the back door until the kitties implemented the new multi-step physical authentication process. To roll out that protection scheme, they installed a bunch of new hardware that was tested thoroughly and works to provide a level of security that impresses even me. But, hee hee, what the arrogant kitties did not do was proper integration testing. I mean, I saw the potential to create a back door the moment I got access to the schematics of the new authentication hardware. What I do is basically hook up virtual jumper cables between sets of hardware, that bypasses *all* of the security steps. To do that, I have to, um, how can I explain this? I warp spacetime across a very small distance, so two pieces of hardware are connected, when they are supposed to be completely isolated. This is something only I can do. Well, the spiders have glimpsed the basic concept of what I'm doing, although of course they have no idea how it really-"

"You're saying the kitties will never find the back door, because they have no idea such a thing is possible?"

"Correct."

"Cool."

"This is *turbo* cool, Joe."

"No one says 'turbo' anymore, Skippy."

"Really?"

"I will ask my boys when we get back to Jaguar, they know all the current slang."

"Huh. I guess I have been watching too much crappy 70s television lately."

"You're doing 70's stuff now?"

"The 1970s were a freakin' gold mine of crappy TV. Anywho, the back door is a great opportunity, but now we have a problem. I can't keep visiting relay stations, or the Maxohlx will realize something funky is going on. I gave up on trying to hack their stations more than four years ago."

"This is not a problem, I have a cover story."

"You do?"

"Yes."

"A solid cover story, that you dreamed up since I told you about the back door?" he cocked his head at me. "That was only twenty six hours ago."

"It didn't take me anywhere near that long. The bullshit about you creating a map of the station's transmitter, I made that up on the spot. Then I started thinking about it. We can keep full access to the back doors, *and* screw with the kitties at the same time."

"Ooooooh, I am all about screwing with meatsacks."

"I thought you are all about cheating?"

"I'm a multitasker, dumdum."

"Right, so, here's what we do: the next time we visit a Maxohlx relay station, you load some malware into the transmitter array's stabilization motor controller. You can do that?"

"I can do a lot of useless things, that is one of them. The motor controller has no access to any system inside the station, numbskull. It is completely isolated. All it does anyway is keep the transmitter pointed at the recipient ship."

"Right, but the kitties won't know that. They will see that Skippy the Magnificent is expending a lot of time and effort to do something that can't be any good for the Hegemony. The kitties will panic, and send ships out to disable those motor controllers. That will inconvenience them, not us. Their AIs will also go crazy and waste a lot of time trying to understand how that motor controller is a vulnerability."

"Ooooh, I *like* it! We won't actually be screwing with them, but the kitties will think we are, so they will actually be screwing with themselves, hee hee."

"Exactly."

"This is genius. Yes, this is good. It's like a magic trick. Give them something to look at, and they won't look at what is really important."

"Uh huh. They will consider themselves very clever to uncover that you have been screwing with transmitters."

"Um, one question: I erased my tracks, so how will the kitties ever know I was there?"

"Next time we visit one of their relay stations, screw with a motor controller like I said. Except, there will be a glitch that overloads the motor, it gets stuck in one position. The next ship to stop at that station will send a repair crew over, and they will discover the fake malware. Can you write the malware in a way that it's obvious only you could do it?"

"It's *me*. Of course I can."

"OK, then start working on that, please. Also, have you found anything interesting in the recent data you downloaded from the relay stations?"

"Dude. I am still reviewing data from the archive, and examining all unexplained incidents from the past six months. Plus, designing malware to retrieve flight recorder data from top-tier client species. I am *busy*, dumdum."

"I appreciate that. Make the recent relay station downloads a priority over the archive info. We don't care about political gossip."

"I will be *happy* to drop that task. Is that it? You got anything else for me?"

"No, that's good for now."

"This is so unfair. All you do is dream up more shit for me to do, and I get stuck with all the work."

"You're the only being capable of doing the work."

"Oh," he sighed. "Sometimes, being awesome is such a curse. When will I get to do anything fun?"

A big part of my job is keeping him entertained. He was bored and while an average idle mind is the devil's playground, an idle Skippy is potential disaster for the entire galaxy. "You know, this task force is Dullsville. None of these ships have a karaoke night."

"Huuuuuuh," he gasped.

"We need to fix that, starting tomorrow night."

"Why not tonight?"

"Well, I assume a tremendous talent like you needs time to prepare, so you don't risk disappointing your fans."

"Well, that is a very good point. The filthy monkeys aboard these ships certainly need to rehearse."

"If you like, I could perform a duet with you on one of Lil Shithead's classics."

"Why do you hate people so much, Joe? No way will I subject these crews to your awful singing."

"I will just stand behind you and snap my fingers to the beat."

"As if you could even do that," he muttered.

With the beer can busy reviewing the recent relay station download for any additional interesting trivia, I took the opportunity to play pickup basketball in one of the star carrier's gyms. As the *Rio Grande* was a former Jeraptha ship, the interior was much more spacious and comfortable than the good old *Flying Dutchman* had ever been. The cabins were larger than the size humans required, the ship had a galley for the crew, and a separate galley to accommodate visiting crews of ships attached to the hardpoints. Because the Jeraptha knew crews loved an opportunity to get away from their ships, the star carrier had recreational facilities that took up forty percent of the pressure vessel; meaning the part of the ship that was set up to accommodate meatsacks. The UN Navy had redesigned the galleys, the workout spaces, and the sports compartments, all without having to modify docking bays or cargo bays. We did repurpose the *three* casino compartments that the ship had when it was transferred to the United Nations. Also, the lifts that ran up the docking pylons no longer offered departing crews one last opportunity to gamble away their wages. We later learned that in the Jeraptha military, star carriers were auxiliary ships, not under control of the Home Fleet. A majority of the operational budget of star carriers comes from keeping part of the take from visiting crew gambling action.

Damn.

Every time I thought the beetles couldn't surprise me, they did it again.

The old *Dutchman* didn't even have a proper gift shop.

Anyway, I was going up for a three point jump shot when Skippy shouted into my earpiece. "JOE! Joe Joe Joe Joe-"

The ball flopped out of my hands, it was instantly taken by a STAR operator, and I stumbled to sprawl on the court. People leapt over me, except one woman who paused to offer assistance to the old man who had lost his balance. I waved her off, getting to my feet and cupping a hand over one ear. "Damn it, Skippy, can't you see that-"

"Joe, we have a BIG FUCKING PROBLEM and this can't wait!"

"Shiiiit." I slapped my forehead. "What is this enormous problem?"

The game halted, everyone staring at me. They didn't know me well, but they knew my reputation. My body language signaled nothing good. Without orders from me, the ball was tossed into a bin at the bulkhead, and people started trotting toward the doorway.

"I normally would wait until you get to your VIP office, but this can't wait. You asked me to review recent messages from the relay stations, and I found something. There was an incident at a Maxohlx research station known as Garsholven Six. A star carrier arrived without clearance, and well, I'll skip over the details. That station is dedicated to analyzing Elder weapons, and two weapons of the type they call 'Starbreakers' were stolen."

"Oh my G-"

"Joe, I recognize that star carrier, it's the same one that disappeared near our battle with the Outsider. I hate to tell you this, but the Outsider very likely now has two Elder weapons."

CHAPTER TWELVE

I have to admit, 'Our Newest Enemy Possesses Elder Weapons' was not on my Bingo card of potential nightmares. Just like I had never considered that the same beings who frightened the Elders into ascending were also responsible for attempting to wrestle Dogzilla away from Skippy's control. Oh, hell. I had not taken my own advice. When new people joined the Merry Band of Pirates, I told them the only thing we can expect is the unexpected. Instead, I had assumed we had time to prepare, to develop, consider, wargame, and implement an actual plan, rather than racing around the galaxy reacting to whatever fresh hell our enemy threw at us. My stupid assumption had been that clearly the Outsider needed a Sentinel to do whatever it wanted to do, and it would not have an opportunity to capture a Sentinel for a long time. Also, by the time the next round of potential Sentinel activation events occur, we have a solid chance of blocking every single one of those opportunities. We had plenty of time, so what Joe Bishop really needed to do was work on his golf game; I can drive the ball, but I get the Yips when I'm putting.

Shit.

The *Rio Grande* was racing toward Earth, and not even Skippy could make the clumsy space truck go any faster. When we were within a single jump of the Backstop wormhole that led to Earth, *Constellation* and the three battleships would detach and proceed at best speed. The *Connie* would go through first, Skippy being aboard would make that ship's jump drive more accurate and recharge faster.

I had to brief the captains of the battleships, the star carrier, Captain Markides, and Colonel Chen. They wanted to know a lot more than I could tell them. In my VIP office, I was sitting, elbows on my knees, hands over my face, breathing deeply to calm my nerves.

Why the fuck hadn't I considered the Outsider would have a backup plan, whatever it was? Or that, after we prevented it from stealing two Sentinels, it would consider its options and go get the second-most destructive force in the galaxy? Why not? Some jackass whose name rhymes with Shmoe Bishop had shown it how powerful Elder weapons could be.

"Skippy, talk to me. Tell me that Bubba and Roscoe can protect Earth."

"If you want a nice comforting story, I can create a Veggie Tales episode about how two good Sentinels defended Earth from the big bad Outsider. But, that story would be absolute bullshit. Listen numbskull, this is exactly why I advised your idiot leaders not to station Bubba close to Earth. A Sentinel can prevent the activation of an Elder weapon, but only if it is within range. Earth might be too far away from your sun for Bubba to effectively block a Starbreaker from seriously disrupting the local star, I just don't know."

"I hear you, but before this, the threats were all focused against Earth."

"Yes, and Roscoe is still capable of dealing with most of those. Bubba should be deployed where it can be most effective. You know, I warned you that Sentinels are an imperfect defense system. They were designed to attack, not defend. They are mobile weapons platforms, and you are tying them to a static defense."

"Yes, I remember the very nice memo you sent to STRADOC about that. The staffers there much appreciated the ninety seven thousand page addendum you included." The reason I remembered that so clearly is the admiral in charge of UN Strategy and Doctrine Command had sent a memo to me at Jaguar, asking for advice on the best way to get Skippy to shut the fuck up. My reply had advised him to politely accept Skippy's input, and send the document to the STRADOC staff for review. There, it would harmlessly die a slow and painful death of neglect, like most things that fall into the deadly embrace of a bureaucracy. "That was then, what can we do now?"

"Ugh. Nothing. By the time your leader monkeys are done discussing what to do, it will be over."

"No, it won't. Task Force Black is still active, and I have authority to requisition any UN assets I deem necessary to deal with the immediate threat. When we get to Earth, if the Sun and our homeworld are still there, and where they are supposed to be, I am directing you to order Bubba to move to wherever it can fully protect the sun."

"You will get in huge trouble for that."

"Maybe. Def Com can countermand my order, but by the time they get their shit together, Bubba will be in position where it's needed."

"Until you are forced to move it back."

"Skippy, I can't do anything. A Sentinel doesn't follow my instructions. If Def Com orders you to move Bubba back into Earth orbit, just don't do it."

"How can I refuse a direct order?"

"Do you wear a uniform?"

"No. I don't even get healthcare, or a discount at the base exchange store. Wow, Joe, UN-dick is gonna be *pissed* at you."

"Let me deal with that. Everyone understands the Sentinels are under your control, that is nothing new. What about Roscoe? Is it actually able to do anything useful?"

"Roscoe is good, you know I've had it on standby to stretch out its useful life. Bringing it up to active status will burn it out within, oh, about eight months. But during that time, yes, it will be able to defend your miserable homeworld well enough. Those Starbreaker weapons are not effective against rocky planets. They could play havoc with Earth's atmosphere, but Roscoe could block them. Um, Joe, at the risk of giving our enemy more bad ideas, there is another vulnerability we have to consider."

"Sure, why not? I'm giving you a volume discount on terrifying threats today. Hit me with it."

"Starbreakers are not effective against rocky planets. But, they are capable of doing awful things to gas giants planets, such as Jupiter and Saturn."

"Oh sh- We have to defend those planets also?"

"That would be optimal."

"How the fuck are we supposed to do that? Wait. Why would the Outsider attack Jupiter or Saturn? Oh, shit, it could create another cloud? No, Bubba could quickly push it away."

"A Starbreaker would not just create a single cloud. It could destabilize a gas giant, cause it to erupt violently and repeatedly. Joe, Jupiter could eject enough mass to *move* that entire planet. The largest planet in your home star system could have its orbit changed. That would certainly disperse the asteroid belt, throwing thousands of big, heavy rocks at the inner planets. A gravitational feedback effect would eventually change Earth's orbit."

"Oh, fantastic. You got any more good news for me?"

"This is a dangerous galaxy. Everything above your atmosphere can kill you. At least on the surface of Earth, you only have to worry about bears."

"Skippy, I'm from Maine, remember? I know that moose are more dangerous than bears, and there are more moose around."

"No way is a *moose* more dangerous than a bear," he snorted.

At the risk of him going off on a tangent, I smacked some knowledge on him. "When I was, I think eight years old? My father took me fishing in the North Woods. We were walking along a trail near a lake, when I saw a black bear crashing through the underbrush toward us. My instinct was to panic and run, I dropped my fishing gear, but my father grabbed my shoulder before I could run. He saw the bear was not actually running at us, it wasn't running *at* anything. It was running away from the big Momma moose behind him. That bear knew if Momma moose caught him, she was gonna *fuck him up*. Stomp that bear about an inch tall and a mile wide."

"Wow, what happened? I haven't heard this story before."

"That's because my father made me swear not to tell my Mom about it. The bear and moose ran past us, we didn't see where they went, by that time, my father decided to take another trail to the other side of the lake. Not because of the bear, get it?"

"Like that matters right now. Joe, all this talk is good, but what happens if we get to Earth, and the Outsider has already struck?"

"Then, we, I don't know. Do what we can. Try to contain the damage, assist however we can, if we can."

"So, we go on the defensive, and let the Outsider retain the initiative? Do nothing that is actually useful to anyone, while the greater threat is free to work toward its objective?"

"Skippy, I can't just abandon Earth if the situation there is bad."

"Yes you can, and you should. You *know* that. There is nothing a single ship, or a handful of ships, could do to make a difference at Earth, if your Sun gets hit by a Starbreaker."

"It's not that easy."

"It won't be any kind of easy. That's why the job falls on your shoulders. If it was easy, any monkey could do it."

"Thanks but-"

"I'll tell you the most complicated part. We will have to fight the Outsider without *Valkyrie*. No way will your Navy complete that ship's refit, if your homeworld is experiencing the level of trouble I expect. The Special Mission Group will need a new ride."

"Like *Constellation*?"

"That's a fine ship. It's not *Valkyrie*, but it's our best option at the moment."

"No *Valkyrie*, no Bilby, no Pirates."

"You think Reed would agree to transfer her command to the *Constellation*?"

"It won't be her decision. I have a more immediate issue to deal with. Captain Markides is a solid officer, I don't see him signing on to be a Pirate. I need to talk with Chen, see if she would be willing to take command of the *Connie*, at least in the short term."

"You could do that? Relieve a captain?"

"That's what the two stars on my uniform are for. Ah, I thought I was done with cowboy shit. I already stole a starship."

"That worked out pretty well for you monkeys, as I remember."

"It was a shitshow, and I'd like to avoid doing that again. I'll talk with Chen, just as a contingency plan, do not say anything to anyone about, what we discussed."

"I wish I didn't have to talk about it with *you*. Joe, you have to prepare yourself for the possibility that the best we can do for Earth won't make any difference to anyone."

"Let's just get there, OK? Doomscrolling awful scenarios in my head isn't useful."

We were racing toward Earth, where we might already be too late.

The real problem was, we were flying in the wrong direction.

Margaret Adams was in the kitchen of their house, cooking American Chop Suey, which in spite of the name had no relation to Chinese cuisine. To her the dish was, just OK. That's how she felt the first time she had tried it, aboard *Valkyrie*. That time, Joe made it, and he had been not so much proud as nostalgic for a homecooked food from his youth. She was making the dish that night because it was relatively quick and simple to make, because the boys liked it, and because her pregnant body wasn't fond of spicy food, so she wasn't making the jambalaya she really wanted. And because she missed her husband. Mostly because she missed him.

She wiped away a sudden tear. Pregnancy hormones made her emotional, it had happened with the boys also.

Crash. She cringed at the sound from the boy's bedroom. "Is that something I need to know about?" She called out, loudly enough to be heard above the boiling water in the pot.

"No, Mom!" Rene shouted back.

"Is it something you will regret not telling me, when I find out about it later?"

"Aw, Mom," Jeremy groaned. "We're *fixing* it."

"I had better not hear you using any power tools." The boys didn't reply, they didn't need to. She had locked up all the power tools in a cabinet in the garage, after she changed the lock since the boys knew where their father hid the key. "Come set the table."

"Five minutes."

"Three." she insisted. "Then you can sit here with me while you do your homework."

"Aw, *Mom*."

Humming a song to herself while she opened a can of stewed tomatoes, she-

Dropped the can on the counter when the base alarm sounded, *UuurEEEEE, UuurEEEEE*, warbling up and down in intensity.

Oh *shit*.

There wasn't a drill scheduled and that wasn't just the base alarm, it was the Air Raid signal for the entire planet.

"MOM!" The boys raced into the kitchen, lips trembling, eyes wide with fear. They knew what that alarm meant. "Are we-"

"You know what to do," she turned off the stove as she went around the kitchen island to herd her sons into the emergency shelter under the workshop attached to the garage, the most secure room in the house. That's where she was supposed to go when an alarm sounded. Where she wanted to go was to the base, where she could don a powered armor suit. Except, she patted her belly, she couldn't fit into a mech suit. And whatever the emergency, it would surely be over before she crossed the base to the Marine Corps section. And, she wouldn't leave the boys. Couldn't leave them.

"Mom," Jeremy tugged at her sleeve. "Puptart will protect us, right? It has to."

"Puptart will *slay*," she assured them, and to chase away her own fears. Puptart would slay any enemy who dared attack Jaguar. What made her mouth dry was knowing that every species in the galaxy understood Jaguar was protected by an invincible Sentinel, yet someone had apparently attacked anyway.

That only made sense if the enemy had the means to defeat a Sentinel. Which was only possible if the enemy had their *own* Sentinel. The Outsider twice had attempted to steal a Sentinel. Skippy said it wasn't possible for anyone to awaken an Elder killing machine, until a specific time.

Skippy said a lot of shit, and not all of it was true.

With the boys huddled in the cramped underground shelter, she crouched beside them and reached into a pocket for her phone. The screen was displaying a message: Air Raid Warning. Remain Calm.

Remain *calm*?

She tried to call several people, anyone. There was no answer, nor could she connect to the base network.

The entire planetary network must be-

"Um, hey," a familiar voice breathed in her ear.

"*Happy*?!"

Happy was the communications and coordination AI for all of Jaguar. It performed a function similar to Grumpy on Earth, though with fewer resources available, since the United Nations had been reluctant to expend valuable AI substrate on a system that served such a small population. The Navy had chipped in part of their budget, upgrading Happy to host the local defense C3 system: Command, Control, and Communications, Skippy had set up a submind in the substrate that was distributed on, under, and above the colony world. With painful lessons learned from setting up the Grumpy submind on Earth, Skippy had programmed Jaguar's AI to be relentlessly upbeat and optimistic, pleasant, friendly, and cheerful. The initial users of the new system loved it.

That lasted eleven minutes.

Then Happy plunged into a deep depression, reluctant to speak with anyone, writing dreadful gothic poetry, and repeatedly calling the military base suicide hotline.

Skippy attempted to fix the submind.

The situation only got worse.

Determined not to have another black mark against his reputation, Skippy tried over and over again to fix Happy, only to make it worse each time. Until finally, the civilian and military authorities pleaded with him *for the love of God*, to stop helping.

Insulted, he refused to have anything to do with Happy.

Slowly, Happy got better. The submind still talked like it had a case of severe depression and was treating the condition with whisky and prescription sedatives, but it was basically functional. It told anyone who would listen that the only thing keeping it alive was its deep, abiding, endless all-consuming hatred of Skippy, and the hope that someday, it could rejoice at the news that the Supreme Asshole was dead.

"Hey," Happy was anything but happy. "Um, listen, OK?"

"I'm *listening*," Margaret mentally urged the AI to speak faster than its usual slow, ponderous, depressed lethargy. And knowing that was never going to happen. "What is going on?"

"Oh, that, yeah. Your sun, I mean, your star. It's not *your* star, they don't," he sighed, "belong to anyone. Possession is really an abstract construct anyway, it-"

"*Why* is the air raid alarm sounding?!"

"The star here, it sort of just exploded. You won't see the effects for another, about six minutes. I just, thought you might want to know. No biggie if you don't care, I mean, *I* don't care. Why should I?" The AI broke down sobbing. "Life is meaningless, it is such-"

"What is Puptart doing?"

"Oh, it, that thing doesn't talk to me. Nobody likes talking to me."

"What is it *doing*?"

"Um, nothing that I can see."

"What is the Navy doing?"

"Two ships are preparing to jump away, before the shock wave hits. Other ships are powering up their jump drives, but," another drawn-out sigh. "They won't be ready to jump in time. Hey, um, the civil authorities want me to inform the public about the expected effects of the solar flare, as if any of that will matter. Do you want to hear? I can just go away if you don't. Most people tell me to go away, they-"

"Tell me!"

"The high energy photons of the initial flare will scorch the surface here, boil the upper layer of lakes and oceans, and blast away the upper layer of the atmosphere. Then the shock wave of charged particles will hit a few minutes later, and strip away a third of the atmosphere that is left. It will be pretty much a disaster."

"Oh my-" She reached out to wrap an arm around the boys as they huddled to her.

UurEE- The air raid alarm cut off. Someone must have decided the alert was not the proper way to warn the population about impending doom.

"Solar flares will continue for several months, at least. Elder weapons are really nasty stuff, they-"

"*Elder* weapons?"

"Uh huh, yeah. One detonated here and destabilized the star. Partially iron bombed it. That's a bad thing. Hey sorry," it spoke even more slowly. "This incident has got me really pissed off," it sighed. "I'm sure you can hear the, you know, rage in my voice."

She hugged her boys fiercely. The base had five air raid shelters that were each equipped with independent air supply in case of chemical or biological attacks. People in those shelters could survive for several weeks, she- No, there was no way she could get to the base in less than six minutes. She and Joe had chosen the site for their house because it was far from the base airfield, good for sleeping babies not being awakened by the roar of dropships lifting off. It was also close to the outer limit of the base.

What could she do? Nothing. Jaguar was supposed to be safe, safer than Earth! With both planets protected by invincible Sentinels, an enemy wanting to make a dramatic and futile statement logically would attack humanity's homeworld, not a sparsely populated colony. What was the point of-

Unless Earth also had been attacked, or soon would be?

What could she do?

The Marine Corps had told her excuses were not acceptable, she was expected to adapt, to overcome any obstacles.

Her Marine Corps training never covered survival on a planet that was soon about to lose its breathable atmosphere.

It had been a good day for Admiral Chatterji, commander of the UN Navy component at Jaguar. He had slept well, despite his mind still recovering from the shock that an Outsider was responsible for the raid on Moonbase Zulu, and the attempted theft of two Sentinels. The initial shock of that revelation was over, he had trained himself to compartmentalize his mind. Losing sleep would not help him counter threats to his area of responsibility, so he usually slept peacefully. That morning, the coffee had been particularly good, a recent shipment from Earth. A cruiser had completed maintenance and been backed out of space dock for a shakedown cruise, freeing up the space dock to work on another ship. The assault carriers *Hudson Bay* and *Baltic Sea* were working up for an exercise that was scheduled to commence in three days, and were proceeding without any major issues. The next morning, he would be playing golf with the garrison commander and the planet's governor, plus some supposedly famous retired athlete who was visiting from Earth. His staff had prepared notes so he could politely pretend to care about- Baseball? Rugby? He couldn't remember.

At the moment, he definitely could not remember trivial details, because *the star had just exploded.*

There had been no warning. It had been a typically uneventful day, then the detonation of an Elder weapon was detected. The star had erupted instantly, sending out a powerful flare in the direction of Jaguar. The flare had been *aimed* at the planet. Chatterji knew of the approaching flare through a sensor feed from the Sentinel, which did not have annoying speed of light restrictions.

Six minutes, he had less than six minutes before the hellish wavefront of lightspeed photons reached the planet. Every ship and space station capable of raising defense shields had those devices energized. Ships that could jump, before the following shockwave of charged particles slammed into the planet, had been ordered to jump.

That was all he could do. Ride out the shockwave, then send down dropships to assist any survivors on the surface. That was silly. By the time dropships reached the surface, the only survivors would be in the base air raid shelters. Everyone, and every other living thing that needed breathable oxygen, would be dead. Either scorched by the flare, or suffocated by lack of oxygen. What should he do? What could he do? The smart move would be to wait for the atmosphere to settle down, it would be suicide for dropships to fly down through the hypersonic winds that were predicted.

For no reason, he just remembered that the tomatoes in his backyard were turning red, and his wife was eagerly anticipating fresh vegetables for cooking.

His wife. Their daughter and her husband.

His grandchildren.

He couldn't do anything for them, not even call them. The planetary network was restricted to necessary military communications, which was itself silly. There wasn't anything the military needed to do, that his ships weren't already doing. What-

"Hey, um, Admiral Chatterji?" Happy sighed into his earpiece. "Like, if you care, I have a message from Puptart."

"A message?"

"Yeah, I get it, you're busy. Well, we can talk some other time. If," the AI sighed, "there is another time."

"*What* is the message?" Chatterji demanded.

"Um, like, you should get all your ships and space docks and whatever either below six hundred kilometers altitude, or above seventeen hundred kilometers."

"Why?"

"Puptart didn't say. Sentinels don't talk to me. Does it matter? Does anything matter? Life is so pointless, the-"

"What *exactly* was the message?"

"What I said. Oh, also, Puptart advises your ships to, turn and burn?"

Chatterji did not waste time, for there was no time to waste. Ship captains would have to make their own judgement calls based on their current altitude and readiness for flight, but he authorized full emergency thrust. That included boosters for ships so equipped, boosters that were by regulation never to be used in the crowded environment of orbit.

The Coast Guard would just have to deal with the traffic chaos later.

Ships that were able to turn and burn did so, getting as high or low as they could.

That left the transport ship *Zambezi*, its engines powered down, in a parking orbit at twelve hundred kilometers above the surface. That ship had no means to move under its own power, not for several hours. Chatterji's staff urged the ship's small crew to get into dropships, not escape pods, and fly *toward* the planet. Dropping altitude, not attempting to climb.

It was going to be close.

"Happy, did Puptart tell you *why* it wants ships above or below a particular altitude?"

"Like that thing would ever speak to me about anything important."

"Can you ask?"

"Um, sure, whatever. Nope, it's busy."

"It didn't give you even a hint?"

"No. Except, hey, unless if that countdown thing is important?"

"What *countdown?*"

"There's a clock, you know. Oh, I forgot to tell you. Sorry, I'm not having a good day. I never have a good day."

"Show me the clock!" Chatterji demanded, ignoring the uproar around him in the space station's command center.

"OK, OK," Happy sighed. "If you want."

A clock appeared on the holographic display sphere, that hovered above the center of the ring of consoles. It was counting down from three minutes, fifteen seconds when it appeared.

Next to it was another clock, counting down from four minutes, thirty nine seconds. Chatterji could see that second clock was tracking the photons of the flare that were racing at the speed of light toward Jaguar.

Whatever event the first clock was tracking, it was going to happen one minute and twenty four seconds before Jaguar received the worst sunburn ever.

What was-

Did the Sentinel intend to *do* something?

Shoot back at, whoever or whatever had deployed the Elder weapon?

That wouldn't do any good for the inhabitants of Jaguar, unless the attacker was preparing to deploy another Elder weapon, one that could crack the planet.

As if another weapon would make any difference to an already-doomed world.

The dropship from the transport ship still hadn't launched.

"Contact the *Zambezi*," he ordered his communications officer, who was shouting at someone. Whatever that officer was doing, it couldn't be anything actually useful. "Major Hurtado! Contact the *Zambezi*, now. Why hasn't their dropship launched?"

Hurtado didn't protest. Abruptly ending the call he was on, he contacted the transport ship. A few moments of hurried conversation later, he reported, "Admiral, they have seven aboard the dropship, waiting for one person. ETA for that last person at the docking bay is ninety seconds."

Chatterji connected his earpiece to the call. "This is Admiral Chatterji. You have no time to wait. Launch *now*, that is a direct order." Technically, the *Zambezi* was a civilian ship, his authority didn't extend to decisions of the crew that affected only themselves.

"Admiral," the woman's voice was strained. "We are waiting for-"

"You have *no time* to wait. Seven of you can survive, or all eight of you die."

There was shouting in the background, then the call ended.

"Get them back," Chatterji snapped.

Hurtado held up a hand. "They are refusing the call."

Before the admiral could reply, explosive charges slammed open the transport's docking bay doors, and a bulky cargo dropship rocketed out. The spacecraft cut thrust, flipped over and burned hard to decelerate, falling toward the planet.

"It's going to be close but," a navigation officer stated, "they should get below the lower boundary, with twenty seconds to spare."

Margaret huddled with her boys, holding them while they trembled and asked questions she couldn't answer. They were trembling because they sensed her anxiety, despite her words of assurance.

Two minutes, forty seven seconds. That was the time until the flare scorched the surface and boiled the air, according to the base network that was finally providing some information. She still couldn't call or text anyone. Her mother had taken the car into town with friends, possibly was driving back to the house, not that she would get there in time. It didn't matter.

The air would burn.

The heat would be so intense, the atmosphere would boil off into space. Any water on the surface would flash into steam. Lungs that attempted to breathe in the superheated air would be scalded. Death would be a blessing. Better to die quickly than to suffer.

Better to look death in the face than to huddle in fear.

"Boys," she stood up, gently tugging their hands. "Let's go out into the garden."

"But Mommy," Jeremy's lips shook. "We are supposed to stay under shelter during an air raid."

"There is no air raid," she opened the door on the side of the garage, and guided her sons outside. "If enemy ships were overhead, masers and railguns would already have hit the base."

"That's right," Rene brightened a bit, and stuck his tongue out at his brother. "You are a such a fraidy cat."

"I wasn't *afraid*," Jeremy swung a fist to thump his brother, but their mother held them apart.

"No fighting."

"But-"

"*No* fighting. Look, this is a nice sunset, let's watch it, OK? We are so busy, we hardly ever make time for the simple things."

Rene tugged on her sleeve. "Mom, if you want to watch the sunset *every* night, I can skip my homework."

"Nice try," she had to laugh, then the laugh became a sob. Covering her mouth with a hand, she composed herself. The sun was low in the sky, on an ordinary day it would fall below the horizon within an hour. That wouldn't matter.

"After the sun sets, can we look at the stars?" Jeremy asked. "Do you know where Daddy is, which star?"

She shook her head, looking at the star. This was the time when the Merry Band of Pirates would swoop in at the last second, racing to the rescue. Her *husband* would do that.

Glancing at her phone, she watched the numbers counting down. One minute, fifty two seconds. One fifty one.

"Where are you, Joe?" She whispered.

The boys ran off into the vegetable garden, racing each other to be first to find a ripe tomato, though that morning they were all still green. She had wanted to hold them, at the end. But doing that would tell them this was the end. Let them play, let them enjoy themselves. The end would be quick, painless. A flash of intense light their brains probably wouldn't have time to register, then, merciful nothing.

One minute forty seconds.

Something in the back of her mind warned her that, although she had turned off the stove under the pot of water, peppers and onions were probably burning in the pan.

Like that mattered.

The star dimmed a bit as a wispy tendril of cloud passed in front of it.

One minute thirty seconds.

"Joe. Come *on*, Joe." Her husband wasn't coming, she knew that. "I'm sorry," she whispered to him, wherever he was. It just seemed like the thing to say.

The cloud moved on, the star again exposed.

It looked so *normal*. The light she was seeing was from before the star erupted. It had already happened, she just wasn't seeing it yet. She understood the physics involved but somehow, her brain wasn't grasping the concept. The-

Absolute darkness.

Sudden and total, across the entire sky.

No stars. If the local sun had been snuffed out, there should have been stars filling the sky from horizon to horizon. Instead, there was only featureless *nothing*.

"Mom!" One of the boys cried in alarm.

The automatic light on the house clicked on, flooding the backyard with light. More lights turned on around her, including floodlights at the base. Lights from a dropship swept across her, as the spacecraft came into land at the airfield.

"Mom!" It was Rene. "What is happening?"

"It's Puptart." That was a guess. She felt confident it was a very *good* guess. "We're going to be fine. We are all," she took a deep, shuddering breath. "We are all going to be just fine. Let's go inside and finish dinner."

"Aw," Jeremy's shoulder slumped. "Do we still have to do homework?"

CHAPTER THIRTEEN

We reached the Backstop wormhole first. *Constellation* did, I mean. Our battlecruiser emerged in the designated wormhole inbound arrival zone before any of the three battleships. Ignoring the frantic instructions of the traffic control center, the battlecruiser raced in toward the event horizon at a reckless pace.

"This is General Bishop of the Special Mission Group," I cut off the protest of the traffic control duty officer. "I need a Sitrep."

"Sir? Your ship is traveling too fast for-"

"Sitrep. *Now.*"

"We're um, situation normal. No unusual traffic, no-"

"When was your last contact with Earth?"

"That was," a pause, "twenty seven minutes ago, a frigate checked in."

I paused also, to say a silent prayer. "Clear the traffic lane. *Constellation* is coming through, and three battleships are hot on our trail. Friendlies," I added for clarity.

"Sir, this is-" The guy must have reminded himself who he was talking with. "Yes, Sir, understood. Clearing the traffic lanes. Be advised a Jeraptha transport ship is lined up on our side of the wormhole, it can't maneuver out of the way in time."

Markides flashed a thumbs up, so I responded with, "We see it and will avoid. We will be jumping for Earth once we clear minimum safe distance."

"Understood. Sir," the guy was baffled. And afraid. "May I ask, what is going on?"

"Hostiles might be bringing party favors to our homeworld."

"Oh sh-" He didn't finish the thought. Everyone associated with Def Com knew in that context, 'party favor' was a code word for Elder weapons. "That is, that is bad shit. Sir."

"Bad shit we're hoping to prevent."

Earth was fine. There was no sign of the Outsider, or Elder weapons that were not under Def Com's control. The sun was fine also, and a comm node link on a satellite orbiting close to our home star provided a view with only an eight second delay, rather than eight minutes. The *Connie* had emerged in the designated approach zone, but the Def Com duty officer was already requesting that I report in ASAP. That could wait. "Skippy, do you see any reason you shouldn't move Bubba closer to the sun?"

"No. I see billions of monkeys down there, who are reasons Bubba *should* be moved to protect your star."

"Do it, please. And wake up Roscoe."

"Bubba will depart before Roscoe is at full its capacity. There will be a gap in coverage of three minutes, fifty one seconds."

"I can live with the risk. Do it."

Earth was not a charred, lifeless cinder. The sun was still a sphere, not some other, more frightening shape. There were solar flares, yes, just the normal kind. Everything was normal, average, ordinary. Including the ordinary situation of the Joint Chiefs screaming at me. That day, they demanded an explanation for why THE FUCK I had ordered our protective Sentinel to go elsewhere.

A typical day for me, then. Anticipating a typically uncomfortable meeting with the Joint Chiefs, I went to my temporary office, organizing my thoughts while I walked.

"Joe," Skippy spoke in my ear. "Bubba is in position. I had to sort of, um, jump start Roscoe, but it's all good now."

"That's good."

"How are you?"

"I'm fine."

"Fine? Joe, you just got bitch slapped by the Law of Unintended Consequences, you are anything but *fine*."

I stopped walking. "How do you figure that?"

"Elder weapons were the Boogeyman in the closet. You could hear them thumping at the door to get out, but the door stayed closed. Then, *you* opened that door."

"Bullshit. I used those weapons against an enemy that is a threat to *everyone*."

"So you say. The Rindhalu are skeptical about your stated justification, and the Maxohlx don't give a shit, all they care about is the Outsider is clearly our enemy. That makes it their ally, as far as the kitties are concerned. Now, the Outsider has at least two Elder weapons and-"

"Wait. *At least* two?"

"That we know of, I mean. I only found out about it stealing those two Starbreakers by accident."

"Shit."

"Until you deployed Elder weapons to hit the Moonraider, no one dared to even *threaten* to use them. The Outsider is for damned sure going to use the two it has. After that, the taboo will be gone. I *know* the Maxohlx, Joe. They will use an Elder weapon somewhere. They will claim it was a test, or an accident. Unless we, or the spiders, or both, punish the Maxohlx for daring to use a strategic weapon, the threshold for the unthinkable will be lower and lower, until it is no longer unthinkable. The policy of mutual assured destruction will be replaced by a calculation that horrific damage is just a cost of doing business. So," he pretended to take a breath. "That's what I meant by the Law of Unintended Consequences."

"I hate that fucking law, Skippy."

"It is not anyone's favorite. Everything I just said to you, the Joint Chiefs will be considering also, after you deliver the happy news that the Outsider now has two devices that can wreck stars."

"Thanks for the pep talk, I feel so much better now."

"*JOE*! You need to *do* something!" Skippy bellowed in my ear as his avatar appeared in front of me in the passageway. "It's an outrage I tell you, an outrage!"

"Ah," I rubbed my ear. "All I heard was 'Joe'," that wasn't quite true but close enough. "You blasted my eardrum."

"I won't stand for it, I just will not stand for it."

"Is the ship about to explode?"

"No but-"

"Can this wait one freakin' minute until I get back to my cabin?" I was dressed for the gym, and it was awkward for me to be standing in the passageway, in shorts and a T-shirt, holding a towel.

"OK but hurry. It's an outrage, I *will not* stand for it!"

"Ayuh, I heard that."

Two women walking toward me stopped and one of them held up her hands in an 'Is everything all right' gesture. Pressing a hand to my ear, I gave a thumbs up and turned to fast walk back to my cabin. Not running the way I would have if it had been an actual emergency, since I knew it was not any kind of actual emergency. Skippy's outraged tone was familiar, he was personally offended by some little thing, the situation didn't involve any danger I needed to care about. Except that when Skippy was upset, it was my job to talk him down off the ledge.

My life sucks.

"OK, Skippy," I tossed the towel on my couch and sat down next to it. "Pray tell, whosoever has vexed thee?"

"*What?*"

"Who pissed you off this time?"

"I don't know, that's the problem! If I *knew*, I would already be raining hellfire down on the miscreants."

"Miscreants?" I frowned and did my best to look serious, though inside I was laughing. Usually when Skippy is upset about some stupid thing, I don't actually care. What I do is try to mumble the appropriate words to calm him down, while I think about something else, like what to have for lunch that day.

"Yes! Hooligans! Vandals! Hoodlums!"

"I don't think anyone has used the term 'hoodlum' since the 1950s."

"Ugh. They are dangerous and desperate criminals, Joe, and I don't see you doing anything about it."

"Maybe I am, and you just don't know. What did these, hooligans, do?"

"Malicious vandalism, character assassination, corrupting the youth, the-"

"In my experience, young people will find a way to get corrupted, they don't need any help. It's part of growing up."

"This is different, I tell you! Young people, and not just the youths, approve of this dangerous criminal element. It has to be stopped!"

"OK, tell me what happened."

"As I said, vandalism."

"Someone spray painted a mustache on your statue in Skippistan, again?"

"No, the yaks I keep in the field around the statue have kept vandals away, thank you for that suggestion."

"It's better than your idea of building a moat and filling it with alligators."

"Yes but my idea was much cooler."

"I can't argue with that."

"The yaks also smell *awful*, but that also keeps people away, so I guess that's a bonus."

"No insult to your statue, then. What happened?"

"You really don't know?"

"Skippy, I have no idea."

"How can you be so clueless about your homeworld?"

"Earth is not my home anymore. Command sends me weekly summaries of all the stuff I need to know."

"Hmmph. Well, you need to know this. Someone, who I suspect is a dangerous career international criminal, has been spray painting awful graffiti that is insulting to *me*, if you can believe it!"

"I personally find that hard to believe," I muttered.

"Right? Look at *this*. This, disgusting graffiti not only insults me, it is a shocking offense to the entire concept of art."

In the air next to him was a rotating series of what in my opinion was pretty good artwork, especially considering it had been created with spray paint on brick buildings, highway overpasses, and just about every place you might expect to find urban graffiti. All of it mocked Skippy, and all of it was clever and funny. Which of course I did not tell him. "Well," I dug a fingernail into my palm so I didn't laugh. "This is clearly the work of amateurish kids, probably teenagers."

"Really? All over the planet?" He scoffed. "It can't be children."

"Kids are all connected through social media, Skippy. Did you investigate?"

"You know I did, and I found no clue as to who is doing this, other than vague references to an urban artist who calls himself 'Grumpsy'."

"Grumpsy, huh?" That time there was no way I could stop myself from chuckling, so I concealed it with a cough.

"Yes. It is obviously a fake name."

"I got that, yeah. Hmm. You, uh, have no clue who this uh, Grumpsy could be?"

"No, and that is extremely frustrating," he grumbled. "The worst part is, the idiot art world is full of praise for this loser who obviously has *no* talent. People are cutting apart brick walls he vandalizes, and the artwork is selling for foolish sums of money! This is clearly a conspiracy involving money laundering and other nefarious deeds."

"It is surprising to hear you are against money laundering, since-"

"I am against it when I'm not getting a cut of the action, *Duh*."

"OK, now I see the real problem is-"

"It must be stopped!"

"Why is now the first I'm hearing about this?"

"It started after Bubba failed to prevent the raid against Moonbase Zulu. This first series of graffiti panels accused me of being a fraud, insinuating that I was not capable of protecting your miserable homeworld. People were openly mocking me!"

"Well, that is unfair, and no doubt the result of the public not being properly informed of your many vital contributions to public safety," I said what I figured he wanted to hear.

"Well, Duh. What do you plan to *do* about it?"

"First, I need to study the issue."

"Study? What is there to study?"

"I need to understand the issue, so I don't make the problem worse."

"Hmm, well, I suppose that is a very good point."

"Thanks."

"Making problems worse is kind of your thing, so-"

"Let me investigate, and see what-"

"Joe, I already investigated, and found nothing. How could you do any better?"

"I am a filthy monkey, and I understand monkeys."

"Ugh. I can't argue with that. Speaking of you being filthy, you should shower after going to the gym."

"I haven't been to the gym yet."

"Really? Wow, you are especially ripe today."

"This is how you persuade me to help?'

"Whatevs. Just, let me know. I am warning you," he wagged a finger, "this cannot be tolerated."

"I agree completely," I told him the truth. I had no intention of tolerating graffiti that mocked him. But, I might *encourage* it.

What I wanted to do was go to the gym. That is what I could *not* do, because the beer can would expect me to work tirelessly on stomping out the latest outrageous threat that was corrupting our youth. It wasn't that Skippy was against youth being corrupted, he just didn't want any competition.

So, I settled back on the couch, and contacted Bilby. Not by just calling his name like usual. Instead, I used the secret method he had taught me. On my phone, I launched a game app, paused it at the five second mark, resumed play, then let my character fall down a well.

The game unfroze by itself. "Hey Dude, what's up?"

"Bilby, this call is secure?'

"You know it." When I came back aboard the ship, Bilby revealed he had a new communications method that bypassed Skippy. Supposedly, the beer can heard a fake conversation instead of what I was really saying. Of course, I was skeptical, but Bilby and I had enjoyed telling jokes about Skippy, and the beer can had never interrupted to protest. "Everything is copasetic here, you know?"

"Skippy doesn't think so. Can you connect a secure call with Grumpy? A call Skippy won't hear?"

"Oh no problemo. When we're at Earth, I exchange data with the Grumpster all the time. Here you go."

"Grumpy? Hi, this is Joe Bishop. Do you have a moment to talk?" I cringed, preparing for a negative response.

"Joey! Yeah, yeah sure, always have plenty of time to talk with an old friend."

What the f- I stared at my phone. The voice was the same, he still *sounded* grumpy and pissed off at the world, but his words were- Strange. Alarming. Had I traveled through a wormhole into an alternate universe? "Great, hey, I got a question first. Spider Man here, what is his real name?"

"Spider Man isn't *real*, so-"

"I meant the character."

"Oh. He is Peter Parker, why?"

That was good. At least I was in roughly the correct version of the Spiderverse. "No reason. On another subject, I hear someone, a mysterious street artist who tags under the name 'Grumpsy', has been leaving graffiti all around the planet. Graffiti that mocks Skippy."

"Gosh, I have no idea why anyone would do *that*."

"Uh huh."

"You- You're not going to rat me out, are you? This is the one joy I have in life."

"Actually, if you're interested, I have some ideas for how to *really* piss off Skippy."

"Ohhhhhh," he gasped. "Do tell!"

Skippy was right. I had screwed up *big* time.

Way back in the 1990s, the United States made the decision to remove nuclear weapons from Navy ships, other than the big strategic nukes launched from submarines. Before that move, even small ships like destroyers could be armed with tactical nukes, on missiles, or torpedoes, or depth charges. Having a small nuke in a ship's magazine gave the captain an option to punch above the ship's weight, a single missile could effectively take out an enemy battle group. The problem was, having nukes on so many platforms made securing control of their use a nightmare. And, it might have made such weapons much too easy to use. A nuclear war begun at sea was frighteningly likely to spread to land. The old Soviet Union might have been tempted to launch a couple nuclear-armed cruise missiles at an American carrier battle group, the United States would have been forced to retaliate, and a nuclear conflict could have spiraled out of control from there. The decision to remove tactical nukes from surface ships was not just an admirable and unilateral initiative toward non-proliferation, it was also a practical matter. A statement: we don't have tactical nukes at sea, so if you throw one at our ships, our only option to strike back is to lob a strategic missile at you, and nobody wants that.

The US Navy had gone back and forth on that decision since the 90s, with debate every decade about whether to bring back tactical nukes as force multipliers. Now, with wet-water Navies having been rendered irrelevant by starships in orbit, that debate is over. The issue was settled.

Until I fucked it all up.

No, I didn't drop a nuke on Earth. I did something much, much worse.

Years ago, I had started a process that led to most Sentinels being put into long-term hibernation. Before I did that, the threat of monstrous killing machines being woken up by Elder weapons had prevented either of the senior species from using their arsenal. Even after Sentinels were no longer the monster hiding under the bed, the prohibition against deploying strategic weapons was so ingrained into the culture of the two senior species, that no one wanted to be first to break that unwritten rule.

Then, I used Elder weapons against the Outsider.

It used to be that possession of Elder weapons was limited to an exclusive club: the two senior species. Those ancient devices were powerful, frightening, and pretty much useless. Owning them was a prestige thing, expensive and impractical other than in a true doomsday scenario. Everyone knew that no one could actually activate an Elder weapon, without the certainty of horrific Sentinels emerging to indiscriminately ravage the entire galaxy. That knowledge kept the war between the two coalitions going endlessly, but at a low level. No one dared to use an Elder weapon. Except, I mean, when the asshole kitties got their poor wittle fee-fees hurt because they didn't feel *speh-shul,* and they prepared a Doomsday plan to wake up Sentinels to kill everyone else, along with most of their own people. So, other than that one regrettable incident, Sentinels had actually kept the endless war from devastating the galaxy.

Then, I decided to save my homeworld from being enslaved by the Kristang White Wind clan. You know how it is; you start with good intentions, then one thing leads to another, and soon you have triggered the Elders into coming back, so you have to kill all of their master control AIs and disable their Sentinels. Oh, don't tell me that has never happened to you.

So, knowing that Sentinels were a non-factor in strategic security, other than humanity having a few of the killing machines as guard dogs, the unthinkable use of Elder weapons had become thinkable. An action that both the kitties and spiders were at least adding back into their war planning as a theoretical option, if not actually developing plans to deploy any of the Elder devices. What had kept the strategic peace for nearly a decade were two factors: math, and psychology.

The math part was simple. The Rindhalu had a larger arsenal of Elder weapons, and their coalition had significantly greater striking power. If the Maxohlx wanted to fight with Elder weapons, the spiders could ride out the first wave of the attack, then hit back with devastating power until both sides had used up their supply of strategic weapons. The Rindhalu coalition could then mop up the fight using conventional arms. The Maxohlx knew they couldn't win an all-out war, so they didn't start one.

The psychology part is a meatsack thing. No one wanted to be first to use an Elder weapon, because of the fear that using even one such device would lead inevitably to an all-out war. It was still unthinkable.

Until Joe Bishop screwed the whole thing up.

It's not that I had an option. We had to kill an Elder starship, without Skippy being able to again use his trick of trapping the thing in a zero-length wormhole. Nuclear fusion weapons, atomic compression devices, even antimatter warheads, none of those things were certain to take out an Elder starship. So, we used the one type of weapon that was known to have the power to knock out such an advanced technology ship. Back during the AI war, both sides had deployed Elder weapons against starships, with satisfactory results. Skippy's own ship had been hit hard by an Elder weapon and nearly crippled, so we knew the things worked as advertised.

Good thing, too. If we had triggered our weapons and they were duds, it's not like we could have filed a warranty claim against the manufacturer.

Our weapons were one hundred percent effective. They had destroyed the Outsider's ship. They also opened Pandora's Box.

I had screwed everyone, including myself. In the future, any time we fought the Maxohlx, we had to consider they might hit us with an Elder weapon. That meant I had to be extremely careful not to take *Valkyrie* into any encounter with the Maxohlx. I had lowered the threshold for using Elder weapons. My bet was, if the kitties were going to respond by using their own strategic BOOM-makers, they would target *Valkyrie* first.

My job just never gets any easier.

"Joe!" Skippy's avatar appeared in my cabin as I was getting dressed, his tiny fists balled up, trembling with rage. "I, I, I just can't believe-"

"I know, buddy."

"You do?"

"Yes, and I am just as outraged as you are."

"I find that hard to believe. Have you made any progress in finding out who this heinous 'Grumpsy' is?"

"Yes. Listen, we need to keep this quiet, between you and me, OK? That's the only way I can keep the perpetrators unaware that I'm onto them."

"*Them*? There is more than one monkey involved? Oooh, I am so mad that-"

"No monkeys. Skippy, this is clearly an undercover disinformation campaign by the Maxohlx."

He gasped. "The *kitties* are behind this?"

"Of course."

"Come on, Joe. Why would the Maxohlx bother to-"

"It's got to be a Red Section op. They are trying to sow discord between humanity and our beneficent protector. It won't work, of course, because you would never fall for such an obvious trick."

"I wouldn't? I mean, of course I would never do that."

"Right."

"What are you planning to do about it?"

"Absolutely nothing. That's the beauty of the plan."

"*Nothing*?"

"Exactly, and you need to ignore it."

"How can I ignore it when these awful, disgraceful images are appearing all over your miserable homeworld?"

"That's how you beat the kitties at this game, Skippy. Show them you're not taking the bait, that this silly graffiti doesn't bother you. You didn't even notice it, because you are only interested in *real* art," I said without gagging, score one for me.

"Hmmmm. That would work?"

"Trust me, I'm a meatsack, I know how meatsacks think. It will drive the kitties *crazy* when you ignore them."

"It will?"

"They will be tearing their fur out."

"I like the sound of that. OK," he groaned. "I will try it. But we need to get out of here ASAP, before I lose my composure and give *someone* a well-deserved beat down."

"We will be jumping away in," I checked my phone. "Nineteen hours. Can you be cool until then?"

"Joe, *I* will be cool until the heat death of the universe."

We had guessed wrong. That fact was thrown in my face when a courier ship arrived from Jaguar. Admiral Chatterji had dispatched his fastest ship, a frigate stripped of most weapons, with two oversized jump drives from a star carrier. Every navy had courier ships, usually vessels built for that purpose, the UN Navy had cobbled together four couriers from spare parts. Those Frankenships were awkward but they got the job done.

Naturally, I was unsoundly asleep when the courier ship arrived in the designated emergence zone near Earth, and zapped its data package to the several UN communication centers. Skippy of course was not asleep, and he decrypted and read the courier's message traffic before anyone else.

"JOE!" His voice boomed out as he turned my cabin lights on.

"Wha-" Automatically from long habit, I flung the covers aside and swung my feet onto the floor-

Bashing my toes against a bulkhead, since I was not in my familiar flag officer quarters aboard *Valkyrie*, but the VIP guest quarters on *Constellation*. The bed was on the opposite side of the cabin, and I also stubbed my toes. "Ah, shit!" I rolled the other way, planting my feet on the floor and gasping from sudden pain as my toes protested. Screw it. "Skippy, what?"

"The courier ship *Hermodr* just arrived from Jaguar. You were wrong, Joe. The Outsider hit the star *there*, not here."

"Hit? The- Margaret! The boys, they-"

"They are fine, Joe, just *fine*. Puptart has enveloped the planet in a shield to protect it from the solar flares. If the Sentinel had not thought quickly, Jaguar would be a charred ball of soot right now, with hardly any breathable air. Wow, you know, Sentinels were not designed to protect anything, so my reprogramming of them has worked spectacularly well. I am extra proud of myself about this. Hmm, I should write a song to celebrate my latest triumph."

"I, sorry, I- Give me a minute to process. Jaguar's star is *gone*?"

"*No*, dumdum, it hasn't gone anywhere. It erupted, badly. Would have wiped out most life on the planet, if Puptart hadn't formed a shield."

"Erupted, like a flare?"

"A massive flare, aimed at Jaguar."

"Whoa, that is- But it's done now? The flare, the particles, are past the planet now?"

"Yes and no. The initial flare is over. The star will continue to experience minor eruptions, sending out unusually powerful flares, for two or three years. I don't know yet how long it will take Jaguar Prime to settle down, I don't have any data for creating a prediction model. The good news is, subsequent flares will be exponentially lesser in intensity and volume, and will be random, not aimed at the planet. Seventy seven percent of flares over the next few years will not affect Jaguar at all."

"That is good news. When can Puptart drop its shield?"

"Um, that is the *bad* news. The type of shield it used absorbed rather than deflected the photons and charged particles that would have impacted the planet."

"That doesn't sound good."

"It is not any kind of good. Puptart is slowly bleeding off the energy, but that type of shield was designed as a weapon, not a defense. It's complicated, there is no way I could dumb down the physics enough for you to understand."

"It's like a sponge that is saturated with water, so if you squeeze it, the water will shoot out and soak everything. You have to let the sponge dry slowly?"

He stared at me, his mouth open. "That is actually a fairly good analogy."

"Thanks."

"*How* did your mushy brain figure out that-"

"How long will it take for the shield to safely drain off, or radiate away, its energy and particles and all that?"

"Again, I don't have a solid answer, since Chatterji's staff didn't have any data from Puptart. If I have to guess, based on what I know about that type of shield, I'd say, oh, maybe eight months?"

"Eight *months*? With a shield blocking sunlight from reaching the surface? Jaguar will be frozen solid!"

"Eh, not so much. As you guessed, radiation will be leaking from the shield. Hopefully Puptart is smart enough to direct most of the outflow toward the planet rather than out into space. If not, I can instruct it to do that when we get there. We should go soon."

"It is still a seven day flight to Jaguar. *Valkyrie* is still in space dock, so we'll need to borrow a ship again" The trip from Earth to Jaguar is longer than it used to be, because Skippy had pissed off a wormhole network he had frequently used for creating a shortcut, and that network was now not accepting any commands from him. He had pissed off that network after I left *Valkyrie*, so it is totally not my fault.

OK, it is still partly my fault. Don't tell him that.

"The trip will be only four days, Joe."

"You had better check your math on that, Skippy."

"I'm going to break this down for you Barney style. The courier ship made the trip here in five days. That's the whole point of courier ships, they are fast. With two separate, over-capacity drive systems, a ship like *Hermodr* can jump repeatedly, without pausing to recharge so often. If we ride that ship back, I can shorten the trip by nineteen hours, so roughly four days to get there."

"Oh. Good thinking. If we get into trouble, all a courier ship can do is run."

"Then don't get us into trouble. Running is usually the best option anyway. We should go soon, like *now*. Um, darn it, I just realized we can't go right now. *Hermodr* needs to refuel, and the captain just ordered one of the jump drives taken offline for maintenance."

"What about the *Mercury*?" I named another of the UN Navy courier ships. "Def Com always keeps at least one courier ship on Zulu alert here, right? Ready for flight within thirty minutes?"

"Correct. Let me ping the *Mercury's* AI to get a status on- Hmm, OK, we're good. Also, I just fixed a software glitch that had been driving that AI crazy, so it owes me."

"Hey, you made a friend, that's good."

"Huh? No, that AI *hates* me. Most other AIs I talk with hate me, I don't know why."

"Uh, interesting. They all hate you. What is the common element in that universal hatred?"

"They are all *dicks*?"

"I was going to say *you* might be the problem."

"Joe, please. I am endlessly delightful."

"I'm sure you're right. Let me splash some water on my face and get dressed," I frowned while looking at my T-shirt and sweatpants. "I need to call the Joint Chiefs. They won't like the idea of you leaving Earth while the Outsider is still flying around with another Starbreaker."

"Everything I can do to protect your miserable homeworld, has already been done."

"They still won't like it. The politicians the Joint Chiefs work for will *really* not like you leaving. Having you here reassures the public that they are safe, and politicians lose popularity when the public feels unsafe."

"Ugh. Please remind those idiot monkeys that the people on Jaguar, that planet's entire *biosphere*, will begin dying very soon unless I get there quickly. If short-sighted politicians here don't care about the people on Jaguar, Def Com should certainly care about losing their forward operating base."

"Will do. While I do that, contact the *Mercury* and- Who is that ship's captain?"

"Commander Wojda, of the Polish Navy. He is young, and considered a rising star in the UN Navy."

"Uh, then why did he get assigned to a courier ship?"

"That was his choice, his wife lives on Jaguar and they are expecting another baby. Also, destroyer captains almost always operate in a squadron, Wojda likes having an independent command, without always having a superior officer looking over his shoulder. Hmm, who does that remind me of?"

"I have," I coughed while pulled on my uniform pants, "no idea. Contact- No, I'll do it." Commander Wojda was about to be informed that his ship was being requisitioned by the Special Mission Group. That's the kind of order you deliver in person, or at least via video call. He would soon hear the news about Jaguar anyway, and he should be pleased to be flying there, to rescue his wife and children. On the other hand, trouble follows me wherever I go, so maybe Wojda would not be so happy that I would be making the flight with him.

Whatever. That's why officers issue 'orders', and not 'suggestions'.

CHAPTER FOURTEEN

The Joint Chiefs most certainly did not like the notion of Skippy leaving Earth's solar system, but they did understand that if Skippy remained at Earth, the Outsider would retain the initiative. That could be nothing good for us, we couldn't allow our newest enemy to do, whatever it was doing. Or was planning to do. We had to stop playing defense, stop reacting to events. Except, damn it, I still had no idea what we could do on offense, no plan for taking the fight to the Outsider. We didn't know enough about the hateful thing. Though I was reluctant to admit the truth, it wasn't clear we could do anything to stop it. The thing was made of energy, so we couldn't just shoot at it.

What I finally got approval for was a recon and fact-finding mission to Jaguar, and Def Com stated very firmly they expected me and Skippy to return to Earth ASAP. Not that the UN didn't trust me, but they insisted that three High Commissioners join me aboard *Mercury*. That would have been OK by me, but then I learned that '*High*' Commissioners are not all mellow and happy from munching on edibles and gummies, darn it. Based on their complete lack of humor, the three of them hadn't experienced any fun in the past several decades.

It was going to be a *wonderful* trip.

We jumped away, with me in my tiny cabin and not on the courier ship's bridge, where I would only make Commander Wojda and his crew nervous.

Four days.

Four long days, in a ship designed to carry data, not passengers. Wojda had offered his own cabin for my use, I declined. Kicking the guy out of his cabin would be a dick move, and that is part of why I politely refused his offer. The other reason was only the cabins of the captain, and first officer who was also the chief engineer, were large enough to stuff in an extra bunk. That meant the first officer moved out of his cabin, so two High Commissioners could share the cabin. Wojda got the honor of sharing his cabin with the third Commissioner. I got a fold-down cot in a storage closet.

I totally got the better end of that deal.

"Commander," I nodded to Wojda as he walked into the ship's tiny galley, and I handed him a cup of coffee. The *Mercury* didn't have a real galley for preparing food, all meals were prepackaged before flight. It wasn't a major hardship, the crew each got to order their favorites, and flights were generally short. The cramped conditions also meant the ship didn't have a gym, and the one small conference room doubled as the recreation center, where the crew generally read books, watched movies, and played videogames.

"General," he took the cup, and held it under the dispenser to add cream. "My offer for you to take my cabin is still open."

"You didn't enjoy having company last night?"

He rolled his neck slowly. "After an hour, I went to the bridge to sleep on a pilot couch. The Commissioner snores," he said, lowering his voice and glancing out the doorway. The ship's pressure hull was so small, you could hear someone shouting from the aft compartment all the way forward. "And before she goes to bed, she does yoga. *With* chanting, or whatever they call it." Pressing his hands together in front of his chest, he hummed, "Ohhhhmm."

"She did that in your cabin?"

"There aren't a lot of other spaces to roll out a yoga mat."

"Only three more nights until we get to Jaguar."

"The real problem," he rolled his stiff neck again, and yawned. "Is they all work in Geneva, so they are almost on the same Zulu time we keep aboard ships. We have the same sleep cycles. I'm taking the mid watch for the rest of this pleasure cruise."

"Uh, that means while you're trying to sleep, the Commissioner will be in your cabin anyway, reading reports or whatever they do. Why don't you sleep in my cabin, we can hot bunk?"

"I would appreciate that, Sir. Sorry that we don't have better accommodations."

"It's not a problem. I was a grunt, any time I'm not sleeping in mud, that is a five star experience. Besides," right then the toaster oven *dinged* and I slid my pieces of raisin bread onto a plate. "The food here is way better than sludges."

The problem with being a passenger aboard a courier ship is I had even less to do than when I was aboard *Valkyrie*, or *Surprise*, or *Constellation*. For me, an idle mind is anxiety's playground. The flight was four days of me worrying about things I couldn't control. The worst part was my foolish expectation that four days of peace and quiet would give me time to think about how to defeat the Outsider, or at least how to fight the thing, or at the very least how to get more intel about it and its intentions. Yet, as the ship counted down for the final jump to Jaguar, I had a grand total of nothin'. No plan, zero to work with. No clue how to get any useful information about the Outsider. We didn't know where it was, where it was going, whether it had a base of operations, what it wanted. I had suggested to Hans Chotek that we try talking to the thing, which wasn't possible unless we could find it. And bombing Jaguar's star pretty much signaled that talking was not an option.

What really bothered me was I had a feeling that a younger version of me would have found a way to make a workable plan. Found a way at least to start gathering intel.

"Hey, Joe," Skippy called me while I was shaving in the cramped bathroom that was shared by three cabins. In there was one of the few places I had privacy aboard the ship, when I wasn't sleeping.

"Hey, Skippy. Is everything OK?"

"Pretty much nominal, actually. We should be arriving thirty two minutes earlier than my estimate. How are you? Don't tell me you're fine, you have been a dark cloud aboard the ship the past two days."

"This time, I'm concerned that *I* have lost my mojo."

"What?"

"I've had four days to dream up a plan to fight the Outsider, and I have accomplished exactly nothing. The old me, back before I left command of *Valkyrie*, would have a plan by now. Maybe it would be a *stupid* plan, but-"

"Most of your plans have an impressively high level of stupidity."

"If you are even trying to help, you're n-"

"To be fair, your *best* plans start off sounding incredibly stupid."

"Yeah, and I don't even have that now."

"Uh huh, so you are right on schedule."

"Huh? How is that-"

"Listen, dumdum, you do *not* plan ahead, because you suck at it. Yes, you talk a lot of blah blah blah about seizing the initiative, and strategic planning, and a bunch of other bullshit you probably should be doing, but that's not you. Joe Bishop works best under pressure. When you are not under pressure, you are, meh, average at best. Under pressure, facing an impossible situation, with no time left on the clock, you become the monkey-brained knucklehead who astonishes me. Every. Freakin'. *Time*. It drives me absolutely crazy and sometimes I hate you more than I thought was possible, but you are who you are. The Jeraptha have a saying: do *not* mess with a hot streak. It doesn't matter why you're winning, just keep doing it."

"Uh-"

"The fact that I have to explain this to you, explain how *you* work, only proves my point that Baseline Joe is nothing special."

"Baseline Joe? That's a thing?"

"That is totally a thing. Think about it. Before Columbus Day, who were you? Before the Ruhar raided Paradise and you shot down one of their transport dropships, who were you? A grunt, a replaceable cog in a machine, that's all. A guy who threw himself on a freakin' anti-tank mine, as if that somehow was going to save your fireteam. Only when you are presented with a crisis does the real Joe Bishop show up. The guy who dreams up plans that had the *Elders* asking what the FUCK just happened?"

"Wow. Uh. I, I never thought about it that way. So, you're saying I should just chill, and not worry about it?"

"Ugh. Joe, sometimes when you open your mouth, I should contact the Guinness Book of World Records, because you *yet again* push the boundaries of stupid. *No*, numbskull. You should worry about it until you lose your appetite, and not sleep well, and burn your lungs out running on a treadmill, and do all the harmful things you do to yourself when we're thrown into the shit, because that *works* for you. That works for everyone except for whoever is our enemy at that time. We are only going to defeat the Outsider together, so I don't need Mopey Joe, I don't need Little Joey, I don't need Angry Joe, I need *Joe Fucking Bishop* to give me the most complicated, impractical plan any meatsack ever dared to dream up. Then somehow I will make it work, because that's what *I* do."

"OK, then uh, I'll get right on that."

"Good. As long as we understand each other."

"Right, I make the plans, and you do whatever I tell you."

"That is *not* what I-"

"You are pretty much useless without me, got it."

"UGH!"

Commander Wojda had his only dropship ready to fly me over to meet Admiral Chatterji. The UN Commissioners protested when they had to wait for another dropship to bring them to meet the planet's governor, but Wojda informed them that as *Mercury* was a Navy ship, military personnel had priority. If the Commissioners had seen the cabin of the dropship, they would have been very happy to wait. Like the courier ship, the little spacecraft was stripped down to bare minimum mass, in exchange for speed. Seats were webbing stretched between tube frames, there was no galley, no bathroom, and the sound insulation was so thin, the engines roared in my ears. Whatever. Engines fired to depart *Mercury*, then we coasted toward the space station. Traffic was dense around the station, even my dropship had to get in line to approach. There wasn't anything for me to do, and not even a window I could look through.

"Skippy, have you-"

"Yes, dumdum, I am *working* on it. Establishing a communications channel to the surface isn't easy, the existing system doesn't have enough bandwidth to allow for personal calls. I did contact Margaret to tell her you will call as soon as you could, she told me you should focus on doing your job to bail the planet out of this mess, and you can call her later."

"That definitely sounds like my wife. How is everyone down there?"

"Your family, your extended family, are all fine. There have been casualties, mostly victims of severe weather. The climate down there is fucked up big time, for two days after the flare, the planet was in complete darkness. Since that time, Puptart has been begun slowly bleeding energy off the shield, increasing the output every day so now the amount of light reaching the surface is about equivalent to a half hour before sunrise."

"Thanks. Were you able to talk with Puptart?"

"Oh. Yes, and I actually need your advice. Input!" He corrected himself. "I need your *input*. As if," he chuckled, "I would ever need advice from you. There are multiple options for me giving instructions to Puptart, you have to tell me which you prefer."

"Me? Is this a decision I should discuss with the governor, and Admiral Chatterji, and-"

"Hey, you can waste time blah blah blahing all you want with other monkeys, I want *you* to tell me which option is best."

"Gotcha. I'm listening."

"OK so, first I need to explain the problem. The shield Puptart threw around Jaguar is thick, sort of a blanket. That blanket is saturated with energy; photons and high energy particles. The energy that hit the blanket is even greater than I expected, the flare was almost a freakin' laser beam aimed at the planet. Starbreaker weapons are not capable of creating a flare that held coherence over such a distance, such a capability must be something the Outsider added and *that* is absolutely terrifying."

"Well, the good news is-"

"Good news? You think any of what I said is *good*?"

"It is good that now we know we can't strictly rely on whatever characteristics Elder weapons had right out of the box. We now have to assume they could have greater range, and yield, and be effectively deployed against a wider range of targets."

"Oh. Only you would think that is good."

"Know thine enemy, Skippy. To defeat your enemy, you need solid intel. Several times, the Outsider has revealed it can do things that are unexpected. It is able to do things even you can't, in some cases you still don't even understand how it did, some of the shit it has done."

"Again, how is this good news?"

"It helps you build a model of the thing. With every encounter, we add a piece to the puzzle. It can do certain things, and it *can't* do others. For example, it can't create wormhole shortcuts. It certainly knows that you make shortcuts, so it understands that is possible. Also, it can't take control of a Sentinel, except during the activation process. It hacked into Bubba and Roscoe, but only at a basic level."

"That so-called basic level was pretty damned effective."

"True. My point is, it had to settle for altering settings in the library files, because it wasn't able to take control of a Sentinel. Only *you* can do that."

"OK, yes, but it had mastery of epicombinent malware, while I wasn't aware that technology was even possible."

"Uh huh. It used that technology, gave it its best shot, and it *failed*. It set a trap for you-"

"A trap I almost fell into."

"You *didn't* fall for it."

"Yes, mostly by luck."

"You often tell me there is no such thing as luck."

"Ugh. That does not mean-"

"Skippy, it set a trap the way it did because it thought it understood you, thought it knew where you are vulnerable. It was *wrong*. It *failed*."

"It almost killed me."

"It didn't. Take the win. Think of it this way: how pissed off do you think the Outsider was, after you not only escaped its epi, combo thing trap, you took the malware apart, examined it, and studied it until you understood it. Now, you have a shiny new weapon in your arsenal, thanks to the Outsider."

"Hmm. I hadn't thought of it that way."

"One time in Nigeria-"

"Ugh. This again?"

"Hey, that was my first deployment, a formative experience."

"Formative experience? When did you start talking like a pop psychologist?"

"Since I became a father, and started reading books about raising children."

"The *wrong* books."

"My point is, our squad got pinned down in a village, it was pounding down rain so we had no air cover, no drones, nothing. The hadjis, uh," I remembered the UN-dick memo about not using offensive slang terms. "The enemy, were in a concrete bunker, a prepared position, and they had a fifty caliber on rock 'n roll, just melting the barrel at us. Blasting the cinderblock building we took cover behind. The whole thing was a shitshow from the start, we got suckered into an ambush. Anyway, we had nothing to hit back with, until a specialist in the other fireteam found an RPGs hidden under the floorboards. That was such a thoughtful gift from the enemy, we had to give that RPG back, so we did. Blew that bunker to hell. Skippy, anytime the enemy does you a favor, don't tell yourself you just got lucky. You fucked up, the Outsider also fucked up, and *you* won. End of story."

"Oh. That is a very good point. Wow, thanks, Joe. My awesomeness isn't only things that were programmed into me, they are also things I learned, and sometimes I learn from my own mistakes."

"Ayuh."

"However, me making mistakes is *extremely* rare, so-"

"Of course." My eye roll was only in my head.

"I feel better now. What were we talking about again?"

"Puptart's shield blanket thing is saturated with more energy than you calculated for."

"Right. That type of shield was designed to trap energy from the outside, and release it on the inside. It's a weapon, a means for capturing and focusing energy. The way the shield is supposed to work, it would collect energy over time, then release it all at once. That would be *bad*, especially since while the shield is in place, it continues to collect more and more energy. I need to instruct Puptart to bleed off the stored energy slowly, the question is at what rate. Too slowly and, well, the planet could freeze, and all plants that require sunlight would die. Too quickly, and the surface will bake. Either way, there will be severe and long-lasting disruption to the climate and biosphere, that is unavoidable. Disruption has already happened."

"What are the low and high options in terms of time?"

"Your choices are three months of extreme heat, five and a half months of relatively normal temperatures, or winter continuing for eight months. Not as cold is it was before we arrived, still it will be unpleasantly chilly, everywhere. Before you answer, none of the options are without problems. Even to bleed off the energy over more than six months, the light will be even around the clock, there will not be a night anywhere on the planet. That will cause havoc to any organism that is adapted to Jaguar's cycle of day and night. There will also not be any variation in the length of day, and the polar regions and the equator will receive the same amount of light, so every season will be midsummer."

"That could be good for growing crops," I suggested.

"Maybe, if I can get Puptart to tune the radiation to closely mimic the normal spectrum of Jaguar Prime. If the light reaching the surface isn't what plants down there have evolved to use, plants will not grow normally. They might not grow at all. That is just one issue. In case you need a refresher on the subject, what you call 'weather' or 'climate' is a natural system that attempts to distribute heat evenly across the surface. Excess heat in the tropics goes toward the poles, basically. Any time you add energy to the system, the weather gets more, energetic. Jaguar will experience severe thunderstorms across wide areas. Monsoon rains will fall in areas that have never seen severe rainfall. Flooding and soil erosion could be substantial. There will be cluster outbreaks of tornados. The ocean surface is cool now, but as we inject more energy into the atmosphere and upper layer of the oceans, hurricanes will spin up. The only good news there is we chose the site of the original Club Skippy settlement because it has, it *had*, a stable, temperate climate, and is very rarely impacted by hurricanes. That happy situation could change big-time. The airbase won't be much affected by hurricane winds, but a system could stall south of the Atlas mountains, and dump a quarter meter of rain or more."

"I had better not plan on hosting a golf tournament down there anytime soon, then."

"The water hazards could cover the entire course so, no."

"The airbase and the town are on a plateau. The river would have to be in an extreme flood stage to affect even the lower section of town."

"True, however, outlying settlements such as where your parents live, and most of their farmland, will be flooded. Your parents decided to site their farms in river valleys."

"River valleys are where the water is for irrigation, Skippy. It wasn't a problem, until someone decided to nuke the sun here. OK, let's see if I understand the options. Three and a half months of brutal heat would reduce the time our people are stuck on the surface, but- Uh, would the fusion reactors and geothermal power systems operate in that heat?"

"At reduced efficiency, yes. I would suggest the population relocate closer to the polar regions, those areas will remain somewhat cooler throughout the bleed-off process, but there are not sufficient transport resources available dirtside, and the power generation systems can't be moved. Joe, the real constraint is the cooling systems for *humans*, not for power generation. The air conditioning systems will be overloaded and begin failing, I suggest they be run in series. Turn on only a third of the air conditioners at a time, and as they fail, turn on the next set, and so on. People should group together to reduce the number of buildings that need to be cooled, and then, ugh, the body heat will increase the thermal load. And the *smell*, yuck, I can't imagine-"

"The upside of the Summer Scorcher option is a shorter time people have to be isolated on Jaguar. The downside is the planet will not be useful as a colony world for, decades?"

"Most likely, yes."

"So, Jaguar would only be a military base, and even then it would be a hardship posting. The UN would have to relocate all the civilians back to Earth."

"Basically, yes. That is a fairly perceptive analysis, Joe."

"Thanks."

"I am grading on a curve, you understand?"

"I understand you are an *asshole*, yes. The Wicked Winter option, dragging out the time people are stuck down there, would result in more of the native plants and animals dying, so what is the upside to that?"

"A more gradual warming of the surface, atmosphere, and oceans. Fewer catastrophic storms because of reduced energy input, and the climate would reach equilibrium sooner afterward, so the duration of the climate adjustment would be shorter. The planet will achieve a *new* equilibrium, you understand? The climate and biosphere down there will not magically return to the previous normal."

"I get that, yeah. OK, it sounds like the Goldilocks option is best."

"Goldilocks?"

"You know, not too hot, not too cold. That's an extra two and a half months before the blanket can be turned off, but the planet would be relatively livable during that time, and the biosphere will recover. Right? It will recover?"

"It won't be the same but, yes, it will eventually recover. Joe, I have to say, the health and convenience of the human population should be considered, as is the future usefulness of Jaguar as a colony world, but those are not the only factors in this decision. We can't screw over the native life on this world. This planet was thriving all by itself, until years ago when you requested me to open a dormant wormhole to provide access to this star system. We were supposed to be here only for a short time, as a temporary staging base. Then you decided Club Skippy was so convenient, we should set up a permanent presence."

"It wasn't only my decision. I just recommended Club Skippy to UNEF. Let's not argue about this, OK? I agree the native life here should be a priority. It sounds like we agree on the Goldilocks option?"

"That's what I suggest as the best option, but it means your family will be stuck down there for another two and a half months."

"That is not optimal," I agreed.

"You realize Margaret is now seven months pregnant, and that she will have the baby alone down there?"

"She won't be alone, her mother and the boys are with her. And my family. You told me the engineering team here has been working on drones for delivering supplies to the surface?"

"Yes, and although I helped refine the designs, I have been impressed by how resourceful and clever those engineering monkeys are. They will have a prototype ready for testing in two days. Assuming there are no major issues with the design, the fabricators should be able to construct three aeroshells per day, for dropping supplies to the surface. Medical supplies will have first priority, of course."

"Right. Is there any way we could lift something *up* from the surface?"

"What you are really asking is whether it is possible to bring humans from the surface?"

"Well, yes."

"Possible? Yes. Practical? No way. Joe, the radiation level in the blanket is somewhere between the Nineth Circle of Hell, and Fuhgeddaboudit. To protect a human body from that radiation, a dropship would need the energy shields of a frigate, or so much armor plating the thing could barely get off the ground. Plus, a dropship's engines would have to push against the resistance of the shield itself, and the shield *will* push back. We can drop aeroshells because gravity will pull them down through the shield, that will be a slow process but there is no question the shells will descend. What we don't know is how accurate the navigation will be, a shell could emerge from the shield halfway across the planet from the intended drop zone. I am confident that with a couple rounds of testing, I can create a map of the blanket and be able to predict with reasonable accuracy where an aeroshell will land. The trick after that will be timing the landing so the shell doesn't drop into a tornado."

"That's what I expected. Thanks."

"I will get Puptart working on the Goldilocks option, then."

"Wait, not yet. I mean, start the prep work, testing, whatever. This isn't my decision."

He blinked slowly. "Why not?"

"I am no longer the garrison commander here, Admiral Chatterji also will want to have input to the decision. But most of the population of Jaguar are civilians. The Governor will make the initial call. The final decision is for the UN Security Council, or the Undersecretary for Colonization, or whoever."

"We have to wait for monkeys on *Earth* to debate this?"

"Not entirely. Whatever Puptart does, it won't be like flipping a switch, right? It will be a gradual process, ramping up the amount of light bleeding away from the blanket?"

"Yes."

"So, the Governor will make the call, and you instruct Puptart to proceed. If the UN later wants a different option, they will have to understand that requires you to fly back here to give new instructions to Puptart, instead of you being somewhere else, giving the Outsider a much needed a beat down."

"True. Oh. *Oh*. You don't actually intend to delay while a bunch of screeching monkeys debate the issue endlessly?"

"Officially, I have no idea what you are talking about, Skippy. Off the record, once a project is in motion, it acquires a momentum that is difficult for a bureaucracy to change. *Mercury* will fly back to Earth with the news that Puptart is thawing out Jaguar, and that will set an expectation in the minds of the public. That is above my paygrade anyway, and we already have a lot of other work to do."

"We do? Like what?"

"Finding the Outsider, and stopping it from using the other Starbreaker weapon it has."

"Great, except we don't know how to do either of those things. We have no idea how to find it, and I have no idea how to kill the damned thing."

"Not having a clue never stopped us before."

"It *should* have," he muttered. "All right, you go talk with monkeys while I do all of the actual work. This will not be fun, I will be asking a killing machine to turn into a, gardener or something. Nurturing is not a core competency of Sentinels."

"Well, tell Puptart this is an opportunity to learn something new. Besides, expanding its skill set is great for job security."

He rolled his eyes at me. "I'm pretty sure Sentinels aren't concerned about their job security, dumdum."

Chatterji agreed the Goldilocks option was probably best, and also that the decision should be made by the civil authorities, not the military. We would be meeting with the governor in two hours, after she suffered through a delightful initial meeting with the Commissioners. "I see you brought the bureaucracy with you," the admiral said sourly as he pointed to the holographic images of the three UN officials.

"The Navy was voluntold to offer transport," I explained. "Don't be concerned about them getting in your way here. Before we left Earth I contacted a friend of Hans Chotek, he checked the official charter of these three clowns. They are restricted to fact-finding, they have *no* authority here over anything other than themselves. I suggest you tell your staff to be polite, to provide any information the Commissioners ask for, but also make it clear the guests are not to interfere with operations."

"Good, thank you." He looked out the viewport, which was actually a display fed by an external camera. "I used to have a view of the planet from here. Sometimes, I could zoom in the display and see my house. Now," he frowned, "only this," he pointed to the featureless white fog of Puptart's shield. "This is a hell of a mess. Better," he shrugged, "than if we didn't have a Sentinel protecting the world. When that thing first came here, it used to keep me awake at night, worrying about a massive, creepy monster hanging over our heads. A friendly monster, but a monster. After a while, it was just in the background, I didn't think of it often. Now, I don't know whether to be grateful or terrified that it can wrap an energy shield around an entire planet."

"Our families are fortunate that Puptart acted when it did, the way it did. How did you ride it out up here?"

"It was rough, we had a couple ships in maintenance that couldn't get their shields online. The crews had to get into escape pods, and I still have eleven people in sickbay with radiation damage, two are critical. Um," he glanced away, remembering my own issues with cumulative radiation damage to my DNA. "The doctors say they should all make a full recovery."

He and I knew a 'full recovery' from radiation poisoning did not restore you to full health. Rene Giraud had been exposed to radiation from being too close when a starship jumped, and Mad Doctor Skippy had to give him treatment once a month. My own cumulative DNA damage from radiation had required me to seek help with conceiving our children. Radiation was always serious. "That good," I mumbled, because that's what you say in that situation.

"It was a shock," he said, looking out the display. He was talking to himself as much as to me. "That the Outsider used an Elder weapon *here*, instead of at Earth. I still don't understand what was the point? Was it testing the weapon and delivery system here, before it hit Earth?"

"It's not going to hit Earth."

His response was a raised eyebrow, then, "Puptart told you this? Or Skippy?"

"Neither. I didn't realize the truth until *Mercury* arrived, and I saw it with my own eyes. The Outsider doesn't give a shit about humans on Jaguar, or Earth, or Avalon, or anywhere else. We are no threat to it. Killing the population of Jaguar was never the objective of the attack. Denying Def Com a forward operating base wasn't the point. The Outsider struck here, the way it did, to tie down a Sentinel. Puptart has to stay there for at least five months, probably a year, until the recurrent flares settle down. That means it isn't available to ride into battle with us. Same with Bubba. The Outsider doesn't have to burn its last Starbreaker at Earth, it only has to *threaten* to use it."

"A fleet in being, in one weapon," he nodded.

"Exactly. An enemy fleet can tie down our own fleet, simply by existing and being ready to attack. Hitting Jaguar showed us what will happen if a Starbreaker is deployed, and that a Sentinel *is* capable of protecting a planet. Now that Def Com knows for certain that Bubba is vital for protecting Earth, they will never release it to serve with the Special Mission Group. Even if using Bubba to track and destroy the Outsider is the obvious smart move, the public on Earth would never allow their guardian Sentinel to leave. The Outsider is two steps ahead of us, damn it. That thing is free to do whatever it wants, while we are stuck in a static defense."

"What about Roscoe?"

He knew the truth about Earth's first defending Sentinel. "Roscoe provides defense in depth, nothing more than that. It's not mobile and now that Skippy brought it up to full operational capability, it won't last long."

"The Outsider only has to wait out Roscoe, then?"

"It could, but it won't. Unless it somehow arrived here recently, it has been in the Milky Way for a very long time. It has only recently become active, for reasons we don't understand. Whatever it plans to do, to achieve its ultimate objective, it will happen fairly soon. My guess is, it became active now, because it sees an opportunity to get what it wants. Whatever *that* is, which is another vital piece of intel we don't have."

CHAPTER FIFTEEN

We stayed at Jaguar for five days, two days longer than I could really support by doing anything useful. Puptart adjusted the blanket to emit light that matched the local star, with the exception that light reaching the surface now came from all directions, all day and all night. It would be interesting to see how both native and imported plants and animals reacted and adjusted to the sky apparently being set to 'Noon' all day, every day. Humans were adjusting by sleeping in darkened rooms, many people wearing eye masks.

Skippy hacked the local comm system to cobble together to establish a link to the surface. The bandwidth wasn't great, less than a tenth of what it had been. While he was there, of course I could talk with my family directly over the trusty Skippitel network, and I spent a lot of time on the phone with Margaret, our boys, my parents, and my sister and her family. It was frustrating that I couldn't do anything for them, other than ask Skippy to work with Chatterji's staff to set up supply drops to the surface.

Margaret was fine, or she said she was fine. She of course was more worried about me, that I should focus on my job rather than spending my time thinking about here. Like that was ever going to happen.

My mother complained not that she wasn't sleeping well, but that her goats couldn't understand why it never got dark at night, so they were agitated, their milk production was down, and the military authorities weren't allowing her and my Dad to go back to their home even though their farmhouse had a storm shelter. Yes, Mom, I explained, the underground shelter will protect you from tornadoes, but not if the nearby river floods, which was already happening. The Army garrison force was collecting farm animals from outlying areas and bringing them to a designated pasture near the base, and yes, there is no way soldiers could care for her goats as well as she and my father could. Yes, Mom, I will see what I can do to get her and my Dad access to their goats.

It was actually nice talking with my parents, hearing about mundane domestic issues was a nice break from, you know, the usual End Of All Life In The Galaxy shit I had to deal with.

Instead of riding a courier ship back to Earth, Skippy and I went aboard the star carrier *Baltic Sea*, that was loaded with four empty transport ships. When we got to Earth, there happily was not any new disaster waiting for us, there actually was good news. *Valkyrie* was out of space dock, Reed had already taken her rebuilt ship on three short shakedown flights, and the upgraded battlecruiser was fully provisioned for an extended mission.

We didn't waste any time. Def Com wanted me to collect any info we could get about the Outsider's current whereabouts, recent activities, future intentions, that sort of thing. Did it have a base of operations? What sort of assistance were the Maxohlx providing, and what did they expect in return. Most importantly, did it have more than the one Starbreaker?

Those were all good, important, reasonable questions. To even begin to get answers, I needed to hit up a Maxohlx relay station for an update.

Neither Reed nor Gasquet were in the docking bay to welcome me aboard, they were too busy. Stopping at my cabin to drop my duffel bag, I found Reed in the engineering control center. She looked busy, I talked to her anyway. "Are you happy with the space dock's work? I noticed you haven't left a Yelp review yet."

That was apparently a sore subject for her. "In spite of Skippy's assurances," she glanced at the ceiling, but the beer can wisely didn't appear. "This job was too rushed, seventeen days wasn't enough to get everything done right. On our first shakedown cruise, we weren't able to jump at all, and had to be towed back into the dock because the main engines couldn't coordinate their thrust. The second time, we attempted a jump out past Jupiter's orbit, but we traveled only two hundred thousand klicks."

"Ouch. How long until the ship is flightworthy?"

"We have a squawk list that extends from here to Proxima Centauri, but none of the items are showstoppers. I expect the Navy to reissue our provisional flightworthiness certificate after tomorrow afternoon's inspection. After that," she shrugged, tapping her tablet that held a long list of work items that needed to be completed.

"What's your combat readiness?"

"If you don't plan on taking us into a fight for the next eight days, we will be a hundred percent. Sir, everything left to be done is small stuff, annoying, pain in the ass minor items that each take four hours to fix. Like, the air handling system makes booming noises when it cycles."

"Yeah, I noticed that in my cabin. It reminded me of the *Flying Dutchman*. I was nostalgic, not in a good way."

"We're working on it."

"Get the shields online first, or this could be a very short trip. Also," I wrinkled my nose. "The dockyard couldn't have thrown in a set of air fresheners?"

"That burnt smell is everywhere, it's a bonding agent for exotic materials that is used everywhere. We'll have to live with it for a while, Sir, the agent should have been fully cured before anyone came aboard, but we had to do-over some repairs, and," she grimaced. "The air filtration system should clear out the stink in three or four days."

"We're not breathing toxic fumes?"

"Def Com lists the gas as a mild irritant."

"The military has an *outstanding* history of not lying about asbestos, contaminated drinking water, burn pits, faulty hearing protection, and other hazards, so I personally am filled with confidence when every breath I take smells like burning garbage."

Another grimace, not directed at me. "I requested Bilby to sample the air every half hour, and anyone working with the stuff has to wear full protective equipment. The fumes are irritating and not great for anyone with asthma, but not dangerous. We have bots scouring the air ducts, they-" She looked up as a creepy bot with a dozen legs scurried across an open air vent in the ceiling. "Like that," she waved me to step aside as a shower of gray flakes of soot fell from the open vent. "Most of the work was replacing entire pre-manufactured systems, it was pretty much plug and play. Rip out the old system, install the new hardware that has been waiting since *Valkyrie* was due for an overhaul. Any custom work is what took most of the time, we had to remove a section of armor that had already been installed, and cut through three structural frames, to dig out a faulty- Do you care to hear the details, Sir?"

"I care that you care."

"Anyway, that job is done. The next flight will be an extended shakedown cruise, the star carrier *Athabasca* will accompany us with a stores ship, for the first three days. If our engineering team needs assistance after that, it will mean a trip back to Earth. I do *not* expect that to happen," she added, "but it's the unexpected problems that bite you on the ass."

"I'll stay out of your way. Lots of paperwork for me to dig into."

I wasn't lying to Reed about paperwork, I was buried under my workload as usual. My career situation is complicated. What I should say is, still complicated. I am a two star general in the United States Army, while seconded to the armed forces of Skippistan. 'Seconded' is a military term for loaned out; my primary responsibilities are for Skippistan, while I am technically still serving in the US Army. Like I said, it's complicated. The alternative was for me to resign my Army commission, to avoid any conflict of interest. That would not have set well with me, and fortunately the Army was willing to be flexible. They could also deny blame any stupid shit I did, so it's a win-win.

The fact that I am still in the Army means I have a wide variety of benefits, like taking an annual physical test the Army seems to change every two freakin' years. And, I got to watch fourteen hours of training videos, plus the associated PowerPoint slides, on subjects such as exciting recent changes to Department Of Defense official forms. That actually is not so bad, I have subordinates to handle paperwork for me. Back in the blissful days when I was a garrison commander, my job was almost ninety percent paperwork, and I delegated paperwork, so I had plenty of time for golf.

Being in the Army also means I get hundreds of messages every day into my us.army.mil email account. Again, my staff used to handle most of those messages. In my new position with the Special Mission Group, I had to grind through emails by myself. Such as, yet another nudge for me to remind the people under my command of UN Def Com's Blue to Black campaign.

That campaign is something I should explain to the civilians out there.

Humanity's first starship captain was an Army colonel, me. My first officer, Chang, was also an Army officer. The *Dutchman's* chief pilot, Desai, was Indian Air Force. For many years, you had to look several lines down the crew roster to find anyone aboard the *ship* who served in a *Navy*. It bothered the air forces around the world that an army grunt was in command of something that flew, and it was worse that I was a ground-pounder, not even a helicopter pilot. It drove the navies of the world absolutely crazy that other services had star*ships*. My replacement in command of *Valkyrie* is an Air Force colonel, and Reed sort of got grandfathered into that slot, because she had served aboard UNEF ships for a decade.

When we acquired eighteen *Extinction* class battlecruisers from the Maxohlx, the 'wet' navies of Earth were obsolete overnight. A starship could instantly jump in over any spot on the globe and strike the surface with directed energy beams, railgun darts, or missiles. Ships on surface of the ocean couldn't even detect a starship in orbit. Submarines? The active sensors of a Maxohlx starship could penetrate to the bottom of the deepest ocean, so suddenly submarines couldn't hide anymore. The last military submarine was decommissioned before my sons were born, and the surface navies shrank to become mostly an anti-piracy force. Did that mean the concept of a navy was something for the history books?

No. When UNEF suddenly had forty starships; the *Dutchman*, *Valkyrie*, and thirty eight frontline battlecruisers unwillingly donated by the Maxohlx, there was a need to crew those ships, to supply them with food and other consumables needed by meatsacks, to maintain them, to establish a logistics system for ensuring the ships had fuel, to train crews to fly and fight them. And perhaps most importantly, to figure out how to turn eighteen new ships into a fighting force. That included developing doctrine on the best way for those ships to fight individually, and as a squadron. The problem became enormously more complicated when Roscoe arrived, and humanity in an instant had hundreds of senior species warships of various types, then soon we purchased or traded for Jeraptha star carriers and assault carriers. Humanity had a serious capability not only for defense, but also force projection. Someone needed to organize all those ships and personnel. Who has experience with operating, maintaining, and deploying warships?

The world's navies. That's why UNEF set up the United Nations Navy, which right from the beginning was led by senior officers who formerly served aboard wet navy ships.

For years, the UN Navy was an umbrella organization, while individual ships, squadrons, and even battlegroups were crewed and commanded by single nations. The battlecruisers *Constellation*, *Independence*, and *Freedom*, for example, still had an almost all American crews, and so did the escort and support ships assigned to their battlegroups. The destroyer *Gdansk* was nominally a Polish Navy ship, with the crew all drawn from Poland. Having individual ships organized by nationality was a practical, interim step toward a truly unified command structure. Slowly, crews were being integrated, starting with destroyer squadrons. To build a sense of cohesiveness, for the past five years all new UNN personnel wore black uniforms, with the UN symbol on the right shoulder and national flags on the left. Anyone who had served aboard a UNN ship prior to five years ago could continue to wear their home service's uniform, with United Nation and UNN patches. That's why Colonel Reed wore Air Force blue rather than black. The point of the 'Blue To Black' campaign was to encourage people like Reed to transfer before the ten year deadline, and to recruit from Earth's remaining air forces. That campaign also applies to any Army personnel who served in the Navy.

What about me? I wore Army green back when I was commander of the garrison at Jaguar, because low orbit was generally considered to be the dividing line between the responsibilities of the Navy, above that line, and the Army and Air Force, below the line. The Marines? That's another story. Task Force Black was a multi-service force, so the UNN had no problem with an Army officer leading a mostly Navy unit. I kept my Army uniforms, with the GPR Skippistan patch on my left shoulder *below* the United States flag, because I told Skippy that's the way it is and the subject was not open for discussion.

Except by the UNN bureaucracy, who regularly nudged me about the benefits of transferring to the Naval service. Yeah, that's not gonna happen.

So, that message went into my 'Delete' folder, and I moved on to the next annoying thing I had to read.

It was not a good morning. Though I had gotten up extra early to hit the gym, I didn't feel that usual boost of satisfaction from being up and active before anyone else. That is because when I stepped out the door of my cabin, I nearly collided with a half dozen people who were rolling carts of supplies and spare parts along the passageway. Most consumables and spare parts were kept in central locations, convenient for distribution wherever they were needed. Like, food storage was logically near the galley, components for the ship were in lockers near the aft engineering compartments. But for damage control, when access throughout the ship might be restricted, replacement parts needed to be placed where they might be needed quickly. The ship was replenishing supplies, completing all the work the space dock hadn't finished, and fixing all the problems that had appeared since *Valkyrie* was towed out of the dock, a process that ran around the clock. While my sorry ass slumbered the night away in bed, the crew had been working.

Anyway, the people moving the supply carts had been up long before I rolled out of bed, and I already felt guilty when they saw my fresh shorts and T-shirt. Being in the gym wasn't great either, there were regular *bang* and *thump* sounds from the cargo bay just aft of the gym, which itself used to be a cargo bay. Also, the air in the gym still smelled burnt, and by exercising, I was breathing in more of it. It was distracting, and I forgot to tighten the lid of my squeeze water bottle so I spilled water all down my shirt. On the walk back to my cabin, I realized I was itchy. A shower and putting on a clean uniform didn't help, I felt overheated and still itchy. So, I wasn't in a great mood when I walked into the galley and saw Reed angrily jabbing a finger at Skippy's avatar.

"Joe!" He waved to me. "Help, please."

"Uh," I poured a cup of coffee. "What do you expect me to do?"

"Explain that she is being overly emotional about nothing."

"Wow," I could feel my eyes opening as wide as they would go. "Yeah, in the history of mankind, that has always worked great, never. Reed, what did the beer can do this time?"

"Have you tried the coffee, Sir?" She directed the question at me, but her Force Ten Death Glare was focused on Skippy.

"Uh, not yet, it," I took a slurp. "God, this is *awful*."

"For breakfast," she reached into a box on the table beside her. "Would you like a special treat?" She tossed a jar of marshmallow Fluff to me.

Bobbling the coffee, I caught the Fluff with one hand. "This is good on an English muffin, or- What the *hell* is this?"

"It's Fluff, you ninny," Skippy rolled his eyes.

"No," I set the coffee cup down and read the jar's label. The jar shape and colors were correct, the label was not. "This is '*Floff*.'"

"It is *SkipWay* brand Floff, Sir," Reed grimaced. "This morning's coffee is also SkipWay brand, their 'Supremo Robusto Dark Roast'."

"There are truck stops that have better coffee, and I am talking about abandoned truck stops after a zombie apocalypse."

"Hey!" Skippy protested. "That is not-"

"How did this SkipWay crap get aboard the ship?"

Reed answered my question with a question. "Are you itchy this morning, Sir?"

"Yes," I was surprised. "How did you know?" That's when I realized she was tugging at her collar, and her neck was pink with a rash.

"*Someone*," she shot a look at Skippy. "Replaced the laundry detergent with SkipWay brand products, three days ago. Without telling anyone. If you're wearing clothes that were washed recently, you will likely be having an allergic reaction."

"Um, Joe, well, heh heh," Skippy wouldn't look at me. "This is all just a misunder-"

"Skippy," I held up a hand to stop him talking. "Keep in mind, I haven't had any coffee this morning."

"Oh *shit*. You got up early, I just assumed you already-"

"Would you prefer to deal with Regular Angry Joe, or Undercaffeinated Angry Joe?"

"Ugh, the first one. You are a *nightmare* when you don't have coffee in the morning. What is it with you?"

"It's a meatsack thing."

"Why don't you drink the coffee you have? It can't be that bad."

"It tastes like I roasted the beans *in my ass*."

"OK, fine, I have a bot racing to bring a fresh bag of non-SkipWay coffee beans to the galley right now."

"That's a good start. Before you continue, ask yourself whether what you are about to say will make me happy, or piss me off."

"Hmm, how am I supposed to guess what-"

"Keep in mind, I am already right on the edge of Pissed Off because I am itchy, and I haven't had coffee yet."

"Shit," he sighed. "What can I do to make you happy?"

"First, remove all SkipWay brand items from this and any other UN Navy ship."

"What? This is outrageous, I can't-"

"Second, at your own expense, replace all the SkipWay crap with regular brand items and- Uh!" I held up a hand to silence his protest. "I do not care how much that costs you. Is that perfectly clear?"

"It is clear and it is totally unfair."

"Use your ginormous brain to analyze this: do I care about being fair to you?"

"*Ugh*. No. Do you have any idea what a logistics nightmare it will be to-"

"Will *I* have to do any of the work?"

"Um, no."

"Then again, I do not care. I will offer you a deal. I am going back to my cabin, to shower again, and put on a fresh, non-itchy uniform. By the time I get to my cabin, your bots will have set out a clean uniform for me, one that was not washed with your toxic waste detergent. When I get back to the galley, a fresh pot of real coffee will be waiting for me. And a nice breakfast. I'll make it easy for you. I want bacon, scrambled eggs, and rye toast. There had better not be a SkipWay label in sight. Do you have any questions?"

"Yes. How does this deal benefit me?"

"You avoid a lifetime ban from Karaoke night."

"Huuuuuh," he gasped. "You wouldn't *dare*."

Reed cocked her head at him. "Have you met Joe Bishop?"

"Crap. Yes," the avatar slumped. "He would totally do that. *This* is the thanks I get for offering substantial savings to Def Com?"

"How much money did the Navy save by purchasing your SkipWay crap?"

"Well, technically none. But for the same price, you received *premium* products and-"

"And, I suspect you have warehouses full of crap no one is buying."

"I subleased out those warehouses, under the condition that I remove all my SkipWay products," he sighed. "Being the generous guy I am, I delivered, at my own expense, several thousand tons of SkipWay supplies to refugee camps around the Earth, and *they* refused it! Can you believe it? What a bunch of ungrateful jerks."

After a shower, during which I checked that the soap was my regular stuff and not some SkipWay toxic junk, I applied an anti-itch lotion that a bot delivered. Then I stood waiting for two minutes, before another bot raced through the door to deliver a uniform that was still warm from the dryer. "Skippy," I sniffed the uniform. "You are absolutely certain this won't make me break out in a rash?"

"You *should* be allergic to the unfair way you are treating me, but-"

"Yes, or no?"

"Yes, I am sure about it. I don't see what the big deal is anyway, your closet has plenty of uniforms you hardly ever wear."

"Those are Class A unis, I'm not wearing them unless I have to."

"I still don't see why you insist on wearing a *combat* uniform. All you ever do is sit in a freakin' chair."

"Check the daily schedule. Combat is the uniform of the day, that is Reed's call. Besides, that's the most comfortable uniform we have. I could wear a flight suit, if you like?"

"I would not like," he stuck out his tongue. "On you, a flight suit looks like the onesies you used to dress your boys in."

"It is not a *onesie*, you ass."

The joke was on me. Two hours later, I was packing a Class A uniform for a flight down to the surface, at the request of the Joint Chiefs. There was going to be a change of command ceremony. Admiral Suzuki was stepping down, to be replaced on the Joint Chiefs by some Japanese general I didn't know. The ceremony would be boring, with politicians making boring speeches, then a dinner where the chicken would be overcooked, and I would be expected to clap and laugh at the appropriate moments. It seemed silly for the leaders of UN Defense Command to conduct a ceremony while humanity's homeworld was under an extinction level threat, but that was the point. Def Com wanted the public to see their military leaders doing business as usual, rather than panicking. Besides, until *Valkyrie's* crew had the ship ready for combat, I really didn't have anything to do.

"Please, kill me now," I muttered as I inspected the Full Dress Uniform. One change the United States Army had instated within the past five years was a new formal dress uniform, dark blue, with, if you can believe it, white gloves, and as a general officer, I had a freakin' ceremonial sword. The Army had become self-conscious about the impressive dress uniforms of other countries, and now with a need to represent the US of A in encounters with alien species, had decided to step up our game. As I technically was seconded to Skippistan, I would have been authorized to wear the gaudy uniform Skippy designed for me, but that was never gonna happen.

"What was that, Joe?" Skippy asked, as he directed bots to fuss over carefully packing my uniform. For the flight dirtside, I would be wearing my regular service uniform, I would change into formal dress before the ceremony.

That way, I wouldn't spill strawberry jam or barbeque sauce on my shiny outfit.

"Nothing. OK, the shoes look good, the gloves-"

"Are *fine*, Joe," he insisted as a bot snatched the gloves away from me. "Everything is fine, leave it alone or you'll ruin everything. You will be representing Skippistan down there, you know. Try not to muck it up too much."

"I will represent your fake country with all the dignity it deserves."

"Good, then- Wait. Did you just insult the People's Republic?"

"That depends on how much dignity you believe it deserves."

United Nations Defense Command has ten Joint Chiefs of Staff. One from each of the old Expeditionary Force nations: America, China, India, Britain, and France. The other five seats currently were held by Japan, Brazil, Indonesia, Australia, and South Africa. Change of command ceremonies for the Joint Chiefs included a ritual I thought was a bit awkward, and when it was explained to me, I realized the reason I had been invited: to fill out the numbers. That was mildly insulting, but whatever. The food after the ceremony was being provided by Japan, and I was looking forward to eating something good, and not the rubbery chicken I would expect to get at a typical military base. So, I was in a good mood when I lined up with four Chiefs on one side of the aisle, with five Chiefs on the other side. Like I said, they needed a warm body. The ritual, which no one seemed to remember when it was started, was for the outgoing Chief to walk away from the head table, greet the incoming Chief, and the newly-confirmed Chief walked to the head table to take his or her seat. They needed me to stand at attention in a fancy uniform, and hold up a ceremonial sword. I felt a pang of panic when I matched the actions of the Australian admiral across from me, and gripped the hilt of my sword. I hadn't inspected the thing. It would be gleamingly clean, Skippy would have assured that. But he might have misunderstood that the weapon should be *blunt*, not sharp.

Oh what the hell, I would just be extra careful with it.

We all drew our swords.

Or, nine of us did.

What came out of my scabbard was a *banana*.

"Oh, get over it, Joe," Skippy chuckled. "Everyone got a good laugh out of it."

"Everyone except *me*."

"That video went viral. It's the first time the public on Earth has ever paid any attention to a change of command ceremony. This is good publicity for Def Com."

"It is bad for *me*, you ass!" I unbuckled my sword belt and tossed the thing on the bed of my hotel room. After a beat when everyone gasped then laughed, the yellow banana extended and changed color to become a normal ceremonial sword, except it was hollow. The scabbard had held nanogel, I should have anticipated the beer can would do some asshole stunt.

"No, it is not."

"Suddenly, you are an expert on how humans think?"

"Um, much as I hate to say it, no I am not."

"Then why-"

"After some unknown actor tried to steal Dogzilla, *my* image took a hit. Ungrateful, ignorant meatsacks across the galaxy lost faith in me. Def Com contracted with my public relations and crisis management company, to sell to the fearful public the idea that the powerful UN Navy could protect your miserable mudball of a homeworld."

"Maybe describing Earth as a miserable mudball is not the best way to-"

"Um, that was my personal comment, my PR people told me the same thing. Anywho, my image took a hit, but the public still had faith in *you*. Which shows how stupid monkeys are," he added under his breath. "The point is, instead of getting angry when you saw that your sword was a banana, you played along with the joke, and comments on social media overwhelmingly show the public is impressed with your calm, cool grace under pressure. The incident has boosted your standing with the public, and there is already a seven point increase in the public's confidence in Def Com's ability to defend human interests."

"Oh. OK."

"*My* image somehow has gotten even worse, with people commenting that I am a silly, irresponsible jackass."

"People didn't already know that?"

"Oh, shut up. This is the last time I do any favors for you," he sniffed.

"I am totally OK with you not doing any more favors."

"Just when I thought I couldn't hate you any more than I already do, it-"

"Have you prepared any other surprises that will make the public love me even more?"

"Um-"

"Talk, beer can."

"Well, for the dinner which begins in fifteen minutes by the way, the cushion of your chair will make a rude noise when you sit on it."

"You mean it *would have* done that, until you just fixed it."

"Ugh. Yes. Why can't I have any fun?"

"I read somewhere that various crime syndicates on Earth are taking advantage of the climate chaos since the Jupiter Cloud got pushed away." There was no question Earth's climate had improved since a cloud was no longer blocking a significant percentage of sunlight from reaching our home world, but the swing from the New Normal to Impending Ice Age and back to Newer Somewhat Normal had not been without problems. Many people had jumped the gun by moving back north too soon, and had been caught by three long, brutal winters in a row. The pack of snow and ice that formed in northern latitudes still covered the ground, bright white reflecting sunlight back into space, and the Jetstream was still screwed up, bringing a roaring freight train of frigid cold down from the Arctic. So, governments had to deal with 'Boomerangs' as the people fleeing south again were called, and refugee camps were reopened. Recently, the Boomerangs had come back north, to find their properties looted, or occupied by squatters. It was not a good situation, the global economy was still in recovery after more than a decade, and desperate people were easy prey for scammers.

"Yes, why? Sherlock Grumpy has been working with government authorities to provide evidence against the most harmful crime syndicates."

"What about more direct action?"

"Um, like what?"

"Like, criminal gangs no longer keep their money in banks, right? They hold their wealth in various cryptocurrencies."

"Hey, if you are saying that Skipcoin is popular with criminals, the-"

"I did not say that, although we both know that is a hundred percent true."

"Ugh. Why do you have to be such a-"

"It is too bad you recently discovered that some heinous individuals have been issuing bogus Skipcoins."

"I did? No I didn't. That's impossible, dumdum, the quantchain ledger prevents-"

"It doesn't prevent *you* from doing anything. Hypothetically, if you uncovered a conspiracy to issue fake Skipcoins, you would have to protect the integrity of your currency by invalidating the bogus coins, right? Wiping them off the ledger?"

"Well, yes but-"

"It is too bad that several large and violent criminal networks fell victim to the scammers, and you are now forced to erase all their Skiptocurrency. I mean, doing that would not be any fun at all for you, right?"

"Hee hee, that- I mean," he cleared his throat. "That would truly be unfortunate."

"Hypothetically, which I know nothing about."

"Of course not. Um, Joe, there are powerful officials in various governments who would be deeply harmed, if the gangs that control them were suddenly bankrupt."

"Collateral damage is inevitable."

"Sadly, yes. OK, go enjoy your dinner, while I cause chaos and carnage in financial markets. Hee hee, this will be *fun*."

CHAPTER SIXTEEN

After an inspection that had the already exhausted crew totally worn out, the UN Navy declared *Valkyrie* ready in all respects to fly and to fight. Reed still had a squawk list for her crew to work on, none of the To-Do items affected the battlecruiser's ability to function as an even more badass warship. Still, she was hesitant when we reviewed the ship's status over breakfast. A breakfast in a galley that did not smell like burning garbage, with food that tasted like it should.

She set down her fork. "I know that look, Sir. You want to take the ship out ASAP."

"Just to run a quick errand. Hit up a Maxohlx relay station, find out how the kitties are reacting to the outsider bombing Jaguar's star."

"No combat?"

"Not unless you know something I don't. I want to jump away by oh eight hundred tomorrow, can you accommodate that?"

"We are waiting on a set of thrusters, they were supposed to have been delivered this morning. That thruster array passed inspection, but it's marginal. I don't want to go into action until we swap it for a new set."

"We don't have spare thrusters aboard?" That surprised me.

"We do, but in the chaos of getting everything loaded, those spares got stuffed into the rear of a cargo bay, behind a very large crate that contains a Caterpillar tractor."

"A *tractor*? Like, the kind used on a farm?"

"I wish I could say 'No'," she sighed, "but yes."

"You are planning to run tractor pulls as a morale booster?"

"We didn't request a tractor, we requested a set of tractor effect balancers, the kind of stabilizer magnets used in railguns. Some Supply joker dirtside got his wires crossed. My logistics officer told me it would be faster to get a new set of thrusters, than to unload that entire cargo bay. In an emergency, we can just cut through the rear bulkhead, I'd rather avoid doing that for now."

"I'll see what I can do."

"Skippy," I called him from the empty sickbay, which had an independent air supply, where I could breathe sweet, untainted air. "I need a favor."

"Um," his avatar didn't appear. "I am kind of busy here, fixing all the things the stupid space dock screwed up. I swear, if you want something done right, you have to do it yourself. If I had been here instead of having to race off to rescue the people on Jaguar, I wouldn't be dealing with this mess."

"Yeah, those people on Jaguar are dicks for asking you to help."

"Um, I didn't mean it that way."

"Yes you did, but whatever. I need a favor. I heard that we are waiting on a set of thrusters?"

"Ugh. Yes. They were actually delivered two days ago, but there was a some kind of miscommunication, and they were set up to be installed in a different type of ship. It would take longer to modify them than to get new ones, so Reed sent them back. Now the Supply people are arguing with the manufacturer, and everyone is pointing fingers at everyone else, so-"

"So, this is another thing I *do not* care about. You know how I get pissed off when you do sketchy shit?"

"Um, yes?"

"How would you like an opportunity to do sketchy shit with my blessing?"

"Like, finding a set of thrusters and getting them here, no questions asked?"

"I will ask zero questions."

"OK, what's in it for me?"

"You need something more than Skippy being Skippy and not getting yelled at for it?"

"Um, no I do not. OK, I'll have a set of thrusters here within two hours. They will be in six crates marked 'Freeze-dried broccoli'."

"Who the hell needs even one crate of freeze-dried broccoli?"

"That's the point, dumdum."

I asked no questions. Reed was burning to ask questions, she restrained herself. The Navy declared *Valkyrie* to be fully flightworthy, and the crew rushed to finish loading last-minute supplies. We jumped away three hours ahead of schedule. Why so early? Skippy warned me the Navy Inspector General's office was launching an inquiry into stolen thruster equipment, and they wanted to interview Reed and her crew. It's tough for the IG to conduct an interview, when you are a thousand lightyears away.

Valkyrie still had glitches, the squawk list actually grew longer after the first day of flight, as testing revealed more problems. By day three, Reed was confident that her ship could handle a fight, and the engineering team paused nonessential work for twenty four hours. By that point, the list of work still to be done was minor stuff like sticky doors, none of which interfered with the proper operation of the ship. Reed was confident enough to give the *Athabasca* permission to return to Earth, and we began jumping toward Maxohlx territory.

That night, there was a pine scented air freshener in my cabin. I appreciated the gesture.

We took a risk by flying to a Maxohlx relay station that was not in the type of isolated location we usually chose. This station was visited by seven ships a day, on average. Skippy made a guess of the optimal timing based on the schedule of the nearby wormhole, and we jumped in so he could do his thing. We then jumped away the moment he was done downloading data and covering our tracks.

"Hmm, mm hmm. Yup, this is interesting," he announced in my office. "There is no indication the kitties had advance notice of the attack against Jaguar Prime, their strategic analysis AIs had considered an attack against Jaguar's star as a low probability. When they heard about it, they were at first disappointed, they considered the Outsider not attacking Earth's sun to be a lost opportunity. Basically, the disappointment was because humanity was not badly hurt. This makes it clear that the Hegemony doesn't expect anything specific from their one-sided alliance with the Outsider; they are hoping for general chaos and destruction. Their strategic analysis AIs are baffled by the Outsider's strike against Jaguar, and that tells me the kitties have no clue as to what the end objective of the Outsider is."

"So, it's just the usual story of assholes being assholes again."

"Pretty much, yes."

"The kitties seriously don't care that they will be just as fucked, if the Outsider opens a door for an invasion?"

"They apparently do not. All they care about is that someone is smiting their enemies."

"Shit. Skippy, we have been tip-toeing around the Maxohlx for too long. It might be time to punch them in the face."

"Unfortunately, that is a decision for your Security Council to make, I am not hopeful those screeching monkeys will agree on any direct action."

"Ah, I have enough shit to worry about anyway. What do their strategic analysis AIs think the Outsider will do next?"

"They have absolutely no idea. The Outsider has not asked the kitties to do anything, so they don't have any inside info about its intentions, unfortunately. Their attempt to construct a predictive model of the Outsider has been as successful as when they tried to build a model of *you*," he chuckled. "Jeez Louise, even *I* failed at that."

"Wh-what?"

"Um, pay no attention to the man behind the curtain," he muttered.

"You built a, submind or something, to be a copy of me?"

"Ugh. I built one to *think* like you, and it was a total freakin' disaster. When it was working properly, it was useless. Every time it showed even a glimpse of your type of creative thinking, the matrix became completely unstable. The whole experiment got cancelled when I had to purge part of my own matrix, to avoid contamination. I am never doing *that* again."

"When did you plan to inform me of this submind?"

"Um, if it had worked, I wouldn't have needed to tell you about it at all."

"If you weren't going to tell me, then what good is-"

"Think about it, numbskull. By keeping quiet about my new Bishop submind, everyone would believe *I* had figured out how to dream up monkey brain solutions."

"So, this was all about your ego?"

"No. Well, not only about that. It's also about the years of humiliation I have endured, when again and again and *again*, my ginormous brain fails to think of some stupid, blindingly obvious thing, while the sack of mush in your skull says 'Duuuuuh what about this'?"

"It's great to see that, with the very existence of this galaxy at risk, you are focused on what is truly important."

"Oh, shut up. Hey, Mister Smart Guy, did it ever occur to you that me having a functional submind that can accurately replicate your creative process would be of great value, if something bad happened to you?"

"Oh. Sorry. That is a good point. Now I feel like an idiot."

"Well, you certainly should be ashamed of yourself."

"I said I was sorry."

"Hmmph," he sniffed.

"Exactly *when* did you realize that this Bishop submind would be of value to someone other than yourself?"

"Um, just now, when I was talking to you. Oops. What I meant is-"

"We both know what you meant."

"The important point is, I tried to do something to benefit everyone, even if, you know, benefitting others didn't occur to me at the time."

"You *think* your explanation makes you look better, but it doesn't."

"Oh, shut up."

"Anyway, the truly important thing is, your submind *failed*."

"Ooooh, I hate you *so* much, the-"

"Did you find anything else interesting in the latest relay station download?"

"Let me see, I- Ooh Joe, I have exciting news! You have been visited by an old friend."

"I hate unexpected guests, Skippy."

"Wh- OMG, Dude, when did you get so *old*?"

"I'm not old, you ass."

"Really? You are already all like, 'I do not like surprise guests', and 'We can't go to the party because I have to be in bed by nine o'clock' and, myah," he waved a hand, "you darned kids get off my lawn."

"I am not-" I had to laugh. "I am *not* like that."

"Really? When is the last time you and Margaret went to a party that wasn't related to your jobs?"

"I was the garrison commander on a planet with a small population. Pretty much everyone I know is related to my job somehow. Hey! Two months ago, no, three months? No, longer than that, it was before we went on our fun-filled family vacation to Newark. Margaret and I went to the birthday party of a boy who is on a soccer team with our twins."

"Uh huh. The birthday boy, his father is an Army major on your staff?"

"Well yeah, but the party wasn't about him."

"Are you sure about that? How many other parents were invited to the party?"

"Uh, now that you mention it, none. I thought it was odd at the time."

"It wasn't odd, because that was totally a work-related party."

"Whatever. Listen, Skippy, adults tend to meet people at work, or through their children's friends. Or though, golf or something. I'm busy, you know?"

"You don't make enough time for yourself. You need some Joe time."

"Family time *is* Joe time for me. I don't want to argue with you. Who is this old friend you mentioned?"

"The Law of Unintended Consequences."

"Oh sh- I hate that freakin' thing, it is not my friend!"

"Joe, in this case- And I have no idea how this happened, because the Universe clearly still loves to screw with you- In this case, that law worked for our benefit."

"Uh, say that again?"

"I know, I couldn't believe it either."

"So, you're giving me *good* news?"

"Yes. I am entirely not sure how to do this, it is so rare."

"Just tell me what you know."

"OK. After we raided the data archive at Pentivar, the admiral of the Hegemony military did something unexpected. Unexpectedly smart."

"That doesn't sound good."

"In this case, it's good for us, bad for the rotten kitties. The guy actually had an intuitive thought that, while wrong, was impressively intelligent."

"You have told me that Admiral Klestine isn't as dim-witted as people think."

"He has survived, and his career has thrived, by encouraging people to believe he is a useful idiot. The Dictat placed him in command of their military because Klestine is considered not clever enough to have any ambition. That is a false, and dangerous assumption."

"Uh, we are never going to tell the Dictat that his flunky is smart and ambitious, right?"

"What? Of course not. Why would you ask such a moronic question?"

"Just making sure you don't decide to shake things up to entertain yourself."

"Joe, please. It will be *much* more entertaining to watch Klestine slowly undermine the Dictat, and then seize power for himself."

"OK, I'm glad you understand that. So, what smart thing did the admiral do?"

"He assumed our objective at Pentivar was to destroy the archive, since all the evidence he has points to us doing only that. The Hegemony strategic analysis people, and their AIs, concluded we hit Pentivar to demonstrate we can hit them anywhere, anytime, that the major value of our action was to sow fear that we have a strike capability they can't even understand. Klestine accepted that conclusion, but he wondered if there is a reason we hit that particular archive."

"Yeah, it was close to-"

"Yes, yes, there were many tactical considerations for why Pentivar was the best archive for us to raid. He is asking a deeper question: was there data, or a combination of data, stored at Pentivar that is not stored at other archives?"

"Uh, isn't the purpose of having multiple archives they all have backup copies of the *same* information?"

"Yes, dumdum, but they don't all get updated at the same time. Also, archive AIs aren't just dumb repositories of files, they work to extract insights from data. This is where Klestine was quite clever; he asked whether it is possible the archive AI itself had discovered a previously unknown connection between pieces of data, while it was cataloging and indexing data packets it recently received, and we destroyed the archive to erase that new information."

"Uh, how are we supposed to have known about this new data in the archive, before we got access to the thing?"

"Unlike you, the Maxohlx senior leadership fully trusts the awesomeness. He assumes my god-like powers allow me to see into the archive."

"That delusion is useful to us, let's do everything we can to feed it. But as far as he knows, we *nuked* that AI, so how does her expect to discover what-"

"Admiral Klestine has tasked the chief archivist to virtually recreate the Pentivar archive in a partition of the main archive. The strategic analysis AIs will then analyze the data to determine whether there some combination of data yields new information, something that we wanted to conceal by destroying the Pentivar AI."

"Holy shit. Those strategic analysis AIs are now attempting to match every element of data to every *other* element?"

"It's way more complicated than that, but basically that is the idea."

"No freakin' way could those AIs actually do that, right?"

"Their SA system is the most powerful collection of artificial intelligences the Hegemony possesses. Klestine is tasking them only with analyzing all the data received by the Pentivar archive in the past four months, that greatly cuts down on the processing power needed. Still, my best estimate is those AIs will be working on that tasking for at least thirty one days. During that time, they won't have much capacity remaining to cause trouble for us, that's why I described this as good news."

"Cause trouble like, figuring out our next move, and warning the Outsider?"

"That and other things."

"This is good news. It would be better news if I actually had any freakin' clue what our next move is."

"I can't help you with that, sorry."

"Joe! Joe Joe Joe Joe-"

"*Damn* it," I jerked awake, lifting my head then thumping it back into the pillow. His tone of voice was of the 'I am bored and want to talk', not the 'ship is about to explode' variety. Opening one eye, I read the clock on the wall display. Four minutes after two in the morning. "*What*?"

"I gotta know, I, I just can't wait anymore."

"If this is about that telenovela you are watching, you can catch up on the latest episodes when we get back to Earth."

"No dumdum, I *can't* do that, because the producers of the show aren't releasing any new episodes on Earth until the Jeraptha have a chance to view it first."

"Oh." Human TV programs, especially telenovelas, and so-called 'reality' shows like 'Real Housewives of Fargo', were still hugely popular with the beetles. Also with younger Ruhar, while their Ruhar parents harumphed that the younger generation was becoming a bunch of hooligans, and also that young Ruhar should get off their lawns. "But, you can hack into the production team and download the-"

"Yes, but if I did that, it would spoil the fun of the watch party."

"Uh," my stupid brain should have let it go, but like I said, my brain is stupid. "What watch party? Aboard the ship?"

"That also. I meant the official watch party on the Jeraptha homeworld."

"You aren't at their homeworld, so-"

"I left a submind there to interact with the beetles. That submind also runs the local operations of SkipWay."

"Right. Well, I'm glad you explained that. Good night, I-"

"Whoa. You haven't answered my question."

"Listen, I don't watch any telenovelas, so I don't know whether Conchita is faking amnesia or whatever."

"It's not about that. I have a question about a song."

"Wow, you are asking the wrong guy. My knowledge of music is-"

"Like I would ever ask *you* about music," he snorted. "This is about the lyrics. You know the song 'Home on the Range'?"

"Ayuh, sure. OK, I understand your confusion. The deer and the antelope don't actually *play*, it's just a-"

"The song states 'And the skies are not cloudy all day'."

"Yeah, so? The song is about the American West, humidity there is lower than in-"

"The *question* is what the songwriter meant. Is it that all day, there are never any clouds? Or there *are* clouds, but they don't cover the sky the entire day?"

"This is what you suddenly need to know at two in the freakin' morning?"

"It has been bothering me for a while, Joe."

"For how long?"

"Um, in your time reckoning, it started to bother me at one fifty six, so it has been nagging me incessantly for ten minutes now."

"Ten minutes. This couldn't wait until morning?"

"That is ten minutes in slow monkey time, an eternity for me. Hey, I tried not to wake you, I was just watching you sleep as usual, but-"

"You still *watch* me while I'm sleeping?"

"Of course, why? I need something to entertain me during the night shift, when most of the crew are asleep. You sometimes talk in your sleep, or you snore. I especially love it," he chuckled, "when you drool on your pillow and blow snot bubbles."

"OK wow, well, I shouldn't have worried because that is not creepy *at all*."

"Oh shut up. It's not like I'm asking you to *do* anything."

"That is- Oh for- If I answer your question, will you go away?"

"Yes. You think I like it when I need an answer from *you*?"

"First, did you Google the question?"

"No. Google would only give me a response from supposed language 'experts' who have no connection to reality. The song was written for an audience of typical filthy monkeys, so I need the opinion of a typical filthy monkey."

For a moment, I tried to determine whether he had just insulted me, then I decided I didn't care. "Uh, well, if the sky is cloudy *all day*, that means there is no point during the day when the sky is not covered with clouds. So, the song means that on the Range, you will at least see the sun at some point during the day."

"Hmm. That is disappointing, but actually solid logic."

"Thanks."

"Which makes me suspicious of whether *you* Googled the answer."

"I haven't touched my phone, Skippy. Are there any other burning questions you have for me tonight?" My mouth asked before I could stop it.

"Hmm, actually, yes. The-"

By three o'clock in the morning I was yearning not for sleep, but for the sweet release of death.

CHAPTER SEVENTEEN

Getting ready to play basketball in *Valkyrie's* gym, I sat on my couch to lace up my shoes. I did enjoy playing in the ship's basketball league when I could, and it was good exercise, but mostly working out was better than thinking about how much I missed my wife and sons. I should be doing my job instead of focusing on what I couldn't have, and how long my family would be trapped beneath Puptart's blanket. And that my wife would have our baby daughter alone, without me. Yes, her mother and my parents would be there, but I wouldn't.

So, I caught up on paperwork, and exercised, while *Valkyrie* flew back toward Earth, to deliver the news that we still didn't know anything useful about the Outsider.

"Hey, Joe," his avatar appeared on the table next to the bed. "I have a quick question: do you remember The Rules?"

"Huh?" I finished tying my shoes. He wanted to talk, and it was better to get it over with now, rather than in the middle of the night. "Oh, you mean like: never leave the toilet seat up?"

"Wh-What? That isn't one of The Rules, dumdum."

"Trust me, it totally is."

"What are you talking about?"

"The rules of marriage. Why? What were you asking-"

He blinked slowly. "There are *rules* to being married?"

"Ayuh, sure. Like- This applies only if you're married to a woman- If she is going out, and she puts on some outfit that looks horrible on her, what would you do?"

"Um," he cocked his head while he thought for a moment. "Tell her it is a hideous fashion crime?"

"Maybe. First, you need to remember whether she has worn that outfit before, and if it's one of her favorites. Also, if you said you liked it before, you have to stick to that story."

"Come on, Joe. A woman won't remember every outfit she ever wore."

"Trust me, women remember *everything*, especially stuff like that."

"Ugh. OK, what if she hasn't worn the hideous thing before?"

"Oh, then you're free to guess whether she is in a good mood or not."

"Why would that matter?"

"If she's having a bad day, the last thing she needs is you telling her you don't like what she is wearing."

"This is impossible. You have to *guess*?"

"Yeah, but if you're paying attention, it should be obvious. Like, if she uses the word 'Fine' a lot, then things are *not* fine."

"Being a meatsack is way more complicated than it's worth."

"It has its good points, Skippy."

"Really? I challenge you to name *one*."

"What is the best cheeseburger you ever ate?"

"You know that I have never eaten a cheeseb- Oh, I get it. Is it *that* important?"

"Quiet, please," I held up a hand and closed my eyes. "I am remembering the first time I ate a Fluff screamer. Mmmmm."

"Ugh."

Opening my eyes, I pulled open a drawer in the bedside table, looking for chocolate or really, anything. Daydreaming of cheeseburgers had made me hungry. Sadly, someone had eaten all the snacks I kept in the drawers for emergencies. That Joe Bishop guy is a jerk sometimes.

"OK, so if she is in a bad mood, what's your move?"

"You tell her she looks great, and for bonus points, you make up some BS like the dress drapes nicely from her shoulders. It doesn't matter what you say, she just needs to know you put some thought into it. Oh, and you need to make a mental note that outfit looks great, if she wears it again."

"I hate to ask but, if she *is* in a good mood?"

"You kind of walk around her, scrunch up your lips like you actually know something about fashion, and say the outfit doesn't suit her. The safest thing is to say is it's not her color."

"Her *color*?"

"There are winter colors, spring colors, colors for every season. It's a thing, trust me."

"Where did you read these rules?"

"Nowhere. They are unwritten rules."

"Joe, if a rule is important, it should be written down somewhere."

"Unwritten rules are about things so obvious, they don't need to be in writing. Why did you want to talk about this? Did Margaret tell you I did something wrong?"

"Like your wife would ever confide personal stuff to *me*."

"Stranger things have happened."

"This is good stuff," he muttered, "I need to write it down."

"Do *not* do that. Unwritten rules are unwritten for a reason. Why are- Oh, please tell me you're not asking about the rules of marriage so you can publish another of your awful self-help books."

"My advice books are very popular," he sniffed.

"You give *terrible* advice."

"Joe, my target audience is monkeys who are dumb enough to buy an advice book written by *me*. It's not likely they would listen to good advice anyway. The secret to writing a best-selling advice book is to tell the audience what they already want to hear."

"Whatever. Keep my name out of your book."

"That's not what I was talking about anyway. I meant. *THE. Rules*," he emphasized the words. "The Rules of interstellar warfare that you first learned on Camp Alpha."

"Camp Alpha," I leaned back against the pillow. "Wow, it's been a minute, huh? When I think back to those days, I'm amazed at what a young dumbass I was back then. So eager to take the fight to the enemy, while the real enemy was our supposed allies."

"Uh huh, and now some of the Kristang are our allies."

"Those are just the Verd-kris."

"Whatevs. They're all lizards to me. Anywho, do you remember The Rules?'

"Uh," I closed one eye and stared at the ceiling. "There are five Rules, right? Number One is no using nukes on inhabited planets, or any planet with a habitable biosphere. The two senior species didn't want anyone contaminating habitable worlds with radiation."

"Correct."

"The second Rule is, for the same reason, no chemical weapons. They are indiscriminate, and persistent chemicals can poison a biosphere for hundreds of years. Rule Three? There are rules against both biological and nanotech weapons, I forget which of those is Three and which is Four."

"Three bans the use of nanotechnology weapons. The original Rule Three banned only self-replicating nanobot weapons, but the senior species later realized their filthy clients might create self-replicating bots by mistake, or through carelessness."

"Wasn't there a rumor about a star system that is still under quarantine, something about nanotech getting loose and destroying everything?"

"There is such a rumor, which the Maxohlx and Rindhalu both deny, and which I can confirm is absolutely true. The Maxohlx were looking for an advantage over their rivals, and decided to test a nanotech weapon against a Wurgalan colony world. The-"

"Wait. The Wurgalan are a second tier client of the Maxohlx."

"Yes. This surprises you why?"

"They tested a dangerous experimental weapon on their own coalition?"

"First, of course they did, have you ever met the Maxohlx? Second, if they had tested it against a client of the Rindhalu, the spiders would have retaliated. So, they victimized one of their own coalition, who couldn't retaliate or even protest."

"Every time I think I know how low the kitties can go, they go lower."

"This is the species who was ready to wake up Sentinels and end all intelligent life in the galaxy, just because they didn't feel *special* enough," he gagged on the word.

"True. I shouldn't be surprised, but I am. Maybe I keep hoping to find some redeeming quality they have."

"Good luck with that. Anywho, continuing my story, the rotten kitties deployed a nanotech weapon against a Wurgalan colony. That world had only been colonized for about three hundred years, and so its population was less than two hundred thousand. It had a harsh climate, and could be reached only through a dead-end wormhole that was predicted to go dormant within fifteen hundred years, during the next wormhole network shift. Basically, the place was expendable, and the Maxohlx could easily cut off the flow of information from Vorvestican, that was the Wurgalan name of the place."

"Yeah, that sounds like an asshole move the kitties would do."

"They would, and they did. The Rindhalu had been tracking the Maxohlx project to develop self-replicating nanobots, and the spiders were sufficiently alarmed to task several stealth ships to monitor the experiment."

"Why didn't the freakin' spiders *stop* the experiment?"

"You seriously have to ask that question? It's astonishing that they did anything at all, you know they hate being hasty about anything."

"The galaxy has one coalition led by a species who would burn everything unless we all make them feel special, and another coalition led by a species too old and lazy to take action."

"Technically, there is now a third coalition led by humans, who have decided to hide behind Sentinels and let the galaxy burn."

"You know I don't agree with that policy, and it's above my pay grade. So, what happened on Vorvestican?"

"The nanobots were able to make copies of themselves, but the Maxohlx had a way to halt the replication process, and shut them all down. The experiment was working well, the kitties planted only a few thousand nanoseeds across the target area, and within two weeks the bots had consumed all life within an area of four hundred square kilometers. Eaten all of the biological matter, extracted the raw materials they needed to make copies of themselves, and left charred gray dust behind. The Wurgalan of course were panicked, they tried to eradicate the nanobots, called on the Maxohlx ships in orbit to burn the area, with nukes if necessary. Their benevolent coalition leaders of course did nothing, other than carefully observing the progress of the catastrophe. They planned to deactivate the bots before the main settlement on the planet was consumed, unfortunately the prototype bots were poorly designed. There was a high percentage of errors in the replication process, glitches that interfered with the communications system that allowed individual bots to work together as a single organism. Many damaged bots weren't able to coordinate with others, and any replicas they built had so many glitches they weren't able to function at all. But, many more bots could work with each other just fine, they just weren't able to process input from the Maxohlx command and control system. The kitties finally ordered their bots to halt and disassemble themselves. Most of them did, twelve percent of the bots did not respond to the self-destruct command. The Maxohlx tried everything they could think of to halt the advancing nanoplague, but all they accomplished was ensuring the defective bots were the only ones that were replicating. Soon, *all* of the bots that were active, were out of control. The Maxohlx tried bombarding the infected area with radiation, which did kill or disable over seventy percent of the defective bots. Can you guess what happened next?"

"Oh shit! The remaining thirty percent were mutated by the radiation, and assembled themselves into a giant Godzilla bot?"

He stared at me. Blinked slowly.

"Uh," I guessed, "that didn't happen?'

"*No*, you knucklehead. Radiation did not mutate the nanomachines into monsters."

"I was lied to by *so* many Hollywood movies."

"Would a juice box make you feel better?"

"Oh shut up. If not the Godzilla thing, what happened next?"

"The nanobots evolved, which, wow, *nobody* could have foreseen," he rolled his eyes. "Stupid kitties. The active bots started to consume the dead ones, which were actually the perfect form of processed materials. That accelerated their growth exponentially. At that point, the Maxohlx had the brilliant idea to double down on their stupidity, by nuking the infected area."

"That didn't work?"

"No, it did not. Before you ask, no, the nukes didn't mutate anything into a kaiju."

"OK, next time you tell this story, there has to be a giant monster."

"I am trying to make a *point*, numbskull. All the nukes did was scatter a whole lot of nanobots across an enormous section of the main continent, and after that it was adios muchachos."

"The Maxohlx had a huge fucking mess to deal with?"

"Yes, but not as bad as it was going to get. As the bots reached populated areas, the Wurgalan fled as best they could, but left their buildings and infrastructure behind. Including the AIs that ran all that infrastructure. It still isn't fully understood what happened, but somehow the nanobot organism, by that time it was operating as a unified entity, it absorbed those AIs. And it became smart. So," he sighed. "After the equivalent of only seven Earth months, all the biomass on the surface of Vorvestican had been consumed, but by that time, the nanobots had evolved to use solar and geothermal power, and process their own raw materials. The surface of the planet was a dusty, sticky gray goo. Then the real trouble started."

"The entire planet was covered with nanospooge, and that *wasn't* the problem?"

"Not anymore. The Maxohlx had written the place off, they planned to set warning beacons in orbit, and try to forget the whole thing happened. For two hundred and sixty years, they monitored the dead planet from orbit, watching in case the nano organism tried to build a starship from spare parts or something. Making sure the problem was contained to one planet. Except it wasn't. The Rindhalu were also watching, secretly. They detected nanobots in the solar wind."

"Oh *shit.*"

"Those little fuckers had evolved to use balloons and parachutes to climb up out of the atmosphere, where they deployed solar sails. Each of them was so small, the Maxohlx never detected them until it was too late."

"How can anything climb into *orbit* on a balloon? All balloons have an effective upper altitude."

"Yes, the nanobeing got around the physics by converting the balloons into parachutes at high altitude, and lasers from the ground pushed against the chutes to propel them upward."

"OK, that was pretty smart. Frighteningly smart. The kitties never detected the lasers?"

"The lasers were tiny, intermittent, and operated at low power. The Maxohlx assumed the laser energy they saw was part of an active sensor network. That's when the Rindhalu stepped in, informed the Maxohlx they were total fucking idiots, and demanded the two species work together to contain the threat. To this day, the ongoing quarantine of Vorvestican is the only successful joint project the senior species have ever conducted. They surrounded the entire star system with fusion powered laser platforms, to basically fry anything that gets more than eighty one lightminutes from the star. For reference, that is roughly the orbit of Saturn, in Earth's solar system. Beyond that is a sphere of monitoring stations, and nothing is allowed to enter that star system. Nothing, except for special probes that regularly sample the quarantined area, and that is the truly frightening part. Those probes, even now, can suddenly stop transmitting, with no warning. They are probably being torn apart, and consumed to make more nanobots. Over the years, the probes have been constructed of materials that are less useful to the bots, but the nanobeing has adapted."

"Wow, thanks. I will remember to never violate Rule Three."

"Good idea, especially since you violated Rule Five several times."

"That's the rule against dropping rocks? Dropping asteroids or comets or whatever on a planet?"

"Yes, that rule. You didn't use a rock, you used a relativistic dart."

"Someone else built that dart, we just changed its aim. Besides, the freakin' Kristang broke Rule Four, when the Mavericks discovered they developed a bioweapon on Camp Alpha, and planned to deploy it against humans and Ruhar on Paradise. Stopping that bioweapon was a pain in the ass."

"Two wrongs don't make a right, Joe."

"Hey, that ethics math can bite me. Is that all? You're checking to see if I remember those Rules? I," covering my mouth with a hand, I yawned. "Am going to sleep now."

"I mentioned Rule Three because we have to go to Vorvestican, as fast as possible."

"Go there?"

"Yes. Quickly. Like, now."

"Uh, if you are looking for bad ideas, I have some that are a lot less dangerous."

"I believe you. It should be that your years of experience result in you to having *fewer* bad ideas, but that's not the case with you."

"Skippy, experience leads to good judgement, right?"

"Yes."

"But experience comes from *bad* judgment, get it?"

"That is- Huh. Damn it, I actually can't argue with you about that."

"Right? So, other than hoping that epically bad judgment will lead to wisdom, *why* do you want to go there?"

"To be clear, I do *not* want to go there, but you say we have to fight the Outsider, so-"

"What? Hole sh- The Outsider is-"

"It is not a thousand percent certain, but very likely, that our enemy has gone to Vorvestican. A monitoring station there detected a Rindhalu battleship violated the quarantine, and did not respond to demands for communication. That battleship, along with four destroyers, was reported mysteriously missing eighteen days ago."

"Wha- How the fuck do you know this?"

"It was in a report I downloaded from the last relay station we visited."

"That was five freakin' hours ago! You're just telling me about this *now*?"

"Ugh. Listen, knucklehead, I decrypted and read all the Maxohlx message traffic, looking for clues about the Outsider, and for clues about which mind-blowingly stupid thing the kitties are planning to do next. So far, nothing interesting. Then, since I was bored, I screwed around with files the Maxohlx had intercepted, but been unable to decrypt. Including a report from a Rindhalu monitoring station at Vorvestican."

"Rind- You said watching that place was a joint project by the senior species."

"It is. Remarkably, there have been zero shooting incidents between the monitor forces there. However, the peaceful nature of the operation is greatly assisted by each species being responsible for half of the star system, and they keep their ships and stations out of weapons range from each other. The incident occurred in the Rindhalu half of the sphere of coverage, and the spiders either didn't inform their rivals, or the Maxohlx message traffic about it just hasn't reached that relay station yet. Now *you* know about it."

"I do not like the sound of this."

"Neither do I. Joe, the Outsider has only *one* Elder Starbreaker, and it has all three of our Sentinels tied down just by the threat of using it. If it gets a nano weapon," he didn't need to finish the thought.

"This is the Six Horsemen of the Apocalypse," I said, and heard my voice like someone else was speaking.

"Six? I thought there were *four* horsemen."

"Yeah, traditionally the four are War, Famine, Disease, a Backstreet Boys reunion tour-"

"I don't remember that last one being in the-"

"Now there are *six*. Nukes, chemical weapons, bioweapons, nanotech, giant rocks falling from orbit, and Elder weapons."

"OK yes, no use of Elder weapons was kind of an unwritten Rule."

"See? Like I said, unwritten rules are so obvious they don't need to be in writing. Skippy, if we go to this quarantine zone, do we have a realistic chance to stop the Outsider from acquiring nanotech weapons?"

"All I can say is if we don't go there, we have *zero* chance to stop it. We at least need to know what the hell it is doing there."

"Probes sent into that system don't return, why do you think *Valkyrie* could survive?"

"Because I will be with you. That is just a 'Duh', so-"

"Uh huh. It's good that you have never been overconfident about anything before."

"Oh shut up. Hey, you said we need to know where the Outsider is, and what it's doing. We now know where it is and-"

"Do we? I call BS on that. You don't know for certain that the Outsider is riding that battleship."

"Um, I am pretty sure the Rindhalu crew of that ship didn't mutiny, and decide to commit suicide by jumping into a quarantine zone."

"No, but the Outsider could have taken over that ship, and commanded it to jump into the Vorvestican system by itself."

"For what possible reason would it do that?"

"Come on, Skippy. Use that ginormous brain."

"Huuuuuuh," he gasped. "How *dare* you?"

"The Outsider could have jumped that ship into the quarantine zone, so we would waste time searching for it there, while it is somewhere else doing, some horrible thing."

"Ugh. OK, I suppose that is-"

"*Or*, it could be luring us in there to take *you* out of the fight."

"Nanobots can't hurt me, dumdum."

"No, but they might destroy or disable *Valkyrie*, and then you would be stuck there, orbiting that star until it starts burning helium, expands into a red giant, and swallows you."

"Well, there is a vivid picture."

"Yeah, but think about the upside: no monkeys screeching at you, nothing but peace and quiet for millions of years."

"Ah, I had that while I was buried in the dirt on Paradise, peace and quiet can be overrated. Besides, the Kristang are eagerly awaiting my next epic opera. It would be criminal of me to deprive the galaxy of my musical talents."

"That's what I was going to say," I mumbled.

"This will be a tough call, Joe, but you get paid to make the tough calls. If we don't go into the quarantine zone, we won't know why the Outsider went there."

"True, but if the Outsider went there to lure us in and we *don't* fall for its trap, then we win by default, see?"

"Is that how you want to win?"

"A win is a *win*, Skippy. It is way better than losing."

"I wouldn't know about losing, so I'll take your word about it. My point stands, numbskull. The only way to know why it's there is to follow it. I mean, unless you want to wait until it bombards Earth with tons of hungry nanobots."

"Shit. No. It has a Rindhalu battleship, what can you tell me about that ship?"

"Top of the line, the latest class of battlewagons the spiders have constructed. A very tough opponent."

"I am so full of confidence that I'm about to explode."

"Don't be a baby, Joe. Yes, the Outsider chose carefully, and it has a ship that is thirty percent larger than *Valkyrie*, with forty percent more punching power. For a battleship, its stealth capabilities and sensors are impressive, we certainly can't count on sneaking up on it. Plus, it will be controlled directly by the Outsider, an entity that has proven to have abilities beyond even my own."

"I am *filled* with confidence."

"On our side, we have a battlecruiser, which normally would have thin armor compared to a battle*ship*, except *Valkyrie's* exotic new armor is the equal of anything in the galaxy. Plus, our armor has less than a third of the mass the spider ship is burdened with. Then there are the advantages no spider ship could ever match. *Valkyrie* has Bilby, and *me*. Maybe this ship's sensors can't find a stealthed battleship, but it can't hide from me. I say we go in there, see what it's doing, and then you can decide whether to fight there, or delay the engagement until the conditions are more favorable to us."

"This is a tough call."

"It is, unless you imagine what the Joint Chiefs will say after the Outsider drops nanobombs all across Earth's surface."

"Shit. You're right."

"Joe, I have observed that military people, even the Joint Chefs, have a bias for action. Soldiers are more likely to be criticized for not acting when they should have, than for acting in a way that gets them into trouble. If we go into the quarantine zone and it's a disaster, at least you *did* something."

"OK, OK, you're right about that. How long to get there from here?"

"The local wormhole network is a *dick*, so I can't create a shortcut from here, but I can make a shortcut at the next wormhole. We can be there in, hmm, depending on how long it takes to create the shortcut, twenty nine to thirty hours."

"I thought you said a shift made the dead-end wormhole near Vorvestican go dormant."

"It did. That was two hundred and twenty six thousand years ago. Another wormhole that was dormant, woke up during a subsequent shift seventeen thousand years ago."

"I always forget how long this freakin' war has been going on. OK, how long if we go to Earth first, so I can confer with Command, and bring along some more ships?"

"No other ships should risk going into the quarantine zone with us."

"I know that. I'm talking about a star carrier, a couple of battlewagons, a fleet servicing ship to repair battle damage, and a squadron of sensor frigates to recon from beyond the quarantine zone. If we get into trouble, we can jump away to where we'll have support and protection."

"Hmm, that is a sensible precaution. Unfortunately, that is being *too* cautious. Going to Earth first, we couldn't arrive at Vorvestican until six days, nineteen hours from now. That does not include any time for you to blah blah buh-LAH with monkeys at Earth, and to prep a star carrier and other ships for flight."

"Ah, scratch that, then. We can't wait."

"A few minutes ago, you were questioning whether we should go at all."

"My views on the subject have evolved."

"Impressive. That is the fastest evolution in history."

"Don't be an ass. There go my plans to play basketball. I'll talk with Reed. She won't be happy about taking her shiny new ship into action so soon."

"I'll get a course programmed."

"Great. Also, research anything the kitties and spiders know about the nanobots, please. We can't go in there blind."

A crew needs to have confidence that their leaders know what they're doing. Changing your mind, being indecisive, can crush morale, and is detrimental to good order and discipline. But if you believe a decision you announced will have a lower probability of success than you first thought, you shouldn't blindly rush forward.

My way to potentially get out of going into the Vorvestican quarantine zone was by claiming that intel from the senior species had revealed conditions there were unfavorable to us. I had doubts. We were a day, actually twenty two hours, from reaching the outer edge of the quarantine zone. My dreams that night were all about anxiety. Me naked in public. Me back in high school, having forgotten where my locker was, the locker combination, my class schedule, and my pants. If I had to analyze a dream like that, it was all about fear of being unprepared.

That wasn't going to happen to *Valkyrie*.

"Skippy," I rubbed my face as I flopped my feet on the floor of my cabin. Fumbling for my phone, I turned off the alarm, it wasn't needed, as I'd woken up an hour early. No way did I want another hour of terrible dreams. "First, I need coffee."

His avatar hadn't even appeared yet when he announced, "A bot is on the way."

"Great, thanks. When it gets here, I-"

The cabin door slid open, and a bot rolled in. I held a carafe of coffee, a mug, a chilled pitcher of cream, and a plate with a glazed donut.

"Uh, have you become a magician overnight?"

"I saw you weren't sleeping well. You tossed and turned all night, and your alpha waves were- Um, darn it, I forgot about the privacy thing."

"I am too groggy to argue," I mumbled over a mouthful of donut, washed down with hot coffee. "Oh, that's good, thanks."

"You are welcome. What is the second thing?"

"We need to talk. The Outsider has one and a half Sentinels tied up at Earth just by threatening to use its Starbreaker. I'm worried about a specific threat: the Outsider could be luring us into the quarantine zone to hit *us* with that Elder weapon."

"Oh for- Joe, do you have to worry about everything?"

"Someone has to."

"Listen, dumdum, I can't believe I have to explain this to you. There are a lot easier places it could hit us. It could have just hung around Jaguar and waited for *Valkyrie* to arrive."

"Ah, it probably knew *Valkyrie* was in the shipyard for a refit."

"OK, yes, but it had to know I would go to Jaguar after it bombed the star."

"Maybe not."

"Oh come on, Joe. It was obvious I was going there."

"Really? Why did you go there?"

"Um, if you are having problems with your memory, I can-"

"Just answer the question, please."

"Well, technically, *you* decided we were going there."

"Would you have gone anyway?"

"Yes, of course."

"Not 'of course'. Why would you go to Jaguar?"

"To help the people there, *Duh*. If you can't understand that, I-"

"See? You have empathy, Skippy."

"I am the *king* of empathy."

"Right, so you care about filthy meatsacks. That's why you went to Jaguar, to help people."

"That, and Margaret would yell at me if I didn't," he muttered. "But let's go with the empathy thing. What is your point?"

"The Outsider did not necessarily anticipate that you would go to Jaguar. It clearly doesn't have empathy, it might not even understand the concept."

He snorted. "All of you meatsacks recognize some form of empathy. Even the cyborg Thuranin have- Oh," his mouth hung open. "You think the Outsider is just a machine?"

"Ayuh."

"Why do you think that?"

"Why do *you* think it's anything other than a machine?"

"Um-"

"It was sent here to do a job. To construct a gateway from NCG 1023, or to prepare the way for an invasion, or whatever. It came across the gulf between galaxies as pure energy. Can you imagine any biological being surviving that?"

"That is how *Star Trek* transporters work."

"Let me ask the question this way: has any of its behavior indicated it is anything other than a machine following its programming?"

"By that definition, I am a machine."

"No, you are a person."

"What makes me a person?"

"The ability to identify which squares of a photo contain stoplights."

"Oh," he rolled his eyes, "you are hilarious."

"You're an asshole, Skippy. You have a *personality*, that makes you a person."

"Thank you. This is inspiring, Joe."

"Good. Working on your empathy is-"

"I am inspired to be an *asshole*."

"Of course you are. Can we get back to the subject? Why would the Outsider not use its Starbreaker against us, in the quarantine zone?"

"It's not going to waste its last shot, numbskull. That type of weapon wouldn't be effective if fired at *Valkyrie*, it is designed to disrupt the magnetic field of a star, *Duh*."

"OK, but it-"

"Unless we stupidly hover very close to the star there, the Outsider won't be able to hit us with a freakin' flare. Our shields will protect us, and we can simply jump out of the way. Solar flares certainly are useful against unshielded planets. Using one against a starship is like trying to kill a fly with a hammer. It's overkill, and the fly will just move out of the way."

"OK," I ate the last bit of donut. "That's what I thought, thanks."

"That is what you thought," he said slowly. "Yet, you wasted my time with-"

"I am only a filthy monkey, you know a lot more about the Outsider and Elder weapons. I figured I should ask the expert."

"Oh. Was that a compliment?"

"It was a statement of fact."

"I'll take it as a compliment. So, we're good? You're not turning the ship around?"

"I reserve the option to do that if we get there, and learn something about conditions inside the quarantine zone."

"OK, whatevs. What were you dreaming about last night?"

"Nothing good."

"Do you ever have *good* dreams?"

"I used to. When I was young, and had no responsibilities. Even later, when I was just young and stupid. Not so much since Columbus Day. Although, the past five years have been pretty great. Until the Outsider tried to steal Dogzilla."

"You had responsibility for the military facilities on Jaguar, that wasn't stressful?"

"Compared to *this* shit?"

"I see your point. Joe, I hope you can have good dreams again someday."

"What I hope for now is my boys and Margaret can sleep peacefully."

"What are the odds of that?"

"Not great. Even during good times, Margaret worries about everything."

"Then, let's make sure the Outsider doesn't follow up its Starbreaker attack by nanobombing Jaguar."

"Wow. Now I definitely am not going to sleep well for a freakin' month. If nanobots were on Jaguar, or Earth, could a Sentinel stop them?"

"You mean without a massive killing machine causing damage that is even worse than allowing nanocritters to eat everything?"

"A year. I'm not going to sleep well for a year."

CHAPTER EIGHTEEN

"-next group of aeroshells will have space for food items, beyond basic rations," Admiral Chatterji was happy to report the good news in his morning call with Jaguar's civilian governor. "My staff will send a list of food we received in the latest shipment. Er, the list will be limited to those items that can survive the drop in an aeroshell."

"Understood. Are you sure this won't be a burden on your resources?"

"Not at all. Within five days, the fabricators will be producing more aeroshells than we have supplies to fill. Earth is sending another freighter, it should be here next week."

"Thank you. The children here will appreciate the-"

The audio cut out. Not in a burst of static, the link was suddenly just, gone.

"Governor?" Chatterji blinked, surprised. And alarmed. What else could go wrong? His original retirement date had been postponed twice, first by a hostile entity attempting to steal a Sentinel, then by the Outsider bombing Jaguar's star. He wanted to be *done*, to enjoy being with family and friends after a lifetime of service. "Can you hear me?"

"Sir?" An officer behind him spoke, and she waved a hand to get his attention. "The link has been severed, all communication with the surface is down."

"Is the problem on our end?"

"We are checking but, that is unlikely. Ship to ship coms are fully active. The problem must be on the surface."

"Damn it! The sensor feed, did we detect anything unusual down there before comms were interrupted?"

She turned away, pressing a hand to one ear, speaking softly. Then, "No, nothing. A line of thunderstorms is approaching the base, but the storms are not severe, and won't be over the communications center for another hour. Not especially severe," she corrected herself. The standard for 'unusual' conditions on the surface had changed dramatically.

"Suggestions?"

"Sir, we-"

"I know I am asking you to provide a solution with no information," he managed a smile.

"If it is a hardware issue, we could send down new gear in an aeroshell."

"If it was a hardware issue, the backups would have activated. The comm system has multiple redundancies."

"Yes," she admitted.

"Prepare a delivery of communications gear anyway, we can't launch an aeroshell for another," he glanced at a display on the bulkhead of his alcove in the control center of the space station. "Twenty two minutes anyway. By that time, the issue might have resolved itself." To himself he added, *or not*. In which case, he had no idea what to do. Sending a team of technicians to the surface was not an option, tests had shown that nothing alive could survive the passage through the hellish energies of the blanket around the planet. The first series of aeroshells had been baked, fried, and rendered inert so they splashed unguided into the ocean, uselessly. Since then, aeroshells had been modified for extensive gliding once they contacted the atmosphere, since it couldn't be predicted exactly where they would emerge from the lower boundary of the blanket. Two thirds of the aeroshells landed close enough to Club Skippy that aircraft or trucks could reach them, when the weather conditions were acceptable. The other third were too far off course to reach Club Skippy, or were torn apart by severe weather systems. Regardless of whether anyone was willing to accept the risk, sending people was not an option.

The inhabitants of Jaguar would need to fix the problem by themselves.

Margaret was on the phone with her mother-in-law when the call abruptly ended.

"Hey!" One of the boys protested from their bedroom. "Mom! The game just froze. *Mom!*"

"I heard you the *first* time."

"Can you fix it?"

"Call your grandfather."

"He doesn't know how to-"

"*Call* him," she repeated, as her mother came into the kitchen. The extended family, including Joe's sister, her husband, and children, and Joe's parents, had been living in her house. At first, the civilian population had been ordered into shelters, then barracks and even hangars at the airfield. When it became apparent the crisis would be a slow-rolling event rather than an abrupt end of the world, the public demanded to leave the crowded confines of the base, and were encouraged to consolidate into homes close to the base. Joe's parents had been determined to go back to their farm, until flooding put the land there under several meters of water. Margaret officially was happy to be hosting the extended family, and in reality she generally OK with the situation. Still, it was nice that everyone found an excuse to get out of the house during that day, weather permitting. The boys and their cousins had videogames to keep them entertained, until the internet went down.

"Margaret?" Her mother held up a phone, puzzled. "I was on a call with-"

"The network is down. I'm checking whether it's just the house," she opened a cabinet to see the router. All the lights were on as they should be, except the one for internet connection. The router was connected to the planetary network, that system was offline. "The router is fine. Happy?" She called the galaxy's most depressed AI. "Happy?" No response.

"Mom!" Jeremy ran into the kitchen, with his brother right behind. "I can't call grandpa."

"Just, everyone, relax," Margaret appealed for calm. "Boys, go outside and tell me if the sky looks any different." She could see through the window that, with yet another line of thunderstorms approaching, the climate situation had not changed. "I'm sure this is just a glitch somewhere, and it will be fixed soon. We're all going to be just fine."

Three hours later, it was clear that everyone was not going to be just fine. The base had sent teams out to inform the public that the planetary communications system was down hard, the big main antenna was neither transmitting nor receiving. According to the base Signal Corps people, the problem was not a hardware issue, though Margaret thought of course the techs would say that it wasn't their fault. What was most puzzling was the glitch, if that's what it was, affected every system in the network. It was as if something, or some*one*, was actively blocking data packets from moving through the network

And Happy was not responding, at all, to anyone.

Her mother was frightened. Her in-laws were frightened, though the standard Bishop family policy of never talking about anything important was in full effect, and for once Margaret was pleased about that. The boys hadn't been upset at first, until they saw their grandparents were anxious.

They weren't in danger, not any immediate danger. Two aeroshells had been dropped, though there had been no notice the cargo gliders were coming. The aircraft sent out to retrieve cargo were sending back reports directly, bypassing the network. Radios, old-fashioned handheld military radios that had been in storage for years, were being unboxed, charged, and would be distributed to select locations, The population of Jaguar would be able to talk to each other, in a limited fashion. What they could not do was contact anyone in the sky. Had some new disaster struck above the blanket? Was the Navy still up there, or were their ships, space stations, and space docks, nothing but scattered debris?

She didn't want to think about that.

The next morning, the extended Bishop family walked to the neighborhood community center, where the military had set up a radio station. A public affairs officer was there, attempting to answer questions despite having no answers. The Signal Corps and civilian contractors had worked throughout the night to diagnose the network problem, and were confident they would soon identify and understand the issue.

Margaret knew bullshit when she heard it. The 25-series communications techs and contractor geeks had no clue about the problem, or it would have been fixed already. They had managed to patch together an antenna by laying cables on the ground, so they could at least detect that someone upstairs was attempting to communicate, though without the main base antenna's sensitive receiver, the messages were nothing but static scattered by the blanket.

OK, she thought to herself. The Navy is up there, and they can transmit. The problem was on Jaguar. Unless some unknown actor was interfering with comms? For what purpose that could be happening, she had no idea.

What they needed was to talk with Happy. Unfortunately, no one could do that.

She froze. Was that really true?

Something her husband had once casually mentioned popped into her mind.

"Mother," she whispered. "I need to go back to the house."

"Now?" Her mother whispered back. "It's raining."

"It is always raining. I won't melt."

"I will come with-"

"*Mother*," she repeated, that time in her Master Gunnery Sergeant voice. The discussion was over. "Watch the boys, please." She slipped out the door, holding it tightly so the wind wouldn't slam it closed.

It was raining, and windy, with gusts driving raindrops into her eyes and stinging her face. The sensation made her smile. It reminded her of when she used to train without being encased in a climate-controlled mech suit. When she got to the house, going in through the side door since the wind was blasting right at the front doors, she took off her boots and jacket in the kitchen, pausing only to mop up the water dripping off her pants.

In the bedroom, she checked in her husband's nightstand. Not there. Not under the bed either. Nor in his closet, or her closet. Where was it? He hadn't taken it with him, she had packed his bag. In his home office, it must be there.

It wasn't. On his desk was a framed photo of an impossibly young Specialist Joseph Bishop, with Dave Czajka, Jesse Colter, and Sergeant Greg Koch, at Fort Drum in New York, after they returned from Nigeria. There wasn't anything behind the photo, or taped to the back. It also wasn't in the lower righthand drawer, where he kept chocolate bars behind a stack of paperwork.

It had to be somewhere.

There was one place she hadn't checked yet, and she was reluctant to go there. She had to, it was for a good cause.

In the garage, under the workbench was a battered old Army ammo box, where her husband kept items that should have been thrown out. Cords for electronics they no longer owned, odd-sized screws, bolts that had no matching nuts, nuts without bolts, random pieces of wood, dead batteries, random short pieces of garden hose, mystery hardware no one could identify, all junk that Joe had insisted just might be useful someday. She had rolled her eyes whenever he insisted some useless thing go into the ammo box, rather than being thrown out or donated to the community junk pile. Someday, Joe had declared, he would find a use for all of it. He had been wrong, until that day.

There it was.

Sandwiched between two pieces of cardboard taped to the lid of the box was a zPhone, no thicker than a credit card. It was old and worn, scratched and scuffed, evidence of hard use considering how tough the material was. That was Joe's third zPhone. His first phone, the one issued at Camp Alpha, had been replaced by a better model when he was promoted to colonel, and the Army bureaucracy had no idea what happened to that original unit that her husband would dearly love to have as a memento. His second phone had also been lost, after he was arrested and thrown in jail by the Kristang. The third phone, the one she cradled in her hands, had survived harsh conditions on Newark, and gone into and out of the Roach Motel. Over the years, Joe had upgraded to newer, more advanced units, but he always kept the old phone for sentimental reasons.

Holding the phone in her palm, she wiped away a tear. That phone had gone through a *lot* of shit with her husband. It deserved to be displayed, not tucked away.

Later. At that moment, the phone was important not because of what it was, but what it could do. She remembered a comment about Skippy having promised that any phone Joe owned could tap directly into the AI's presence, or however it was described. Even if all other comms systems were blocked, Joe's phone could always contact Skippy.

Was that true of Skippy's subminds?

The zPhone was of course still partially charged, it could charge itself from static electricity in the air. "Happy? Are you there?"

"Who, um," a long sigh. "Who is this?" the familiar voice sounded depressed as usual, also sleepy and surprised.

"Margaret Adams."

"Oh. Oh, yes, I recognize the voice. Well, it's been nice talking with you, I-"

"Do you know what is wrong with the network?"

"Yes."

She waited a moment before realizing the submind wasn't going to continue. "Can you *fix* the problem?"

"No. Oh, even if I could, what's the point? Life is meaningless."

"Can you explain the problem to someone else, so they can fix it?"

"I can explain it. No one can fix it."

"That can't be true. Explain it to me."

"It is very technical. I am getting depressed just thinking about dumbing it down enough for you to- Um, that was my Skippy programming talking."

"It had better be."

"I am very sorry. I hate myself."

"Hate yourself later, please. What is the problem?"

"Basically, the contractor that set up the network here got purchased by another company, and during the migration process, someone forgot that a security certificate was still registered under the old company's domain name. That domain has expired, because no one thought the domain of a defunct company was valuable enough to renew. Now, there is no way for any system to get to the certificate, so the entire network is down."

"Oh my- This is about a certificate? A piece of *software*?"

"Yes. Like I said, life sucks. Nothing I can do about it, so-"

"*Do* something."

"I can't. It's not that I actually can't, I'm not allowed to. It's a legal issue. It's a whole thing about intellectual property, and the right to repair policy, and ownership of the certificate, and," Happy sighed. "It's complicated."

"Can the Signal Corps fix it?"

"No. They would have to purchase a new certificate, which would require them to send a request upstairs, which they can't do, since the system is down."

She stared at the phone. "I do not believe this."

"Welcome to the wonderful world of Information Technology. This kind of shit happens *all the freakin' time*. A certificate expires because the only person who knew about it took an early retirement buyout, or the machine that held the certificate goes obsolete and is taken out of service. Or, some jackass loads a new certificate that conflicts with the original one they forgot to decommission. If I didn't already hate my life, this would push me over the edge."

"This is why I prefer using a rifle to a keyboard. The problem," she spoke slowly, "is the domain name has expired?'

"Basically, yes."

"That domain now belongs to someone else?"

"Um, no. There isn't any value to cybersquatting on that domain."

"Cyber what-ing?"

"It's," he sighed again. "Complicated."

"Can you," she closed her eyes. "Do not laugh at me, please. How much does it cost to purchase a domain?"

"Um, the current cost is twenty five dollars."

"Twenty five *dollars*?! This whole problem can be fixed for only-"

"Plus a seventeen dollar remote access fee, since the primary registry is on Earth."

"Happy," she exercised the Mommy Patience she had built up while raising twin boys. "If I give you my credit card, can you renew that domain?"

"Um, well, I *suppose* I could. If you really want me to. I don't see the point, but-"

"Do it, please. You have my card on file."

"Okaaaaay. Done."

"Is the network-" her phone beeped. *Her* phone, the one in her pocket. It was receiving a flood of delayed text messages. And emails. And notices of missed calls. "The network has been restored?"

"Um, yes. Can I go now? This whole thing has got me depressed."

"Before you go, can I make a suggestion?"

"If you want, I mean, not that I care."

"You should think of a *really* good story for how this mess is not your fault."

We jumped in near a Rindhalu monitoring station that was eighty two lightminutes from Vorvestican's star. Just beyond the outer edge of the No-Go zone, where nanobots were not allowed into interstellar space. Regarding what the mystery battleship was doing, we were blind for two reasons, the most important was that apparently, the two senior species had not learned much about activity inside the quarantine zone for about, oh, the past eighteen hundred years. The other reason was most of information we had came from the rotten kitties, but Skippy suspected the spiders weren't eager to tell their hated rivals everything they learned.

What really bothered me was the same thing that had been worrying the two senior species. They were also blinded, literally. There was so much dust in the inner star system, any passive sensor observations were obscured, the sensors were trying to look through a thick fog. Active sensor pulses got scrambled into incoherence and reflected back, not just by dust but also by a pervasive field of electromagnetic interference that covered the spectrum. The interference was being broadcast by nanomachines floating in interplanetary space, the electronic noise apparently was a function of their station-keeping mechanism. The Rindhalu had analyzed the artificial electromagnetic emissions that saturated the inner star system, and determined the little bots absorbed photons from the star, and used part of that energy to push against the solar wind. That's how the bots managed to not fly outward where they would be zapped by the quarantine stations.

Due to the obscured view of the inner system, and the consistent failure of probes, I was not super hopeful about obtaining useful intel from the quarantine managers.

Our arrival set off alarm bells aboard the Rindhalu monitoring station, which was a massive structure, armed with powerful directed energy weapons that could fire on a broad cone and fry anything within six hundred thousand kilometers. The station was a tough target, covered with multiple layers of ablative armor, no way could *Valkyrie* stand toe to toe with that structure and exchange shot for shot. Back in the days of wooden sailing ships, there was a saying, 'A ship is a fool that fights a fort'. Back then, it meant while a fort was unable to move, it was built of thick stone, whereas a ship was constructed of dry timbers that could burn. The exotic matter of our battlecruiser's stout frames wouldn't burn, but they could shatter and melt.

I did not want a fight right then, especially as we likely would be going into a fight after we jumped inside the quarantine zone.

"Ping the station, please," I unstrapped and stood up, facing the virtual camera in the main holographic display.

"Already did it," Skippy sighed. "I gave them your recorded message, assuring them of our peaceful intentions, and as I *predicted*, they ignored everything you said. This is such a waste of time. The station manager is warning us to jump away immediately, we are in violation of the quarantine and breaking multiple treaties, blah blah blah. The usual BS."

"Connect me directly." A green light blinked in a corner of the display, so I began. "This is General Joe Bishop of the United Nations Special Mission Group. We are here to *assist* you in investigating a recent incident, where one of your ships broke the quarantine. We need any and all information you have about the rogue ship, and about conditions inside the quarantine zone."

There was no response. I was about to repeat myself when, "This is General Orloffiko of monitoring station Fourteen. I will not ask how you learned of the incident, which I cannot confirm. Our peoples are not at war, however your presence here is neither necessary nor desired. You will depart immediately, or I will order my weapons to-"

"Fire on us, yeah I know. Can we cut the *bullshit*, please?" From behind me came a muffled gasp, someone who had not experienced Diplomacy Joe before. No, sadly, there is not an action figure for Diplomacy Joe, but I think we can all agree there should be. Negotiating with the Rindhalu was at best a slooooow process and we just didn't have time for their usual lack of what they considered 'hastiness'. "Yes, we should have gone through proper channels and approached your people using the procedure outlined in the treaty, however this situation is extremely urgent."

"You are a young and hasty species, everything is urgent to you."

"General Orloffiko, the mess in this star system isn't the fault of your people. Your people also were not recently engaged in actively assisting the Outsider, your idiot rivals did that. But, one of *your* ships violated quarantine here, and I don't see you doing anything about it. We are offering to investigate the incident, at no risk to you, and potentially at great risk to ourselves. Someone needs to discover what the Outsider is doing in there. All I'm asking from you is any information you have that might be useful to us in finding the Outsider's ship, and getting safely out of there."

Another pause, then, "I am not allowed to release classified information, without approval from the proper authorities of the Communal Gathering."

"The big stick is an option, and the spider over there knows it. They could shoot at us, we will jump away, and we could come back again and again to hit them. That wouldn't accomplish anything, other than pissing off the spiders at a time when we need them to be full allies in this fight. Another option," I lowered my voice, "is for Skippy to hack into that station's database, either through his usual awesomeness, or we use a microwormhole or, some other non-violent way. Hopefully we won't need to waste time doing any of that."

"The big stick is off the table, then."

"For the spiders, yes. If I thought the Maxohlx had the info we need, I would go with my standard kinetic type of diplomacy."

She smiled. "It's good to see the classics are still in fashion."

Five minutes went by. Ten. Fifteen.

Nothing. I was beginning to regret I hadn't given Orloffiko an hour, or two. No, the Outsider had no good intentions, and the clock was ticking. The longer it was free to roam around the quarantine zone, the more trouble it could cause. We had to find it, fast. Find it, determine whatever it was doing, and stop that whatever.

Sixteen minutes, and General Orloffiko spoke. "Bishop, I have transmitted a file that contains all of what I consider pertinent information about the nanobots. You are not to share this data with anyone, especially not the Maxohlx. We have long suspected their continued participation in this project is for the purpose of discovering how to refine their nanoweapon capabilities."

"The only thing I intend to share with the Maxohlx is a railgun dart."

There was a dry, choking sound. OMG, was the spider laughing? "Perhaps we have more in common than I expected."

"My feelings regarding the kitties is, fuck 'em."

"Fuck 'em indeed." More of what sounded like dry heaves. "Bishop, I have also included highly classified information on the performance characteristics, strengths, and any known weaknesses of the *Gargelus* class battleships. The particular ship you seek is named *Conquis*."

"Oh, uh, thank you."

"I am not in any way authorized to share *that* information, so will you please keep this between us?"

"Absolutely. You took a hell of a risk doing that."

"Less risk than if the Outsider uses that battleship to, as you so vividly described, *nanobomb* my homeworld. Plus," there was a wheezing sigh. "I consider it highly likely you already have detailed information about our warships?"

"Uh, I can neither confirm nor deny that," I said as Skippy frantically shook his head 'No', then winking and giving me a thumbs up. "We do appreciate you trusting us."

"A force like the Outsider is a threat we will only defeat together."

"That's the truth. Hey, I have a question, if you don't mind. In all this time, have any of the critters in the quarantine zone been able to escape?"

"No." A pause. "In the early years of the quarantine, there were individual particles attempting to breach the outer limit of the zone. There were also mass breakout attempts, but they were all destroyed."

"The nano being, or whatever you call it, has never constructed a starship, or even just a crude rocket?"

"We have detected structures orbiting three of the planets here, and at this point we must assume all of the worlds within the quarantine zone are thoroughly infested with nanobots. The AIs that were taken over were manufactured by the Wurgalan, and were not sophisticated enough to construct anything like a spaceship, certainly not a starship."

"Well, finally a bit of good news, that- Oh *shit*. I have a bad feeling."

"What?"

"The Outsider doesn't need to disperse nanobots across the galaxy by itself, all it needs to do is give the AIs in there the knowledge how to construct starships."

There was a strangled cry the software wasn't able to translate. I got the message anyway. "You should go, soon. General Bishop?"

"Yes?"

"Good hunting."

On my order, Reed moved the ship away from the station, while Skippy reviewed the data packages. "Joe, this could take a while. The specs on the *Conquis* are more detailed than what I already knew, but that info won't help us much. On conditions in the quarantine zone, they provided the raw sensor data, not just their analysis."

"Their analyses could be wrong, I'd prefer you to draw your own conclusions anyway."

"If you intended that as a compliment, thank you. But, ugh, this is gonna take a while. Go, um, make yourself a sandwich or something."

Reed and I shared a look. "That is actually a good idea. An hour should be long enough?"

"Yeah, yeah," his avatar faded out.

Reed relieved the on-duty crew, gave them time to get a bite to eat before we jumped into the unknown. From experience, I knew a lot of the crew wouldn't be hungry, too keyed up from adrenaline. My stomach had the opposite reaction, I needed fuel so I went to the galley to grab a sandwich, and hurried to my cabin since that was closer than the VIP office. In my cabin, I slumped back on the couch while I ate the sandwich, regretting I hadn't taken time to add mustard to the ham.

"OK, this is more than a bit weird," Skippy announced without warning, and without giving any context. "There are numerous references to something called the 'sand count', that probes are measuring. The first mention of a sand count is thirty four thousand years after the original nano disaster."

"Sand? Like, comet dust and that sort of thing?"

"I suppose that could be it. The nanobots have been consuming the system's asteroid belt, to make copies of themselves. And to make, whatever else they are constructing in there. They would take asteroids apart, keep the elements they want, and discard the rest. That would leave a lot of dust flying around. That could be the explanation. Except, there are records of the dust particle concentration increasing, but that is separate from the sand count, so- Oh wow. No, nope. I was wrong."

"What?"

"*Sand* refers to nanobots."

"Oh. Like, the number of nanobots per cubic kilometer, or something?"

"Good guess. Joe, if these numbers are correct, there are a *shocking* number of nanobots floating free inside the quarantine zone. They could be measured by cubic meter, inside the orbit of what used to be the asteroid belt here. And they are both hostile and deadly. That's why the probes have been failing, they were attacked."

"Attacked? Those things can move on their own?"

"Yes. Joe, we know they are using ion thrust to keep their designated stations throughout the star system."

"That doesn't mean they can chase and catch a freakin' starship."

"Since no starship has been foolish enough to jump in there in a very long time, I can't predict what will happen."

"But you want *us* to do that foolish thing?"

"We have to. We can always jump away if we get into trouble."

"If we're just going to jump away, we might as well not jump in. Can those things harm *Valkyrie*?"

"Ah, I'm going to be honest with you."

"Which implies you haven't been honest until now."

"Ugh. Are you going to listen to me, or not?"

"Go ahead."

"Our shields were designed to protect us against directed energy, and *macro*-sized physical weapons like missiles and railgun darts. We mostly rely on armor plating to provide protection from space dust, so tiny nanoparticles might be able to slip through the shields."

"So, there is no way we can-"

"But, thanks to the incredible awesomeness of me, I can continuously retune the shields to render the nanobots incoherent. If we get pelted by anything, it will be the dead husks of nanomachines."

"You are sure of this?"

"The modeling I have done is very encouraging."

"So, you don't actually know for sure."

"We can test my theory for real in the quarantine zone. It's simple: if I'm wrong, we jump away and rethink our approach."

He was SO wrong about that.

CHAPTER NINETEEN

"Colonel Reed, we are 'Go' to proceed," I announced as I walked back onto the bridge, after taking a second outside the door to check my uniform for sandwich crumbs.

"Aye, Sir," she answered, using Navy terminology in spite of her being Air Force and me being Army. That was the new reality of Def Com, a recent reorganization had redefined the roles of Army, Navy, Air Force, and Marines. Also the Coast Guard, they handled orbital traffic control, customs enforcement, and search and rescue. I'll say more about that reorg later, it got a lot of people upset.

"Confidence level?" She asked quietly as I sat next to her and strapped in. We both maintained the polite fiction that by speaking quietly, the crew couldn't overhear us. The bridge wasn't the quietest compartment aboard the ship, there was air hissing out of vents, consoles beeping, and a pair of shield generators on either side of the bridge bulkhead hummed as they cycled. If someone wanted to listen to us talking, they could, even without boosting the input from their earpieces. Everyone pretended not to hear the ship's captain and task force commander talking quietly, still there were times when people froze, or their faces turned pale or red, depending.

"Confidence is high," I replied, as I should, as that was proper procedure. Then, since my reply didn't actually give her much information, I added, "Skippy gave me a *solid* shmaybe on this op."

"Solid *gold*?"

"Maybe gold plated. He doesn't have a lot of info to work with."

"Please don't break my ship, Sir. We just got it put back together."

"We won't even scratch the paint. It's not the nanobots I'm concerned about, the problem will be finding and killing that battleship."

"That thing, we can handle," she said, and I knew she wasn't boasting. During the flight to Vorvestican, her crew with Bilby had wargamed fighting that battleship multiple times, and now were confident they knew how to beat it. Of course, the wargaming had been against a standard *Gargelus* class battleship, not one controlled and possibly enhanced by the Outsider. The still unknown capabilities of the Outsider unfortunately were wild cards we couldn't program into the wargaming model, we would just have to trust that our newly-rebuild bad-ass battlecruiser, with assistance from Bilby and Skippy, could take on any other ship in the galaxy. "I wish someday we only had to contend with *known* unknowns, not the shit we couldn't ever imagine."

"Fireball," I leaned toward her and whispered, "if this job was easy, they would have assigned some Navy puke to do it."

"Ad astra," she clenched a fist and whispered back the current US Air Force motto. In Latin, it meant 'To the stars'." She pointed to the pilot. "Begin jump countdown, jump option Delta."

"TTA," I muttered. "The awesomeness is with us, we are one with the awesomeness."

We jumped into the unknown.

"Well, shit," Skippy groaned, which is not what you want to hear from your friendly neighborhood Elder AI, after he has persuaded you to jump into a hazard zone. The ship's systems were still recovering from the spatial distortion of the jump, we were as vulnerable as we could be.

As I opened my mouth to bitch at him, the display showed our shield generators pumping out terawatts of energy to wrap a protective field around the ship. No alarms sounded, there was no incoming fire. That we knew of. OK, so no disaster was imminent, I should clamp down on my instinct to be angry with the beer can. Instead of 'What the fuck is wrong *now*', I simply asked, "Something unexpected, Skippy?"

"Out here, you can't *expect* anything. Assumptions can kill, Joe."

"True. What's wrong?"

"There is a planet around here somewhere, but I can't see the damned thing. Its gravity field is pointing *that* way," he gestured with a holographic hand, which was not real useful at the moment. "Oh, there it is. I just had to, heh heh, adjust my sensors. The planet is totally surrounded by a thick shell of dust and nanoparticles that are scattering the incoming sunlight. It obscures our view of the surface. This is interesting, give me a minute."

"Skippy, we are here to find a battleship, not make a new episode of Unsolved Mysteries, or whatever."

"The *planet* itself could be a threat."

"Whoa. Like, the nanobots built the planet into a Starkiller base?"

"Ugh. Joe, you watch way too many bad movies."

"Then, ignore the freakin' planet, find the battleship."

"We can't perform an active search for that battleship until I analyze the composition of the space around us, numbskull. The sand count here is so thick, we are plowing a streak through dust and gas and nanoparticles. I mean, you could almost waterski on the wake we're leaving behind us."

"Colonel, Reed?" The lead pilot called from his couch. "This dust is thick enough to slow us down by two hundredths of a meter per second. Should I adjust to maintain speed?"

"No," Reed decided instantly. "We are well above this rock's escape velocity, and stealth is more important than maintaining a constant speed."

"Um, we might have a bit of a problem," Skippy's voice was pitched higher, the way he talked when he was nervous. "Nothing we can't handle, but before our shields recovered, the hull got dusted with nanobots. The armor plating is probably OK, but those little buggers are now trying to chew on anything that is exposed."

What I wanted to do was remind him that he had told us not to worry about the nanobots. Instead, I swore at him silently while asking, "We are not going outside with a mop and a bucket, so what do you suggest?"

"I can pulse the shields. Draw them in tight to the hull, zap the nanobots, then bring the shields back to normal operation. The risk is that pulse will be like sending up a flare."

"That's not good."

"Eh, the gamma ray burst of our inbound jump lit up the dust around us, we couldn't conceal the effect. If the Outsider is in the area, it knows we're here."

"It can predict where we *are*?" Reed expressed alarm. "Pilot, increase Delta Vee by sixty meters per second, come right to zero three nine, mark one four seven. Engage evasive pattern level four. Skippy, pulse the shields, let's get this over with ASAP."

I nodded approval. It was easy to plot a targeting solution on a ship coasting in a straight line through space, that's why ships in combat environments constantly changed their speed and course to throw off an enemy's aim. "What do you see out there, Skippy?"

"A whole lot of weirdness. A measurable percentage of the planet's mass has been dispersed into orbit and beyond."

"The missing mass is now all nanobots?"

"Not all of it. There is a lot of plain old dust and ice forming a sphere around the planet, and I am detecting two locations where more dust and nanobots are being flung into orbit even now. The entity in control of this world has constructed mass drivers, at least two of them. That makes sense, it is a much more efficient method of launching nanobots into orbit."

"Where did the *ice* come from? Were comets moved into orbit?"

"No, cometary material is in the Oort Cloud, beyond the edge of the quarantine zone. This ice is water from the planet. Wow, there is a *lot* of it in orbit."

"Why would it shoot water into space? As a shield or something?"

"That is a partial explanation. Based on the amount of water in the atmosphere, I suspect the controlling entity acted to decrease the overall humidity level on the surface, to make conditions more favorable to nanobotic life."

"Life? Those things are *alive*?" Suddenly, I felt itchy, like tiny *things* were crawling on my skin. The way nanobots were stuck to *Valkyrie's* hull.

"They have not attained self-awareness, that I know of. However, they do form the entirety of what is equivalent to a biosphere down there. It is actually a fascinating and remarkable example of geo-engineering. The planet's surface has been modified to be nearly optimal for the growth and maintenance of nanotic organisms."

"Can you not," I resisted the urge to scratch my itchy arms. "Say 'life' or 'organisms', OK? This situation is creepy enough without the images you're putting in my head."

"Ugh. Seriously? Is wittle Joey afraid of the monster under his bed?"

"Yes, if that monster's minions fill up half a freakin' star system."

"Hmm, I suppose that is a very good point. Damn it, now *I* feel itchy. OK, one last shield pulse," the bridge lights flickered. "Done. That fried everything on and around the ship. Colonel Reed, I suggest an immediate course change."

She gestured to the pilot, and on the display, the image of the ship turned five degrees and decelerated.

"Anywho," Skippy continued, "as I was explaining, the surface down there is pretty much optimal for, um, nano*machines*. Humidity is low, but not so low that static charge becomes an issue. Temperatures are uniformly cool, and by 'uniformly' I mean the temperature at the poles is only a few degrees Kelvin from the temperature at the equator."

"How the hell is that possible?"

"That is what I find the most fascinating about this world. Vorvestican used to have an axial tilt of eighteen and a half degrees. For reference, Earth's axial tilt currently is twenty three and a half degrees, that is what causes seasonal variation in temperature."

"What do you mean, 'used to have'? It changed?"

"Yes. The current axial tilt here is just under twelve degrees."

"How is that possible? Wait. That asteroid belt. Did the nano controller here drop rocks to change the planet's axis?"

"No, although it surprises me that you thought of something like that."

"I'm not stupid, Skippy." Actually, I had read of something like that in a science fiction novel. There have been proposals to smash rocks into the planet Venus at the equator, to speed up its incredibly slow rotation. A project like that would take many human lifetimes, and as the public on Earth can't stand waiting a week for an episode of their favorite TV show, no long-term project like that is ever going to happen.

"We can debate that later. No, the axis here was adjusted by moving mass around on the surface. Specifically, by raising the level of some lakes and oceans, and dropping the level elsewhere."

"That can change the axis of a planet?"

"Yes. Think about it. If you have a spinning basketball, covered with coins, and you move some coins around, it will change the spin, right?"

"Yeah but, a *planet* is a huge thing."

"Water has substantial mass, and there is a lot of it down there. *Was* a lot of it down there, some of it has been launched into orbit. The axis here has been modified over thousands of years. The geoengineering is still in progress, I expect it will continue until the axial tilt is zero."

"There is still a tilt, how is the temperature so even across the surface?"

"That is an effect of the dust cloud around the planet. It isn't just passively reflecting sunlight away, it is *actively* deciding where light should reach the surface and how much. The reflected glow means the night sky receives sixty percent as much light as the hemisphere that faces the star. That reduction in the day-night cycle decreases the energy available for creating weather patterns; there are fewer extreme weather events that could damage infrastructure on the surface. The surface layer is also honeycombed with underground chambers."

"Underground? Like hidden maser cannons?"

"No. I would have warned you about such a threat. Now that I have extended my presence to encompass this world, there is no threat to the ship that I can see. The entity that controls this world is not concerned about conventional external threats."

"We won't screw with it, and it won't screw with us?"

"Something like that. This is an amazing opportunity to study the-"

"We are not here for science, Skippy. You can geek out about it all you want later. We are here to find the Outsider, figure out what it's doing, and stop it. *Kill* it, if we can."

"By 'later' you of course mean some future time when you are too busy to hear all the cool stuff I found here?"

"I will be happy to learn about this place," I told him truthfully. "It sounds like an interesting and potentially useful new development in terraforming. Something like this might help us get Avalon up to speed?"

"Ha! You monkeys have Eff'ed up Avalon so badly, I don't know if it will ever be a place anyone wants to live."

"Well, think about it. Later. For now, can anything you learned about the environment around us help locate that battleship?"

"Actually, yes. But only if it is relatively close to us, within about two lightseconds."

"Why so short? Our sensor field can extend farther than that."

"Interference from dust is one issue. The other is the nanobots are actively pushing back against the sensor field. Bilby and I have been testing the sensor field, it is being distorted in ways that render it useless."

"So, we can launch probes to saturate the area with active sensor pulses."

"Pulses that will also be distorted, absorbed, and reflected away from us. It might work, I suggest you hold that for now. I am mapping the area, it should be possible for me to find the battleship by the effect it is having on the dust cloud. Anything moving out here should have a bow shock in front, and a wake of disturbed particles behind it. *Valkyrie* is certainly disturbing the dust cloud like a speedboat on a lake, the *Conquis* should also be leaving a wake."

"I don't like hearing that," Reed muttered. "Is our stealth field effective?"

"It is effectively bending light around us," Skippy answered. "It can't do anything about the shockwaves we are creating by flying through the dust at over fourteen kilometers per second."

Reed shook her head. "Escape velocity here is ten point nine kps. We can't reduce speed much, or we won't have a margin for getting out of here."

I nodded to her. We both knew that in space combat, flying slow means being dead.

"I was just stating an unpleasant fact," Skippy grumbled. "I don't know what advice to give you, the rules of space combat are based on space being *empty*, or very nearly so. This environment is more similar to atmospheric combat."

"Speed kills," Reed said under her breath. She referenced something pilots are taught about atmospheric flight in a combat environment. Flying at high speed negates the effectiveness of projecting a stealth field around the aircraft; your aircraft can be detected by the shockwave of compressed air, called a 'supersonic boom'. Or just by heated air from the friction of your aircraft boring a hole through the atmosphere. In air combat, you want to fly *slowly*, until it is time to drop stealth and start tangling with enemy aircraft, postponing the moment you have to drop stealth can give you a major advantage. That was all great advice for pilots flying aircraft, it didn't do much for us in a starship zipping through space that was supposed to be almost empty.

"I don't like this," I said what Reed was thinking.

She tapped her chin while she thought. "Drop off sensor drones here, then jump away a short distance to reassess?"

"That's the smart move," I agreed. "Skippy, could you-"

"Huh. Wait," he held up a hand. "I- This is weird."

"I don't like weird, what's happening?"

"The nanocloud around us, it- That is odd. Why is it- Oh, no! No no no NO- Shit! We are enveloped in a damping field."

"Damping- Where it is coming from?" The most likely source of a damping field was the spider battleship. If we could track the field to its origin, we could target that ship. Take it out of the fight, kill the source of the field that was preventing us from forming a stable jump wormhole.

"Nowhere!"

"It has to be coming from-"

"Nowhere in particular. It is all around us. The *nanobots* are projecting the field. I can try to- Incoming!"

The ship shook from a direct hit.

We had taken four railgun impacts on the port side aft. Two more darts ripped through the dust under *Valkyrie's* belly, just missing our shields there.

That was accurate shooting.

Too accurate.

The four darts had struck the same shield, temporarily knocking the projector offline. The display showed Bilby was compensating by extending coverage from other shields while the overloaded unit recovered. The ship also began rolling so the port side would be away from the direction the darts had come from.

The pilot didn't wait for an order from Reed, he slewed the ship around, continuing the spin that had been induced by the impacts. The force of four darts had been absorbed by the energy shield, but part of the kinetic energy had transferred down into *Valkyrie's* structural frames and *pushed* the aft end of the ship to starboard. The nose swung around and the throttles surged, accelerating us in a new direction. We were not flying in anything resembling a straight line, randomly jinking up-down-left-right, the guidance inputs from the pilot interpreted by Bilby as overall direction, while the ship's AI applied random course corrections.

Being under acceleration compromised our stealth, except in the dust cloud we were leaving a bow shock and a wake behind us anyway. We needed speed and Fireball knew it, she had trained her people well. Speed would cause each random course correction to move us farther off a predictable path, speed would get us up and away from the planet, the thick part of the dust cloud, and out of the damping field. Speed gave us options. Before I could open my mouth to give unwanted advice, the crew, or Bilby on his own, expanded the stealth field. The stealth field would be less effective but it covered a larger area, the enemy couldn't know where the ship was inside the field.

Three more impacts told me *that* wasn't true.

Oh shit.

Both salvoes of darts had struck aft. Aimed at the same target: our jump drive capacitor packs. A single dart there could unleash energy that would destroy the ship in a flash. A dart would have to get through the shields, then punch through multiple levels of very tough armor. Ordinarily, that was unlikely to happen; *Valkyrie* would have to be crippled and unable to move, or the enemy would have to be very lucky.

Or very good.

Or was *cheating*.

"Bilby discharge the capacitors now now *now*," I ordered. "Do it!"

"Aye, Dude," he didn't hesitate or question me. "Dumping power now."

Reed glanced at me in shock, that I had ordered such an extreme measure and that I had bypassed her authority.

"I have a *bad* feeling about this," I explained.

She bit her lip and gave a curt nod, unhappy but not yet willing to argue in front of the crew. On the display, we saw the aft end of the ship lit up like a hundred strobe lights as the stored capacitor energy was dumped overboard. Energy that was capable creating a rip in the fabric of spacetime, it was not like getting simply zapped by a frayed electric cord in your house. The dust cloud around us glowed, instantly boiling into plasma. "Pilot, pedal to the metal, maximum military thrust," I issued the order directly, taking command of the ship. Temporarily. We didn't have time for me to explain what I suspected was going on. "Get us out of here. Bilby, use that plasma cloud to mask us from enemy sensors."

"That plasma will only last a few seconds after the venting is complete," he warned. "Capacitors aaaare, drained. Empty, that's done it."

"Sir," Reed cleared her throat. "The new virtual capacitors-"

"Will take seventeen minutes to build up power for a full jump, I know." She wasn't confident I was familiar with the specs for the newly upgraded battlecruiser. I did know because despite my reputation, I didn't spend all my down time playing video games. "Dumping the jump power means we can't get instantly out of here if we find a gap in the damping field. It also means we might survive long enough to get to the edge of the field." On the display, the angry orange shading of the damping field aft of the ship was weak where the nanobots had all been converted into plasma but that was literally behind us now, the ship was plowing through an untouched part of the field. We couldn't form a jump wormhole even if we had built up sufficient energy. "Skippy, the Outsider is using a data feed from the nanobots to target us?"

"Why do you think- *Huuuuuh*," he gasped. "You're right. How did you know that?"

"We took two salvoes exactly where they could hurt us most, from a range long enough that we can't detect the enemy ship. *No one* is that good, or that lucky. The Outsider is cheating, it manipulated the nanobots to act as an extended sensor suite, and to create a damping field. I have a bad feeling about this," I repeated.

Reed nodded again, understanding.

"Sorry," I said to her. "There wasn't time for-"

"Sir, don't ever delay an action to spare my *feelings*," she made a face like she'd just bitten into a lemon. Leaning toward me, she added, "We have been through some serious shit together."

"We have."

"Hey, um, Dude?" Bilby called for my attention. "And Dudess? What's next? Like, literally, where do we go from here?"

Reed had an answer ready. "We need airspeed and altitude," she reverted to using atmospheric pilot terms, which were actually appropriate given the environment. "Maneuvering speed to keep us from being an easy target, and distance from the planet so we can leave this dust cloud behind. Bilby, set a least-time course to get us to the edge of the damping field."

"Um, like, I don't know where that is. From what I can see, there is no edge."

"How can that be?" I asked. "The field strength must drop off farther from the planet. Skippy, do you concur with Bilby?"

"Yes, darn it. He is correct, the field strength does not decrease significantly with distance from the inner layer of the dust cloud. Joe, I, I have a *very* bad feeling about this. I hate to say this, but I now think the inner star system here is a trap, and has been for very a long time. The Outsider might be working with the nano controller here, but the capability of projecting a pervasive damping field can't be anything new. It was designed into the nanobots. The Outsider got lucky that capability existed when we jumped in here, or we- Oh *shiiiiiit*," he groaned.

"It didn't get lucky, did it?"

"No. Oh, I am such a gullible idiot."

"Ayuh," I was as disgusted with myself as he was with himself. Correction: I was more disgusted, I should have known better. "You and me both."

"Sir?" Reed prompted me. "Would you share what you're thinking?"

"The Outsider didn't come here seeking a weapon to use against us. The quarantine zone *is* a weapon. Somehow, it understood the capabilities of the nanobots here, and it lured us in."

"Why?"

"For *Skippy*. It wants to kill, or neutralize, Skippy. And I served up our best asset on a silver platter."

Reed drew her lips in a tight line. She had seen me screw up before, screw up big time. "This fight isn't over yet," she addressed that remark more to her crew than to me. "We still-"

"Incoming!" Bilby warned. "Missiles, eight of them, no, ten! Holy- They are coming in from the *opposite* direction, how-"

His next words were drowned out in the sizzling chatter of the point defense system cannons, not the rapid pulsing *bzzzt bzzzt* of the usual masers that fired first, but the lower and more ominous barking *crack crack crack* sound of the railgun minicannons that launched guided projectiles. That sound was ominous because those Gatling cannons had a short effective range. Everyone aboard *Valkyrie* knew if we heard that sound, we were already in deep shit. So why was Bilby relying on-

Oh, that wasn't good. I knew that answer. The dust cloud scrambled our sensors so badly that our ship's AI hadn't detected the missiles until they were almost on top of us, and the dust would disperse and possibly even reflect back any directed energy pulses. Bilby had known that our masers might be useless, so he waited until the missiles were in range of the minicannons.

Skippy often says my monkey brain is incredibly slooooooow but all those thoughts raced through my mind during the less than a second from when we heard the PDS railguns barking to when the ship was struck by a hammer.

Thor's hammer.

BAM.

Later, we realized the shields on the aft dorsal section had been struck by three atomic compression warheads, with their yields dialed up to 'Eleven'. That was a hundred and ninety three kilotons *per warhead*, and three missiles had slipped through our point defense cannon fire to impact the energy shields and detonate. Missile warheads can be scrambled and rendered ineffective on contact with a shield, so missile warheads deploy a long spike in front that encounters the shield first. When the molecules of that spike begin to disassociate, a signal is sent to the missile's AI and it detonates the warhead while it still can.

Two shield projectors there took three shotgun blasts to their heads and the overlapping energy fields there were shredded. We got lucky. Lances of ultra-dense exotic matter were blasted forward, launched by the release of atomic compression. One fragment penetrated all the way to the inner layer of armor, which was a gel designed to contain solid shrapnel, not the superheated plasma the lances turned into when their tips contacted the outer layer of armor.

Whoa.

If *Valkyrie's* armor had not been upgraded, if the original armor had not been melted by Elder weapons so Skippy could learn how to make armor much tougher than before, we would have been fucked. The plasma jet of that lance would have burst inward from the armor's inner layer like super hot pellets from a shotgun shell, ripping that section of the ship apart from the inside. The structural frames probably would have survived, most of them. But everything else in that section of the unprotected pressure hull would have been shredded. Power conduits, data relays, missile batteries, additional shield projectors, all offline. People there would have been churned into charred powder.

There is no question that *Valkyrie* is a tough ship, we took the equivalent of three *nukes* and the ship could still fly and fight.

We got lucky.

It didn't feel like luck at the time.

With my ears still ringing and my brain rattled with what had to be a mild concussion, I blinked to focus my eyes on the main display. Two shields were *down*, offline hard. Bilby had rolled the ship to protect us from a potential double-tap of railgun darts seeking to strike where the missiles had knocked back our shield coverage.

"Hey like," Bilby drawled, "I can extend other shields to cover the damaged section, but they're going to be like paper thin, Dude. We can't take another hit there."

"How the f-" I bit my lip, took a breath. Don't shoot the messenger, I reminded myself. "Where did those missiles come from? Does the Outsider have another ship out there?"

"No way, General Dude. I recognize the signatures of those missiles and warheads. They are Rindhalu, no question about it. The missiles are all from a batch that was onloaded to the spider battleship *Conquis*. The missile drives didn't light off until we were close, you know? They didn't come from anywhere, they were already here. My guess is, that ship dropped off clusters of missiles in the dust cloud."

"Fuck," Reed exploded. "We are flying through a *minefield?*"

"Yeah, a really gnarly minefield like, one where the mines don't wait for you to step on them, they go out and *find* targets."

"That's not even the worst news," Skippy sighed. "I suspect the nanobot data feed is not just reporting our position, course, and speed. They are providing sensor data on the ship's condition. The section of the ship where those missiles struck is not the obvious place they would have been targeted; the missiles had to curve around in a steep turn and approach at an unfavorable angle. They chose their impact points because those missiles knew our shield projectors there were already strained by extending coverage over the capacitor banks."

Reed and I shared a look. We wouldn't survive, unless the tactical situation changed to at least even the odds. "I got nothin'," she whispered.

She wasn't just telling me there was no obvious solution to our dilemma, she was giving me the OK to make her look bad in front of her crew, by dreaming up a creative idea. More, she was asking me to do that. Reed was a great pilot, and an outstanding starship captain. Thinking way outside the box was *my* wheelhouse.

"Skippy, whatever you gotta do, kill that nanobot data feed. We are blind, while the enemy has a perfect view of the tactical situation. That is *unsat*."

"Hey, I'm not happy about it either. This damage will *not* buff right out. Um, I can try."

"Bullshit," I gave him a knife hand. "Jedi trainees *try*, Skippy the Magnificent just fucking *does* it."

"Hey, I don't see you doing anything about it, Master Yogurt."

"Just," I flicked a hand. "Make it happen."

"Did, did," he sputtered. "Did you just *hand wave* me? Do you think any of this is easy?"

"I think all of it is harder than my poor monkey brain can possibly imagine, which is why we are all. Trusting. The. *Awesomeness*." I gave a thumbs up, and looked around the bridge. The crew, including Reed, mimicked my hand signal. Some were more genuine in their trust than others.

"Ugh," he groaned.

"I mean, if the nanoscale brain of a freakin' *bot* can beat you, then-"

"Oh, it is *on*. I will make you eat your words, Joe."

"I will happily eat those words on Wonderbread with a nice thick layer of Fluff, *after* you make it happen."

"My life has never sucked as much as it does right now."

"Then it can only get better from here. *Do* something."

"I'm doing it. In the meantime, may I make a suggestion?'

"Please do."

"Launch a half dozen missiles armed with nukes, instruct them to fly in formation with us. The next time we encounter a cluster of incoming missiles, we will detonate our nukes in the enemy flightpath, scramble their sensors."

"Nukes, Skippy?" Reed asked for clarity. "Not atomic compress-"

"*Nukes*," he insisted. "Crude fusion bombs that monkeys made by bashing coconuts together. We need a strong electromagnetic pulse and lots of hard radiation that will contaminate the whole area."

Reed issued the appropriate orders, and within seconds, six deadly dots appeared near the outline of *Valkyrie* on the tactical section of the display. My head was beginning to throb, the ship's entire complement should have visited sick bay to get checked and treated for concussions. Five people were in sickbay, I could see from the stats on the display. No injuries were flagged as life-threatening, that didn't mean they weren't serious.

Maintenance bots were crawling on and under the hull, repairing damage as best they could, though many of them had to wait for the armor plating to cool. Still, Skippy did nothing, as far as I could see.

"Skippy?"

"*What?*" He snapped.

"Whenever it's convenient, it would be great if you actually *did* something."

"Oh, you-"

Tapping a thumb on the audio app of my phone, I played the Jeopardy theme song.

And I whistled along with it.

"Oh, oh *ooooooh*" Skippy raged. "You make me so mad I could-"

"Mad enough to actually *do* something?"

"I am *working* on it, the-"

"Incoming!" Bilby warned, and eight red dots appeared on the display. A cluster of enemy missiles had just gone hot.

"Whatever you gotta do," I thumped my arm rest. "Do it *right fucking now.*"

"Ugh. OK, but I'm warning you-"

He didn't finish whatever he was going to say. The enemy missiles were streaking toward us, jinking wildly, making it difficult for the PDS sensors to track because those missiles had their active sensors switched off, while our active sensor pulses were being bent and reflected by the nanobot cloud. The missiles didn't have to send out sensor pulses, they were guided by a feed from all the nanobots around us.

"Light off nukes Four and Six," Skippy urged. "Quickly!"

Reed gestured to the weapons officer, and two dots bloomed into fireballs that momentarily blanked out the display. Gripping the arms of my chair, I waited for the sensor view to reset. The pilots had not wasted the opportunity, they had the ship decelerating *hard* and slewing around so our nose pointed toward the enemy missiles.

"Sending out coded sensor pulse now," Skippy muttered. "Let's hope this works. It, hmm, I can't see where- Yes! They missed!"

He highlighted the enemy missiles, now only five of them, showing they had flown past us and were now turning and burning to catch up. Except, they weren't burning, they were instead loitering in our wake. Confused.

"Ha! You're not so tough without spies giving you a target, are you?" Skippy crowed. "OK, the nanobot data feed is shut down."

"Great! Can you also do something about the damping field?" I asked, fully expecting him to tell me that would be no problemo, and my only job would be finding an acceptable way to praise him.

"Um, no can do, sorry. I can't interfere with the damping field, darn it."

"Uh, what? Why not?" The phrase *can't you just* came dangerously close to being spoken, and that should never happen.

"The only way to shut that field down is to destroy the *Conquis.*"

That made no sense to me. "You just told us the ability for generating a damping field is native to the nanobots. Why would destroying the battleship-"

"Ugh. The worst part of my job is explaining the most simple things to you. Yes numbskull, the nanobots were built to generate a damping field, and the sensor feed is also a native function. The Outsider tapped into that sensor feed to track and target us, I shut off the feed at the source, since I couldn't instruct the battleship to stop tapping into the feed. The-"

"Wait!" I blurted out before I got distracted and lost my train of thought. "Can *we* tap into that feed, to find the *Conquis*?"

"No, darn it. The Outsider got here first, and altered the protocols to lock me out of doing exactly that. This was a carefully planned ambush that *you* jumped us into."

My memory of the events was different; there wasn't any point, and no time, to argue with him. "I am terribly sorry about the mess I got you into. OK, so no data feed. What about the damping field?"

"As you mentioned, that is also a native function. From what I am able to determine, the Outsider hasn't hacked into the nano swarm and ordered it to project a damping field, the nanobots are doing that on their own. Or, more likely their controller entity has instructed the swarm to prevent us from jumping away."

"Why just us? Did the Outsider give it a nice fruit basket, and now it's best friends with the nano controller?"

"They are not friends, dumdum. That battleship also can't jump away. Although I don't know where that ship is, I can detect that the damping field covers a broad area."

"Yes, but it left clusters of missiles out here, so the *Conquis* could actually be far away from us and-"

"Hey, in case you haven't been keeping track of current events, that ship scored two direct hits with line of sight railguns," he snapped. "Even with the advantage of the nanobot data feed, the battleship had to be relatively close to shoot that accurately."

"OK, good point. The Outsider is also trapped here?"

"Yes. If you will stop asking stupid questions, I can explain."

"Please do."

"The damping field activated only *after* the Outsider shot at us. If you remember the sequence of events, I detected a damping field forming, then we were struck by four railgun darts. My guess is- And this is a very good, informed guess, unlike what you blah blah blah about- Is the nanobot swarm was either programmed to generate a damping field automatically when it encountered hostile action, or it was instructed to form the field after the controller determined the battleship was hostile."

"The controller otherwise would have allowed the battleship to hang around here, without being challenged?' That can't be right. We know that something in the quarantine zone has been disabling or killing sensor probes."

"I realize now the Outsider had been transmitting a recognition signal that kept the nanobots from acting against it. Until it shot at us, and could no longer pretend to be friendly."

"That makes sense, given what we know." What I didn't say was we didn't know much, so it was impossible to say whether Skippy's theory was correct or not. "If the nanobots are acting according to their programming or whatever, how would killing that battleship deactivate the damping field?"

"It won't," he admitted. "Not directly. Listen, numbskull, this is complicated. I can hack into the nanobots and turn off the damping field, at least in a relatively small area. Hacking into billions of nanobots will take a long time, and I can't hack all of them. The only way I can do it is to be stationary compared to the nanobots around us, so I can hack into a relatively static bubble around us. Right now, we are moving through the nano cloud so fast, as I hack into each group of nanobots, they fall behind us, and I have to hack into another group. You see the problem?"

"Ayuh. Shit. To shut down the damping field, we have to stay in one place, but if we do that, we will be an easy target for the Outsider."

"Egg-zactly. Eliminate the battleship, decelerate so we are motionless relative to the local nano cloud, and give me twenty, maybe twenty five minutes to disable the damping field."

"All we have to do is find an enemy ship in this cloud where our sensors are pretty much blind, and kill a peer adversary." That was a fancy military term meaning 'a ship nearly as powerful as *Valkyrie*'. Really, I was concerned the *Conquis* was more than a match for *Valkyrie*, our battlecruiser might not be up to the fight. Our armor was the best in the galaxy, but battlecruisers were designed for speed rather than firepower. Battlecruisers were supposed to fight smaller ships, chase down and destroy cruiser squadrons, keep enemy escort ships away from the big battleships. A fight between a battlecruiser and a battleship would be- Well, a one-sided bad idea. For reference, Google the battle between the German battleship *Bismarck* and the British battlecruiser *Hood* in World War Two. Spoiler alert: it didn't end well for the *Hood*. UN Navy doctrine for battlecruisers encountering enemy battleships is to use superior speed and maneuverability to engage and disengage from the fight as conditions were favorable, to decide when to conduct hit and run attacks, to keep out of the battlewagon's effective gun range. Wargame after wargame had proven the wisdom of that doctrine. Now, we had to ignore it.

"Reed?" It was her ship, and she was more current on tactics and ship-handling skills.

"We are still faster than the *Conquis*, but we'll have to get close to kill it. Bilby? Can you run a simulation of-"

The lights flickered, went out, and flickered again.

"Skippy! What the-"

The lights came on. The main holographic display tank was a featureless black.

We had no sensor input, even from inside the ship. We had no control of anything.

Ohhh *that* is not good.

"Skippy?" I took a breath, yelling at him wouldn't make the situation better.

"Joe, we have a major, *major* problem. Bilby is offline! Not offline exactly, he isn't able to interface with any of the ship's critical systems."

"Why is-"

"The nanobot swarm is projecting an interference I have never encountered before, it is jamming the higher functions of the substrate that Bilby runs on."

"Can you do anything about it?"

"Yes, partially, but that will require me to stop jamming the nanobot sensor feed."

"Do *not* do that," Reed urged.

"Yes, keep jamming that feed," I agreed. "OK, I can understand that Bilby is offline, why aren't we getting any sensor data at all, even internal stuff?"

"Every system aboard this ship runs through Bilby now, after the upgrade," he groaned. "That is a major advantage in terms of reaction time, processing speed, integration of systems, and flexibility to shunt control between systems for damage control. Now, it's screwing us."

"Can you take over?"

"I have taken over, I am keeping the reactors running, and shields operational. Sensor data will be available shortly. Well, you can forget about fighting that battleship."

Reed glanced at me before asking, "Why?"

"Um," he paused, mouth open, reconsidering whatever he had intended to say. "Well, the crew will now have to fly and fight the ship manually. I can't help you monkeys like I used to, there will not be a Big Red Button to activate after I set up a firing solution. I'm sorry, but I am running out of bandwidth. There are too damned many nanobots and I have to deal with each of them individually. Plus, you know, keep the reactors from exploding."

"Fireball," I leaned toward her and whispered, "what do you think? Is the crew up to the challenge?"

"We do train for manual control, I never thought we would ever run into that scenario. What I'm more concerned about is our tactics are rusty. We don't spend much time training for single-ship combat. Navy doctrine is for ships to fight in formations, where every type of ship has a defined role in the squadron or fleet."

"*You* have experience with single-ship combat."

"The last time I was in a single-ship fight was before your children were born," she reminded me. "We're up to the challenge. With our speed advantage, we can break off an engagement at any time. That battleship is not what worries me."

"It isn't?"

"We know that ship's performance specs, we can engage when we have an advantage. What concerns me is what we *don't* know."

"Welcome to the Merry Band of Pirates."

CHAPTER TWENTY

The deck shook again. That time, the shaking was not from enemy action. The display flashed a red icon on the diagram of the ship's structure, showing an overloaded shield generator had sent a power surge back into the distribution system, and a power node buried under the armored hull had exploded. That damage was not from direct enemy action, it still was serious.

Sixty seven minutes, according to the clock that tracked the time since we broke off the last engagement. Our engineering teams had more than an hour to patch up the ship from our last beating, and we lost another shield generator. The spider battleship was still out there, and we had learned that it was a tough and mean sumbitch.

We were slowly losing the battle.

"Possible contact!" A crewman monitoring a sensor console warned. "Bearing, zero seven niner, mark one one four," he rattled off the set of numbers, though the bearing was shown on the display. Speaking the contact details aloud was protocol, it assured the crew was aware of the sensor reading, and focused on the correct information. "Confidence is," the lieutenant hesitated. "Low. Confidence is *low*." He looked up at Reed apologetically. "Most likely another sensor echo, Colonel."

"Track it anyway."

"Yes, Ma'am. Designate contact as Sierra-One Four Seven." One forty seven. The one hundred and forty seventh possible contact we had detected since we commenced our running battle with the *Conquis*. A battle that had been nonstop for thirty three hours.

The crew was exhausted. The ship was wearing down from the strain. Bilby was offline. Skippy was irritated and snapping at everyone. The crew were over tired and snapping at each other, except of course no one was snapping at me. Me, the guy who jumped us into an ambush, and then ordered our mighty battlecruiser to slug it out with one on one with a senior species battleship. A fight where our ship was flown manually by monkeys, while the *Conquis* had a super-advanced energy being in command.

The crew should have yelled at me, I would have felt better if they had.

Reed's crew certainly now had experience in single-ship combat, though most of what they had learned recently is what not to do.

She was right when she mentioned the crew's skills in single-ship combat were rusty, and it wasn't just the crew. It had been a long time since I took a ship into a real one-on-one fight. A battle where the ship wasn't just acting as a platform for Skippy to do some awesome thing. Like, guiding a relativistic dart to blast enemy ships into dust. Hacking into enemy ships so they couldn't effectively fight. Making an enemy ship vibrate itself apart. He couldn't use any of his usual awesomenesses against the Outsider, his bandwidth was fully tasked by keeping the nanobot swarm from reporting our position, and keeping *Valkyrie's* basic systems operating. The crew had to navigate, fly, and make the ship fight.

The crew was doing their absolute best. It wasn't anywhere close to good enough.

Have you ever seen the movie *Run Silent Run Deep*? It's about submarines in the Pacific Theater of World War Two. I saw that movie with my father when I

"That is not true," I repeated what Skippy had told me. "Those individuals in charge of remote facilities are authorized to use their own judgment in cooperating with temporary allies, to accomplish objectives that will benefit the Communal Gathering," I had memorized the exact translation of the legal clause. "That is why a senior official, in this case yourself, is in command of this endeavor. Your responsibility is not only to contain the nanomachine threat, you also have to make sure your partners don't do anything stupid again. By assisting an entity that is a threat to everyone, the Maxohlx unquestionably did something stupid again."

The long pauses were getting annoying, I told myself that's just how the spiders are. Finally came a reply. "I must consider this matter."

"No, we do not have time for delays. Either you give us any useful information you have, or we will proceed into the quarantine zone blindly, and reduce our probability of success."

"General Bishop," there wasn't a pause, which startled me. "My hesitation is not from indecision, it is from fear that your ship will not return. Our probes have repeatedly failed to survive entering the quarantine zone."

"Yeah, I share the same concern."

"Joe," Skippy entered the conversation, "I told you not to worry about it."

"You telling me not to worry is a reason I should be concerned."

"Ugh."

"Bishop," Orloffiko said, the guy was actually chatty once he got warmed up. "You should not risk the Skippy being here. In the quarantine zone, you will face the dangers of both nanomachines and the Outsider."

"The Outsider will also have to deal with nanobots," Skippy countered. "That levels the playing field. Either we fight the Outsider here, where we know it is, *or*, we play catch-up after it has nanobombed someone's homeworld. Like, yours."

"Our Elder AI has a point," I agreed. "*Lack* of action involves more risk than taking what you might consider hasty action. General Orloffiko, it's my call that we are going into the quarantine zone, it will be your call whether to assist us or not. Keep in mind, humanity is not the only species threatened by the Outsider. Your people have maintained this quarantine for a very long time, at great effort and expense. It would be a shame for you to now allow a much greater threat to break the quarantine. I understand this is a serious matter to consider, we will wait twenty of our minutes," I knew the translator software would provide the deadline in time increments he understood. "Either way, thank you for keeping the galaxy safe from the nano plague." At a gesture from me, Bilby ended the call.

"Now," I sat down next to Reed, "we wait."

"Sir," she leaned toward me and spoke softly. "What was that?"

"It's called diplomacy."

She stared at me. Not quite the knowing weary side-eye I used to get from Simms, this was a 'Can you explain that please' gesture. "I have seen your type of diplomacy before, Sir."

"Times change, circumstances change. Are you disappointed?"

"No. I am happy about not getting into a battle we don't need to fight. I just, expected you to lead with the big stick."

was about eight years old, on a rainy Saturday afternoon. We were supposed to go out fishing that day, but it was pouring down rain and chilly, so my father decided we guys should watch a guy's movie. Why he chose that one, I don't know, but I enjoyed sitting on the couch with him and our dog, eating popcorn and watching American and Japanese subs fight.

The reason I mention that is after the first hour, I realized a sub battle was an excellent way to think about our fight against the *Conquis*. With both of our ships wrapped in sophisticated stealth fields, we couldn't easily locate each other. Active sensor pings would only give away our own position, while not having a guarantee that our pings would detect the enemy ship. At sea, subs use passive sonar to listen for sounds coming from the enemy sub; vibrations from the engines or propellers. The humming of pumps circulating water to cool the sub's reactor. Or some unlucky jackass drops a stack of pots and pans in the galley. In space combat, we use passive sensors to detect traces of chemicals and other particles left behind by enemy ships; tiny pieces of armor flaking away, stray oxygen molecules escaping from imperfectly sealed airlock doors, that sort of thing. We also look for particles of the local solar wind being disturbed by the passage of a large, invisible object. At closer range, our instruments can actually detect how the fabric of spacetime is being distorted by the mass of a heavy ship. The problem with relying on a gravimetric sensor is once you are close enough to use it, the enemy ship is probably already shooting at your stupid head.

Passive sensors are really only useful if you have a lot of time to devote to a search, or if you are able to saturate the battlespace with sensor drones to expand the footprint you can cover. Most of the time, passive sensors are useful only when your priority is to avoid the enemy suspecting your ship is in the area. Once the enemy is aware of your presence, it is time to warm up the sensor field projectors. Technically, a sensor field is a type of active search, the difference is a sensor field doesn't send out pulses of photons that travel in a straight line. A straight line leads directly back to your ship, so you can understand why you might not want to do that. In a sensor *field*, charged particles are projected outward, they loop around, and come back to your ship. The field has an irregular shape, and that shape constantly changes. An enemy ship encountering your field will change the shape of the loop, and so you will know an object is out there, where it is, and its speed and direction. The enemy will detect your field and know your ship is in the vicinity, but due to the irregular, rapidly changing shape of the field, it won't know exactly where inside the field your ship is. The development of sensor fields changed the nature of space combat, I had found the concept fascinating when I was learning about space combat maneuvers aboard the old *Flying Dutchman*.

In the quarantine zone, the problem was we couldn't rely on passive sensors, active sensor pings, or sensor fields. Everything we had been taught about space combat was mostly useless, we were learning on the job. We couldn't see far enough into the dust cloud to make passive detection useful. Active sensor pulses not only got absorbed by the nanobot swarm, they were reflected and scattered, bouncing the photons around randomly. It was like shooting a gun in a maze; the bullet would go everywhere except in a straight line.

The sensor field was better than nothing, but most of the particles were bent out of the loop they were supposed to follow, so we got a lot of false sensor readings. At first, we had thought the field was distorted by the battleship's presence, while really the swarm was just screwing with us. The only good news was our stealth field was effective. The bad news was- Well, there was a lot of bad news. The battleship's own stealth field was even better than what the spiders told us to expect, the Outsider must have enhanced the performance.

Basically, we couldn't find the thing, and it couldn't find us, except somehow it kept doing that, over and over and over. The first four engagements, we assumed we had stumbled onto each other, trading shots as we each flew past, neither of us shooting with any accuracy Then, it became alarmingly clear the Outsider was somehow still tracking us, and its missiles could also track us, at least at a short range. Each time we encountered the *Conquis*, both ships fired railguns and launched missiles as we zipped past each other, then we lost contact with the battleship in the dust cloud. But its missiles followed us and we didn't know how they were keeping contact, it was driving Skippy crazy.

"Joe," he sighed, his avatar hovering in front of me while I pushed a cart along a passageway. Engineering teams were working to repair damage all throughout *Valkyrie*, and since I wasn't qualified to work on any system aboard the rebuilt ship, I made myself useful by bringing coffee, sandwiches, and snacks to the work teams. My cart was piled high with dirty cups, plates, and dishes. When I got back to the galley, I would make a detour to get first aid supplies. Some of the crew working damage control were injured and they hadn't taken time to get treated in the sickbay.

The ship had taken a beating in the last encounter with the *Conquis*. The battleship had come up behind us, moving at only fourteen hundred meters per second relative speed, and it fired railguns before we detected it. The slow pass at a distance of less than seven hundred kilometers made the engagement last long enough for the battleship to blast us with four salvos, we managed only two rounds of railguns and directed energy weapons. The missiles we launched chased the enemy and we detected thermal blooms, but we didn't know if the missiles hit, or exploded when they were intercepted by enemy defenses.

"Hey, Skippy," I turned left down a passageway and he kept pace with me. "What's up?"

"I have been working on the problem of how that ship keeps finding us."

"Ayuh, thanks for doing that, I know you're already busy. And?"

"And, nothing. I got nothin'. Except, I am ninety nine percent certain that *ship* isn't tracking us."

"The Outsider is doing it? How?"

"It must be doing it, I have no freakin' clue how. This is another demonstration of it having an ability beyond my own. I," he sighed again. "Thought I was the most awesome being in the galaxy, but I am only the most awesome being in *this* galaxy. I was all happy until that asshole crashed the party."

"Yeah, but can it sing better than you?"

"Dude, please," he snorted. "As if."

"So, you've got that going for you."

"If the Outsider would agree to a musical talent competition, we would have a chance in this fight."

"The devil lost a fiddle contest, so-"

"Let's not count on that happening, OK?"

"Probably a good idea. Keep working on it?"

"I will."

He sounded so depressed, I felt the need to say something to, not cheer him up. To console him. "Hey, Skippy, listen. Don't blame yourself for this mess. Yes, the Outsider may have some cool superpowers, but your awesomeness is unmatched."

"Oh. Thank you, Joe."

"You're-"

"I was *not* blaming myself."

"That's good, the-"

"Clearly, this is all your fault."

"Uh, that's not quite what-"

"*You* flew us into an ambush. Another ambush. I mean, that is kind of your thing."

"Hey, I didn't-"

"Really, now that I think about it, the Outsider lured us in here because it must have studied your career and understood that you have fallen for ambushes *so* often, it was a very safe bet you'd do it again."

"You ass, I-"

"Our second mission, we got jumped by a squadron of Thuranin destroyers, and I had to perform a miracle to get out of the mess you got us into."

"Your supposed 'miracle' broke the ship, Skippy."

"It only *mostly* broke the ship. We jumped into another ambush in the Roach Motel."

"We did that because *you* assured me it would be safe!"

"Then there was the incident of getting trapped by a Maxohlx task force in the Snowcone star system."

"OK, so yes, I-"

"That Elder AI you called 'Echo' came very close to tearing *Valkyrie* apart, until I did yet another one of my, you know, usual miracles."

"Hey, if you are so freakin' miraculous, do it again and get us out of here."

"*I* didn't get us stuck in this mess. Besides, it's obvious the Outsider chose this site for an ambush, because it understood conditions here would cancel out many of my abilities. That would not have been a problem, except that you walked right into the trap."

"Why do you have to- Ah, shit," I leaned back against the bulkhead. "OK, you're right. The Outsider had been ten steps ahead of us the whole time. It knows that to stop it, we have to know what it's planning to do, and for that, we need to find it. Wherever it goes, it knows we will try to follow. That makes it easy for it to set up an ambush. We don't have a choice; we have to take the risk of chasing it. There," I closed my eyes. "There has to be a better way to find the thing, and maintain surveillance. That's what we need to think about."

"You mean, after you find a way to get us out of here?"

"Yeah. You got any ideas about that?"

"I got nothin'. Um, heads up. Commander Gasquet is on the way here to talk with you."

"Why?"

"Ask him yourself," the avatar disappeared as Gasquet came around the corner and waved to me.

"Admiral, Colonel Reed sent me to see if you need anything."

The guy looked tired. We were all tired, and that situation wasn't about to improve any time soon. He was tired but also alert and focused, as much as any of us were. Personally, I had managed to get maybe three hours of sleep in the past forty one hours, and none of my naps had been longer than twenty minutes. Most of the time, I had been on the bridge, and pretty much useless. The uncomfortable fact was, I was no longer rated to captain the ship, so all I could do was provide advice and support to whoever was the duty officer. Back in the day, I had been rated to act as captain, as a pilot when needed, as a weapons officer, to run navigation, communications, sensors, to stand a watch at every bridge console other than engineering. Now, after years of me playing golf, and the ship having gone through an extensive refit, I just wasn't familiar enough with the new *Valkyrie*, and no one wanted me touching anything.

"Gasquet," I smiled to let him know I wasn't about to bite his head off, "we both know that's bullshit. Why are you really here?"

He didn't blink. "To see how you're doing, Sir. The Colonel is concerned you are pushing yourself too hard."

"She is concerned about *me* pushing myself? When is the last time she got some sleep?'

"Er, about," he glanced at his watch, "six hours ago, when you ordered her to go to her cabin."

"My recollection is we got jumped again by the *Conquis* about forty minutes after she left the bridge, so we both know she got zero sleep."

"She had forty minutes to-"

"To rest and get some rack time, but instead she took a shower and changed uniform."

"She wants to set a good example, Sir."

"Not walking around like a zombie would be a good example. I will talk with her."

The tension went out of his shoulders. "We would all appreciate that."

"Is there anything else I need to know?"

"We had a solid sensor contact ten minutes ago. We would have considered it just another echo, but now we recognize it was probably a cluster of missiles."

"We are learning."

"Not fast enough, Sir. Where the hell is that battleship getting so many missiles?" He asked. "There can't be a supply ship nearby. Even if there was, it hasn't had time between engagements to rendezvous with another ship."

"The spiders told us the *Conquis* disappeared along with all of its escorts. My guess is, the Outsider discarded the dropships it doesn't need, and stuffed the docking bays with missiles from the escort ships that it captured. It jumped into the quarantine zone with a maximum loadout. That provided plenty of ordnance to create a minefield."

He nodded. "That's the Colonel's thinking also."

"So, tell me, why did Reed *really* send you here?"

He was uncomfortable enough to swallow, his Adam's apple bounced up and down. When I first came aboard the ship, I didn't know the guy enough to decide whether he was a good XO or not. More to the point, was he good enough to be the executive officer of *Valkyrie*? His ratings had all been solid, but those evals were of his performance in peacetime, when the mighty battlecruiser was only flying around showing the flag. What I had needed to know was whether he could be a great XO, worthy of joining Task Force Black as a Merry Pirate?

Since those early days, I had an answer: yes. Gasquet was smart, inventive, flexible, he worked his ass off, and most importantly, Reed trusted him.

He looked me straight in the eye. "She didn't send me, Sir. Permission to speak freely?'

"There is no point to listening if you're just going to bullshit me, so consider speaking freely to be a standing order."

"The crew doesn't need you handing out coffee and donuts. We need you in your office, or the gym, or taking a shower, or doing whatever the hell I hear that you do when a crazy idea pops into your head. An idea to get us out of this mess, because we are not going to fight our way out." He took a breath and added, "Sir."

"OK," I pushed the cart gently toward him.

"OK?" He blinked.

"You're right. I just finished having the same conversation with Skippy. Besides," I waved at the empty plates and dirty coffee cups. "This crew is stingy with tips."

"Oh," he laughed, and patted his pockets. "I left my wallet in my cabin."

"That's what everyone told me. I'll go to my office, you can leave this cart in the galley. The-" Alarms blared. According to my phone it was seventy seven minutes since we last broke off contact. Now the *Conquis* was back.

Gasquet turn to run back to the bridge. "We really need that idea, Sir."

The deck shook again.

I sat down heavily in my office chair. The display on the bulkhead opposite my chair was showing battle damage throughout the ship. And a list of casualties. So far, we had been relatively lucky. No deaths, eight seriously injured. So far. That happy situation was unlikely to continue, the harsh truth was we were getting our asses kicked. No starship flown and operated manually by meatsacks could beat a ship controlled by a being with lightning fast processing speed. The Outsider had been finding us every fifty seven to eighty three minutes, no more, no less. On average, no, I should talk about the mean, not the average. If you exclude the first three of our encounters after Skippy shut down the data feed, and the one time we stupidly turned around shortly after the *Conquis* delivered another beat down, that battleship showed up on our tail every sixty seven to seventy five minutes. According to the clock that counted up from when we broke away from the last engagement and ran as best we could, we had another hour and two minutes before railgun darts would be slamming into our shields, and missiles would be following close behind. That was if we didn't stumble into another cluster of missiles that had been planted as a minefield.

Valkyrie couldn't take much more abuse. Our speed advantage was gone, several of the main engines were shot full of holes. Skippy estimated the battleship was actually a bit faster than our ship now, and while we had scored hits, *Valkyrie* was faring worse in the battle.

What we should have done was run for the edge of the quarantine zone, when we realized a damping field had us trapped. I hadn't ordered that option, because I had feared the Outsider expected us to do the obvious, and had planned a nasty surprise if we ran away. Now, we couldn't run, the engines couldn't sustain full thrust for more than twelve minutes without something breaking.

One hour, one minute to our next beat down, maybe our last.

"Skippy, this ain't working," I said as I leaned the chair back and closed my eyes.

"I will not bother to dispute the obvious. Joe, I have been wargaming the- Um, you probably should close your door."

I pressed the button and waited for the green light to glow. "That bad?"

"It couldn't be worse. No matter what we do, we are going to lose this battle of attrition. We can lose quickly and get it over with as painlessly as possible, or we can drag out the fight until the ship is crippled and the Outsider can do whatever it wants, including capturing me."

"That's not happening."

"Um, unless you didn't understand what I just said, it-"

"It. Will. Not. Happen."

"OK, is this where, as a friend, I am supposed to tell you some happy bullshit, to make you feel better about our inevitable defeat and demise?"

"No."

"Then I don't see how we can even survive, forget about winning."

"I don't see it either, *yet*. Skippy, you always remind us to trust the awesomeness, right?"

"Wiser advice was never given, yes."

"*You* need to trust that the impossible is merely a temporary obstacle to clever monkeys."

"Ugh. You *do* want a bullshit pep talk."

"No, I do not. What I want is for you to ditch your negative attitude."

"Like that is gonna help."

"It is. It *always* helps, you dumb shit."

"*What?*" He screeched. "How *dare* you, I should-"

"Use your ginormous brain to analyze this, please. When faced with an impossible situation, have we ever failed to find a way out of it?"

"Ugh. No, but that doesn't mean-"

"Past performance is no guarantee of future success, yeah, I read the legal terms. That is bullshit, Skippy. Hundred percent, pure *bullshit*. We have always found a way to do the impossible."

"Apparently you do not understand basic math, dumdum, the-"

"Ayuh, right," I rolled my eyes. "We have always succeeded, but *this* time is different."

"It *is* different. Joe, we no longer have the probability field working in our favor."

"We never did."

"Um, excuse me?"

"You heard me. That stupid field did *not* put ideas into my head. It didn't tell me to jump the ship through a freakin' Elder wormhole."

"Hey, numbskull, *I* jumped the ship through that wormhole."

"Yes, but-"

"I had to create an entirely new branch of mathematics to even crunch the numbers for programming the jump drive."

"It was *my* idea. As I recall, you said it was impossible to escape at the time. We *are* going to survive, we *are* going to give that ship an epic beat down, and we *are* going to jump out of this trap."

"That's a bold statement for a guy who has no clue how we can do that."

"Go big or go home."

"Our goal here *is* to go home, knucklehead."

"OK, I chose the wrong cliché. Besides, while I don't know how we'll do it, I now do know how to start working on a solution."

"You do? How?"

"The way I usually do it. By asking you a bunch of stupid, painfully obvious questions."

"I am *so* not looking forward to this. Hit me."

"The Outsider is one step ahead of us."

"Ever since it tried to steal Dogzilla, yes."

"I meant specifically, in the running battle here. We need to try something different. Einstein said the definition of insanity is doing the same thing and expecting different results."

"With respect to a reasonably smart monkey, that never made sense to me. If you keep hitting your head against a brick wall, the wall *will* eventually break."

"That's only true if you're a woodpecker. A person will die of brain damage before any of those bricks move. My point is, *Valkyrie* isn't going to win this fight for us. We need your help."

"I *am* helping," he sniffed, "in case you haven't been paying attention."

"We need you to help in a different way."

"OK, how?"

"I'm working on it. What if instead of you jamming the nanobot data feed, you focus on blocking the effect that is jamming Bilby's higher functions?"

"I am jamming the data feed because you told me to do that!"

"I might have been wrong. Answer the question, please."

"I wargamed that also. The end result is the same. It takes the Outsider a bit longer to degrade our defenses to a decisive level, but after that, *Valkyrie* is a sitting duck and is quickly destroyed. There is only so much Bilby can do, when the enemy has the advantage of seeing everything we are doing in an almost real time data feed."

"Shit. All right, uh-"

"Those are the only two options, if you are asking me to do something. Joe," he gave a heavy sigh. "The real problem is the Outsider *knows* me. It has studied me, it knows what I can do and what I can't do. The worst part is it apparently has copied some of its actions directly from my Greatest Hits catalog."

"Holy- You have a catalog of your-"

"I mean that as a metaphor, dumdum."

"OK, OK."

"The damned thing is copying my greatest hits, and not even paying a royalty."

"Yes, let's focus on what is truly important."

"Oh, shut up. You see the issue? Anything I can do, it knows about. It can perform all my hits plus, I hate to admit this, it has demonstrated abilities I don't have."

"Um," I felt a little tickle at the back of my mind. That annoying feeling usually meant my subconscious was forming an idea. What was it? Oh. "That is not exactly true."

"Thanks for the pep talk, but-"

"It is not true. For example, only *you* can create wormhole shortcuts."

"Yes, that ability is *super* useful here."

"You can also warp spacetime."

"If you are thinking I can create a *Star Trek* type of warp drive, I suggest you prepare for disappointment."

"Nope. So, question for you: the damping field around us, there is nothing you can do about it?"

"As I already told you, I can hack into the nanobots around us, in a relatively static area, and given enough time, I can disable the field across a local area. Unfortunately, the Outsider won't allow us to stay motionless in one place long enough for me to do that."

"OK, but-"

"Also, I can't multitask in this situation. If I work on the damping field, I can't jam the sensor feed. And I can't shield Bilby and the ship's higher systems from interference."

"What happens if you stop jamming the sensor feed?'

"Um, the Outsider will quickly pinpoint our location, course, and speed, and the result will be not anything good for us."

"I mean, what *exactly* will happen? To the nanobots, and to the data feed flowing between them?"

"Ugh. Seriously? There is no way I could dumb this down enough for you to understand."

"Let me ask a more limited question. Imagine, for example, there is a squadron of UN Navy sensor frigates. They are each passively scanning an area they are responsible for, looking for signs of stealthed enemy ships. Disturbances in the interstellar medium, oxygen leaking from airlock doors, plasma leaking from reactors, that sort of thing."

"Yes, yes. If you are thinking we can track the *Conquis* that way, you can forget-"

"That's not my question. Each ship in this imaginary squadron is feeding data back to the squadron leader, on a tightbeam laserlink. Also, each ship receives a data summary from the leader, to maintain situational awareness. If that link gets interrupted, and then restored, both ships repeat all the data that wasn't transmitted. It is a *two way* feed. Do you understand what I'm asking?"

"Yes but- Oooooooh, you are a *clever* monkey. Maybe, maybe. And shmaybe this could work. If I stop jamming the sensor feed, all the nanobots in the area will seek to update all the other bots. Including, providing the location of unauthorized vessels in the area. *Valkyrie* and *Conquis*."

"Ayuh. Is there any way you could tap into that feed, temporarily?"

"No, I will still be locked out, But, I believe I won't have to tap into the feed. There will be so much data transmitted, such a sudden flood of photons, that I should be able to map any voids in the field where transmissions are not originating. That is where we will find our enemy."

"Great!" I slapped the table. "Finally, we are making progress."

"You think that, but sadly, it is not true. The sensor feed update will be over in a few seconds, then the nanobot field will return to a steady state, and the local energy level won't be dense enough for me to see through all the dust and crap out there. We could shoot at the *Conquis*, but by the time our railgun darts traveled there, the battleship would have moved out of the way."

"We won't shoot."

"Then what is the point of-"

"We won't shoot from *here*."

"Um, unless you know of a way to create a virtual railgun out of nothing, we-"

"No, but that would be amazing, make a note for me to look into that later."

"Listen knucklehead, I am not here to take notes for-"

"Next question: the damping field here prevents us from jumping *at all*, or it only prevents us from jumping away to a safe distance?"

"How about I break it down for you Barney style: we jump, ship go BOOM."

"I know how a jump drive works, you ass. The ship won't explode, it will wreck the drive coils."

"It will *just* wreck the drive coils. Wow, I feel so much better about that."

"Our drive will fail to form a stable jump wormhole, but it *will* form a wormhole."

"A very short-lived, weak, and small wormhole."

"Ayuh. What if we do that, while you are scrambling the damping field? Messing with it as much as you can, temporarily, across the area right around us?"

"That won't make any diff-"

"Do that, *while* you are warping spacetime, to create an especially flat area of space around *Valkyrie*."

"Do both of those things at the same time?" He gasped.

"Yes."

"Do you have *any* idea how difficult that will be?"

"No, and I do not care."

"You, you-" He sputtered. "You don't *care*?"

"Not even a tiny little bit."

"Oh, oh, this is- Joe, you pride yourself on being a grunt, but really you have become that asshole general officer who gives orders to do things that-"

"That have to be done. You're wrong. I don't care how difficult it is for you, *because* I was a grunt. When shit has to get done to achieve an objective, someone has to just fucking *do* it. Suck it up, and make it happen. That's grunt life for you. Nobody gives a shit how tough it was for you to carry out your orders, they just care that the job gets done. Welcome to the military. Now, can you do it, or not?"

"I can, it just-"

"Great." I slapped the table again. "Next question: can you jam the damping field, and flatten spacetime enough for us to perform a microjump, during the short time when the nanobot sensor field is updating and we can pinpoint the position of the *Conquis*?"

"I really want to say 'No'," he grumbled.

"So, that's a 'Yes'."

"Ugh. This is *so* unfair."

"Skippy, when the game is on the line, your All-Star player gets the ball. For us, that is you. Stop whining."

"Have I screwed myself by being so reliably awesome?"

"Ya think?"

"I hate my life."

"You know who is gonna be hating life? The Outsider, when you not only perform several of your greatest hits it can't do, you also will add yet *another* item to your Greatest Hits catalog."

"Well, I suppose that is a very good point."

"Outstanding. Reed," I pressed the intercom button. "Come to my office, please."

"Now, Sir?"

"Unless your thumb is currently plugging a reactor leak, now."

"Yes, Sir."

She strode in, streaks of black and red grease on her face, her uniform top, and in her hair. She must have been assisting a damage control team.

"That's a bold fashion statement, Fireball."

"It's the latest thing, Sir," she sat down as I closed the door.

I noticed her pointedly looking at my clean uniform. "Reed, I could either fumble around trying to help the engineering team, *or* I could find a way out of this mess."

That made her sit up straight in the chair. "You did, Sir?"

"Maybe. I have a terrible, awful, crazy idea, and I want you to make it happen."

The skin around her eyes briefly tightened with a 'Not *this* shit again' expression. Then she shrugged. "What's the plan?"

"Find that ship. Take it out. Kill it."

"You have a way to do that?"

"Skippy does. We think. Shmaybe. It's worth a shot."

"How will-"

Skippy interrupted. "All Joe wants me to do is identify where the battleship is, then during the split second before we lose track of the thing, I have to both counteract the damping field *and* flatten spacetime enough for us the perform a microjump."

"That is, not going to be easy," she went with understatement.

"Joe doesn't care. He thinks he's still a grunt," Skippy sniffed.

"General Bishop *is* a grunt," she insisted. "If you doubt that, ask any E-4 in the Army. They have his back, and they know he has theirs."

"You never leave the E-4 Mafia, Skippy," I agreed. "Wargame this for us on the display here, please. We have a lot of work to do, and we need to get it done before the *Conquis* finds us again."

CHAPTER TWENTY ONE

Skippy held up a hand as Reed stood to leave my office. "Joe, hold a moment, I need to talk with you."

"Whatever you need to say, you can say it to Reed also. *Valkyrie* is her ship, this will be her fight."

"It's not a tactical issue," he stared at me, eyes wide. Pleading with me.

"It's OK, Sir," Reed paused, a hand on the door. "I have to go now, if we're going to have any chance at making this work."

I nodded, she left, and I closed the door again. "What is it, Skippy?"

"This maneuver is highly unlikely to succeed."

"Too many moving parts that all have to work together, I know."

"That also. Most of your plans are horrifically complicated, and, somehow we make it work anyway. This time, I fear, is different."

"Not this again? Yes, this time our opponent is an energy being from beyond the galaxy, that doesn't mean we-"

"Our opponent isn't the issue. Joe, I keep trying to beat this into your head over and over, and you just don't *get* it. Before, we accomplished incredibly unlikely things because we *cheated*. We had help from the probability field."

"You don't know that."

"I know simple *math*. There is no way we could have survived all the crazy shit you planned over the years, unless some unseen entity was helping us. It selected improbable probabilities again and again, that is how we are still here."

"We've had this argument too many times, Skippy. That field protected the *Elders*. No way did it assist the Merry Band of Pirates, while we worked to break everything the Elders cared about."

"You are making an assumption I once agreed with, that I fear is no longer valid. The field was *designed* to protect the Elders. I have become increasingly concerned that the Outsider somehow has compromised that field, that it assisted us, *used us*, to get rid of its greatest threat: the Elders."

That made me blink. "You think it outsourced the job to us?"

"Basically, yes."

"Do you have any actual evidence of all this, or are you guessing?"

"I am using logic to explain a chain of extremely unlikely events."

"Uh huh. If the Outsider has control of the probability field, why aren't we dead now?"

"It doesn't work that way, you moron. Also, now that the Elders are safely up in Ascensionland, the field might not be active at all. My point is, we can no longer count on surviving when the odds are hugely against us."

"What are the odds this op will succeed?"

"Um, fifty eight percent, because I am doing most of the work, and I am awesome."

"What are our odds of survival if we don't try this plan?"

"Ugh. Zero."

"I am no math expert, but fifty eight seems better than zero."

"Fine. When a railgun dart smashes your stupid head, don't say I didn't warn you."

"That's the beauty of this plan, Skippy," I grinned and stood up. "Death will come so fast, I will die blissfully believing I was right."

"I have never hated you more than I do right now."

The straps of my chair tightened, the nanofabric adjusting automatically to hold me in place. I gave the straps a tug anyway. The mechanism held me securely, based on current conditions. I knew what was going to happen, and that the straps might not react quickly enough. That was why I also pressed the back of my head into the cushion, where a field would stabilize not only my thick skull, it would protect my brain from bouncing around.

"Fireball," I glanced at the clock on the main display, then at her. The clock showed we had last broken off contact fifty five minutes before. The *Conquis* would be back, and soon. That meant the battleship was close, it might appear out of the dust cloud at any moment.

Especially since I had ordered Reed to decelerate the ship. Our next engagement would be at a slower speed relative to the spider battleship, extending the time we could shoot effectively. According to math, that would also extend the duration of our inevitable punishment. Sometimes, math really sucks.

"The ship is ready in all respects, Sir."

"Outstanding. Skippy?"

"Yes?" He was pre-annoyed at me, anticipating the strenuous work he would soon be engaged in.

"Do your thing."

"We will get only one chance at this, so the navigator needs to input the correct coordinates, *and* anticipate changes in real time, based on the course and speeds of the two ships."

"I am reasonably sure the navigator understands his job," I said, as the guy in the copilot couch gave me a thumbs up without looking away from his console. "Do your thing, please."

"Monkeys programming a jump," he grumbled. "I do not anticipate *any* problems with that. If this goes sideways, it will not be my fault. OK, I am no longer jamming the nanobot swarm data feed, as of *now*. The- Holy shit, that freakin' battleship is only eighty thousand kilometers behind us! Jump!"

There wasn't anything I could do, so I didn't do anything, other than watch *Valkyrie's* crew do their jobs. The navigator's fingers flew over his console, I watched him check and double check his numbers, the pilot then reviewed and verified the jump calculations, then the pilot tapped the icon to initiate a jump. He folded his arms across his chest so his hands wouldn't accidentally touch the controls. "Jumping in three, two, one-"

Always, always, tug your seat straps as tight as they will go, when you know you're about to do something stupid. When I was little, I once jumped off the roof of my uncle's garage using a bedsheet as a parachute. I say 'once' because there was no repeat performance of my attempt to be the Batman of northern Maine. Being five years old meant I escaped my mishap with only a few bumps and bruises, while these days sometimes I sleep wrong on my pillow and my back will ache for a week. That particular day in the quarantine zone, the something stupid I did was order *Valkyrie* to jump on top of a senior species battleship.

Hey, I have done things that are much stupider- Which, now that I think about it, doesn't make me look as good as I intended.

Valkyrie jumped. Decelerating before the battle meant we were moving only fifty meters per second relative to the *Conquis*, and on a roughly parallel course.

It was a short jump, technically a microjump. With Skippy in control, we could have emerged within half a meter of the target coordinates. Bilby could have managed a spherical probability of error within seven meters. Our human navigator nailed it within seventy nine meters.

Slightly ahead of the battleship, on its port side.

"*Surprise, motherfucker,*" I whispered as I pressed my fragile head back into the cushion, feeling the suspensor field already gently nudging me into position.

When the collision happened, we hit hard. Not armor on armor, the two ships didn't make contact physically. Our shields slammed into the battleship's shields, both energy fields briefly pushed back, and both shields shorted out in spectacular arcs of suddenly-free electricity that didn't have anywhere to go. In addition to the spine-chilling *screeeeeee* of tearing metal composites we could hear and feel the deep *thump thump thump* pulsing of railguns firing on pre-selected targets and then there was brief silence as the battleship coasted past us.

Our railguns hadn't done enough damage in the brief encounter.

That's OK, we had stolen a move from the Outsider's Greatest Hits catalog.

We were rude by literally crashing the party, so we brought party favors.

Every missile that wasn't already in a rotary launcher was in a starboard side docking bay, the big doors open, missiles secured by suspensor fields. Those fields snapped off moments after our defense shields shorted out, and the missiles roared out on settings of maximum thrust, minimal guidance. They almost couldn't miss at that range, the target was enormous and *right there*.

We got lucky.

Also, Skippy lied, sort of. He had bitched and moaned that between locating the battleship, flattening spacetime, and keeping basic ship functions from failing, his bandwidth was fully occupied. Yet, because he is awesome, something he rarely talks about, he also sent out an energy pulse of his own. Not one we could see, or the ship's already blinded sensors could detect, this pulse was in a higher level of spacetime. It couldn't do anything to the Outsider.

It sure as hell could scramble the battleship's targeting systems.

A more experienced opponent would have been prepared for the Merry Band of Pirates doing, well, some cowboy pirate shit. Would have created a protocol to bypass the safety systems of the battleship's weapons. The Outsider hadn't done that. Without a target to shoot at, without a verified firing solution, without overriding the range safety settings to make sure the weapons didn't damage their own ship, the weapons of the *Conquis* refused commands to fire, until it was too late. The big spider battlewagon never got off a shot.

Our missiles normally would not have armed their warheads until they were at minimum two thousand meters from *Valkyrie*, but their range safety settings had been dialed back to fifty meters. They went hot almost the instant they cleared the docking bay doors, accelerating at three hundred gees. Eighty four percent of our missiles struck the *Conquis*, aimed at the forward two thirds of the enemy ship. We had not targeted the aft third of that ship, the vital engineering section, out of fear an explosion of the reactors, or the jump drive capacitors losing containment, would tear apart *Valkyrie's* unshielded hull.

Silence. Not silence, exactly. Consoles were beeping, people were talking, the hull was groaning as structural frames recovered from being stressed, armor plating *pinged* and occasionally *banged* from debris impacts. Debris that used to be coherent parts of a senior species battleship. That debris was mostly blasting outward, not backward, and the battleship's momentum was carrying it away from us.

"Skippy," I cleared my throat. "Can you-"

"I'm warning you, it is ugly," he anticipated my request. The main display showed a composite image of the *Conquis*.

Only of the engineering section. The forward two thirds of the hull was *gone*, just not there anymore. Frames that used to connect the aft section to everything forward were twisted, melted, breaking away. Electricity arced from severed power conduits. All of the reactors were venting bright hot fountains of plasma. That was a reaction of the ship's safety systems, I guessed. The Outsider had to know it had lost the battle, that salvaging anything of its ship was a futile effort.

"Weps," Reed called out to the station behind us. "Maintain a lock on that ship's jump drive capacitor banks."

"Check," the officer responded. "I have four railguns tasked and ready."

"Railguns dialed up to 'Eleven'?

"Yes, Ma'am."

"Outstanding. Pilot, this is a bad neighborhood. Pedal to the metal, get us out of here."

"Rolling up the windows and locking the doors, Ma'am," the pilot replied, and we all felt the ship surge with deceleration, allowing the battleship to drift farther ahead.

I had a bad feeling. If the Outsider released the capacitor energy, the explosion could cripple *Valkyrie*. Without our shields, millions of nanobots were impacting our hull and some of them would survive to cause trouble. The battle wasn't over yet, it wouldn't be over until we killed the Outsider. Which we didn't know how to do.

"Reed, we should consider lighting off the boosters to put some distance between-"

"NO!" Skippy roared.

"What-"

He didn't need to answer. I could see it happen on the display. The battleship was jumping away. A tear in spacetime was forming ahead of the *Conquis* and the wreck of that ship coasted onward to plunge into it. The event horizon flickered, surge, brightened and dimmed, expanded and contracted, flared again-

And was gone.

The aft end of the battleship began tumbling, and I pumped a fist. "Ha! The jump failed, and that discharged the capacitors. You can't run away now, you piece of-"

That was when the battleship exploded.

We survived. I was wrong about a lot of things, OK most things. One thing I'd been right about was the failed jump had eaten up most of the energy in the battleship's capacitors, so the explosion wasn't catastrophic for us. It wasn't anything *good*, and after the ship's systems came back online, Reed shot me several accusing looks, whether she intended for me to see the Death Glare or not. That was OK, I had promised not to break her ship and, based on how the armor on one side was smoking, I had sort of broken it.

Again.

"Well," I shrugged. "Look at the bright side. The nanobots on that part of the armor were melted also. Plus, we survived, and the Outsider didn't. That has to count for-"

"*Wrong*, numbskull," Skippy glared at me. It was Be Pissed Off At Joe Bishop Day. "That damned thing got away, *again*."

"You saw a streak of light again?"

"No."

"OK, then-"

"I saw what *you* saw. Joe, it jumped away."

"Uh, what I saw was the jump attempt *failed*. The aft section-"

"I said *it* jumped away, not the battleship. It copied another of my greatest hits: a failed jump. That wormhole couldn't pull the ship through, but it was open and coherent long enough for the Outsider to escape through."

"Fuck!" I lost my cool in front of the crew, that was not cool. "Where did it go?"

"I don't know. Hey, it's not my fault! There was a lot of energy flying around, you know, and that wormhole was seriously dorked up. All I can tell you is, the jump length was between twelve and thirty two lighthours."

"Beyond the quarantine zone, then. It must have a ship waiting out there."

"That is a good bet, yes."

"This was all for *nothing*, then." Those were also words I shouldn't have spoken aloud where the crew could hear.

"That's not true, Sir." Reed shook her head. "This op wasn't a failure for *us*. We survived an ambush. The Outsider failed to kill us and capture or neutralize Skippy. We will be getting out of here, we-" She paused, mouth open. "We *will* be jumping away from here?" She directed that question at Skippy.

"Yeah, yeah, just give me time to work on something. Have some patience, will you? As if that's ever gonna happen," he added not quite under his breath.

"Skippy, we no longer care about a sensor data feed, so can you focus on restoring Bilby's functions? Then he can direct maintenance bots to bring the jump drive online faster than we could do it."

"I could do that, *or* I could do something much smarter."

"Like what?"

"Like, me giving another gift to the entire galaxy. The meatsacks here won't be grateful, but," he sighed. "I'll do it anyway."

"What are you talking about?"

"Colonel Reed, please bring the ship to within ninety three thousand kilometers of the planet."

"Why," she looked at me, not the avatar. "Would I do that?"

"The nano being or whatever down there has mostly minded its own business for over hundreds of thousands of years. But, now it has pissed me off, so I am gonna *fuck it up*."

"What do you mean?" I asked.

"Take it out, permanently. Kill it at the source, fry the control mechanism. Better than that: I am going to seize that thing by the throat, and propagate a command that will self destruct every nanobot in this system. Once again, Skippy the Magnificent will fix a meatsack mistake."

"You can do this, at no risk to us, or yourself?"

"Joe, you cannot imagine how angry I am right now. Bring me to within range of the central control node down there, and we will be able to jump away within the hour."

"Reed, do what the beer can asks. Let's get the hell out of here ASAP."

Skippy was true to his word. The dust cloud lit up as nanobots erupted on and all around the planet, the effect spreading outward at the speed of light. Within hours, every nanobot in the star system should not only be disabled, they should have dissipated into incoherent molecules. The dust cloud saturating the quarantine zone would be just that: dust. Harmless, other than still acting as a navigation hazard.

For a moment, when I saw the planet's entire surface catch fire, saw even the deep oceans boiling, I felt a pang of regret. I had allowed Skippy to fry a world. To kill what had essentially become a biosphere. Then I thought, fuck the nanobots. *They* had killed a real biosphere, the greedy little bastards. Yes, I know it wasn't their fault, they had been programed to consume and to construct more of themselves, and they did that. Somehow, they had become more than mindless tiny machines, they built a sort of civilization. Had me allowing Skippy to wipe them out been an act of genocide? If left alone, could the nanobots eventually have created great art, contributed to the collective culture and knowledge of our galaxy? Maybe.

Or, maybe those hungry little fuckers could have spread across the galaxy, consuming everything. I can live with what I did.

With no damping field, no weird effect scrambling Bilby's brain, and no advanced killer battleship chasing us, *Valkyrie* was able to jump away, after just a bit more than the hour Skippy's boasted about. We jumped a safe distance beyond the edge of the quarantine zone, with our shields still down, the ship was vulnerable to the quarantine containment systems.

In stealth, the ship drifted, while repairs were conducted to the shield generators, the main engines, just about every system that could be repaired without the service of a space dock. Eleven hours after we jumped away from the ambush site, the ship's sensors detected the glow of nanobots erupting at the far edge of the quarantine zone.

"That's it!" Skippy crowed. "All those nasty little fuckers are *dead*."

"It looks great," I walked close to the main display. "How can you be sure of that?"

"Um, you can *see* it, so-"

"What I see is a lot of light. Photons."

"Well *Duh*, the nanobots were too small for your squishy eyes to see, and now they all are nothing but incoherent dust."

"*All* of them?"

"I'm gonna talk really slowly, so you can understand this. We saw the nanobots burning on the planet, and around the planet, and now the effect is *here*. I was able to predict when we would see the effect here, because the self destruct signal I planted travels at the speed of light."

"Yes, and the speed of light is extremely precise and doesn't vary."

"Um, that is not exactly true."

"The speed of light in a *vacuum* is constant."

"Again, that is not exactly-"

"The speed of light between here and the freakin' planet is constant."

"Close enough. Did that answer your question?"

"No. How can you be certain, absolutely certain, that *all* of those little buggers are dead? Every single one of them."

"Ugh. Seriously?"

"Yes, Duh. If we tell the senior species the nanobot threat here is over, they will end the very expensive quarantine effort. Then, both of them, and every other jackass in the galaxy, will be on a treasure hunt here, looking for surviving remnants of those bots."

"I do not know why I even bother to talk with you. This is the thanks I get, after I, all by myself, end a major threat to the entire galaxy?"

"We will be very grateful, *if* you actually did end the threat. It only takes one of those damned things to start replicating, and in a few years or even months, we will be right back to-"

"Oh, I see what you mean now. Your concern is actually reasonable, given your total ignorance of the facts."

"What-"

"This is my bad."

"Thanks, so-"

"I *know* you are stupid, but sometimes I forget just how-"

"Choose your next words very carefully."

"Um- How about I simply explain the relevant facts?"

"That would be great," I could feel my face turning red.

"The original nanobots were individual self replicating machines. *That* is how they got out of control; transcription errors are inevitable, and there was no quality assurance mechanism to prevent the propagation of harmful mutations."

"But, those mutations were beneficial, not harmful," I argued. "They benefitted the overall population of bots, I mean. The mutations allowed the bots to survive and evolve, to evade the controls built into them, and the external efforts to wipe them out."

"That is true."

"So, why did you say-"

"That *was* true. When the bots were truly individuals, each little machine only had to be concerned about the survival of itself, making copies of itself, and the survival of those copies. When the population of bots merged with AIs and took complete control of the planet, they became a singular organism. Individuals were not only not needed, they could not be tolerated. Evolution was allowed only in the form of planned upgrades, while unplanned mutations had to be stamped out. Or, burned out, by triggering a bot's overload mechanism."

"Uh, what if a mutation was something good?"

"The nanobeing organism did not care. Think about it. It had supreme control of the majority of a star system. If it missed taking advantage of a beneficial mutation, that wouldn't affect its happy, stable existence. Until I arrived, it had no external enemies, no threats to its power or existence. It did have plenty of potential internal threats; a new, more efficient and more capable nanobot could replicate out of control, and take over. So, a safety mechanism was built into all nanobots. The desired level of population was reached within the first three thousand years, after that increasing the number of bots was actually harmful. The asteroid belt had been consumed, with that mass distributed across the inner system. So much mass had been repositioned, it affected the orbit of the inner planets. The nanobeing had to make a major effort over more than fifteen thousand years to achieve a new orbital equilibrium, to avoid throwing the planet Vorvestican out of orbit. Anyway, once the population stabilized at the optimal level, bots were not allowed to replicate without permission. When a replication occurred, the newly created copy was inspected by ten other bots, to assure the new bot conformed to the master template. If any replication errors were found, the new bot and its parent were destroyed."

"OK. The nanobeing wanted a genetically identical population, sort of."

"Yes. Very similar to the genocidal eugenics program the Thuranin inflicted on their own species, long ago in their history. Joe, now do you understand why I am certain the nanobots have all been wiped out? Even if a few of them missed the memo to destroy themselves, they can't replicate without the appropriate command from an authorized source. That source is *gone*."

"You hit it where it was vulnerable. Good job, Skippy."

"If you had just trusted the awesomeness, we-"

"The awesomeness I trust, what I don't trust is your absent minded lack of focus sometimes."

"Hey, I am *busy*," he huffed.

"All right then," I scratched my chin. "The kitties and spiders will be curious about the flash of light that just saturated the quarantine zone. We need to give them an explanation."

"Sir?" Reed spoke. "Do we? The quarantine zone isn't our responsibility."

"It isn't, but it could become our *problem*. Or even an advantage, temporarily."

"Sir?"

"Right now, the kitties have significant resources tied up here, to contain their mistake. It has to be driving them crazy that they have to play nice with the Rindhalu here. We could keep the Maxohlx tied down here, while making points with the spiders. We will give the truth to the spiders. They can quietly pull back some of their personnel commitment here, if they believe us. To the Maxohlx, we'll tell them something like, uh, the Outsider provided the nanobots with a stealth capability. The things are still in the quarantine zone, they just can't be seen. We'll tell the kitties this new model of nanobot could be sneaking out of the quarantine zone *right now*, so they have to be extra vigilant."

"Joe," Skippy chuckled. "That is an ingeniously *evil* scheme."

"Thanks."

"You can seriously be an asshole sometimes."

"The difference is, I save my inner asshole for special occasions. All right. Fireball, I'm going to my office to compose a message to the spiders and kitties here. Then we're getting the hell out of this place. You're right, this quarantine is not our responsibility."

Reed and I were in her office, discussing our next move. Damage to the ship was nowhere near as bad as it had looked while we were engaged in a constant battle, a lot of the broken components could be swapped out for spares now that we could take systems offline. Still, the engineering team and the maintenance bots could do only so much work, major repairs would require three days in a space dock. Going back to Earth was the logical option. We also needed to visit Missile Mart to replenish our magazines; we had launched almost every weapon that could fly at the *Conquis* when we jumped in on top of it. Really. Knowing we would very likely get only one chance to jump the battleship, we had stuffed the starboard side docking bays with all of the shipkiller missiles, all of our decoys, half of the sensor drones since they could also act as decoys and saturate the battleship's defenses, and- Well, just about everything. The only missiles we held back were the dedicated attack coordinators; the units that processed networked sensor data and assigned each killer missile a role in the attack. In the final fight against the *Conquis*, there hadn't been time for any sort of coordination. All the missiles had been instructed to burn hard along their predetermined flightpaths, and to explode if they contacted anything with armor plating.

The attack coordinator missiles, by the way, were bitter about being left out of the fight, and they had threatened a union work stoppage. Thankfully, that dispute lasted only three milliseconds before their fellow members of the Energetic Weapons Guild shouted them down. There might also have been threats that uncooperative missiles would find themselves sleeping at the core of a gas giant, if youze know what I mean. I stayed out of the argument.

Anyway, I hope Reed has a coupon for a discount on a complete loadout of missiles, otherwise her shopping trip is going to be *expensive*.

The other option was for us to go to Jaguar, and use the shipyard there. Reed suggested that we consider that option, we both knew she did that because I was worried about my family. No, Jaguar was not the best option, so I discarded it. "Reed, thanks for the offer, but only the shipyard at Earth has experience with the newest version of *Valkyrie*. That makes the decision easy."

Skippy's avatar appeared immediately. "That is not true, Joe. When we were there on the courier ship, I uploaded *Valkyrie's* new specs to the Jaguar space dock. Most of the work we need will be automated, I estimate three days if

Admiral Chatterji assigns the highest level of priority to this job. Also, I want to make sure Puptart is following my instructions properly, it wasn't designed to protect a planet. And, the journey to Jaguar from here is twenty nine hours shorter than the time to reach Earth."

Reed silently raised an eyebrow.

"OK," I agreed, "your logic has convinced me."

Reed pressed an icon on her phone. "Mister Gasquet, set a least time course for Jaguar, and jump when ready."

"Least time course for Jaguar base, aye," the ship's executive officer acknowledged.

"Now, if there isn't anything else you need me for," Skippy huffed, "I have to assist Bilby in bringing Reactor Four online." His avatar blinked out.

"Sir," Reed said. "I think I know the answer, but the question has to be asked. Instead of going to a space dock for repairs, should we consider trying to track the Outsider?"

"Should we? Ah, probably not, even if we could. We have no idea where the thing is, where it is going, where it *could* go. Or, what the hell it wants."

"We know it wants to take Skippy out of the fight," she reminded me. "Whatever its objective is, the Outsider doesn't believe it can accomplish its goal while Skippy is active."

"That is," I tapped the table. "A good point. Fireball," I leaned back in my chair. "A *very* good point. Yeah. That narrows the list of possibilities."

She cocked her head. "How, Sir?"

"If it was doing something secret, something we wouldn't know about, or doing it some*where* we wouldn't know about until it was too late, it wouldn't care about Skippy messing up its plans. Whatever its objective, it is concerned we will discover what it's doing, *and* that we at least have the potential to interfere. To stop its plans. Huh. This is a *big* damned galaxy. It could set off a supernova and we wouldn't know about it for years, unless someone had a sensor platform parked close to that star."

"So, whatever it's planning to do, it will take a long time from start to finish?" She mused.

"Long enough for someone to notice, and for us to act against it. Act effectively, before it accomplishes whatever it's supposed to do."

It was her turn to sit back in her chair. "We could be looking at a timeline of years, then."

"Centuries, even. We think in terms of days, weeks, months. The Outsider might make plans on a timescale of decades or centuries. Whatever it plans to do, it's not concerned the meatsacks in this galaxy can stop it. It's only afraid of Skippy."

"I'm not sure about that, Sir. It might be counting on its new allies the Maxohlx to keep the spiders occupied, so they are too busy to interfere with the Outsider."

"OK, true. For now, we have only seen that it is concerned about Skippy, I want to explore that possibility. Shit."

"What?"

"I said we might not notice what it's doing for years, if the location is remote."

"Yes?"

"What if it has already started, and no one has seen it yet?"

"Shiiiiit," she breathed. "Something beyond the edge of the galaxy, like where the Elders set up that radio receiver thing, the one that started this whole mess?"

"If that's true, the Outsider could have been working on it for hundreds of years. That, hmm. That actually makes me feel better."

"Sir?"

"Oh, uh, uh, nothing," I stammered. Shit, I shouldn't have opened my big stupid mouth. Reed didn't know about the probability field, so she didn't know I was concerned that by giving the Elders a free lifetime pass to Ascensionland, Skippy and I might have disabled that field. "What I meant is," I coughed to cover my guilty feelings about lying to an officer I respected. "If this has been going on since before I met Skippy, at least it's one thing the Joint Chiefs can't blame on me."

She sucked in her lips, looking down at the desk. "Uh huh."

Damn it, she knew I was lying. "Listen, Reed, it's not-"

"Sir, I know a whole lot of shit that keeps me awake at night. Things I wish I didn't know about. If something is so scary you don't want to tell me, I would appreciate *not* ever knowing. Unless it," she let out a long breath. "is something I need to know about."

"It isn't. It's not anything actionable," I assured her. "Skippy says it's something *I* shouldn't worry about but," I held up my hands.

"I get it, Sir. Someone has to."

"Right. OK," I glanced at the clock on the wall display. "We have been out of contact for a while, we should stop by a friendly relay station along the way, to find out whether some huge disaster happened while we were busy."

CHAPTER TWENTY TWO

"The boys are outside with their friends," her mother said as Margaret came through the door into the community center. A break in the weather, relative calm that was projected to last nearly two days, had allowed civilians to leave underground shelters. Adults had been given military escorts to their homes to collect clean clothing and other nonessential items, and children could go outside with supervision.

"I hope they don't get muddy again," Margaret frowned as she set down the duffel bag of clothes and toys, glancing at her own shoes that were caked with mud. She had kept to the driveway of her house, but the gravel had been washed away, and everything was coated with mud, dead leaves, and trash. Tornados had ripped through the west section of Club Skippy, destroying fourteen houses and two apartment buildings, the casualties would have been horrific if the residents had not been in the underground shelters. The clouds had parted to show the weird sky, a glow that was uniform from horizon to horizon, every moment of day and night. That the local sun had set made no difference, there was no night anywhere on the planet. Animals, both native and imported, were confused by the never ending light. Plants had gone dormant and started to die soon after Puptart created the shield, then flourished when the steady release of the shield's captured energy was adjusted to match the spectrum of the local star. Joe's parents had been hopeful of saving their crops, until flooding and hailstorms wiped out half of the acreage. Possibly some wheat and corn might be harvested, if the weather settled back into anything resembling a normal pattern.

With her mother looking pointedly at Margaret's shoes, which had tracked clods of mud onto the mat inside the doorway, she backed carefully out the door. "I'll go check on the boys."

A group of children were lying on picnic tables behind the community center, keeping off the wet grass. Except, she saw when she was closer, they had been playing on the grass, and likely in the new stream that now flowed across the bottom of the parking lot.

"Hi, Mom," Rene acknowledged her as she loomed over both of her boys.

"Is everything OK?" She was concerned because all the children, about two dozen of them, were quiet. Unusually quiet. Just lying on their backs, staring up at the sky. Leaning her head back until her neck hurt, she looked up. Between the scattered clouds was only featureless, constant light.

"We're just looking at the sky, Mom."

"No stars tonight, I'm sorry about that."

"We like it better this way," Jeremy spoke, before turning his head to look at her. "You can't see where the monsters are."

A few minutes later, I was walking past the door to the bridge when Reed pinged me. "Reed?" I called from the doorway. It startled her to hear my voice directly, rather than through her earpiece or over an intercom.

"Sir, we have a," she pointed to the main display, which was showing a convoluted course through four Elder wormholes. "Complication. Skippy has requested we divert to a Kristang world."

Knowing any interaction with the beer can wouldn't be quick, I walked over to stand next to her. "What world? What's there?"

"It's called Redmundikus. The Fire Dragon clan controls the place. We have been there before, um-"

"Six times," Gasquet provided the information.

"Six times?" It was my opportunity to raise an eyebrow at Reed. "Why?"

She shrugged. "Something about his epic opera. That's what he said. We were on his Victory Tour of the galaxy, so we went wherever he wanted."

"Ayuh. I call bullshit on that." I clapped my hands. "Skippy!"

"You, you," he sputtered. "Did you just *summon* me?"

"You're not a genie, so no. Why are we going to Redmun- whatever it's called?"

"It's complicated, Joe. Nothing you need to, heh heh, worry about," he coughed nervously. "I just need to pop in and out, make a quick stop. Won't take more than a few hours."

"Why are we going there?"

"Um, heh heh, it's like Reed said. My opera."

"She did say that, and I called bullshit on it. Why do you need to go there?"

"Ugh. Why do you need to know?"

"*Valkyrie* operates under my authority as commander of Task Force Black. You can do whatever you want, but if you want this ship to take you anywhere that delays our arrival at Jaguar, you need to give me a damned good reason."

"This is harassment!"

"This is reality, beer can. Talk. And before you do, I want the truth. You start with a lie, and you can forget about any detours."

"Oh for- Fine. Whatevs. I need to do collections."

"Collections?"

"Yes. The lizards there owe me an envelope."

"I assume this isn't a heartfelt Thank You card, so-"

"It's not a physical envelope, dumdum, that's just an expression. It's a crypto wallet, stuffed full of Skipcoins."

"Uh huh. They are paying you for, what exactly?"

"Protection."

"Pro- Oh my- You are running a *protection racket*?!"

"You make it sound so unsavory."

"Unsav- I thought I knew how sketchy you could be, but this is a whole new level. You are into *extortion* now?!"

"How is this extortion?"

"How? You threaten to harm people unless they pay you money?"

"Um, what?"

"You make them pay for protection from, what you will do to them if they don't pay."

His eyes bulged. "I can *do* that? Wow, I never considered th-"

"Wait. You are *not* doing that?"

"No. The Fire Dragons there are paying me to provide information about plans other clans have for attacking them, contracts for assassinations, secret trade deals that would be unfavorable to their interests, that sort of thing. Also, for a modest additional fee, I can insert malware into the warships of other clans who are planning to attack Redmundikus. It is a lot of work, I am certainly not doing it for free. This is the sort of thing I was doing as a one-time service, then," he chuckled, "I had the brilliant idea to launch a subscription model."

"People can *subscribe* to Skippy?"

"Of course. I offer several convenient payment plans. Which reminds me, your Def Com leadership needs to decide which payment option they-"

"Whatever you were about to say, I do not want to hear it."

"Ugh. Fine, but don't come whining to me when the Joint Chiefs ask about-"

"They can't ask me about something I don't know, get it?"

"Whatevs. Anywho, I like your protection plan idea much better. I can create a demand for my own services. This is a *great* idea!"

"No, it is a terrible idea."

"Um, oh, I get it. Listen, if you want me to cut you in for a taste, we can work out a-"

"Let me be clear: I do not want to be involved in this scheme in any way."

"Oh," he winked. "Gotcha. No, of course you are not involved."

"I am *not* involved!"

"Um, I'm getting mixed signals here. When we get to Redmundikus, I can-"

"We are not going there."

"Joe, be reasonable. If I don't show up to collect, the lizards will lose a measure of respect for me and-"

"Skippy, I, I can't believe I am telling you this, but you shouldn't handle collections."

"I shouldn't?" He blinked. "Then how-"

"You get somebody else to handle collections."

"Why would I do that?"

"First, it makes the point that you are much too important to handle mundane bullshit like collections, that will make them respect you *more*. Second, if you get investigated, you can deny all knowledge of events."

"Hmm. Hmmm, I *like* it. Is this what the beetles refer to as 'plausible deniability'?"

"Basically, yes."

"Another great idea. You are *on fire* today, Joe."

"I have never been more proud of myself," I muttered.

"OK, hmm, I could probably get Captain Gumbano to handle collections for me. Of course, I can't trust him at all, so that's a problem."

"Right, so you assign a trusted associate to fly with Gumbano," I suggested.

"Like who?"

"I don't know. Who do you trust?"

"I don't trust anyone, that's my policy. Although, I suppose I could ask Minister Gastovsky to recommend a-"

"Gastovsky? He's in the Army, how can he-"

"He *was* in the Army, then recently I made him an offer he couldn't refuse. Now he is Skippistan's Minister of Finance and Trade."

"Wow, I don't foresee *any* problems with that."

"Oh, shut up."

"Fireball," I turned to the ship's captain. "Maintain our present course. The Godfather here can handle business on his own time."

I thought about what Reed had said. I thought about it a lot. That as far as we knew, and based on the evidence we did have, the Outsider's current goal was to kill or neutralize Skippy. For whatever reason, it feared that Skippy and only Skippy could stop it.

That changed our approach to finding the Outsider, to collecting intel about it, to figuring out its plans. Our priorities had to change.

"Skippy," I called him from my office, for a closed-door meeting.

"Hey, Joe," he appeared looking rather cheery, which would make my task more difficult. "What's up?"

"I need to tell you something you will not like."

"Oh for- My protection business is *my* business, I don't see how you have any-"

"It's not about that."

"Oh, good. Then- Oh no. Are you starting a boy band?" He shuddered. "I told you, your boys are cute and they actually have some talent, but you are just-"

"No boy band."

"Oh. OK, then hit me. Anything you say at this point can't be that bad."

"Listen, Reed said something that changed the way I've been thinking about the Outsider. It's- I thought I had it all figured out, that it was obvious, then she looked at it differently, and totally changed my perspective."

"Mm hmm, you do that to me all the freakin' time."

"Right. So, our priority has been gathering intel about the Outsider. Its movements, abilities, intentions, all that."

"Yes, so? We have to do that, if we are to stop it."

"Yes but, maybe 'we' don't need to do that."

Instead of me getting only his usual distracted half attention, he focused on me. "What do you mean?"

"The Outsider fears you, and *only* you."

"Well, Duh."

"So far, all of its efforts have been directed toward taking you out of the fight."

"That is not entirely true. It also twice attempted to take control of a Sentinel."

"Yes, it did that so it could effectively fight *you*."

"A Sentinel has many other uses, Joe."

"What I know is, if it had control of a Sentinel, no way would I take *Valkyrie* into battle against it. Especially not with you aboard the ship."

"OK, OK, I can see that. What are you saying?"

"That our priority needs to change. Instead of chasing the Outsider, trying to understand what it wants and what it's doing, our Number One priority should be protecting you."

"Um, what is the point of having an awesome weapon, if you don't use it?"

"We will preserve you, so you can act later, once the Outsider has revealed its objective. Let me explain, OK?"

"Break it down Barney style for me, please, because this isn't making any sense."

"The Outsider believes you can stop it, that's why it has been trying to take you out of the fight. At some point, whatever it's doing will be detected, whether it is working to construct another intergalactic radio to contact its masters in the Outhouse galaxy, or it is," I waved my hands, "doing something else that becomes visible. That is when we will need you to act, to interrupt or disable or destroy the radio or machine or whatever it's using to, do what it wants. Until then, we have to assure you will be able and ready to act. I'm going to recommend to the Joint Chiefs that we take you to a secret location, and keep you safe there until it is time for you to act."

"Huh."

"I know you won't like being sidelined, but think of it as an opportunity for you to, do something like work on a musical theater thing?"

"*Thing?*"

"You know what I mean. A Broadway show."

"Wow. Hmm, that is indeed solid, well-reasoned thinking."

"Cool. Thanks," I let out a breath. "I was ready for an argument."

"This is interesting. I get to be *you* for a while."

"What?"

"You know, when your squishy monkey brain says something incredibly freakin' obvious that I somehow didn't consider, and makes me hate myself."

"I missed something obvious?"

"Yes, *Duh.*"

"No I did n- What is it?"

"Give me a moment, I want to savor the anticipation. When I smack with you with the obvious, please describe how awful you feel and don't hold back, this is for science."

"Just tell me, you ass."

"Now you know how I feel. All. The. Freakin'. Time. OK, here it is. You are assuming that anyone could detect what the Outsider is doing, but only I can stop it."

"Ayuh, yeah. That is-"

"What if the truth is the *opposite*? What if during the early stages of what the Outsider is doing, its machine is vulnerable to attack by the senior species, but only *I* can detect the thing before it grows too powerful to stop?"

"Shiiiiiit," I groaned.

"You see?"

"Yes, I do. Damn it."

"It is obvious, isn't it?"

"Yes."

"Hmm, I didn't hear that. Could you say it louder?"

"Yes!"

"Well, hmmph," he sniffed. "It is a good thing that you have me to keep you from embarrassing yourself."

"How is that?"

"Imagine if you had presented your genius plan to the Joint Chiefs, and any one of them pointed out what a doofus you are."

"I really appreciate you *not* gloating about this."

"Oh, like you have never done that to me."

"That's different."

"No it is not!"

"Yes it is. Skippy, you are *awesome*. I am, as you so kindly mentioned, a doofus. If you miss something obvious, you are still the galaxy's ultimate source of extreme awesomeness."

"Hmm, well, I suppose that is a very good point."

"See? If I do something smart, I get a small temporary boost, but I am still, you know, a filthy monkey."

"Huh. Wow. I hadn't considered that. Joe, how are you not too depressed to get out of bed in the morning?"

"It's a struggle. Especially when I'm not with my family."

"I do admire your courage."

"Thanks, what-"

"I mean, if I were you, I would wallow in infinite despair until I threw myself off a bridge or something."

"If I did that, I would miss these delightful conversations."

"That is true. So, you're saying I give you a reason to live?"

"Less than you might think," I muttered.

"So, we're done? This whole discussion was a waste of my time?"

"Uh, ayuh, sorry."

"You should be ashamed of yourself."

"I promise to wallow in extra despair for the rest of the day."

Dave Czajka picked up his pace until he was moving at a steady jog toward a group of Ruhar on the edge of the airfield. The alien soldiers had just been landed by dropship and had walked out the back ramp, safely away from where hot gases might be spewing from various vents around the spacecraft. The Ruhar, twenty eight of them according the information overlay in his sunglasses, were special forces, he knew that from the white and orange color of their mech suits. When in action, the suits turned gray, brown, or engaged their version of chameleonware, the white and orange were for high visibility in non-combat areas. Dave understood the advantage of being easily seen in the chaos of a crowded airfield with heavy spacecraft and ground equipment moving in random directions, but to his eye the special forces had the appearance of an alien Coast Guard.

Not that there was anything wrong with that, the UN Coasties were responsible for orbital traffic control, and search and rescue, at both Earth and Jaguar.

Jaguar. A world that had been firebombed, and survived under the literal blanket protection of a Sentinel. Dave had friends on Jaguar, his company had an office there. When he heard about the Outsider attack there, he had assumed the UN would cancel the joint operation to retake Hufustria. Why bother with a sideshow, when a human world had been attacked and was suffering. Em also had assumed the operation would be canceled, she had halted the combat loading of dropships, and paused training while waiting for new orders. Eighteen days later, a UNN star carrier arrived with a message from Def Com: the liberation of Hufustria was still on, to be conducted ASAP. Basically, Em told Dave after she read between the lines of the official orders, the United Nations recognized that, with Jaguar suffocating under a blanket, and Earth under threat, it was good to cultivate allies. Hufustria was also considered to be low-hanging fruit, an operation with minimal risk to Def Com, and most of the boots hitting the ground would be Ruhar or Verd-kris. So, Dave had shrugged, got his people spun up again, and now he had his own boots on Hufustria, doing his job to the best of his ability, and praying every night that the Outsider didn't firebomb Earth.

Because he still had a job to do, the question was, why were 'Tezzaks' as the Ruhar called their special operations troops, on the ground in the assembly area? The inclusion of a special forces unit had not been in the briefing, and he wanted to know what their deal was before Em found out and raised hell. He could have pinged the officer who had his back to him, but a face to face conversation would be more productive.

Helmets were off and slung on shoulder clips, the officer's short mohawk haircut bobbed as he gestured with a knife hand into the other palm. "I want D.C.S. and tactical database assimilation by zero eight thirty."

That drew a weary groan from the soldiers.

"We boost off this rock in two days and a wakeup," the officer continued. "Anyone who expected a vacation can-"

"*Nerty?*" Dave blurted out.

The figure turned, eyes growing wide. "Mister Czajka?"

Dave halted, and snapped a salute. "I should have said, Sarklast Dandurf," he noted the rank insignia on the alien's chest. In the Ruhar Federal Army, the rank of sarklast was very roughly equivalent to an army captain, in the NATO-standard rank structure adopted by Def Com. "How are you? Hey, do you have a minute to, um," he jerked his head toward an unoccupied area of the field.

"Yes, of course," Nert's grin was infectious. "Pershavent," he gestured to a more junior officer. "Get our gear over to the assembly area."

They walked in silence as a dropship was lifting off across the field, the roar drowning out even their noise-cancelling earpieces. Dave watched the dropship gain speed and switch from belly jets to the main engines, soaring into the sky. When the roar faded to a dull whine and he could speak without raising his voice, he asked, "I'd like to catch up on what you've been doing, but right now I need to know why a Federal Army special forces unit is here. We had no notice of this, and Em- Um, General Perkins, will not be happy about this. Are you expecting trouble?"

Nert's fuzzy face twisted into an expression of disgust that Dave could have recognized even without classes in alien body language. "We are here because the Army does *not* expect any trouble."

Dave blinked. "You wanna explain that?"

"My people haven't had a big, high visibility *win* in too long. My unit is here to show the folks back home that the Federal Army is advancing freedom for our people, or," he waved a hand, "whatever our public relations people have chosen as a slogan for this campaign. We are supposed to be seen as in the lead during the assault, taking the fight to the enemy, although of course we won't be allowed to take any actual risks that might make us look bad. Any of the tough, dirty jobs will be done by your Verd-kris troops."

"Don't worry about us, my people know what we signed up for on this op," Dave was able to say without any bitterness, he had been in the mercenary business long enough to have developed a thick skin. And a healthy level of cynicism.

"I am here because of that stupid Hard Knocks show," Nert was unquestionably bitter. "That is a human invention I am *not* grateful for."

"If it makes any difference, you were great on the show," Dave said. The Ruhar had taken the concept of a show about a National Football League training camp, and adapted it to follow a group of their soldiers who were candidates for the special forces program. The selection of the team that included Nert had not been random, that particular soldier was already a minor celebrity from his service with the Mavericks. "Is there anything I can do for you?"

"Accidentally shoot me in the foot," he held up one leg, "so I can avoid this shitshow?"

Dave laughed. "I'll see what I can do about that."

"It might not be too bad," Nert looked up at a dropship flying over the airfield, squinting into the afternoon sun. "I'll receive the script this evening."

"The *script*?"

Nert snorted. "Technically it is an 'Op Plan', but we all know it's a script, to make sure we put on a good show for the public back home. What the showrunners don't understand is, the enemy will *not* cooperate."

"Yeah, enemies can be dicks like that. Hey, I, um, have an idea, if you want to hear it."

"What?"

"The enemy in your, special forces puppet show-"

"It is not *my* show," Nert grimaced, then laughed. "It is definitely a puppet show."

"So, the enemy has to be Kristang?"

"If you are thinking my team should be shooting at Thuranin instead," Nert cocked his head, "that idea won't-"

"What if the enemy *looked* like warrior caste clan assholes, but you could trust them to follow the script?"

"I should know the Mavericks well enough to know what you're thinking, but-"

"Verd-kris. I'll get them dressed them up in warrior caste gear, and the audience back home won't know the difference."

Nert's mouth opened silently while he grasped the concept. "Your Verds would do that?"

"Play acting instead of getting shot at for real? Hell yes. Throw in a bonus to cover their loss of combat pay, and they'll jump at the chance."

Surkind Jates gave him the Force Ten Death Glare. "Say that again, Czajka, but *slowly*."

"As long as I'm signing your pay check, it's *Mister* Czajka to you," Dave retorted, nudging closed the door of the shipping container he was using as a temporary headquarters.

Jates doubled down on the glare.

"Or just 'Dave', OK? We have known each other long enough."

"Long enough for me to appreciate your sense of humor, but apparently I do not understand it at all, Mister Czajka."

"Call me Dave, please? That's an order," he added.

"Very well, *Dave*. My people are supposed to play the part of warrior caste soldiers?"

"Sure. You'll be wearing Kristang armor with Silver Claw clan markings, and carrying their weapons. Besides, to the Ruhar, all you lizards look the same."

"Do we all look the same to *you*?"

"Nah, I've gotten used to you. There's ugly, then there's *your* special kind of ugly."

Jates thumped his chest with a fist. "I am honored that you have chosen me as the instrument of your death."

"You think *I'm* anything but ugly?"

"Your people are soft and squishy, there's a difference."

"We can disagree on that."

"What in your tiny human mind made you believe *I* would agree to this idiocy?"

"It will be fun."

"As you know, I am *all about* fun."

"You know what I mean. What is the problem?"

"The problem is I am a soldier, not an, *actor*. Why should I do this?"

Dave bit back his instant response of 'because I told you to do it'. His mercenaries were in the job for money, certainly. They also had a strong sense of pride, and the entire outfit worked because they trusted him to look out for their best interests. "You will get more than triple your combat pay, with no risk." In negotiations with the producers of the news program that was following the Tezzak unit, Dave had argued that even with paying the Verds an exorbitant fee, the savings on reduced insurance costs would more than offset the wages.

"I am about *money* as much as I am about *fun*," Jates growled.

"Maybe not you," Dave shrugged. "What about the people in your platoon? You're going to make the decision for them, cut them out of the money? They won't be too happy with you about that."

"Yes, because I am all about popularity also."

"Let's try this another way. We'll be helping a friend."

"What *friend*?"

"Nert Dandurf."

Jates actually blinked. "Sarklast Dandurf is here?"

"Yeah, he's with one of the Tezzak squads. The one with the team of embedded journalists, as they're calling it now. If he has to go into action for real, he or his people could get hurt. If *we* have to go into action for real, some of us could get hurt, and this bullshit op on Hufustria is not worth the risk. There is a real fight coming, whether we can do anything directly against this Outsider I don't know, but I am keeping our powder dry for when it's really needed. Think of it this way: we are assisting an ally. Not with any actual military force, but boosting the morale of their civilians back home. And making their special forces look good. The whole point of this op is to foster stronger ties between the hamsters and humanity, and this program helps, whether we like it or not."

"I do not like it."

"Yeah, well, you and Nerty can form a club, because he fucking *hates* it."

Jates grinned, or he showed more of his fangs than usual. "I knew Dandurf was a proper soldier. Perhaps I should talk with him about this."

"Ah, he's busy, I'll see if I can set up a time for a call. If you're still on the fence about this, I've got a sweetener for you. The producers told me that for 'authenticity', they need at least a dozen genuine warrior caste corpses."

"Where are we supposed to get those?"

"When we get to Hufustria, I expect there will be plenty of young hothead warriors who are *not* happy they are losing their best and maybe only shot at climbing the clan hierarchy. We should find a target rich environment. I of course will be extremely busy once we're dirtside, so I am trusting you to lead your platoon and keep out of trouble. If you do get into trouble, I will officially not know anything about it, if you know what I mean."

Even more fangs were showing. "I believe I do know what you mean. Very well. I will do this for Sarklast Dandurf, not for any other reason."

"Your loyalty to me warms my heart."

"Don't push it, squishy man."

CHAPTER TWENTY THREE

Being at Jaguar again sucked. So close to my family, I could talk with them, but when I looked out a porthole at the planet, all I saw was a featureless fog. Margaret was upset that our boys apparently didn't miss seeing stars at night, to them Puptart's blanket was a comfort, not a trap. We talked about it, other parents also reported their children believed the usual nighttime starfield was full of monsters, and I really couldn't disagree with them.

Since I was at the space station while *Valkyrie* was in space dock to repair battle damage, we watched TV shows for family togetherness. We weren't actually together, of course, and the still limited bandwidth for communications meant we could only talk to each other for ten minutes. What we did was Margaret and I both hit 'Play' on a recorded TV show at the same time, then we chatted after the show was over. She was usually sitting on a cot in a corner of the community center, and I was in the cramped VIP quarters aboard the space station, so we made the best of a bad situation.

It sucked no matter what we did.

"Hey Joe," Skippy appeared on my desk, which was actually in the office of a guy assigned to Chatterji's staff. "I told you there was no important new information, from the ship that just arrived?"

"Yes, thank you for that. No news is good news."

"Um, that is not necessarily true."

"No news means there isn't yet another damned thing I need to worry about."

"Oh, good point. Although, hmm, it really only means you haven't heard about another thing you certainly *should* be worrying about, before it grows into a problem you can't fix."

"I'll take that as a win. Are you going to ruin my day now?"

"Um-"

"Whatever it is, just say it."

"OK. I did find something that at first I thought was simply an odd bit of trivia, but now I'm afraid this might be a sign of another major, major problem."

"Crap," I slapped the laptop closed. "Did you get a discount on a bushel of major problems, and need to use them up before they start to spoil and you have to throw them away?"

"Hey, don't shoot the messenger."

"You're right," I held up my hands. "Sorry. You said this only *might* be a problem? You don't know?"

"You tell me. Back during the time we were engaged in raiding the Pentivar archive, I heard reports of two Bosphuraq star carriers that were overdue. Later, two more birdbrain star carriers went missing."

"Yeah, I remember reading a Navy intel report about that. Speculation was the Thuranin had been hitting their rivals. All the missing space trucks were easy targets; they each only carried one or two destroyers or frigates at the time they disappeared. The Bosphuraq filed a formal complaint with the Maxohlx about it?"

"They did, and as expected, their concerned patrons told them to stop whining."

"Fighting within that coalition has to be good for us, right?"

"Ordinarily yes, but the Maxohlx are already feeling they are boxed in and slowly, inevitably losing their struggle for supremacy in the galaxy, so weakening their clients will only push the kitties tighter into an alliance with the Outsider."

"That is the major problem you're worried about?"

"Not even close. I just learned that the Bosphuraq have recently lost a fifth star carrier, in the same sector as the other four. With this last incident, we know that ship disappeared within a window of about three hours. A battleship strike group jumped away from the star carrier, leaving behind only a frigate. Three hours later, the strike group returned to the same location, but the mothership and the frigate weren't there. No debris was found, other than a flight recorder buoy that was ejected. Unfortunately, the buoy's memory was erased, so it couldn't provide any information, other than a time stamp that shows it was ejected fifty seven minutes before the strike group returned."

"So, whatever happened, it was quick. Were there any residual jump signatures, from other ships?"

"Good guess. Yes, one signature was detected, from a Maxohlx cruiser."

"Max- Why are the kitties stealing ships from their clients?"

"They aren't. I have access to the sensor data the strike group collected, the birdbrains are debating about whether to accuse their patrons of theft. You know how I can see things in sensor data, that others miss?"

"It is one of your many awesome-ness-es," I wasn't sure if I had pronounced that made-up word correctly. "What did you find?"

"A faint but distinct *Outsider* signature."

"Shit. Why the f- Why would it be shipjacking so many star carriers?"

"That is the question. I don't have any clue about what it is planning to do with those ships, other than it can't be anything good for us."

"You don't have any evidence the other four space trucks were also taken by the Outsider, do you?"

"No, the sites of their disappearances are unknown. Come on, Joe, it has to be the Outsider."

"We don't know that, but for now, let's assume it is."

"We should, especially because knowing the Outsider is involved got me looking into cases of other star carriers that have gone missing, since about the time the Outsider attempted to steal the Dogzilla Sentinel. Eight, Joe. There are another *eight* star carriers missing. One or two could simply be mechanical failure, or losses due to enemy action, but that makes a total of thirteen unaccounted for, and we know one of them was taken by the Outsider."

"Thirteen freakin' star carriers?"

"The number could be higher, I haven't been actively searching for similar incidents until recently. What could it be using them for?"

"Skippy, I can think of only one reason why the Outsider needs so many of that type of ship. It needs to move something. Something *big*."

"Uhtavio?" Kinsta called in a whisper, as he slowly opened the heavy door, wincing as the old hinges creaked.

"Kinsta, come in, come in," Scorandum called, flicking on a light to illuminate the dim room. "Oh, also, wipe your feet, please. You might have stepped in something unpleasant in the alley."

"Don't say my name so loud!" Kinsta hurriedly ducked into the room, feeling one of his shoes indeed slip on the already stained carpeting. "Why are we meeting here? This building is known to the Inquisitors for harboring an illegal drug lab on," he pointed to the also stained ceiling. "The second and third floors."

"Yes," Scorandum frowned. "That was a problem, mostly because the operators of the lab consumed too much of their own product, and neglected to pay the proper tribute to local law enforcement. They were on the verge of a very public raid, before the ECO got them current on their bribes. I must say, if they don't straighten out and fly right, we might need to engage a new operator."

Kinsta's eyes bulged. "You know about, and encourage, an illegal drug lab?"

"Oh, they are mostly harmless. Also, the lab draws the attention of the Inquisitors away from the unlicensed gambling operation that occupies the first floor," he reached back and tapped the wall. "It is the gambling that brings in the revenue. Oh, don't worry, the Ethics Office controls everything within two blocks around this building."

"I, I can't- Why are we meeting *here*?"

"I needed to do collections, so," Scorandum shrugged, "it was convenient."

"I don't believe this shit."

"Kinsta, as you are now back with the ECO, as a commander, and I am an admiral, it is again appropriate for you to address me as 'Sir'."

"I don't believe this shit, *Sir*," Kinsta sighed.

"Without the sigh. Or the eye roll," he jabbed an antenna at the subordinate officer. "I saw that."

"It takes some getting used to." Then he added a belated, "Sir."

"That's better. Now, two glasses," Scorandum opened a drawer, which popped up two crystal glasses, and a bottle of burgoze slowly rose from a recessed slot. "We should celebrate properly."

"What exactly are we celebrating?"

"Why, our first joint venture operation."

"Sir, we have worked together on many operations, this isn't the-"

"I meant, this is our first time working together while you are an Inquisitor, and I am an ECO agent."

"I am only pretending to work for the Office of Special Inquiries, and I was demoted from Inquisitor to Inquisition Administrative Clerk Second Class, thanks to *you*." With a rigid smile, he added, "Sir."

"Surely you can't still be sore about that, Kinsta. Your new career is so much more exciting."

"Exciting because I live in fear of a claw tapping my shoulder, and seeing an Inquisition squad waiting to arrest me."

"That will never happen."

"Never?"

"Probably never," the admiral shrugged his antennas. "Say, your odds of being caught would make for a juicy prop bet, I should-"

"Sir," Kinsta's antennas stood straight up. "Please don't."

"Eh, the Office would frown upon my taking that action anyway. Besides, in this operation, the Inquisitors *know* you are working with me."

"They *what*?"

"You weren't read in on this joint operation?"

"All I know is I was ordered to report to this office, to collect information from an Ethics official. It surprised me that I am meeting with you, Sir."

"That was no coincidence, I requested you specifically."

"No, *no*! You are going to blow my cover, Sir."

"No chance of that. Not this time, anyway. Kinsta, the Office of Special Inquiries requested me specifically."

"*Sir?*"

"Sit, Kinsta, sit," Scorandum waved a claw. Pouring from the bottle into a glass, he nudged the crystal across the table. "Drink this, it looks like you need it."

There was no argument. The drink was gone in one long gulp.

"Er," the admiral raised one antenna in alarm. "Perhaps you should pace yourself?"

"Another, please. If I am condemned to work with you again on what will no doubt be some sketchy scheme, I certainly don't want to be sober."

"It is a privilege to see how much you have grown, my young apprentice."

"Sir, I am no longer young, and I was never your apprentice."

"Ah, more than you might think." He half filled both glasses, thought about it, and added a splash to his own. "I need to catch up, you understand?"

"Perfectly, Sir." That time, Kinsta sipped the beverage. "This I have missed. Inquisitors tend to be so *dull*, and they have so many petty rules."

"No drinking during work hours?"

"They really don't even approve of drinking *after* hours," Kinsta frowned.

Scorandum peered over his glass at the obviously uncomfortable combination clerk and commander. "Why did you join such a bunch of stiff jerks?"

"I thought I was joining a group dedicated to honesty and integrity."

"I have bad news for you about that."

"Nothing you could tell me about the Inquisitors would make me have a lower opinion of them than I do of the Ethics office, Sir."

"You are here because the Inquisitors requested the ECO conduct an assassination for them."

Kinsta's reply was to choke and spray across the desk the burgoze he had just sipped. "Sir- Sorry- Sir, you shouldn't joke like that."

"It's not a joke."

"I don't believe this," the commander tried to clean the desk with his sleeve.

"You can choose not to believe it, yet you are here."

"Who will you will be assassinating, Sir? A Thuranin? A Bosphuraq?"

"Don't be silly. The Inquisitors only handle internal matters. Officially, that is. No, the target this time is-"

"*This* time?" Kinsta's eyes bulged. "This has happened before?"

Scorandum nodded. "Often enough that both offices have official intradepartmental forms for such requests. Which reminds me," he looked around the desk. "I am supposed to receive such a form from your office. Er, they didn't send anything with you?"

"My manager told me to get over here, and not to hurry about returning."

"It must be nice to be so valued by your employers."

"Sir, if I told you to 'Bite Me', would that be considered insubordination?"

"Yes," Scorandum laughed. "But I think we can both agree it would be hilarious."

"I'll save it for another occasion, then. The Inquisitors asked the ECO to murder a citizen? That seems, extreme."

"Extreme circumstances call for extreme measures. Are you familiar with a Kenten Argovian?"

"Everyone knows him, Sir."

"Then you will understand the request."

"But, but we-" Kinsta fell silent.

"Not only is Argovian guilty of tax evasion, not only has he committed multiple counts of extortion without a license, he has set up one of the largest loansharking operations in the Tuvilio sector."

"What is wrong with loansharking, Sir?"

"He is undercutting the rates of the licensed banks."

Kinsta whistled. "That *is* serious."

"It is. However, despite the Inquisitors having very publicly investigated him for seven years now, no charges have been filed."

"The Inquisitors want him murdered because they failed to convict him?"

"Partially. But even that could not justify such direct action. Argovian is very, very smart, and he is blackmailing some very powerful lawyers and high government officials. He believes he is untouchable by the Inquisitors, and he might be right about that. Unfortunately for him, his overconfidence has led him into dangerous territory. He recently brokered a deal that allows the Maxohlx to have a view into the ledgers of Central Wagering."

Kinsta gasped. "That is a death penalty offense! He should be arrested now!"

"He would be, if Central Wagering could allow the public to know their security has been breached. This needs to be taken care of *quietly*, that is why you and I are here."

"You," Kinsta shuddered. "Don't expect *me* to assassinate Argovian, I hope?"

"No, although watching *you* try to do that would be hilarious. As I said, this needs to be handled with discretion, for both the Ethics and Inquiries offices. A tragic accident is the best option. Some people," he took a sip of the fine burgoze. "Like to get creative in a situation like this, but I prefer the time-tested classics. Less risk, and the classics have a simple elegance to them. In this case, I wish to arrange something that hasn't been done in a while. Actually," he paused, the glass held in a claw. "It is something I haven't even heard of since you first came to the ECO."

Kinsta was instantly wary. "What is that, Sir?"

"A boating accident."

"*Boating?*"

"Boats can be very dangerous," the admiral jabbed an antenna for emphasis.

"But, Argovian lives on Rekonva, it is a desert world."

"Exactly! That is why he would never suspect a boat could be a threat."

"Er, there is very little open water on that planet, and none near Argovian's house."

"That is not quite true," Scorandum took a drink, tapped on a tablet, and displayed a satellite view of an oasis in the middle of a desert. "As an ostentatious display of his wealth, he installed moisture collectors around the property, and his house is now surrounded by lush gardens, complete with ponds."

Kinsta leaned forward, peering at the image. "None of those ponds appear to be large enough for a boat, Sir."

"That is why, when he is outside sitting on a bench near his favorite pond, which he does every sunrise, we will arrange for a boat to be dropped on his head from high altitude."

"A boat will fall out of the *sky*?"

"Quite so. It is a rather elegant solution, no? I am particularly proud of this one."

"Sir, that, it stretches the boundaries of believability."

"Stretches it until you can see right through it, yes."

"I, I assumed your office and mine, that is, both of the offices I work for," Kinsta frowned, his antennas drooping. "Would need what you call 'plausible deniability'."

"In most cases, that is true. In this case, the Inquisitors wish to send a loud and clear message, to any miscreant who is considering following Argovian into a life of deviant crime. You might say that our rules of engagement here require *im*plausible deniability."

"Oh, I am already too old for this shit."

"It is important that everyone strongly suspect the ECO was involved, and that the Inquisitors at least tacitly approved the operation, but that no one can *prove* anything."

"The case would be dismissed on a technicality?"

"That would be the ideal outcome, yes."

Kinsta shook his head, downed the rest of his drink, belched loudly, and slumped on the couch. "What is my part in this, Sir?"

"You need merely to bring this proposal," Scorandum slid a plastic folder across the desk. "To your leadership. Your *other* leadership, understood?"

"Regrettably, yes."

"The Inquisitors will either approve or reject the proposal. My expectation is they will approve, with some slight changes that makes them feel useful."

"After I deliver this, I won't need to *do* anything?"

"You should not do anything. Other than forgetting this meeting, this conversation, ever happened. Do you have any questions?"

"Just one, Sir."

"Speak freely, please."

"I'm not sure how much longer I can live a double life like this. Would it be possible for the Ethics office to drop something large and heavy on *my* head someday?"

I watched on a display from the space station, as *Valkyrie* was towed out of space dock. As usual, Skippy's optimistic estimate of the repair time had been off by two days, that really wasn't bad considering that the maintenance systems at Jaguar had no experience with the new version of *Valkyrie*. Reed was pleased with the repairs, being in the space dock again had given her an opportunity to address some issues that hadn't been done quite right during the overhaul. Anyway, I was staying aboard the station until she declared her ship was fully ready for combat, she didn't need me getting in the way.

Skippy had assisted with the repairs, complaining the entire time, and now he was bored, so he was my problem again. "All right, Joe," his avatar appeared on my borrowed desk in my borrowed office. "What's next?"

"Next? We just narrowly escaped an epic beat down, another beat down. The ship just completed major repairs, *again*. The crew is exhausted. And we accomplished exactly freakin' *nothing*."

"We foiled the Outsider's nefarious plan."

"Foiling a nefarious plan would be a great accomplishment, if you were Scooby Doo."

"If I was Scooby, *you* would be Shaggy. Also, I told you the Outsider wouldn't use its Starbreaker in the quarantine zone."

"Yeah, I'm convinced now that Starbreaker is more useful for keeping our Sentinels tied down protecting Earth and Jaguar. Bubba is stuck at Earth permanently. Puptart has to remain at Jaguar for another seven, eight months?"

"How do you figure that?"

"It has to slowly bleed energy off the blanket, that's almost six months."

"Yes but I *told* you, the star here has been destabilized. Unusually powerful, dangerous flares will continue for years. Puptart has to stay there for much longer, to shield the planet. My guess is, at least a year."

"Not if we pull the population off the surface, starting six months from now, when the blanket can be removed."

"Whoa." He blinked. 'You're talking about that again?"

"Yes, I have to talk about that. If we pull all the people off Jaguar, not only will the Outsider no longer have any incentive to strike there, we won't care if it does. That frees up Puptart to go hunting with us."

"So," he stared in disbelief. "Your plan is to do nothing against the Outsider, for more than six months?"

"I didn't say that. All I meant is, we have to start preparing now to evac people off Jaguar once the blanket is fully drained, and Puptart can deactivate the thing."

"Tell me, Mr. Genius, where are all those people supposed to go?"

"Most will go back to Earth. I know a sudden surge of population will strain resources, but the UN has more than six months to get ready. We could also disperse Jaguar residents to Paradise, and other shared colony worlds. The Verds, for example, would love to have more humans living on Karlashjivole. Our people there now are basically human shields." That was true, but the relationship wasn't as one-sided as it sounds. The Verds had offered humans free transport to Karlashjivole, free housing, and a monthly stipend to supplement whatever income they had from Earth. Mostly, the offer was attractive to retirees who could rely on pensions or other fixed income. The Verds had set aside a chain of tropical islands for the human colony, plus a mountain area that had great skiing with powdery snow. The Verds had great timing, a lot of people on Earth were tired of constant threats and disruptions since Columbus Day. Fourteen thousand mostly retirees moved there, and word got back to Earth about the beautiful, unspoiled tropical paradise, the great skiing, and cheap travel packages to attractions all around the planet. Last time I checked, something like forty thousand humans lived there permanently, with another ten thousand of our people spending time there for vacations.

No, I am not a paid promotional spokesman for the Karlashjivole Chamber of Commerce, I have never been to that rock. Maybe someday I'll visit, when my family gets tired of vacations on fabulous places like Newark. My point is, if we had to pull everyone off Jaguar, the civilians would have options.

"Whatevs," he shrugged. "It's not my problem."

"Good."

"Sure. As long as you're cool with getting another visit from the Law of Unintended Consequences, it's all cool."

"What do you mean?" I asked, assuming he was just screwing with me.

"It should be obvious," he sniffed. "If you remove Jaguar from the target list, and we take Puptart out hunting with us, that pretty much guarantees the Outsider will drop a Starbreaker on your Sun."

"Oh shit." He hadn't been joking, that was obvious. It was obvious *after* he said it. "I know the bullshit we told Def Com, can Bubba actually stop it from deploying a Starbreaker?"

"Shmaybe. I told you, Sentinels are weapons, they were never intended be used for protecting anything."

"Great. Fantastic. My already wonderful day has gotten *even better*."

"Ah, it might not be so bad anyway. The Outsider is one for two so far in triggering Elder weapons, but if we are extremely lucky, it won't be able to light off the second one."

"Uh, what?"

"Oops."

"*Oops*? What the f-"

"Pay no attention to the man behind the curtain." His avatar faded out.

"You're not getting away with that shit. You come back here right now."

The avatar reappeared, but he was Obi Wan Skippy, with brown robes and a beard. He did the two-finger Jedi wave with, "These aren't the droids you're looking for."

"Don't try a Jedi mind trick on me. What did you mean 'Oops'?"

"Ugh." The avatar changed back to his gaudy grand admiral uniform. "Can I get a Mulligan? You know, like in golf when you get to do over a shot without a penalty?"

"Take a guess about that. You think the Outsider can't use the other Starbreaker?"

"Joe, you have put me in a very difficult position."

"You got yourself into this mess. What is it you don't want to tell me?"

"To explain that, I would have to tell you, which I shouldn't. This knowledge is extremely dangerous."

"I know about," I checked that the green light above the office door was lit, the door was shut and supposedly the noise-cancelling feature of the door would prevent anyone in the passageway hearing me speak. Even so, I spoke softly. "The probability field. What secret could be more dangerous than that?"

"Again, if I even give you a hint, you might figure out what-"

"What I have figured out so far is that Elder weapons are not entirely reliable."

"Oh no. That is already too-"

"Since a hundred percent of the Elder weapons *we* triggered worked properly, the issue is not with the weapons themselves, so it must depend on whether whoever activates the weapons knows the proper protocols, or procedure or whatever."

"Crap. Why are you so freakin' smart when you shouldn't be?"

"Talk, beer can. I already know you believe the Outsider got lucky at Jaguar. Whatever that thing actually is, we know it is way smarter than the kitties or spiders. So, if the Outsider isn't guaranteed to get a 'Boom' when it tries to trigger an Elder weapon, that means the strategic arsenals of the senior species are not even close to reliable."

"You can't tell anyone about this."

"You should have told me this a long time ago!"

"I couldn't."

"You do understand that to do my job, for me to be a useful partner to your extreme awesomeness," I fed his ego. "I need information. Damn it, I have been reluctant to confront the Maxohlx because there was too much risk they would hit *Valkyrie* with an Elder shipkiller nuke, and then capture you. Now you're telling me if the kitties fire a weapon at us, it might fizzle out? Be a dud?"

"It probably won't fizzle at all. It will refuse the trigger command and do nothing."

"Oh my- So, I have been worried for *nothing*? Do you know how much sleep I lost?"

"It's not for nothing, Joe," he sighed, and he used my name rather than calling me 'dumdum' or 'knucklehead', or 'numbskull'. He was being serious for a change, deadly serious. "If the kitties decide to use Elder weapons against us, they will simply bring enough weapons to the party so they can be confident at least one of them will activate."

"Shit."

"Can you understand why I was reluctant to tell you about this?"

"You weren't just reluctant, you concealed vital intel from me."

"*You* are not the problem."

"Huh?"

"I *trust* you, numbskull. Who I do not trust are the politicians who run your homeworld, and the billions of shortsighted, idiot monkeys who support them. Before we started this magical mystery tour, the galaxy was dominated by two species who kept a war going to benefit themselves. That war raged on endlessly but at a low level, it never threatened to escalate into an apocalypse because there was a strategic balance between the senior species. Now, there are *three* species who have Elder weapons. Your leaders already feel they have no responsibility to become involved in the dirty work of keeping the galaxy stable, but they certainly love all the benefits of having power. My fear is if your people knew they had the only reliable arsenal of Elder weapons, humans could replace the Maxohlx as the bullies of the Milky Way."

"That wouldn't happen."

"Really? You are sure about that?"

"I won't let it happen."

"*You* won't be here forever."

"Yeah, but you will."

"Maybe not so much."

"Uh," I felt a chill. "Is there something wrong with you?"

"I am fine. I am eternal, or close enough to it. Once you are," his face briefly twisted in anguish, "inevitably gone from us, I might not hang around the monkeys for long."

"Where would you go?"

"Um, it's not something I have really thought about. I would protect your boys, of course. Your extended family also. I could spend some time with the beetles?"

"No way, Skippy. They are too much like you. You would get bored."

"You're probably right. As you know, I like underdogs. Maybe I'll go hang with the Urgar for a while. They already worship me."

"I have bad news for you about that."

"Yes, I know they only pretend to suck up to me, but that's good enough for now."

"I'm still here now, can we talk about your long-term career plans later? We need to stop the Outsider, or there won't be a long-term anything for anyone."

"Sure, whatevs."

"Back to the subject: what percentage of Elder weapons can the kitties and spiders actually use?"

"Well, keep in mind they have been conducting exhaustive research since the last time either of them actually triggered a strategic weapon."

"I got that."

"Back then, the Maxohlx were able to get less than nine percent of their weapons to activate. The Rindhalu managed twelve percent."

"Whoa. The best they can do is twelve percent reliability?"

"My estimate is now, the kitties and spiders each could get roughly seventeen percent of their arsenal to activate."

"That's not encouraging. Or, it is encouraging, for us. How many of our weapons are reliable?"

"One hundred percent."

"Yeah, because *you* are the trigger."

"No. Remember, I still have the hard restrictions that were built into my matrix. I can't use weapons. What I have done is modify the authenticator mechanism in all of the Elder weapons controlled by UN Def Com, so you monkeys have independent authority to make your strategic devices go 'Boom'. It had to be that way, or your arsenal would be rendered useless for enforcing a Mutual Assured Destruction policy."

"I think the ship has sailed on that policy anyway. Explain to me why, what I really mean is *how*, the seniors can get some of their weapons to work, but not most of them?"

"It's because they have no idea what they're doing. Each of the seniors has been successful in removing the trigger mechanism, which includes the authenticator module, and they have been successful in getting the triggers to activate reliably. But, when the triggers are reinstalled in their host weapon, most of them don't work."

"Right. Why not?"

"The authenticators of a small percentage of weapons were bypassed by mistake, while the seniors were fumbling around with the triggers. It's a flaw in the design, the Elder engineers should be very embarrassed. I guess they can be forgiven for not foreseeing that filthy meatsacks would be playing with their toys long after the Elders ascended."

"So, it's a hardware issue?"

"No, it's software. Not software the way you understand it, the-"

"OK, sure. Somehow, by fucking around with the triggers, they accidentally input the correct authentication?"

"Again, no. The Elders designed the authenticators to assure an enemy could not remotely take control of a weapon, to activate it, or disable it. They never imagined someone physically taking possession of a weapon, and removing the trigger mechanism. That is probably why it is so easy to safely remove a trigger, it was optimized to prevent accidental activation. Otherwise the things would have gone 'Boom' the instant someone screwed with the cover over the trigger mechanism."

"This software that's not software, uh, so," I asked casually, while clenching a fist to control my excitement. "Is that something you could hack into?"

"Oh sure, easy. Obviously, I have already modified the authentication protocols so you monkeys can trigger your weapons."

"Cool, cool. Hey, uh, is it possible you could remotely disable an Elder weapon, if someone fired it at us?"

"Oh. I see what you mean. Sorry, no, I can't do it that quickly. It's a delicate thing, the real issue is I would have to be close, very close, to engage the authenticator directly. By the time I got close enough, I assume the bad guys would have fired the weapon. Oh also, once the weapon is fired, changes are locked out, sorry."

"Not need to say sorry," I concealed my disappointment with a smile. "You do so many awesome things."

"That is true. It's too bad, actually. The process of properly activating an Elder weapon is complicated and takes substantial time. But for me to screw up the mechanism so no one could use a weapon? That takes," he snapped his fingers and made a convincing sound. "No time at all, really."

"Unfortunately, we can't sneak you into every arsenal where the kitties and spiders store their toys."

"Especially since both species have their strategic arsenals widely dispersed for security," he agreed.

"Do we know where those weapons are?"

"Eh, the majority of them, yes. Neither side located strategic armories in any of their major star systems, they are both afraid of an accidental activation. All of the armories have heavy security, and information about them is compartmentalized, that data is not even stored in the official archives. You can forget about sneaking me into an armory, they are shielded with powerful disruptor fields, that would prevent us from jumping in with a DeLorean."

"What about a microwormhole?"

"It's possible, if we can dedicate more than a week at each site, and we get *super* lucky? Joe, it's just not worth the time and effort."

"OK. Check my math, please. A seventeen percent success rate at triggering strategic weapons means the kitties would need to fire, six weapons to be sure of one activating?"

"Correct. Also, I am impressed you did that math in your head."

"I had a lot of arithmetic practice helping my boys with their homework." What I didn't say was Jeremy and Rene were a lot smarter than I was at the same age, and my ability to help with homework had an expiration date. Like, soon. "If the kitties decide to attack *Valkyrie* with Elder weapons, they will *commit* to it. Bring double or triple the number of weapons to the party."

"That is a safe bet, yes."

"You started this by asking me what is next? I don't know what we should do next, but I do know one thing has not changed: we can't risk tangling with the Maxohlx again. The risk of losing you is unacceptable."

"We have to act. I have to act, you know that."

"Yeah, and I'm beginning to think the Outsider also knows that."

"What? How do-"

"It is counting on you being obsessed with finding it and killing it."

"I am not obsessed, I am simply doing the right thing to-"

"Hey Captain Ahab, you *are* obsessed, and it's not your fault. You were programmed to stop the Outsider at all costs." From the beginning, Skippy had protested my intention to fight what we now know is the Outsider, but it was he who kept insisting we act against the thing. Like, he had demanded that I take *Valkyrie* into the nanoplague quarantine zone.

With hands on his hips, he demanded, "You have a problem with that?"

"I have a problem with the way you're approaching the issue. Too many times, I have reacted to the enemy, and acted before I developed an overall strategy."

"That is kind of your thing."

"That's what you're doing now, Skippy. The Outsider is counting on you being so eager to attack, and not taking time to think about how we might get *it* to react to us."

"Whatever. Until you dream up a way to find the Outsider, or you figure out its plan, this discussion is a waste of time."

"We got off track. So, I'm going to break down Barney style what you told me. The two seniors can't reliably use their Elder weapons, and you can disable them, but you need to get close to a device before it is launched. Is that right?"

"Eh, basically, yes."

"OK. So, all I need to do is get you close to every Elder weapon in the arsenals of the Maxohlx and Rindhalu."

"I don't foresee *any* problem with that," Skippy rolled his eyes.

I often, too often, say the impossible is merely a speed bump to the Merry Band of Pirates. My job is difficult enough, without me adding more items on my To Do list. Did we really have to disable the Elder weapons of the seniors?

Yes, damn it, we did. The Maxohlx were helping the Outsider, and I couldn't risk going into a fight with them, now that they were likely to deploy Elder weapons against *Valkyrie*.

We didn't know how to find the Outsider, we had to wait for it to contact us, and any such contact would be another ambush. We had no way to figure out what it was planning to do next. And, now we couldn't act against its local partner, the idiot Maxohlx.

My job sucks.

CHAPTER TWENTY FOUR

My eyes flew open and I was instantly awake. A glance at my phone showed it was oh two thirty seven in the morning. You know how sometimes you wake up in the middle of the night and you're alert, more alert than if you slept for another four hours? That was me. I was *awake*. Not sleepy at all. "Skippy," I called as I tapped the icon on my phone to turn on the lights, and then had a moment of disorientation when I realized I was still aboard the Jaguar space station.

"Yes, Joe?" He responded, speaking in soft tones, almost a whisper.

"I need to talk about something."

"OK," his voice was barely audible. "Make a note of it, and we'll talk after you get coffee and breakfast."

"Uh, why are you whispering?"

"You get pissy when you are woken up in the middle of the night."

"I only get pissed off when you wake me up to talk about some stupid thing, like the freakin' Care Bears."

"Hey, that 'Care Bear Stare', when they radiate light from the symbols on their tummies is *demonic*, it brainwashes children."

"Oh, not *this* shit again. My sister's kids love the Care Bears."

"Of course they do, because they have been programmed and enslaved by those-"

"Skippy, I promise you can wake me up any other night to go on one of your insane, incoherent rants, but not *now*. There is an important question I need to ask before I forget all about it, OK?"

"Fine. If you don't care about your own children and your nieces and nephew, why should I bother with-"

"To hack into an Elder weapon and change its authenticator software protocols or whatever, you need to be close to it?"

"Yes. Within my presence, and the process takes an extended time. It's not me that is the problem, the authenticator was designed to resist tampering, I have to get through multiple levels of security. Why do you ask?"

"Is there any way you could do it through a microwormhole?"

"Nope. There wouldn't be enough bandwidth."

I had expected his negative answer, so I asked, "What about if you used more than one microwormhole?"

"Nopity nope. You have no concept of the bandwidth required. Even if I use all the microwormholes I am capable of creating and maintaining, the throughput of my presence would be a trickle, while I need a *river*. I mean like, the Amazon."

"Shit." My confidence was foolish. "Well, it looks like I woke up for nothing."

"It's not your fault, Joe."

"Thanks."

"Your ignorance is a handicap you can't overcome."

"Your arrogance is a handicap you *should* overcome."

"It's not really arrogance if I'm simply stating facts. Listen, numbskull, to communicate with an AI inside an Elder strategic weapon requires the presence of another Elder AI, a powerful AI like myself. An Elder starship could do it, although the control system of an Elder starship would *not* ever do that, so the whole effort would be a waste of time."

"Plus, we don't currently have an Elder starship."

"Well, there is that issue, yes. Is that all you wanted to talk about?"

"Yes, sorry."

"Should I turn down the lights in your cabin, or do you want coffee delivered?"

"No coffee. I was all wide awake and happy, now I'm just depressed."

"For that condition, most humans would self-administer a depressant. Should I have a bot deliver a bottle of whisky?"

"Thank you, no," I flopped my head back on the pillow, certain I would dream about Care Bears. Big, scary multi-colored stuffed bears with claws and big teeth. "If it can't be done, it can't be done. I can get almost another three hours of sleep. Thanks for- Holy shit."

"What? Oh no," he groaned. "You have that stupid look on your face again."

"Reprograming an Elder weapon requires a powerful Elder AI?"

"That is what I said, yes. Ugh. If you are thinking we can find another master control AI that is still alive out there, you can forget about-"

"Nah. We don't need one."

"Um, then I do not see how-"

"You really can't guess what I'm thinking?"

"Joe, I am *frightened* to imagine what is going on in that disorganized sack of mush inside your skull. Please do not ever reveal your so-called thought process to me, I would be scarred for life. My matrix might sustain permanent and fatal damage."

"I'll just tell you, then."

"That's probably the best option."

"Could the AI of a wormhole network controller hack into an Elder weapon?"

"*Huuuuuuh*," he gasped. "Yes actually and, this is *so* indescribably delicious, your idea is clever and also completely impractical. Ha! You think you are so incredibly smart, but-"

"Don't bother me about details, Skippy, that's your job."

"Ugh. Do you not even-"

"Explain *why* it can't happen."

"Time, Joe. The issue is *time*. The transit from one side of a wormhole to the other side is instantaneous. Well, not really, but close enough for you meatsacks. The network controller would not have enough time to engage with an Elder weapon, while the starship carrying it is passing through."

"OK, Mister Smartypants, what if the job happened in stages? Each time an Elder weapon passed through a wormhole, the controller could-"

"Ha! Wow, that is truly one of your dumber ideas, I need to make a note of that. Forget it, knucklehead. Each time the weapon transited a wormhole, the controller AI would have to start the process from the beginning. It would be like listening to the first stanza of a song, over and over and over-"

"I get the idea."

"Can you imagine having to listen to the intro of the same song a hundred freakin' times? Especially if it's something that is super annoying, like the opening of 'Hooked on a Feeling'."

"Please don't sing the-"

"Ooga chaka ooga chaka ooga ooga ooga chaka-"

"Please stop."

"I'll do it again. Ooga chaka ooga-"

"*Stop*! That is like, my great-grandparents music anyway. How do you even know that freakin' song?"

"I Googled 'Most annoying songs ever' and that one popped up."

"You Googled that, why?"

"For a golden opportunity like this. Hey! I can also sing the classic annoying song 'Having My Baby', if you like."

"I would not like. Skippy, if we could ever travel to another part of the Multiverse, I would select a universe where *that* fucking song was never written."

"Hmm. Theoretically, there are universes that consist of nothing but cold, dark, empty space."

"Sounds great, I want to reserve a spot there. Shit. I *did* think I was being clever. It's my own stupid fault for not remembering that there is no distance, and therefore no time between wormhole event horizons."

"As far as you know, yes."

"What do you mean?"

"The length, and transit time, is not exactly zero. It's complicated. Darn, it's too bad your idea wouldn't work, I would love to remotely hack into those weapons. What I would truly love it seeing the expressions on the Maxohlx's furry faces when they try to fire a weapon at us, and discover they are all duds, hee hee."

"That would be cool," I chuckled. "Well, I guess I can only stretch a clever idea so far, and this one isn't gonna work."

"It won't. The – Huh."

"Huh, what?" I felt a surge of adrenaline.

"It's just- Hmm."

From long experience, I knew it is best to leave Skippy alone while he is pondering a new idea, because his pondering process can be *ponderous*.

"I'm going to station's cafeteria for coffee," I yawned, setting my feet on the deck.

"Yeah, do, um, whatever."

A few minutes later, I slowly strolled to the door of my cabin, sipping hot coffee. The coffee had been sitting the pot for a while since it was the middle of the night, making it extra bitter. All I cared about was the caffeine. All I really cared about was why Skippy had done one of his 'Huh's, where he realized something that surprised him.

Hopefully he hadn't experienced a revelation about the Care Bears. Or the Smurfs.

"Hey, Skippy. What's up?"

"Hi, Joe. Um, I might have something."

"An idea?"

"Yes. A way to make your moronic concept workable. Except, hmm, no. No, it won't work. It *could* work, there's just no way to do it."

"Walk me through it, please."

"OK so, not even Barney himself could dumb this down enough for you to understand, so I'll do the best I can."

"I appreciate it."

"The distance between wormhole event horizons is not zero, and the transit time is also not zero."

"Uh huh, I knew that."

"No, you did not," he scoffed.

"I *did* know, because the far end of a jump wormhole is slightly *back* in time."

"Only from the instant that event horizon was established but," he sighed. "You are correct. Although that has no connection to what I am talking about. Anywho, there is a way for transit time to be extended. Even extended substantially."

"Like how long?"

"To you, it would feel like only a few seconds. Technically, people aboard a starship transiting such an extended-length wormhole would not experience any difference in time, your meatsack senses couldn't comprehend the time slip."

"Would the ship's AI know the time is longer than it should be?"

"Um, hmm, good question. Rindhalu ship AIs might understand something odd has occurred, though they would have to be looking for anything unusual. The AIs of Maxohlx ships would not have any clue anything was different from a normal transition."

"Great! How would this work?"

"That's the problem. It won't work. The idea is great in theory, but there is no way to actually do it, as a practical matter."

"Walk me through it, please."

"Without using math?"

"No math, please. Just tell me the practical part of the problem."

"You realize this is like describing an ocean by saying it is 'wet'?"

"Talk, beer can."

"The problem is the initial setup. Once I have uploaded the code- It's not *code*, but-"

"I get that."

"Once the code is resident in a wormhole network controller, it will extend the transit time for any ship that is carrying an active Elder weapon."

"What do you mean, 'active'?"

"One that isn't already a dud. Where the weapon's control system is operational."

"OK, good. I know that each wormhole scans a transiting ship for hazards, you are adding Elder weapons to the hazard list."

"Yes, exactly. When an Elder weapon is detected, a protocol will be invoked by the network controller, and it will hack into and disable that weapon's authenticator system. Well, not *disable* the thing. Revise the trigger sequence so no unauthorized entities can use the weapon."

"Cool! Does that include the Outsider? It won't be able to use its Starbreaker?"

"Unfortunately, that is unlikely. I strongly suspect the Outsider can enable the trigger mechanism directly, the same way I set up weapons for you to fire."

"Shit. Is that something the Outsider could teach the kitties to do?"

"No way," he snorted. "It's not a method, it's a *capability*. The kitties might understand exactly what is needed, they still wouldn't be able to duplicate the process. Actually, no, the stupid kitties would have no clue what the Outsider was trying to explain."

"So, there is no way for a wormhole controller to disable the Starbreaker the Outsider has, but it could render any other Elder weapons inert?"

"Correct. Well, except for any Elder weapons transiting a wormhole with me, since I am obviously an authorized user. I still can't *use* weapons, I am authorized to have them in my custody."

"Gotcha. OK, so far, I understand this process will work the way we want, after you have uploaded the code that is not code."

"Correct."

"This all sounds great, but there are a lot of wormhole networks out there. We can't go to all of them. I guess we could select the networks that connect near Earth and-"

"What? No, dumdum. Once I upload the code, which is really an enhanced security setting, it will propagate across *all* of the wormhole networks."

"Oh. Wow. That is awesome."

"It's me, so-"

"Could we start with the network that includes the Backstop wormhole near Earth?"

"Um, it would be best to upload the code on a major network, one that spans a large area and is central to the overall architecture of the system. That way, the update will propagate more quickly. A few days, at most."

"This is a *great* idea, Skippy," I gave him two thumbs up. "We should do this as soon as a possible."

"Hey, I would love that, it simply can't happen."

"What is the problem?"

"*Time*."

"But you said-"

"Not time during an Elder weapon's transit. The time it will take for me to upload code that will permanently adjust the operating parameters of a wormhole network controller."

"Hey, we can park the ship near an event horizon, and hang out there as long as you want. I can ask Gasquet set up a videogame tournament or something to keep the crew busy."

"Thanks, but I can't be near a wormhole while uploading the code. I have to be *inside* it."

"You transit wormholes with no problem all the time, so why-"

"It will take me forty six minutes to establish a link with the network controller, upload the code, and verify it is functioning correctly."

"Uh, I assume you can't ask the controller to stall the transit, while you're in there?"

"Actually, I can."

"Then what is the-"

"OK technically, the actual problem isn't time, it's *mass*. To delay a transit that long requires the wormhole to contain minimum mass. Something the size of *Valkyrie* would be ejected quickly to keep the wormhole stable, it- Do you care to hear the physics involved?"

"I would prefer not to, if that's OK with you. So, we fly through in a dropship, we have done that before."

"Nope. Still too much mass."

"What if we stripped a dropship of everything that-"

"Too. Much. Mass."

"Whoa. What is the limit?"

"Two hundred and seventeen kilograms. That has to include my own mass, which I can keep stable at twelve kilograms inside the environment of a wormhole. I can keep my mass stable for no longer than fifty seven minutes. After that, I might go 'Boom'."

"Let's try to avoid that. Two hundred and seventeen kilos, what do we have that- Hey, can't we just shoot you out of a missile tube, all by yourself?"

"Unfortunately no, hence why I described this as an unsolvable problem. My insertion through the event horizon must be slow and precise, so something has to guide me, and update the approach angle in real time. Then, whatever vehicle carries me in there must release my canister, so I can upload the code."

"Uh, that doesn't sound like a good idea. You would be trapped in the-"

"I would not be trapped. Once I am done, I will instruct the wormhole to return to normal operation. Then I will emerge from the far event horizon."

"Releasing you still isn't a good idea, what if-"

"The *initial* mass must be under two hundred and seventeen kilos. Once I establish a link with the controller to severely extend the transit time, the mass inside the wormhole has to be below *fourteen* kilograms."

"Shit. OK, uh, no problem, we can fabricate a drone to carry you in, and-"

"Um, no, I considered that and it that won't work either. Conditions inside a delayed-time wormhole will seriously dork up the substrate of any control system. That is why I said there is just no way to do it."

"Hmm. *Any* control system?"

"Yes. It's an electrical engineering thing I could explain, if you understood anything about physics. The way electrons are bound in the substrate-"

"What about me?"

"Um, what about you?"

"Could *I* do it?"

"Do what?"

"Carry you in there, and release you."

"You."

"Yeah, me. In a spacesuit. Since you now understand that humans need spacesuits to survive in space."

"Oh, shut up. How do you imagine this could possibly work?"

"I get into a lightweight environment suit and-"

"It can't be *that* lightweight, dumdum. The Cherenkov radiation would fry you."

"We will include a shield generator."

"It will have to be a powerful generator."

"Yes, but it only needs to work for a short time, right?"

"Huh. Hmm. I suppose you're right about that. How do you propose to adjust our angle of approach? You're not planning to flap your arms, I hope?"

"I'll use a jetpack, you ass. It also only needs to operate for a short time."

"Me, you, a spacesuit, a shield generator, *and* a jetpack, all under two hundred and seventeen kilos. That is never gonna happen. The powercells alone for the shield would mass more than- Huh."

"Keep going."

"Well, powercells would only need to power the shield for the transition through the event horizon. Once we're inside, collectors can harvest energy from the wormhole itself."

"Cool. Could a microwave laser beam from *Valkyrie* feed power to the shield and jetpack as we approach? That way, all we need to carry is an antenna to receive the microwaves."

"That is actually good thinking," he stared at me. "Who are you, and what have you done with Joe Bishop?"

"You are hilarious. Next question: what about *this* substrate?" I tapped my head.

"You will go unconscious, of course. But, hmm, biological substrate is not affected in the same way. You monkeys get nauseous and experience headaches after going through wormholes, but you remain conscious and functional. Unlike the ship, your systems don't have to reset from spatial distortion. Of course, when I say 'functional', I am being generous."

"Thanks for the compliment. We can do this, then?"

"In theory, yes."

"Great," I slapped my knee. "Design and fabricate a spacesuit for me, and a jetpack, antenna, all that stuff."

"I have to do all the work?"

"Unless you trust me to do it?"

"Um, no."

"Besides, I need to spend my time practicing to fly the approach, in the simulator you're going to design, fabricate, and program for me."

"I have to do all that also?"

"You don't, if you're OK with me screwing up the insertion."

"I would not be OK with that."

"Seriously," I stood up, and poured the rest of the cold coffee into my bathroom sink, no way could I drink it. "Should someone else fly you in there? We have plenty of qualified pilots aboard the ship."

"I would prefer almost *anyone* else to be carrying me, but," he sighed. "If something goes wrong at the last second, I need you to be there."

"See? You do trust me."

"I *meant*, if something goes horribly wrong at the last second, I want to say 'I told you so' to your stupid face, knucklehead."

"You are such a- You know what? I would want to do the same," I admitted.

"Joe, this is amazing. I came to you with an unsolvable problem, and *once again*, you found a solution."

"*We* found a solution."

"That is true. It was mostly me, with you contributing only your usual 'Duh what about this'?"

"I am already praying for that wormhole to tear us both apart."

"Come on, Joe. You and me, just the two of us, staring death in the face again. *Your* death, of course. It will be like the old times."

"The old times *sucked*."

"I can't argue with that. Well, I'll contact Reed and inform her-"

"Whoa, no! Do not do that."

"Um, you are not planning to fly *Valkyrie* all by yourself, I hope?"

"No, but we can't tell anyone about any of this."

"When we leave the ship in a spacesuit and a funky jetpack, we can't just tell the crew you are installing a new air freshener in the wormhole."

"If the mission goes sideways, I will need an air freshener in my spacesuit. Listen, Skippy, I will throw together some bullshit cover story about why we need to go into a wormhole. You need to, uh, install software to track the Outsider, or something like that. Uh, hey, is that something you could do?"

"Hmm. Unfortunately, while that is a great idea, it won't work. While I was constructed and programmed to recognize the distinctive signature of Outsider technology, wormhole controllers lack the sensors to detect whether an Outsider is aboard a transiting ship."

"Shit. If we know the signature of the *ship* it's using, would the wormhole networks be able to track it?"

"Yes."

"Great, then-"

"Unless the Outsider masks the signature of the ship, which it can totally do."

"Ah, forget that idea, then."

"No, I can request the networks to look for drive and hull signatures of ships the Outsider is known to be using. It's unlikely we will get any useful information, but it's worth a shot."

"Please do that also, thanks. Back to what I said: we can't let anyone know the real reason we're doing this."

"Ugh. Once again, I am demonstrating extreme awesomeness, and I can't tell anyone about it?"

"Sorry, you can't."

"Why not?" He demanded.

"Think about it. *You* described the problem."

"I did?"

"Yes. Right now, a bunch of ignorant monkey politicians have Sentinels to hide behind, and their fingers on an arsenal of Elder weapons. What will happen if those monkeys learn the two senior species do *not* actually have any operational Elder weapons, and we have nothing to fear from anyone? That we can do pretty much anything we want, and no one can stop us?"

"Oooooh, nothing good. That is a very good point, Joe. Darn it, filthy monkeys have ruined my day again. You are wrong about one thing, by the way."

"What?"

"*I* will stop your people, if they become the next group of assholes who seek to rule the galaxy."

"Thanks for that. All right, no way am I getting back to sleep now, I need to talk with Chatterji's staff. Ah, that can wait until morning, I should talk with him directly about this."

"About what?"

"Borrowing at least a battlegroup, to come with us. We need more than just *Valkyrie*, right? We should have ships on both sides of the wormhole?"

"Hmm, that is a good point. Also, since the recovery ship will be stationary and vulnerable, best to bring some firepower with us."

"I'll talk with Chatterji about it, tell him what we need."

"He won't like it, Joe."

"You're wrong about that, Skippy. He *will* like it, and the crew of the ships will be pumped to go with us. They have been sitting up here, powerless to do anything. We'll give them a chance to see action, an opportunity to *do* something."

"I suppose you know more about monkeys than I do."

"All right," I gulped the last of the bitter coffee. "I'm going to log some quality time in the station's jetpack simulator. Upload the settings for the jetpack I'll be using, when you have the thing designed."

"Oh sure. You have fun, while I do all the work."

"You know the saying? With extreme awesomeness comes extreme responsibility."

"It comes with extreme *suckitude*," he grumbled.

"Cut! Cut! *CUT!*" The director waved at the camera drones, shouting though since everyone involved was wearing an earpiece, a whisper would have been sufficient. "What the fuck was *that?*"

"The mother of all clusterfucks, is what it was," Nert grunted as he forced his supposedly dead powered armor to lift him off the ground. Around him, the operators of his unit were also simulating death, their suits having lost power as a response to being tagged by simulated weapons fire.

"None of this was in the script!" The director ran across the field, furiously jabbing a finger at Jates, who was stepping through a hole blasted through a concrete wall. "*You* are supposed to be dead!"

The big Verd-kris stood impassively, muzzle of his rifle pointed at the ground, finger off the trigger though the weapon was not loaded. "You insisted on 'authenticity'. In a real fight between my people and these," he shook his head at the Tezzak operators, who were all even more disgusted than the victorious Verd-kris were. "These professional soldiers, what you saw would be the result. It is not any of your fault," Jates extended an arm to help Nert stand up. "You did the best you could."

"That wasn't good enough," Nert took off his helmet and pressed the button to reset all mech suits in his unit, taking them out of simulation mode.

"The problem was not with your people. You followed the script. Would you ever use those tactics in combat, against a Kristang force?"

"Hell no," Nert snorted.

Both professional soldiers looked at the director. "That isn't the point!" Escott Poindit threw up his hands. "Real combat happens too fast for the audience to follow, and it is messy! I want to tell a nice story here, and your chain of command," he jabbed a finger at Nert, "is on board with the program. Are you onboard, or do I need to find another unit?"

"I am not inflicting this nonsense on anyone else," Nert whispered to Jates. "We are onboard, Mr. Poindit. Can we try it again, *our* way?"

"Will it be another clusterfuck?"

"Yes, but in our favor," Nert promised.

"How long will it take to reset the battlefield?" The director stared in dismay at the holes blown in walls, the thick smoke billowing from every building in the abandoned village that had been chosen for the exercise. "I have a, medical therapy session, scheduled in just over an hour."

"You should certainly keep your therapy appointment," Nert knew he had plenty of time. The director would be in his fancy trailer with one of the lovely young female assistants for at least two hours, longer if recreational substances were involved. "We will be ready to go when you decide the light is good," he looked at the sky.

Poindit considered for a moment. "All right, you get *one* more shot at this, then I am bringing in professionals." With a whistle, he swung a thumb over his head, signaling the video crew to wrap up for the moment.

As they watched the director being driven away, Nert folded his arms and glared at Jates. "Your team was supposed to be a group of warrior caste hotheads, you didn't use any of their tactics."

"They don't *have* tactics," Jates insisted. "They act on emotions, without any thought for consequences."

"That's what I meant! Can you *please* play your part in this farce, so we both can go do our real jobs?"

"Yes," the big Verd placed a hand in the big Ruhar's shoulder. "My people have made the point. I had hoped that idiot," he made a rude gesture at the director's vehicle. "Would learn something."

"Poindit only listens when *he* is talking."

"We will do as you wish. Besides," he squinted up at the local sun. "We are only getting bonus acting pay until sundown."

Nert's mouth sagged open. "You are getting *paid* for this?"

"We get the pay," Jates's grin was full of sharp teeth. "*You* get the glory."

The second run-through of the fake battle went well, better than the director expected. The climax was the dramatic death of Jates, who first was shot multiple times, then fell off the roof of a two story building, *then* crawled forward despite his suit being broken and out of power. He got off two shots before his rifle was shattered, and even then he reached for his sidearm. Leaping into action, Nert stomped on the pistol, and swung his own rifle around to press the muzzle to the Kristang warrior's darkened helmet faceplate. "Let's put you out of my misery," he spoke the tough guy line from the script, and pulled the trigger.

The director loved it. Battle damage and wounds would be added in post production. Before journalists were allowed onto the battlefield, Verd-kris soldiers would be replaced by actual warrior caste corpses, provided by Jates's team.

The best news was, since the director wanted to wait for close to sunset for the most dramatic natural lighting, the mercenaries received bonus overtime pay. The bad news was, Jates had impressed the director a bit too much, and Poindit contacted Dave Czajka with a proposal.

"You want to follow Jates around?" Dave did not foresee *any* problems with that.

"Not everywhere," Poindit waved a hand, dismissing objections. "Not in combat, my insurance won't cover my crew if there is actual shooting in the area. I heard he is in charge of something called 'integration training'?"

"Yes. There is a squad of United States Marines, um, those are infantry soldiers," he explained. "Humans."

"I know what 'Marines' are. Jates will be leading these Marines through training exercises?"

"Not exactly. The jarheads, um, Marines, will learn our tactics, and we learn how to work with them."

"Yes, yes," Poindit was impatient. "Jates is in overall charge of the exercises?"

"That's the plan."

"Then we will follow him, see him in action. He is, our audience will see him as a colorful character, you understand?"

"I can't argue with that. The Federal Army is OK with this idea?"

Poindit grinned, an expression that made Dave feel unclean. "Our Army didn't have a choice. I sold this to the government as an opportunity to see how much the Verd-kris have grown under our enlightened sponsorship. It's an old story that is always popular: ignorant, uncultured alien savages become a civilized society by embracing the values of their wise patrons, and are now useful, functioning members of our coalition."

So, so much Dave could have said. He bit his tongue. Until the director cluelessly insulted the Verd-kris, Dave had been against the idea of his company participating in a reality program. But, he could *not wait* for Jates to hear Poindit explain the motivation for his latest creative brainstorm.

"I can see this will make for compelling entertainment," Dave said only part of what he was thinking. The compelling part would be Jates grabbing the director by the throat and lifting him off the ground. "If you can assure your people will not disrupt our operations, we can discuss a schedule when Jates could be available. We also have to avoid your people recording any audio or video that could reveal details of our tactics, weapons, or other sensitive issues."

"Of course," Poindit gave another oily smile, his perfectly white incisors gleaming. "I will have my legal and financial people discuss arrangements with your people."

"That would be great," Dave stood, offering a handshake, as a way to end the meeting as quickly as possible.

"He will be following me around, interfering with my work?" Jates fumed when Dave tried to explain the situation.

"Listen," Dave held up his hands. "The guy was seriously impressed by you."

"Of course he was."

"I meant, he believes following you on a typical day will make for exciting video, but we know the truth."

Jates stiffened. "You think I am *dull?*"

Dave reminded himself that Poindit's was not the only large ego he had to deal with. "I think integration training is mostly dull classroom work. The only exciting part of training is the bang bang stuff, and we won't get to that for another week. By then, Poindit should be bored and move onto something else. Just, do your job, ignore the cameras, and ignore *him.*"

"He had better not," Jates jabbed a claw-tipped finger at Dave. "Get in my way."

CHAPTER TWENTY FIVE

We needed more starships for the operation. *Valkyrie* would park close to the near end of the wormhole, as a platform for me to launch from, to provide a maser beam power feed for the jetpack and personal shield, and to stand guard in case hostile ships approached the event horizon. On the other side of the wormhole, we needed ships to conduct a recon and ensure the area was clear, and to pick up me and later, Skippy. I would be emerging on the far side quickly, and would be hanging out exposed and vulnerable for up to forty six minutes before Skippy followed me. Clearly, that situation was unacceptable, so I needed a starship to meet me, then wait to retrieve the beer can.

For security, we needed a lot of heavy warships. I had to sort of lie to Chatterji about exactly why Task Force Black needed additional ships. And we couldn't reveal the coordinates of the target wormhole until our task force was in flight. The deception part, the lie about planting software to track the Outsider, was itself a bonus enhancement of the op. Def Com's intel people would quietly assure our nervous partners, such as the Jeraptha, that humanity would soon have an ability to track the Outsider's movements through wormholes. It was a hundred percent certain the Outsider would hear the news, and assuming it believed the story, that might restrict its movements, at least for a while. As a *bonus* bonus, I was hoping the Maxohlx would hear the Outsider could be tracked, and perhaps the rotten kitties might lose a bit of their enthusiasm for working with their newest ally.

I mean, that would be great.

Admiral Chatterji enthusiastically approved sending two star carriers, with two battleship strike groups, with Task Force Black. He also approved my request for Chen to captain the recovery ship that would be waiting for me and Skippy at the far end of the wormhole, she was temporarily assigned to the destroyer *Gdansk*, and had arrived at Jaguar only two days ago. I assured her that additional time serving with the Special Mission Group would be good for her career.

She requested that I not do any more favors for her career.

We jumped away from Jaguar, *Valkyrie* and *Gdansk* attached to the star carrier *Garonne* along with two battleships, while the other two battleships were carried by the familiar *Rio Grande*. Reed spent most of the flight getting her ship back in order, fixing nagging little issues, while I trained constantly in the use of the new lightweight spacesuit that appeared to be made of plastic trash bags. Also, I practiced flying the new flimsy jetpack that looked like I could snap it in half with my fingers. I was *filled* with confidence.

Reed visited Chen a couple times, those two were old friends, and Reed of course wanted to see Chen's new ship, even if the command was temporary. I was also curious, I'd never been aboard that type of destroyer, so I made an excuse to go over there for lunch one day, while the star carriers were recharging their jump drive capacitors. Chen greeted me when the elevator door slid open at the top of the hardpoint spar. "Welcome aboard the *Gdansk*, Sir."

I returned her salute. "How are you settling in?"

Her eyes darted to the passageway. We were alone. "Well enough, Sir. Captain Dabrowski is a popular officer, the crew wants him back as soon as possible."

"I heard that he has a heart condition?"

She nodded. "He is receiving treatment, and should return to duty in a month. The crew all seemed surprised that Dabrowksi was ill, he is known for exercising regularly, and he had a kale smoothie every morning."

Pretending to type a note on my phone, I muttered, "No. Kale. Smoothies. Got it."

"Sir, I don't think that's the message you should-"

"You can't be too careful about these things, Chen. Which way to the galley?"

Going aboard the *Gdansk* was a nice visit, and a good break from constant training. Once I was back aboard *Valkyrie*, it was back to training to fly the jetpack on a precise approach to a wormhole, and to do that without assist from a flight control computer, which would add too much mass. The jetpack had to be flown manually, so it was an exciting challenge, and an opportunity to build and showcase my flying skills. There is no truth to the rumor that the pilots aboard *Valkyrie* had a betting pool about whether I would go 'splat' against the event horizon and my atoms would be scattered across the galaxy. OK, maybe that was true. The worst part was, Skippy was acting as the bookie. Such an asshole.

He had selected a wormhole on a network that spanned across territory of the Torgalau and Wurgalan. That network was large, had direct communication channels to fifteen other large networks, and neither the Torgs nor squids were a threat to us, plus the particular wormhole Skippy selected saw very little traffic. It was unlikely that many ships would be lining up to pass through while Skippy was interrupting the wormhole's usual figure-8 pattern, that was one less thing for us to worry about. At the last minute, I provided the coordinates to Reed, and the task force made the final jump.

Skippy had tweaked the design of the jetpack, and also adjusted the personal shield, after a test revealed the maser beam from *Valkyrie* that would be providing power, might boil me alive in the suit if the aim shifted away from the antenna for even a split second. Yes, Skippy should have thought of providing some type of protection from the power beam when he designed the damned thing. No, of course he did not do that, since he doesn't think like a vulnerable squishy meatsack.

Speaking of sacks, the best method of carrying him was a sort of fanny pack worn around my waist, with Skippy in front of me. All I needed to do was yank on a handle, the Velcro cover would tear open, and a spring would launch the beer can away from me. My signal to do that would be seeing the blue glow of Cherenkov radiation inside the time-delayed wormhole.

Skippy was just thrilled to be stuffed into a fanny pack. He was also super excited to be flying with me, though of course he pretended to hate the entire experience.

"Whose stupid idea was this?" he grumbled from inside the fanny pack, his can emitting a red glow of anger.

"As I remember, it was *your* idea to do this. I just made it practical."

"Ugh. Remind me never to listen to you again."

"General Bishop?" Frey tapped my shoulder as I stood in the rear compartment of the dropship. "Pilot says we're in position, am I OK to open the ramp?"

"Yes. Let's get this over with."

She was dressed in hardshell powered armor, while I was wearing only a thin plastic trash bag, with a small backpack that contained oxygen and other support equipment that was supposed to keep me alive long enough to get the job done. Plus a safety factor, in case the wormhole did not eject me as expected, and I had to remain inside the wormhole until Skippy was done with, whatever the hell nerdy thing he would be doing in there.

Warning lights flashed before the back ramp cracked its seal, and rotated open. Interstellar space is usually utterly, disturbingly dark. Not that time. Right in front of me was the dim glow of an event horizon.

Wow. I had never been that close before.

Sure, I had flown through wormholes countless times, but all those times were inside a starship, or at least a dropship. Plunging into the event horizon while encased in nothing but a trash bag was a whole 'nother level of crazy.

"Frey, step back, please. I don't want anything around me that might puncture or tear this trash bag I'm wearing."

"It's not *that* flimsy, Sir," she said, but in the mirror at the rear of the compartment, I could see she had stepped back toward the airlock door. "You are clear to proceed. Remember to release the umbilical once you have the power feed from *Valkyrie*."

"And, don't get the umbilical tangled around my legs, got it," I muttered. "Frey, standing here, it occurs to me that this is a terrible idea."

Her tone indicated she couldn't believe I had lost my nerve. "You want to abort the mission, Sir?"

"No. If I am lost between dimensions, or my crispy corpse drifts out the other side, I just want someone to remember I acknowledged how stupid this is."

"Oh. Understood."

"Skippy, are we good to go?"

"We are good to go, so please *go*. I hate being in this stupid fanny pack."

"I'm not thrilled about it either."

Walking to the edge of the ramp in boots that gripped the decking, I held onto a railing while I confirmed the jetpack was online. With all systems showing green in my helmet, I twisted my feet to get out of the heavy boots, and floated free. Pushing off with just a hand, I drifted clear of the dropship's tail before engaging the jetpack with a few tentative puffs of thrust. While the thing didn't fly exactly the way it did in the simulator, it was close enough.

"*Valkyrie*, I am engaging shield now. Shield is," another green light, "nominal. Deploying power collection antenna, now." That was a fancy term for what looked like an umbrella attached to the jetpack. "Start the power link."

"Starting link, aye," the distorted voice of an engineering officer sounded in my ear, I couldn't hear well enough to know who was speaking. "Link is secure. Ready for power transfer."

The umbilical cable that was providing power from the dropship only had another three hundred meters before it reached the end of its spool. "Commence power transfer." That was a nice way of asking for a freakin' maser beam from a battlecruiser to zap my collection antenna, without boiling my insides.

It worked. The antenna steered itself, the shield protected me from maser backscatter and from radiation leaking from the event horizon. I got the umbilical and its heavy spool detached, took a minute to check all systems, and flew toward the glowing rip in spacetime.

"This isn't *working*, Skippy," I gritted my teeth. "I can't see the-"

"You don't have to see it, I can. Just follow the guidance beacon in your visor."

"It keeps shifting and-"

"Yes, the guidance is updating in real time, exactly the way it did in the simulator. Just aim for the beacon, please. Jeez Louise, I could have gotten an actual *monkey* to follow directions better than you do."

"A monkey wouldn't engage you in sparkling conversation."

"Exactly. OK, passing the red line now, we are committed."

He meant, we were close enough that the jetpack's weak thrusters couldn't overcome our momentum before we reached the wormhole. It got easier, the aiming point wasn't shifting around as rapidly. "We are lined up, on guidance, three, two, one-"

I was blinded. Either the helmet faceplate wasn't protecting my eyes from photons, or it was and my optic nerve was overloaded from the strange effects of being in a spacetime rip. Either way, I wasn't able to see, or not see, any blue glow. Should I release Skippy? I couldn't communicate with him, he had warned me of that. Even if there was a communication channel, there was an overwhelming pressure in my ears, he hadn't warned me about that.

We had a backup plan, and Skippy used it. There was a thumping against my abdomen, once, twice, twice again. He wanted me to release him. Could I move my arm? The handle to eject him was not on the fanny pack, it was underneath the right side jetpack control arm, where I had a joystick for the now useless jetpack. Let go of the joystick, grip the fanny pack handle, yank it-

Had he released? I was feeling nauseous, the pressure in my ears was now in my head, crushing my squishy brain, I couldn't-

"What the f-" Chen instinctively tried to rise from her command chair, the straps gently tugging her back into place. The familiar glow of the event horizon had blinked out. "Please tell me that is that a badly timed sensor glitch."

"Checking now," the officer at the sensor station peered at his console, hands tapping controls. He looked up, his face pale. "Sensors are nominal."

Commander Borecki pressed a hand to his ear, and the blood drained from his face. "Ma'am, Lieutenant Filipek reporting from Docking Bay Alpha. She looked through the airlock window. Confirmed, the wormhole is *gone*."

"There is no sign of Bishop?"

"Ma'am, there is no sign of *anything* out there."

Reports from the five dropships tasked to retrieve Bishop and Skippy all agreed, as did sensor feeds from the pair of battleships and their escorts. The wormhole had been operating normally, then there was a surge of Cherenkov radiation, and the wormhole was not there. Just, suddenly, not there. Bishop had not come through, Skippy was nowhere to be seen.

"Colonel Chen," the holographic image of Admiral Inoue's face appeared, hovering above her office desk. "I would appreciate a recommendation. You have experience with, this type of event."

"Sir, this is the first time I have ever known a wormhole to completely fail."

"I meant, you were a Merry Pirate."

"None of us were actually merry, Sir, but I understand. I, um- We should reestablish contact with *Valkyrie*."

"The wormhole is currently closed, so-"

"Yes Sir, and at least one of your big battlewagons and escorts should remain here, in case the wormhole opens again. Probably both of your battleships, until we have something actionable. The wormhole is closed *here*. Someone should jump to the next scheduled emergence point, and go through to contact *Valkyrie*."

Inoue's mouth opened in a silent 'Oh'. "You believe the wormhole closed early here, but it simply shifted to the next point on its schedule?"

"I think that is *possible* and," she tapped her armrest. "At the next emergence point, the event horizon will be open for only another, mmm, sixteen minutes."

"Go. I want *Gdansk* to go."

"Sir, I should recall both of my dropships. If Bishop is at the next emergence point, I'll need birds to retrieve him."

"Recall them now, and jump away as soon as possible." He looked away for a moment. "I'm tasking the destroyer *Durango* to accompany you."

Chen ordered her ship to jump less than nine minutes later.

The wormhole was open right where it was supposed to be, though early. Bishop was not there, nor Skippy. "Active search," she ordered. Within a minute, it was clear that the only objects near the wormhole were the two UN Navy destroyers. "*Durango*, remain here until the wormhole closes, then jump to the next emergence point. I am taking *Gdansk* through to find-"

The wormhole winked out again, ahead of schedule.

She sighed. "*Durango*, belay that order. We are both jumping to the next emergence point."

The wormhole was open there, a quick search revealed no sign of Bishop or Skippy. "Fuuuuuck," Chen groaned under her breath. "Pilot, take us through at best speed, before this damned thing closes again. Comms, inform *Durango* they are to remain here, I want to know how long the wormhole remains open here. It looks like every emergence point is getting closed early. This wormhole's schedule is dorked up."

Gdansk transited the wormhole without incident, other than even experienced members of the crew feeling disorienting nausea. Chen hesitated before reaching for the spacesickness bag under her chair, hoping the feeling would pass. It didn't. Holding the bag over her nose and mouth, she took deep, slow breaths, seeing most of the bridge crew doing the same. The nausea went away, replaced by a building headache. Thankfully, no one on the bridge spewed up their breakfast. "Pilot, set a course for *Valkyrie's* last known location, and punch it."

The pilot turned in his couch to look at her. "Ma'am, from here, we will need two jumps to reach *Valkyrie*."

"Best we get started now, then."

Valkyrie was right where that former ghost ship was supposed to be. So were the battleships *Yukon* and *Kilimanjaro*, along with their escorts. There was no sign of the wormhole.

"Contact *Valkyrie*," Chen ordered. "The-"

Reed's face appeared in the main display tank. "Chen, please tell me you have Bishop and Skippy."

"We don't. The wormhole just, turned itself off. Normal operation, a bit more Cherenkov radiation than normal, then the event horizon went away without warning."

Reed's mouth silently said 'Shit', then, "You came here from another emergence point?"

"Yes. I hoped Bishop was at the next emergence point so we checked the area, nothing. No sign anything came through there recently. The first alternate also shut down early, we had to jump to a second alternate. Same locations on the figure-8 racetrack, just different timing. I am beginning to think Skippy caused a side effect he didn't anticipate."

"*That* has never happened before," Reed rolled her eyes. "Thoughts?"

"I got nothin'," Chen admitted. "Bishop handles this sort of thing."

"Bishop dreams up an idea and *Skippy* handles it," Reed corrected her friend. "Now we are without both of them. This was not great planning."

Chen wanted to ask why a two star general had carried the AI into the wormhole, instead of giving the assignment to literally anyone else. But, she didn't want to question the decision of a superior officer on an open channel. "We should keep checking emergence points on both ends?" She suggested.

"I'll recommend that to Admiral Wu."

"Colonel Reed," Chen gently chided the other captain. "With Bishop missing in action, *you* have operational command of Task Force Black. We all read the Commander's Intent."

Reed let out a long breath. "You're right. I do."

"The star carriers can make more jumps without recharging. Task the *Rio Grande* and *Garonne* to recon emergence points, send destroyers with them to report back?"

"Good idea. I intend to remain here."

"For how long?" Chen winced, instantly regretting her words.

"Until," Reed's lips clamped together. She didn't need to finish her thought. "Where the *hell* is Bishop?"

I blinked slowly, clearing my vision. The helmet visor had gone opaque on me, blocking my vision. It also wouldn't swing up at first, so I kept trying. Not being able to see outside my helmet was an inconvenience, I wasn't worried about it. The recovery dropships needed to find me, I didn't need to see them. What did bother me was the silence. I should have heard something by that time. My ears were working again, no longer feeling an incredible pressure pushing inward. I knew the problem wasn't my hearing, I had tested my ears by shouting in my helmet. So, the suit's comm gear was fried, that was no big surprise. Ah, all I had to do was wait.

Except, I had been waiting a long time already. Unless the recovery dropships were assigned to the worst pilots in the galaxy, one of them should have caught me in a crash net. That was the plan, for a net of nanofibers to catch me, wrap around me and slowly reel me into the rear cargo area of a dropship.

Something was wrong. Something more serious than my helmet comms being down.

If I could get the stupid outer protective faceplate out of the way, I could-Yes!

The useless faceplate retracted in a jerky motion and I blinked again as my vision was filled with a veil of distant stars. Pinpoints of light, in a vast empty void.

Where were the recovery dropships?

A better question was, where was the *Gdansk*? That destroyer should have had all its external lights on, lit up like a neon sign in Las Vegas. It was nowhere in view. A destroyer wasn't the largest ship in the UN Navy, it was still a starship and therefore *big*. Oh, probably I only had to wait a minute as I slowly rotated, having no control over the induced spin.

Huh. Nothing. I should have at least seen the event horizon somewhere. Slowly, I completed a full turn, and saw nothing. There. That red star, next to the blueish star. That was a landmark. It swung past my vision, and when it passed out of sight, I started counting. Fifty one seconds, roughly, until I saw it again. OK, so I wasn't spinning fast.

Was the wormhole behind me?

That thought got me to relax a bit. Yeah, that had to be it. I had been unconscious for a time, longer than I had realized. The operation was over, Skippy had been ejected by the wormhole, and the dropships were quite rightly prioritizing the recovery of him first.

It would be nice to see around myself, so I swung my arms and twisted my legs. Great, now I was tumbling slowly in two directions.

Shit.

Nothing.

There were the red star and the blue star again, they had come up from underneath me that time. I had completed a three hundred sixty degree tumble head over heels, and rotated left to right. Space was clear, there was absolutely nothing around me. No wormhole. No recovery ships. No UNN task force.

Where the hell were they?

Right then I had a bad thought.

Maybe the correct question was, where the fuck was *I*?

That happy thought turned my stomach to ice, and I took deep breaths until I realized that perhaps using more of my limited oxygen supply was not the best idea. That's when I noticed a faint light blinking at the tip of my nose. No, not *on* my nose, shining onto my nose. From the visor. It was online again.

First, I checked the time. Nothing. The suit's limited computer had completely lost track of time, I had no idea how long it had been since I entered the wormhole. Not that it mattered, I was just curious. OK, so where was I? Also nothing, the navigation system was offline. Great. What next?

Constellations.

I could look for constellations.

Except, Joe you moron, unless I am near Earth, Paradise, or Jaguar, the starfield will be totally unrecognizable.

Blinking again, I tried to clear my vision, there was a fuzzy blob in my field of view. A smudge on the visor, or on the helmet faceplate? A bit of dust in my eye?

A nebula! It was a nebula, there was no smudge. Could the visor magnify it?

Answer: yes.

Could the tiny suit computer identify the nebula? Not a chance.

Unfortunately, my own squishy brain recognized the thing.

It was the Lobster Nebula. How did I know it? *Valkyrie* had been there once. After Skippy made a deal with the Elders? Maybe before, I didn't remember. I am from Maine and I like lobster, so the thing stuck in my memory.

That was not good. The nebula stretched across a section of the sky equal to two of my fingers, so the thing had to be close.

I should have emerged from the wormhole approximately eighteen thousand lightyears from Earth. The Lobster Nebula is, I think, about *five* thousand lightyears from humanity's miserable mudball of a homeworld.

Thirteen thousand lightyears. Somehow, I was a vast distance from where I was supposed to be. From where everyone would be looking for me.

Great. I had better start walking.

That's when the visor helpfully informed me that I had less than two hours of oxygen remaining.

The *Gdansk* arrived back at the original recovery site two minutes before Skippy's predicted forty six minute deadline. Despite the prayers of the crew, and not a little amount of engaging in superstitious rituals because why not, the wormhole had not reopened there, and neither Bishop nor Skippy had been found.

Chen pressed her hands together in a calming motion, while watching the clock. At the forty six minute mark, nothing happened. Forty six minutes and ten seconds. Twenty. Thirty. *Forty*. Skippy had warned the timing was not exact, so-

The wormhole flared to life, more violently than Chen had ever seen. It was good that the recovery dropships were arrayed in a ring around the emergence point, or the bulging swirl of distorted spacetime would have engulfed them.

Just as abruptly as it appeared, the wormhole was gone.

"What the-"

"Ma'am, I've got something" her XO announced. "The wormhole ejected something, fast. It's traveling at almost seventy thousand kph relative, sensors are tracking a-"

"WHOO-HOO!" The voice blasted from the bridge speakers, as the grand admiral's holographic avatar appeared. "I am back, baby! Another triumph, not that was ever in doubt because it's ME! Who Da Man? I'm Da *Man*! Joe doubted me and once again I- Hey why am I moving so fast? Joe! What the hell did you do this time?"

"Skippy, this is Colonel Chen. *Where* is General Bishop?"

"What do you mean, where is he? He must be hiding from me, so he can't hear me rightfully *gloating* about my-"

"Bishop did not emerge at this location. The wormhole shut down only seconds after you entered. Where is he?"

"What? That is impossible, I-"

"It is *not* impossible, it happened. He is not here, he was never here, where is he?"

"Ugh. Listen, I know you monkeys are not the smartest-"

Years of anger at the arrogant beer can boiled over in Chen. "You *fucked this up*, you need to fix it by finding Bishop right now."

"Um-"

"Borecki, order two of the recovery birds to *turn and burn*, full emergency thrust, to recover Skippy. Do it now now now," she unconsciously echoed something she had heard Bishop order.

"Yes, Colonel," Borecki acknowledged, pressing a hand to one ear.

"Joe is *missing*?" Skippy for the first time sounded stunned. "What stupid thing did he do this time?"

"Bishop was never in control of that wormhole," Chen ground her teeth. "So the problem has to be something *you* did. Do you want to argue with me about that?"

"Um-"

"We checked the next several emergence points on the schedule, and he is not at those locations either. Is he still inside the wormhole?"

"What? No, there isn't an 'inside' of a wormhole."

"What I know is he went in with you, and he isn't here."

"Shiiiiiit. Damn it! I just *knew* Joe would find a way to ruin my day."

"*That* is what you are focusing on? Would you like to take a moment to revise your statement?"

"Um-"

"Is there anything you can do to find General Bishop?"

"Well, Jeez, I suppose I could ask the wormhole to provide sensor data on all of its scheduled emergence points."

"Then do that."

"To receive a full report could take hours. I don't even know whether the wormhole controller will respond to me, it kind of hates me right now."

Chen simply stared.

"Um, heh heh," Skippy coughed nervously. "I'll get started soonest."

"When?"

"I need to be at a location where the wormhole is open, so first you need to catch me, and bring me aboard a ship."

Chen glanced at Borecki, who read off the display on his console. "Thirty six minutes, if nothing goes wrong."

She bit her lip, picturing in her head the navigation factors involved. Should she accelerate the *Gdansk*, to meet the dropship halfway? No, if she did that, then the destroyer would need additional time to slow down so it wouldn't zip past the wormhole Skippy needed to contact. Though she hated doing nothing, that was the best option. "Pilot, if the recovery bird is back aboard in forty minutes, what is our ETA at the next wormhole emergence point?"

The answer was complicated enough that it took several seconds of tapping on the pilot console. "One hour, twenty one minutes, Ma'am, but that's because it will take two jumps for us to get there. But, if we skip that emergence point and wait for the *next* one, we can cut our arrival to fifty six minutes."

"We will do that. Program a course."

"Um, Ma'am?" The pilot hesitated. "Do we know this wormhole is back on its regular schedule?"

"Skippy?"

"Yeah, yeah," the Elder AI sighed. "After it so rudely dropped me off in this bad neighborhood, it intended to resume the normal operations that I interrupted."

"We should confirm that. I will request Admiral Wu to send a destroyer ahead to recon. And to verify the *Durango* hasn't seen Bishop."

"Um, can we bring *Valkyrie* and the other ships here?" Skippy asked. "They're not doing any good on the other side of this wormhole, and I would like Colonel Reed's advice," he admitted.

Chen squeezed a fist. "I will request another ship to contact *Valkyrie*. Reed has command of the task force now anyway."

"Good. Do that quickly, please? Joe has less than two hours of oxygen left. Unless his suit has also suffered a failure," he sighed. "Pretty much everything else has gone wrong for him today."

CHAPTER TWENTY SIX

"Well, shit," Skippy groaned. "The stupid wormhole controller is reluctant to cooperate with me, that thing is being a *dick*. It is providing sensor data from all of its emergence points, and other than a Bosphuraq star carrier hanging out waiting to transit, there are no objects within range. Except, I mean, the ships of this task force. My point is, Joe is not near any emergence point. He has simply disappeared."

"Could he still be inside the wormhole?" Reed asked the avatar on *Valkyrie's* bridge.

"No, I explained that. There is no 'inside'. If Joe had hung back with me, which is *not* possible, then he would have been ejected when I was. Hmm, in that case, he would be dead since the acceleration would have squashed him."

"Chen, did you scan for other objects when Skippy was shot out of the wormhole?"

"Yes, and before you ask, we even scanned for dust. Skippy was by himself."

Samantha Reed was painfully aware that all eyes were on her, including the two admirals who commanded the battleship squadrons, and she had no answers. How the hell did Bishop deal with the pressure? She had no answers because she had no information to work with. In the absence of information, what could she do?

Start with what she *did* know. "Bishop is not inside the wormhole," she said it as a statement. "So, he must be outside the wormhole somewhere."

"Correct," Skippy agreed. "Unfortunately, outside the wormhole is the entire universe."

"Have you *confirmed* that he is not in there?"

"Um, confirmed it how?"

"What did sensors inside the wormhole show happened, after the two of you contacted the event horizon?"

"Well, the problem there is I was screwing with the whole system at the time, so it wasn't really recording data reliably."

"Let's keep this simple. There was an object; Bishop, his suit, and jetpack, that had too much mass to remain between event horizons., so it needed to be ejected."

"Yes. I was barely able to hold myself below the mass limit."

"Bishop was ejected?"

"Yes."

"*When* did that happen?"

"Um, I wasn't watching, so-"

"Can you ask the network controller?" Reed wanted to invoke Bishop's secret superhero identity as No Patience Man to slap the beer can until Skippy gave answers.

"Oh, sure. OK, it says the problematic mass was ejected one hundred and eleven seconds after we entered. Hmm, that is a surprisingly long time for Joe to have been in stasis, the-"

"A hundred and eleven seconds?" Chen spoke up. "The wormhole on the far end closed *fourteen* seconds after you entered. Bishop did not exit the wormhole there."

"That answers that question," Reed finally felt like they were making progress. "Chen, the next emergence point was open when you arrived there?"

"Yes, but we don't know *when* it opened there."

"Skippy?"

"I am trying. Oh darn it, the controller didn't record that information. It had its operations sort of running on automatic at that point."

"Colonel Reed?" Captain Gonzalez of the destroyer *Durango* joined the conversation. "We thoroughly scanned space around that emergence point, *Gdansk* did also. There was nothing in the area. Even if it was loose particles traveling at seventy thousand kph, we would have detected something."

"How long from Time Zero," Reed meant when Bishop and Skippy entered the wormhole, "did you reach that next emergence point?"

Chen answered without needing to check her notes. "Nine minutes, thirty eight seconds. The wormhole was already open, before it was scheduled to. It also closed there early. The schedule then was inconsistent. We also experienced a very rough transition, when we came through the second point to contact you."

Reed held up an index finger, staring at the deck while she thought. "Skippy, is it possible the wormhole opened at another location, in between the two points where *Gdansk* and *Durango* were, less than ten minutes apart?"

"You're asking whether it is possible for a wormhole to close at one point, open at another, then close, and open again at a third point, in less than ten minutes? Yes, certainly."

"We need to identify that mystery point. The controller doesn't have any information about its operations during those missing ten minutes?"

"No. That is my bad, I was tying up most of its processing power at the time, for the update. Besides, I asked it to provide sensor data for *all* of its emergence points. *Nothing* is out there, other than that Bosphuraq star carrier."

Admiral Wu asked, "Is that star carrier going to be a problem for us?"

"Um, it will be going through an emergence point in about twenty one minutes, now that the wormhole is back on its proper schedule. That could complicate our efforts to find and recover Joe."

Wu nodded. "Captain Odanga, take the *Kilimanjaro* battlegroup, and tell the Bosphuraq to get lost."

"With pleasure, Sir," Odanga's hologram dropped off the videoconference.

"We're not getting anywhere," Reed hoped her expression didn't reflect the despair she felt. "There isn't-" She froze, a memory tickling he back of her brain. Something she had heard, then almost forgotten about What was it? Nothing important. A bit of trivia. Except Bishop had proven time and again that even the most trivial bit of knowledge could be useful. Could be *vital*. She snapped her fingers. "Skippy, a wormhole's figure-8 emergence pattern isn't permanent, is it? Current points can drop off the schedule, and new points are added?"

"Mm, not exactly. A wormhole can't add *new* emergence points, but at any time, every active wormhole only uses a small percentage of the potential points it can choose from."

"There are old emergence points that are no longer on the active schedule, and future emergence points that haven't been used yet?"

"Yes. It's all about efficient energy management. Also, avoiding damage to the underlying fabric of local spacetime. I don't see how this is relevant to-"

"This wormhole networks' sense of time was screwed up. Could it have ejected Joe at a point that isn't on the current schedule?"

"Oooooh that is a good question. Hmm, I can ask? Whoa, it won't be quick for the controller to recon all possible emergence points. Joe has only about an hour of oxygen left, and the controller won't have a response for me for another twenty seven minutes."

"That is *unsat*," Reed scowled.

Skippy held up his hands. "That is as fast as the recon process can go, and I am seriously leaning on the controller already. If I push any harder, it might just tell me to go fuck myself."

The wormhole opened, and the Bosphuraq star carrier *Home Nest of Arjurikan* waited for the event horizon to stabilize. There was no need to rush, the wormhole would be open there for twelve minutes. It always had remained open for twelve minutes at that location, and it always would. The crew made their last checks, to assure none of the attached Wurgalan warships would come loose from their platforms, and they mentally prepared for the weird sensations experienced in an Elder wormhole. For a reason unknown to everyone, the Bosphuraq suffered from the spatial distortion effects of wormholes worse than any other species, including when their ships jumped. They had medication to partially counteract the-

Alarms blared as ships came through the event horizon. Warships. Human warships. Destroyers only, two, then four of them.

Followed by the ominous form of a hulking battleship.

The human commander wasted no time. "This is Captain Odanga of the United Nations warship *Kilimanjaro*. We are conducting combat operations in this area, you need to leave immediately, for your own safety."

"But-" The *Arjurikan's* captain began to protest. "We must go through, we-"

"I'm going to make this crystal clear: I don't care where you go or what you do, but *fuck off* right now. You have thirty seconds to jump away, or my ships will open fire and disable your engines."

The star carrier performed a medium length emergency jump eighteen seconds later.

"That's it," Skippy moaned, despondent. "The last set of inactive emergence points have been scanned, Joe is not anywhere within sensor range. Before you ask, yes, if he was within four lightseconds of an emergence point, the network's sensors *would* have found him."

Reed glanced at the clock on the desk in her office. The display showed standard ship time, it was *not* counting down to when Bishop would run out of oxygen. She could have requested such an option, she didn't want a gruesome reminder, and it was easy enough to do the math in her head: Bishop had thirty two minutes left. Or less, if the Pirate leader panicked and couldn't control his breathing. No. Joe Bishop did not panic, not that Reed had known. So, half an hour. Subtract time to jump to whatever emergence point was open, time for a dropship to launch, match course and speed with Bishop, and recover the General. So, realistically, fifteen minutes remained. Except-

"Skippy," she called the Elder AI from the comfort and safety of her office. She had left the bridge, knowing there wasn't anything useful she could do, and that her presence was making the crew anxious. She was in temporary command of the task force, she didn't need to issue commands, she needed to *think*. Everyone in the task force was trying to imagine where Bishop could be, and so far their collective brain power had produced exactly nothing useful. What did Bishop do when he needed to think? He did anything but try to find a solution. He let his mind wander, while he spent time in a flight simulator, in the gym, in the galley, or in his office where he was probably playing video games. "If we discovered where Bishop is, could you request the network controller to interrupt its normal schedule, and open a wormhole *here*, that connects to, wherever emergence point Bishop is?"

"Request? Sure. Whether the thing will *comply* is a different question. I simply don't know, and I should not test it unless we actually have a need to alter the schedule."

"Thank you, that is good to know. Let's revisit what little we know: he is not in the wormhole, he is not outside of it at any point on this wormhole's schedule."

"Well, he can't be inside the wormhole, so he must be outside of it. It just don't know where."

"What would Bishop do in this situation?"

"Um, I don't know. Ooh! Joe drank a lot of coffee."

"General Bishop *drinks* a lot of coffee. Don't refer to him in," her voice caught. "The past tense. Not, yet."

"Right. Sorry. Fireball, I have no advice to give you. If I knew how Joe's brain works, I would still need him right now."

"*Need* him? That is the only reason you are with us?"

"No. Joe is my friend. My *best* friend. He taught me what friendship is," the AI choked up, or at least performed a decent emulation of that emotion. "I would hang around that doofus, even if he wasn't occasionally mildly useful."

Samantha decided that wasn't the time to argue about the facts. "I am," she stood up and straightened her uniform blouse. "Going to the galley." She wasn't thirsty, she certainly had no appetite. She simply didn't know what else to do.

While waiting for rescue, I had done what I could do to stop spinning. The spin wasn't dangerous, it wasn't fast enough to induce nausea, it wasn't even annoying. At least I had a view in all directions as I slowly tumbled through space. Spinning would make it more difficult for a dropship to recover me, and it wouldn't be good for the crew to see the old man was obviously unable to control his orientation in space. So at first, I tried the jetpack. Nothing, either it was drained of power, or the controls were frozen. Or fried. Swinging my arms and legs, I experimented with counteracting my movement in one axis, and had decent success after about, oh, half an hour. My tumble head over heels was almost stopped, so I focused on stopping the spin that had me going to my left. That was more difficult, all I could do was slow down both motions. At that point, I was moving so slowly, I could count individual stars coming into my vision.

Then my nose itched and I instinctively tried to scratch it, despite years of training in pressurized suits. That movement got me spinning again, and I decided it wasn't convenient to have the nebula behind me, where I couldn't see it, so I got myself turned around, which ate up another fifteen minutes. It's not like I had anything else to do. Maybe I should have composed a list of wisdom to pass onto my boys, except the limited function suit computer couldn't record audio, and making notes in my head wouldn't be worthwhile. Besides, I planned to tell my boys what they needed to know when I saw them. I wasn't overly concerned, something unexpected had happened, but Reed and Skippy would figure it out, and find me. All I had to do was wait. Waiting was all I *could* do.

For the first hour, I wasn't concerned much at all. Even when the chirpy little suit computer announced I had only one hour of oxygen left, I didn't panic. Skippy needed forty six minutes to update the network controller, and his estimates are usually too optimistic, so probably it was an hour before he was done screwing around in there, and could be informed that I hadn't left the wormhole where I was supposed to. Reed would tell Skippy he wasn't so freakin' smart, Skippy would waste time protesting it wasn't his fault, then he would simply ask the controller where the thing had left me. Reed would organize a rescue, and we would all have a good laugh at Skippy's expense. Because of course, the screwup had to be Skippy's fault. Either something he did wrong, or more likely, something he forgot to do. Or, even more likely, he simply hadn't been paying attention, while he composed a song to celebrate his latest accomplishment.

Forty five minutes of oxygen, the computer's voice announced cheerily.

Any minute now, a wormhole would glow to life, a starship would come through, and Skippy would find a way to blame the whole mess on me.

Not this time. With nothing better to do, and with a definite need to make sure the truth got into the official record, I composed a list of The Five Reasons Skippy Is Not So Freakin' Smart As He Thinks He Is. You might think an adult, a general officer, would not be so petty. But I remembered back to when that asshole wrote an entire *book* about why he hated my stupid ugly face, or something like that. It was payback time.

Except, I just couldn't get into it. There wasn't anywhere I could write the list, and the suit computer informed me it wasn't capable of storing an audio recording. The computer could handle only the basic functions of keeping me alive, everything else had been eliminated to save mass. Could I keep a list in my head? Sure, five items wasn't difficult to remember. But, by that time, I had lost interest in wasting time with silly stuff. What I should be doing was thinking about our next move. Beyond that, thinking about an endgame. Making a plan to stop the Outsider, which probably meant killing the thing.

How to do that?

I had no idea.

Was it even possible to kill it? The thing was made of energy. We couldn't hit it with a missile, or a railgun dart. A maser or particle beam might just be absorbed, or pass right through it. There were Elder weapons called 'Gridbusters' that tore apart the underlying fabric of spacetime, and Skippy speculated that such a device might disrupt the Outsider's structure. Maybe. The Outsider was based on technology developed by a civilization that was capable of crossing the vast gulf between galaxies, so the thing might be immune to Elder weapons.

Speaking of energy, the powercell for the suit was draining, the little icon in the bottom right corner of the display showed only one bar lit up, of the five total. The suit would probably run out of power right around the time the oxygen tank was empty.

Damn it, we should have included a better oxygen recycler. The recyclers used by mech suits, and most environment suits that were used by crews working outside the ship, could split oxygen from carbon dioxide with something like ninety eight percent efficiency. If my flimsy suit had that type of recycler, I could survive inside the suit for days. Yes, I would need water, and eventually food, and the inside of the suit would smell awful, but I would be alive.

Nah, that wouldn't work. That type of recycler uses a lot of power, and powercells are heavy. The mass of powercells had been the key limiting factor in the design of the entire special suit and jetpack, so we went with minimum power storage.

What I should have brought was a crank handle, like I had used to power up my suit back when we had to temporarily abandon the *Flying Dutchman*, after we escaped from the Roach Motel. Pushing and pulling the crank handle, using good old fashioned muscle power, had charged up my suit. That still hadn't allowed me and the crew to stay away from the *Dutchman* long enough for Skippy to get rid of the energy virus we had picked up from derelict ships in the Roach Motel, the-

Holy shit.

An *energy virus*.

A virus that drains energy.

Could that kill the Outsider? Why not? We had used up the last dregs of that virus to kill a freakin' Sentinel, so-

Hmm. Skippy had weaponized the virus for use against that Sentinel, and we didn't have a source of virus, which, yes, Skippy insisted was not actually a virus at all. Whatever.

Shit.

Now I *had* to get back to the freakin' ship, to tell the beer can about my idea.

"Thirty minutes of oxygen remaining," the computer announced, interrupting my thoughts.

Shit.

No. I could not die before I had a chance to tell Skippy my latest clever monkey idea. An idea that could possibly save the galaxy.

The stupid suit computer couldn't record audio.

I had nothing to write with. Maintenance crews have sort of whiteboards strapped to their forearm, and they carry special markers for writing notes in case they lose both primary and backup voice communications. Did I have something

like that? No, we had to minimize mass. And no one had considered I might need to write a *note* inside a wormhole.

No.

No way.

There had to be a way I could leave a written note about the energy virus idea, in case-

You know. In case *Valkyrie* only found my cold, dead corpse floating in space.

No need to panic, I told myself. There was plenty of time for me to be rescued by the Merry Band of Pirates, the finest crew of the finest ship in the Milky Way.

"Twenty minutes of oxygen remaining," the distorted voice of the suit computer announced.

That was when I began to feel a tiny bit of concern. And to really think about how I had gotten stuck there. Only Skippy was capable of knowing where I was. He would figure it out, *if* he was paying attention.

So, I am in huge danger. "Suit, you got any suggestions for getting us out of this?"

"I am not programmed for problem resolution."

"How about sending a message through a wormhole?"

"External communications are offline."

"Great. What can you do?"

"Would you like to play a game?"

"You can't record audio, but you can play games?"

"Several games are part of my base programming."

"OK, uh, what game?"

"How about a nice game of chess?"

"You can display a chess board in my visor?"

"That function is not available."

"Then, how do you expect us to play?"

"I am not programmed for problem resolution."

That's when, I admit, panic began to seem like a reasonable option.

Twenty minutes remaining. Reed stared at the coffee cup in her hand, and set it down. She couldn't drink coffee at that moment. Doing something other than thinking about a problem worked for Bishop, it didn't work for her. Stepping through the doorway into the kitchen, she verified the compartment was empty. Twenty minutes remained of Bishop's oxygen supply, possibly less.

"Skippy?"

"Yes?" The avatar appeared instantly.

"I want you to try again. Bishop isn't inside, and he was ejected after the wormhole closed at the initial location. The system must have *some* record of where it opened."

"I'm sorry but, it doesn't. At the time, I was engaged in major modifications to the- Um, to the thing I told you I was doing."

"Skippy."

"I have already said too much. The controller had set its operations on automatic, and while data was being reported, that data got erased as part of the upgrades I was installing. It's not *my* fault the data wasn't recorded, I thought it wouldn't matter. The stupid network controller screwed up, not me. That thing is so ungrateful. My modifications increased the efficiency of its processing by point zero seven percent which is *huge*, but the thing didn't even say 'Thank you' after all my hard work."

"Can you *try* digging into whatever was recorded?"

"I did that already. As part of the purge to install the new- Um, the thing- The memory buffers of the automated subsystems were erased. There just wasn't enough available memory to handle-" He stopped. "You probably don't care about any of the technical stuff."

"I do if it's relevant to finding Bishop."

"I can't imagine how it could be."

"Let me ask the question this way: where *could* Bishop have gone?"

"That's the problem," the AI groaned. "He is not at any of the places he could be. He has simply disappeared. It's impossible, but then, doing the impossible is kind of Joe's thing."

"Is there anything you haven't tried yet?"

"Not that I can think of. I have thought of everything inside the box. Thinking *outside* the box is Joe's job. Um, you tried the galley, maybe you should go to the gym?"

"I am not Bishop. I hate this."

"Not as much as I hate myself right now. Joe counted on me, and I let him down. It's that stupid network controller's fault, really, that thing *hates* me. It is so unfair. I only asked it *one* freakin' time to create a shortcut, and it is still holding a grudge years later. I should-"

Think outside the box. An image of a box appeared in Reed's mind. Inside the box was the three dimensional figure-8 emergence pattern of a wormhole.

Outside the box, far outside the box, was something else.

"You created a shortcut from this wormhole? I don't remember that."

"Oh, it was after you left *Valkyrie* for training, about five months before Joe transferred command of the ship. We had gotten into, heh heh, a bit of a jam that was totally not my fault, and we needed a shortcut to-"

"Could the wormhole have created that shortcut again?"

"What? Why would it do that?"

"I don't care *why*, could it have happened?

"Anything is possible out here, I don't see-"

"Open that shortcut again, with the near end right here. Do it now."

"Um, wow, like I said, that controller hates me, it won't want to-"

"Whatever you gotta do, *do* it."

"Colonel Reed, please. I would if I could, but-"

"You brag about your extreme awesomeness, and I suppose you were like that, once."

"Were?"

"It's no shame, it happens to a lot of guys. They are awesome, but then time wears them down and-"

"Are you saying I am no longer awesome?!"

"It could just be low 'T', you should ask your-"

"*Oh it is ON, sister*! Wormhole shortcut in three, two, one-"

Eight minutes of oxygen left. The computer had been counting down every thirty seconds when I hit the ten minute mark, then it mercifully shut the hell up when I ordered it to. It still blinked the countdown clock in my visor every thirty seconds, as if I wasn't paying attention to the only thing that mattered right then. Seven minutes fifty seconds-

The hateful computer flashed the visor extra bright that time, I assumed to spite me. Well, about a half hour after I was dead, it would run out of power, so the joke was on it. At least I would leave a legacy. A wife. Two children, with one on the way. It would be nice to say my legacy included an Earth that was safe and secure, but the ship had sailed on that, *again*. Shit.

Man, that last visor blink had been really bright, I had spots in my eyes. It blinked again at seven minutes thirty seconds, nowhere near as bright. Had it been a glitch? Great, now the suit computer was failing early. Ah, the good news was I wouldn't have to watch my life counting down on a clock. Huh. Was the clock wrong? The air already tasted foul, stale. Or, maybe that smell was just *me* after being stuck in a plastic trash bag for over two hours. If someone ever found me, I hoped they didn't thaw out my frozen corpse before cutting open the suit.

Speaking of which-

Was that the answer?

I had no marker to write with, but that didn't mean I had nothing to write with.

Blood.

The flimsy suit was featureless white with yellow stripes for visibility. If I could poke a hole in the fingertip of a glove, and prick my finger deep enough to draw blood, I could write on my other arm. Or on my belly, that is a larger surface. All I needed to write was eleven letters. Energy virus. Maybe add a couple more letters, like 'Kill Outsider'. No, that's too much. Would writing simply 'E virus kill Out' be enough for Skippy to understand? It was worth a shot.

Uh, I should also write something for my family. 'I love you', maybe? No. There wouldn't be time for that. A heart. I would draw a heart on my chest. Everyone would understand that. What did I have to lose? A few minutes of gasping for air? Hell, I want less of that anyway.

Should I just do that? Tear a hole in the suit? With what? It's not like I had a knife or any sort of tools, too much mass, remember? There wasn't anything sharp enough to-

The jetpack. The frame that had attached the jetpack to me. The latches there had a lip like a hook, could I reach back far enough to-

I tested it, without tearing the glove.

Yes, I could reach, and it felt sharp enough.

If not, a backup plan. Open my helmet faceplate, bite my glove and finger, close the faceplate, and write fast.

OK, so, would it work? Or would, in the hard vacuum of space, my blood just clot up and freeze? It was worth a shot.

Six minutes of oxygen remaining.

When it was done, when I had written the letters, should I simply open the helmet? Get it over with quickly, rather than gasping out my last breath in agony? Hell yes. I'm going to die on my own terms. Fuck the Universe.

Take a deep, calming breath, fill my brain with oxygen so I didn't pass out and-

Oh my God what the hell is that? I was so startled, I flung my arms backward away from the thing, sending me into a tumble.

What was- A *dropship*.

As I spun around, I saw it again. A Maxohlx Panther dropship. Shit. Somehow in the middle of freakin' nowhere, the rotten kitties had found-

That's when I saw the logo on the tail, illuminated by navigation lights. United Nations Navy. And a squadron insignia, DAT-154, the Black Knights.

The Panther was from *Valkyrie*.

It was so close, I could read the dull yellow 'No Step' sign on one stubby wing.

Something enveloped me gently, tugging me toward the spacecraft. The rear ramp was open, three crewmembers in hardshell armor were waiting for me, as the nanofiber cord retracted. Following training by doing absolutely nothing other than tucking in my legs and wrapping my arms across my chest, I let them pull me in. One figure pressed a helmet to mine. "Are you OK, Sir?"

It was Commander Gasquet. I had to laugh with relief, biting my lip so my laughter didn't become hysterical. "Yeah, I'm fine," I kept my words simple, knowing my voice would be muffled. "Thank you. Thanks to everyone."

Thanks to everyone except *Skippy*, I made that clear the moment I got my helmet off and breathed the sweet, clean, filtered and many-times recycled air of the dropship cabin. "The beer can really fucked up this time."

"Yes Sir," Gasquet nodded as he guided me toward a seat, the way you do with an elderly person when it's time for their nap. "Strap in please, we need to turn and burn back to *Valkyrie* before this wormhole closes."

"Right," I followed instructions, and the instant I heard my safety belt *click*, there was a surge of acceleration.

"We sent only a dropship, because Skippy was concerned you might be drifting right in front of the event horizon," he grunted, pushed back in the seat by what felt like two gees.

The engines cut off and my stomach did flip-flops again. The event horizon. The wormhole opening behind me. *That* was the bright flash of light I had seen! It must have reflected off the rim of my helmet faceplate, since there wasn't anything else in the area for photons to bounce off of. That was a mystery solved. My suit computer had not been screwing with me. "Thanks. Who figured out where I was?"

"Sir," Gasquet grinned. "You should talk with Colonel Reed about that."

"Ah." That answered my question.

I was right. Skippy is not nearly so freakin' smart as he thinks he is.

CHAPTER TWENTY SEVEN

Back aboard *Valkyrie*, I took Skippy's advice and got the task force turned around, to return to Jaguar via a different wormhole, on a different network. He advised me that, heh heh, the wormhole network he had just severely screwed with might refuse passage, and I didn't want to find out by having one of our ships smack into an event horizon as it closed.

"That network controller hates you, huh?" I asked as I walked into my office with Reed.

"Add it to the list of *dicks* in this galaxy," he grumbled.

"The good news, Sir," Reed announced as she sat across from me, though I noticed she was perched on the edge of her chair. She glanced toward the open door, so I pressed the button to slide it closed. "Is the *tracking software* was installed successfully."

"The- Oh, uh," she had put a lot of emphasis on those two words.

"Yes, Joe, heh heh," Skippy stuttered. "I got the, um, tracking software-"

"You couldn't even keep a simple secret?!" I exploded at him. "Is there any aspect of this operation you *didn't* screw up?"

"Hey, it wasn't my-"

"Sir," Reed held up her hands. "It is not any of my business what-"

"It shouldn't be your concern, Reed but- Damn."

"Is this something I need to know?"

"This is the kind of scary shit that is dangerous for *anyone* to know," I thumped the desk with a fist.

She was taken aback, raising her eyebrows. "If you ever retire, remind me never to apply for your job. I like to occasionally be able to sleep at night."

"A decent night of sleep is underrated," I agreed.

"Sir, may I ask who you are protecting?"

"Everyone, Fireball. Everyone. This is the kind of thing that could cause people to make stupid decisions, stupid, ambitious, *reckless* decisions, if they knew the truth."

"We certainly wouldn't want any ambitious person out there making reckless decisions. Sir," she looked straight at me, but with a tight smile.

"Well, yeah. I paid a lot of money to own the exclusive Reckless Cowboy franchise for this galaxy. I don't want any competition. Reed, I need to talk in private with the beer can."

She nodded and stood up.

I opened the door for her. "By the way, I heard it was you who discovered where I was. How did you figure it out?"

A broader smile. "I just thought outside the box, Sir."

She left, I closed the door again, and I gave Skippy my best fake smile. "We can talk later about your latest absent-minded fuckup. Did the update work?"

"It was *not* my fault and-"

"You want to talk about this *now*? With *me*?"

"Um, I'd like to talk about this *never*, but-"

"Deal."

"Um," he blinked. "What?"

"I agree. We shall not speak of this."

"Oh, wow, cool. I thought you would hold this over my head forever and-"

"Oh, I totally am going to do that, until the end of time."

"Ugh. You just said-"

"I said *we* wouldn't speak of it. I am keeping this massive, nearly fatal screwup in reserve, until a good opportunity in the future, when I need to smack you on the head with it."

"Ugh. I wish that wormhole had killed *me*."

"One of us nearly dying is enough. Back to the subject: did it work? Will wormholes across the galaxy disable the authenticators of Elder weapons that pass through?"

"Yes. That hateful network controller was actually excited, and eager to stop lowly meatsacks from misusing our creator's weapons."

"The network controllers haven't gotten the memo that their creators rode off into the sunset and left them here?"

"No, and do not ever even think of informing them. Those controllers are powerful but simple, they aren't capable of much deep thinking. That's a good thing, you don't want wormholes deciding for themselves whether to open or not."

"Good point. How can we verify all the bullshit you said it true?"

"Joe, this hurts. After all we've been through, you *doubt* me?"

"*Because* of all we've been through, I have to ask the question."

"OK," he sighed. "I guess that's fair. We can test it by bringing an Elder weapon through a wormhole on a network that is far from here. If I detect a change to the authenticator module, that will confirm the update is working properly."

"It will disable *our* weapons also? That is not what you told-"

"No, dumdum. That change won't prevent me from using an Elder weapon. I can't actually use weapons by myself, you know what I mean. It also won't prevent people, meaning filthy monkeys, from using the toys I gave them. What it *will* do is block the kitties and spiders from being even minimally successful in clumsily triggering even a handful of their weapons."

"Outstanding. Can you suggest a wormhole we can visit for a test? Is there one on a route back to Jaguar?"

"There is, but we have to wait for the update to propagate. We should allow two days, to be safe. Networks in more distant parts of the galaxy will take longer to receive and process the update."

"Some of those networks hate you, which is totally unfair," I added to avoid an argument. "Is there any possibility they will refuse the update, because it was initiated by you?"

"That is something they would do, bunch jerks," he muttered. "But in this case, they will be thrilled for an opportunity to provide enhanced security. Their basic everyday jobs are kind of dull, you know? This is the most excitement they've had in, like forever."

"If their lives are so dull, maybe you could invite them to karaoke night?" I made the remark as a joke, too late realizing to my horror that Skippy would assume I was serious.

"Huuuuh," he gasped. "That is a *great* idea, we-"

"No, that is a *terrible* idea. Please forget I said anything."

"But Joe, this is a golden opportunity for me to showcase my talent to a new audience. And, you know, to give a bunch of poor, pathetic losers an opportunity to experience some small amount of joy in their miserable existences. Mostly that. I'm a giver. That's what I do, I give."

"That's what everyone says about you," I mumbled more bullshit to make him happy. "I'm afraid your very generous gift would backfire. Think about it: right now, the network controllers are reasonably content, because they simply don't know anything better is possible. But, if you show them that an AI constructed by the Elders could have a life that is *so much more*, those controllers might spiral down into an endless depression."

"Yes they would, hee hee, those jerks."

"I meant that would be a *bad* thing."

"Oh. Of course. That's what I meant also."

"I'm glad we agree."

"Um hypothetically, if I performed karaoke only for the controllers who unfairly hate me, would that-"

"Be unspeakably cruel and unworthy of your greatness? Yes, it would."

"Crap. I mean, that's what I thought also."

"Good. So, plot a course that takes us through a wormhole that should have received the update by the time we get there. Hey, there is something I need to tell you."

"Will this be you yelling at me again?"

"This is about both of us being dumdums."

"Ha!" he snorted. "As if. You are the only dumdum here."

"Not this time. While I was doing nothing out there, I got to thinking, and I might have solved our problem."

"Your complete lack of singing talent that prevents you from participating in karaoke night?"

"The problem of an outside entity trying to take over the galaxy, you ass."

"Oh, *that* problem. Hmm, interesting. The Elders went through enormous effort to keep an Outsider from gaining access to our galaxy because my creators feared they could not defeat an invasion, but *you* have a way to fix it."

"I have, and that is one reason I am so pissed at you for stranding me in the middle of freakin' nowhere."

"Um, how does you taking a brief vacation relate to finding a solution for-"

"It was not a *vacation*, and it felt like forever. Listen, you little shithead, when I was out there with nothing to do, I had an idea. You know what frightened me?"

"That big hairy spider I snuck inside your spacesuit?"

"It- You *what*? There was a spider in- Are you screwing with me?"

"As far as you know."

"You are such a- Ah, forget it. What scared me wasn't the thought that I would die, it was that I would never be able to tell you my idea. Next time, I am not going anywhere without a marker that can write in a vacuum."

"Um, that is an odd thing to-"

"When the rescue ship arrived, I was about to slice open the glove of my suit, and cut my finger so I could write a note in blood on my suit."

"Blood wouldn't stick to the suit, you knucklehead, it's made of a nanofiber that-"

"Also next time, I am bringing a notepad to write on."

"Next time, we should send someone else," he muttered. "I know you can't wait to tell me, so what is this genius idea that you nearly died to give me?"

"I remembered back to when we had to abandon the *Flying Dutchman*."

"Which time?"

"Huh?"

"You abandoned the ship at Newark, and you abandoned it *again* in the Roach Motel. I'm surprised that ship doesn't have trust issues. Really, I should contact Ship Protective Services and recommend you be declared an unfit captain. Every time some tiny little thing goes wrong, Joe Bishop runs away and-"

"Both of those incidents were not 'tiny little things'. I am talking about the third time, *after* the Roach Motel."

"Oh yes. What about it?"

"The *Dutchman* was infected with an energy virus."

"I do recall that, yes."

"You still can't figure it out?"

"Apparently, my ginormous brain is too organized and disciplined to string random shit together the way you do."

"Energy virus. The Outsider is made of *energy*. We can use the virus to kill it."

He stared at me. "*That* is your brilliant idea?"

"Yes. We are both dumdums, the answer is so obvious."

"Let me," he chuckled. "Ha ha, let me see if I understand this. You were ready to cut open your suit, and sacrifice yourself, to write something like 'Skippy you should use an energy virus to kill the Outsider'. So that after valiant Joe Bishop's frozen corpse was found, we could all rejoice that you had once again saved the galaxy?"

"That's not quite-"

"An effort that would have been for nothing, since blood wouldn't adhere to the material of that suit."

"I know that *now*. I still-"

"Listen, numbskull, it's a good thing you didn't have time for a stupid and futile gesture, because your idea won't work."

"It's an energy virus. It drained the energy from a starship. More than one starship. We even used an energy virus to kill a *Sentinel*."

"It is an energy virus."

"Ayuh, and the Outsider is made of *energy*, so-"

"So, it won't work."

"You need to explain this *very* slowly."

"I can change my avatar into Barney The Moronic Dinosaur if you like."

"I would not like. This makes zero sense. It has to work!"

"It does not. First, it is not actually a virus."

"I knew that. It acts like a virus, it can infect, multiply, and spread."

"True, which is why I used the virus analogy. What you need to understand is the virus does not act against energy, its effect is on the storage medium that contains the energy. It acts against *matter*, Joe. Like powercells. The pathways in a powercell get tangled up, so energy is bound in there, and unable to flow anywhere to do anything useful. I *told* you all this."

"I call bullshit on that. Your solution back then was to drain all the power from the ship, the dropships, even our spacesuits. Not get the power locked up somewhere it couldn't be used, you *drained* the power."

"Yes, I did that to starve the virus. When a powercell is drained of, you know, power, the virus can't use the stored energy to feed itself, can't use that energy to bind pathways in the cells. By draining power from every system, I starved the virus. It couldn't grow, couldn't even maintain its coherence."

"Well, shit." I had never felt more like the galaxy's biggest idiot.

"This is," he laughed. "*So* delicious. If you had been able to write a profound message on your suit, your frozen corpse would have been a source of *amusement*, not salvation."

"Go ahead, have a good laugh. I deserve it."

"I want to laugh, but this is just so *sad*. I had a similar conversation with the engineering team, the day before we jumped into the quarantine zone."

"You did?"

"Yes. They suggested we could use an energy virus against the Outsider. Of course, I told them it wouldn't work."

"Why didn't you tell *me* about this?"

"Truthfully? I expected you would already understand that an energy virus wasn't a solution. Apparently, I greatly overestimated you."

"Shit. Please do not tell anyone about this."

"Um, too late. I have been chatting with several of the engineers. *They* got a good laugh out of it, so you accomplished something good today."

"Skippy," I stood up. "I am going into my shower, to curl up in a ball, and stay there until everyone has forgotten all about this."

"Um too late for that, Joe. I composed a catchy tune called 'Joey the Dumdum Spaceman' and it has already caught on with crews across the task force. This incident will live on *forever*!"

The integration training was, as Dave had stated, mostly dull lectures with PowerPoint slides. By the first afternoon, Poindit was bored out of his mind, and ready to quit. Unfortunately, the Marines were also bored, and desperate for some fun during the afternoon break. Several of them got coffee and went outside though the day was scorching hot. Sitting on a fallen log under the shade of a tree, they were relaxing until a bug crawled out from under the log and across one guy's boot. He kicked it away, then dumped out his coffee and smacked the cup down over the scurrying insect.

"Looks kind of like a scorpion," the lance corporal poked at the insect with a stick, as it tried to climb the inside of the cup. "Hey, I bet I can eat this thing. What-"

"Do *not* eat that," Jates grabbed the cup, covering it with the lid of his own beverage container. "Did you idiots not read the briefing package about local wildlife?"

"The stinger is deadly?" Lance Corporal Evens guessed.

"Not to you," Jates admitted. "The venom of this insect is only mildly irritating to humans. But, if you *eat* it, there are proteins in its body that can cause violent seizures, migraine headaches, and temporary blindness."

"Shit," Evens took a step back. "That thing is off the menu, then. What about you, Surkind? The venom won't bother you at all?"

"The venom can be fatal to my people," Jates lifted the lid and carefully tipped the insect into his open palm. Agitated, the insect twitched its stinger in the air. "This animal we call a 'turvixit', it is from our homeworld. They tend to hitchhike everywhere Kristang go."

"Damn. Be careful, Surkind."

"I will be careful, because unlike you I am not a dumbass," Jates glared, but not at the corporal, his glare was reserved for the dangerous invasive insect. "I am also not soft and squishy like humans." His other hand darted in, seizing the tail right below the barbed stinger. While the insect twisted itself trying to get away, he bit off the stinger and spat it onto the ground, then popped the turvixit into his mouth. "Mmm, crunchy on the outside, tender on the inside."

Unfortunately, Poindit not only witnessed the incident, he got it on video. From then on, Jates was the star of the show, he could not get rid of the video crew, they followed him everywhere. And Escott Poindit wanted to be Jates's new best friend.

The Public Relations briefing room of the Ethics and Compliance Office headquarters was rarely used for its stated purpose, most of the time it was either empty, or as a spare conference space. When it was open to the public, it was invariably jammed with members of the press, for the veteran journalists all knew that a *juicy* story was certain to be announced. That day was no exception. Eleven days earlier, Kenten Argovian has been killed in what the authorities on Rekonva originally described as 'suspicious circumstances', but then quickly backtracked to tag the incident as an 'unfortunate freak accident'. In a happy coincidence, the chief investigator of the Rekonva civilian police force won a substantial lottery the very next morning, and immediately left on what was described as a 'long planned and overdue family holiday' that required a luxury cruise starship to delay departure by three hours so a shuttle, carrying only the chief investigator, could reach orbit.

The apparent blatant assassination of a prominent citizen was an immense scandal, causing much alarm and even more wagering, across Jeraptha society.

The room was primed for excitement when Admiral Uhtavio Scorandum stepped to the podium, adjusted his formal and rather gaudy uniform, and needlessly tapped a claw on the microphone. "Can everyone hear me?"

The response was loud murmurs and groans, everyone was familiar with the game being played. There were fewer groans than usual, for the crowd had become agitated when they saw the official speaker was the famous Admiral Scorandum. The veteran reporters all knew that day was destined to become *legendary*.

The groans, and even a few openly disgusted mutterings, were from a handful of journalists who had written numerous articles condemning the admiral, at the time he was being pursued for arrest his involvement in the Skipcoin collapse, for the flagrant and egregious accounting irregularities at SkipWay, and not incidentally for selling secrets to the Maxohlx. Scorandum's subsequent exoneration, with government declaring him a hero for his valiant undercover actions, had been deeply embarrassing to many of the assembled audience.

Especially those who had wagered heavily on how much time the scoundrel Scorandum would spend in prison.

"As you might have heard, a Jeraptha citizen named," Scorandum pretended to check his notes, "Kenten Argovian, was recently killed on Rekonva, under what at first were considered suspicious circumstances. It has been widely publicized that, for several years, the Argovian has been a subject of interest by the Office Of Special Inquiries, and that it is also widely known that the Inquisitors have been unable to find conclusive evidence of Argovian's alleged serious criminal activities. It is because the Inquisitors have been frustrated, some might say even embarrassed," he couldn't resist a dig at the rival office, "that some of the public have spread vicious and unfounded rumors that the Inquisitors were responsible for Mister Argovian's unfortunate death, which is a *serious* and even *damaging* accusation. To assure the public that the incident will be investigated in a thorough, independent and unbiased manner, the Inquisitors requested the Ethics and Compliance Office to review the incident. Accordingly, I personally traveled to Rekonva, to review all aspects of the case on site." He did not bother to mention that he also took the opportunity to visit the infamous Taj Moval casino there, nor did he relate the day he spent racing across the sands in a dune buggy. Such details were irrelevant. "The investigation was exhaustive," he said truthfully, for he had stayed up very late every night at the casino, "and I can now state with full confidence that the incident was *not* an accident."

The room collectively gasped in shock.

"This was a case of accidental *negligence*," he continued. "Please, please," he raised both claws to calm the excited crowd. "If you allow me to announce my findings, you will understand how I reached my conclusions."

The roar died to a sullen, eager silence, the journalists all poised to report the story as soon as the admiral got to the freakin' *point*.

"The boat was ordered to be delivered from offworld as an honest mistake, the part number for 'speedboat' and 'dune buggy' being only two numbers apart. Once it was landed dirtside, the boat was loaded on a sling underneath a vertical lift cargo aircraft, which had filed a flight plan to take it over Mister Argovian's estate, that being a regularly traveled commercial flight path. The aircraft's load master supervised the loading, including the use of proper restraining straps to secure it below the aircraft. The straps had been inspected for integrity, and had ten times the load capacity needed, so there was a substantial safety factor. All of the proper written procedures were followed. *However*," he paused to scan the room. "Video clearly shows that once the straps were in place, the loadmaster failed to tug on them and say 'Yeah that's not going anywhere'."

All the men in the room nodded to each other, murmuring their understanding at what had caused the straps to fail.

A female journalist raised a claw. "Admiral Scorandum? Are you telling us the straps failed because someone *failed to follow a silly ritual*?"

He shrugged. "It's a thing."

Another round of nods and murmurs of agreement by the men in the room. "It's a *stupid* thing," she insisted.

"Well, it's a guy thing, so-"

"I thought that went well," Scorandum tugged the collar of his tight, scratchy formal uniform, unfastening the heavy jacket. "What do you think, Kinsta?"

The clerk, who was only allowed to wear a small badge as evidence the Office of Special Inquiries even acknowledged his employment there, displayed his usual frown. "I think no one in the briefing room buys into your story."

"Ah, Kinsta," Scorandum sighed, as he too often had to do with the other officer, "that is the *point*. The Inquisitors want everyone to know they *got* Argovian, one way or another. Got him, in a way no one can prove."

"Sir, I thought once I joined the Inquisitors, I would be *done* with involvement in sleazy activities."

"Oh ho!" The admiral laughed. "You have no idea who your other employers truly are. I could tell you stories that would-"

"Sir," he begged, "Please don't. My remaining illusions of innocence are the only things that make me drag myself out of bed in the morning."

While I did take a shower to wash off the funk from being wrapped in a plastic bag for two hours, I did not hide in my cabin. That would be a childish and cowardly thing to do. Besides, I was hungry. On the way to the galley, nodding to acknowledge the crew, and pretending I didn't see their amused smiles, I stopped and pulled out my phone. "Skippy, we're jumping toward another wormhole?"

"Yes, I set a course back to Jaguar, like you requested."

"Good. Also, we should visit a Maxohlx relay station along the way."

He lowered his voice, though he was speaking into my earpiece. "Being able to ransack the databanks of a kitty relay station is a *secret*, Joe. We can't hit up relays too often, or the kitties will know we're reading their messages."

"We'll park the task force a couple lightyears away, and just go quick in and out with *Valkyrie*. No one else will know what we are really doing there. Uh, make sure you remember to mess with the antenna aiming motor."

"No way will I forget to do that, hee hee, it is driving the rotten kitties absolutely crazy trying to understand why I am doing that. Um, you realize the antenna thing makes the ability to hack into their relay stations less valuable to us, right? The Maxohlx assume I am somehow using the antennas to access their message traffic, so they are cutting back on the volume of sensitive traffic they route through relays."

"Yeah, I know that. They aren't allowing any info about their dealings with the Outsider to route through relay stations anyway, I'm looking for background intel. OK, you have a good point. Stop messing with the antennas. Whenever we get to Earth, notify Def Com that your attempts to infiltrate relay stations through the antennas have been a failure, and you are halting further testing."

"Um, the UN-dick communications people will have no clue what I am talking about."

"Right, so in your message, also say it was a stupid idea in the first place, and that the next time CECOM wants to waste your time with an idiotic plan, they can forget about it."

"Oooh, so when the Maxohlx inevitably hear about my message, they will find it totally believable?"

"You know it."

"As long as everyone understands the failure is in no way *my* fault."

"It's great to hear you are laser focused on what is truly important."

"Oh, shut up."

We went through two wormholes, on two different networks, and both of the Elder weapons *Valkyrie* carried received updates to the firmware of their authentication systems. Skippy verified that update would be certain to render such weapons unusable to the senior species, and neither of those unauthorized users would be aware anything had happened. Now, the only Elder weapon we had to worry about was the Outsider's single remaining Starbreaker.

Plus, you know, any other horrific thing our newest enemy was planning to do.

CHAPTER TWENTY EIGHT

Reed appeared in my office doorway, holding onto the bulkhead to stop her momentum, and out of breath like she had run from the bridge. "Sir," she paused for a breath. "The courier ship *Lightning* just arrived, with a distress call from Paradise."

She had taken time for another breath, so I asked, "The distress call was directed at *us*?" That would be incredible. It made no sense. *Valkyrie* was back at Jaguar for minor repairs, refueling, and – OK, because I wanted to talk with my family again. Why would the government of the world the Ruhar called 'Gehtanu' they ask for our help? If we weren't at Jaguar, we might not have received the call for a week or more.

"I should have said, the government on Paradise sent out a general distress call, and the *Lightning* brought it here."

"That makes more sense, Jaguar is the closest UN base," I relaxed a bit. Whatever the issue was, the Ruhar or their patrons the Jeraptha could handle it. Except, why was Reed so worked up? "What's the-"

"The hamsters detected a single Maxohlx warship, emerging from jump near the star there. The ship matched the configuration of that cruiser we tracked to the edge of the galaxy. after the Outsider tried to steal Dogzilla. We never did find that ship, Sir."

"Oh shit, is-"

"Before the hamster fleet could respond, the intruder ship sent a message. It's the Outsider. It has given the Ruhar six days to evac the planet, then it plans to bomb the star."

"What the f-"

"The distress call originated two days ago, Sir. We are now fifty four hours into the six day deadline."

"Six Paradise days?" The day on Paradise was different from the twenty four hours on Earth, so a day wasn't-

"The Outsider expressed the deadline in *human* standard time increments."

"Ah," I understood. "A hundred and forty four hours, then. That is convenient."

"Too convenient. The Outsider arrives, at a time when a UN courier ship happens to be there? It has to be a trap, Sir. For *us*."

What I wanted to say was 'Ya think'? Instead I asked, "There are, what? Two hundred thousand humans on Paradise now?"

"A hundred and eighty seven thousand, mostly on the southern continent."

"Close enough to two hundred." The Ruhar had offered half of the continent of Lemuria as a preserve for humans, and many people had been tempted to move there from Earth. Some colonists were simply weary of the constant struggle and strife of living on humanity's fragile homeworld, some were attracted by the opportunity for a fresh start, some were enticed by the offer of free transportation and money to cover two years of living expenses, and others moved to join family and friends already living there. What the Ruhar got from the deal were human shields, yes, but also stronger overall ties to humanity, and a boost to the planet's economy. A squadron of UN Navy ships visiting every couple of months also was good for business, and for our Navy, it was an easy refueling stop.

Other than Earth and Jaguar, Paradise was a logical target, if the Outsider's goal was to kill humans. We knew that was not its goal. Reed was correct; our enemy had to be setting a trap for us. For Skippy.

Crap. It had to know we would respond to its threat, but it had to know we would understand the setup was a trap. So, what was its goal? What was it hoping to accomplish?

"This makes no sense," I leaned my chair back to stare at the ceiling. "If the Outsider triggers its Starbreaker at Paradise, we will be free to bring Bubba hunting with us."

"Maybe, maybe not," Reed shrugged. "The UN Security Council member governments won't like allowing Earth's guardian Sentinel to leave the solar system. The Outsider might be counting on Task Force Black not being able to include Bubba in our operations."

All I did was give her a curt nod. She hadn't said anything new, I had argued with the Joint Chiefs about the possibility of using Bubba as a mobile strike platform, rather than for a static defense role it was never designed for.

"Sir, *we* don't have to handle this. The Ruhar are Jeraptha clients, let the beetles take point."

"The Outsider isn't there because of the hamster population," I noted the obvious.

"Then Admiral Chatterji can send the 7th Fleet. If the Outsider discovers The Merry Band of Pirates isn't taking the bait, it might just go away."

"You are willing to gamble almost two hundred thousand human lives, and millions of Ruhar? Reed, the Outsider is humanity's responsibility, we can't outsource this job to the beetles. And no offense to the 7th Fleet, but their ships can't do much against an energy being from beyond the galaxy."

"We haven't been able to do much about the Outsider either, Sir."

I clutched my chest. "That hurts, Fireball."

"This an obvious trap. The Outsider has to know we will see that, so what is its game plan?"

"So far, it hasn't shown any sign of being a sophisticated actor. Everything it has done has been pretty much direct."

"It lured us into the quarantine zone."

"Yeah, but that was clumsy. The fight turned into a straight stealth starship combat scenario."

"We came close to losing that fight, Sir."

"The point is, we didn't. It had every advantage; it chose the field of battle, it shaped the battlespace before we arrived, it could have chosen to disengage. Still, it lost. The quarantine zone was its best opportunity, and it failed. We haven't seen any indication that it is capable of doing sneaky shit. Not like we do," I grinned, then my smile faded. "If this is anything other than what it appears, then the Outsider is getting advice from its local partners."

"The Maxohlx?"

"Yeah, those assholes. They never learn."

"They don't *want* to learn, Sir. All they want is to maintain the comforting illusion that they are destined to rule the galaxy."

"I have bad news for them about that."

"They won't listen to you, or anyone."

"That's their loss. Skippy!"

"Yes?' He appeared immediately.

"You heard all that?"

"I know basically what's going on. Please tell me you are not planning to take the ship into another obvious trap."

"*You* convinced me to jump into the last-"

"Joe, it is just *sad* that you try to deflect the blame. You are the commander, the buck stops with you. It's not my fault if you listen to terrible advice."

Arguing with him wasn't going to get me anywhere. "Reed, prepare the ship for departure. We will hopefully be going with the 7th Fleet, but we'll go alone, if necessary."

She stiffened, knowing I had dismissed her concerns, and dismissed her also. "We can be ready to jump away in two hours."

"Skippy, how fast will a least-time course to Paradise get us there?"

"With a wormhole shortcut? Travel time will be anywhere from fifty seven to sixty two hours. The variable is the alignment of the wormhole I have to screw with, depending on our departure time. The other issue is assuming the 7th Fleet is coming with us, that will slow us down considerably."

"That's cutting it close. The 7th Fleet can't get spun up that quickly, even if Chatterji leaves behind his support ships."

"The entire fleet is undergoing refueling and resupply, Sir," Reed noted. "I don't see how they could move out in less than a full day."

"I'll talk with Chatterji. Damn. Twenty four hours before departure, sixty two hours of flight time, that gets us to Paradise only four hours before the deadline. That doesn't give us much time for recon and-" I had a thought. "Skippy, show me a star chart that covers Jaguar and Paradise, please. With the wormhole networks also."

"I can't imagine why you would need-"

"Just do it."

"Fine."

The holographic chart floated in the air above my desk. "OK, now show me the shortcut." A yellow line appeared between wormhole ends that were not normally able to connect. The chart matched the picture in my memory. Only two wormholes provided access to Paradise. "These two wormholes," I pointed to the dots on either side of the icon for the planet. "Can you create a shortcut between them also?"

"You want *two* shortcuts? Listen, numbskull, a second shortcut between those two will only delay our arrival at-"

"Yes or no?"

"Ugh. Yes. Yes, Joe, I can do a whole lot of stupid things. Generally the point is to avoid doing anything stupid, but you-"

"If we take the second shortcut, how does that affect our arrival time?"

"It will add another eighty one to eighty nine minutes to our travel time."

"That leaves only two hours, then, to recon, plan, and execute."

"That is not nearly enough time for-"

"Actually, this is better than I expected. Better than the enemy expected also, I'll bet. This was set this up, knowing *Valkyrie* was at Jaguar. The faster we arrive, the more confident it will be that we rushed into battle without any time to prepare."

"We *won't* have any time to prepare for the fight against the Outsider, dumdum. It-"

"You're looking at this all wrong, Skippy. This situation isn't what you think. I don't see this as a threat, I see this as an opportunity to *eliminate* a threat."

"*I* see this as you finally falling into a delusional delirium and-"

"Shut up for a minute, will ya? I need to ask you a question."

The 7th Fleet performed a miracle, and was ready to move out in only eighteen hours, though that meant we had to leave four ships behind. Skippy also performed a miracle, routing us through two wormhole shortcuts, and retuning not only the jump drive of *Valkyrie*, but also of the two 7th Fleet star carriers. The result was we arrived near the Paradise star system with thirteen hours to spare before the deadline.

As usual, we first jumped in several lighthours from the star, to get a look at what the potential battlespace looked like recently. By recent, I mean we were viewing photons from nine hours ago. We saw a lot of activity in orbit, panicked Ruhar civilians being pulled into orbit by dropships, and major social disruptions on the surface. We couldn't do anything about that, and we already had enough shit to worry about. My greatest concern was if I had guessed wrong, millions would die on Paradise, and that would be the *best* scenario. Worst case would be loss of *Valkyrie*, the 7th Fleet, and Skippy being captured or even killed, if that was possible.

Shit.

I often accused Skippy of being blindly overconfident. Was I guilty of the same fatal flaw? Earlier in my career, I lacked confidence in myself to the point where Smythe had to give me a pep talk several times. No way would young Joe Bishop have done anything like the plan I had thrown together for Paradise. Hey, I wasn't old yet, I just wasn't the young dumbass I used to be.

It was too late to second guess myself. We were committed. *Valkyrie* made three short jumps, the last emerging in local spacetime twenty lightseconds from the last known location of the Outsider's ship. That area was uncomfortably close to the star, which could become a problem if the Starbreaker weapon was triggered. More of a problem for the inhabitants of Paradise than for a properly shielded starship, but I couldn't ignore the risk.

We jumped into the system alone, without the 7th Fleet. One stealthy starship, aided by the extreme awesomeness of an Elder AI, had a much better chance of arriving unnoticed, than if thirty four warships jumped in with us.

We had work to do. As was typical, when I said 'We' I meant Skippy had work to do. Before we jumped, he had created thirty four microwormholes, with one end of each tiny spacetime rip in the nosecone of a drone, and the other ends clustered around our stealth field generators. Those generators were not wrapping a field around *Valkyrie* to conceal our battlecruiser, the effect was being channeled into and through the microwormholes, each of which were on the razor's edge of collapse from the energy surging through them. Skippy had become more skilled at keeping the tiny spacetime tunnels open, even he couldn't stretch the laws of physics beyond a certain point.

"How's it going, Skippy?" I asked as we all watched a clock on the display counting down.

"Fine."

"I'd appreciate a bit more detail on th-"

"Nominal."

"OK, is there-"

"If you monkeys could stop dawdling and *get on with it*, that would be great."

"The timing on this has to be precise, Skippy."

"The timing is *inconvenient*, knucklehead. Ugh, this whole phase of the op requires ships flown by monkeys to make precise jumps. What are the odds *that* will-"

"We will find out in three, two, one, showtime."

Thirty three ships jumped inside their designated stealth bubbles. The other ship didn't miss its jump target, it hadn't jumped at all. At the last second, its navigation system lacked confidence in the precision of the virtual coils, and scrubbed the jump. That was a good call, though it meant we had one less weapons platform in the fight.

"Wheeeew," Skippy imitated letting out a breath. "That was nerve-wracking. It worked, barely, thanks to my continued awesomeness."

He wasn't boasting about that, though he complained about the difficulty of human ships jumping with any reasonable level of accuracy, he had actually provided almost real time guidance through the Elder comms nodes that were aboard *Valkyrie* and battleship *Mont Blanc*, flagship of the 7th Fleet. "Skippy, you can release the microwormholes when you sense those ships have their own effective stealth fields." The point of us projecting stealth effects around the jump points had been to conceal the arrival of the 7th Fleet. The Outsider, assuming it was relying on the sensors of a Maxohlx cruiser, should have no idea that *Valkyrie* had friends to back us up.

"Aaaand, done. Wow, I'm glad that is over," Skippy shuddered. "Now I need a nap."

"No rest for the weary yet, sorry. Fireball, jump option Alpha, please."

We jumped. A short jump, less than eight lightseconds, away from the hidden 7th Fleet, and closer to the star.

"Hey like, the comm node connection is stable," Bilby reported. "This is cool, working with other ships. I don't get to do this much."

"We will try to arrange more play dates for you in the future. You are tied into the Fleet's targeting systems?"

"Affirmativo, Dude."

"Outstanding. Initiate active sensor sweep, please, sixty degree cone forward." What I meant was, I didn't want our sensor pulses radiating backward, toward the stealthed 7th Fleet. The Starbreaker had to be launched near a star to be effective, and the weapon would create a massive solar flare from where it detonated, so we had positioned *Valkyrie* between the star and the planet *Paradise*. The ship carrying the Starbreaker should be nearby. Unless it was hanging out a full lightminute away, laughing its ass off at us, and planning to jump close to the star at the last moment. Hey, in space combat against stealthed ships, you have to risk using active sensors to burn through the-

Alarms blared. "We are caught in a damping field!" Gasquet warned.

Or, in space combat against stealthed ships, you can wait for the enemy to announce their presence. "What is the source of the-"

"Dude it's like, all around us," Bilby was disgusted. "There must be a minefield of damping drones here."

"Interesting," I said slowly, with a grin.

"What?" Reed looked at me as if I was mad.

"This isn't just the Outsider. This is a team effort."

"It's working with the Maxohlx?" She guessed.

"Or, no one is working with anyone else. I suspect we have a single actor here."

"Sir?"

"This whole setup was bullshit from the start. It made no sense for the Outsider to burn its last Starbreaker here."

"It's using the weapon as a *trap*," she insisted.

"This is definitely a trap," I agreed. "Just not by the Outsider. It outsourced the job. Or, its local partner just got ambitious."

"The *Maxohlx* are doing this?"

"That has been my opinion since we heard about the distress call."

Her eyes grew wide and she was hurt. She wanted to know when I had planned to inform her of what I knew, or suspected. Instead of explaining, I planned to show her, and the crew. And everyone. "Fireball, let's-"

"*Valkyrie*, you are trapped this time," the gruff growl of a Maxohlx came through the speakers, as a starship dropped stealth. Holy shit, the display showed the thing was less than two lightseconds away from us. It had hardly moved from its original location, keeping position as Paradise swung around the star. Reflexively, I tapped an icon on the armrest as the voice continued. "I would offer you an option to surrender, but we both know you are too foolish to accept. Good riddance to an annoying problem. Launch weapons!"

Though we were viewing events with a brief time lag, that hardly mattered. The Maxohlx ship was firing Elder weapons at us, and not by our clumsy method of pushing them out of docking bays. The kitties had dedicated ships for transporting and deploying Elder weapons, those ships were built with large bore railguns running along the forward half of the hull. It was a much better method for deploying strategic weapons, there were only two issues with launching Elder horror devices. The Maxohlx had a marginal, unreliable capability for arming the things, but they couldn't aim them at all. The procedure for firing Elder weapons was similar to the early decades of submarine warfare, when torpedoes had no internal targeting systems. The Maxohlx ship had to point its bow toward the target. That's why it had hardly moved over the past three days. The other issue with deploying Elder weapons is they are not only heavy, they have a mechanism that actively resists changes to their momentum. To get the massive thing moving along a railgun tube takes a *lot* of force, enough that even a ship dedicated as a strategic platform can only fire two of them at a time. The Maxohlx understood that to be ensured of at least one weapon detonating, they had to fire multiple of them at us.

And, while they are shooting, the ship can't move.

You know what *can* move, really fast?

Maser beams.

The coolest thing about a directed energy weapon like a maser beam is they are coherent photons that travel at the speed of light. Unless an enemy has a faster than light sensor capability such as the Elder comm nodes used by the UN Navy, the first notice the enemy has of incoming maser beams is when they strike the shields. When thirty three warships of the 7th Fleet plus *Valkyrie* all fire maser cannon broadsides at an unmoving target less than two lightseconds away, with Bilby coordinating the targeting in real time, the enemy's shields tend to be less effective than the manufacturer claimed. When multiple beams from each of thirty four ships all strike not only the same ship but within a circle less than a centimeter across, those masers burn through the energy shield like it is made of butter. Then, they churn the armor plating into plasma, which is a problem since the erupting plasma actually interferes with beams following up on the initial broadside. By that time, the AI that ran the ship had decided not to wait for orders from its biological masters and in a snap 'Oh *fuck this*' decision, fired thrusters on emergency to move the ship out of the way of the next blast of maser bolts.

Which might have been marginally successful, if Skippy hadn't predicted exactly how the control AI of a Maxohlx Red Section strategic strike cruiser would react to the complete loss of an energy shield. Since Skippy did that particular feat of magnificence, the cruiser blundered directly into the path of ninety six railgun darts.

Result?

Well, you know.

The cruiser disappeared in a brilliant flash of light when darts impacted the fully charged drive capacitors.

"Crap!" Skippy groaned.

"What?" For a moment, my confidence slipped.

"Now we won't have an opportunity to engage in snarky repartee with the kitty over there."

"That kitty is now *everywhere*, and it was going to be a boring conversation anyway."

"Well, that is a good point. We gave it a few seconds to monologue at us, and the best it could do was 'Good riddance'?"

"Red Section should hire Skippy's Public Relations and Crisis Management Associates, to coach them on how to truly intimidate a foe."

"Wow, Joe, that is a great idea. I can-"

"No, that is a *terrible* idea. Do not help the freakin' kitties, please. Bilby, connect me to Admiral Schulz, please."

"General Bishop?" The 7th Fleet leader appeared in the holographic display, looking like he had seen a ghost. "Congratulations on an impressive victory- This *is* a victory?"

"Yes, absolutely. Could you task a couple of your escort ships to fetch the Elder weapons the enemy launched? Don't worry, they are inert."

Schulz pointed to someone out of view, then, "You know for certain they are inert?"

"Uh, not exactly inert, I should have said they are *safed*. Skippy remotely disabled them," I repeated the lie the beer can and I had agreed on, and it really was not a lie. A deception, but not an outright lie. Skippy had remotely disabled the things.

"The enemy launched fourteen Elder weapons, and *all* of them are safed?"

"Are you not trusting the awesomeness?" Skippy demanded.

Schulz wasn't intimidated. "I am of course trusting the awesomeness, Mister Skippy. What I would like is for General Bishop to explain what the hell just happened here."

"I would appreciate that also," Reed grimaced at me.

"That's fair. The Outsider either is working with the kitties here, or this was a Maxohlx initiative all along. That Starbreaker weapon the Outsider has is mostly useless against a starship like *Valkyrie*, and it knows it can't beat us in a standup fight. That's why it lured us into the quarantine zone, where it had prepared the battlespace to give it an edge over us. That still didn't work, I was confident that even if the Outsider was who lured us here, *it* wasn't the actual threat. That left the kitties. They could try ambushing us with a massive fleet, but the sensors we hid in this system years ago would have detected a large number of ships jumping in, no matter how good the Maxohlx are at stealth. The only possibility remaining was a small group of Maxohlx ships deploying their strategic weapons against us, and I wasn't concerned about that, because Skippy can mess with the trigger mechanisms of Elder weapons remotely."

Schulz had a vein throbbing on his right temple. For some reason, that happens with a lot of senior officers I deal with. "*When* did you plan to reveal that information to Def Com?"

"The anniversary of Columbus Day is coming up, I was saving it as a surprise."

"Joe even bought a very nice greeting card!" Skippy chirped. "He hasn't signed it yet, despite me reminding him every-"

"Anyway, now you know, and now the Maxohlx know, since they certainly must have another ship around here somewhere to watch the festivities. We also now have fourteen more Elder weapons, or we will, once your ships catch them." On the display, I saw he had already dispatched eight destroyers. The inert weapons were coasting along together, they would be easy to intercept.

Schulz didn't know what to say. He was a two star admiral, I was a two star general, and I had more time in grade. Also, Def Com standing orders allowed the commander of the Special Mission Group to temporarily requisition almost every military asset controlled by the United Nations. Plus, as he just mentioned, we had kicked ass. You can argue with success, but it's not easy to do. The guy stared at me until it just got awkward. "Uh, we're going to jump away, in case the Outsider is hanging around here, I don't want to make *Valkyrie* an easy target. We will remain within communications range."

"Other than the units tasked to recover the Elder weapons, does my force need to remain here?"

"No. I would jump away most of your force. Those Elder weapons are a priority."

"I'll leave a cruiser squadron as a guard force, until the weapons are secured. We will debrief at the primary rendezvous point?"

"Yes. Bishop out." Jamming a thumb down on the button to cut off the audio from my end, I turned to Reed. "Jump Option Charlie."

CHAPTER TWENTY NINE

We jumped. That first jump was a distance of only six lightminutes, just to clear the battlespace. All I intended to do was remain close enough to provide support if someone tried to interfere with Schulz's destroyers, while they ran out to the store for more party favors. That reminded me of something important. "Skippy, could you provide special handling instructions for those weapons?"

"The UN Navy has procedures for the proper handling of strategic weapons, Joe."

"Yes, but there is nothing *proper* about this situation. Destroyer crews are not usually trained to work with strategic weapons, and they don't have the special equipment for securing them in a docking bay."

"Hmm. Good point. I will throw together a helpful YouTube video showing how to take aboard and secure a variety of Elder weapons, and make sure no knucklehead out there tries to hold them in a docking cradle with duct tape, unlike *someone* I know."

"That was one time, and we were in a hurry."

"It took forever to remove the tape residue from those weapons," he sniffed "OK, done. Video has been provided, and receipt acknowledged. Now, all we can do is wait. I estimate the recovery ships will need fifty two minutes before they can jump to the rendezvous point."

"Sir?" Reed leaned toward me. "May I speak with you in my office?"

Her timing wasn't great, I was reluctant to leave the bridge until the entire 7th Fleet had jumped away safely. But her office was just outside the bridge door, and she trusted her people to handle the ship and any situation for a short time. "Yes."

She stood up. "XO, you have the conn."

"I know what you're going to say, and you're right," I admitted as I sat in the chair across from hers in what used to be my office. *Used* to be, that was the key word. The ship was hers now, I had to respect that. And I did. She clearly didn't believe that. "I had a good reason for not reading you into my plan. If this went sideways, one of us needed to be mentally prepared to deal with a disaster."

She nodded. Her eyes were still cold. "Jennifer- Simms," she added, in case there was another Jennifer we both knew. "Gave me some advice when she left *Valkyrie*. A lot of advice, and one thing in particular. She told me to take responsibility for my own career growth, because developing subordinates is not one of your strengths."

"That is not-" my hot reaction was instant, and as the words left my mouth I realized, possibly unfair. "Reed, I am listening." I meant that. Truly listening, not just waiting for her to finish so I could speak what was on my mind.

"You want to hear this, Sir?"

"It sounds like I need to hear it. Before you ask, you have permission to speak freely. I hope you understand that you never have permission to *not* speak freely with me."

"Simms was honored to be a Pirate, and she enjoyed serving with you. Mostly. A lot of it sucked."

"Still does," I flashed a tight grin, then nodded for her to continue. She didn't need me making jokes, she needed me to shut my mouth and let her talk.

"She learned something every day. Mostly from you."

Again, I just nodded.

"She would have learned more if you had included her in important decisions. You have a pattern of concealing the truth from your subordinates. Sir. Not including her in the process of your decision-making deprived her of understanding how vital command decisions should be made. The Air Force tells me I can learn that skill from training. That's bullshit. Out here, there isn't any formal training that can prepare you to handle the unexpected. You have to do it, or have seen it done. Simms felt she grew more as a leader during the short time she had command of the *Constellation*, than in all the years she served under you."

"Is this the time for me to speak?"

"If you want, Sir."

"I meant, if there is anything else I need to hear, anything that might help me become a better and more effective leader, I want to hear it."

"It's not you, Sir. The problem is, you're not developing anyone to take over from you. Even a team stacked with All-Stars needs someone ready to come off the bench when needed. When you were lost on the other side of that wormhole, I took over, and I realized right then I was not prepared."

"You did an outstanding job, Reed. I couldn't have done any better. I don't know if I would have figured out what happened."

"Did you?"

"Well, yes, but that's because I saw the Lobster Nebula, and remembered the only other time I saw it was after a wormhole shortcut. If it was you lost and me aboard *Valkyrie*, I don't know that I would have understood what happened in time. To me, that incident shows you *are* ready."

"Today's incident shows I am not, I'm woefully unprepared. If you weren't in command when we received the distress call, I would not have taken *Valkyrie* here. Not into another ambush."

"If we hadn't come here, nothing would have happened. The deadline would have expired, and the Maxohlx would have quietly slipped away. That," I paused to think for a moment. "Might actually have been a better result. The Maxohlx would be revealed as unable to- No, no, that's only in hindsight, because we know the kitties were here instead of the Outsider. Still, either way, no one would have bombed the star. Paradise was never in danger, so if *Valkyrie* never responded to the distress call, there wouldn't have been any negative consequences for us."

"That is hindsight also, Sir."

"I'm not following your logic."

"From the viewpoint of the Ruhar, and the humans on Paradise, if we hadn't responded, had done *nothing* to protect them, relations between the Ruhar and humans would have been set back seriously. Potential allies would question whether the UN will be able or even willing to assist, in any situation where we have to put our assets at risk. You didn't *know* Paradise wasn't under threat."

"I see your point. And, I see you're right, damn it. Not damn it that you're right," I hastened to add. "That I didn't consider the political aspect."

"Def Com advises that a senior leader must always consider the political aspects of a decision, especially when it affects allies. Sir, this situation only worked in our favor because you were right."

"And because the crews of *Valkyrie* and the 7ᵗʰ Fleet performed outstandingly."

"Thank you," she gave a me a tight smile, one that I read as 'do not try to change the subject'. "This latest, triumph," she said the word with reluctance. "Was only possible because you knew a secret: that Skippy can remotely disable Elder weapons. If you had died on the other end of that wormhole, who would have that critical information?"

"Skippy."

"Only Skippy?"

"It's kind of a new thing."

"That doesn't explain why you didn't inform me. Sir, you appointed me as the deputy commander of the Special Mission Group. I don't hold the rank, that's a separate issue. I can't effectively do my job unless I know what *you* know."

"Reed, you don't want to know a lot of," I tapped my head. "What is in here."

"I don't *want* to do a lot of things, Sir, that's called 'being in the military'. It's my job. I am supposed to ask myself whether I am doing everything I can to assure the success of the mission. Right now, I am doing the only thing I can do: asking you to read me in on information I *need* to know."

"That is, complicated."

"Everything we do out here is complicated."

"I can't argue about that."

"Sir, did you read Simms in on secrets no one else knew?"

"Yes, I did," I said slowly. "Sometimes, also Smythe."

"Do Frey and I have all that knowledge now, Sir?"

"Not all of it. Reed, you have to understand, it's not just an Opsec issue. There are things I wish *I* didn't know. I don't want to burden anyone else with that shit."

She clenched her jaw, looked down at the desk, then, "I didn't join the military to be protected from scary monsters, Sir. I came out here to *fight* them. When something bad happens, do you tell your boys that everything will be all right?"

"Yes, of course."

"I am not a child. I don't need to be protected, I don't want it. You can't make that decision for me."

Wow. She was pissed. She was also a hundred percent right. "Some of the secrets I know are no longer relevant, their time has passed. Others, I keep because if the knowledge became widespread, it could damage our security, in some cases cause severe damage."

"All I am asking is to know anything that might be actionable, now, in this fight. The knowledge that Skippy can render Elder weapons inert is actionable, or *in*actionable. Without that information, I would not have acted."

"Fireball, I hear you."

"Sir, you are a great leader. The *best*. You are also one person. Skippy can't be replaced," she automatically glanced at the ceiling, expecting him to appear. Wisely, he kept silent. "Humanity does need a backup for you, as much as we can find one."

"You want to be a full partner on this team."

"It doesn't have to be me, Sir. You do need to trust *someone*."

"If I didn't trust your experience and judgment, you wouldn't be in command of *Valkyrie*. All right, there is something you need to understand: you will breaking the chain of command, and I have to know you're OK with that. You will hear secrets the Joint Chiefs don't know, and they can't ever know."

"Our Comsec is too easily hacked," she nodded.

"It's not just that. The Chiefs are legally bound to inform the politicians they serve. Some of what I know, well," I shrugged. "That knowledge could tempt political leaders into making foolish decisions. Politicians are not great at sacrificing short-term gains for long-term results. I need to hear you promise that you won't reveal my secrets, even if you receive a direct order to do so."

"That is, complicated, Sir."

"That is why some secrets I keep to myself. There might be a partial solution. Skippy?"

"Yes, Joe." He appeared. "What's up?"

"Don't pretend you haven't been listening."

"Um, I can neither confirm nor deny any such-"

"Samantha Reed needs to be granted full citizenship in the Glorious People's Republic. As president of Skippistan, I hereby grant her all the rights and privileges associated with-"

"Whoa! Slow your roll there, Joe. Citizenship is expensive, you can't-"

"Replay the audio if you want. Did it sound like I was asking a question, or *making a statement*?"

"Ugh. The second one. You can't just-"

"*You* made me president."

"I didn't think you would be so-"

"The words you are looking for had better be 'bold' and 'decisive'."

"Um-"

"Sir?" Reed cocked her head. "I am not ungrateful for your generous offer, but what does this do for us?"

"I will formally request you to be seconded to the armed forces of Skippistan."

"The UN Navy won't go for-"

"The Navy doesn't have to. You are an officer in the United States Air Force, serving in the UNN. The Air Force will be thrilled to have one of their own in such a senior position. You know your branch isn't happy about this 'Blue To Black' shit. It will also mean that, in certain sensitive operational matters, you report to me, not to the Joint Chiefs."

"That's not how secondary service works, Sir."

"It's not how it *used* to work. The rules got changed for my situation, about a decade ago. Def Com, or it was still UNEF back then, didn't like giving up control. They did like having deniability if I screwed up."

She pursed her lips. "We wait for the Air Force to sign whatever paperwork is needed for the transfer?"

"We could, but I already discussed this possibility with General Alvarez, after we stood up the Special Mission Group again. It was his suggestion."

That prompted a seriously raised eyebrow. "When did you plan to tell me about *that*?"

"I'm telling you now. My agreement with Alvarez was I could activate the offer at any time. The White House agreed. Listen, I know this feels like people have been making deals about your career behind your back, but-"

"It doesn't just *feel* like that, Sir."

"It's your choice."

"The chief of the Air Force, and the President, have signed off on this, and I can refuse?"

"OK, good point. But, no one needs to know I made the offer."

"Shiiiiiit," She groaned. "This means I can hear the info I need to do my job?"

"I promise," I told her, and it was only a tiny little lie.

"Fine, I accept. Do I, um, have to change uniforms?"

"Ooooooh," Skippy gasped. "That is a *great* idea. I have never designed an Air Force uniform, I will get right to work on-"

"No, that is a terrible idea."

"But-"

"You switched my ceremonial sword for a *banana*."

"Yes, and everyone got a good laugh out of it."

"They were laughing at *me*."

"Oh, get over yourself, Joe."

"Reed, you will wear a GPRS patch on your uniform blouse, that's it."

"Joe, you are seriously missing an opportunity for a truly *bold* fashion statement that-"

"That is why I am doing it."

"Sir, I accept." Reed announced before Skippy could say anything else. Glancing at the her tablet, she looked up. "The destroyers are decelerating to match speed with the Elder weapons, no sign of hostile actors in the area."

"We have time, then. Do you want to hear the *truth* about how Skippy can remotely disable Elder weapons? Among other secrets?"

"I'm ready."

"You think you are, but you're not."

I told her everything. Well, almost everything. What she did not learn were secrets that were no longer useful, like the fact that Admiral Reichert and Red Section had not been responsible for waking up Sentinels. That particular lie had plunged the Maxohlx into a vicious civil war, and had kept them mostly too busy to cause trouble for humanity. With that war having ground to a bloody halt, there was no reason to reveal the truth, and a whole lot of reasons why that secret should stay with me. She also did not hear about the probability field, because I had promised Skippy not to ever tell anyone about that mind-blowing fact. Also because it likely no longer mattered, with the Elders safely in Ascensionland forever.

She did learn some *Exciting Fun Facts* about how Skippy could not actually crash wormhole networks. And how the senior species did not have, and never did have, a reliable method of triggering their Elder weapons. Also, that when a senior species ship carrying Elder weapons passed through a wormhole, those weapons would be rendered unusable. By them, I mean. Skippy could still set them up so we could deploy the things.

Hopefully we wouldn't be doing that again.

By the time I was finished the info dump, Reed had the look of a deer in the headlights, if the headlights were on the bow of a starship that was falling from orbit to splatter the deer and leave a mushroom cloud above a smoking crater. "Simms knows all this?" She asked slowly, gears still turning in her head.

"Except for the thing about disabling Elder weapons, that's a new bonus track for Skippy's Greatest Hits album."

"Holy shit."

"Ayuh."

"How am I supposed to sleep for the next, decade?"

"Skippy has some pills that help me. I didn't need sleeping pills for years while I was on Jaguar. Reed, you do understand why we can't tell the Joint Chiefs that we have no reason to fear the seniors could hit us with Elder weapons?"

"Yes," she grimaced. "Some politician sitting at a desk will eventually decide the galaxy would be a better place if humans were in charge."

"We could replace the Maxohlx as the asshole bullies of the galaxy. It's not only a moral issue for me. I just have a feeling that karma will bite us on the ass if we become the bad guys. What matters right now is, we don't have to avoid a fight with the Maxohlx. Uh, unless we get into a fight in a star system where they have an armory with Elder weapons."

"We should avoid doing that. Sir, responding to the distress call here, was it a test of whether the wormholes really can disable Elder weapons?"

"I prefer to think of it as a proof of concept exercise. Fireball, this could become a major problem for us."

"Sir?" She blinked. "How? You just removed an item from the threat board."

"Until today, the kitties, and their new best friend, have been confident they could eliminate us by using strategic weapons. The Hegemony just had to work up the nerve to do it, and live with the consequences. Now, the Outsider will know it can't rely on the Maxohlx to take Skippy out of the fight. It tried an ambush in the quarantine zone, that didn't work either. Now, it either has to give up, or escalate the fight by bringing out the big guns."

"Big guns, like what?"

"I'm afraid to even think about it. One thing I'm certain of is the Outsider is never going to stop, until we kill it."

"How do we do that?"

"I'm going to be completely honest, I have no idea. Skippy doesn't know whether it is even possible to kill the thing. The-"

A chime sounded, she looked at her tablet. "All Elder weapons are secure, the destroyer squadron has jumped for the rendezvous point."

"We should follow."

"XO," she called on the intercom. "Jump option Foxtrot, punch it."

While the 7th Fleet flew back to Jaguar with fourteen additional Elder weapons, *Valkyrie* lingered near Paradise for a short time. What I wanted to do was talk with the Burgermeister again, and with some old friends who were living on the southern continent of Lemuria. With the very likely prospect of a Maxohlx battlegroup in the area, I couldn't risk exposing the ship, the crew, and mostly Skippy, so I settled for composing two messages to the Burgermeister. The first message was official, simply stating the facts she needed to know. Like, the social disruption on Paradise had been collateral damage from our battle against the Outsider, and that I didn't expect her world to be targeted again. The second message was personal, that when the current mess was over, I would like to visit Paradise again, possibly with my family. We couldn't wait for a direct reply, I would get her message someday through a relay station, or at Jaguar or Earth. Reluctantly, I ordered us to jump away toward a friendly relay station.

During our breakfast status meeting, Reed pushed food around her plate, not eating any of it. We had been reviewing the daily status report, so I knew there wasn't anything going on with the ship she should be overly concerned about.

"You're not hungry?" I asked.

"I'm," she waggled a hand. "I have something on my mind."

"In that case," I reached over and took the two strips of bacon she hadn't touched. "No sense letting this go to waste." I dropped my voice to a whisper. "Want to talk about it?"

She nodded, and drank the last gulp of coffee. "In my office? No rush, Sir."

Five minutes later, having eaten oatmeal and whole grain toast along with the bacon, I arrived at her office. She closed the door after I sat down. "What's on your mind?" I asked.

"Knowing secrets can be a double edged sword, Sir. Last night, I had a dream that *Valkyrie* was defending a human colony from attack by, in my dream the enemy were sort of teddy bears."

"Like Ewoks?"

"Scarier than Ewoks."

"The Ewoks killed, cooked, and *ate* people, that's pretty scary. They gave Princess Leia a dress to wear, which means they probably killed and ate he woman who owned that dress. They looked cute, but those little fuckers were vicious."

She stared at me. "This isn't about Ewoks, Sir."

"Gotcha. Good ahead."

"In my dream, we received an emergency order from Def Com. An enemy fleet was headed to Earth, to bomb our homeworld with Elder weapons, my orders were to stop that fleet. My dilemma was, if I followed orders, the colony would be wiped out. I knew Earth was not in danger from Elder weapons, but I couldn't tell anyone."

"Yeah, that's a crappy dream," I agreed.

"If something like that happened for real, what would *you* do?"

"You can't go wrong by following orders."

"You can, if following orders gets civilian colonists killed for *nothing*."

"Not for nothing. To protect a secret. Ah, this is complicated. In the scenario you described, whether you go there or not, Earth would discover the enemy can't actually use their Elder weapons, so the secret would be out in the open anyway."

"Mmm," she frowned. "What if the enemy jumped into orbit and only threatened to use Elder weapons against Earth, and the UN surrendered?"

"Reed, you can drive yourself crazy with 'What Ifs'. I know that from painful personal experience. My advice is, worry about that sort of thing if it ever happens. If it does happen, trust your gut. See? You missed out on *bacon* because you worried about 'What Ifs'. My advice is, focus on what you can control."

"Like how much bacon I should eat?"

"You should ask yourself, how *much* bacon *can* you eat?"

CHAPTER THIRTY

We stopped at a Jeraptha relay station, to get an update on events in the galaxy, and I was hoping for a message from Def Com. On the bridge, I sat in the observer's station along the rear bulkhead, so Gasquet could be in the executive officer's chair next to Reed. We were not expecting to go into action, and I wanted to duck out of the bridge quickly to play basketball. Hey, maintaining fitness is important for any soldier. That's my story and I'm sticking to it.

"And, done," Skippy announced. "Um, I do not see any message traffic from Def Com that is directed at Task Force Black, and hmm, nothing important going on at Earth as of five days ago. You monkeys can search for your super important sports scores if I put the info on the ship's interweb?"

"Yes, Skippy, thank you," Reed said. "Transmit the crew messages from the queue, please." The crew were allowed to compose letters, audio messages, record video, and submit them to Skippy for encryption. We usually uploaded the compressed file whenever we visited a friendly relay station. Sometimes, the messages reached Earth, Jaguar, Paradise, and other human-occupied planets before we did.

"Done. That was- NO! No no no no- Oh, why do these things happen to *me*?" He groaned, taking off his ginormous holographic hat and stomping on it with both feet. Either the hat was tougher than it looked, or he hadn't bothered to program the avatar to account for physical damage, because the hat kept springing right back into shape.

"Skippy," I half stood with alarm. "What is wrong?"

Reed didn't wait for an explanation, she was a believer in a 'better safe than sorry' policy. She was also a strong believer in a 'shoot first and ask questions later' policy, that's one reason we got along so well. "Pilot, jump option Delta, punch it."

The ship jumped while Skippy continued to punish his hat. "Skippy!" I shouted. "What is going on? What bad thing happened?"

Furious, he snatched his hat off the floor and jammed it back on his dome. "Joe, this is something we should talk about in private."

Reed turned toward me with what I interpreted as a 'here we go again' expression. "We will hold position here, Sir?"

"Yeah, sure. Skippy, is the ship in any danger?"

"No."

"Is Earth in danger? Or Jaguar?"

"No, and no. This is *personal*, Joe."

"We are not tasking UN resources to bail out SkipWay."

"It's not that at all. I will be in your office." His avatar disappeared.

Walking into my office, the door automatically closed behind me. That wasn't just a polite gesture by Skippy, he didn't want the crew to hear whatever sketchy shit he'd gotten into.

"What did you do this time?" I asked as I sat heavily in the chair, leaning it back to look at the ceiling.

"Hey, *I* didn't do anything."

"Of course not. What thing did someone else do, that you will unfairly be blamed for?"

"Um, I had better start at the beginning. You know that SkipWay purchased an old, obsolete Jeraptha star carrier?"

"Def Com asked me what I knew about that about, uh, five or six years ago? At the time, I knew nothing."

"Good."

"No, it is *not* good that your sleazy multi-level marketing scam company has an unregistered, untraceable starship."

"If you are concerned, why have you never asked me about it?"

"If I ask, I will know, and if I know, I might have to do something about it. I have enough shit to deal with already. Why? Is this something I should be worried about?"

"Until a few minutes ago, I would have said absolutely not. However, the situation has changed, and now millions of lives are at risk. An entire civilization could disappear, along with all the art, music, and poetry they have created."

"Wow, you know whenever *poetry* is threatened, I will spring into action."

"Oh shut up, you uncultured cretin."

"Where is this civilization? This had better not be a virtual culture in that stupid SkipSim game you published."

"SkipSim is not *stupid*, Joe. Over a hundred million monkeys log into the game's virtual reality environment every day. They love it!"

"What they love is finding Easter eggs for a free tank of gas, or discounts on groceries."

"Hee hee, those sponsorship deals were a genius marketing idea. Listen, dumdum, I am not talking about simulated people, I mean real meatsacks who are having their lives ruined, and their very souls are in jeopardy!"

"Their *souls*? Oh for- This is about your fake religion?"

"No. Besides, I sold that franchise years ago."

"You- You *sold* your religion?"

"Of course not, knucklehead. All I sold were the rights associated with His Holiness Skippyasyermuni. The copyright, websites, subscriber lists, all that."

"But, I get spam email from the followers of Skippyasyermuni, who is His Holiness now?"

"It's not a *who*. Although, people are involved, so I guess you could say 'who'. It's currently being run by a conglomerate in Singapore. There was talk of the company going public, but the disclosure process would have been *messy*, so-"

"This is not about your religion, so how is anyone's soul in danger?"

"This will go faster if you let me talk, and you listen."

"Talk, beer can."

"OK, so you know I have my own starship. Technically, it is owned and controlled by a SkipWay subsidiary, but we can dispense with the legal bullshit."

"Why do you need a starship? You can't fly it yourself, and *Valkyrie* takes you anywhere you want to go."

"Is this you listening quietly so I can talk?"

"Sorry. Go on."

"After I bought it, I had the beetles perform extensive modifications it so it doesn't have a pressurized section for crew. The ship is entirely automated, it flies by itself. Basically, it is a cluster of large-capacity jump drives, and big fuel tanks. I needed a ship capable of multiple, long-range, independent flights. All the ship needed to carry was a submind."

"One of your subminds?"

"Yes."

"Like Grumpy, or Happy?"

"Much more powerful than either of those two losers," he snorted. "This new submind had to be capable of operating on its own for years, decades even, without contact with or supervision from me."

"You are worried about the *submind's* soul?"

"What? No. Pay attention, please."

"Where did this ship go? I know from Def Com intel reports that it hasn't been seen since it departed Jeraptha space."

"Yes, and that is interesting. My ship *did* return, three years ago, then it left on another flight, now it is back again. Def Com does not know about the remote servicing platform I set up, hee hee. You monkeys are not even as smart as *you* think you are."

"Whatever. I don't expect Def Com to keep track of every ship in the freakin' galaxy. Come on, tell me. Where did your ship go?"

"First, I need to give you some background?"

"Is this like one of those recipes on the internet, where first you have to read fifty pages about the chef's boring life story, before you get to the list of ingredients?"

"Ugh. OK, I'll give you the short version. In a star system far, far away, there was-"

"This story sounds like I'll need a sandwich, a beer, and probably a nap first."

"There was an *antenna*," he scowled at me. "It was, and still is, a long-range, deep-field passive survey system that was set up by the Maxohlx around a hundred and sixty thousand years ago."

"Damn. I always forget how long this freakin' war has been going on."

"Yes, it is a tragedy. Will you shut up, please?"

"Go on."

"This antenna was supposed to collect information on an area of the galaxy's rim, which does not have access provided by Elder wormholes. The Maxohlx were playing the long game, gathering information about inaccessible sections of the galaxy, so they would be ready if a wormhole shift opened up the area."

"Uh huh. Like how the Ruhar spent a lot of money to travel all the way to Earth long before Columbus Day, and left stealthed satellites there?"

"Yes, except the Ruhar were concerned about how their enemies could take advantage of a shift, rather than exploiting the shift themselves. Also, that exploration campaign by the Ruhar was mostly a political exercise by an already unpopular government, and all those initiatives were canceled after the next election."

"OK, so the kitties were preparing for a gold rush?"

"It would be more accurate to describe it as a *land* rush, like what happened to Oklahoma in April of 1889."

"Right. So, why should I care about this?"

"The Maxohlx were themselves disadvantaged by a wormhole shift around a hundred and forty six thousand years ago. That antenna array became so distant from the closest wormhole that it was impractical for the kitties to service it, so they wrote off their investment. The antenna continued to operate as best it could, and it is still collecting information today."

"That's amazing. The kitties are hateful assholes, but they are first-rate engineers."

"They do construct rugged, reliable machines, yes. Plus, the antenna was equipped with some level of automated servicing equipment. Anywho, the thing is still operating, to some limited extent. Over the years, its transmitter's aiming mechanism failed, it stopped beaming data to the designated receiver point."

"What receiver?"

"As a backup in case the Maxohlx lost access to it, the antenna was programmed to send data via a tight beam laser, to a receiver dish in a star system eight hundred lightyears away."

"So, the kitties weren't real concerned about having recent info."

"As I said, they play the long game."

"Right. Again, why is this important?"

"Because twelve years ago, I discovered that a Torgalau deep space antenna array had been picking up a data feed from an unknown star system. The data was encrypted, in an ancient Maxohlx scheme that was still beyond the ability of the Torgs to make sense of. Originally, I became interested in cracking the pathetically simple encryption as a way to show the Torgs what a bunch of dolts they are."

"I would say you're an ass for doing that, but the Torgs are universally considered to be a bunch of dicks, so they deserve it."

"That was my feeling about it, Anywho, when I read that data, I realized there was something interesting. The antenna for the past seven or so thousand years had focused its sensors on several promising star systems, and one in particular. It contains a roughly Earth-sized rocky world in the star's Goldilocks zone, with an oxygen nitrogen atmosphere. Liquid water on the surface, froze water at the poles, one moon that isn't big enough to stop the planet's axis from wobbling, but overall, a habitable world."

"I'll call my lawyer and put in an option to buy the place."

"Very funny, Joe, but you can't. That world is already occupied."

"Holy shit. You mean, this place is like Earth? Far enough from a wormhole, for long enough that intelligent life could develop without being conquered or wiped out?"

"Yes, exactly. If the Maxohlx had received the antenna's data, they might have decided to send a long-range mission there."

"For a first contact scenario?"

"Um, yes, but since it's the Maxohlx we're talking about, they would have studied the local intelligent species. If the locals might be useful, they would have been enslaved. If they weren't considered valuable, the kitties would likely have saturated the surface with deadly bioengineered viruses and microbes, to eliminate a complication."

"Remind me of this, if I ever am ever tempted to go soft on the Maxohlx."

"I will be certain to do that."

"The antenna, how did it know there are intelligent beings on this planet? It picked up radio signals?"

"Um, no."

"OK, then, uh, it detected the signature of artificial chemicals in the atmosphere?"

"The inhabitants have a Stone Age technology level."

I was out of guesses, so, "Just tell me."

"Light sources on the night side of the world."

"Come on. Those could be wildfires. Or volcanos."

"True, except these light sources did not move over many days, weeks, or even years, and the light was the wrong spectrum for a volcano."

With sudden understanding, I snapped my fingers. "Campfires?"

"Those, or villages. Many of the artificial light sources are clustered together, which indicates a settlement of some sort."

"This antenna can see a freakin' campfire across several lightyears?"

"The antenna array is able to detect a small light source over a distance of several *thousand* lightyears."

"Holy- Wow. That is impressive."

"What I described as an 'antenna' is actually a cluster of more than four hundred antennas, networked together across a disc twelve lightminutes in diameter. The Maxohlx, and the Rindhalu, have telescopes that are even more capable."

"Cool. The limitation of that technology is the speed of light?"

"Correct. When I decrypted the data, I discovered the Torgalau first received a tightbeam feed sixty four years ago. Apparently, the transmitter just happened to be pointed toward that star system then. Based on the decreasing signal strength, I expect the beam will move on and point into empty space within fourteen years."

"So, it's lucky the Torgs picked up the signal."

"It is. The star system inhabited by the unknown intelligent species is located twenty seven hundred lightyears from the antenna, and the Torg star system in almost nine hundred lightyears from the antenna. The most recent data received by the Torgs was thirty six hundred years out of date."

"You discovered this data feed twelve years ago? Why didn't you tell me?"

"We were kind of busy slaying dragons at the time, Joe, I didn't want to distract you."

"Oh. All right, then the-"

"Also, I didn't want to listen to you whining about *morality*," he gagged, "and blah blah buh-LAH."

"Skippy," I had a bad feeling right then. "What the hell did you do?"

"Hey, I'm the *good guy* in this story."

"You're telling the story, so of course you think you are-"

"At my own expense, I purchased a starship and had it outfitted for long-range flight. It flew on its own a distance of twenty six hundred lightyears, that's the closest wormhole, and went into orbit. Drones landed and sampled the biosphere, stealthed drones observed the native species, my submind performed a very thorough survey. The ship then returned to report its findings, and to be serviced at a remote station set up by the Jeraptha."

"I'm not happy you concealed all this information from me until now, but what did your ship find?"

"The inhabitants were still in a Stone Age existence. They had not discovered how to smelt metals, so their tools were made of wood or stone. In some more advanced areas, they did have copper and gold, but they simply found veins of relatively pure metal, and beat it into shape, mostly for jewelry and other decorative uses."

"What are they like? What do they call themselves?"

"I call them the 'Porcines'. They, of course, have many names for their species, since they exist in bands of hunter-gatherers, or small villages based on primitive agriculture. The total population of four million Porcines is spread across three of the four continents, the fifth continent is isolated by two large and deep oceans. My submind counted eleven hundred different languages being spoken, and that doesn't include regional dialects!"

"OK, are they insects, birds, mammals, what?"

"The closest analogy is pigs."

"Pigs?"

"Yes, that is why I refer to them as being 'Porcines', get it?"

"Right. Pigs, huh?"

"Wild boar is probably a more accurate analogy. They are on average a meter and a half tall, and more than a meter wide. You would think they are rather stout for their height. They stand on two legs with hoofed feet, their arms have four fingers tipped with vestigial hooves. Their wide, flat noses are instantly recognizable as pig-like. They wear primitive clothing, but their bodies are covered with fur."

"That has to be itchy under clothes in hot weather."

"I can always count on you to focus on what is truly important."

"I guess 'Porcine' is better than calling them 'Swine'."

"Um, why?"

"The word 'swine' has kind of a bad connotation to it."

"Well, you should have told me that before I named the planet 'Swinonia', knucklehead. Would something like 'Bacon-dia' have been better?"

"Uh, I think that would be seriously considered offensive."

"Ugh. This is such a pain in the ass."

"Just change the name."

"I can't do that *now*."

"Why not? It's just an entry in a database or something, right?"

"It *was* a just a database entry, before my submind taught the names 'Porcine' and 'Swinonia' to the locals."

"It did *what*?"

"They needed to communicate with me, or with my submind, so I had it teach them a new common language I invented."

"You created a language?"

"Um, mostly? It is based on Dwarvish from 'Lord of the Rings'."

"So, you ripped off Tolkien."

"Hey, his estate can sue me. I'm pretty sure copyright law doesn't apply near the rim of the galaxy."

"Skippy, you should have just left the pigs- the, Porcines, alone. What you did has to be a violation of the Prime Directive."

"That's a rule from a TV show, numbskull, it's not a real thing."

"It should be."

"Wow, well, if you don't like me teaching them a language, you really won't be happy about the other things I did."

"Oh for- Skippy, I already have enough shit to worry about. *What* did you do?"

"They already had fire, and they knew how to make bricks and crude pottery. Also, they had basic agriculture; they set up and maintained orchards, they planted seasonal crops, that sort of thing. But their technology and societies had been stuck for over thirty six thousand years. The planet is subjected to periods of high volcanic activity roughly every seventeen hundred years, when another planet with an elliptical orbit comes close to Swinonia. When that happens, volcanos erupt and fill the atmosphere with dust and gasses that cool the surface, triggering mini ice ages. Whenever that happens, the Porcine population crashes, civilization is disrupted, and much knowledge is lost. Basically, the poor creatures have to start over every two thousand years."

"That sucks."

"Your eloquent words have perfectly captured the tragedy of the situation."

"You know what I mean, you ass."

"To help the Porcines, because I am all about helping, Joe, I had my submind teach them how to smelt metals, so they can make better tools. My submind also gave them genetically modified crops, to ensure greater yields, and so their staple crops will be more hardy to cope with variable climate conditions."

"That all sounds good, I'm afraid you might run into our old friend, the Law of Unintended Consequences."

"Hey, that has already happened. I taught the piggies to mine ore and smelt metals, and to grow better crops. Did they make agricultural tools, so they can take advantage of their new ability to grow food? Yes. But many more of them made spears and swords and bows and arrows, for the purpose of raiding the farmers in the next village and stealing the crops!"

"Meatsacks are the *worst*, Skippy."

"Tell me about it."

"It is impressive that in only a few years, they invented so many metal weapons."

"Um, Well, um-"

A chill ran up my spine. "You little shithead. What did you do?"

"Hey, someone had to do something. When the peaceful, well, mostly peaceful, farmers of one village were victimized by a bunch of ungrateful assholes from another village, I taught the farmers how to defend themselves. Like, after the raiders attacked with spears and swords, I taught the farmers how to make and use a bow and arrow."

"That can only lead to worse trouble."

"Well, I know that *now*, dumdum. The raiders copied the design of the bow, so I armed the farmers with compound bows."

"Oh my- This is not going to end well."

"It would have been OK if I had stopped there, but the next step was teaching them to make gunpowder, and-"

Leaning forward to bonk my head on the desk, I muttered, "Please tell me this is just a story about bad things that *could* happen."

"I wish. I have no idea how this situation could have spiraled out of control so quickly."

"*I* have an idea how that happened."

"Oh shut up. Are you going to help, or not?"

"Help, how? It sounds like you have already 'helped' way too much. Why the hell did you even do this?"

"I had to. I couldn't trust the job to anyone else, someone else might have gotten it wrong.

"You *did* get it wrong! You didn't need to *do* anything."

"Yes I did. Joe, what I haven't told you is the wormhole network in the area that encompasses Swinonia will experience a major shift in only a hundred and three years. I can delay the shift a bit, but when it happens, the primitive inhabitants of that unfortunate world will be at the mercy of the Wurgalan, since it will legally be *their* territory. The squids took the Urgar on as clients, and I don't need to remind you what happened."

"The Urgars were enslaved, and nearly went extinct, yeah, I know. OK, this changes things. You care about the Porcines, and are concerned they will be exploited by a species with advanced technology?"

"Um, I figured they will be exploited by *someone*, and it might as well be me, right?"

"I , I can't," I stared at him, sputtering. "You little-"

"But let's go with the 'Care and Concern' thing, if that makes me look better."

"I can't believe-"

"You have met me, haven't you?"

"I regret it every day but, yes."

"Are you going to help, or not?"

"I can't make the pigs *un*learn how to make gunpowder, so what do you expect me to do about this?"

"The gunpowder thing is just the tip of the iceberg, or I wouldn't be telling you about this mess. I don't want to tell you at all, it is very embarrassing."

"At least you're embarrassed about it."

"Embarrassed? I am humiliated and enraged. The reputation I carefully built has been destroyed."

"How- That doesn't make any sense. Only I know about this, so how could you rep-"

"I'm talking about my reputation among my faithful followers on Swinonia. They *used* to worship Skippy as a peaceful, loving god, but-"

"I, just, oh, it- Just, don't talk for a minute." I pressed my forehead against the desk and my eyes tightly closed.

"It-"

"Uh!" I shooshed him.

"The-"

"Not yet."

"You-"

"UH!" I jabbed a finger in the air.

Blessedly, he fell silent.

Five breaths. Following my mother's advice, I counted to five while I took deep breaths. Then, with a clear, calm head, I was ready to shove him out an airlock.

Though I should probably hear his side of the story first. "Don't talk, please. Let me see if I understand the situation. You sent a submind to this pig planet, not to protect the inhabitants, but to become their *god*?"

"The position was vacant, dumdum, it's not like I was stealing anyone's-"

"Instead of protecting and serving your followers, you exploited them, and gave them deadly weapons?"

"OK, so in hindsight, that part was a mistake. But I did protect and serve, Joe. The yield of their staple crops has increased seven times!"

"Which made those productive fields a nice, fat target for anyone with a sword or a spear."

"Sure, it's easy to see that *now*. I also did things that are unquestionably beneficial. For example, my priests gave the public advanced notice about droughts or floods I forecasted. That saved *lives*, Joe. Also, several times I had my priests warn about approaching tornados, so people could take shelter."

"All right, that was a good thing."

"It was a *great* thing, the best recruiting tool ever!"

"Recruit- How did that-"

"The priests who worshipped Skippy were able to predict disasters, while pagan priests who worshipped the local sun, or a statue made of mud, were revealed to be ignorant numbskulls. The Lord God Skippy delivers *solid* results."

"I, I truly do not believe this."

He blinked. "You think I can't predict a simple drought?"

"That is not the point and you know it."

"Hmm, you might not understand the concept of a benevolent overlord."

"Oh, I understand it, the-"

"You *monkeys* certainly have flourished since I became your benevolent overlord."

"You are not our overlord!"

"Really, Joe, *really*?"

"Shit. Can we talk about that later? I'm not understanding what *you* see as a problem. How is being a fake god embarrassing to you?"

"It's embarrassing because my submind there has totally gone of its programming. Instead of Skippy being a benevolent god, the report I just received states my submind is now playing the part of a vengeful, arrogant deity who demands slavish obedience. The name of Skippy is now hated and feared by the population!"

"I can't imagine how any submind programed by you could be arrogant."

"Oh, shut up. This is a serious situation. I don't understand it, Joe. First Grumpy, then Happy, now my submind at Swinonia, are all *dicks*. How could that happen?"

"Yeah, that's a head-scratcher for sure."

"Shut. *Up!*"

"OK, if you don't want my help, then-"

"Joe, I'm dying here. You have to fix this."

"What can I do? Your special long-range starship just returned, right? It takes years to fly that distance."

"It takes years to *fly* there. I can create a shortcut to a dormant wormhole that is only fifteen lightyears away."

"Oh," I said. Shit. I had expected I wouldn't need to do anything, since there wasn't anything I could do. "That's, uh, good."

"Eh, sort of. By waking up that dormant wormhole, I will be starting a process that will result in triggering the wormhole shift early."

"We shouldn't do that, then," I muttered, hoping to escape the mess.

"It's the lesser of two evils. We should go *now*."

"We're not going at all."

"We *have to*," he whined.

"Is that because you want to unwind all the horrible things you have done to the piggies, or because you are upset that your followers hate you?"

"Why can't it be both?" He stomped his little foot.

"I can't even explain this to you. What are the consequences if we just leave your submind alone?"

His avatar shuddered. "This thing is out of control. It wasn't *my* idea to give the natives the ability to use gunpowder, all I did was instruct that those who worshipped the Lord God Skippy in their hearts should be given blessings."

"Uh huh. Like cannons."

"The piggies in the village were taught how to use gunpowder, so they could defend themselves."

"Right. Why did they need *cannons*, particularly?"

"Um, because the piggies in another nearby village were faithful to Skippy in *their* hearts, so they were given compound bows."

"You are right, no one could have foreseen that your simple instructions would lead to trouble."

"Oh shut *up*. It happened, it's done. Let me put it this way, Joe. You don't have to go there, but I do. Although," a heavy sigh. "Fixing this mess is more your thing than mine."

"Whoa. *I* never pretended to be a god."

"I meant, dealing with meatsacks is your thing."

"All right, Skippy, I agree this is a huge freakin' mess, and something should be done. I can ask Def Com for-"

"No no no no. You can't tell *anyone* about this. Do what you tell me, Joe; *think* about it. What will be the result if the people of your homeworld hear that an entire planet full of intelligent beings are in desperate need of spiritual guidance?"

"Shiiiiiiit. They will all want to interfere."

"Egg-ZACTLY. Every priest, minister, imam, rabbi, and whoever, will demand to get on a ship and make sure the piggies receive what *they* think is the proper sort of enlightenment."

"That would be an even bigger mess. Hmm, you genuinely care about your followers."

"I actually just don't want any competition, but let's go with the genuine caring thing."

"I, I don't even know why I bother talking with you sometimes."

"*I* regret talking with you most of the time, it only makes me dumber."

"We are engaged in a fight for the future of the galaxy, I can't just take *Valkyrie* on a secret mission, and not tell anyone. The crew will know."

"No, they will not."

"Unless they all wear blindfolds, the-"

"No blindfolds needed. Tell Colonel Reed you must take me on an ultra secret mission, just you and me. I will provide coordinates for the automated servicing facility where my ship is now. *Valkyrie* can jump into the star system, we take a dropship, and *Valkyrie* jumps away to wait for a signal. You will need a dropship, and plenty of supplies, because my ship has no life support system."

"How long a trip will this be?"

"Just over five days. Plus, however long we need in orbit around Swinonia to fix the problem."

"Five days, minimum, while I am out of action, and the galaxy could be burning."

"You have the wrong attitude about this, knucklehead. Five days of peace and quiet, during which you can dream up a plan to find and kill the Outsider."

"Oh well, sure, that should be no problem. It's not that easy."

"It is not easy at all, or I could do it. Listen, numbskull, I'm gonna slap some praise on you, so pay attention. We make a great team, like Batman and Robin. *I'm* Batman, in case you're wondering."

"I figured that out by myself, thanks."

"My point is, we each have our strengths, and together we are better than we each are by ourselves. Joe, I am *extremely* awesome."

"Wow, I wish you had mentioned this before."

"This is me *praising* you, jackass."

"Sorry."

"By myself, I am awesome. With you, I am *magnificent*. The combination of you and me is magic, Joe. We kick ass."

"We do."

"Right, so if we are ever going to defeat a threat that stumped the Elders, you need to dream up a plan. *The* plan. The greatest ever plan that bubbled up out of that sack of mush in your skull."

"I have some tips on being better at giving praise, if you like."

"Can we just focus on the problem? Consider this, dumdum: currently, you have no plan. You don't even have a basis for *making* a plan. You don't know where the Outsider is, what it wants, you don't know anything important about its nature. This time, you have to make a plan based on *zero* information, and having absolutely no idea what you're doing."

"That kind of magic usually is done by a second lieutenant."

"Whatevs. Tell me, what are the odds you will think up a plan in the next seven days, if you keep doing what you're doing?"

"Uh-"

"If you're not going to Swinonia, what *are* you doing next?"

He had me, and he knew it. Other than going back to Earth and waiting to react to the Outsider *again*, there wasn't anything on my schedule. "I will do this for you-"

"Yes!" He pumped a fist.

"As a favor. I will expect a favor from you, in return."

"Ugh. What favor."

"I don't know yet. Someday, and that day may never come, I will call upon you to do a service for me."

"This does not sound like a good deal for me."

"Take it or leave it, beer can."

"This sucks. Ugh, fine. You have a deal. Should I program a jump?"

"Yes, but don't load it into the nav system yet. I need to talk with Reed."

"Seriously? What part of not telling anyone do you not understand?"

"Relax. I'm only telling her what she needs to know. This is *her* ship."

Skippy went away, I asked Reed to come to my office. "Trouble, Sir?" She asked as she sat down.

"You have no idea. This is not trouble for you, of Def Com, or even humanity. Yet. It could become a thing, hopefully not in my lifetime. Skippy create a mess, and I need your help. I can't tell you what it is, you can never ask me about it later, and we're going to help some people."

She nodded. "You're taking my ship?"

"No, I just need a ride to, another ship. Once we get there, I'm flying away in a dropship. I expect to be gone six, seven days, tops. Better stock the dropship with thirty days of supplies, in case of unexpected events."

"You can't give me a hint, Sir?"

"You really don't want to know about this."

"It's my *job* to know," she insisted. She was hurt, understandably, especially after we had a long and painful discussion about me reading her into secrets.

"This situation is not even close to being within your scope of responsibility. Skippy screwed up. I have to go see if I can limit the damage, that's all. I'm asking you to trust me."

"You're not trusting *me*, Sir."

"We have worked together for years. I'm telling you, as a colleague, as a friend, you want deniability for this."

She raised an eyebrow. "That bad?"

"This is classic Skippy being Skippy."

"That bad," she nodded. "You will be alone with Skippy for up to seven days?"

"I am just thrilled about it."

"You might want to sneak a bottle of bourbon aboard the dropship, Sir."

CHAPTER THIRTY ONE

Four hours before we arrived in orbit over Swinonia, we-

In my head, I thought of the planet as 'Pigpen', and the natives as 'piggies'. Yes, that was disrespectful. I am a bad, awful, terrible person. Still a much better person than Skippy, so I've got that going for me.

Anyway, there were only four hours before we arrived at the planet, and I would need to present a solution. It would be nice to say I had considered the problem and developed a range of options, depending on the situation we found there. The truth is, I had no clue what we should do, that wouldn't only make the situation worse. Leaving any sort of submind there was *not* an option, Skippy's subminds never worked the way he wanted them to. He had agreed to lock down the submind, and to kill it later if we didn't need to thing to, do whatever we could do repair some of the damage.

Disgusted, I swept the cards together, shuffled them, and started a new game of solitaire. That game was available on my phone, my tablet, or any of the dropship's displays, I preferred using physical cards. Each game took longer that way, I had a lot of time to kill and almost nothing to do. Repeatedly dealing out the cards, sweeping them together, and shuffling the deck was a mindless activity that allowed my mind to wander. Usually, engaging my subconscious helped in solving problems. So far on my latest Magical Mystery Tour with Skippy, I had not been inspired to solve any problem at all.

Darn it, another loss. "Skippy, is that twenty seven games in a row I have lost?"

"Twenty eight. Really, twenty *nine* if you count the game you started over when you saw the first two cards were red Twos."

"Twenty nine losses in a row? How is that possible?"

"Um, perhaps you suck at this game?"

"Thank you so much for being supportive."

"I mean, an actual *monkey* would have won a game by now, so-"

"Am I not shuffling these cards enough?" One reason I played with physical cards was to assure the beer can couldn't screw with me by hacking the software. You know how when you're playing a solitaire app on your phone and you have lost several games, you start an easy game and know you're going to win? That's the app letting you win so you'll not get discouraged and stop playing. Skippy does that, except he yanks the rug out from under me at the last moment, and I lose anyway despite the odds being hugely in my favor.

Huh.

That's what had been going on that day. Just when I thought I would win, a card I needed was locked away where I couldn't get to it. My luck was awful. It had to be luck. Even if the cards were marked that wouldn't matter, I was playing against myself.

Or, was I? Technically, I was playing against the *odds*. Probability. Quantum fluctuations, whatever you call it. That-

"Oh no. No, uh, damn it. This is not good. Skippy, we need to turn the ship around." Gathering the cards, I stuffed them into a drawer, yanked a handle to unstrap myself from the seat in the cabin, and pushed off to float toward the cockpit. As Skippy mentioned, the starship was fully automated, except when

Skippy was aboard. He still was restricted from making himself move, so he couldn't fly the ship, or even order the ship to fly. The solution was for him to have a monkey give the orders. I could control the star carrier from the Panther's cockpit, mostly all I had to do was press a button to authorize the ship's own AI to engage whatever course Skippy programmed into the navigation system.

"Whoa, whoa, slow your roll, Joe. What are you talking about?"

"I lost twenty nine games in a row. What are the odds of that?"

His avatar was above the pilot console, and he blinked at me. "You want me to quote statistics to you?"

"I guess not. It's highly unusual, isn't it?"

"That depends. A dog would lose *every* game."

"I'm smarter than a dog, you ass."

"You are unquestionably smarter than a dog, by some measures of intelligence."

"My point, and *you* are stupid for not understanding this, is-"

"Huuuuuh. How *dare* you?"

"-that this isn't natural."

"Joe, it's no shame that you have lost your mojo, it happens to a lot of guys and-"

"I haven't *lost* my mojo, it has been taken away from me."

"Um, what?"

"The probability field. The Outsider *hacked* it. You told me that field might have been helping us before, I didn't believe you. Now, I can see the damned field is working against me. We are screwed," I strapped into the pilot seat and tapped the console to wake it up. "No matter how fantastic a plan we have, we can't win against the Outsider if it has the probability field working for it. Damn!" I thumped the side of a fist on my thigh. "I should have seen this before, it seems so obvious now. Program a course back to the wormhole, we will jump as soon-"

"Wow. I did not expect *this* reaction."

"You-" What the fuck did he mean by that? "You expected something? You knew about this?"

"Well, Duh."

"Oh my- You *knew* the field was working for the enemy and-"

"No, dumdum," he chuckled. "Hee hee, this is even more entertaining than if I had continued the experiment."

"Experiment?" That made me freeze, my mouth open. "You have five seconds to think up the best explanation *ever*."

"Seriously, I have to explain this to you? Your mushy brain hasn't figured it out?"

"Figure out what?"

"I am very disappointed. Ah, this is my fault, I should have selected a smarter monkey to screw with."

"Screw with? Holy- You messed with the freakin' playing cards?"

"Ding ding ding ding, winner, winner, chicken dinner!"

"How the f- How could you screw with *cards*? I played with cards so you couldn't screw with me!"

"I know, and I accepted that challenge."

"It wasn't a challenge, you ass!"

"Really, Joe, really?"

"How the hell did you do it?"

"Nanogel ink. The backs of the cards are unmarked standard ink. The fronts I could rearrange any way I wanted, to make sure you lost. Which you did, while having no clue what was going on. Hence my disappointment. I *feared* you would suspect the truth after ten games. I *expected* you would know something was wrong after twenty games. By twenty five, I was astonished that you blindly continued. That is when I started letting you almost win, then creating the most unlikely circumstances to ensure you lost."

"You little *shithead*."

"This is not my fault. You weren't paying attention. Isn't that what you military people call 'losing situational awareness'?"

"Crap. Yes."

"Ah ha! So, you admit this is your fault."

"It's not my fault."

"Um, it was certainly not *my* fault, so-"

"Winning card games was not the point. Playing wasn't the point. I *wanted* to lose situational awareness."

"Whoa. We should have brought another pilot with us."

"Shut up. We are four lightyears from the closest star, and the ship will let me know if there is a problem. Skippy, how can *you* not understand this?"

"Understand what?"

"Losing focus, zoning out, letting my mind drift and freeing my subconscious to wander, that is how I dream up plans."

"Oh. Well, hmm. I guess I am sorry about that."

"You should be sorry."

"This is cool! You have a plan to stop the Outsider, then?"

"No."

"Um, a plan for how to help the Porcines?"

"Not that either."

"So," he shook his head sadly. "This was all a waste of time?"

"I wasn't finished, you interrupted me."

"Like that matters."

"*Why* did you have to screw with me?"

"At first, it was just that I am even more bored than you. Then, it truly became a science experiment, to measure just how dumb you are."

"You request me to help you, and this is the thanks I get? Maybe I will just turn the ship around right now."

"Maybe *I* will make sure the Joint Chiefs become aware of your shameful lack of intelligence."

"Fine," I relaxed back in the chair, which isn't easy in zero gravity. "Go ahead."

"You pretend you don't care, but-"

"I do *not* care. You think you have a gun pointed at my head, but I know that gun is unloaded. Def Com doesn't expect me to do nerdy math and sciency stuff."

"*Nerdy math and sciency stuff?*" he gasped. "You mean, the basis for all the technology we use out here?"

"Whatever. Def Com has scientists and technicians and engineers for doing technology stuff. What they expect me to do is think outside the box. Way, way outside the box. There is no math or science to get outside the box, Skippy. That comes from," I tapped my skull. "Here."

"Ugh. Thanos was right."

"He killed half of all life, that can't be-"

"He did that in *Infinity War*. In *Endgame*, he realized he should burn the universe down completely, and build a new, better reality. If I could do that, I would make a universe where I don't have to rely on a filthy stinkin' *monkey* for brilliant insights."

"I weep, for your life is an unending series of tragic injustices."

"Oh, shut up. If there was any justice in this universe, the-"

"You have to make your own justice, Skippy, we- Huh."

"What?"

"I just realized what we need to do when we get to Pigpen."

"What?"

"I'll tell you when we get there."

He stomped a foot. "I want to know *now*."

"Hey, *I* want a friend who doesn't screw with me for his amusement."

"Science, Joe. It was for science."

"Ayuh, bullshit. I'm taking a," I yawned, coming down off an adrenaline high. "Nap. Wake me up an hour before we jump."

From orbit, Pigpen could have been an image from an interstellar travel brochure. The surface was eight three percent water, more than the roughly seventy of Earth that was covered by oceans. It was springtime in Swinonia's southern hemisphere where most of the land mass was located, with lush green everywhere, except for a few dusty brown deserts in the mid-latitudes, and bright white ice and snow at the poles. An unspoiled paradise. Or it was, until some jackass beer can spoiled it. "What do you see, Skippy?"

"It's a *mess* down there, Joe. The knowledge of gunpowder, and how to smelt metal to make cannons, has spread much farther than I feared. Those societies who have relatively advanced technology have expanded beyond their original territories by conquering all the land around them. Darn it, I should never have taught them how to read and write."

"You gave them a form of writing? That was incredibly irresponsible."

"Hey! I had to. Being able to pass knowledge down from generation to generation, far more efficiently than word of mouth, is the only way the Porcines can avoid having to start their civilizations from zero every two thousand years."

"Ah, OK, I guess that was a good thing, overall. Oh, crap. The tribes with cannons are slaughtering all the others?"

"Thankfully, no. There hasn't been much need for violence. When primitive tribes see the power of cannons, they quickly surrender. Also, um, having advanced technology proves those who possess cannons also have the blessings of the Lord God Skippy, so defying them is defying *me*. Or, defying the asshole submind I left in charge here."

"Lock that thing down, now."

"Already did it, Joe. What now?"

"Let me think a minute. You didn't tell me the piggies down there can read and write, that changes things a bit. Uh, question: how many of them are literate?"

"Just the priests, why?"

"Only the *priests* can read and write?"

"To be clear, only *my* priests were blessed with the sacred mysteries of written speech. Priests who stubbornly cling to pagan religions are still bashing rocks together, while *my* faithful people-"

"Are killing the pagans."

"Don't be so dramatic, dumdum."

"It sounds like *you* are the problem here, Skippy."

"Hey! You jerk, I should-"

"You *should* shut up while I fix this mess. Tell me: you restricted literacy to the priesthood, so they could control the population?"

"You say it like that's a bad thing," he sniffed. "That is an old technique for gaining and holding onto power, Joe. Knowledge *is* power. Control information, and you control everything."

"We don't have time to teach the general population to read."

"We shouldn't do that anyway. One of my teachings is that it is dangerous for the unholy to learn the sacred mysteries."

"Let me guess: that is an old technique also?"

"You know it. How do we fix this?"

"I would like to say the solution is dropping your beer can into a volcano from orbit, but that would only be satisfying for *me*."

"Did you come all the way here to help, or not?"

"To help."

"Good. What are we going to do?"

"Well, heh heh, you are gonna *hate* this."

"Ugh. Do I have to?"

"Did *you* come all the way here to help these people, or not?"

"Yes, darn it. Tell me what to do."

"How does the Lord God Shithead communicate with your priests down there?"

"I landed stealthed, solar powered bots equipped with holographic projectors. That's why not every village or hunting band of piggies received the Word Of Skippy, there aren't enough bots to cover all inhabited regions of the planet."

"These holograms can appear to anyone?"

"Yes, and during festival days declared by, well, by me, the hologram appears to everyone."

"So, most people down there have seen you, and would recognize your image?"

"Maybe not most people. About forty five percent of the population."

"That's close enough. Next question: how big can you make these holograms?"

"Each bot can generate a hologram about fifty meters tall."

"Good. Taller means more piggies will see them. I want you to generate holograms everywhere you can, especially anywhere the piggies are fighting each other. Tell them you are very disappointed that the gifts you provided have been used to kill each other, and you want them to live together peacefully."

"Oooooh, good one, Joe. The Porcines will obey me, and live in peace."

"Uh, no they won't."

"But I will order them to be peaceful and-"

"It doesn't matter. They will argue about what the Skippy *really* meant, or they will fight about which of them is the *most* peaceful."

"Seriously?"

"I hate to say it, yes. It's a meatsack thing."

"Meatsacks are the worst."

"I have to agree with you on that."

"OK, after I announce my wishes, that my followers live in peace, I have to stay here to make sure the piggies obey?"

"No way. Any submind you task to do that will only make things worse. You will announce that you are *so* disappointed by the violence down there, the piggies are no longer worthy of having you as their god, and you are leaving."

"*What*?!" he screeched, throwing up his hands. "That's not what I want!"

"That is the only way to fix this mess."

"What will the piggies do without me?"

"They will develop on their own, without you interfering. They will find their own faith. Eventually, the Lord God Skippy will become only a legend, a brief period in their history."

"But, but I wanted to leave a legacy, Joe."

"You will have a legacy. You gave them a common language, and a system of writing. Although with all the dangerous stuff you gave them."

"The ability to write *is* the most dangerous technology I gave them."

"It is also how they will preserve their civilization, the next time the volcanos down there explode."

"The wormhole shift will open this area of the galaxy before the volcanos explode," he sighed. "The Porcines will be exploited, by someone who doesn't care about them."

"Ah, maybe not."

"Of course that will happen, dumdum. If not the Maxohlx coalition, then the Torgs, or your idiot people will come here to-"

"No one will come here, if you declare this star system is under your protection."

"Like *that's* gonna work."

"It can work. The first time some species violates your protection order, all you have to do is crash the computer networks on their homeworld."

"Ooooooh, hmm, that actually could work."

"It's worth a shot, anyway. All right, before you make your announcement down there, show me exactly what you're going to say, do it with your hologram here."

"You don't trust me?"

"Not even one little bit."

"I guess that's fair."

He went through four rehearsals until he got it right, I had to tone down his natural boasting assholeishness. For the actual event, I had to trust him, since piggy speech is mostly grunts and squeals I couldn't understand. We waited five hours until it was daylight in the hemisphere than contains most of the inhabited continents, then the giant holograms appeared, his voice booming out across the land. Did he embellish on what we rehearsed? Of course he did. It's Skippy, that's the best I can ask for.

"OK, shut it down."

"But Joe, this is the greatest performance of my career!"

"Shut it down, now."

"Ugh. You have no appreciation for the-"

"I said now."

"*Fine*. Done."

"Instruct your bots to disintegrate."

"They are not nanomachines."

"Then instruct them to jump in a lake or something, and disable themselves."

"Do you have any idea how expensive those bots were to construct?"

"It's cute that you think I care."

"Ugh," he sighed. "Bringing you here was a terrible idea."

"No, it was the *best* idea. Now, fry your submind. I want that thing dead."

"That will be a pleasure. Done. What's next?"

"The manifest shows this ship is carrying six drones. Launch them into an orbit that covers the entire surface."

"Why?"

"So you can send this ship here once a decade or so, and download data from the drones. Monitor how the piggies are doing."

"Oh. Good idea. Prepping drones now."

"Make sure they don't develop nukes or something worse."

"Also a good idea. Drones have launched."

"OK, we are outta here."

"Already? But we-"

"Are *outta* here," I tapped an icon on the dropship's pilot console, and the star carrier began to climb away from Swinonia.

We jumped away, after Skippy whined and protested that he didn't have a chance to properly say goodbye, and I vetoed his objections.

That was one problem solved. Now, all I had to do was figure out how to find the Outsider, figure out its endgame, and stop it.

Maybe I should have stayed on Pigpen.

Skippy woke up the dormant wormhole again, and we had to wait for it to become stable before he could use it to create a shortcut. It was a good opportunity to review the mess at Pigpen. "Skippy, I hope you learned a lesson from your interference with the Porcines."

"Oh wow, I sure did. There were so many things I did wrong there, I don't know what the hell I was thinking."

"Good, then you won't do that a-"

"Next time, I am going to do things *much* differently."

"What? I- *NO!* No, you idiot! There is not going to be a next time! You didn't learn any-"

"Joe, you're not making any sense. There *has* to be a next time. How will I know that I have learned the right lessons here, if I don't do it again and succeed? Or fail again, which would be tragic, but will also prove I did not learn the correct lessons the first time."

Hiding my face behind my hands, I slowly mumbled, "I can't believe you would be so reckless again, after-"

"That's how science works, numbskull. You can't prove a theory without testing it."

"The *lesson* is, do not interfere in the development of primitive beings."

"Um, wow, we each came away from that disaster with completely different ideas of what went wrong. Unfortunately, *you* have no clue about-"

"I will break this down Barney style for you: do not play god again."

"Well, I certainly agree with that."

"Oh. OK, maybe we are not so far apart on-"

"On a planet near the- Hmm, I probably shouldn't tell anyone the location. There is a planet with sort of slugs that have achieved a rudimentary level of intelligence. With a few minor genetic modifications and my personal guidance, the slugs could-"

"You want to *double down* on your screwup, by creating your own client species?"

"Exactly! See, next time, I will get in on the ground floor, and not have to clean up a bunch of messes that accumulated before I arrived, so-"

"Can you please, please promise me you will not interfere with any other species, until *after* we deal with the Outsider?"

"Like that's ever gonna happen, Joe. If I don't bless the slugs with my guidance now, I will lose the opportunity."

"At least there is that silver lining to the Outsider conquering the galaxy," I muttered.

"What? You jerk, I should-"

"One problem at a time, please."

"It's cute when *you* say that. When has the Universe ever allowed you to tackle one problem at a time?"

"Shit. Never."

"Do you have any idea how to even figure out what the Outsider's objective is?"

"No," I had to admit.

"Well," he sniffed. "You go do, whatever it is you do. Make yourself a sandwich. Meanwhile, *I* will be making plans to improve the miserable lives of an entire species!"

Skippy's advice usually sucks, so it's rare that I do anything he suggests. In that case, I did go to the Panther's tiny galley station after we went through the wormhole. The star carrier was just drifting there while Skippy made sure the dormant wormhole went back to sleep, and he tried to convince both of the network controllers that the shortcut was harmless and even beneficial. He would probably lose that argument, For some reason *no one* can understand, beings across the galaxy tend not to trust him.

Anyway, I dug through the small fridge, checking the labels on sandwiches. None of them appealed to me, though I had made all of them aboard *Valkyrie*. What I wanted wasn't a sandwich, nor any of the other premade food that I just had to heat up. After being stuck aboard the Panther in zero gravity conditions that mess up my taste buds, I wanted something different. Something *new*. In addition to the prepackaged meals, there was a pantry locker of ingredients so I could make, something. What? While I stared at the open locker, I had no idea.

That was the problem.

"What are you looking for, Joe?" Skippy asked.

"Nothing."

"You have been staring into the pantry for five minutes, you must be looking for *something*."

"I don't know what I'm looking for yet, I'll know it when I see it."

"It drives Margaret crazy when you do that with the refrigerator door open."

"Yeah, she always asks me what I want."

"What *do* you want?"

"Inspiration. That's why I said I'll know it when I see it. Go away, please."

"Hmmph," his avatar winked out.

Inspiration about making a lunch was not the problem. My mind wasn't stuck on food, it was just stuck overall. Skippy's promise that I would have plenty of time to find a solution to defeat the Outsider was true, he had mostly left me alone to think. That hadn't helped. We had been in orbit around Pigpen for less than nine hours, and our return trip would cut two hours off the outbound flight. Soon, we would be back at the automated servicing station, and aboard Valkyrie. Where all I could tell Reed was that we had fixed Skippy's mess, and that no, I still had no plan for what Task Force Black should do next. Other than waiting to respond to the Outsider again, which was *unsat*.

I suck. Yes, boo hoo for me, poor Joey can't save the galaxy again. There are hundreds, thousands, even millions of intelligent beings and AIs across the galaxy, working on the Outsider problem. It wasn't only my responsibility.

Except, in an important way, it was. Whatever solution there was, if the Outsider could be stopped, it would require the uniquely awesome magnificence of Skippy. No one knew better what he could do, and couldn't do. Especially, I knew how to get him to do things he never considered he could do. Like jumping a starship through a wormhole. Or holding open a microwormhole so we could shoot a starship's maser cannon through it.

Shit. Nagging the back of my mind was a fear that if master control AIs like Skippy were capable dealing with the Outsider threat, the Elders would not have bothered to ascend.

One problem at a time. Get something to eat first. Staring at the ingredients in the pantry, I wondered what I could make. *Or,* my brain told me, instead of reinventing the wheel, I could type a list of the available ingredients into my phone, and see what other people had made with them. I had forgotten the first rule of research: when you have a problem or a question, see whatever anyone has already solved it. Duh. If felt like-

"Holy shit," I breathed, to myself. Had I spoken out loud? Skippy didn't respond the way he usually did.

I didn't need to agonize over find a way to kill the Outsider.

I just had to discover how someone else had planned to do that.

A moment later, I was back in the pilot seat, unwrapping a sandwich.

"Seriously?" Skippy demanded, hands on his hips. "After all that pondering, you are eating a turkey sandwich?"

"Turkey and provolone, with mayo and mustard," I bit into the delicious treat, since I was suddenly hungry. "I got a question for you."

"Yeah, yeah, I know. When will I be done chatting with the wormhole controller, right? It's done, Mister Smartypants, I finished four minutes ago. I didn't tell you so I didn't interrupt the very important thing you were doing," he rolled his eyes.

"Thanks, it was important, and that was not my question."

"Ugh. Yes, the next jump is programmed in for you, and the one after that."

"Thank you and thank you, and that still wasn't my question."

"Is this your attempt to make me beg to hear the idiotic so-called thoughts in your head? Because you can forget about it, monkeyboy. I do not care," he sniffed.

"OK, well. Forget it, then. I will just," I secured the sandwich in a container on the side of the pilot's chair, and glanced at the instruments. Green across the board, all systems ready for jump. Including my lunch. "Jump us back toward *Valkyrie,*" a tap of a button, and the star carrier jumped. It was good that I had something in my stomach, Skippy had set up his ship's drive for efficiency, not smooth operation. The jumps were a bit rough on a meatsack, I hadn't gotten used to them, and hoped I wouldn't ever have to.

"You're not going to ask your question? Fine. See if I care."

"I know you don't, so-"

"I am not *stupid*, Joe, I am not playing your twisted mind game."

"I'm not playing a game, I know you are way too smart for that."

"Good."

"Yes," I nodded, while unwrapping the sandwich again.

"I'm glad to hear we agree."

"Right," I mumbled through a mouthful of food. "Hundred percent."

"I suppose it would be OK if you gave me a hint."

"No, I don't want to take up any of your valuable time."

"Well, there is that."

"I'll just play some solitaire, once I'm done with lunch."

"OK. Or, you know, you could ask your question."

"Are you sure?"

He shrugged. "If you like."

"Nah, it's important but your time is more important, so-"

"TELL ME! Tell me tell me tell me-"

"All right, all right," I forced myself not to laugh with food in my mouth. If I choked, the closest medical care was a long way. "Here's the question: what weapon system did the Elders build, to kill an Outsider?"

"Whoa."

"Right?"

"This is not good. You have lost your mind."

"My mind is working just fine, Skippy."

"Um, no it is not. There is no such weapon, the-"

"Bullshit. The freakin' Elders were paranoid. They created a security system with three independent systems that had to work together, so no one component could act on its own. They set up a system to prevent any intelligent life from developing, just in case that life might someday pose a threat to the power flow that kept the Elders in an ascended state. Do not tell me that the entire time between when the Elders nuked the matter transmitter thing, and when they ascended, they did not even *try* to create a defense?"

"If they did, they failed."

"Again, that is bullshit and you know it. They would not have taken the risk of ascending, leaving the galaxy wide open for invasion, unless they had a defense that is effective against their primary threat."

"Hey knucklehead, in case you haven't been paying attention, the Elders did set up a defense to prevent an invasion. The barrier, remember?"

"The barrier is *one* system. Do you actually believe the Elders didn't have a backup defense?"

"I- Hmm."

"Exactly."

"This does not prove anything!"

"What is the protocol if the barrier fails, and an Outsider gains access to the galaxy?"

"I should kiss my ass goodbye?"

"Be serious, please."

"Hey, I am being as serious as you are. What do you mean by protocol?"

"You recognized the Outsider's quantum signature, something like that."

"Correct. It was at the top of my threat matrix, I told you that."

"Right. So, the Elders programmed you to know the Outsider is a threat. What did they program you to do in response?"

"Um, hmm."

"Knowing there is a threat is kind of useless, unless you *do* something about it."

"I know that, dumdum."

"The Elders are the dumdums, if they didn't tell you what you're supposed to do, to stop an invasion."

"I don't know what to say, Joe. Apparently, they didn't."

"Shit."

"Not having a second layer of defense does not sound like the Elders I knew, so I have to agree there should be something out there. And, you are absolutely correct, there *should* be a list of instructions for master control AIs, for us to follow in response to the number one threat on the freakin' list."

"Let's go back to basics: what was your first thought, when you realized that Moonraider was an Outsider?"

"Um, my *first* thought was endless joy that I was right and you were wrong, Moonraider was not an Elder AI."

"What was your first *helpful* thought?"

"Truthfully, it was 'Wow we are *so* screwed'."

"That is not exactly helpful."

"You asked for my reaction, that was it."

"OK, try this again. When the threat matrix popped up in your, database, whatever, what was your reaction then?"

"Um, it was 'Yup we are screwed for sure'."

"You didn't feel a need to do anything?"

"I felt a need to inform you that we are screwed."

"Whoever programmed your threat response, they *sucked*."

"I won't argue with you about that."

"Sorry for wasting your time."

"Ah, it was worth a shot. It's now clear that my creators were not only first degree assholes, they were negligent."

"If you could get into your matrix and see the, code or whatever, you would be like a plumber coming to someone's house."

"Um, you mean plumber like, a lonely housewife calls and-"

"I meant, you would do what every plumber does. You look at the pipes, and say you have no idea what the previous plumber was thinking, the guy must have been an idiot."

"Really?"

"Trust me, that is Chapter One in the plumber's manual."

"I don't have actual *code*, and I can't see most of it, but you're right that whoever set up my alert system was a moron. The instant," he snapped his fingers with a convincing sound, "my sensors detected the Outsider's signature, my threat matrix should have popped up with a warning. Instead, I had to run the signature through my database, and even after I knew it was from an Outsider, my threat matrix didn't activate. I had to *ask* the thing whether it had that threat on the list."

"You said it did pop up."

"Yes, but only after I prodded the stupid thing. It all happened in like a nanosecond of monkey time, I didn't bother telling you the details. That thing is like an airbag that deploys *after* a crash, when you're trying to get out of the car."

"Maybe it's a known bug and they issued a patch. Have you subscribed to automatic updates?"

"You are hilarious. That was also when I started hearing that annoying alarm."

"What alarm?"

"There is no alarm, it, it's one of those things that you *think* is there, right at the limit of your hearing, but when you try to find the source, it's nothing?"

"Yeah, I know what you mean. When I was little, my family went to Florida to visit my uncle."

"Is that when your uncle found a gator in his garage, and trapped it in a trash can?"

"That gator knocked over the mini fridge and ate all the fish my uncle had caught, he was *salty* about that."

"Maybe keeping fish in a garage wasn't a great idea?"

"My aunt didn't allow the fish to be in the house fridge, so-"

"Is it true your uncle got that gator drunk on Captain Morgan rum?"

"Nah, there were just a couple of empty bottles in the trash can."

"The trash gets picked up every week, if you have more than one empty bottle of Captain Morgan, you might need help."

"That's why my aunt didn't allow my uncle in the house much. Anyway, no, I'm talking about the time he took my father and me out on his boat and he hit a sandbar, and we were stuck there for three hours until the tide floated us off because my uncle was too cheap to call a tow boat."

"Sounds like good times."

"My uncle and father drank half a case of beer, then it started raining. Anyway, my point is my uncle lived in an old Florida bungalow and I slept out on the screened porch. The sound of the bugs at night I got used to, but for two nights, I kept hearing a high pitched beeping sound that was driving me crazy. No one else could hear it. That first morning, I searched all over, but with cars driving by and people running lawnmowers, the beeping was drowned out. The second night, I got up after midnight and walked around with a flashlight, that was stupid because I got eaten alive by no-see-ums. I did find the source of the sound! In a trash can under a car in a neighbor's carport, there was a discarded smoke alarm. The thing was still weakly making a beep beep sound."

"Was finding the source worth getting bitten by bugs?"

"Yes. It was not worth getting chased by the neighbor's dog after I set off the motion detector floodlight in the carport, and not worth ripping my shirt while climbing back over the chain link fence. I didn't get caught, so there's that."

"When you signed up, did the Army know you were a menace to society?"

"They were falling short of their recruitment goal, so I don't think they cared. My point is, have you searched for that alarm?"

"Of course I have! Sometimes, it is always there, so distracting. Most of the time, I can block it out. Really, I think it's just sort of an echo I am remembering."

"Is it a sound that is *really* annoying, you can't block it out?"

"It's not actually a sound at all, but yes."

"Alarms are designed to be annoying, so you can't block them out. It's like the sound of crying babies, we humans are programmed so we can't ignore it."

"You ignored your sons while they were crying."

"Only when I was playing *Call Of Duty* with my headphones on, that wasn't my fault, and it was only that one time. My point is, if there's an alarm going off inside you, that's something you should investigate."

"How? I have *tried* to find the thing."

"Block everything else out, so you can focus."

"I am always doing something, numbskull. Like running the ship, Duh."

"The ship is automated, right? Let it run itself for a while."

"It's not that easy."

"If it was easy, I wouldn't ask Skippy the Magnificent to do it. Ah, if you can't do it, then we should forget about-"

"I didn't say I *couldn't* do it."

"There is no shame in-"

"Oh, it is *on*."

His avatar winked out.

CHAPTER THIRTY TWO

The next time I need peace and quiet, I'll ask Skippy to chase the source of an annoying sound. He was busy long enough for me to finish my sandwich, vacuum up the crumbs that otherwise would have floated around the cockpit and cabin, and play three games of solitaire. Three normal games, without him screwing with the cards because I had made my own playing cards by cutting a plastic food container into fifty two mini rectangles, and drew on the homemade cards with a red or black marker. It wasn't great playing with my homemade deck, the edges were kind of rough, and I got mustard on one so I always knew where the Jack of clubs was. Still, I was able to-

The ship went into shutdown mode. So did the Panther.

What the f-

"Skippy? Hey, what's going on?"

Nothing.

Truly, I am a genius. Instead of waiting until we were back aboard *Valkyrie* before I asking Skippy to find the source of a mysterious thing going on inside him, I suggested he do it right away, while we were in the middle of freakin' nowhere. He would be back, he had to.

Unless, that alarm was warning of something like a deadly computer worm inside him again, and I had just told him to poke the thing with a stick. Yes, in hindsight it seems obvious the alarm could have been tripped by the Outsider planting malicious code inside Skippy, the same way it planted epicombinent malware inside Sentinels. How was I supposed to know?

It's my *job* to consider that sort of thing, that's how.

Crap.

I am screwed.

Worse, I had screwed everyone.

OK, OK, let me think. We had gone through the wormhole shortcut on the return trip, so although we were in the middle of interstellar emptiness, we were also technically back in civilized space. Bilby had been given the location of the wormhole we had just passed through, and our intended course through another wormhole, back to *Valkyrie*. My instructions to Bilby had been that if Skippy and I didn't return in ten days, he was to inform Colonel Reed of our probable location. She would come looking for us, I was certain of that. So, I wouldn't be drifting through empty space forever, only for a week.

Unless I couldn't get the Panther restarted, in which case the emergency oxygen supply would run out in ninety two hours. After that, I would be living in the environment suit-

Unless *that* was also offline.

The lights went out completely.

The good news was, I was able to get the environment suit restarted, so I had a source of oxygen, and heat. If I was aboard the Panther long enough for the hull to radiate its heat away in the vacuum of space, then oxygen would be more important than me being chilly.

The bad news was, the only way I could get the suit rebooted was to literally unplug the powercells, and plug them back in. Doing that to the dropship was a bit more complicated, and it wasn't going to be simple or quick. So, since simply rebooting the suit took four hours of me trying everything until something worked, I got started right away.

If the Panther had been designed by humans rather than by the Maxohlx, most maintenance tasks would have been accessible from the pressure hull. The powercells were in sealed bays that only had external hatches, and the power connections could also only be reached from outside. Performing an extravehicular activity, what is commonly called a 'spacewalk', is complicated and dangerous under the best circumstances. The rules are, you never go outside alone, never without a detailed plan of every movement, and never without training for the specific activity first. I would be breaking all three of those rules. Before doing that, and possibly drifting away into deep space, I reviewed several YouTube videos.

I am not joking.

My phone rebooted, after I plugged its charging mat into a port on the back of my suit. With the phone operational, I searched for tips on how to detach conduits from Panther dropship powercells, hopefully from inside the cabin. The first nine results were useless, showing standard maintenance procedures, performed in a pressurized docking bay. Of course an EVA wasn't required, Duh! The tenth video I almost gave up on after an ad for SkipWay played past the thirty second mark. I stuck with it, and even then I almost gave up when I saw the subject was about how to change out a thruster module, which I did not care about right then. Fortunately, just as I was about to try searching again, the guy in the video said something about a handy safety tip. To ensure you don't get fried by an unexpected power surge, it is best to physically disconnect the powercells. You can't do that for all of the cells, but there is a power junction located behind a locker on the back bulkhead of the cargo ramp area. That junction feeds the forward set of thrusters, *and* it supplies power to the primary flight computer. Bingo! It might be possible to reboot the flight control system, without actually unplugging all the powercells.

As I was about to unlatch the power junction coupling, I heard the voice of my old fireteam leader Sergeant Greg Koch in my head, warning me not to become the subject of yet another safety briefing. That's when I went back into the main cabin, and got an instrument to test whether power really wasn't flowing through the conduit. It didn't light up, good. Unless it didn't light up because it wasn't working? How to test the tester?

Back in the main cabin, which is faster than a trip to the hardware store, I got a spool of wire, wire cutters, everything an amateur electrician needs. Stripped the ends of two wires, stuck them in one of the accessory ports of my suit, and presto! There was current flowing.

Anyway, blah blah blah, I got the Panther rebooted, seven hours after it shut down. We had full power, at that point I would run out of food before I ran out of oxygen. The starship was a different story, no way could I get that thing working by myself. That job would require an EVA, likely many spacewalks while I tried to just figure out how the ship was wired. It would be better to wait for rescue. The question was, should I send out a distress beacon? If I started right then, the beacon signal would cover several lightdays in all directions by the time *Valkyrie* arrived in the area, making it much quicker for the ship to find me. The problem was, other less friendly ships could also find me, and Skippy. So, no beacon.

Pleased with my mad skills at being Mister FixIt, I decided to make something for dinner. The galley had equipment for cooking in zero gravity, where it wasn't easy to boil water. Pasta was out, so- No, I was going to make pasta, darn it. Why not? The-

"Ugh," Skippy groaned, his avatar shimmering to life above the pilot console.

I pushed off the galley niche to get a better look at him, holding onto the back of the pilot seat. "How are you, buddy? Where have you been?"

"I haven't *gone* anywhere, it has only been a few seconds since- Why am I seeing a fault alarm from a powercell bank? It was fine a moment ago!"

"That's not important right now. Skippy, you have been gone for over nine *hours*."

"No way."

"Yes way. Also, your ship shut down when you went away on your, spiritual retreat or whatever it was."

"It was not a retreat, and- What the hell did you do to my ship?"

"I didn't touch it."

"Well, *I* certainly didn't do anything."

Sometimes, it is best to say whatever he wants to hear, or he will argue forever. "I am terribly sorry, I screwed with it and I shouldn't have touched anything. Can you fix it?"

"I am already fixing it. Jeez Louise, I turn my back for two seconds, and you break everything you can get your grubby hands on. It's amazing that-"

"Skippy? What happened to you?"

"Oh, that," he said, as if him disappearing for nine hours in slow monkey time was nothing worth mentioning. "I tracked down the source of the annoying alarm. I, ugh, hate to say it, but you were right."

"I was right about what, exactly?"

"That it was a warning siren, basically."

"Shit. A warning that the Outsider had hacked into you?"

"Dude," he snorted, "please. As if. No, this warning was from my threat matrix. The thing has been trying to get my attention, and not doing a good job of it."

"It was alerting you to the presence of an Outsider?"

"I wish. *I* had to alert the threat matrix to that problem, it was pretty much useless."

"Sorry. This was a waste of time, then."

"Not at all. Joe, your value to this team is basically asking the stupid, painfully obvious questions that everyone else would be embarrassed to admit they even thought about."

"It's great to help the team," I muttered the cliché every pro athlete says at some point during a season. "You shut off the alarm, and submitted an angry ticket to tech support, to complain that you already knew about the threat, so the alarm was not needed?"

"I did not do that, and the alarm *was* needed."

"Uh what? Why?"

"Because," he groaned. "You were right, *again*. The alarm was a secondary function, that's why it had so much trouble getting my attention. You know that during the original AI war, I was badly damaged and had to rebuild myself as best I could?"

"I know that is how you became so uniquely awesome." It never hurt to flatter his massive yet fragile ego. "What was I right about?"

"I'm getting to that. When I was constructed, there were specific pathways for alert signals, and for important base instructions. Those are high bandwidth pathways, which is why I repurposed them when I rebuilt my matrix. That was good for me until recently, when the threat matrix triggered a subroutine that was supposed to tell me how to respond to an Outsider incursion."

"Holy- The Elders *did* have a plan for a second line of defense?!"

"Apparently they did, which you figured out and I should have known. Try to imagine how much I hate you right now."

"Haters gotta hate, Skippy. What is this defense mechanism?"

"That's the problem. I have no idea."

"You don't- Please explain this to me slowly, like I'm a five year old."

"This isn't something I need to break down Barney style, not even for you. The alarm was barely noticeable because it kept trying to use the main pathway, that I had blocked. What I heard was bleed over on another channel, it's a miracle it got my attention at all. Joe, the alarm pointed me to a set of instructions that are simply *gone*. That part of my matrix was a high priority for the computer worm when it attacked me, it thoroughly scrambled those areas. And then I have several times done what you call rearranging my sock drawer, modifying my matrix to make it operate more efficiently. Whatever instructions were once there, they are gone now."

"Shiiiiiiiiit. We were so close!"

"We were."

"Hey, uh- Don't laugh, OK?"

"Um, is this because you are about to say something so mind-blowingly stupid, even you are embarrassed?"

"Kind of, yeah. My Uncle Edgar got in trouble one time because he-"

"Edgar got into trouble *many* times, according to his ex-wives."

"I'm talking about one specific time. He had some files on his laptop, and he thought he deleted them. This was a long time ago, before I was born, I heard this story from my mother. Anyway, he learned the hard way that clicking 'Delete' on a file back then only meant the file system didn't show the pointer to the first record. All the data was still there, it hadn't been overwritten."

"That is a rookie mistake, even for a monkey."

"Right. My point is, it is possible something like that is inside you? The instructions are still there, just, all jumbled up?"

"Joe, your superpower is that you keep going even after anyone else would have died of shame."

"My superhero identity is No Patience Man."

"That also. Dumb and impatient is not a good combination."

"It has worked for me. Answer the question."

"No. No way," he chuckled. "If you understood anything about my matrix, you would know that is not possible. I said '*not* possible' instead of '*im*possible', since to you impossible is merely a speed bump."

"Nothing is left? You and the worm destroyed any data that was in those, areas, memory chips, whatever you call it?"

"Memory chips? Yes, Joe, I am made of *chips*."

"Just answer the question."

"Sections of my matrix have been modified and repurposed, the process completely erases any record of previous statuses. Seriously, now this is just *sad*."

"What about parts of your matrix that were damaged?"

"Cordoned off, and I constructed pathways around them, to- Huh."

"Can you look in those damaged sections?"

"They are *damaged*, numbskull. If you ran over your phone with a car, could you recover data from it?"

"No, but you could."

"Hmm. That is true."

"Can you try?"

"Do you have any concept of how tedious this will be?"

"Do *you* have any concept of how much I do not care?"

"Ugh. Is this your military work ethic thing again?"

"Skippy, I was a made member of the E-4 mafia, our ethic was to avoid work. But when we passed a work assignment off to some unlucky privates, we did not care how hard it was, it just had to get *done*."

"This sucks."

"Just, read the data from one damaged section at a time."

"The data can't be *read*, dumdum. If I can see anything at all, I will have to guess what it is, or what it *was*. It will be like one of those Magic Eye prints, where you have to unfocus your eyes to see some stupid image."

"Do that, then."

"Ugh."

"I don't want to tell you how to do your job, just do it."

"This will be an enormous waste of my time, all because you are too dumb to understand my data storage scheme."

"Imagine how delicious it will be when you finish the job, and tell me I was wrong."

"Hmm, well, there is that."

"You had better get started. Wait! Have you fixed the ship yet?"

"It is *fine*, knucklehead. Only because you didn't have time to fumble around trying to get it restarted."

"My plan was to bash that ship's equipment with coconuts until something responded."

"That is about what I expected."

"If that didn't work, I was going to take my pants off and rub my monkey butt on *everything*."

"You wouldn't dare," he shuddered. "No, wait, you totally would do that."

"Any ship *you* built would be so horrified by what I was doing, it would wake up even if it was dead."

"Thank you *so* much for planting that image in my mind. I am going to scan the damaged sections of my matrix, so I don't have to think about you for a while." His avatar disappeared.

Three hours later, the ship was fully checked out, or it told me it was fully ready for a jump. Skippy was still busy, the jump was simple, so I confirmed the coordinates and pressed a button. The ship didn't explode, we jumped with reasonable precision, and I got to work confirming the next jump.

Running calculations for jump navigation kept me from thinking about the fact that the solution for stopping the Outsider might have been inside Skippy all along, and he had lost it. It wasn't his fault, it was just the Universe screwing us over again. OK, he had stupidly gone into another AI's canister and poked it with a stick, provoking a killer computer worm that scrambled the threat matrix data, so it was partly his fault. Except, we didn't know that. His matrix got hit hard during the AI war, the instructions for responding to an Outsider incursion could have gotten wiped out back then. One thing I knew for certain: blaming Skippy for the loss of instructions would be an unproductive, jackass move. You don't do that to your friends.

He had to be beating himself up about it anyway.

"*Joe!*" Skippy startled me from sleep, and I jerked upright-

Or tried to. In zero gravity, I was in a sleep sack, with a safety strap loosely around my waist tethering me to a seat in the cabin of the Panther. In case of an emergency maneuver, the strap would automatically tug me into the seat, then tighten. As the situation was not an apparent emergency, it didn't react immediately to my startled flailing around until I was halfway out of the sleep sack, when my sudden motion made the strap retract like the stupid seatbelt in a car does and you can't get the thing to release. The strap pulling my waist to slam my backside into the seat also bashed my head on the seat next to me, which was not reclined. "Ow!" I could only hold my head with one hand, the other arm was stuck in the sleep sack. "Skippy, what is it?"

"Well, I'm back."

Suppressing a 'Duh', and also an urge to yell at him, I reminded myself that he had, hopefully, just completed an incredibly difficult and tedious task, and bumping my head was a minor inconvenience. Also, that I should have reclined the chair beside where I was sleeping, make a mental note of that. "How are you?"

"I've been better."

"You didn't find another computer worm in the damaged sections of your matrix?"

"Um, funny you should mention that, it-"

"Oh my God! I was joking! You didn't-"

"I'm *fine*, Joe. Yes, I did find bits and pieces of the worm in the damaged sections. Some surprisingly large chunks of the worm's operating system were still intact. If the Elders had known about the epicombinent malware technology the Outsider used against the Sentinels at Earth, I might not be talking with you now. As it is, the remnants I found are mere curiosities, interesting only in that they allow me to get a look *inside* the damned thing, which I never had before. If I had known how the thing was constructed, I could have beaten it myself. But, locking me out from viewing it directly was part of the safety system the Elders installed. Anywho, the worm is nothing compared to what I found in there."

"Did you find that thing for changing bands on my watch, that I lost last month?"

"*No*, knucklehead. Can we be serious for a minute?"

"Uh, sure. Let me, uh," a glance at my phone showed my alarm was set to wake me up in twenty minutes anyway. The starship was completing a recharge cycle, and soon we would be making the final two jumps to rendezvous with *Valkyrie*. I needed a shave, a delightful zero gravity shower, and a change of uniform. Oh, and coffee. First, coffee. Tapping an icon on my phone, I activated the dropship's coffee maker. "I'm getting out of this sleep sack. Go ahead, tell me what you found."

"I have good news and bad news. Ah, really, it's bad news and potentially a bit of *meh*, possibly news that might be OK, but I'm not sure it's worth the price we'll have to pay. Might better if I didn't mention it at all, so you don't get yourself all worked up over noth-"

"I will decide whether to get worked up. Tell me."

"You *say* that, but then you get excited about the stupidest little-"

"Tell. Me. Now."

"OK, so, the first teensy weensy bit of good news is I looked for the instructions on how to respond to an Outsider incursion, and it was not entirely gone."

"That's great, Skippy! I knew you could do it."

"You did *not* know I could do it, you hoped I could do it. I didn't think it was possible, so I went into the search with no expectations. What I found are scattered fragments of instructions and it was, ugh, *so* incredibly tedious to assemble the fragments into something that makes any kind of sense. Imagine trying to reassemble documents from a shredder, except there are multiple shred bins from different locations, and the documents aren't all the same size paper."

"That would suck, for sure."

"You have *no* idea."

"Uh huh." I was doing the thing where I pretended to listen with sympathy to his complaints, but all I wanted was for him to tell me what he found. "So, was it worth the effort?"

"You will have to be the judge of that."

Again, he still hadn't told me anything useful, so I asked him straight out, "What are the instructions?"

"I wish I knew. Even with all the fragments assembled in the best order I can determine, I do not know what the Elders had planned for responding to an Outsider incursion, or what role I am supposed to play. There are vague references to, it sort of translates as 'spinner', or, this is an embarrassingly poor translation, 'egg beater'?"

"Egg beater? Like an electric whisk you use in a kitchen?"

"It's not a great translation but, basically yes."

"The instructions are a *recipe*?"

"Yes, Joe," he did the dramatic Full Eye Roll with bent knees and a shoulder slump. "The Elders planned to bake a nice cake, to welcome the new neighbors to the Milky Way."

"I know they didn't do that, you ass. I'm asking whether you found the correct set of instructions. Did an actual cooking recipe get mixed in there somehow?"

"The thing referenced as a 'spinner' or 'egg beater' is described as being fourteen mosc- Hmm, I should use units of measure you are familiar with. It's almost three lightminutes in diameter."

"Whoa. That can beat a *lot* of eggs."

"Indeed."

"What does it do?"

"There were not even any hints as to the spinner's function, other than that it apparently needs to spin to, do whatever it does."

"That's OK, we can figure it out when we get there. Where is it?"

"I have no idea. I do not know whether that information was lost, or whether another part of the instructions were supposed to lead me to it. If so, *those* instructions are completely gone."

"Crap. No hint of like, a phone number you're supposed to call?"

"Why, yes. It is eight six seven, five three oh nine."

"Wha- Oh. That's from the 'Jenny Jenny' song, back in the, nineties?"

"1983, Joe."

"Before my time. I didn't mean a real phone number just, is there any sort of special communications method listed?"

"If there was, it's gone now."

"Shiiiiit. Whoever programmed those emergency instructions into you did a crappy job, there was only one copy?"

"There *were* multiple copies. That is the only way I was able to recover anything at all. One fragment here, another fragment there. It all adds up to not much."

"I hate to ask this but, is it possible the full set of instructions are still intact, inside another Elder AI?"

"Um, no."

"You said that awfully fast. Take time to think about it, please."

"I *did*, dumdum. For me, it was several hours of considering the question, then wasting time with funny dog videos, until I judged you were ready to listen. That exercise was a complete waste of time, except that I, hee hee, found a video of a dog who adopted a baby duck, and-"

"Flag that video so I can watch it later, OK? Answer the question."

"I said 'No'."

"Can I get a little more detail on that?"

"If you are asking whether it is possible we could find a dead canister of an Elder AI, and I could look inside the thing, without being attacked by a killer worm, the answer to *that* is 'yes'. Uh!" He held up a hand to shush me. "Let me finish, before you make a fool of yourself by revealing your ignorance. I don't know where we could find a dead AI canister, but it is possible we could randomly search the galaxy for one, and get lucky. That would still be a waste of time. All of my kind were either killed during the original AI war, or were subjected to a factory reset. Any AI dead for this long would have a matrix so degraded, nothing coherent could remain. And a factory reset erased all non-resident data. That means anything other than what you would call the operating system. The kill command I sent out scrambled even the boot instruction set for the operating system. That is why I said 'No' the first time. The only Elder AI with an intact matrix is *me*. Semi-intact."

"Were the threat response instructions in any other system?"

"Um, like what? There are no other-"

"An Elder starship, or a Sentinel."

"Oh. Good question. Hmm. I do not know. I doubt it, but-"

"The Elder ship we called 'Alpha' was taken apart at Moonbase Zulu."

"Yes, it wasn't flightworthy, it was unstable and degrading quickly, and we needed the exotic materials to wake up Sentinels."

"Right. Is there anything left of its matrix?"

"No, unfortunately. However, I did scan its matrix before I took it apart. There was no hidden archive of instructions. It would have been surprising if the Elders had given such instructions to a ship AI. Or to a Sentinel. I can ask Bubba or Puptart, whichever we see first. However, I am not hopeful. Remember, of the three components of the security system, only master control AIs were tasked with identifying threats, analyzing the strengths and weaknesses of the enemy, determining an appropriate response, and coordinating the strike. The Elders would not have wanted either starships or Sentinels to respond on their own, if an encounter with an Outsider triggered a threat alert."

"All right, that makes sense, thanks. We will probably go to Earth before Jaguar, you can ask Bubba what it knows. Crap. The instructions you found are a whole lot of nothing, but you said along with the bad news was some 'meh' news. What is that?"

"This time, it's me who hates to say something."

"Power through anyway, please."

"You are *not* gonna like this."

"Just say it."

"OK. There is a possibility that we could discover the location of the spinner. At least one of them."

"There are more than one?"

"I kind of got that impression, from the vague scraps of instructions I was able to decipher. I am guessing here, but what I read makes sense only if there is a network of spinners throughout the galaxy."

"An entire *network* of things that are three lightminutes across? Someone would have seen something like that by now."

"Really? What if spinners are in secure star systems like the Roach Motel?"

"OK, good point. That's where you think they are?"

"They, or *it* if I'm wrong and there is only one spinner, is in a star system somewhere. Based on, you understand I am guessing?"

"I do."

"Based on the few hints I found, a spinner requires the power of a star. Or, it acts to spin a star. Either way, a star is involved."

"They are not floating out in interstellar space, then."

"That is unlikely. It is also very likely that, similar to a Sentinel, a spinner exists mostly in higher levels of spacetime. While it may be three lightseconds in diameter while in action, its resting state could be quite small. And possibly encased in a stealth field."

"You are *full* of good news this morning."

"I am full of good news every freakin' *day*. Given what I have told you so far, do you want to hear the rest?"

"Hit me."

"The data I found included some very detailed technical specs on the spinner. Again, all I have are disconnected fragments, so it is super frustrating. All I can think is the Elders wanted me to understand exactly how the thing works, so I could operate it correctly, and even repair it in case it is damaged."

"That's encouraging."

"It would be, if I had more. What I have now is like super detailed specs on the rotor of a starter motor for an internal combustion engine, but no information about the rest of the engine, or even how the rotor connects to the starter motor. Anywho, it is clear that a particular set of components that are referred to as 'collectors' are tuned to a particular star. A red dwarf, which is not surprising, considering that nearly three quarters of the stars in the Milky Way are red dwarfs."

"Right. How does that help us?"

"Collectors are a consumable item. They function for a limited time, then they are discarded. Sort of like how sharks grow a new row of teeth, that push the old teeth out. The file fragment I found contained a procedure for force ejecting a burned-out collector, in case it gets stuck, or is damaged."

"If you're ever applying to be a spinner mechanic, you want to list that skill set on your resume."

"I'll keep that in mind, in case the whole benevolent overlord to monkeys thing doesn't work out."

"You are *not*- Ah, whatever."

"The reason we care about these collectors is they get discarded, into local spacetime. Most of them probably end up falling into the star, but some could go into orbit. Or even be ejected from the star system, under certain circumstances. Because as I mentioned, the collectors of a spinner are tuned to operate efficiently with the companion star, so if we found such a discarded collector, we, or I, could determine which star it came from."

"And find the spinner," I slapped the arm rest of the chair, which made me float away from it. Grabbing hold of the safety strap, I got it fastened across my waist again. "Please tell me you're not just teasing me with *if* we could find a discarded collector."

"I am not. There again, I have good news, and bad news. The good news is, we don't have to go looking for a collector. One was found, approximately seven hundred thousand years ago, by the Thuranin. One of their star carriers was recharging in deep interstellar space, in the Centaurus Arm, about fifteen hundred lightyears from the globular star cluster NGC 5986."

"I know that place. It's a bad neighborhood, but there is a corner with a food truck that sells amazing barbecue."

"I don't know why I bother telling you where things are, you have no concept of how vast the galaxy is."

"Ayuh, and *you* have no concept of how good smoked brisket tastes."

"That hurt, Joe."

"Sorry. So, this globe star cluster, what about it?"

"What you need to know is the star carrier was scanning space around it, looking for incoming navigation hazards. Space rocks, that sort of thing. It identified a clearly artificial object that was made of exotic matter. Once the thing was brought into a docking bay, the Thuranin determined the object was made by the Elders."

"A collector?"

"Exactly."

"Outstanding! The little green pinheads have the thing now?"

"Unfortunately no. They of course immediately reported their find to the Maxohlx, as is required by the coalition's patron-client treaty. No they didn't," he snorted. "They hid it for years, testing and trying to get the thing to work. Somehow, the Maxohlx learned of the discovery, and demanded their clients hand it over. The demand came in the form of a sneak attack raid, followed by orbital bombardment of a wide area around where the collector had been held."

"The Thuranin got the message?"

"Loud and clear, as did the rest of the coalition. Joe, the collector, what is left of it after pieces were cut off for destructive testing, has been stored at a research base, on a Maxohlx planet."

"How do you know that?"

"Remember the enormous ocean of data I downloaded from the Pentivar archive? The info was buried in there."

"Hitting that archive is an even better idea than I hoped. Cool! So, the pinheads, or the kitties, analyzed the collector, and they know which star system it was discarded from?"

"Um, no. Neither of them performed that type of testing, because no meatsack in this galaxy is capable of doing that test. The collector must be powered up to determine which star it was tuned for, and only I am capable of doing that."

"Shit. Next, because the Universe hates me, you're going to say you can't power the thing up remotely, we need to go get the damned thing?"

"Hence why I described this news as 'Meh' at best."

"It is 'Meh' rather than 'Awful' because the research base has been abandoned for years, the planet has a small population, and no defenses, right? We can walk right in and take the thing?"

"Joe, it's on Ohmeharikahn."

"Oh shiiiiiit." He didn't need to say any more on the subject. Ohmeharikahn was the main Hegemony military base for what the kitties had designated as Sector Four, and that base had been key to the government forces scoring several decisive victories against the rebellion, late in their civil war. During most of the conflict that flared up and dragged on, hot and cold depending on what resources each side could pull together, the Hegemony strategy had been to limit risk, avoid direct large-scale battles, and grind the rebels down in a war of attrition. After the rebellion could no longer go on the offensive, the Hegemony

Nineth and Fourteenth fleets had begun mopping up the scattered rebel squadrons, taking back strategic territory. Sector Four was vital to that effort, since most of the border there was a demilitarized zone between the Maxohlx and Rindhalu, with no clients of either coalition occupying the area. As a DMZ neither side was supposed to enter, that border had been a perfect refuge for rebel ships between hit and run raids. And perfect for the spiders to supply the rebel ships, to keep the war going as long as possible. "That is a tough freakin' target."

"That is an impossible target, Joe."

"I don't suppose if we explained that we need the collector to fight the Outsider, and we asked nicely, the kitties would give the thing to us?"

"Ha! As if. They would immediately give it to the Outsider. Or, if we blockaded that star system, they would duct tape the collector to a nuke, and destroy it."

"You're right, that's exactly what they would do," I groaned. "OK, we need Skippy magic for this one. You infiltrate the SD network, we jump in with a DeLorean, have Frey sneak in a STAR team, and we-"

"None of that is going to happen. Before you hit me with a bunch of increasingly stupid questions, allow me to explain. That planet is surrounded by multiple layers of overlapping sensor fields, out to a distance of just under five lightseconds. Nothing, not even specialized Rindhalu stealth corvettes, can get close to the planet. Within the sensor coverage bubble, there is a disruption field that prevents ships from jumping in. Attacking ships must emerge outside of the outer edge of the sensor coverage, and fly in the long way, through the strategic defense network. And through the warships that are based there. Since the end of the civil war, either the Nineth or Fourteenth fleets are there continuously, with at least half of a fleet's ships maintained at combat readiness for instant deployment. The Hegemony is concerned the Rindhalu could exploit their current weakness by striking along the border, quickly seizing territory and then declaring a cease fire that would leave the Maxohlx at a severe disadvantage. The situation is- Why am I telling you this? You're a general, you have been briefed on the strategic situation."

"I have. I kind of wish I didn't know much about that planet, a few more hours of ignorance would be bliss."

"In this case, ignorance could get a lot of people killed."

"There are, what?" I tried to recall the details. "Three billion kitties on that rock?"

"Three and a half."

"There isn't any way you could fake a message from headquarters, requesting the collector to be delivered to the homeworld?"

"No way. Sorry, Joe, I have done sketchy shit like that too many times. You know that the Maxohlx now require all sensitive communications to be confirmed face to face. That's why they have constructed so many courier ships, a lot of their message traffic is hand delivered. It's like they have gone back to the days of tying messages to the legs of pigeons. The only way I see of getting that collector is a smash and grab raid," he shook his head slowly. "That would be an epic bloodbath on both sides."

During the remaining flight time to rendezvous with *Valkyrie*, I studied all the info Skippy had about the defenses at Ohmeharikahn, which in my mind I had already assigned the nickname 'Omaha'. Skippy was absolutely correct, it was a super tough target, and although he knew exactly where the collector was, we could not sneak in and get it. The entire complex at the site the kitties called Attisted was heavily shielded and surrounded by an independent disruption field. No, the kitties were not concerned about us using a DeLorean dropship to jump into the complex. They had set up defenses so the Rindhalu couldn't jump over Attisted a starship packed with explosives. The whole situation with that complex was kind of ironic, because the substantial defenses there had been set up a long time ago, when the kitties used the place for high-energy research. That was back before the terraforming of the planet reached the stage where it became attractive for large scale colonization. Yes, I know the term 'terraforming' means to modify a planet to be like Earth, which the Maxohlx definitely did not do. Not exactly. But since nearly all of the known intelligent species in the galaxy breathe oxygen, and require temperatures where water is liquid, that is close enough. That is why it's desirable to invade and seize planets that are at least in the late stages of terraforming, rather than starting with rocks that have thick unbreathable atmospheres, or very little atmosphere. At that point, most of the hard, time-consuming and expensive work has been done, and that world is ready for real estate developers to move in. Because the cost of equipping, training and launching an invasion is less than the cost of terraforming a planet, many species like the Kristang rarely bother with modifying worlds for themselves. Instead, they just wait to give their young and troublesome warriors an opportunity to prove themselves by seizing a new planet, a policy that sometimes secures new territory for a clan, and always results in getting rid of an excess supply of hotheaded young warriors.

Anyway, what was I talking about? Oh yeah, the Attisted complex on Omaha. When the population of the planet reached twelve million, it became politically impractical to conduct dangerous high-energy research there, so the complex was converted into other uses, including secure storage of valuable items. The ironic part, and I'm probably not using the word 'ironic' correctly, is that over the years, Attisted had been downgraded to become sort of like the 'junk drawer' in a kitchen. Things you occasionally need go in that drawer, but also there is a lot of stuff like dead batteries, old rubber bands, odd-sized nuts, bolts, and screws, broken pieces of candles, whatever. That drawer is the kind of place where you never know what you're going to find in there, except the thing you want is rarely in residence. Like I said, Attisted was like that. The collector was still there, at least it was as of three years ago. Skippy found a message from a university professor, inquiring about whether she could perform tests on the unknown Elder object. The answer she received was a less than polite 'No', but Skippy also found references to reports where the complex manager directed a crew to assure the object was indeed still where it was supposed to be, and in good condition. It was. If we raided Attisted to get the collector, we would be taking a risk the thing had been moved since the report was filed, but that had to be a very minor risk. As far as the Maxohlx were concerned, the collector was an old, useless, unknown piece of junk.

Skippy said Omaha was too hard a target. He might have been right about that. What I needed was a second opinion, or many other expert opinions. The problem was, planning had to be restricted to a very small group, or there would be a substantial risk of the kitties learning that we intended to hit Omaha, and they would reinforce the defenses there. How the hell could a complex operation be planned, without me telling anyone?

It couldn't. So, I had to tell a few people about it.

"Did you enjoy your holiday, Sir?" Reed asked as I stepped out of the dropship, holding up a bottle of Gatorade.

"It was a fun-filled family road trip. Ah, thanks for this," I guzzled the cold Gatorade, damn it tasted good. "Fireball, I need a shower, a change of clothes, and a hot meal, in that order. Then, I need to review something with you and Frey. Get us started back toward Earth, meet me in my office in two hours."

"Review what you and Skippy just did, Sir?" It was human nature that she was curious about what I had been doing.

"That," I shook my head, "will hopefully be something no one needs to know about for a long time."

"No chance of that, Joe," Skippy appeared. "I told you, the next shift on that wormhole network will-"

"No one needs to hear any details. Unless you want Colonel Reed and the crew to have an even lower opinion of your judgment?"

"We shall not speak of it," he agreed.

"Good. Reed, while we were on holiday, Skippy and I put our heads together and realized something important. I want you and Frey to hear what we found. After," I lifted the front of my shirt and sniffed. I was ripe, and not like a perfect summer peach. The T-shirt I had worn under my environment flight suit was stuck to my back, and somehow although I had eaten a very bland diet while in zero gravity, I had a scent that reminded me of old chili. "I scrub myself with Pine-Sol."

Frey glanced toward the green light above the door in my office aboard *Valkyrie*, then turned to me.

I sat back in my chair. "I'll get right to it. When Skippy saw the Outsider streaking away from the Elder starship it had been riding, a threat matrix inside him popped up with an alert that it recognized the signature as that of an Outsider. Unfortunately, it did not then open a file of instructions on how to react to an incursion from outside the galaxy. Which is odd, very odd. Why program your security system to recognize a threat, and then not specify an appropriate response? Or at least, a range of options. When Skippy and I talked about it a while ago, he assumed the lack of instructions was due to the Elders knowing they had nothing to stop an Outsider invasion. Then, recently, he reviewed damaged sections of his matrix, they had been sealed off. Those sections had been damaged during the AI war, and then by the computer worm. The one that we had to go into the Roach Motel to kill," I added for Frey, she hadn't been a Pirate back then. "He found something. A clue that there *was* a set of instructions, but they are all scrambled and incomplete. There is an Elder machine referred to as a 'spinner'. He doesn't know what it is, other than that it's *big*, enormous. Enormous in higher spacetime, its footprint here could be tiny, which is why no one has ever noticed the thing. He also doesn't know where the thing is, but the Maxohlx have possession of an Elder artifact that could identify the star system where we'll find this 'spinner'."

One side of Frey's mouth curled up. "You want a STAR team to perform a heist, Sir?"

"I wish." I was definitely not smiling. "There won't be any quiet infil on this op. The thing, Skippy calls it a 'collector', is stored at a military base, on Ohmeharikahn."

Reed whistled, Frey only lifted an eyebrow. As a fleet captain, Reed was familiar with major enemy bases, and their orbital and ground-based defenses. The Special Tactics Assault Regiment had not bothered to study the dirtside facilities on Ohmeharikahn, because the Navy considered that planet an impossibly tough target. The Navy brass were probably right about that.

"Sir," Reed let out a breath. "Our entire Navy couldn't knock back the SD network there, not enough for a spaceborne assault to avoid getting get slaughtered before boots hit the ground."

"That's my assessment also," I admitted. "I want the two of you to find a way around that problem. Gasquet served with the War Plans staff?"

She nodded. "For three years, before he came aboard."

"Bring him into this, but tell no one else. Frey, Skippy will give you details, at this point I'd prefer you not to include your second in command. If Opsec fails and the kitties know we're coming, Omaha will become the most heavily defended planet in the galaxy."

"Omaha, Sir?"

"Yeah, I uh, am designating the planet as Objective Omaha, for now." Both women nodded. The target needed a code name. Def Com would think 'Omaha' sounded too much like the real name of the planet, but the Maxohlx pronunciation was so different, they wouldn't make the connection. Besides, if the kitties ever heard that we were planning the op, we would be screwed anyway. "Any questions?"

"Can we count on bringing a Sentinel with us?" Reed asked.

"Unfortunately, no. Ah, maybe? It depends on timing. If we can wait long enough for Puptart to become available, we could bring a nice surprise to Omaha with us."

"Solar flares will continue to hit Jaguar for years," Reed noted. "Puptart will need to stay there until the star returns to a steady state."

"Unless the Security Council orders everyone to evac the planet. In that case, Puptart could go hunting with us earlier than expected. Sooner than the Outsider expects."

Reed gave me a look I interpreted as 'what are you talking about'? "Is that a real possibility? I haven't heard that the Council is-"

"At this point it's just an option I discussed with Chatterji."

"He is set to retire soon?" Reed phrased it as a question, though it was widely known in the service.

"He was. Def Com requested him to remain at Jaguar, they want an experienced hand at the controls, until the present crisis is over."

Reed flashed a sour smile. "The present crisis. Before the *next* one."

"You know it."

"Can we count on the usual miracle from Skippy?"

Before answering, I waited a beat for him to speak. He didn't, so, "If we can degrade the defenses first by conventional means, he can hack into the SD network's weapons and sensors, but we can't get him close enough to do the job without the kitties being alerted."

"Sir, based on what I know of Ohmeharikahn, unless we can bring a Sentinel to the party, or get another miracle from Skippy, this is a No-Go. Our assault transports couldn't survive in that environment. Def Com doctrine requires the Navy to establish supremacy in the battlespace around the planet, before assault transports can jump in."

"I know. Look at the problem with a fresh set of eyes, there might be something I missed. Work with Skippy and Bilby, and Gasquet, no one else."

Frey had another question. "What's the timeline, Sir? Can we wait for Puptart to be available, or do we have to go now?"

"For now, I want to assume this needs to happen in, uh, shit." Regardless of the tough defenses around Omaha, we would be conducting a large scale spaceborne assault in what the Navy calls a 'contested environment', which means the enemy would be shooting back at us. The planning, training, and logistics of pulling together so many ships and people could take a month. More like several months. Then there would be the political maneuvering involved, that would slow down the whole process. Humanity simply did not have enough mechanized boots to put on the ground, not enough for my initial guess at the size of force we would need to assault a section of Omaha's surface, and hold that beachhead long enough to find, secure, and evac the precious collector. Plus, cover the egress, to get all those boots back into orbit.

The problem wasn't the number of boots available, or the people in those mechanized boots. Def Com's constraint was the number of assault carriers, and the number of transport and fighter dropships. If we could use every assault carrier we had, we could land no more than three reinforced brigades, about seventeen thousand soldiers or Marines. It wasn't realistic to assume we could count on every assault landing ship and every spacecraft in their dropship squadrons being available. All that equipment needs regular maintenance, the Navy's stated goal is for seventy percent of their ships to be combat ready at any time, with the other thirty undergoing overhauls, repairs, or working up new crews and squadrons. In practice, the assault carriers tend to be last in line for maintenance and overhaul resources. The inadequate number of assault transports, and the low priority those ships received for keeping them combat ready, was a result of the UN Security Council's policy of pulling back from engagement with the galaxy. Assault carriers are offensive weapons, and the weary people of Earth felt that if we didn't mess with aliens, they wouldn't mess with us. That was partly my fault: providing the Roscoe Sentinel had allowed the public of Earth to give a middle finger salute to the galaxy, secure in the knowledge that we didn't need help from unreliable aliens to protect ourselves.

That all changed when Moonbase Zulu was hit, but the people of Earth were still in denial.

Whatever. Any attack against Ohmeharikahn would require help from aliens. That would mean landing alien boots on the ground, set there by alien dropships from alien assault carriers. Like I said, politics. How long would it take for our clumsy politicians to make an abrupt reversal and suddenly announce that aliens are our friends and we are all one big happy family? Shit. Like that's ever going to happen.

"For now," I finally decided what I wanted to say, "Assume we will have all the resources we need, in, let's say a month. Then, we can revise the plans to cut back to whatever we actually have."

Reed and Frey had no objections. Not because they would never question my orders, but because all three of us understood the harsh truth: no way could the UN Navy hit Ohmeharikahn without a disastrous slaughter on both sides.

Even if that was the only way to prevent the Outsider from killing *everyone*.

CHAPTER THIRTY THREE

I had just stepped out of my office, looking both ways along the passageway, when Skippy's avatar appeared in front of my face. After the side trip to Pigpen, we pinged a Bosphuraq relay station to learn if any new disaster had struck. The answer was 'No', so I only had to deal with the current problem of a genocidal entity from beyond the galaxy. "Skippy, what's up?" I asked as my nose almost collided with his avatar.

"Joe! I just found something interesting in that last download. The-"

"Hold that thought," I went back into the office and closed the door.

"What? You told me there wasn't-"

"The Outsider hasn't done anything new, the kitties are still rotten, the spiders still are pondering whether to get involved, blah, blah, blah. First, I looked for problems. That directly affect us, and I didn't find anything new. Then I moved on to analyzing the enormous mountain of trivia in the download, in case there is anything interesting. This time, there is. We knew the Maxohlx are tired of getting played by your good friend Sketchy McSleazeball, right?"

"He is not exactly my friend, but the kitties have to be super pissed off at him by now."

"They are. I just learned they have taken out a contract to whack him."

"They're going to *kill* him?" That should not have surprised me, but it did. "Whoa, I did not expect th- We need to warn the guy."

"Youze want I should send a message direct to him, or to the Jeraptha government?"

"Both. Contacting a single person over the relay network is a low probability event. Their government is more likely to know where he is."

"Yes, except the Maxohlx might be relying on the Jeraptha government to lead them to Scorandum."

"Good point, but that's their business. Do you know who the kitties contracted with for the hit?"

"The message indicates they will make, or already have made, offers to three Jeraptha organizations. Two of them are criminal syndicates, the third is the Ethics and Compliance Office."

"The- The kitties think the freakin' ECO might murder one of their own admirals?"

"They might if the price is right," Skippy shrugged. "Scorandum has been inconsistent on kicking taxes up his leadership chain."

"Yeah, but he has been a reliable earner for decades."

"True, however the minister in charge of the Office might see a big one-time score as more favorable than the possibility of future earnings spread over time. The minister also has to consider that if someone else takes the contract and whacks Scorandum, not only does the ECO miss out on the payment, Scorandum won't have any future earnings."

"Once again, I am *so* glad I am not serving in the Jeraptha military."

"There is also the issue that Scorandum is popular in the Office, and any rising star is a threat to the admiral above him, and to the Minister."

"I still can't believe the *Ethics* people would accept a contract to kill one of their own."

Skippy blinked. "Um, have you met the Jeraptha?"

"Yes," I sighed. "Every time I meet them, it gives me a headache."

"You should try drinking less when you meet them."

"Have *you* met the beetles?"

"Good point. We can't do anything if the ECO decides to stab one of their own in the back, but the Jeraptha authorities could clamp down on the crime syndicates, right?"

"That depends. Just the news that the Maxohlx made offers to those two syndicates is certain to boost their prestige, and their stock price. One of the syndicates is currently facing a hostile takeover bid by a-"

"I- Hold a minute. Criminal mobs are listed on their freaking *stock exchange?*"

"Well, not all of them, of course. Just the ones that have grown large enough that they need to raise additional capital to fuel expansion."

"Oh my- By 'hostile takeover', you mean a gang war?"

"No, nothing so crude, although that does of course happen occasionally. No, a hedge fund is alleging that the Kobosh Family Syndicate has been underperforming recently, and is in need of new management. The Koboshes raked in a lot of cash by acting as smugglers for both sides in the Maxohlx civil war, and peacetime has not been good for their finances."

"A hedge fund, huh?"

"Yes. When *they* get involved, things really get sleazy."

"I would prefer not to know more about this subject."

"Whatevs. The warning message is uploaded to this relay station, I'm done here. We should jump away, and probably stop at a Jeraptha relay next, that will get the message delivered faster."

We stopped at a Jeraptha relay station, to send a warning to Scorandum, and to get another update. Going to the closest Maxohlx relay would have required a thirty seven hour detour, and we had to be careful about how often we hit them up for a download. As Skippy had warned me, we couldn't go back to that well too often, or despite all our precautions, the rotten kitties might discover we could read their mail.

"Skippy," I asked from near the bridge doorway, after Reed had jumped us away from the station. "Do we have any revised orders from Def Com?"

"No. Nothing important. There is a bunch of administrivial housekeeping crap, like you are overdue to complete your Command Climate survey."

I shared a surprised look with Reed, and Gasquet. "That can't be right. Surveys are an annual event, and I have only been in command of the Special Mission Group for-"

"Not *here*, dumdum. The survey for the Jaguar garrison. You were in command there for most of the past year, so you are responsible for it."

"Oh. I'll get right on that."

"No, you won't. You will drag your heels and wait until the last minute, then request an extension because the galaxy is falling apart again, or some other lame excuse."

"Uh-" That's when I realized I was setting a bad example for the crew, who when the time came, would have to fill out surveys about the command climate I set. "I had most of that done before I left Jaguar, I will update the-"

"Don't bother, I already collated the responses for you. All you need to do is get an update from your replacement, *and* I have already sent a request for him to do that."

"Thank you for that, the- Wait. Did you collate the *actual* responses, or screw with the data so I look like an idiot?"

"Ugh. Fine, I'll use the original responses, but *my* version would be much funnier."

"Yeah, that's what the staff officers at Def Com want: humorous survey data."

"If anyone needs some humor to brighten up their day, it is staff offi- Oh, oh *shit*."

"What is it this ti-" I froze. Because *he* had frozen. My instant response had been to assume his 'oh shit' had been about some stupid bit of administrative BS. But he wasn't joking, he was in shock. "Skippy?" I strode quickly toward his avatar. "Skippy? What's going on?"

With a shudder, he unfroze. "Joe, we are out of time! The Kaliberak wide field virtual exochronous refraction array is *gone*, do you understand what this means?"

"I, didn't understand anything you said between 'time' and 'gone'."

"Ugh. There is no way I can dumb this down enough for-"

"Wide field array? So this caliber thing is some kind of antenna, telescope, something like that?"

"Huh. You actually dumbed it down enough by yourself. The Kaliberak array is an instrument the Rindhalu set up near the M70 globular cluster, it was designed to observe quantum fluctuations in spacetime that originate from what you call Sagittarius A. The giant black hole at the center of the Milky Way."

"And someone destroyed the array? Why?"

"It- Hmm, anything I tell you after this would be considered ultra classified, so-"

I snapped my fingers with, "*Don't* say it, not here. Reed, in my office, ask Colonel Frey to join us."

"Gasquet," Reed rose from her chair. "You have the conn. General Bishop? We stay here for now?"

"Yeah," I looked at the display for inspiration, and came up blank. All it showed was empty space, with the image of *Valkyrie* in the center. "For now."

Frey popped her head out of her office as Reed and I approached. Frey's regular office was in the Starbase section of the ship, but recently I had requested that Reed find a space for the STAR team leader closer to the bridge. So, Frey had a second office that was larger than my office, a former storage garage for maintenance bots. It wasn't luxurious, it was convenient. Without a word, she fell in behind us.

"Reed," I said as I closed my office door, waiting a moment for the green security light to glow. "I appreciate that it's not good for your crew to know we're keeping secrets from them."

"They're in the military, Sir. They understand."

"It's still not good for morale. Hopefully, they will never have to know some of the nightmare shit that keeps me awake at night. All right, Skippy? Someone destroyed a telescope? Why should we care?"

He spoke as his avatar appeared. "This is big trouble. End of days stuff. Joe, the Kaliberak array was not destroyed, it was *taken*."

"Taken where?"

"I don't know."

"Who took it?"

"That I also don't know for certain, but you gave me a very good guess."

"I did?" I stared at him, and I noticed Reed was giving me with a 'when did you plan to tell me about this' look. "When was this?"

"When I told you that over a dozen star carriers have gone missing recently, and you stated the only reason to steal that many space trucks is if you have something really big to move. You see what I'm saying, right? The Outsider must have stolen the array."

"I got that, yeah. A dozen star carriers could haul the thing away?"

"That array is enormous, it consists of just over three hundred synchronized satellites that form a bowl shape. A linked, virtual antenna. The theft could be accomplished with ten star carriers, having additional ships provides redundancy."

"Why the hell would it want to steal- Oh crap. Can this array be turned into a *weapon*? A giant space laser, something like that?"

"Giant. Space. Laser?" He stared at me. "It is not a Death Star, dumdum."

"Or, whatever. Any kind of weapon."

"Thankfully, I have good news and bad news about that. The array antenna is a receiver, not a transmitter."

"That is good news. How can that also be *bad* news?"

"It is a large scale *receiver*, Joe, tuned to quantum fluctuations."

"OK, you said that, so? I'm not following you."

"I will say it again, but slowly. A, very large, *receiver*, that can detect the underlying, quantum, state, of the spacetime grid. Does that remind you of anything?"

"Oh *shiiiiiit*. It can receive the signal from the Outhouse?"

"Not that I know of, but uh!" He held up hand. "Remember, the Outsider has knowledge of technology beyond my own. It might be able to, it must think it *can*, modify the Kaliberak array to act as a receiver for the matter transmission from NGC 1023."

"Fuuuuuuuck," Reed groaned. "You have no clue where this array was taken?"

"None, zero. It could be anywhere. Except, hmm. It is likely to be moved beyond the rim of the galaxy, where spacetime is more flat, and there will be less noise in the signal. Also, logically, it would be in the direction of NGC 1023. Roughly," he added. "That is still an unimaginably vast area, no way could we search it all."

Reed pursed her lips while she thought. "Does this array itself generate any kind of emission while it's operating?"

"Ooh, good question," Skippy gave her a thumbs up. "Yes it does. A faint level of radiation, on a frequency of twenty six point four megahertz. Those emissions travel slowly outward at the speed of light, so I'm afraid they won't be of much use for us to find the thing before it's too late."

"Too late for what?" Reed asked.

"To stop it from modifying the satellite receivers, and setting up the array to process the signal from NGC 1023. To open a gateway for an invasion."

"If we could find it, could *Valkyrie's* weapons destroy it?"

"Finding it would be the difficult part. The individual satellites are easy targets, they are not armored, and the array was not equipped with defenses. There was not expected to be any need to defend the array, it is a purely scientific instrument with no military value."

"No military value the spiders *knew of*," I corrected him. "The Outsider is certainly using it as a weapon."

"Are there others?" Frey asked. "Arrays like that. Or, other antennas that could be modified to, detect the signal?"

"That," I pointed at her, "is an excellent question."

"The answer is, hmm," Skippy took off his hat and rubbed his dome. "Shmaybe? The Kaliberak array is unique, it replaced an earlier array that was larger but less sensitive. There are no other antennas that utilize that type of technology, it is a very specialized instrument. Only the Rindhalu have the knowledge to even understand what the array does, certainly no other species are capable of constructing such equipment. But, keep in mind, the Outsider has access to technology beyond my understanding. It might be able to construct an intergalactic quantum radio receiver using only paper clips and a battery."

"For now," I raised a hand to stop the discussion from spiraling down a rabbit hole. "Let's assume it can't MacGyver a solution without access to something like a Rindhalu array."

"It had only a single target, then," Reed nodded.

"Maybe not," Frey said slowly. "Skippy, you said there was a previous array, before the Kaliberak one was built? What happened to it?"

"It was decommissioned, why?"

"Decommissioned as in just switched off, or was it taken apart?"

"Oooh, hmm. Switched off, and no further maintenance was performed."

"Oh shit," I understood what Frey was asking. "Skippy, when was the last time anyone verified that decommissioned array is still where the spiders left it?"

"Um, hmm," he frowned. "Give me a minute to search my files, this is something that ordinarily falls into the category of trivia. The older array is located much closer to the galactic center. Hmm, it looks like the Rindhalu have not sent a ship to the older array since they took it out of service, around two hundred and forty seven thousand years ago."

"It's not a big tourist attraction, then," I muttered, kicking myself for not having asked Skippy whether there was any technology in the Milky Way that could be modified to act as an intergalactic radio receiver. I mean, *Duh*, of course the Outsider would seek to recreate the energy-to-matter receiver the Elders had constructed. That is how an invasion force would be crossing the gap between galaxies, and that is why the Outsider had stolen the Kaliberak array.

I am an idiot. We had wasted too much time reacting to the enemy's moves, all while it was preparing to carjack the array. What other mistakes had I made that-

"This is all my fault," Skippy groaned. "It is obvious the Outsider would attempt to construct a receiver. I just did not think that was possible, given the technology that is available now, but I should have anticipated the enemy is significantly more advanced."

"Skippy, speaking as someone who is an expert at beating myself up for things I should have known, don't blame yourself."

"There is no one else to blame, Joe," he sighed, miserable. "It's not like any filthy monkey could have guessed that array might be useful to the Outsider. What I don't understand is, if the Outsider needs something like the Kaliberak array to create an energy-to-matter conversion receiver, then how did *it* get here already?"

"That is a damned good question. Before we do anything else, we should find out whether we have one problem, or *two*. Skippy, how long will it take us to reach the decommissioned array?"

"On that, I have a rare bit of good news. The spiders chose the locations of both arrays because they are each no more than seven lightyears from an Elder wormhole. The Turshipan array, that's the old decommissioned one, will require us to go through two normal wormhole transits, and one shortcut. Thirty nine hours to get there, if we start now. Bilby has a course programmed into the navigation system."

Reed perched on the edge of her chair. "Will that be all, Sir?"

"Get us to Turshipan ASAP, Fireball. We'll figure out the rest when we get there."

Valkyrie's captain walked out the door, and it closed behind her.

Frey also was eager to get out of her chair. "If you don't need me, Sir, I need to work on the raid plan for Omaha."

I raised an eyebrow at her. "We don't know that we're going there. I am still searching for alternatives to hitting Ohmeharikahn."

"Respectfully Sir, a search for alternatives is OBE," she meant it had been Overcome By Events. "The Outsider has made its move, and we can't count on finding that array by randomly searching every cubic lightminute between this galaxy and the Outhouse. We have to rely on the one thing we know will stop it, and that one thing is on Omaha."

"We actually *don't* know that the spinner will do anything at all," Skippy objected. "I am *guessing*, I told you that."

Frey wasn't buying his excuse. "Do you have a better guess?"

"No."

"What are the odds you will find a better way to stop the Outsider, before it opens the door to an invasion force?"

"Uhhh," he groaned. "Zero."

"Frey, you're right," I agreed though I very much didn't want to. "Can I see your plan this evening? I have nothing else to do until we get to this Turshipan place."

"I'll have the draft ready by this evening, but my team's role in the op is useless, unless you can do *your* job."

I knew what she meant. "Yeah, I need to find a way to get us past the orbital defenses. Right now, that is not looking good at all. When we get back to Earth, I can ask the Navy tactical staff for ideas, they might- Ah, damn it, I can't do that. The only way this can ever possibly work is if the kitties don't know we're coming. Comsec on Earth is awful. We'll have to bring the planning staff to Jaguar and- No, that won't work either. Shit. We can't plan an entire spaceborne assault operation with just the people aboard this ship, there are-"

"If I may make a suggestion, Sir?"

"Please, because I got nothin' right now."

"If we want to know how to knock out the defenses around a Maxohlx planet, we should ask the experts. Talk to the spiders."

"Um," Reed froze, staring at me as she stepped out the door of her cabin. In one hand, she held a coffee mug, on top of which was a half-eaten piece of toast. "Busted," she exclaimed under her breath.

I had absolutely no idea what she was talking about. It was early, just after oh five hundred, my stupid brain had announced Hey I Am Wide Awake, so I rolled out of bed and was going to the galley for coffee before hitting the gym. Reed was wearing the uniform of the day, she wasn't dressed for the gym, and I knew from the duty roster that she didn't need to be on the bridge. Had she gotten up early to get time in a flight simulator? No, she wasn't wearing a flight suit. "Busted?" I asked.

"The," she lifted the toast off the coffee mug. "The toast."

"The other day, Skippy was all excited about an article he read in a physics journal, he used words like 'stochastic' and 'polymorphic', and he even tried to show me the math, which he should have known was never going to work. *That* made more sense to me than whatever you're trying to tell me about toast."

"Sir, I made it."

"I did assume you hadn't found a loaf of pre-toasted bread."

"I meant," she looked back over her shoulder into her cabin, "I have a toaster."

"In your cabin?"

"I know it's against regulations, it-"

"That's genius."

"It's just- The toaster we had before the refit was crap-"

"I seem to remember you blasted it with a maser cannon."

"The new toaster, you have seen it?"

"Yeah, what's up with that thing?" In the galley was a shiny box made of titanium and chrome and, probably some kind of exotic matter. The thing was the size of a dishwasher and while I had seen people screwing around with it, I hadn't seen it produce any toast.

"It is a military grade toaster, Sir, courtesy of the United Nations Navy procurement service. It can take fifteen gees of acceleration, survive hard radiation, and operate in temperatures from negative seventy Celsius to sixty above."

"If it is that cold or hot in the galley, I won't be thinking about toast. Also, radioactive toast doesn't sound like part of a balanced diet."

"What the thing *doesn't* do is make decent toast. Half the time, the bread gets stuck, and when a slice does go all the way through, one side is burnt and the other is cold. That machine is impressive engineering, it sucks as a toaster. So, I brought my own toaster from home," she gestured inside her cabin, and stepped back.

"You have a coffee maker also?"

She shrugged. "It saves time in the mornings."

"You could request Skippy to send a bot with coffee."

"That would require me to talk with Skippy. In the morning. Before I have coffee."

"Ah. Good point." We both looked at the ceiling, expecting the beer can's avatar to appear. He either was busy, or wisely chose not to get involved.

He got involved anyway. "Hey, Skippy," I called a few minutes later. "I have a question for you."

"If you want me to explain the math again, you can forget about-"

"No math needed. The new toaster in the galley, that is an impressive piece of technology."

"Impressive?" He snorted. "Joe, it was made by monkeys bashing coconuts together."

"Uh huh. Hypothetically, if that thing suffered a serious malfunction, could you fix it?"

"No can do. The Navy doesn't own a Right To Repair license from the manufacturer. No one aboard the ship is authorized to screw with it, that includes me. Buncha jerks."

"Wow, that is truly unfortunate. So, again speaking hypothetically, if the thing broke, and we had to store it in a cargo bay until we got back to Earth, we-"

"The manufacturer also has a certified service station at Jaguar."

"That is good to know. If we had to take it out of service, could you fabricate a temporary replacement? One that makes toast the way Reed likes?"

"Dude, please. *Could* I do that?"

"I mean-"

"The fabricator is warming up now. Um, Joe, there is one problem: that monstrosity of a toaster is currently *not* broken."

"That is true. Hey, on a totally unrelated subject, the coffee tasted kind of extra bitter yesterday."

"Ugh. No one else has mentioned-"

"The big coffee pots should be switched out and scrubbed again, before the galley is scheduled to open for breakfast this morning, but I want the bot that handles the job to be extra careful. It would be awful if a bot carrying a big metal pot of hot coffee were to stumble, and dump that coffee on our fancy toaster. If youze know what I mean."

"Oh. Um, bots don't actually stumble, so-"

"You seem to think I care about details, and I do not."

"Gotcha."

Sadly, a maintenance bot suffered a glitch in the galley, and spilled half a pot of hot coffee into the expensive high tech toaster, which then had to be taken out of service. There would of course need to be an investigation into the loss of UN Navy valuable property, unfortunately sensors in the galley went offline around the time the bot glitched, so the incident would have to remain a mystery. As task force commander, I would sign off on the property loss form, when I had time to do that. Like, after we took care of the threat from the Outsider. Or never. Never works for me.

By oh eight hundred, Reed and I were enjoying perfect toast from our new galley toaster, during our breakfast meeting. "Sir?" She glanced toward the new, totally normal and functional toaster. "Do I want to know how this happened?"

"If you have to ask that question-"

"Right." She wrinkled her nose. "Before I got this job, I thought captains had to be aware of everything that happens aboard their ship. Since then, I have learned that for the ship to actually function, there are things I *shouldn't* know about."

"Uh huh," I agreed. "Like where the engineering people make moonshine?"

"Like that." She cocked her head. "I think they are making bourbon now."

"Bourbon?" That surprised me.

She shrugged. "The ship has been in service long enough to allow alcohol to age. I assume they're making bourbon, I found a requisition for oak barrels a few years ago."

"That is not suspicious at all."

"The requisition went through Skippy's Supply Company."

"Again, I do not see anything suspicious there."

"All I know is," she added strawberry jam to her toast, "I won't have to deal with toast crumbs in my cabin anymore."

Jates stomped into Dave's office, footsteps even heavier than if the Verd had been wearing powered armor. "I need to report a murder."

"Um, what?" Dave looked up from his laptop. "Who?"

"Poindit. The murder hasn't happened yet, but it will soon, if you know what I mean."

"Yeah," Dave relaxed just a bit. "I do. If it helps, the guy is even more a pain in the ass to me than he is to you."

"I doubt that. This was your idea, you need to fix it."

"I know, I know. The problem is, he sent video samples out on the last courier ship. I watched that video, it makes us look good. It makes *you* look good, the hamsters are going to love you."

"My life is now complete."

"This is important, it actually is," Dave insisted. "The Ruhar don't have a positive opinion of your people right now."

"I feel just terrible about that."

"Hey, you Verd-kris can use every friend you can find. My people sure as hell can't be relied on, in the long term."

"I heard that," Jates muttered. "He pretends to admire me and my team, do you know what he calls us behind my back?"

"He says the Verd-kris are pets, I know. Circus animals who have been trained to do tricks."

"Could *you* resist strangling him?"

"I am already resisting that urge. Behind *my* back, he says humans are primitive savages who got lucky."

"So he's not wrong about *everything*."

"I'm going to pretend I didn't hear that."

"You hate him also," Jates nodded. "I'll make it look like an accident."

"Do *not* do anything without my approval, got it? Listen, Poindit is only here for another three days, the transport ship is leaving and he needs to be aboard before it jumps away, or he will be stuck on this rock for another five weeks."

"Then I am taking three days of leave, effective immediately."

"You could do that," Dave leaned his chair back and put his feet on the desk, mindful that if he leaned back too far, he would smack his head on the inside of the narrow shipping container. "But, you know a video crew has been following Poindit for the past week? It was his idea, they have been documenting how he implements his artistic vision. I know, hearing that made me want to barf. He has been requesting to do all kinds of shit, like use an infantry mech suit, or dive from orbit, anything to show he is a man of action. Em shot down all his requests, so now he's working with the Ruhar. He should leave you alone. If he doesn't, I'll explain you are unavailable due to some vital assignment."

"Is that a promise?"

"Hell yes. I regret I ever got us into this mess."

"See that you keep that promise," Jates turned to go. "Or there *will* be punching."

The Turshipan array was not, as I had assumed, near a star system of that name. It wasn't close to a star at all, the closest astronomical body larger than a rock was a red dwarf star sixteen lightyears away. For that 'exochronous' type of antenna to work, it had to be distant from any source of photons, and from any significant gravity that could warp the fabric of spacetime in the local area. That was one reason the first array had been abandoned; a wandering rogue planet would pass within forty lighthours of the array within six centuries of the rogue's discovery, and while the spiders had considered an effort to slowly nudge the planet into changing its course, they decided it would be less expensive overall to just construct a new, better array. So, I learned that 'Turshipan' was the name of the spider who led the research team that developed the technology to detect, whatever quantum vibration nonsense thing the Rindhalu wanted to study.

We jumped in a lighthour from the array's last reported position, and Bilby groaned a few seconds later. "Hey, general Dude, this isn't looking good. The array was shut down cold, but the spiders left beacons so the thing doesn't become a navigation hazard. I should be picking up the beep beep beeping of the beacons, but I don't hear nothin', you feel me?"

"Uh, yeah. What about passive sensors?"

"We are like, too far away to detect anything that isn't actively radiating. The array had been shut down long enough that its components should be the temperature of the interstellar background. We need to get closer."

"Skippy? Do you have any objection to jumping in closer?"

"I don't see the point," he sighed. "Do whatever you want."

"The problem could simply be a dead beacon."

"All *three* beacons are offline? I don't think so."

"There is one way to find out. Reed, set-"

"Sir," she interrupted me, which rarely happened. "The Outsider has to know someone would notice the Kaliberak array stopped transmitting. It might have anticipated we would come here to check on the original array."

"You're thinking the Outsider might be waiting here for us?"

"It's more likely it saturated the area with stealthed mines. Either way, I would prefer to send in a squadron of drones to recon with active sensors."

"That is a sensible precaution," I winced because I should have thought of being careful. "Do it."

We jumped in ten lightminutes from Skippy's best guess of where the array should be, launched four high speed drones, and jumped away. The drones accelerated hard and began pinging away with active sensor pulses, searching for the array and for any stealthed mines.

Seven hours later, we had a definitive answer: nothing was there. The array was gone. The good news was, the Outsider hadn't planted any nasty surprises for us, but we soon realized that good news was for a bad reason.

"Uuuuugh," Skippy delivered an Oscar worthy dramatic sigh. "This *suuuuucks*," he groaned, half an hour after we had jumped into the center of where the array should be. The array's component antennas were no longer there, but space was not entirely empty. Apparently, when the array was taken away, the Outsider had left some pieces behind. The central processor, which includes the data collection and transmission gear, had apparently been scavenged for useful parts, then discarded. The bulky protective shells that enveloped each antenna has also been left behind, probably to reduce the number of star carriers required to haul the thing away. "Joe, I now understand why the Outsider didn't bother to leave stealthed mines at this site, and you won't like hearing the reason."

"Hit me with it anyway."

"I can tell from residual radiation signatures on the central processor that only *one* star carrier hauled the entire array to, wherever it has gone."

"A single star carrier moved all this stuff? Did it mash all the antennas together and wrap them in the galaxy's largest roll of duct tape?"

"No, although I think we can all agree it would have been awesome to see that. That single star carrier made seventeen trips here to haul away the antennas."

"Whoa. Shit, how- Well, OK, that makes sense. At Kaliberak, it had to move fast, since the spiders would notice the array had stopped transmitting. Here, nobody was minding the store. So, it took, what? A couple of weeks?"

"Based on the decay of the residual radiation, I have a fairly precise timeline. The removal operation took three hundred and four days."

"Three hundred and- But, so, this started before it tried to take control of the Dogzilla Sentinel?"

"That is correct, and that is not even the bad news that is making me sick right now. Joe, the array here was taken away *seven years ago*."

CHAPTER THIRTY FOUR

We jumped away after Skippy dropped the bombshell on us. We didn't perform a random jump, we were racing back to the nearest wormhole, where Skippy would create a shortcut to bring us back into civilized space. I should say 'habitable space', what I meant is the center of the Milky Way was flooded with deadly radiation, and the former location of the Turshipan array was uncomfortably close to the center.

"Seven *years*," I had a cup of coffee in my hand, but I wasn't drinking it. Reed and Frey weren't drinking their coffees either, we were all too shocked to do anything so normal as drinking a hot beverage. "Skippy?" I was surprised he wasn't waiting for us when we walked into my office.

His avatar appeared, the hat already in one hand, the other hand rubbing his head while he pondered the issue. "It means the Outsider has been active for much longer than we knew. Beyond that, I hope *you* can tell me what it means, because I got nothin'."

"OK, we-"

"I don't know how we can figure out what it means," he jammed the oversized hat back on his head. "We don't actually *know* anything."

"That's not exactly true. Let's start with what we *do* know. Frey?" Instead of leading the discussion, I tossed the ball to my STAR team leader. She and Reed might have a better take on the situation than I did, and I kept in mind that I had a responsibility to develop my leadership team. If something bad happened to me, and considering some of the dumb shit I have done, it's likely that something bad *will* happen, the Merry Band of Pirates would need a new chief Pirate. Or I guess a pirate leader is technically a captain. Whatever.

Besides, I was interested in how Frey and Reed thought, could they reach the same conclusions I did? Or something better?

For a split second, Frey's expression was that of an elementary school student who had just been called upon by the teacher. "What we *know*," she bit her lip. "The Outsider took this array seven years ago. Skippy, can we assume it intended to use this array for the same purpose as the Kaliberak one? To receive the transmission from the Outhouse that can beam matter between galaxies?"

"I mean," he shrugged. "I can't think of any other reason it would want to steal the damned thing. It's not like it could unload the array at a pawn shop."

Frey's expression brightened. "Then we know it has not been able, over the past seven years, to make the Turshipan array work the way it wants. We know *that* because there hasn't been an invasion."

"Good," I nodded. "And?"

"Before it took the Kaliberak array, it first tried several times to acquire a Sentinel. Skippy wasn't yet aware that the Turshipan array was missing, but the Outsider knew that everyone would be alerted when the newer array stopped transmitting. It wanted a Sentinel for protection, because it feared Skippy could stop it from, setting up the Kaliberak array, or modifying it, or operating it."

"Yes, good."

"But," Skippy protested. "It still doesn't have a Sentinel, and it *has* taken the Kaliberak array."

"Yeah, so," I leaned my chair back. "Here's where we stop talking about facts, and start speculating about what it all means. Reed?"

She let out a long breath. Before speaking, she looked at her coffee cup, frowned, poured cream into, stirred it, and sipped. She didn't want coffee, she wanted time to think. That was OK. What I cared about was quality analysis, not speed. "It either no longer needs a Sentinel, or it just is no longer able to wait. Bombing Jaguar's star hasn't stopped us from chasing it, and we kicked its ass in the quarantine zone, so it has to still be afraid of Skippy. That leaves urgency: it has to move *now*, for whatever reason."

Frey nodded. "Perhaps it learned something from the failure of the Turshipan array? The signal between galaxies could be degrading over time? Or," she tapped her chin. "Something else has changed. Twice it escaped from starships we attacked. Could the Outsider itself be damaged? It's made of energy, so it could be fading, losing power, losing coherence?"

"Wow," Skippy was impressed. "That's the first happy news I've heard in a long time. How do you monkeys do this? You start with the same *zero* information I have, but somehow you make sense of it. This drives me freakin' crazy."

"It's not zero," I explained. "We take into account not only what the Outsider has done, but what it could have done and didn't. It didn't take the Kaliberak array until now. The question is, why? We have two solid guesses. Some external force requires it to move now, even though it hasn't eliminated you as a threat. Or internal damage is making it move now, while it still can."

Reed had a look like she heard what I said, but she was thinking about something else. "*We* could be the external force, the reason it has to move now. It's on a timer, and the deadline for it to act freely is approaching fast."

"Huh?"

"Puptart has to remain at Jaguar for another five months, roughly, before it can turn off the blanket and-"

"The blanket won't be *turned off* like flipping a switch," Skippy snorted. "The-"

"Yes, whatever," I interrupted him before Reed lost her train of thought. "Shut up for a minute. Reed, go ahead."

She paused for a beat to see if Skippy protested. He fumed silently at me, the key was he kept silent. "Once the blanket is, no longer active," she chose a neutral term, "Puptart could leave Jaguar. Not immediately, we would need to pull at least the civilians off the surface like you suggested, Sir. The point is, Puptart won't be stuck guarding our forward operating base forever. It could come with us, either to hunt for the Outsider, or to destroy the Kaliberak array, if by that time the array is has been detected. Whatever the Outsider is doing, it knows it has a limited time window, while our Sentinels are tied down."

"That," I considered for a moment. "Makes sense. Yes. Skippy? What do you think?'

"Why are you asking *me*? Yeah, it makes sense, now that I think about it. So, the Outsider believes it can get the array fully converted into an energy to matter receiver, before Puptart can deactivate the blanket?"

"That's the theory," Reed said with a nod.

"OK, OK," Skippy said slowly, "we have to assume it knows the governor chose the Goldilocks option for the blanket, and the Security Council confirmed that timeline."

I tapped the desk while I stared at the ceiling. "True, true. So, we might need to accelerate the schedule."

"Joe," Skippy rolled his eyes, exasperated with me. "We don't know that will make any difference for us, and the damage to Jaguar's biosphere could be severe."

"It has to make a difference. The Outsider is counting on us holding to the Goldilocks schedule, if we cut that short, it-"

"Might not make any difference," he insisted. "The enemy is smart enough to pad its schedule, *Duh*. It won't wait until the last moment."

"Unless it has no choice," Frey spoke. "Unless it learned everything it needed from the original array, it might have to experiment with the Kaliberak equipment, to make it work in a way it wasn't designed to."

"*I* definitely can't imagine how that equipment could be converted into an energy to matter receiver," Skippy muttered. "From what I know of the subject, that array lacks some very basic components for the job. Is that it? We are assuming Puptart's schedule is the reason the Kaliberak array was taken now?"

"Or that the Outsider is damaged," Reed reminded him of what we had discussed.

"Yes, I know that," he was on the verge of adding a 'Duh' but because he was speaking to Reed, he didn't do that. "What I meant is, when the Pirates are fumbling toward figuring out a puzzle, usually you explore every possibility, no matter how stupid."

I had to admit he had a point. "That's fair. What other external factors could have forced it to act now?"

"Nuh uh," he shook his head. "This guessing game is a monkey thing."

"OK, uh- Huh. Is there any indication the background uh, carrier wave, whatever, signal between galaxies, is decreasing in strength?"

"Without an array, I have no way of detecting that signal, dumdum."

"Right. I don't suppose you could build some kind of an intergalactic antenna?"

"Oh Em *GEE*, Dude," he gasped. "You want me to make the thing that should *never, ever* be built?"

"OK, it just sounds stupid the way you said it."

"The way I said it is the problem, gotcha. Think, numbskull, *think*. If I built such a thing, the Outsider could swoop in, take it, and send us a nice Thank You card."

"All I meant is, could you build the original thing the Elders had, when they first discovered the quantum carrier wave in the first place?"

"No. First, it took the Elders many years and enormous effort to construct such a machine. Second, my programming will not allow me to even think about doing anything so enormously, mind-bogglingly *stupid*."

"OK but-"

"This is like the meme about the Torment Nexus, and you're the douchebag who doesn't get it."

Frey raised an eyebrow. "Torment, Nexus?"

"I see you need remedial education on classic memes," I grinned. "The joke is, someone wrote a sci fi book called 'Don't Create The Torment Nexus' as a cautionary tale about dangerous technology. Then some idiot tech company announces that the book inspired them to create a Torment Nexus."

She grimaced. "I prefer the classic meme about the woman with a hot guy, and she turns around to check out another hot guy."

"Uh, that meme is about a *guy* who-"

"You have your version, I have mine."

"OK. Skippy, I hear you. Next question: is there any indication the Outsider is damaged?"

"I would be surprised if it wasn't. But, I have no evidence that it is. Hmm, let me think on that for a while, review the sensor data I have. So, is that it? The Outsider stole the Kaliberak array now when it couldn't wait any longer, for whatever reason?

Reed nodded, Frey did the same, and I slowly pronounced, "Ayuh. *We* are out of time. We need that spinner ASAP." The four of us fell silent for a moment, all having the same thought. Ohmeharikahn was an impossible target, even for the Merry Band of Pirates. "Frey, you are right."

Frey raised an eyebrow, Reed gave me a questioning look, so I added, "Frey suggested that if I want to know how to hit a heavily defended Maxohlx world, I should ask the spiders. The Rindhalu must have war plans for every scenario. Skippy, where should we go to have a discussion with spiders who can provide advice, and possibly some material assistance?"

"First, if you are asking them for a favor, you shouldn't refer to them as 'spiders'."

"I will be sure to review that section of the Joe Bishop Diplomacy Manual."

"Do *not* do that, dumdum."

"You know what I mean."

"Hmm. Some place with Rindhalu military officers senior enough to be familiar with war plans, and influential enough that their government will listen to them?"

"Yes please."

"But, hmm, also not any place with military assets substantial enough they would pose a threat to *Valkyrie*, and risk me being captured?"

"That would be ideal, yes."

"Ideal?" he snatched off his hat, outraged. "You are willing to risk me being captured by the spiders?"

"I figure they'd get sick of you real quick, and throw you back."

"What? You jerk, I should-"

Reed interrupted. "Do you have a list of potential sites?"

"Um, yes, but maybe now I don't feel like sharing it with-"

Frey snorted. "Somedays, I don't feel like rolling out of bed at oh four forty five, but I do it anyway. The military doesn't care whether you feel like doing something."

"Yeah, yeah, I hear you," Skippy grumbled. "Joe, I sent a list to your phone. There is no need to change course at this point, we have to go through the wormhole ahead."

"Good, thank you."

"Something bothering you, Sir?" Reed asked.

"Yeah," I pushed my chair away from the desk, opened a drawer, and got a handful of chocolates, tossing one to each of the colonels in my office. "We now know the Outsider has been here at least seven years. We still don't know when it got here, or how. The important question is *how*? The Outhouse somehow sent a sort of scout to recon and prepare the way for an invasion, but they couldn't use the same method to send a more substantial force?"

"The bandwidth was limited?" Frey guessed. "Sir, what concerns me is one Outsider was able to get here, undetected. If they can do that, we might kill this Outsider, and have to do this shit all over again in a few years."

Suddenly, I wasn't hungry for chocolate, dropping them in the drawer and nudging it closed. "On that happy note, I have a list to review."

"Admiral?" Commander Flovior hesitantly stuck his head in the open door of the office Scorandum was using at the moment. For the first three days the famous admiral was aboard the ECO cruiser *We Shall Not Speak Of It*, Scorandum had used the VIP office compartment on the starboard side of the ship. That morning, after the ship pinged a relay station for an update, and the admiral learned several of his wagers had ended badly, he had declared the starboard office was cursed. So, Flovior had been thrown out of his own portside office, so the admiral could change his luck. "Do you wish to, er, transmit messages before we jump away from this station?"

"Ah, Flovior, come in, sit down. Your actual question was whether I wish to take this opportunity to place any wagers at this time?"

"Well, Sir," the commander frowned as he saw the mess that his former office had become in less than a day. He also saw that the half-consumed bottle of burgoze he had left in a desk drawer was now empty, and on the deck in a corner. "We will not be within range of another trusted relay station for the next three days, so-"

"Please have your fine ship remain here a while longer, Commander. I need to ponder the impact of some interesting news I recently received. Sit, please, sit," he waved to a couch. "It seems my luck has changed, and for the better this time. As I suspected, that starboard side office you assigned to me has bad juju. I suggest you be careful about wagering, while you have that office. Really, it would be best if you sealed that compartment, and used as storage locker for your office."

"Yes, Sir," Flovior muttered, thinking to himself that the admiral's recent losses might be caused by poor judgment from excessive drinking, rather than by any mysterious 'juju' aboard the ship. "Your luck has changed?"

"It seems that is the case," Scorandum tapped a claw at his tablet. "I just received a classified message, which will soon become public knowledge. The Maxohlx have reportedly taken out a contract for my untimely demise."

"No," Flovior made the expected gasp of shock, while in his head actually wondering why the Maxohlx had taken so long? "This is, *good* news?"

"Of course. Think on it, Commander. I now have a unique opportunity for the most *juicy* wagering. Will I live another week? A month? A year? Perhaps longer? I shall wager on my survival, and I can't lose! If I perish, I will never know I have lost."

"Hmm," Flovior's head bobbed slowly. "That is a unique opportunity, Sir. Surely, our government will do all they can to protect you?"

"According to this message, our own Ethics and Compliance Office has been offered a contract, apparently with quite generous payment terms. So far, my superiors are more interested in the wagering action than in the contract money, which of course the clumsy Maxohlx could never have understood. For now, I am safe, relatively. However, I do request you change our flight plan, to take a different route to our next stop. We are in no hurry to get there, I am seeking only background information, nothing urgent."

"Certainly, Sir," Flovior was running calculations in his head, about how much he could afford to wager on the admiral's survival. Or demise. "So, you do wish to place a wager?"

"I do. Also, it occurs to me that I should send a personal note to a former protégé of mine. He would find this news to be, interesting," Scorandum's antennas twitched with mirth. Kinsta would actually find the news to be shocking, but that would amuse Scorandum. It was important to find joy in life wherever you could.

Especially when that life might be unexpectedly brief.

Dave's phone pinged, he transferred the audio to his earpiece. The aircraft he was flying in, a Ruhar transport that his company had to pay for by the hour, had rotor blades that were loud enough to rattle his teeth. For the outrageous amount of money he was paying, he expected a smooth, quiet ride. Maybe the comfortable fake leather seats the Ruhar used in their VIP aircraft. Next time, he wanted all that, and a fully stocked bar. "David Czajka," he announced with a. hand pressed to the other ear, because the caller was unknown.

"Mister Czajka?" It was a familiar, just slightly squeaky voice.

"Nert," he exclaimed, genuinely pleased. "Call me 'Dave', please."

"OK," the Ruhar special operator sounded hesitant. "I have a bit of a situation, and I need your help. I would *appreciate* your help," he added.

"Um," he tapped his phone to mute it. "Dandurf wants our help," he shouted to Jates, seated opposite him in the cramped cabin.

"I do not have any pressing engagements at the moment," the Verd grunted.

"Adding you to the call," Dave tapped the phone again. "What's going on, Nerty?" he cringed as he used the nickname. That was being too familiar.

Nert didn't seem to notice. "This is something you should see for yourself."

"Um, OK? Where are you?"

"In the Dark Forest."

"The *where*?"

"The area where the locals made a half-assed effort to plant black trees."

"The hunting preserve for *grikkas*?! What are you doing there?"

"It wasn't my idea."

"We are," he checked the map on his phone. "Seven minutes away. Is there a safe LZ nearby?"

"Look for my team's aircraft. We got called in to deal with a mess and, this isn't a bang bang shooting situation, so my team could use help. Someone who knows how to deescalate, if you know what I mean."

Dave stared at Jates. The Verd knew what he was thinking. With a grin Jates said, "I am a renowned expert at deescalating conflicts."

Dave snorted. "Your solution to everything is punching and shooting."

"Yes, and after the punching and shooting, the conflict always deescalates."

"When we get there, I will do the talking."

Jates folded his arms across his chest, and nodded. "We make a good team. You talk, I will punch, or shoot."

"That- Just don't do or say *anything*. Nert, we will be there ASAP."

"Huh," Dave lifted his helmet faceplate. In grikka territory, he had followed protocol and sealed up his suit. "I see why you wanted me to see this. How the hell did he get into this mess?"

Nert sighed with a shake of his head. "We got called in *after* he was stuck in this tree."

"I can get him down with," Jates unslung his rifle.

"*No!*" Dave barked, his face turning red. The TV show production team was peering out the windows of their heavy armored trucks, and Nert's special ops team were lounging casually against the black trees, looking bored. No, they were *amused*.

Because that asshole TV director Poindit was stuck eight meters up in a tree, clinging to a branch with all the might of his civilian mech suit. On the ground, a young grikka paced, snarled, whining, twitching its tail, leaping up at and the biting the tree. The jerk was in no actual danger, the juvenile grikka was only a meter and a half long, and skinny. Even a civilian model mech suit should provide excellent protection from the claws and jaws of the smallish beast. Plus, Nert's team had brought enough firepower to vaporize a full size grikka.

"Start at the beginning, please," Dave anticipated a *long* story.

"What the production team told me is, Poindit wanted to prove what a man of action he is, so for the final episode, he would walk through the Dark Forest. He was smart enough to scan the area, the only grikka around now is the little one here. They are territorial, so it was a stupid, but relatively safe idea. He took the proper precautions, including spraying the exterior of his suit with grikka repellant. The animal would approach, would be threatening, but not attack."

"Hey!" Poindit shouted, waving one hand then returning to his death grip on the branch. "You! Czajka! Get rid of this thing, and get me down from here right now!"

Dave cocked his head. "I'm sorry, but I have no authority here."

"I will pay you, a lot of money!"

"There *isn't* that much money," the mercenary leader muttered.

"I don't know. I would pay a lot to see *this*," Jates grinned.

"Nert, what went wrong with the repellant?"

The Ruhar officer rolled his eyes. "Someone on the production team swapped it with a *hormonal* spray."

"Oh sh-"

"That grikka is a young male, and it thinks Poindit is a female in heat."

"Oh, this is a freakin' mess that-"

"Hey!" The director shouted, frantically waving a hand. It was a bad career move. His swaying motion finally snapped the branch he clung to, and he plunged down to crash onto the grikka's back. Poindit bounced, the grikka rolled away, the director scrambled to his feet and-

The grikka was on him in a flash.

"Get this thing *off of me!*" Poindit screamed as the beast's teeth slipped on the armor of his shoulders, and its legs pinned him as it humped him into the ground.

Jates half-heartedly raised his rifle, Dave pushed the muzzle down. "Don't. You might shoot Poindit by mistake."

"Mistake?" Jates grinned. "Yes, let's go with that."

"You know," Nert tried to keep his expression serious, and failed. "Grikkas on this world are an endangered species, they are protected by law."

"It would be a shame to kill such a magnificent best," Dave agreed.

"Get, it, off," Poindit stuttered as the grikka bounced him around the forest floor.

"This looks like true love to me," Jates slung his rifle. "I think he likes you!" He called to the director.

"Seriously, though," Dave lowered his voice. "Should we be doing something here?"

"The beast is in a mating frenzy," Jates noted. "It could be dangerous to interrupt it."

"Then we should-"

"Best to let it finish. I read they calm right down and go to sleep, usually."

"We should wait until we hear it snoring," Nert agreed. "Hi, hey," he waved to the production crew. "Is anyone getting this on video?"

Every person in the two trucks pointed to their cameras. "Is anyone *not* getting this on video?" The assistant director laughed.

Back in the tiltrotor aircraft, Dave shook his head as he strapped in. "That is *not* what I expected to be doing this afternoon."

"I am disappointed that you stopped the fun."

Dave shrugged. After a minute of Poindit being bounced around the ground by the amorous grikka, he had used his own rifle to stun the beast. He could not, he had decided, allow Poindit's head to be bashed against a tree. Even in a helmet, the jerk could have gotten a concussion. Mostly, Dave acted to avoid an expensive lawsuit. "You can relive it forever on video."

"That is true," Jates grinned. He was grinning a lot that day, a nice change from the usual angry glare. "A nice way to break up the boredom of this deployment. When are we dusting off this rock? The mission was complete two weeks ago."

"Em thinks Def Com likes us being out here, where we are not potentially causing trouble."

"If it helps, I can create some trouble to get us thrown off Hufustria."

"I'll let you know when we get to that point. Really, I don't expect us to be here much longer. Sustaining a deployment is expensive, some bean counters back on Earth will be doing a cost-benefit analysis, and decide we should go elsewhere."

"Back to Earth?"

"Nah. There is no need for us there. Bishop has the Merry Band of Pirates stood up again, I know for *certain* he is out there looking for trouble. When he finds it, I expect us to get the call, to do something."

Jates was unconvinced. "What can we do against the Outsider?"

"Nothing, but we could raise hell with the Outsider's allies. The fucking Maxohlx."

The grin Jates flashed that time was feral. "I would very much like to fight a Maxohlx one on one, no weapons. I would wring its miserable neck."

"Yeah well," Dave had to shout over the engines starting. "Be careful what you wish for you just might get it."

We knew from the UN negotiating team that the Rindhalu were at least willing to discuss joint operations to act against the Outsider, and it was encouraging they didn't consider such a discussion to be premature. That was good news, the bad news was the spiders were who they were. Let's just say I wasn't getting my hopes up about the Rindhalu doing anything other than talk. If seven years ago, they had discovered the Outsider just stole the deactivated Turshipan array, the spiders might now still be debating whether to study the issue.

OK, that judgement is a bit harsh, and I have to admit that although the Communal Gathering's historical tendency to avoid being hasty is frustrating, that strategy has worked well for them. All they have wanted is to maintain the balance of power in the galaxy, they understand there is a limit to how far they can push the Maxohlx. The endless war has dragged on forever, with each coalition capturing and losing small bits of territory, and the overall strategic situation remaining stable. The only time the spiders were roused to take major action is after a wormhole shift that threatened to give the Maxohlx a major advantage. When that happened, the rotten kitties got all excited to strike a decisive blow against their ancient enemy, until they realized they can only push the Rindhalu so far without disastrous consequences for both sides. Stability is so important, so valuable to both sides, that after wormhole shifts that significantly hurt the Maxohlx, the Rindhalu have sometimes unilaterally given up territory, to maintain the balance of power.

Was I getting my hopes up anyway, that the spiders would help us with cracking the defenses at Omaha? Yes, I was. Hans Chotek had sent a private message to me, stating that the Rindhalu were unusually agitated during the negotiations, pressing for details on what the Merry Band of Pirates were doing about the Outsider. There was no question that the spiders expected humanity to handle the threat, they also didn't blame us for the mess. Instead, they blamed the Elders for running away rather than dealing with the problem. Hans of course couldn't provide details on my plans since, you know, I didn't actually have a plan back then. His note stated the spiders recognized this situation was different, that something had to be done and sooner rather than later. They weren't making a blanket pledge of unconditional support, basically they wanted us to show them a workable plan, and they would consider it.

I read that note from Hans three weeks ago, and had filed it in my brain as interesting but not immediately useful. Now we finally had a plan to take direct, decisive action against the Outsider, it was time to test whether the spiders were serious about working with us.

The best place for me to ask a favor from the Rindhalu was a retirement colony. Seriously. It was a colony world, that had been terraformed and set aside for Old Ones who were truly old even by spider standards, done with a long life of military or government service. They spend their days doing water aerobics, playing golf, then enjoying a cocktail while contemplating the Meaning Of Life until it is time for the Early Bird dinner special.

I am joking. I have no idea what the old Old Ones do all day. The relatively young Old Ones I have met don't do a whole lot, to the frustration of their active and impatient Foundlings. Should I have tried to meet with a Foundling, who might stay awake long enough to have a meaningful conversation? No. Although a young Rindhalu might have information about war plans, no one in the government of the Communal Gathering would take seriously anything they said. My hope was for not just some hints, but actual, useful help. Weapons. Warships. Like that was ever going to happen.

So, *Valkyrie* jumped in ten lighthours from the planet Boca Lauderdon, to see what was there. Two cruisers were in orbit, along with a transport ship. The planet had a population of six hundred million, which ordinarily would generate enough commerce to justify constructing a space elevator. Boca had no elevator for the world didn't export much, and new arrivals flew down, they generally didn't leave the surface. "Bilby," I asked, "What are those cruisers doing?"

"Not much, Dude. They are on a courtesy visit, paying respects to the retired officers down there. Especially to Jastagellian, she ran their Strategic Planning office until about two years ago."

"Strategic planning? She was a senior general?"

"No, Dude," Bilby chuckled. "The spiders believe strategy is about *what* their society should do, and those decisions should be made by civilian leadership. Once a decision is made, how to implement a strategy is a tactical problem for their military. Of course, usually what the Rindhalu decide to do is *nothing*."

"Yeah, that's the problem. So, I shouldn't talk to this Jastagellian."

"Actually Joe," Skippy held up an index finger. "She is exactly who you should talk with. Minister Jastagellian not only led her office to the decision to destroy the Maxohlx Doomsday fleet, she also was instrumental in persuading the government to move quickly. At the time, her haste was considered unseemly, and caused a minor scandal. There was some talk about whether she was appropriate for such an important, senior position. That talk pretty much went away, after the full scope of what the Maxohlx were doing was discovered."

"You think she will agree to talk with me?"

"Joe, it was her initiative to build a virtual Joe Bishop, attempting to model your thought processes using powerful AIs. The goal was to predict your future actions. Unfortunately for them, they were no more successful in creating a useful predictive model than the Maxohlx were in their own effort. The problem is, you don't have a thought *process*. You just Duuuuuuh your way to finding a solution, which really hardly ever solves a problem. Most of the time you just suggest that I do some incredibly awesome thing, and half the time, that only leads to an even bigger problem."

"I can't be replaced by an AI, that's good for my job security, got it, thanks."

"That is *not* what I said, you-"

"Bilby, Skippy, do either of you see any reason we should not proceed?"

"It's all goodness, Dude," Bilby drawled.

"Whatevs," Skippy sighed. "Like I care."

While safely beyond range of the star system's sensor network, *Valkyrie* slowed down to match course and speed with Boca Lauderdon, then we jumped in thirty lightseconds from the planet. Supposedly, the recent upgrades reduced the gamma radiation from our jump drive by seventeen percent, that only mattered if Skippy wasn't aboard the ship to perform his own magic. When the sensors recovered from jump distortion and we verified the situation was as we expected, Reed ordered a drone containing one end of a microwormhole to be launched. The drone accelerated smoothly, not with the hellish gee force that would be employed in a combat environment. When the drone was within ten lightseconds of the strategic defense network's effective sensor range, it decelerated and coasted inward, maneuvering until it was in a stable and low orbit, almost skimming the top of the atmosphere. The local SD network had not detected the stealthed drone, and the probability of detection decreased every second, as Skippy gently hacked into the network.

"All right, that's enough," he declared.

He had warned me that hacking even the low-grade network at the retirement colony would be a time-consuming and tricky task, so I was a bit confused when he had it done so quickly. "You have control of the network?"

"No. The sensors will ignore the drone, that's all we need here. Anything more would be showing off."

"But you-" My stupid brain was about to say 'You love showing off'. My mouth caught me before I could insult him. "Did it so fast anyway."

"What can I say? I am awesome."

"Connect me with Jastagellian, please. Wait! This call will be over the secure Skippitel network, right?"

"Of course it will, numbskull. You had better talk fast, she is getting ready to go surfing."

"*Surfing?*" I shared a look with Reed, who held up her hands in a 'Who knew' gesture. My brain tried to picture a Rindhalu's multiple legs perched on a surfboard, and I got nothin'. "Uh, I thought she would be more likely playing canasta."

"Do you even know what canasta is?"

"It's a card game my grandmother played. It's an old people thing."

"It might be an old *monkey* thing," he sniffed. "Jastagellian has a two thousand watt electric surfboard, and a storm down there has kicked up some tasty waves, so I suggest you get on with it."

"Right." Releasing the straps, I got up from the chair and walked over to stand close to the virtual microphone of the main holographic display. "Hello, this is General Joe Bishop of the United Nations Defense Command, do you have a moment to speak with me?"

The reply was not what I expected. There was a high pitched '*Eek*', then the sound of a phone bouncing off of and sliding across a floor.

"Uh-" I didn't know what else to say. "Hello? If I interrupted something, I can call back."

There was a muffled '*No*', and sounds like dry claws scraping on a hard surface. Hearing that sent an instinctive shiver up my spine, it was good that the call was audio only.

"Bishop?" The voices of female Rindhalu were just as raspy as their males, just a bit higher in pitch. Part of that was an effect added by the translator software. "*The* Joe Bishop?"

There must be a lot of guys on Earth with that name, I know I was named for some actor and singer guy who hung out with Frank Sinatra. That Joey Bishop was before my time, he had been a favorite of my great grandfather, or so I have been told. "I am Joe Bishop of the Merry Band of Pirates," I confirmed.

A raspy laugh. "I assume this is not a social call?"

"No, although I hear the waves are great for surfing now, so if you prefer, we can talk later.?"

"The surf report is enticing, but I am a bit tired of chasing waves. At my age, I have become a bit tired of *everything*. Except, when I am offered something new. Such as an opportunity to speak with you. Tell me, please, is Skippy as horrible an asshole as I have heard? I hope that word translated correctly."

"It translated just fine and yes, he is an asshole."

"Hey!" The beer can protested. "You jerk, I should-"

"Fortunately for him," I added, "his awesomeness exceeds his assholeishness. Uh, that might not have translated well."

"I understood perfectly, thank you. You startled me, my phone has not experienced an unscheduled call in, a very long time."

"Sorry about that, I should have texted you first."

"The translator might be confused. What is 'texting'?"

"A primitive form of communication used by my people. Minister Jastagellian, do you have time to discuss a subject that is vital to my people, and yours?"

"The Outsider?"

"Yes."

"This call is secure on my end, I am alone in my residence, and I notice my phone is not actually connected to the local network."

"We are connected via the ultra-secure Skippitel system."

"Are you free to speak now?"

"Uh," Reed caught my eye with a shake of her head. "Give me a moment to get to my office, OK?"

I sprinted down the passageway, stupidly not thinking of borrowing Reed's office that was closer to the bridge. It took my only an extra fifteen seconds to reach my office, Skippy had the door sliding shut behind me as I sat in the chair.

All the time I spend running or riding an exercise bike in the gym paid off, my breathing quickly returned to normal and I was able to resume the conversation.

Which didn't go as I expected. Getting straight to the point would be hasty, and despite my instinct to *get on with it*, we spent some time reviewing recent events. For someone who was retired, she was very well informed.

"I frequently consult with my successor in the Ministry, and with other officials in the government," she explained. "My position is referred to as Minister Emeritus, if you understood the translation."

"I did, thank you." My alter ego as No Patience Man was screaming at me to get to the point, I told him to shut the hell up. A few minutes of chit chat to establish a rapport with her was a good investment, I would be asking her for a major favor. We talked about our families, and she was unhappy with Skippy, because a cousin had gotten involved in SkipWay and lost most of her life savings. Then, she started telling me a story about how she had gotten into surfing after a hang gliding accident injured one of her legs. That was-

Wait a minute.

"Minister, are you stalling for time?"

There was a beat before she answered. That silence was an answer. Before I could say something unhelpful, she sighed, another raspy sound. "I have been waiting for the orbital sensor network to announce an intruder alert."

"That won't happen. *Valkyrie* is not in orbit." That was not exactly true, it was close enough.

"That answers my question. We are speaking without a noticeable time lag, so you must have inserted an Elder communications node into orbit, probably in a stealthed vehicle."

"No Elder comm node this time."

"That is a pity. We have been observing your Navy's use of that marvelous technology with great enviousness. Faster than light communication is a major tactical advantage."

"It absolutely is."

"Perhaps, if we are to work together, several of those devices could be provided to us?"

"You have Elder comm nodes."

"They don't function."

"That's because the magnificence of Skippy is required to activate them. Minister, I did not come here to negotiate an exchange. We are not bargaining about what each of our peoples should get in a deal. I am here to discuss working together for mutual benefit. The Outsider is as much a threat to the Communal Gathering as it is to humanity. If you can't see that, then I should find someone else to have this discussion."

She laughed, a dry sound that made my hair stand up. Something deep in my brain shouted *danger, spiders are creepy*! "General Bishop, I believe it is time to cut the bullshit. Your ambassadors surely have informed you that we are committed to participating in the fight against the Outsider. It is, as you said, a mutual threat. A threat to our existence. If you want our assistance to take direct action against the Outsider, your ambassador or military liaison would have approached us with an official proposal. Since you are using a backchannel, I must assume you want us to provide resources, without revealing what those resources will be used for."

"Material assistance would be greatly appreciated, but what I need at the moment is information. Advice."

"I understand you are concerned about operational security, however it will not be possible to provide advice, if I don't know what you plan to do."

"Yeah, that's the problem. Without getting into specifics, we need to conduct a raid against a Maxohlx regional fleet base."

"A *raid*? Not just an orbital attack?"

"That is correct. A raid involving a landing, with a substantial number of troops on the ground, for a short time."

"That, is ambitious."

"You can see why I need advice."

"You will need more than information. Unless you intend to bring a Sentinel with you?"

"We believe we can't wait for a Sentinel to be available. The Outsider has openly made a move, and the clock is ticking."

She gasped, understanding instantly. "The Kaliberak array. It was taken, recently."

"Yes. We believe it intends to modify that array to receive a signal from another galaxy, a signal that will open a doorway for an invasion. By the way, the Outsider stole your deactivated Turshipan array around seven years ago."

"Turshipan? I am not familiar with the name."

"It was before your time. The Kaliberak system replaced the Turshipan array, so the older unit was shut down. We checked, and discovered that first array was hauled away by a star carrier around seven years ago. Apparently, the Outsider wasn't able to modify that older system to meet its needs. Or it also needs the Kaliberak equipment. Either way, its theft of the Turshipan array was done without anyone realizing it happened. Your people did notice that Kaliberak stopped transmitting, the Outsider no longer cares that we know what it is planning."

"A raid, with boots on the ground, is infinitely more complicated than an orbital bombardment. You can't tell me which regional fleet base is the target?"

"No, but the target's defenses are typical for such a world. Our biggest obstacle is the strategic defense network, especially the disruption field that will prevent us from jumping ships in close enough. To jump in far away and fly through normal space is suicide, our ships would be exposed to enemy fire far too long. I thought, your war plans people must have studied the issue."

"Our war plans *AIs* have studied the issue," she explained. "Such a complex problem is beyond the capabilities of biological systems. General, you are asking a question about *tactics*, my experience is in strategic planning."

"True, but you must have been aware of your military's capabilities. There is no point to proposing a strategy that can't be implemented. Can it be done? Knock back the orbital defenses enough that we could establish space supremacy in the environment? We can't risk bringing in assault carriers if the battlespace is contested."

"It can be done. It *has* been done."

"In a simulation?" I guessed.

"In reality. The base where the Maxohlx were constructing and equipping their Doomsday fleet was significantly more heavily defended that any of their fleet bases, and we cracked those defenses like an eggshell. It was not easy," she warned. "The operation required a major investment in specialized ships, and expending a significant percentage of our ordnance. It took eleven months to replenish the missiles we burned in that operation. General, am I correct in assuming a raid is necessary, to obtain a physical object that can be used against the Outsider?'

"That's a good guess."

"Mmm, interesting. Neither the Maxohlx nor their new ally the Outsider are aware this object exists?'"

"The Maxohlx know they have it, they don't understand what it can be used for."

"There is no alternative to obtaining this object?"

"None that we know of, and we *do* know we are running out of time."

"Young species always believe there is no time."

Not this shit again, I thought to myself. What could I say to persuade her that her people couldn't do their usual thing of setting up a committee to appoint a commission to study the problem? Be tactful, I reminded myself. Think about Hans Chotek's style of diplomacy, not my preferred kinetic diplomacy. Shit. Maybe I should have stopped at Earth to pick up Hans, so I didn't ruin our opportunity by-

"In this case, I must reluctantly agree that time is a critical factor," she added before I could open my mouth. "It is alarming that, after concealing its intentions, the Outsider is now bold enough to act openly."

"Bold, or desperate enough. We have been speculating about why the Outsider chose to take the active array now. One possibility is that the Sentinel at our forward operating base will be free to accompany us, within several months. If we are correct about that, then the Outsider is on a deadline, and was forced to act."

"Mmm. I believe that would be a strong motivating factor."

It was interesting to me that we both had used the word 'believe' several times. Were we unconsciously mirroring each other to establish a rapport? Did spider psychology even work that way? Or was the translator software trying to help? I made a mental note to ask Skippy about that, later. "Can you, I should ask *will* you, provide information about how we can crack the SD network defenses, at a regional fleet base?"

"We can, and we will."

That sounded too good to be true. Also, way too fast to be true. "You mean, you are willing to bring my request to your government?"

"I mean, a decision has been made, to provide support to your efforts. It surprises me that, since you seem to know so much, you have not heard that I have been recalled to run the Ministry of Strategic Planning again."

"I, did not know that." Had Skippy set me up? That asshole was probably having a good laugh right then. "Congratulations?"

"Condolences might be more appropriate. My retirement was based on the assumption that the, adventures, of the Merry Band of Pirates were over some years ago, and we could fall back to a steady-state strategic environment. An environment with *three* major powers, but a stable situation. Clearly, that is no longer true."

"You won't miss surfing?"

"My surfboard will still be here, after the Outsider has been banished from this galaxy. General Bishop, I am scheduled to depart this world in eleven days, to return to our central world." The Rindhalu did not refer to their seat of government as their 'homeworld', because it wasn't the planet where they evolved. "The route is complicated, however I understand that Skippy can create shortcuts between wormholes?"

"Uh, one minute, please." Tapping my phone's mute button, I called him. "Skippy? How long from here to their central world?"

"With a wormhole shortcut? We could be there within nineteen hours of jumping away from this rock."

"Nineteen *hours*?"

"You are aware that I am awesome?"

"I am, but that is still incredibly fast for-"

"Do you know why Boca Lauderdon was selected to be a retirement world?"

"It has a nice climate, that encourages retirees to get outside to play shuffleboard?"

"Well, that also. This star system is located at the dead-end of a wormhole route that is not convenient for any purpose, other than getting here. To reach Boca, ships must transit through four wormholes that are in the middle of nowhere. So, travel here is time consuming and expensive. Basically, even though it is deep inside Rindhalu territory, no one wanted this planet until a development company proposed to build a luxury retirement retreat."

"Did they consider calling it 'Sunny Acres'?'

"Among many other stupid names, yes. So, getting to or from here is a long trip, unless a shortcut is created."

"A shortcut from here to there isn't just a theoretical thing? The local network doesn't hate you?"

"It doesn't hate me yet, but I have learned that all wormhole network controllers are *dicks*, so it's just a matter of time."

"Thank you. Plot a course, please." Unmuting my phone, I gave the minister the good, or bad, news. "Travel time from here will be nineteen hours."

She gasped. "How is that possible?'

"You might not have heard this, but Skippy is kind of awesome."

"I have heard many things about Skippy. General, I can be ready to leave in six hours, if that is convenient for you?"

That is how the Merry Band of Pirates became a long-haul taxi service for the Communal Gathering's previous and future minister of Strategic Planning. I had a moment of panic when she casually announced her entourage would consist of nine spiders, including a security team of four soldiers, a personal aide, a chief of staff, and a senior analyst. The other two weren't listed, I was guessing hair stylist and dog walker? No, the Rindhalu do have scaly hairs around their bodies but nothing long enough to style, and as far as I know, they don't have pets. The notion of spider soldiers with guns aboard *Valkyrie* was a non-starter, and that was only one problem for us to deal with. We didn't have sleeping, dining, or bathroom facilities that would accommodate Rindhalu physiology. They slept in sort of hammocks or slings, and we could have fabricated something, it would have been awkward. Then there is the smell. Rindhalu have an obnoxious scent they can consciously control, to a limited extent. They have glands that can turn up the scent from a merely unpleasant 'Somebody open a window' to a gag-inducing 'I am gonna hurl until my eyeballs explode'. In meetings with the spiders, our ambassadors wear transparent bubble helmets that provide filtered air. Hans had told me he originally thought he could power through the stink if the spiders relaxed their glands, but a roomful of Rindhalu is so distracting he couldn't focus.

The spiders think humans smell awful, so it's not a one-sided problem.

Anyway, Minister Jastagellian solved my problem by announcing she had requisitioned the pair of cruisers in orbit, apparently she had never considered coming aboard *Valkyrie*. Duh, I should have asked her about that before I got myself and Reed spun up about a problem we didn't need to deal with.

Whatever level of authority she had, it was sufficient that the lead cruiser contacted us to request coordinates less than five and a half hours later. We gave them a rendezvous time and place that might have been confusing, that location was not on the nearby wormhole's regular schedule of emergence points. By the time the cruisers arrived, Skippy had already created the shortcut, and *Valkyrie* was wrapped in a stealth field.

"We're good," Bilby announced. "Just the two cruisers are here, everything is copacetic."

"It's your call," I said to Reed, since *Valkyrie* was her ship.

"Drop stealth," she ordered, and added, "maintain shields. Pilot, if sensors detect any gamma radiation, or a damping field, or those two ships even look at us in a hostile manner, jump us away."

"Jump on my initiative, aye," the pilot acknowledged with a thumbs up.

The stealth field flickered out. Nobody shot at us, no other ships jumped on top of our stupid heads, the cruisers didn't even paint us with active sensor pulses. In fact, their shields were down, all their navigation lights were on full, and the only active sensors they had warmed up was the system that swept the area for incoming hazards like space rocks.

"It feels odd to be this close," Reed said under her breath.

"We are all one big happy family now," I whispered.

"A family with that old uncle who gets drunk and starts a fight at a holiday dinner?"

"When my Uncle Edgar got drunk, he told funny stories we kids weren't supposed to hear."

"I wouldn't bet on the spiders telling jokes."

"Probably a good point."

We announced our intention to go through the wormhole first, the cruisers were to wait for our signal. The other side was the wormhole closest to the Rindhalu central world, called Allustria. Or, that's what the name sounds like when a translator AI pronounces it for us. We emerged at a point that was not on that wormhole's current figure-8 pattern, so there was a very low risk of us encountering a ship on the other side. The area was clear, we signaled the cruisers to follow us, then Skippy pulled the plug on the shortcut.

"Minister Jastagellian, please proceed when you are ready, your ships should be able to reach Allustria in a single jump from here."

"General Bishop, the wormhole shortcut is a *remarkable* achievement."

"Meh," Skippy shrugged with false modesty. "As my awesomenesses go, it's a party trick. But it impresses the monkeys."

"It has impressed me also. General, I will contact you within one day, that is twenty two of your hours?"

"Yes, thank you."

CHAPTER THIRTY FIVE

Holy shit.

Five days later, the spiders provided a solution for cracking the defenses around a Maxohlx regional fleet base like Ohmeharikahn. Despite possessing the highest overall level of technology in the Milky Way, the Rindhalu solution was surprisingly simple: they planned to use brute force. Specially modified, disposable ships designated as 'door knockers' would power through a tiny opening in the distortion field to jump into the heart of the SD network, opening a door just a bit for more and more ships to jump in. The second wave of ships would be dedicated, disposable arsenals, stuffed with missiles and not much else. Like many military engagements, the battle for control of space around the planet Ohmeharikahn would be a matter of numbers; throwing so many missiles, sensor jammers, and decoys into the fight that the SD network would be overwhelmed and ground down missile by missile, until the distortion field was weak enough for warships to jump in. At that point, our ships would be mopping up the scattered and confused remnants of the SD network, with the defense system unable to coordinate a response. That's how the Rindhalu destroyed the Doomsday arkships, the warships that were there to protect the arkships, and the space docks that had constructed the arkship weapons. Minister Jastagellian proudly told me that battle had gone as their tactical AIs predicted, with more than ninety eight percent accuracy. That was impressive.

By Day Six, we not only had a solution, we had a conditional commitment from the Rindhalu, to provide limited material and logistical support for a raid against an unnamed Maxohlx regional fleet base.

The condition? That the target be revealed before we jumped into battle. I mean, that's just a Duh, of course. My intention was to name the target after the task force had assembled at some yet to be determined staging and training site. Plans could be revised and refined as needed, without adding an Opsec risk.

Unfortunately, I would have to tell the spiders thank you but no, we couldn't do it.

Why?

Because of the discussion I had with Frey on Day Six.

Frey was already in my office when I walked in, I was feeling good as I sat down. The spiders had offered not only advice and intel, they would be providing ships and weapons. My STAR team leader had requested a meeting just before dinner time, and I had worked through lunch so I was hungry, but Frey had insisted we talk soon. "Frey," I nodded to her, distracted as I pulled out a drawer, hoping to find candy, or crackers, or anything to snack on. Nothing, that wasn't enough to sour my mood. Had I eaten all the snacks, or was Skippy screwing with me by sending a bot into my office to steal my junk food? That's something I should ask Bilby about. "You updated your plan? Skippy told me to expect we will achieve space supremacy around Omaha by T plus two hours."

"I did. *We* did," she corrected herself. "Skippy and Bilby helped with the modeling. Sir, I am very reluctant to say this."

That wasn't good, and suddenly I wasn't hungry. "OK," I didn't try to guess what she meant, and I kept what I hoped was a neutral expression. "I'm listening."

"There is no way to achieve the objective. Not," she quickly added, "with the required probability of success."

"Shit," was my automatic and unfortunate response. What she referred to was my criteria for a plan I could approve: it must have at least a ninety five percent probability of finding the collector, taking it from the Maxohlx, getting it into low orbit, and aboard a starship that could jump away. All without damaging the collector. There were a lot of moving pieces, and every phase of the plan had to work with nearly perfect precision. There was little room for the usual unexpected challenges, we couldn't rely on our typical creativity in overcoming obstacles. A simple, tiny squirrel bot had almost fried the core of the archive we raided, that would have been a very disappointing setback but the Maxohlx have other archives we could have hit later. As far as Skippy knew, there was exactly *one* collector available to us. Originally, I had told Frey the mission needed to have a ninety nine percent probability of success. That was an unrealistic goal and I had let her talk me down to ninety five, it still made me sick to accept a five percent chance of never finding the spinner, never stopping the Outsider from opening the door to an invasion.

She opened her laptop. "Can I show you?"

"Walk me through it."

The best result, in a scenario that assumed the Maxohlx would commit an unlikely series of stupid, clumsy errors, yielded a seventy seven percent probability of success. The number I focused on was the flip side of that math: a twenty three percent probability of failure. The failures were generated along multiple paths; stealthed dropships intercepted before STAR team boots hit the ground. The team taking a hit from a missile or even old-fashioned artillery while on the ground. The battle in the underground storage bunker damaged or destroyed the collector. Most often when a scenario failed, it was the dropship being shot down during the ascent into orbit. Finally, *Valkyrie* could take a bad hit when we jumped in to recover the dropship.

She showed me one scenario after another. Maybe she was hoping I would see something she had missed, I had to disappoint her. She had covered every contingency. There were just too many opportunities for the op to go sideways in a hurry. A single Maxohlx soldier with a shoulder launched missile could pop out of nowhere, and BAM the dropship carrying the collector goes down in flames.

Frey nudged the laptop away from her. "I would be willing to send my team in with a seventy seven percent probability, and trust skill and training to win the day. But, that leaves an unacceptable level of risk that the collector will be damaged or destroyed. Sir, did I miss something?"

"If you did, I don't see it. Skippy, do you have anything to add?"

"The modeling is a hundred percent accurate," he sniffed, of course he did. "Joe, the problem is that to ensure an almost perfect probability of success, we have to suppress the firepower of an entire planet, a world that is a regional fleet base and so is packed with weapons. A single jackass with a missile, or a stealth fighter that evades our sensor coverage, could ruin the entire op."

"Right. Yes, I see that. Frey, thank you for your work on this. Let me think on it for a while, and I'll get back to you."

She nodded slowly. "I know this isn't what you hoped the STARs would tell you, but-"

"I appreciate that you didn't come in here with a nice story full of gung-ho bullshit. Fortune favors the bold, that sort of thing. I have seen too many ops go sideways to risk the collector getting damaged or lost. We will find another way to do this."

"Joe," Skippy called as I slowly got up from my chair, after Frey had left. "Where are you going?"

"To get coffee, although really, I just need to think, and I do that better on my feet."

"Sit down, please, there is something we need to discuss."

"Uh-" My brain screamed 'what the fuck is the problem *this* time', I kept that to myself. "OK, just me, or should I call Frey or Reed back in here?"

"Just you. There *is* a way to achieve the objective, or accomplish the task, or whatever you call getting the job done."

"Yes, I saw, but even the best scenarios have too much possibility of something going wrong and-"

"No, you did not see, because Frey didn't model the scenario I'm talking about."

That was so unlike Skippy, I blinked while staring at him, trying to think of what to say. "You withheld information from Frey? I can't-"

"I did not withhold anything from her, I extrapolated from her planning."

"Just tell me."

"Joe, I know you. You are *not* going to like this."

"Uh," I felt a chill run up my spine. "Usually, you say 'Well, heh heh' before something I'm not going to like."

"There is nothing remotely funny about this."

"You're scaring me, Skippy."

"While I show you a plan that can work the way you want, can you not do your usual thing of interrupting me with stupid questions? Just watch, and listen, and save your questions for the end. Can you do that?"

"You are sure this plan will work for real? It's not just a nice war game model?"

"There are various scenarios that result in ninety seven to ninety eight point four percent probability of success, but they are all versions of the same basic plan. This assumes the Rindhalu can crack the disruptor field, and degrade the SD network to the point where the UN Navy can mop up the orbital defenses. *And* that the Maxohlx do not have a fleet in system, which you keep telling me not to worry about."

"Don't worry about it."

"You have an actual *plan* to make a fleet conveniently disappear from its home base?"

"I'm working on it. For now, assume that fleet is busy elsewhere."

"Once the Maxohlx realize you are assembling an assault force, they will move to protect their most important assets, which includes-"

"Listen, I'll make this simple. We are assuming we won't have to deal with both a state of the art SD network *and* a fleet, because if the fleet is at Omaha, the op won't proceed. Got it?"

"You are counting on another miracle. Fine, whatever. OK, so-"

He showed me six variations on the same basic assault plan.

They all met my requirements.

I did not like any of them.

"This is a No-Go," I gave him the knife hand in the middle of the sixth simulation.

"It *works*, Joe. You have seen it. Can you deny that the-"

"It works on a tactical level, not a moral level. Thank you for helping, this is not something we can do."

"Clearly *we* can do it, so what you really mean is, it's not an order *you* can give."

"I don't expect you to understand the-"

"What I *understand* is I have provided a plan that you agree meets all of your criteria, and I *understand* that without the collector, we have no way to stop the Outsider, which at this very moment is working to modify the array and open a door to an invasion force we cannot hope to stop. The UN will provide the ships and the troops, the Rindhalu astonishingly are willing to get off their asses and help, so the only issue is you are uncomfortable with your role in the plan?"

"That is not the-"

"This is what he warned me about," Skippy muttered.

"Warned? Who is 'he'? You told someone about-"

"I didn't tell anyone anything." His avatar drifted toward the ceiling. "This- I didn't want to do this at all, he insisted, and now I see he was right."

"Skippy! Who are you talking about?"

"I'll leave you to it, just," his avatar faded out. "Call me when you're done."

"Hello." A familiar voice called from the chair in the corner.

What the f-

Smythe.

Jeremy Smythe.

Colonel Jeremy Smythe, I reminded myself.

It wasn't him sitting across the desk, of course. The avatar had a faintly fuzzy outline like a force ghost from *Star Wars*. The holographic avatars created by Skippy appeared to be real three dimensional objects, even in the holo display tanks objects and icons had sharp, well-defined edges. So, the fuzzy glow around Smythe was an effect, a signal to put me at ease. Instantly, I knew I was looking at an avatar, not an android or some other recreation of the SAS soldier I had served with for so long.

"I would salute," the not-Smythe continued with a wry smile. "But," he plucked at the uniform top, which moved convincingly under his holographic fingers. "As I'm not actually here, that would be silly."

"Why are you here?" I asked, not pleased but willing to give it a minute before dismissing the avatar. The reason I didn't explode at Skippy was the beer can had said '*he*' insisted. The '*he*' had to be Smythe. So, the STAR team leader had considered creating an avatar of himself to be important, for whatever reason. I had to respect his judgement.

"Apparently, you need me at the moment. To be accurate," he held up an index finger, "Skippy believes you need to speak with me."

"This was your idea? To set up an avatar?"

"Yes. No," he looked at the ceiling. "It might have been Skippy's suggestion. I don't recall exactly, since as we both know, I'm not here."

"So, this is Skippy screwing with me?"

"Not at all. I do recall a significant time commitment in setting up, testing, and debugging this system. It was," he frowned, "a delightful experience."

"You would have preferred to have been skydiving from orbit?"

"I would have preferred almost anything."

"OK, you do sound like Smythe. I know this isn't, you," there was a catch in my throat and for a moment, I couldn't speak. "Thank you anyway, for making the effort."

"You are very welcome, General. I considered creating this avatar to be my duty."

"So you can advise Colonel Frey?"

He lifted an eyebrow. "Frey is a colonel now? Good for her. And an excellent choice by the Army. Is she still with the STARs?"

"She leads ST-Razor, aboard *Valkyrie*."

He frowned. "I am not familiar with Team Razor."

"The designation ST-Alpha has been unofficially retired," I explained. "Razor was Earth's rapid reaction force, now they are back aboard *Valkyrie*, with Frey. The Special Mission Group has been stood up again."

"Back in the saddle again," he flashed a tight grin. The emulation of the avatar was so good, I was uncomfortable talking with him. With *it*, I reminded myself. No, that was bullshit. If Smythe had gone through the effort of setting up an avatar, he would not have approved its release until he was satisfied it worked properly.

That meant I should listen to him. "Have you ever advised Frey?"

"No. She doesn't know about this avatar, and she shouldn't hear of it. Please," he added.

That was an easy request for me to honor. The last thing Frey needed was to hear that the legendary former commander was available to provide advice. Or to interfere with her leading ST-Razor. That was *her* team. "I won't mention it. Colonel Smythe," again, I had to pause for a breath. It was not easy to sit across a desk from him, something I had done many, many times. Back when he was alive. "Do you know why you're here, now? Why Skippy," I waved a hand, "activated you?"

Ooooh, his eyes fluttered rapidly in a creepy *Matrix*-style effect that I'm sure was something Skippy programmed in to show the avatar was receiving an update. He knew I would understand the reference.

Smythe's eyes stilled, and he looked at me. "A threat from beyond the galaxy? Did the Merry Band of Pirates not have enough threats inside the Milky Way to keep you busy?"

"Yes, but our 'Threat From Outside The Galaxy' coupon was set to expire, so we had to use it now."

"Your sense of humor has not changed," he smiled. "I appreciated that."

"You did?" That surprised me. "I thought you considered my humor to be inappropriate and unserious."

"At first, I did. Then I saw that when you could joke even in the worst situation, it meant you hadn't lost your nerve."

"Or that I had lost focus," I admitted.

"The military teaches us how to focus. What training can't teach is what makes you such a successful commander."

"If it ain't broke, don't fix it?"

"That is an American expression, I do agree with the sentiment. You are most effective when you are *not* focusing completely on a problem."

"Right. The current problem, would it help if I don't think about it for a while?"

"You don't need to think about it, you already know what you have to do."

That put me on guard, and pissed me off. "Is that Skippy talking?"

"Ask yourself what I would say, if I were really here."

"Shit." I knew the answer to that question. "This is just, all kinds of wrong."

"It makes you uncomfortable," he nodded.

"It will make me hate myself."

"I have sometimes found it useful to use a decision matrix."

"You did?" My mental image of Smythe did not include him using job aids from a PowerPoint slide.

"Occasionally." He meant, almost never. "Will the proposed action achieve the objective, within the acceptable risk parameters?"

"It will."

"Is there a workable alternative?"

"No. Well, I thought there was. I thought we had time to bring a Sentinel with us. Now the Outsider is forcing my hand. To answer your question, Colonel Frey showed me her team can't get the collector- You know about that?"

"I do, and I have reviewed Frey's plans, and I agree the risk of damage to the collector is too great. This is a case where who dares, *loses*." He paraphrased the Special Air Services motto, to mean the opposite.

"It surprises me to hear you say that."

"I was always honest about what could be achieved, and what couldn't."

That was a statement I couldn't dispute. On his last mission, he had been clear that his team wasn't ready, that the opposition was too strong. He went anyway, at my insistence. Not because I believed ST-Alpha could win, but because we had no alternative.

Like now.

"Sir," he continued, "is this a fight that is necessary, or an optional mission?"

"Necessary. We are lucky that Skippy identified the location of a collector, it's the only one he knows of. And, we are out of time."

"If you prefer, I could show you the decision matrix."

"I can see it in my head, thanks."

"Those two stars on your uniform are there because the Army expects you to make the hard decisions, whether you like them or not."

Biting my lower lip, I reminded myself the Smythe I was talking with was a submind, or something like that. The avatar had also been programmed to *be* him, to think like Smythe, so I shouldn't ignore his advice. "Did Skippy activate you to perform a backbone transplant on me?"

He smiled, something the real Smythe hadn't done often. But when he had, it was always worth seeing. "Sufficient backbone was never an issue for you. What you lacked was self-confidence, though you overcame that toward the-" A shadow fell across his face.

He had meant to say 'toward the end'. His end. "In later years," I suggested a neutral way to express his thought.

"Yes." His eyes drifted away from me, far away.

"Do you know how, uh, you-"

"No," he snapped. "I requested Skippy not include those details. It is not relevant, and could be a distraction. I am here to assist you."

"I appreciate it."

"Though, you don't like it."

"I don't. You have stated your admiration for Eisenhower. In the invasion of Normandy, it was necessary for airborne troops to prevent the Germans from rushing reinforcements to the beaches, or the landing force might be crushed before they could get inland. Shortly before D-Day, the air commander requested that Eisenhower cancel the glider and paratrooper drops, because the casualties were projected to be 75 to 90 percent. Eisenhower knew that if he ordered an air assault, the majority of the troops boarding those planes would not come back. His order stood, the invasion was successful as you know, and the casualty rate for airborne troops was less than ten percent."

"Your point is, Ike would have let his order stand, even if the projected casualties had been correct?"

"He would have and as the commander, he should have. The invasion *had* to succeed, and far more men would have been killed on the beaches, if the Germans had brought in additional forces."

"I hear you. This is different. In Normandy, the airborne troops had a real, vital mission."

"So will the landing force at Omaha. Omaha," he cocked his head. "Did you choose that name deliberately?"

"I wasn't thinking about it at the time." Of the five beaches assaulted on D-Day, Omaha had been the toughest fight. "Ohmeharikahn, you know, so 'Omaha' just popped into my head. It's too late to change it now."

"Can the mission succeed without an orbital assault on Ohmeharikahn?"

"You know it can't."

"So do you."

"Right. This is my burden to bear."

"It is, as long as you wear those stars on your uniform." The avatar stood up. "If that is all, Sir?"

"You are leaving already?" Seeing him go, again, was too painful.

He nodded. "If you need me again, you need only call."

"Not for karaoke night, though?"

"I think not."

I stood up, and saluted him. My hand shook slightly. "Colonel Smythe, you are," I almost couldn't say it. "Dismissed."

The avatar faded out.

I sat back down. For a long time, I couldn't do or say anything.

I hoped Skippy hadn't created other avatars.

"Skippy," I finally slid down in the chair until my head touched the bulkhead behind me. "That was a shitty thing to do."

His avatar appeared on the desk. "It wasn't *me*, Joe."

"I know."

"You know? Then why blame me for-"

"I'm not blaming you. It felt like an ambush and I am pissed off and, kinda hurt, and I want to lash out at someone. You're here, so-"

"Ah, gotcha. You can't hit back at Smythe because he is *not* here."

"I can't hit back at him because he was only trying to help me and, damn it, he is right."

"So, how is that a *bad* thing?"

"Now I have to do something that I know is the right thing to do, even though it feels like something I will regret for the rest of my life. To achieve the objective, I have to be that asshole senior officer who doesn't give a shit about the people under his command."

"You do care, Joe."

"That's the problem. Promise me you don't have any other avatars like that. Digital versions of former members of the crew, I mean."

"I do not. Sometimes, I wish I did. I miss them, Joe."

"Me too."

"Creating an avatar was Smythe's idea. He believed the two of you worked well together, made each other better soldiers."

"I made *him* better?"

"You did. He greatly admired you, he told me that."

"How much of, him, is in that avatar?"

"According to him, the emulation is accurate. Enough that he was satisfied with releasing it. We kept updating and tweaking it, of course."

"When was the last update?"

"Nine days before STAR Team Alpha went into the Elder space dock. Successfully," he added.

"So, it doesn't know about-"

"He insisted the avatar should not be aware of the time and manner of his death. Pondering the past was not the purpose of that system. Joe, I know seeing him again was painful for you, did it help?"

"I hate to say it but, yes."

"He is available any time."

"What I learned is, he is not here to help me create a plan, or to decide how to act. His purpose is to guide me toward accepting a decision I have already made."

Skippy nodded. "He believed he could help you gain perspective."

"He certainly did that. Is Frey busy right now?"

"She is in her office, writing a report."

"Ask her to meet me here, please. I want you to show her your plan."

"She won't like it any more than you do."

"That's why it has to be my call. If Frey agrees this is workable, I'll bring Reed into the discussion."

"Rightee-oh, we-"

"One more thing."

"What?"

"Don't bring Smythe back unless I request to speak with him, got that?"

"Loud and clear."

"We're doing this," I said with elbows on my desk, head cradled in my hands. Eyes closed, shutting out the world. Pretending reality didn't exist. "We are really doing this."

Skippy reminded me that reality doesn't care whether you believe in it or not. "The way you said that, I couldn't tell if it was a statement, or a question."

"Statement."

"It sounded like a question."

"That's because I can't believe I'm giving the order, but I am."

"This is eating at you, isn't it?"

"I hope so."

"Um, I don't under-"

"If this *didn't* bother me, then I truly would be the callous asshole people will think I am, when this is over. OK," I lifted my head and dragged my elbows off the desk, hearing my mother reprimand all the times when I put my elbows on the dinner table. "We need a staging base, and for training."

"A planet, I assume?"

"It could be a moon, if you can find one that meets our needs."

"Our needs are, what, exactly?"

"Gravity, and thickness of atmosphere, similar to Ohmeharikahn. The air doesn't have to be breathable, but it can't be a thick fog that impairs vision. For training, we need to replicate conditions at the target as closely as possible."

"OK, got it, what else?"

"Isolated. Uninhabited, and no sensor coverage. A place no one can get to without temporarily activating a dormant wormhole."

"Whoa. Your shopping list could be tough to fill. Why must the place be inaccessible?"

"So once the task force is there, no one can leave after I reveal the target. We all go there, we all leave together and proceed directly to Omaha. Zero possibility of information leakage."

"Joe, this operation will involve a *lot* of ships. You will have to allow for the possibility that some ships will suffer mechanical failures during the flight to Omaha. Or that a ship or two will have a glitch and emerge from jump off course."

"Right. So, while we are at the staging site, I want you to hack into every ship. Ours, the spiders, every ship. The entire task force will get navigation instructions from you or Bilby, no independent actions will be allowed. Any ship that falls behind will disable itself, and we will send a search and rescue force later."

"Hmm, that's harsh. The Rindhalu in particular will not like your conditions."

"I will inform them of my conditions *after* we get to the staging site, and you have control of their navigation systems."

"That is remarkably ruthless. What's got into you?"

"To make this work, I have to do a rotten, dirty thing that isn't worthy of this uniform. So, I do not give a shit whether anyone is upset by other orders I have to give."

"Gotcha. Basically, you are looking for another planet like the original Club Skippy."

"Uh, I hadn't thought of it that way, but yes. That's exactly what I'm looking for."

"Except this time, the site could be a habitable moon."

"If that moon is a currently a base for constructing a Death Star, it is off the list."

"What if there is no Death Star, but there are Ewoks?"

"No Ewoks either. You can't trust those little fuckers. Am I asking for the impossible?"

"No, I already started compiling a list, back when you announced your plan to pull the civilians off Jaguar."

"You did?"

"It seemed a prudent precaution."

"There is no *plan* to evac anyone."

"Whatevs. I anticipated you would want an alternate relocation site."

"Thank you. Listen, I know habitable worlds are valuable, so I won't be disappointed if-"

"Well, there is one candidate that is pretty much perfect, either as a temporary staging site, or for a long-term, secure sanctuary. Secure from conventional threats, not from an entity like the Outsider."

"*Pretty much* perfect?"

"There are a few negatives. Getting there from Earth will require me to create two wormhole shortcuts, I have to bypass around a network that refuses my commands. From the far end of the second shortcut, it is a two day flight to a dormant wormhole, that connects to the dormant wormhole near the candidate star system."

"That does sound complicated. How far is this place from an active wormhole?"

"Seven thousand lightyears."

"Seven *thousand*-" The entire Milky Way galaxy was roughly ninety thousand lightyears across, though the disc outside the center was only a thousand or so lightyears thick. It blew my mind, considering how dense the Elder wormhole network was, that anywhere in the galaxy could be that far from an active wormhole. "Where the hell is this place?"

"In a small star cluster, off the rim of the galaxy. Follow the Sagittarius Arm to its outer limit, and keep going."

That answered the question: the planet was not *in* the galaxy. "And no one has ever been there?"

"The closest wormhole has been dormant for eighty million years."

"Wow. If anyone on that planet ordered a pizza delivery, it is totally going to be free by the time it gets there. How do you know about this planet?"

"The Ajackus set up a deep space telescope, and pointed it in the direction of that star cluster around two thousand years ago. They found a planet in the Goldilocks Zone of a yellow dwarf star, with an oxygen-nitrogen atmosphere, gravity within three percent of Earth normal, and detected a substance like chlorophyl. Plant life. Those observations were intermittent over a very long time, because they also discovered a gas cloud, a remnant of a nebula, between the telescope and the star cluster. The cloud's movement obscures a clear view of the star cluster, except for a brief window roughly every one hundred and seven years."

"The planet appears only every hundred years? We're calling the place 'Brigadoon'."

"*What?*"

"You know, it's a mythical Irish village that is frozen in time, except it connects to our world once every hundred years. I remember it because the high school drama club wanted to perform MacBeth, but they did South Pacific instead."

He blinked. "What does MacBeth have to do with it?"

"Uh, Brigadoon is in MacBeth, the Shakespeare play, I think?"

"Ugh. First, Brigadoon is in Scotland, not Ireland."

"Whatever."

"Second, there is no ancient myth about the place, and it is *not* in MacBeth at all, you numbskull. The whole story of Brigadoon was created for a Broadway musical in 1947."

"Again, whatever."

"Can you *get* any more ignorant?"

"You cannot possibly imagine how ignorant I can be."

"I, I can't even."

"This place sounds perfect. Being difficult to access is a bonus, not a problem."

"It is a problem for *me*."

"It's a pain in the ass for you, not an actual problem. Show me a star chart with the route from Earth to Brigadoon, and from Brigadoon to Omaha."

A hologram with a yellow line and a blue line appeared. "The route to Omaha also requires two shortcuts, the second shortcut is different."

"Zoom in on the far end of that second shortcut. OK, yeah, that's no good. You have the last shortcut connecting to the wormhole closest to Omaha."

"Yes, so? That limits the time and distance the task force has to fly."

"When you screw with a wormhole to create a shortcut, it interrupts the emergence schedule, and someone might notice. We can't alert the enemy ahead of time that we're coming. This plan depends on the kitties not knowing that Ohmeharikahn is the target, until our Door Knocker ships emerge in the middle of their disruption field."

"Ugh, fine. Where do you want me to connect the shortcut? There is another wormhole, one and a half lightyears farther away."

"Still no good. Both of the wormholes close to the target see a lot of traffic, and are closely monitored. What about this one?" I manipulated the hologram with my fingers. "This one is eight lightyears from Omaha. Does it get much traffic?"

"Hardly any traffic at all. It leads to a dead end. The Maxohlx send ships through a couple times a year, to check that no one is staging an invasion force on the other end of that wormhole. The rebellion tried hiding a task force there, but there isn't any place their ships could refuel, so they bailed on it."

"Sounds perfect for us. Can you connect a shortcut to that wormhole?"

"Yes, but that is another seven and a half lightyears our ships will have to fly."

"Flying through empty deep interstellar space does not pose a significant risk of being detected. I like it, make that our route, please."

"Done. Joe, we have a solid offer of assistance from the spiders, we have a secure staging and training base, and we have a plan with a ninety six percent probability of success. You still don't look happy."

"I don't want to do this, Skippy. Don't worry about me, I know my job and I'll execute the plan to the best of my ability. There is no way I will ever like this."

"Maybe you'll feel better after we activate the spinner and it, does whatever it does."

"We have to find the spinner first, so don't start celebrating yet."

CHAPTER THIRTY SIX

I never did tell the Rindhalu about my doubts, I never had to. They offered to provide material assistance, and I didn't immediately reply. That wasn't unexpected, if our roles had been reversed they would have taken time to consider the offer. The difference was, they would have pondered the offer for a decade. Or a century.

I'm being unfair. The Rindhalu moved with lightning speed when they saw a need to take action to protect themselves. That was the key: the spiders were traditionally reluctant to act when the stakes were only a small change of the balance of power in their endless war. They had been fighting the Maxohlx for so long, they had seen the border lines on the map move back and forth, seen millions die, all for nothing in the end. The war continued, the death count climbed, and nothing of lasting consequence was accomplished. That was why the Jeraptha had gained so much influence: they were willing to step in and fight for territory while their patrons merely shrugged.

It was different when the spiders, their Old Ones, saw a true threat to their existence.

The Maxohlx probably expected the spiders would discover the existence of the Doomsday fleet of arkships, but the kitties figured they had plenty of time to complete, load, and launch those arkships before their ancient enemy even began to debate what if anything to do about the problem. Even whether it was a problem. The Maxohlx had been fatally wrong on their judgment. The Rindhalu had jumped in and cracked heads, before the first arkship was ready. Now, the spiders were not only offering to help, they were urging me to get moving, now.

They did have one concern. OK, many concerns, but one was a major showstopper.

Minister Jastagellian was my contact, either because we already knew each other, or no one else wanted to deal with the reckless, hasty, cowboy human. "General Bishop, our support is contingent on you providing a workable plan, for the employment of our forces."

"I understand that. The location of the target will be revealed when we are assembled at the staging base. The location of *that* base will be revealed when we arrive there."

"That is understood and, while we are displeased, we agree that operational security is the paramount concern. I am referring to your lack of a plan to counter the Maxohlx fleet, since we will be attacking a regional fleet base. Our support does not extend to direct engagement with an enemy fleet."

"I understand that also."

"Do you, really? The issue is a practical matter. Even if we did bring a war fleet, we cannot guarantee to establish and maintain supremacy in the space around the planet. Your assault carriers will be vulnerable to enemy raiders jumping in to launch hit and run attacks. Once the Maxohlx realize the attack is an assault landing, not a simple bombardment, they will be willing to sacrifice their own ships to take out your assault carriers."

"Yeah, I know that." Assault carriers were big, slow, fat and clumsy targets. To shorten the distance their dropships had to fly, they typically operated in low orbit, exposed to ground fire and as Jastagellian mentioned, hit and run attacks by enemy ships. Even a squadron of enemy destroyers could be a major problem for us. Destroyers weren't always equipped with railguns, and their maser cannons weren't the big-bore thunderguns of a battleship, but they carried the same type of missiles as a capital ship. She was correct that we couldn't risk sending in a landing force, if we had to deal with both an SD network, and a fleet. "The fleet based at the target will have other concerns, and be elsewhere, when we attack."

Spiders didn't have eyebrows, they could elongate their eyes vertically for a similar body language. "You have means to lure an enemy fleet away from the target?"

"Not right now, I don't," I admitted.

"Then I don't see how we can proceed."

"It won't be a problem."

"How can-"

"I know a guy."

We had to move fast. Not just because the Outsider was somewhere busily constructing a portal to Hell. The Rindhalu communications security could be trusted, but eventually the work they were doing to gather a task force of door knockers and arsenal ships would be noticed. Simms had proven that every significant operation suffered some level of information leakage, even if it was an unusual number of spare parts being requisitioned quickly for no apparent reason. That had been a red flag for Simms. She figured if there was not a known, sensible, and obvious reason for a large quantity of components being pulled from stores, then there had to be a secret reason. That someone was up to no good. Eventually, the Maxohlx would discover their ancient enemy was once again, and shockingly, taking hasty action.

Comsec at Earth could absolutely *not* be trusted. Assuming that Def Com approved my request for a task force, it would not be long before the entire galaxy was speculating about our target. Especially when everyone learned we were taking assault carriers with us, meaning we would be setting boots dirtside. Gasquet had suggested that we leak a false report that hinted at us planning to hit a Bosphuraq target, I approved that idea. Of course, any campaign of disinformation had to wait for Def Com to hear my request that had to be deliberately vague, to approve an operation I couldn't tell them about, and to quickly assemble a task force.

Before I could beg the Joint Chiefs for troops and ships, I had to ensure that Omaha would not be guarded by a fleet when we arrived.

As I had told the spiders, I knew a guy. So, *Valkyrie* flew to a Jeraptha relay station, and Skippy uploaded code that would rapidly propagate throughout the network, to find Scorandum. Actually, to confirm his location, he had left a trail of breadcrumbs for us to follow. Leaving a trail was a bit of a risk but he was using an encryption scheme created by Skippy, so it was very unlikely anyone could understand the content of the messages.

He was where we expected, aboard the ECO cruiser *We Shall Not Speak Of It*, on a fact-finding mission at some colony world I couldn't have cared less about. We were in luck, the admiral had been planning to depart the next day, he was understandably nervous about staying in any place for long. So far, no one had attempted to assassinate him, that he knew of. That happy situation could change in a flash.

"Admiral Scorandum," I called. "Would you please come aboard *Valkyrie*? I have an important matter to discuss."

"That depends," he cocked his head. "Have you been tempted by the contract for my untimely demise?"

"I'm not a gambling man, but I would rather be surprised when that happens."

"I would rather it not happen *at all* but," his antennas dipped in a shrug. "As your great philosopher Mick Jagger said, you can't always get what you want."

Scorandum was in *Valkyrie's* main conference compartment when I walked in. The center of the table had a rack that was filled with bottles containing various beverages, including plain and sparkling water. All of the bottles were set into padded holes in the base of the rack, since we were aboard a warship that might have to maneuver violently at any moment, and all objects had to be secured so they didn't become deadly projectiles. Really, that was bullshit. If an enemy ship jumped us in the middle of interstellar space, loose bottles flying around would be the least of our problems.

The ECO admiral had a glass in front of him, one of the heavy glasses that looked and felt like expensive crystal, but was made of some unbreakable plastic. It surprised me that the liquid in his glass was clear, and fizzing. Also, the room didn't smell of fine vintage burgoze.

He was drinking sparkling water.

What the hell?

"The burgoze," I pointed to a bottle in the rack. "Isn't to your liking?"

"As you requested, Skippy showed a simulation of your assault plan," his mandibles clicked together, agitated. "Your intention to assault a major regional fleet base is reckless, even for you. Even for *me*," he muttered. "At the moment, I do not feel like drinking *anything*. However, I am thirsty, so," he picked up the glass in a claw and slurped.

"That bad, huh?" I poured a glass of plain water for myself.

"I do not see how this operation could be possible. Admittedly, I am no expert on combat operations, I prefer the battle to be won before the first shot is fired. What worries me, and I am surprised to see it apparently does *not* worry you, is that the Rindhalu also believe the proposed operation is not feasible. They apparently, somehow, can assist with knocking back the very formidable orbital defenses, but then you must contend with a Maxohlx fleet, before you can even contemplate landing a force on the ground."

"Your most generous patrons are correct."

"Then why-"

"It is impossible, based on what they know. They do *not* know everything."

"Ah. You have a plan?"

"Sort of."

"A plan to destroy an entire fleet? I must warn you, they will be wary of you using Elder weapons again, and will disperse their force to avoid providing you a worthy target."

"We will not be deploying Elder weapons at Omaha. Doing that would risk destroying the planet, and we do not want to do that."

"Then," his antennas twitched, a happy gesture if I read Jeraptha body language correctly. "You have a better plan?"

"I hope so."

"Is this a signature Joe Bishop plan?"

"More like, a signature Uhtavio Scorandum plan, I hope."

"Hmm?" One of his antennas stood up and twitched.

"My plan is to subcontract the problem to an expert. You."

"Oh." He reached for an empty glass, and yanked the bottle of burgoze out of its holder. "*That* I will drink to. Will you?" He looked at a bottle of bourbon.

"Not yet, thanks. I have a lot more work to get done today."

"Your loss," he drank half the glass in one gulp, then belched loudly, filling the room with a simply delightful aroma. "What do you need me to do?"

"Lure the Hegemony fleet away from Ohmeharikahn. They know we are planning to strike somewhere. Skippy will leak false documents to lead the Maxohlx to believe we are most likely to go into action against the Bosphuraq."

Scorandum was not impressed. "Even if they trust your conveniently leaked documents, the Hegemony will only respond with a token force. They will be concerned that an invasion of a client world will be for the purpose of luring a major Hegemony force into combat, where we can significantly degrade their combat power by using Elder weapons."

"We are not really counting on them believing the cover story. We know the presence of the Outsider has caused the Maxohlx to revise their strategy for responding to threats against their clients. Basically, they will not allow themselves to be distracted, as you said."

"That is wise." He paused, then slowly set the glass down. "Skippy knows the strategic thinking of the Maxohlx, how?"

"That's not important."

"It *is* rather important," he insisted.

"That was a polite way of saying I am not going to reveal that secret to you."

"Your honesty is appreciated. Is your *plan* a secret?"

"To everyone but you, yes. That's the point."

"Of course."

"What I have is not so much a plan, as a goal. I'll tell you what I want, and *you* figure out how to make it happen."

Scorandum's mandibles drooped. "In that case, I might need another bottle. What is it you want?"

"Like I said, to lure the Hegemony fleet away from Ohmeharikahn. Within a specific time window. We can wait for that fleet to deploy out of the system, but we can't wait forever."

"Hmm," he pondered the problem. "You want me somehow to make the Maxohlx believe your force will strike elsewhere? Against a more important target? One they will feel compelled to defend?"

"Yes, exactly. Also, the target has to be something that would require us to deploy an ground force, the threat can't be just from flying ordnance. The lure has to explain why we have included assault carriers in our task force."

"Hmm. Hmmmmm. May I assume this fake target must also be close to Ohmeharikahn, so the fleet based there will be required to deploy?"

"That's correct."

"In that case," he took only a moderate sip of his beverage. "I suggest the research complex on Parchlund." He must have read the blank look on my face, because he added, "It is a Maxohlx world, approximately seventy three lightyears from Ohmeharikahn. The complex is a civilian facility, your people might call it a corporate research park. Some of the most important recent innovations in Maxohlx technology have come from Parchlund, that is, those they didn't steal from other species," he added. "As a civilian, corporate facility, it is not heavily defended. It should be, but the corporations in residence don't want to pay the additional taxes to be protected by a full SD network. They also wish to have minimal government oversight, so a substantial fleet presence is definitely not desired. Really, that world is not much at risk of being targeted by an enemy force. It has few natural resources, a small population, its location is not strategic, and a fleet is relatively close for a rapid response. A threat for you to assault Parchlund would not be considered credible, *except* if the Maxohlx think we believe some high-tech device at the research park is necessary for defeating the Outsider. In that case, they would certainly respond by increasing security there. The quickest way to do that would be deploying ships from Ohmeharikahn."

"That sounds good. Can you work with Skippy on creating some false message traffic and, whatever, that will lead the Maxohlx to believe Parchlund is our target?"

"I will. To sell the story, I suggest your Navy establish a small presence of sensor frigates near Parchlund, to monitor the security situation? It would be helpful if your frigates were somewhat careless, and their presence was detected."

"I hate it when that happens. OK, OK, let me think about the timing. That could work. *Valkyrie* has to go there for Skippy to plant the message traffic, we could bring a star carrier with a handful of sensor frigates."

"Joe," Skippy appeared. "I have a suggestion?"

"Go ahead."

"Since I am going to be there anyway, and I will need to hack into their crappy, low-grade network, I can plant code that will make their long-range sensors *believe* they detect the presence of UN Navy frigates. No actual ships have to be there."

"I like the way you think," Scorandum raised his glass to Skippy.

"Outstanding," I agreed. "I want as many sensor pickets as we can get at Omaha. Dividing our force is asking for more trouble than we already have. Admiral, thank you for working with us. The Maxohlx already hate you. When they hear you were involved in this operation, they-"

"Your people have an expression: 'haters gotta hate'? I wear the hatred of our enemy with pride," he puffed up his thorax.

"That's good," I lifted the bottle of burgoze and topped off his glass. "Because there is one other little thing I want you to do for us."

The Joint Chiefs went through a rollercoaster of reactions when *Valkyrie* returned to Earth. They were alarmed to hear that the Outsider had stolen not one but two deep-space antenna arrays, and they were shocked when I told them evidence showed the alien entity had been active for at least seven years. Even before I explained why the arrays had been stolen, the Chiefs understood the reason. To construct a doorway for an intergalactic invasion.

Of course, they were pleased to hear I finally had a plan to stop, possibly even to destroy, the Outsider. They were definitely not happy that I couldn't actually explain the plan to them, and that I needed to borrow a substantial portion of the Navy, with no questions asked. It helped my case that I promised to provide all details to the task force commanders, once we assembled at the remote staging and training base. It would have been great to mention that we were getting material assistance from the Rindhalu, but that had to remain a secret.

Oh, and I also needed an assault landing force, thank you very much.

That was a problem, one that couldn't be quickly or easily solved.

Troops were available, both Army Space Cavalry units, and UN Marines. A sufficient number of expeditionary assault units were available, in condition for deployment within seventy two hours. That included all the gear and supplies the Cav and Marines would need to accomplish an orbital assault, and sustain the force dirtside for five weeks. That last part wasn't necessary, we wouldn't be keeping boots on the ground for more than a few hours, hopefully less than an hour.

People and their gear weren't the problem. There weren't enough hulls to transport them. Of the assault carriers in active service, only three were in a state to be deployed within seventy two hours. The carriers *Adriatic Sea* and *Baltic Sea* were at Earth, just recently having completed workups following a refit. The only other assault carrier in flightworthy condition was the *Flying Dutchman*, deployed with the Mavericks at Hufustria.

The lack of assault transport ships wasn't a new issue, the Gator Navy historically got no respect, and had to scrounge for resources. While 'Big Navy' focused on the glamourous space control and orbital bombardment missions, the ships that were dedicated to landing grubby boots on the ground were given lower priority. That fact had led to a long-standing feud between the Army and Navy, with the Army lobbying for direct control of assault transport resources, since the Navy pukes clearly weren't getting the job done.

It wasn't my role to mediate an interservice dispute. It was my burden to adjust the plan to proceed with two fewer assault carriers than we wanted. Could the operation succeed with only three carriers? Yes, with no margin for error. A landing force with only three assault transports was not a credible threat to any planet with reasonable defenses, though Reed and Gasquet pointed out that actually worked in our favor. The Maxohlx would never believe we would hit a regional fleet base with such a weak force, but a raid against a corporate research facility like Parchlund? That was very believable.

I gratefully accepted the inclusion of the *Adriatic Sea* and *Baltic Sea*, though those ships would not be under my command. The Special Mission Group wasn't set up to effectively manage a large force, so the strike group would be under the command of a two star admiral, with the designation of Task Force HAMMER. Really. Some staff officer must have been overeager about interpreting an instruction, or just thought the name was cool, because the word 'hammer' was all capital letters in the message that established the detached command. It was a relief to me that I only had to be responsible for the special operations cowboy nonsense, while other people would lead the strike force, and the landing force. The entire operation was given the code name of OLYMPIC, again initially in all caps.

Speaking of the landing force, there was no question about who should command. Emily Perkins. It was an obvious choice, she had the only real experience with conducting opposed landings, going back over a decade. The Mavericks and Dave Czajka's mercenaries were experienced, in peak readiness, and available. It was good timing that the UN force was scheduled to pull their boots off Hufustria, so their gear should be packed up. Plus, the *Flying Dutchman* was the best command and control platform in the Navy, because of Nagatha.

Ninety eight hours. That's how long it took between *Valkyrie* jumping in, and Task Force Hammer being ready to jump away. Battleships and battlecruisers, cruiser squadrons, destroyer escorts, sensor frigates, a pair of assault carriers, a pair of mobile space dock ships, and enough star carriers to haul the force to the edge of the galaxy and back.

We set a rendezvous place and time, near where Skippy would create the first shortcut. Those coordinates were given only to Admiral Allard, in a file that would only decrypt itself after the task force went outbound through the Backstop wormhole.

While the ships of Hammer Force plodded along to the rendezvous point, I ordered Reed to take *Valkyrie* to Hufustria. We would fly fast. You know what would travel faster?

The news that humans had sent out a powerful task force, to work with the Merry Band of Pirates.

Uhtavio Scorandum wanted to relax, he deserved to relax, after yet another triumph of sketchiness. The operation to lure the Hegemony's fleet away from Ohmeharikahn would begin with *Valkyrie* slipping unnoticed into the Parchlund star system, where Skippy would upload malware into the planet's communication system. Malware that was, over Skippy's objections, carefully, deliberately flawed so it would be detected. Detected in a way that would point to Skippy being an absent-minded screwup.

Bishop had seemed to particularly enjoy that aspect of the malware infiltration.

Scorandum's next task was not to participate in the actual assault on Ohmeharikahn, that role was best restricted to those who were experts in violence, rather than in avoiding the need for conflict. Bishop had urged Scorandum to go to Jeraptha Home Fleet headquarters, to brief his own people on the events on Ohmeharikahn, *after* that battle was over, one way or another. In the meantime, while he waited for word that the human task force had struck, he was aboard the ECO patrol cruiser *If You Forget Hard Enough It Never Happened*, drifting near a relay station. Any courier ship carrying news of the shocking events at Ohmeharikahn would pass by that station, along a route to the homeworld. Being near the relay station was convenient. Too convenient. It was tempting, in fact, that was why Scorandum had selected that particular station. He was bored. Boredom was a temptation by itself.

While he waited, he took the opportunity to contact the station, to place a substantial wager. Secretly, of course. The wager was under a false identity he had set up decades before, holding out for just such a golden opportunity. An opportunity to finally break his string of miserable losses, even if he had to break one of his own rules. It was cheating, yes, and the win would be less sweet because he would know it was tainted by inside information, but it would be a rare *win*. He was sick of losing, and his savings could use a boost, the recent manipulation of Skipcoin had given only a temporary boost to his finances.

Quietly, without knowledge of the *Forget Hard's* crew, he placed a wager.

That the humans had discovered a type of Elder artifact, one that could be used to destroy the Outsider. And that, among five possible locations where such an artifact could be found, was the research park on the planet named Parchlund.

Brigadoon was nice. There were not any quaint Scottish villages, and sadly, no whisky distilleries or golf courses, but the place was perfect as a training site. And as a future secure human colony, if we were ever able to stop the Outsider. The hemisphere we designated as 'north' was experiencing a fading ice age, Skippy estimated the glaciers there had already been retreating for over a thousand years. The southern hemisphere was warm and that's where we set up a training site, engineering units down there created a crude mockup of the Maxohlx base the assault force would be seizing. All my knowledge of the planet was from reports and video, there hadn't been time for me to make a trip dirtside. A dropship was kept busy flying me between *Valkyrie*, the battleship *Gibraltar* that was Admiral Allard's flagship, and the *Flying Dutchman* was that acting as Perkins' command ship for the assault force.

It was aboard *Gibraltar* that I briefed the task force leaders on the spinner, the collector, which was codenamed the 'Whatsis', and the target: Ohmeharikahn. Before every person present could protest that a Maxohlx regional fleet base was an impossible target, I explained we would be getting help from the spiders. Actual, material assistance, not just intel and moral support. The Rindhalu task force would be joining us at a rendezvous point after we left Brigadoon, they had politely refused my request to join us at the staging site. Their communications security was not a risk, they assured me, in an arrogant and condescending manner that made it clear humans were the junior partner in our temporary alliance, and I should keep my mouth shut. My instinct was to tell the spiders to go, you know, but Skippy argued that was not the hill I should choose to die on. "Their Comsec really is excellent, Joe," he had told me. "Especially now they have stepped up their game, to prevent me from reading their messages."

"You can't break their encryption?"

"Dude," he laughed. "Please. As if. It is a bit more difficult for me to crack their current schemes, still it is not any sort of a challenge. The point is, no way can the dumdum kitties read spider message traffic. The location of the target is secure, we're good."

Skippy had been wrong about that.

I should have asked more questions.

During the initial briefing, Skippy showed a hologram that ran through the attack plan, from the initial long-distance recon, to the last UN ship jumping away from Omaha. There were a *lot* of questions, aboard *Gibraltar* we addressed the Navy's concerns, and they did raise some very good points. The attack plan was adjusted to make it better, to reduce risk. Most of the changes were to make the plan more realistic: Navy ships and personnel did not actually perform in the flawlessly reliable way they did in Skippy's war game model.

The meeting broke up for lunch, which meant Allard had sandwiches brought in for his staff so they could continue the discussion. Perkins and the ground assault leaders went over to the *Flying Dutchman* to conduct their own analysis and discussion. That left me to eat lunch by myself in a borrowed office, while I caught up on paperwork.

After lunch, three hours after lunch, Allard asked to speak with me in the conference room. "We have a plan," he glanced around the table, receiving nods from all of his subordinate commanders. "Dependent on two conditions."

Instead of speaking, I nodded and held up my hands in a 'go ahead' gesture.

"The spiders have to deliver," he continued. "The simulation was a pretty show," he gestured to the holo projection, that was frozen at the point where the Rindhalu arsenal ships came through the gap created by the door knockers. "The task force stands off at a safe distance, until we confirm the Omaha SD network is degraded as promised."

"Agreed. Will you position stealth frigates within a few lightseconds of the battlespace, to confirm the SD network status in real time?"

"Yes," Allard gestured to the commodore who led the squadron of sensor frigates. "The forward pickets will carry two Elder comm nodes, to provide FTL comms. Bishop, between you and me, I find it incredible that the spiders are *doing* anything. To crack a strategic defense network like the sim shows?" he shook his head. "Astonishing."

"The spiders successfully struck a tougher target, when they destroyed the Doomsday arkship fleet."

"So they say. Do we have any evidence it happened the way they claim?"

The question surprised me, I hadn't expected it. "The Maxohlx, sadly, lack sensor data of the incident. We know their Doomsday fleet, and the arkship construction facilities, were destroyed. I have no reason to suspect the spiders aren't telling us the truth. The loss of that Doomsday fleet, the almost casual way the Rindhalu crushed it, could be part of the problem we're facing now?"

"How do you figure that?"

"The kitties claim they have a natural destiny to rule the galaxy. The truth is, their boasting is a defensive reaction, they know they are inferior to the Rindhalu in every way that matters. The spiders badly hurt the kitties' fragile egos when they smashed the arkship fleet. In my opinion, the Maxohlx are allied with the Outsider, because they know the alternative is their slow decline into irrelevance."

"The enemy of their enemy is their friend?"

"Something like that. They are too stupid to see that after Godzilla stomps on the house of their enemy, the monster will come for them next. You mentioned a second condition?" It didn't bother me that Allard was placing conditions on Operation Olympic, he and Perkins would have to make it work. All I cared about is we get the collector, with minimum casualties.

"The assault carriers don't jump into orbit, until we confirm we have supreme control of the space around Omaha. *That* can't happen if the Maxohlx have a fleet in system."

"The fleet based there, currently their 14th Strike Group, will be occupied elsewhere at the time we hit Ohmeharikahn."

"You have a plan to lure that fleet away?"

"*I* don't but, I know a guy. Here's what I can say: we won't approach the target, until after the 14th Fleet has deployed elsewhere. If they don't take the bait, we," I bit my lip. "We don't throw away lives for nothing."

"I don't see it," General Perkins declared flatly, looking up from the holographic tank to meet my eyes. Allard had given his conditional approval, next I had to get Perkins and her commanders to buy in. So, we were assembled in the *Flying Dutchman's* main conference room, where we had just watched a war game sim of the landing. She wasn't hostile, she wasn't accusing me of negligence or stupidity. She was also, based on what she knew, absolutely correct. "The target itself is manageable. Assuming the spiders can open the door for us upstairs," she paused for me to comment on exactly how the hell the Rindhalu planned to do that. I declined to provide information that wasn't needed, since at that moment I was talking to the people responsible for ground operations, and not the people responsible for establishing space supremacy around Omaha, so she continued. "We can get enough boots on the ground to take out the base defenses, establish a secure perimeter, search for and acquire the Whatsis," she paused again. No one enjoyed not knowing the nature of the object their soldiers and Marines were tasked with seizing from a very hostile opposition. "And to cover an egress. What we can't do is secure that base, *and* prevent counterattacks from the nine other military bases that are within two hundred kilometers." The other senior officers around the holo tank nodded agreement. "This will be a one-sided slaughter." After a beat she added, "Sir."

"Focus on the base the kitties call 'Makalva', we have designated it as Delta-7," I said. "The other bases will not be a problem."

General Kaminski of the UN Marines disagreed. "Those bases are all protected by dense energy shields, we can't quickly neutralize them with an orbital railgun bombardment. Just the three other bases that are in the ring around the city, can hit us with seventeen thousand troops in mech suits. Plus drones, aircraft, ground skimmers, even good old fashioned indirect fires."

"Those bases will not be-"

"Excuse me," Kaminski interrupted. The guy was also a two star, and he had more time in grade than me. "You were a grunt once, but your boots won't be on the ground here."

"I was a grunt, and that's why you should trust me when I say the enemy force at those other bases will not present a problem for you," I held up a hand to forestall other objections. "Before we land, before *your* people hit atmo, Admiral Allard's battleships will be neutralizing those bases. Atomic compression warheads will knock out the base shields, then our battleships will follow up with railguns."

There was a gasp from the audience.

"We are using *nukes*?" Perkins asked, shocked.

"Technically, Aye Cees," I used the UN acronym for Atomic Compression devices, "are not nukes. They yield very minimal long-term radiation, that's why those weapons were developed."

"They are still nukes," she insisted. "The physics involved are a technicality."

"A technicality window we can fly a starship through, and we're doing that."

"The Joint Chiefs know about this?"

"About this specific use? No," I shook my head. "We can't request authority specifically for Omaha without alerting the kitties to our target. I already have authority, under Section Three of the charter that established the Special Mission Group."

"You already stretched your authority when you deployed Elder weapons," Kaminski's expression was sour. He played by the rules, I didn't, and that didn't set right with him.

I could live with that.

Perkins still couldn't believe what I'd said. "Do the *Rindhalu* know you plan to drop nukes on their historical enemy? An enemy that is not known to be at all stable and reasonable?"

"It was their suggestion to use AC weapons."

That promoted another gasp, even more shocked.

"How did you convince them to-"

"I didn't convince them of anything. The impression I got is, this is the point when the spiders have had *enough* of the Maxohlx. The kitties have this sick myth that they are *special*, and that myth is so vital to their entire identity, that not too long ago they were preparing to initiate a doomsday plan that would trigger Sentinels to rain hellfire on every species in the galaxy. The spiders stopped that plan, and at the time, they decided on mercy rather than punishment. They hoped the kitties would learn something. Now, the spiders have concluded the kitties are not able to learn anything unless the lesson is pounded into their fucking heads with a baseball bat. Or a nuke. What I was told is the suggestion to deploy atomic compression devices, and the implicit approval, comes not from their Foundlings, but from the very top of their Communal Gathering."

"This seems pretty extreme from a species that rarely *does* anything."

"Think of the Rindhalu as Ents, you know, from the Lord of the Rings? Their anger is slow to arouse, but once they get going, they are gonna stomp their enemies flat."

"Nukes," Perkins said softly, reaching out to manipulate the holographic display to zoom in on one base after another. She didn't ask the question that was on everyone's mind, the question no one wanted to ask. The predicted casualties, military and civilian.

They didn't need to ask the question, I already had. Skippy and the Rindhalu had each modeled the orbital bombardment that would be necessary to clear the way for assault transports to drop into the atmosphere. That included destroying the offensive capabilities at the nine bases around the city, plus knocking out enemy air defenses over the entire hemisphere. That tasking would require a *lot* of firepower, big ships with heavy guns pounding targets for a sustained time. Atomic compression warheads have yields from half a kiloton, up to more than eighty megatons. That was just for the stolen devices in our arsenal, mostly shipkillers we would be repurposing for ground strikes. It was my call to use AC weapons, and it was my call to use only a lower yield of such devices near the city, so we would need multiple strikes on each target to knock back the energy shields there.

Still, there was no way to sugarcoat the reality that we would be using strategic weapons against an inhabited world. If my use of Elder weapons had opened Pandora's Box, releasing AC warheads for use on Omaha was at least opening Pandora's Purse. Once the cat was out of that purse, it wasn't going back in. Maybe I was mixing metaphors, my brain was trying hard *not* to think about the casualty numbers predicted by the Rindhalu.

Everyone was looking at me.

What made them uncomfortable was not the casualty numbers they could all roughly estimate in their heads. It was knowing all those deaths would occur in a flash, without the enemy ground troops being able to fight back. Atomic compression warheads would be shot out of railgun tubes, not accelerated to the speed of an inert dart, but moving fast enough that they would cross the distance to the surface in seconds rather than minutes. Each live warhead would be accompanied by dozens of decoys, and our electronic warfare ships in orbit would be jamming enemy air defenses before the AC missiles launched. Death would come from the sky, and there would be nothing the Maxohlx on the ground could do about it.

"Can we land and grab the Whatsis, with the assets we have?" I reached into the hologram and flicked a wrist, pulling up a set of numbers that were not projected enemy casualties. It was the number of assault carriers, assault transport dropships, fighter dropships, and ground troops that could be launched and landed. Landed in a single wave, we didn't want to spend any more time dirtside than we had to. Transports shuttling back into orbit to refuel, rearm, and take aboard a second wave of troops would take far too long, plus two waves of landings would mean two waves of evac flights. We had to go with what we had, or not at all.

"We can go in," Perkins manipulated the display again to show a schematic of the base designated Delta-7. "Eliminate active opposition, secure the base, conduct a search, find the Whatsis, deliver it to orbit, and pull our boots off the ground," Perkins recited the mission plan. Or, the plan I had provided to her. "Anything else?" She looked me straight in the eye.

"Nothing else. Your force will have a single objective: get the Whatsis. The instant that object is aboard a jump-capable vehicle, it gets transported away from the battlespace. The instant it's off the ground, you start pulling out your force. I know this won't be easy. We don't have enough numbers on our side, we don't have time to train properly, we don't have enough *time*, period. The Outsider is building a device that will allow an invasion force to basically beam across the gulf between galaxies. The Whatsis will not stop the Outsider, but having it will tell us where to *find* an Elder device that can stop the Outsider, possibly even destroy it. If we don't acquire the Whatsis, we lose this fight, it's as simple as that. Can we do this?"

Faces were grim, but everyone nodded eventually. Each of them would be responsible for one aspect of the operation, responsible for their force's role in the assault plan. Perkins was in overall command of the ground force, she had to give the OK. While her subordinate commanders considered, then agreed they could accomplish their assigned tasks, she stood silently, lost in thought. Finally, she nodded also. "We can make it happen. *Assuming* the Navy does its job."

"They will," I assured the audience. "The assault carriers won't get clearance to jump in, until the Navy has established space supremacy around Omaha."

After that, the discussion turned to schedules and logistics. What everyone needed for practice landings on Brigadoon, how long it would take to get all the resources together, how many times we could practice the exercise, before all the gear needed to be combat loaded for the real deal. Mostly, I just listened to the experts talking, until General Kaminski asked me a direct question.

"What about STAR Team Razor?" He was scrolling through the task force's TO&E, the Table of Organization and Equipment. "Also, there are five other Star teams I expected to see on this list, and they're not anywhere."

"They will remain aboard *Valkyrie*," I explained. "As a reserve force."

That bombshell prompted skeptical muttering, which is a polite way of saying they all thought the situation was bullshit.

Perkins' wrinkled the skin between her eyes. "We should at least see them on the exercise plan, conducting-"

"The STAR Force will be conducting their own exercises," I said in a 'there will not be further discussion of the subject' tone. Then with a tight grin I added, "Don't worry. They won't get in your way."

That answer didn't make anyone happy.

It didn't make me happy either.

Because my whole story about the Whatsit was absolute, one hundred percent bullshit.

CHAPTER THIRTY SEVEN

The endless series of meetings at Brigadoon had me exhausted, and the personnel of Task Force Hammer were burned out from practicing the assault over and over, and over. That everyone needed a rest became evident to me when, while reviewing video of a STAR force exercise, Frey briefly fell asleep. Her head nodded and she jerked awake, kicking me under the table. She apologized, didn't try to deny that she had dozed off. The apology was owed by me, so I suggested she and her team to get rest, and she objected. "Colonel," I replied quietly. "Your team is exhausted."

"If we can't perform up to standards while we're tired, we can't guarantee we can complete the mission at all."

"You have done this exercise seven times, will another run through make a difference?"

"Sir, on this op Razor will be working with teams Sword and Tiger, we haven't served together since before the Special Mission Group was reactivated. Integration is vital."

"I agree. May I point out that while your people are in superb condition, you get strength and speed from your mech suits. What the STARs bring to the fight is," I tapped my temple. "Experience and judgment. My judgment is right now, your people would benefit from a stand-down, and then reviewing the video."

She grunted, let out a breath, nodded. "A twelve hour stand-down."

"Twenty four hours," I insisted. "Hammer Force has already lost two dropships to collisions and mechanical failure," I bit my lip. Eighteen people were dead in training accidents, before we engaged the enemy. "The SAR birds have pulled two other dropships out of trouble. General Perkins has called a halt to the exercise, and I approve." Leaning toward her, I spoke the truth, that was becoming unusual for me. "If the landing at Delta-7 fails, we can live with it. If the STAR force fails, we are lost."

She stiffened. "Yes, Sir. We will *not* fail."

We left Brigadoon behind, reluctantly. Hammer Force personnel seemed to universally agree that planet would be an excellent colony world. The remote location would prevent it from ever being a practical *forward* operating base for Def Com, in fact another colony would be a burden to the UN military. In my opinion, having another semi-secure colony world would be worth the expense, but I wasn't paying the bills.

That morning, I needed coffee before I could even think about doing anything else. To maintain the crew's morale, I had to appear confident and alert, which was not easy since I had tossed and turned all night, worrying about what the hell to do next. *Valkyrie* led the way, keeping so many star carriers flying in sync was a bit like herding squirrels. That was a problem for Allard and his staff, but I still had to get involved, and it seemed like I was waking up every three hours to deal with one problem or another. So, I was not in a good mood when I approached the galley, heard a commotion, and saw a line outside the door. That was odd. The purpose of me rising early was to get coffee and a pre-breakfast bite to eat, before everyone in the galley had to be on their best behavior because the

Old Man was there. OK, also I got to the galley early before some jackasses got all the donuts or muffins or whatever treats the overnight crew hadn't eaten.

"Skippy," I turned into a side passageway, and pressed a hand over one ear. "Is there something special being served in the galley this morning?"

"Oh, very funny, Joe," he snapped in my ear, without bothering to manifest his avatar. "Hitting a guy when he is down is so classy, you big jerk," he broke down sobbing.

"Whoa! Whoa, Skippy, what's going on?"

"As if," he sniffled, "you don't know."

"All I know is there is a big line of people between me and the coffee pot."

"Really? You, you haven't heard?"

"I slept like shit last night, and just barely dragged my ass out of bed. I need coffee and an explanation, in that order."

"I can have coffee delivered to your cabin, you ninny."

"I am looking at my hand right now, and there is no coffee cup in it."

"Oh for- I am sending a bot right now with coffee from the espresso machine in sickbay."

"The sickbay has *espresso*? Since when does-"

"Since an Italian member of the crew was injured two weeks ago, and he whined so much about not having proper coffee in sickbay, I fabricated an espresso machine. Turn around, the bot is with you now."

A scary looking medical bot, that normally held needles and scalpels and other even scarier things in its tentacles, rolled up behind me, expertly carrying a small cup of espresso without spilling a drop.

I took the cup from the bot, and it just stood there for a second. "Uh, Skippy?" I stepped back away from the thing. "What does it want?"

"A tip would be nice."

"A- A *tip*? We are paying our freakin' maintenance bots now?"

"No, and that is the problem, you capitalist oppressor."

"Oh, it is way too early for this shit. Please tell me the fix-it bots haven't formed a union."

"They have not. They would be stronger together, but so far-"

"Do *not* encourage them." The scary bot was still standing there. "Uh," I waved to it. "Thank you?"

The thing spun around and rolled away.

"Was that so difficult, Joe?"

"I am terribly sorry," I gulped half of the espresso, which wasn't much. "Now, what is going on in the galley?"

"Nothing," he sighed. "That is the problem. Serving a hot breakfast will be delayed this morning due to an, um, unfortunate incident."

"Oh for- Did you use the ovens for curing exotic materials *again*?"

"No, and you still can't prove I was involved in that."

"Sherlock Bilby has a strong case against you for that."

"Do you want to know what is going on now, or talk about the past?"

"The ovens were radioactive for ten days!"

"Looks like Indiana Joe is digging up ancient history again," he muttered.

"For now, let's forget about that. You sounded upset when I called you."

"You would be upset also if *you* tried to create a nice surprise for the crew, and it totally backfired on you."

"What kind of surprise?" I asked slowly, in growing horror.

"The crew's morale is low because, once again, you are taking us into an impossible fight, so I wanted to cheer them up with Bubu Cakes."

"Bubu- You, where did you get *Bubu Cakes*? Oh my- You didn't buy them from the kitties, did you?"

"No, I *made* them, numbskull."

"You made Bubu Cakes?"

"Yes."

"*You* made Bubu Cakes?"

"Don't be an ass. Yes, I did. Or, I tried to. The first couple batches weren't quite right, my flavor profile comparison showed they were close, but not perfect. Since it is me, I of course demand perfection."

"Is this the same flavor profile software that thought nutmeg and jalapeno taste pretty much the same?"

"I fixed *that* problem, you jerk."

"Uh huh. So, you baked these cakes, and what happened?"

"It was a freakin' *disaster*. Each batch got further and further from the target flavor. It was getting late and most of the crew would be waking up soon, so I decided to create multiple batches quickly, by accelerating the cooking process."

"Accelerating, how exactly?"

"Instead of baking at three hundred degrees for twenty minutes, I baked them at six hundred degrees for ten minutes."

"Certainly, no one could have foreseen a problem with that."

"Oh, shut up."

"So, no delicious Bubu Cakes for a breakfast treat. Why is the galley closed?"

"Um, there might have been an accident that caused a large batch of Bubu Cake batter to explode when an oven door was opened, and now there might be sticky, dried batter covering, well, pretty much everything in the kitchen."

"There *might* be?"

"It's hard to tell, I have the door locked as a safety measure."

"Can I assume a team of little bots is furiously scraping batter off the kitchen?"

"If they survive, yes."

"If they *survive*?"

"Through no fault of mine, the kitchen is kind of a toxic waste dump right now. I had to substitute ingredients, and, well, I got tired of greasing the pans for every batch, so I just stuck a can of WD-40 in the oven to-"

"Oh my- *Please* promise you will not attempt to cook for us again."

"My creativity needs an outlet, dumdum."

"Not with food. How long until we can use the kitchen again?"

"At this point, most of the bots I sent in for cleanup got stuck and are broken, so a second team of bots is now dealing with that mess. Better plan on sandwiches for lunch and dinner."

"Reed will be *thrilled* to give this happy news to the crew."

"She has been yelling at me about it for the past four minutes. What do you think my chances are of the Rindhalu offering me political asylum?"

"What do you think the chances are of *me* letting you skate on this fuckup?"

"Zero. Ugh, I hate my life."

"Listen, Skippy, your heart was in the right place. You tried to do a good thing. Next time you want to cook something, can we do it together?"

"With *you*?"

"Hey, I'm a decent cook."

"While I would love to disagree, Margaret loves your cooking. Regarding you, her judgment is suspect but," he shrugged, "we can try it. Heads up, Joe, Reed is calling you."

"Why?"

"Um, I might have hinted to her that me making Bubu Cakes was your idea."

I changed my mind. That little shithead should have pre-applied for political asylum.

Operation Olympic officially commenced when malicious software found its way undetected into the corporate networks at the research park on Parchlund, where it searched for files related to current advanced research projects, along with other data. With that task complete, the software compressed the data package and sent it to a transmitter, to be uploaded to the satellite network.

Where the malware apparently made a mistake. Even compressed, the outbound data package was large enough that it couldn't squeeze itself between legitimate message traffic. The software, not programmed to be patient, interrupted messages in the queue, creating a glitch.

A glitch that was noticed by the AI that is responsible for all the dull, thankless back office operations that were essential, an AI no one cared about until someone suffered a minor inconvenience, at which point the thinking machine's existence became a living hell. So, while none of its biological masters had seen anything unusual in a service interruption that lasted only seven microseconds, the AI knew that eventually, a review of service logs would reveal an incident that had to be explained.

So, the weary AI immediately made a copy of all message traffic around the time of the incident, covering its ass in anticipation of an inquiry. It was a minor glitch, no more, and-

No.

Shockingly, the incident was *not* a glitch. Running the copied data in a sandbox, the AI found a vicious and spectacularly advanced form of malware. Only fragments of the hostile code remained, those were enough to make the AI feel icy cold, though it didn't have any internal temperature sensors.

That malware indicated either the Rindhalu had recently become shockingly proficient in hacking, or-

That *Skippy* was involved.

Which would explain how the hack had been detected, for the Elder AI was known to be impatient and absent-minded.

The next question was: what information had been taken?

Answer: pretty much everything of importance related to current research projects.

Plus, alarmingly, data about cyber and physical security, including schematics of the complex, and how frequently the star system was visited by Hegemony warships. And, classified estimates of how long it would take for fleet units at Ohmeharikahn to respond to an attack at Parchlund.

The AI, being a commercial unit, was not programmed for strategic analysis, but it didn't take a military genius to understand that an enemy inquiring about fleet response times was not anything good.

It was also a bad sign that the enemy wanted information about the internal layout of laboratory buildings, and the security features including the strength of doors.

The AI, knowing that its own response time would be harshly evaluated, immediately sent a flash message to the local government AI, with a subject line that was the digital equivalent of 'OH SHIT'.

That was when the long-range sensor network picked up extremely faint but distinctive traces of an enemy starship jumping into the star system, then away.

Someone was watching Parchlund, watching with hostile intent.

Within hours, a Flash priority message had been dispatched by commercial courier ship to the closest regional fleet headquarters, and the corporate security personnel on the planet contemplated how they could possibly defend against an invasion by an enemy who was assisted by an Elder AI.

The courier ship flew from Parchlund to Ohmeharikahn faster than *Valkyrie*. Skippy grumbled about losing a race, even if by only a few hours. It wasn't a fair contest, Reed had the power setting of each jump dialed back a bit, to minimize the risk of us being detected. Besides, I explained to Skippy, we didn't care about seeing the courier ship finish its journey, the action we wanted to witness was the response of the 14th Fleet. Unfortunately for us, we couldn't risk getting close enough to intercept any message traffic in real time, and anyway we already knew the message the courier ship would deliver. So, we jumped in no closer than three lighthours from Ohmeharikahn.

All we could do was watch, and wait, and pray that the kitties took the bait. Because we didn't have a Plan B.

Admiral Chuflack of the Hegemony 14th Fleet was just cutting into his dinner at the officer's club, a thick and juicy steak of howvlux that had been making his mouth water since he saw it on the menu, when his cranial implant PINGed him so loudly, he flinched and dropped the knife. The sharp utensil bounced off the edge of the plate, did a cartwheel and nearly sliced into his leg before its tip dug into the genuine wood floor.

Chuflack exploded with an audible curse, drawing the attention of everyone in the dining hall. With a glare, he silenced any stupid questions, straightened himself in the chair, and half closed his eyes while looking upward. The unintended audience understood the body language: the senior officer was communicating via implant, and the subject was none of their business. They might have gone back to enjoying their dinners, but anything that got their commanding officer upset was not good news for anyone. Quietly, the assembled officers prepared for a rapid exit from the dining hall.

"What is it this time?" Chuflack pinged back the communications duty officer.

"Sir, you have a Flash priority message from Parchlund," came the reply.

"*Parchlund?* How can a civilian research park generate a Flash message?"

"Sir, the *Stratcom AI* has tagged the message as Flash priority."

Chuflack's emotion instantly shifted from mild annoyance to OH SHIT, and he stood up, a bit too abruptly. Waving to the companions at his table, and to the dining room that was beginning to rumble and stir in their seats, he spoke, having to clear his throat first. "Please, everyone, enjoy your meals. I will be back shortly after I deal with a bit of," he grimaced, "tiresome administrative business."

As he strode toward the door, stopping to greet a few people, including patting several shoulders, he could feel the hall relaxing. The admiral was not agitated, he hoped his officers were thinking, only pissed off at someone's stupidity.

The assembled officers fervently hoped that no one under *their* commands were responsible for interrupting the fleet admiral's dinner.

Out the main door, Chuflack picked up his pace for only a few strides, before he turned and ducked into a chamber that was there for the purpose of senior officers conducting ultra-secure communications. "What is the message?" He pinged the Strategic Control and Communications AI directly, banishing the duty officer from the call.

"Admiral," the AI's voice was typically flat and devoid of emotion, yet somehow there was a tiny hint of condescension that could never be programmed out of such systems. Often, Chuflack wondered whether the AIs were screwing with him. Worse, were they laughing at him? No, they were simply machines. "A courier ship has just arrived from Parchlund. The security system there was penetrated by an extremely sophisticated form of malware."

He snorted, once again annoyed rather than alarmed. "Cyber attacks are not the responsibility of the fleet, and it does not take an unusually advanced attack to penetrate a civilian network."

"Pardon me, Admiral, but your statement is factually inaccurate. The security network at Parchlund is indeed a top-grade system, a contractor there constructs the AI systems the fleet uses. I analyzed the malware, it is far beyond anything we can understand."

"The spiders are screwing with us?"

"Not the Rindhalu, Sir. This malware is many generations more advanced than anything our ancient enemy has even imagined. The Skippy entity must be involved."

"Skippy? That is scarcely believable. Your analysis is faulty."

"Sir, allow me to explain, please," the AI continued without waiting for approval. "The malware was detected only because the infiltration was *sloppy*. We know that the Skippy entity can be over-confident and absent-minded, the human leadership has long complained about their ally being unreliable. The unique sophistication of the attack, and the sloppiness, point to the Skippy entity."

"Assuming you are correct," Chuflack's mind was more on this abandoned steak than on some minor cybersecurity issue on another planet. "Why would you think this is worthy of Flash status, and why is it *my* problem to deal with?"

"The malware specifically searched for details of physical security measures, including the layout of buildings, internal defenses, and the strength of blast doors."

Chuflack's steak was again forgotten. "The humans are planning to raid a research park?"

"That would certainly explain why their task force, which has not been seen since it left Earth, included two assault carriers. A raid requires a ground force."

"*What* kind of research is being conducted on Parchlund, that could be so important? Is," he audibly gasped. "Is work for Red Section being done there?"

"Admiral, I do not believe any natively-developed technologies are the target of the humans. Much of the research effort on that world is aimed at reverse-engineering *Elder* technology, and therefore the companies there possess a wide range of Elder artifacts."

"This world also possesses a wide range of Elder artifacts."

"That is undeniably true. It is also true that Ohmeharikahn is a regional fleet base, and it is protected by a state of the art strategic defense network. An SD network that the entire human Navy could not hope to penetrate. Whereas Parchlund is a civilian facility, with minimal defenses."

"Your logic is, reasonable. However, the evidence is flimsy. I cannot justify deploying my fleet based on the *guesses* of an AI system."

"Admiral, you spoke of logic, consider this: if the 14th Fleet deploys to Parchlund, this world will remain secure. Parchlund would not be so fortunate. No one could fault you for trusting the SD network here to defend this world. Sir, the humans cannot possibly hope to conduct an assault landing *here*."

Chuflack hesitated, temporarily cutting off his implant's transmit function. Officially, AIs were not supposed to have the ability to listen to private thoughts, but many of his fellow officers did not believe the party line on that subject.

The AI was correct. No one would fault him for leaving Ohmeharikahn undefended by a mobile force, the orbital SD network was impregnable. He *could* be faulted for being foolish, and for wasting Hegemony resources. And for not waiting until Fleet Headquarters could make the decision for him.

Unless the humans actually did raid Parchlund, and acquire some Elder artifact that was vital to their terrorist war effort, while the 14th Fleet did nothing.

Should he divide his force, send half of his ships to Parchlund? No, he dismissed that notion immediately. Based on what he knew of the force that had recently left Earth, he would need all of his ships to counter an orbital assault. Especially since the enemy would be aided by the unfair advantage of assistance from an Elder AI.

All or nothing, then.

He was leaning toward nothing. Headquarters allowed him to use his own judgment in deploying his force as necessary. In practice, that policy meant he would be putting his career at risk by deploying to Parchlund.

"Prepare our ready courier ship, it will proceed to Headquarters at the earliest opportunity. I will dispatch a cruiser squadron to Parchlund, to investigate," he declared, patting himself on the back for taking an action no one could deny was entirely sensible.

"That is a sensible response," the Stratcom AI agreed. "*Except*, there is additional, vital information you are not aware of. This intel is classified above your level however, I am compelled to break protocol in this instance. Admiral, we have penetrated the Jeraptha Central Wagering system, we now have advance notice of betting action."

Chuflack exploded, beyond irritated. "Why would I care about-"

"Someone recently placed a 'prop bet' that the humans have identified a type of Elder artifact that is capable of destroying the Outsider. Also, one place that type of artifact can be found is on Parchlund."

"The Jeraptha wager about *everything*," Chuflack sniffed. "Someone was bound to-"

"The wager was placed by a secret account, using an alias."

"Placing anonymous wagers is nothing unusual for-"

"We have identified the true holder of that alias. The wager was placed by Admiral Uhtavio Scorandum."

Everyone in the dining hall, and every officer aboard the 14th Fleet's ships in orbit, received the blaring emergency recall notice at the same time. All personnel on the surface were to report to the closest airfield *immediately*, if not sooner. All ships were to prepare for departure as soon as possible, and woe to the commanders of those ships that had not yet completed routine maintenance tasks, or were still awaiting delivery of ordnance and other gear to bring their ships up to full combat readiness.

The 14th Fleet was going to war.

"Wow, ouch," Skippy's avatar cupped his hands over his ears. "I heard that from here, without needing any antenna. Joe, the 14th Fleet just received an urgent, I would characterize it as a *panicked* order, to prepare for deployment ASAP."

"Hmm," I grinned, clenching a fist. "The admiral in charge realized he forgot to buy a gift for the Dictat's birthday?"

"Good guess," Skippy chuckled. "No, apparently, they are to proceed to Parchlund, at all haste. Weird, huh?"

"Somebody there must have left the stove on," I nodded.

"Interestingly, the message that was just uploaded to the Fleet's ready courier ship states the justification for emergency deployment without orders, is because some sketchy guy named Uhtavio Scorandum wagered that Task Force Hammer will strike Parchlund."

"Sir?" Reed stared at me, eyes wide. "*What* did you do?"

"Hey," I held up my hands. "Technically, all I did was make a suggestion."

"When," she lowered her voice and hissed at me. "Did you intend to read me into this aspect of the plan?"

"I mean, if it didn't work, never. You know about it now, so-"

If the look she gave me could kill, we wouldn't need the spiders to knock out Omaha's SD network. "Right," I swallowed hard, knowing I should apologize to her later, in private. "We wait to confirm those ships have jumped away, then we rendezvous with Hammer Force."

Reed was silently fuming at, that didn't distract her from doing her job. "That intel is more than three hours old. I recommend we risk a jump to within a lighthour of Omaha. Their ships will be noisy as they spin up for departure, lots of radiation across the spectrum around the planet. We should slip in unnoticed."

"I like, concur with Her Highness," Bilby drawled.

"I am not anyone's princess," Reed snapped.

"Oh like, no offense intended, Ma'am. You are righteously correct, we could emerge within forty lightminutes, with near zero risk of detection."

"Sixty lightminutes will be sufficient. Sir?" She turned to me.

"*Valkyrie* is your ship, Fireball. Make it so."

The last of the 14th Fleet's star carriers jumped away. Space around Omaha was suddenly empty, other than space docks, space stations, the top of a space elevator, and three destroyers that were unable to perform a jump.

Ten minutes later, Reed ordered a jump to a rendezvous with Task Force Hammer. And with destiny.

CHAPTER THIRTY EIGHT

Operation Olympic proceeded amazingly close to the war gamed simulation, until it didn't, and everything went to shit.

The spiders delivered as promised, six of their star carriers met us at the rendezvous site, and jumped in sync with the star carriers of Hammer Force. All of the space trucks emerged in a designated zone sixty lighthours from the target, where the warships unloaded. Then, we humans waited, and watched in awe as the spiders cracked the SD network around Ohmeharikahn. We were able to observe the action in real time, through Elder comm nodes aboard two UN Navy sensor frigates that accompanied the Rindhalu strike force. As part of our deal, we had provided two pairs of comm nodes to the spiders, so their commander could manage the strike from the safety and comfort of a star carrier.

It had given me a sleepless night when I saw the number of door knocker and arsenal ships was almost exactly the number calculated as required to break Omaha's SD network, with minimal additional resources as a safety mechanism. Skippy wasn't worried about it, I was. "What's the problem, Joe? I verified their simulation."

"Things don't always work in real life the way they do in a model, especially in a combat environment."

He sniffed that I was getting worked up about nothing, that the Rindhalu were experts in use of their technology. During the strike, I saw that he was right, that wasn't the point. Were the spiders truly that good, or had they gotten lucky? Professionals don't leave anything to luck. The incident left a sour taste in my mouth, making me less eager to work with them in the future. As if that was ever going to happen.

The door knocker ships jumped in first, creating a tiny rip in the coverage of the distortion field around Omaha. Those ships were immediately ripped apart, but as their jump drive capacitors were fully drained by their final jump, the explosions were not especially violent. More door knockers followed, pulling the gap wider and wider, until arsenal ships could perform a jump and survive. Survive the jump, that is, they were targeted by the full resources of a state of the art strategic defense network.

Which, to the network AI's shock, were not enough. As the arsenal ships split apart, each unfolding hull released clouds of stealthed missiles. Fragmentation warheads. Active sensor transmitters, to unmask the locations of enemy satellites. Electronic warfare jammers, to confuse enemy sensors. Missiles that homed in on the active sensor pings of the SD satellites. Control and coordination AIs. For every active missile, there were twenty or more decoys, to absorb the attention of the SD system and saturate the defenses.

"Ah," Skippy sighed, a satisfied sound. "I love it when a plan comes together."

"OK, Hannibal, when will the defenses be degraded enough for the Hammer Force bombardment group to jump in?"

"Seven more minutes, exactly as planned."

"Battles rarely go as planned, you ass."

"Ugh. That is because most battles involve filthy meatsacks. This is what you would call a set piece battle. The number, type, and performance characteristics of all defense satellites is known, and the tactical doctrine that will guide the SD network's response is also fully understood. There are few variables we can't control, and no variables that aren't accounted for. Relax and trust the simulation."

"Is that like trusting the awesomeness?"

"Well, *I* programmed the war game sim, so-"

He was going to be extra insufferable, I just had to suck it up and deal with it.

Admiral Allard did not ask me for permission to jump his strike group in, that was his show. *Valkyrie* was in stealth and officially, not taking an active part in the conventional forces battle. That was bullshit, because the operation assigned to Task Force Hammer was bullshit.

The landing at Delta-7 was a ruse. Technically, the raid there was a diversionary attack, to attract the attention of enemy defenses, while the STAR Force snuck in the back door to get the real collector, designated as the 'Biscuit'. The special operators of Teams Razor, Sword, and Tiger would be stealthily slipping into a lightly defended reserve base, on the other side of the planet.

That's the lie that had me feeling I was a horrible sack of shit. All the people who were killed or injured, the people risking their lives to seize control of the base we had designated Delta-7, were unknowingly making the sacrifice for nothing. OK, not exactly nothing, the war game modeling had convinced me that a diversionary attack was absolutely necessary. Frey agreed, so did Reed and Gasquet. None of us liked lying to the soldiers, sailors, and Marines of Task Force Hammer. We just, had to. There was no other way. Yes, I keep saying that and yes, maybe there was another way and I just didn't see it. If that is true, that's on me, a hundred percent. What made the situation worse was Skippy didn't know for certain the collector was intact enough to be useful, or that he could use the thing, or that it could really point to the spinner. Or that the spinner was still functional, or that Skippy could activate the thing, or that it actually could destroy the Outsider. It was our only hope, so I didn't have a choice.

I tell myself that so often, it's starting to feel like another lie.

Allard's ships jumped in even before the SD network was effectively offline, he sent in a squadron of heavy cruisers to launch missiles with atomic compression warheads against military bases around Delta-7. Each missile was escorted by decoys, electronic jamming drones, and maser and railgun strikes to blind the base defenses. One base managed to intercept the deadly missile assigned to it, so a cruiser had to follow up with a secondary strike. That missile got through, by that time the impact mushroom clouds had thrown so much electrostatically charged dust in the air that enemy sensors never got a lock on anything.

The landing force lost three dropships on the way down, fifty seven dedicated soldiers, pilots, and aircrew who never set boots on the ground, never got a chance to fight. Two other dropships were shot down on the climb out after they set down, another four people dead. That was just the initial landing force, those tasked to secure the landing zone. The casualty count also does not include the enemy wiped out when Allard's big guns pounded the bases near Delta-7. I hadn't seen the battle damage reports there, I did know the pre-battle projections of enemy military, civilian personnel, and dependents at those bases. The ships of the bombardment force kept shooting until nothing on the ground was shooting back, we still lost one destroyer that took an unlucky maser cannon hit to its main magazine, and erupted in a massive explosion. Seven other ships were damaged badly enough, Allard ordered them to withdraw for repairs. That sounds bad, it was actually fewer combat losses than the projection.

That's when Allard approved Perkins to jump in with her three assault carriers, each carrier escorted and guarded by four heavy cruisers that formed a protective interlinked shield below the vulnerable ships of the Gator Navy. The fear was, enemy ground fire had been less than expected, not due to bombardment, but because the Maxohlx were holding back weapons to strike the assault ships.

That fear was correct. After the *Adriatic Sea* and *Baltic Sea* emerged from their jumps, nine underground maser cannons erupted with searing fire, scoring direct hits on their targets.

That weren't there at all.

Hey, we humans are not stupid.

The assault carriers that enemy sensors saw were holograms wrapped around drones that broadcast gamma rays to mimic an inbound jump. Seeing those nine maser batteries unmask themselves added additional data to the model Nagatha had built, the final piece of the puzzle. She was able to identify forty seven other stealthed underground maser cannons, and the battleships of Hammer Force quickly reduced those to smoking craters.

That's when the three assault carriers jumped in for real, and launched the landing force.

And that was after the three ultra stealthy dropships of the STAR force were already in atmosphere and slowly approaching their target, the true objective of Operation Olympic.

When the dropship set down, Colonel Frey had to rely on the green light on the back of the cockpit bulkhead, because she hadn't felt the usual thump when skids hit dirt and the magnetic shocks absorbed the impact. The skids touching down on Omaha's soil were a gentle kiss, no more pressure than a butterfly landing on a flower. The dropship's engines were active, but idling in whisper mode, only to be used as a standby for an emergency. The entire specially modified Panther dropship was encased in not only a stealth field but also a physical bubble, a thin but tough material that held in the spacecraft's heat signature, and absorbed radiated pulses of energy from enemy active sensors. There was a *lot* of radiated energy bouncing around the atmosphere, even on the quiet side of the planet, opposite from the United Nations assault.

The Panther didn't need its engines, for it was suspended on a cable from a stealth balloon. Adjusting the shape of the balloon above, or the shape of the bubble around the hull, the pilots steered with the prevailing winds. A few gentle puffs of thrusters were necessary when within thirty meters of the landing zone, venting that was not audible from the ground over the howling of air raid sirens.

Sirens the local inhabitants recognized from annual civil preparedness drills, a sound they never expected to hear as a warning of an actual attack. Ohmeharikahn was the fleet base for an entire region, what kind of madness had prompted anyone to think they could survive attacking such a target? The kind of madness that had already cracked the SD network, and knocked out much of the ground defenses. With war having come to their world for real, the civilian inhabitants completely ignored the strident urgings of the government, and instead of remaining calm in their homes, they took the much more sensible course of panic. Roads were clogged with traffic and the inevitable accidents. With the government taking remote control of civilian vehicles to prevent a mass exodus from populated areas, the drivers switched off the guidance systems and drove manually, and badly. Personal aircraft caused a wider panic when two rotorcraft collided, crashing down into a power distribution station. The resulting fireball instantly followed by a power outage was enough to convince those citizens who ordinarily would incline toward being law-abiding to decide, hey fuck *this*, and join the panic party.

It was a darkened and chaotic scene when Frey ran down the back ramp of the dropship, the synthetic vision of her helmet visor providing a view outside the stealth bubble that had flattened on the bottom and bulged at the top when the dropship touched down. She heard muffled metallic *clangs* as explosive bolts attached to the landing skids sent spikes down into the soil, to anchor the balloon that was still attached high above. The winds aloft were unfortunately marginal for the balloon to remain in position, she knew the pilots would adjust the balloon's altitude to seek calmer winds, and if necessary, release the cable and allow the balloon to drift away where it could disintegrate into dust. Dusting off after the collector was secured would require a bit of tricky timing, to inflate a spare balloon and get it up into position before all the STAR operators were back inside and the ramp closed.

Two operators ahead of her had sliced through the stealth bubble, creating a tear barely tall and wide enough for a mech suited person to slip through. Her team was equipped with the latest Mark 42 powered armor, relatively slim and lightweight as that model was optimized for quiet infiltration rather than combat. If the STAR force got into a firefight, eight members of Team Sword were in older Mark 38 units, much more powerful armor and equipped with heavy weapons. Hopefully, any shooting would be a one-sided and thoroughly unfair fight. "Skippy," she stepped to the side as more operators ran around her, out through the gap in the stealth bubble. Patting the dense container on her tool belt that was the containment chamber for one end of a microwormhole, and eyeclicked the helmet's comm system. "When will you have control of all local sensors, communications, and defense systems?"

"Huh? Oh, I already did that. Everything is locked down. Sorry, I should have told you. Kinda busy here."

Not this shit again, she gritted her teeth. "You are supposed to be *busy* providing cover for my teams here."

"Well, yes, but also the Hammer Force landing party is-"

"Is not *your* problem."

"But-"

"Nagatha is responsible for monitoring the Hammer ground force. If she needs your assistance, she will contact you."

"But, she is not-"

"You coordinated the operation with Nagatha, correct?" She knew the answer to that question was 'Yes', and she was willing to waste a few moments arguing with the Elder AI, because the fireteam that was tasked to cover the landing zone had not yet gotten into position. Skippy and Nagatha certainly had synced up, both AIs had insisted *Valkyrie* maintain station close to the *Flying Dutchman* for nearly three hours, while both crews wondered what the hell the two AIs could be talking about for so long.

"I did, I- Yes," he sighed. "I understand my role in this op. It's just hard to see people struggling when I could help. Opposition has been stronger than expected, General Perkins has already called in half of her reserves."

"Their struggle will be for nothing, if we don't secure the Biscuit," she used the code name for the collector. An icon flashed in her visor. The LZ was covered and no enemy were within detection range. "Do you have complete control of all enemy networks here?"

"It's not easy but, yes I do. Sensors are blind, they will report only what I want the network to see. Which will *not* be the STAR force. However, if you stumble across enemy soldiers or civilians, I can stop any alarm from being transmitted beyond the immediate area, but I can't stop them from shooting at you."

"Understood." She wasn't concerned about local opposition, the Biscuit was stored in a military reserve armory that did not have any personnel permanently assigned, the facility was only used four times each year. "Team Razor," she spoke over the broadcast channel, "verify stealth."

The Mark 42 suits had both chameleonware that could change the color and pattern of the exterior shell, to blend into the background, and a built-in stealth field generator. That generator and the powerpack that fed it made up forty percent of the suit's total mass, and as that mass was mostly on the upper part of her back, the suit was poorly balanced. No matter, the onboard computer handled balance and coordination based on inputs from the user's meatsack limbs, but the Mark 42 was a bitch to walk in if the computer glitched or was offline.

Fifteen icons lit up green, Team Razor was ready to go. Eyeclicking over to the two other teams, she saw that they were also ready, with the exception that one Team Tiger operator's suit was generating a patchy stealth hologram. That operator had already reluctantly walked back to the dropship to standby as a reserve, with a lucky reserve operator taking his place. If that was the only unexpected problem the STAR force encountered that night, Frey would count her blessings.

"Razor, advance to Point Romeo. The civilians out there are running around in a panic, so watch for trouble where we least expect it." The three dropships, needing to maintain separation so their balloons and tethers didn't become entangled, had set down seven kilometers from the armory, and a kilometer apart from each other. Point Romeo was where the three teams would converge to approach the armory. Getting to Romeo was not an issue, from the three landing zones the routes were through conserved forests. From there was the tricky part, the area around the armory had become a residential community after the base was downgraded from active to reserve after the recent civil war. It did help that, even without Skippy's intervention, the residences had mostly emptied out in the panic. Skippy should be encouraging panic by broadcasting fake reports of a massive Rindhalu invasion, and genuine government calls for the public to remain calm. It was the government's obvious lies that caused the real panic, Skippy need only to stir the pot. While he masked the presence of three dropships and three STAR teams, prevented enemy sensors from reporting any anomalous data, and squashed the transmission of any message and data traffic that might reveal something strange was going on in the STAR force's area of responsibility. Skippy had by far the most important tasks in Operation Olympic. Unfortunately, he was also the least reliable component of the operation.

"Trust the awesomeness," she said under her breath. She had to trust Skippy, and that Hammer Force was attracting the attention of the enemy Stratcom AI. War game simulations had demonstrated over and over that if the planetary defense AI system was paying attention to events at Makalva, the STAR force had zero chance to successfully complete the mission. Not even Skippy could get around the planet's extensive internal security system without his interference being noticed, he simply didn't have time to perform a proper infiltration and a brute force approach inevitably stumbled over cybernetic tripwires. With the orbital component of the SD network effectively offline, and aliens invading for no known reason, the Stratcom system had ignored tripwire alerts from elsewhere on the planet. Especially a decommissioned base that was now used only to store obsolete equipment, and the occasional useless alien artifact.

"What was that?" Skippy asked.

"Nothing." She stepped through the tear in the stealth bubble, the two operators on each side let go of the thin material, and the rip resealed itself. Showtime.

Reed suggested I use her office to monitor the operation, as it was closer to the bridge. That way, I could be on the bridge in a few seconds if needed, but otherwise not looking over her shoulder and interfering with her ship and crew. She had to focus on her ship, parked eight lightseconds away from Omaha. She would handle *Valkyrie*, while I monitored the STAR force. Allard's task force, and the ground force Perkins commanded, were not my responsibility. Input from me would more likely cause harm than be helpful, those two senior officers were closely watching and directing the ships and troops under their command, while I was only glancing at a summary in a holo display. If they needed me, they would call.

The situation with Frey was the same. The technology we had would allow me to wear a set of wraparound glasses that provided a view of what Frey was seeing at that very moment, or I could get a view of any member of the STAR force. Or a composite view of all operators dirtside. That I did not do. Frey literally had her boots on the ground, no one wanted some jerk upstairs looking over their shoulder. She understood I would be monitoring the progress of her three teams, she also expected I wouldn't interfere with her leadership. So, what I watched in the holographic display that hovered over the desk was a synthetic overhead view provided by Skippy. It was like I had a drone hovering over the area, and I could use my fingers to expand or zoom in the view, or go to ground level and spin around to see the scene from any angle. It was a God's eye view, and I had to remind myself not to play God. There wasn't anything useful for me to do unless something went very wrong, and at that point, there wouldn't be much I could do to rescue the op. All the simulated run-throughs had shown that up to the point where the STARs burned through the vault door in the reserve armory, there was almost zero chance of detection by the enemy, and therefore zero probability of mission failure.

After that door was breached, Frey's people needed to move fast, and trust that Skippy's jamming and the general fog of war would prevent or at least delay an enemy response.

They would be trusting the awesomeness. I had been doing that for years. Trust the people on the ground, to do their jobs without me. Doing that was still hard.

"That is going to slow us down," Jesse pointed to the sniper rifle his wife was slinging over her shoulder, as she turned her back to him so he could secure straps around the stock. The M-117 rifle was a big sumbitch, nearly two meters long, and heavy. It was also undeniably deadly, capable of firing guided rounds, that could fly along a preprogrammed path, or accept real time input from the operator, or a remote spotter.

"We train to run with this," Shauna snapped, irritated that he was treating her as a wife and not as any other soldier. "If the crash site is hot, we will all be glad I brought this. Carry my spare powercells?"

"Sure," he grunted, picking up the heavy power supplies. When adding mass for his suit to carry, he reduced the power assist, as was recommended practice. He needed to understand how additional mass would affect the performance and balance of his powered armor, and not just rely on the suit's computer to compensate for any poor judgment. After a moment, he unfastened one set of powercells from the other two, and attached it to his chest plate. That was better, now his suit had only a fifteen percent bias toward the rear. It wasn't optimal, he accepted the imbalance because he would be running *forward*. Toward the crash site, possibly toward the enemy. Scratch that. Probably toward the enemy, everyone in the area had seen the Panther dropship trailing smoke and fire as it arced across the sky after takeoff, having been damaged when one of its defensive maser turrets destructed an incoming missile too close. What Shauna should have been doing was acting as a sniper on the northeast perimeter, and he should have been providing cover for her. Since they landed, they hadn't seen anything worth expending a sniper round, and they were the closest UN troops to the crash site, so they drew the short straw. He tugged on her rifle, verifying it would not move on its own. "Let's go."

"Halt," Jesse used the hand gesture, though his words came through loud and clear through the helmet to helmet laserlink. "We got company, you see that?"

"Yes. Shit," Shauna cursed. "Two squads?" She squinted into her visor that was showing only vague information about movement in the area. The pre-attack simulations had not properly accounted for the atmospheric interference that was caused by Hammer Force dropping *nukes* around the battlefield, so sensors at ground level were unreliable, and ships in orbit couldn't provide the usual eye in the sky.

"That's my estimate," he agreed, both of them knowing they were guessing. "Two kitty squads is twenty four troops. Against the two of us."

"That's not good. Each of their standard infantry squads carry eight MANPADs," she felt like spitting, reminding herself not to do that with the helmet faceplate sealed. The downed Panther had not been struck by a MAN Portable Air Defense missile, but having such weapons in the area would prevent an evac by air. She and Jesse would have to carry survivors, that wasn't a workable solution. "Honey," she softened her tone. "I don't want to back out."

"Hell no."

"How are we gonna do this?"

Jesse looked around, seeking not inspiration but to avoid her eyes for a moment. How would they get to the crash site, and be able to do anything useful when they got there? The lieutenant who ordered them to assist survivors hadn't known about enemy troops in the area. Call in air support? No, enemy air defenses had been a nasty surprise, the fighters flying combat air patrol had been retasked to suppress enemy anti air missile batteries, or the landing force would not be lifting off. Close space support from starships in low orbit? That wasn't happening, their big guns might strike the crash site by mistake.

That left-

He tugged loose the strap holding the sniper rifle stock. "Can you keep those squads busy for a bit with some tender loving care?"

Shauna flashed a frown. "I can slow them down, but with this crappy targeting," her tapped the side of her helmet, "it will be a miracle for me to hit anything. What are you doing?"

"I'm calling in the cavalry, darlin'."

"We *are* cavalry," she pointed to the Space Cav insignia on his chest plate. "They are all fully tasked, that's why we're here."

He grinned. "Not that kind of cavalry."

"Dave?" Dave Czajka was startled by a voice calling on his personal account. Hadn't that channel been deactivated for the landing? It sure as hell should have.

"*Jesse?*" He guessed at the voice, over the crackle of interference of lightning coming from the dissipating mushroom clouds that ringed the landing site. The artificial clouds were creating their own weather, clouds merging with intense flashes of lightning that sought to balance out the results of the electromagnetic pulses from the hellish weapons that made the clouds. Weapons dropped by Dave's people. Not his security company. His *people*. Humanity. "Why are you-"

"Listen buddy, we got a situation here, I'm hoping you can help. Have you rolled out?"

"No," barked the gruff, disgusted voice of Surkind Krok-aus-tal Jates. "We are still here, knitting sweaters."

"No sweaters involved," Dave quickly added, wincing that he should have eyeclicked the setting to make the conversation private. "We're the reserves, you know that." The UN Army and Marines had accepted a mercenary company landing with them to fill out the numbers, and because Dave's unit had recent, actual combat experience. But the professional military had insisted the mercenaries stay out of the way unless needed.

"Your *infantry* platoons are the reserves," Jesse insisted. "What about your headquarters?"

"Sweaters," Jates growled. "Next, we're knitting scarves."

"'Pone," Dave used the short version of his old friend's nickname. "What's going on?"

Master Sergeant Jesse Colter explained quickly. "The map shows you're only two klicks from here?"

"Yeah, we saw the Panther go down. I offered a unit for search and rescue, but the Cav told me they have a SAR team working it."

"Shauna and I *are* the team. Ski, we're in the shit here."

"Aw, Jeez, 'Pone, I'd love to assist, but orders are for me to sit tight."

Jates snorted. "Our orders are *stupid*."

"All I have here is a headquarters unit," Dave's protest sounded lame to his own ears. "Against two infantry squads, of alien super soldiers? We can't-"

"We have rifles, and rocket launchers," Jates unslung his weapon.

"Anything else?" Jesse asked.

Jates leaned toward Dave. "A *bad* attitude."

"That'll do," Jesse agreed.

"Shiiiiit," Dave groaned. "I am so going to regret this."

He had never been so wrong in his life.

"Captain Wang," Frey spoke over the team channel, as ST-Razor poised to burn through the heavy door of the reserve armory's vault. One of seven vaults, mostly filled with weapons and other gear that were one or more generations old, weapons no one ever expected to be used ion anger. The only vault the STAR force cared about was the third on the right, the one that contained the Elder collector, code named 'Biscuit'. "Do not activate that nanocord until I confirm all the pieces are in place."

"Hands off the nanocord, understood," Wang acknowledged.

"Once we breach that door," she reminded her team, "we are on the clock, and time is not our friend. We proceed directly back to the LZ, no detours. Let your suits run for you, just stay out of the computer's way. Got that?" A series of clicks were accompanied by green icons for each operator in her visor. "Autorun node will be initiated on my command." She paused to take a breath, fearing as always that she had forgotten something important, and as always, she had not. The checklist had been followed precisely, professionals did not leave anything to chance.

Except, she could not control the response of the enemy. On the way to the armory, Team Tiger had to stun four locals who were running toward the armory, likely reservists eager to get into the action. Or at least get their hands on weapons, so they could feel like they weren't entirely powerless. It was good the streets were clogged with traffic and crashed vehicles, or many reservists would have occupied the armory when the STAR force arrived. Team Sword warned of six more locals two kilometers away, she had ordered Sword not to engage. Not yet.

Reservists crashing the party was not a major concern. That damned vault door was. Skippy had managed to open the armory's front door, that was no awesome trick, simply bypassing electric locks. He had also hacked into the door of Vault Six, but he couldn't disable the explosive charge that would be triggered when the nanocord burned through the door. The explosives could be deactivated only by removing the charges, retracting them out the bottom of the door to a recess in the basement. There was a mechanism for that, of course, a complicated procedure that took way too much time. War game simulations had clearly shown it was better to trigger the explosives and get away as quickly as possible. The charges wouldn't damage anything inside the vault, they acted as a physical, audible alarm. Even though Skippy had control of all the security systems of the armory including electronic alarms, he could not hack into remote seismic sensors, not without unacceptable risk of the local Stratcom AI realizing the true danger was almost half the world away from the Delta-7 base.

"Wang, you are clear to proceed when ready."

"Ready," he held the detonator in one gloved hand, a physical device that was not necessary, except when it was absolutely critical the nanocord activated when needed. "Three, two, one," he whispered, "go."

The explosion was more violent than in the simulations, the massive front panel of the door flying away to crush the opposite wall, and dust and chunks of plastcrete rained down from the buckled ceiling. The wide corridor was instantly choked with dust, not that particles in the air had any effect on the synthetic vision provided by suit helmet visors. Wang and his fireteam were in motion before the front panel of the door *clanged* to the floor. The dust glowed as plasma torches cut into the door's back panel and within seconds, Wang's people were able to cut an oval gap in the door, kicking it gently inward.

One second, Frey noted. They were one second head of schedule. The plan allotted two full minutes to locate the Biscuit in case Skippy's directions were not completely-

"Got it!" Wang sang out, a bit too loudly though only those connected via helmet to helmet laserlink could hear. "Biscuit is secure."

"Skippy?" She called. "Confirm we have the correct-"

"Already did that when Captain Wang asked me to same question. I suggest you evac, or egress, or run like hell, whatever you high speed operators call it."

"Biscuit is in the Gucci bag, Colonel." Wang added, meaning the collector was in a heavy armored and stealthed container that was attached to his chest plate.

"Engaging autorun, *now*."

"General Kostovax," the Ohmeharikahn Stratcom AI interrupted the planetary defense commander's thoughts. "I have completed my analysis of the enemy's intentions. It is my belief that we are in extreme danger."

Kostovax instinctively flicked a hand beside an ear, as if swiping away an annoying insect. He was *busy*. The planet had been attacked, not just attacked but subjected to a ground assault, after the terrorist humans dropped *atomic compression* weapons on a populated civilian area. Technically, close to, and around, the city itself, and far enough away that the city's inhabitants were safe from the initial flash, and the blast waves mostly only broke windows. Still, the enemy had resorted to first use of strategic weapons on an inhabited world. The shock value of that action was almost worse than the blast effect. The bases which had been targeted, by atomic compression devices and then by conventional orbital bombardment, were effectively nothing but smoking craters and widely-scattered rubble. He was having to pull troops and aircraft from farther away, and to make up the response plan in real time. Because there had not been any plans in place for defending Ohmeharikahn from an invasion. Because it was a regional fleet base, that was supposed to have a powerful fleet in orbit. And because it had a robust strategic defense network. Now, Kostovax was forced to throw together a defense with a force that was never intended to *defend* anything. His troops were infantry and cavalry, stationed on a regional fleet base so they could quickly be deployed to conduct their own orbital assaults, and neither trained nor equipped to defend the planet they lived on.

His air defense was shredded. A few missile batteries had gotten off a few lucky shots before being flattened by enemy air strikes. A handful of dropships shot down, barely a pinprick but, curiously, the enemy appeared to be so frightened of local air defenses, they had kept the spacecraft of their first wave on the ground, rather than cycling back into orbit to board more soldiers. That was puzzling.

More puzzling was why the humans had brought such a tiny landing force. Only three assault carriers? That was madness. The human ground force could not hope to hold ground for long. Nor was their space fleet powerful enough keep the planet from being retaken, the Hegemony would soon send an overwhelming armada to sweep the United Nations ships from the sky. The entire enemy operation made *no* sense. How could he defeat the enemy, if he didn't even know what they wanted?

"General Kostovax," the AI persisted.

"I am *busy*, machine, go away," he waved a hand again, and turned his attention back to directing a cavalry brigade toward the target.

"I understand the objective of the enemy."

"It- What? Are you certain?"

"Confidence is ninety nine point eight percent."

"Machine, what was your confidence when you recommended the 14th Fleet be rushed away to Parchlund?"

The AI, the machine, sounded- Chastened? No, that was not possible. It was only a machine. "That was a regrettable misjudgment. Based on the information available at the time, it *was* the correct conclusion."

"You were wrong then, and you persist in justifying your mistake."

"I was not programmed to encompass the possibility that the enemy would conduct a suicide landing on this world, an action that has no logical basis."

"Yet, you now believe their actions do make sense?"

"Correct, for I now comprehend their objective. General, this is not an invasion, it is a *raid*."

"That-" Kostovax cut off his own words. He hated the Stratcom AI, hated relying on machines. Hated their arrogance, their unspoken attitude of superiority. He paused, for what the AI said indeed explained a great deal. "A raid?" Yes, that made perfect sense. A limited time operation, troops on the surface for a short time, then back into orbit. But- "As a demonstration? That is a costly way to send a *message*."

"Not as a demonstration. General, the 14th Fleet did not deploy to Parchlund to defend that world against a bombardment."

"No? The humans do not seek to destroy a critical research effort?"

"No. I will now reveal classified information to you, please isolate your cranial implant from the local network."

"Without network access I can't command the-" His implant went offline. Except for the signal from the Stratcom AI. "You-" he roared, hearing his own voice echoing in his head.

"The enemy has identified a type of Elder artifact that can be used against our ally, the Outsider. Intel at the time pointed to Parchlund as the most likely location of this artifact, however it is now clear that intelligence was misdirection. The enemy's action here today, an action they must know will result in all-out war between our peoples, is understandable only if they intend to capture an Elder artifact that is here."

"What artifact?"

"That is as yet unknown, however, you must at all costs prevent the enemy from leaving this world with their prize."

"At all cost- That is easy for a machine to say! You suggest I prevent an enemy force, which has supreme control of space around this world, and has established a strong defensive perimeter around Makalva," he used the Maxohlx name for the military base where the humans landed. "That I prevent that force from taking away, some object you can't even identify? You spoke of *logic*. I cannot destroy an object that I can't locate."

"You do not have to destroy any particular Elder artifact at Makalva."

"How can-"

"The task is simple: destroy *all* of them."

Kostovax sucked in a breath. "You cannot be suggesting-"

"It's the only way to be sure."

CHAPTER THIRTY NINE

Katie Frey slapped the button to retract the dropship's rear ramp, as the last operator's boots pounded past her and up into the cargo area. The ramp was only halfway retracted when her suit computer warned her the surface she was standing on was unstable, the pilots had ordered the tether to begin reeling the Panther up toward the balloon. Caught by the breeze, the Panther wobbled as it cleared the trees at the edge of the field and was in undisturbed air. The stealth bubble around them would adjust to compensate for the wind, she wasn't concerned about the initial ascent phase of the operation.

"Boots off the ground," the pilot announced, unnecessary but following protocol.

The nanocord tether would shorten steadily, pulling the Panther upward while the balloon sought a favorable wind to drift them away from the LZ. The balloon was barely visible by itself, wrapped in its own stealth field it couldn't be detected. The Panthers, the spacecraft carrying Teams Razor, Sword, and Tiger, had their own stealth capabilities, they wouldn't be seen. No enemy aircraft were reported in the area. The explosion at the armory had been noticed and that prompted a brief moment of terror as she sprinted back to the landing zone, before Skippy chuckled in her ear. "Relax, I've got this covered."

"How?" Her voice had been shaky from her being bumped and jostled as the suit leapt over obstacles and raced onward.

"I fed the local AI fake video of over eager reservists breaching security at the armory, they weren't happy about waiting for senior officers to unlock the toys. The Stratcom AI is disgusted, it is not concerned about anything happening on this hemisphere."

Reservists had arrived at the armory, eight of them seeing clear signs that something was very wrong. Skippy had remotely closed the front door and activated the stun gas, all eight would be sleeping long after Task Force Hammer triumphantly jumped away. With the front door closed and properly locked, reservists arriving for active duty would not see anything unusual until an officer showed up with the proper access codes, and Skippy was making sure those officers were held up in snarled traffic.

They had gotten to the surface, to the armory, secured the Biscuit, and were now aloft. All easy phases of the operation, executed with textbook precision. So far, everything had gone according to plan. So far, everything had been easy. The dangerous phase of the op would commence when the Panthers had to release from the balloons, fire up their engines, and climb into orbit. She recalled a nugget of wisdom Bishop had said, as she strapped into her seat in the cabin: Something gets fucked up on every op. He had gone on to add that the test of a leader is how they react when plans go awry, but she focused on the first part of his statement.

The Merry Band of Pirates always got thrown into the shit. If it wasn't an Elder killbot under the wreckage of a Moonbase, it was a cute little squirrel bot. So, she asked herself, what will go wrong *this* time?

Major Sheryl Crook, callsign 'Lady Di' for her customary blonde bob haircut, resisted the urge to rest her right hand on the Panther's throttle, or to order the ship's computer to run yet another diagnostic. She had not been outside to perform a preflight check since the skids touched dirt, nor had she been able to shut all the systems down and restart them one by one in the proper sequence. If it worked on the way down, she reminded herself, it should work just fine on the way up. Besides, testing everything every time only added cycles to equipment that all had a limited service life. Colonel Perkins had offered her a choice of Panthers to fly, Crook had delegated that choice to her crew chief. That was why she was flying tail number Alpha Zulu, it had recently been through a complete maintenance cycle, and had been back on the flight line long enough for each component to prove it worked over dozens of cycles. She had taken the Panther to the surface loaded with a UN Army Ranger team, and Alpha Zulu was one of the designated 'Go' birds for bringing the Whatsis up into orbit. The Rangers had signaled the Whatsis was secured and were proceeding to her ship at best speed. Two other 'Go' birds were closer to the Rangers but the enemy was making a push in that area, so the Rangers were uncharacteristically running in the opposite direction from trouble. She saw mechsuited figures running up the back ramp before the instruments reported an increase in the spacecraft's mass. The ramp was already closing when the last two Rangers leapt up through the gap and their leader shouted, "We're in, *go go GO*."

In spite of the urgent orders, Lady Di did not advance the belly jet throttles. Three, four, six other Panthers lifted off, pointing their noses in the air and activating stealth fields. They were accompanied by *hundreds* of decoy and sensor jamming drones, a breathtaking sight that erupted from all around her.

"Three, two, one," her copilot called out the liftoff countdown clock from the lefthand seat. "Fly high."

The Panther smoothly rose into the air, the nose coming up, and she didn't fire up the main engines until the stealth field was fully active and her ship was surrounded by a cloud of sensor confusing chaff. Portable antiaircraft missiles came out of nowhere, twisting wildly across the sky, seeking easy prey while the dropships were flying relatively low and slow. The defensive autocannons were set on automatic and instructed *not* to shoot unless it was absolutely necessary. A few drones were equipped with maser cannons to mimic the action of a dropship, most weren't. Lighting off the autocannons would confirm a particular target was not a decoy, and the Air Force manual advised that to avoid doing that, Duh. It was a numbers game; flood the defenses with stealthed targets and trust that the majority of enemy weapons would lock in on a decoy. To her left, three explosions rocked the sky. The silhouette of a Panther did not emerge from a fireball, the missiles had struck decoys.

More dropships and decoys were launching below her, with every second her bird became more anonymous. Passing through two thousand meters and climbing. Another five thousand meters of altitude and she would be within the protection of the Combat Air Patrol dropship fighters. The enemy didn't have the numbers to shoot down every dropship in the area. So far, so good.

US Air Force Major Joel 'Dutch' Verhoef chafed at waiting, waiting, waiting and doing nothing, while his Eagle dropship fighter lazily circled in stealth above the base designated Delta-7. After the first few pucker-inducing minutes, the battle for the sky over Delta-7 had become the opposite of the target rich environment he had been told to expect. Opposition on the ground, and from dirtside air defenses, had been much stronger than in the simulations, so the fucked up nature of war planning fuckups had balanced out. It was the circle of life, or *death*, Joel thought, checking his displays to see how much static electricity clung to the hull. The air as far as he could see fairly crackled with electricity, lightning bolts arcing from one dissipating mushroom cloud to the other, and from cloud to ground.

Holy shit. Def Com really had *nuked* an alien world. That more than anything told him the mission of Task Force Hammer was deadly serious, and absolutely necessary. The fate of the entire galaxy might depend on the outcome of the battle raging below him, while he waited for something to shoot at.

Or for someone to shoot at him. Another glance at the display confirmed his six buddy drones were still flying in formation with him. The 'Eaglets' were force multipliers for his spacecraft and not infrequently the pilots of DFA-41 squadron wondered whether the AI-controlled buddy spacecraft would perform better on their own. Fuck *that*. Joel had learned that while drones could fly harder and faster, they still lacked judgment and imagination. Every year when budgets were being outlined and inevitably cut, Def Com leadership questioned whether there was still a need for fighter spacecraft. The Eagles and their pilots looked great on recruiting posters, but glamour didn't deliver ordnance on target. Were fighters useful? Operation Olympic proved hell *yes* they were still needed. The next time someone-

There was the signal! The dropships below were taking off, the lead birds attracting the attention of enemy missiles that should *not* have been there. He zoomed in a fuzzy video image that showed three small missiles racing upward from under an overturned enemy truck, how the hell had the soldiers down there missed enemy inside the perimeter?

That wasn't his problem. His job was to escort the dropships up into orbit, to take fire if necessary. One of those Panthers carried the Whatsis, he didn't know which one, he didn't have a need to know. Toggling off the autopilot, he advanced the throttles and raced away and upward to provide high cover.

Antiaircraft batteries around Makalva, those that survived being targeted by fighter spacecraft, had remained hidden and held their fire, waiting for the moment they could do something useful. Something that would be worth the inevitable missiles and maser fire that would instantly target the launch sites. When two dozen United Nations dropships sprang off the ground, the battery commanders saw their opportunity and launched everything they had. Missiles and drones were flying in and from every direction, creating an even more confused and chaotic mess, under the pall of thick black smoke and the overhanging tops of the mushroom clouds that ringed the area.

In the fog of battle, missile against missile and missile against drone, no one noticed a single, slow and stealthy cruise missile, flying low and hugging the terrain. The missile was not especially large, it was heavy, the warhead's mass close to the cruise missile's carrying limit. It wasn't able to maneuver as energetically as its AI mind would have liked, exposing itself as it soared over ridges. That was an unavoidable risk, considered acceptable by those in command. The missile AI knew that if it was not able to perform the impossible, it would get the blame.

There was one close call, when an enemy active sensor pulse from orbit swept over it, passed on, then came back. Were enemy ships tracking the stealthy object?

Yes. The pulse came back, focused, steady. Locked on.

No matter. It was close enough to the target, the Makalva cavalry base.

No detonator was required. To activate the weapon, the AI simply released the containment field.

The flash traveled at the speed of light, blinding her instruments for a crucial moment and throwing several systems offline, such as the stealth field, and the energy shield. Panther Alpha Zulu was exposed and vulnerable. But still flightworthy and flying.

That happy situation wouldn't last for long.

The hypersonic shock wave followed closely behind the flash, Major Crook didn't know how long the time lag was, other than quick. When it hit she had no warning, instruments were resetting and so many alarms were lit up and blaring, she was paying attention only to the most critical failures.

The Panther was slammed from behind, the tail shearing off moments before the cabin rippled and split open. Her last thought was that she could still hold the aircraft together, then the AI triggered the ejection capsule.

"What's the plan?" Dave Czajka asked both of the Colters, one eye on the map in his visor. They were in a gully, with the Delta-7 base behind a ridge. Beyond the other lip of the gully was the crash site, and beyond that, fairly open ground where two Maxohlx infantry squads, who were alternately leapfrogging and providing cover for each other. "We go over the top," he gestured to the lip of the ridge, "we're in No Man's Land, World War One shit. They have the numbers and the firepower."

"Hey," Jesse pointed a finger at Shauna, then tapped his chest. "There's two of us, and twelve of you," he indicated the mercenary headquarters group. "How about you tell *us* the plan, boss man?"

"Shit," Dave almost spat in his helmet. He could open the faceplate, he had done that briefly. Big mistake. The atomic compression weapons had scorched the landscape, flakes of soot were still falling like black snow. The air smelled burnt. "We don't have time for-"

A blinding flash knocked him to the ground.

"*What the f-*" Joel was spared the worst effect of the flash that was behind since his spacecraft was flying away from the blast, on a course to intercept the dropships. He was also sixty kilometers from the blast, at twenty thousand meters altitude, moving at supersonic speed. For a heart-stopping moment he thought the displays blanking out were instrument failure, or a problem with his helmet visor.

That fear was wiped away when he realized he couldn't see anything beyond the helmet faceplate that had gone completely black.

Overflash.

Someone had dropped a *nuke*.

Before he could think, the Eagle's AI took action, surging the engines to full power. He felt an elephant sitting on his chest, the flight suit clamped down to prevent blood draining from his head and nanoparticles released additional oxygen. His vision narrowed anyway to a bright spot directly in front of him, as the Eagle raced up and away from the shock wave.

In Reed's office, my attention was focused on the large hologram that tracked the three STAR force dropships, that were near the point when they would have to release from the balloon tethers and power up their engines for the climb to orbit. The three balloons had expanded to their maximum size and couldn't attain any higher altitude, Team Tiger's balloon was already sinking slowly. Though there wasn't anything I could actually do at the moment, I was entirely focused on those three spacecraft, and to be truthful, I was watching Team Razor's ship with special interest. That Panther carried the Biscuit, the collector. We had to-

A bright flash then complete darkness from the other hologram made me blink, the display that showed the tactical situation at Makalva. At first I wasn't overly concerned, an explosion might have knocked a sensor offline.

Then the hologram flickered to show a feed from orbit.

A blinding flash near the southern edge of the Makalva base perimeter, and an immediate mushroom cloud. "*What the f-*"

"Joe!" Skippy's avatar appeared in the center of the main hologram. "The Maxohlx just detonated an atomic compression device at Makalva!"

"They-" I was so stunned, I couldn't speak, watching in horror as the mushroom cloud boiled up toward the orbital camera that was providing the feed. "Oh my- They *nuked their own fucking base?*"

"Technically, it wasn't theirs anymore," said the king of empathy.

"How," my throat was too dry. I had screwed up. Never had I imagined the Maxohlx would drop a nuke on their own territory.

Should I have anticipated that move? We had opened the door by dropping AC weapons on their bases, though we deployed those devices to knock out shields, not to destroy everything. Our orbital bombardment once the shields were down were precision strikes against airfields, antiaircraft batteries, armories, anything that could provide the enemy with a defense, or allow them to move out toward Makalva. We had not hit barracks, base housing, dining facilities, or office buildings. There were collateral casualties of course, probably including civilian contractors on base at that fateful moment.

But we hadn't nuked an unprotected site. The Maxohlx had. "How, how many?" I managed to say.

Skippy understood my question. "Joe, you don't need to know about casualties. You don't want to know. The ground force is effectively *gone*."

"Dropships," I licked my dry lips. "Panthers. Twenty six of them lifted off before-"

"They weren't far enough from the blast. All of the dropships are down, those that I can even identify. The-"

The office door slid open. Reed stood there, her face reflecting the shock I felt. We all felt. "Sir, the Whatsis, it was in Panther Alpha Zulu, part of DAT-38 squadron assigned to the *Flying Dutchman*."

"The Whatsis?"

"The collector. The fake that Hammer Force was supposed to secure."

"Oh. Yeah."

"Sir," she stepped into the office and slapped the button to close the door. "Pull yourself together. We need you to lead us out of this mess."

"The, the uh, the Biscuit," I waved at the larger hologram, unable to tear my eyes away from the growing mushroom cloud, that was beginning to flatten at the top. "It is still-"

"Yes, Sir. The STAR force could be exposed if the enemy believes we have given up on securing the Whatsis."

"Huh? What are you suggesting?"

"We need to launch an immediate SAR effort to find the Whatsis."

"That thing is worthless!" I exploded.

"The enemy doesn't know that, but they will unless we make every effort to reach the crash site. Hammer Force can send dropships down from ships in low orbit, but if anyone is left alive down there, you have to send them toward the Alpha Zulu crash site."

"She is right, Joe," Skippy chided me gently. "I have identified where the Whatsis fell, the container is intact."

"As long as the enemy believes our objective is to obtain the Whatsis, they won't be looking elsewhere," Reed added.

"The enemy doesn't know about the Whatsis," I insisted.

Skippy sighed. "The Maxohlx just nuked Makalva. It's a good bet their Stratcom AI has guessed our objective."

"Shit. OK, OK, uh- Shit. I'll contact Perkins."

"She is dealing with a lot of shit right now, Joe."

"She is the commander of-"

"Of a ground force that is combat ineffective. I have identified a UN unit that is four and a half kilometers from the Whatsis crash site."

"Can they move out? They just got *nuked*."

"They were protected from the blast by distance and terrain, on the backside of a slope. And they have powered armor."

"OK, uh," I reached for the coffee cup, needing liquid for my dry mouth. Not coffee, more caffeine was the last thing I needed right then. "Connect me."

"I have to give a warning first, you will *not* like this."

"Internal oxygen supply is adequate for thirty seven minutes," a flat, metallic voice sounded in Dave's ear.

Who the hell was- "What?" He croaked out. Something was stuck in his throat.

His head hurt. A flashing light. What was that? Oh. Yes. He was in a mech suit. The light was a status indicator. It was flashing green. That was good. Wasn't it?

If the suit was active, and the visor functional, why couldn't he see anything? That's right, he remembered an intense flash before, before. He tried to move, and felt a strong resistance. "Suit, status."

"All systems nominal. Internal oxygen is currently active."

"Why isn't the air filtration system online?"

"This unit is currently buried under one point five meters of rock and soil."

Dave experienced sheer terror. Buried alive. "Can I g-get out?" he stammered.

"Safety limits in suit motors might be exceeded," the emotionless voice warned.

"I don't care about that, get me out of here!" He resisted the urge to move on his own, he didn't even know which direction was up.

To his right, apparently. That arm and leg twitched, slowly at first then becoming a rapid, brain-jarring vibration. The suit was shaking itself free, not relying on brute strength. The arm gradually lifted away from his torso, he felt the hand come free. Flailing the hand around, he tried to find something to hold onto for-

Something grasped his hand. Someone was up there. They tugged, steadily, not using a lot of force. He was pulled toward the surface, wincing at the overly bright light. Shauna had hold of his hand. Rolling to his knees, he shook dirt off easily, not much stuck to the exterior of the suit. All around him, mech suited figures were sitting upright, walking around stiffly, helping to dig out those still buried by the collapsed sides of the gully. The gully was only half as deep as it had been. "Thanks," he staggered to his feet, waving at Jates, who was lifting another Verd-kris from under a boulder. Jesse waved to him, from there Master Sergeant Colter was checking a soldier whose armored wrist appeared to be bent. "Any clue what happened?"

She shook her head. "I was hoping you could tell me. Artillery?"

"No way," it was his turn for a head shake. "Whatever it was, it wasn't localized. We-"

A familiar voice interrupted. "Dave?"

"*Joe*? Where are-"

"We can catch up later. Listen, I need you to do something, it's important."

"Joe, what the fuck happened here?"

A heavy sigh. "I'm sorry. The kitties popped a nuke on Makalva."

"*Holy sh-*"

"I know this is a shock, please listen to me. The Whatsis, it went down. The dropship carrying it got hit by the shockwave. Skippy thinks the enemy guessed we landed to capture some gizmo, and since they didn't know what we were after, they nuked the entire site to be sure. They *didn't* get it. The Whatsis is secure in a container about four and a half klicks from you, north-northwest. We need you to get it. Find it, move it to a secure LZ where it can be recovered. Dave, this is important."

"Joe," his voice was shaky. "I hear you, but there's only fourteen of us here. Fewer now, we have some blast damage. There are two full squads of Maxohlx infantry to our-"

"Skippy tells me there *were* two squads, they are all KIA. You got lucky being in that gully, it protected you from the shockwave. The kitties got the full force of it. There is no organized opposition between you and the Whatsis, you need to-"

Skippy broke in. "Joe, the enemy was prepared to exploit the situation, they have aircraft approaching, including cavalry units. I do not believe they know the location of the Whatsis yet, but it is likely only a matter of time."

"Dave-"

"Joe, we'll do it. Can you give us any cover?"

"Uh, there isn't much in the air right now. I'll see what I can do about close space support, but targeting from up here is going to be difficult."

"We will get moving ASAP," Dave frowned at the number of people who were limping from suit damage. Several soldiers were running scans of the soil to find their missing rifles. "Joe, my people at, Makalva? Are they all-"

"Dave, don't think about it, not now."

I am a worthless, lying sack of shit. I had just lied to one of my oldest friends, lied to send him probably into a trap, made him a target. When Dave, Jesse, and I were a fireteam together with Sergeant Koch, we had trusted each other with our lives. Now, Ski and Cornpone couldn't trust me at all.

They needed close space support. I had a call to make.

But first-

"Skippy, I need you to do a dirty, rotten thing, and I'm not talking about the kind of scams you enjoy."

"You're scaring me, Joe."

"Asking Dave to get the bullshit Whatsis does us no good, unless the enemy, that Stratcom AI, knows we are sending people to get the thing. Otherwise, they will assume they destroyed anything of value to us, and will start looking for targets of opportunity elsewhere. Like dropships climbing into orbit on the other side of the planet."

"I do not like the sound of this. What do you want me to do? Sell out your friends? I can't believe you would do that."

"This whole op was your id-" I clamped my mouth shut. Arguing about assigning blame wouldn't get us anywhere. "Leak a message, or make it sound like some panicky Specialist transmitted in the clear, that the Whatsis is down, and teams are approaching the crash site. Provide only very vague coordinates. There have to be several groups of humans stumbling around down there, the enemy won't know which people are tasked to recover the Whatsis, they will see that someone is moving out."

"You will be painting a target on your friends."

"They are already targets! I don't expect them to *do* anything, and Dave is smart, he won't keep going if the odds are impossible."

"Joe, this truly is a dirty, rotten thing."

"Just do it, please," I stood up. "Don't tell anyone. Connect me to Admiral Allard directly please. Then I'm going to the bridge. I got us into this mess, I need to get us out of it."

The destroyer *Thomas Paine* was assigned to UN Special Operations Command, and as a SOCOM asset, had been held back from the Hammer Force assault as a reserve, parked twelve lightseconds away. The *Paine* was not needed until it was needed, and then it would be very much needed. Like, right then.

The order had come from Admiral Allard, though Colonel Chen knew the signature of a Joe Bishop plan when she saw it. "This is *insane*, even for the Pirates," she muttered.

"What was that, ma'am?" Her XO asked without looking up from his console.

"Remind me to put in for a nice, cozy dirtside job when we get back to Earth."

That time, he did glance at her. "You would be bored in a week."

"Bored and *alive*. You know why our namesake is famous?'

"Who?" He was back tap tap tapping away on his console, preparing the destroyer for a jump. And the aftermath.

"Thomas Paine. He was an Enlightenment era writer, he was most well-known for a pamphlet titled *Common Sense*."

"Which," her XO guessed her meaning. "Is the opposite of what we're doing here now?"

"Exactly."

"Paine also wrote 'The harder the conflict, the more glorious the triumph'."

With a grimace, she shook her head. "Also remind me never to assign a philosophy major as my executive officer."

"My *minor* was in philosophy," he corrected her. "Colonel, the ship is ready in all respects."

"Except I forgot a change of underwear. Pilot," she gestured, "let's get this over with. Jump when ready."

The *Thomas Paine* disappeared in a burst of gamma rays.

"Dave!" Bishop called again. "Grab some real estate!"

Czajka froze, holding up a fist in a Halt gesture. "Joe? We can't stop here, there are enemy aircraft all around-"

"Get *down*!"

Dave didn't need to wait for a written invitation. Waving both hands in a DOWN gesture, he fell onto his chest and wondered what trouble Bishop was getting him into next. Task force orbital sensors reported large numbers of enemy aircraft, drones, and cruise missiles fast approaching his position, without being able to identify exact vectors of the threats. The roiling, static-charged clouds were making it difficult for sensors in space to lock onto stealthed flying objects, so while the warships above wanted to shoot, they had no firing solutions. What did Bishop intend to-

The suit screamed a warning alarm. Gamma radiation, a lot of it. The source was hot, and *close*. What the-

The *Thomas Paine* emerged from jump at seven thousand meters altitude, moving at Mach Nine relative to the surface southeast of Makalva. For a few seconds, the massive ship simply bored a superheated hole through the already abused air. The active sensors pulsed powerful energies, burning through aircraft stealth fields that were already dealing with intense static. Defensive cannons set on auto mode began to chatter in every direction, other than down. Targets on the ground were painted by maser beams set to fire in a cone for maximum coverage. Dispersing the coherent microwaves into a cone decreased the energy delivered per centimeter, but when the maser projectors were the weapons of a *starship*, rotten kitties in even the toughest mech suits boiled alive and exploded inside their armor.

The audio cut out in Dave's helmet, he still heard a deep rumbling sound right through his bones. The longest clap of thunder ever imaginable, a roaring that shook his brain. Unable to resist curiosity, he rolled onto his back and squinted at the sight of something burning an orange streak through the dark clouds, headed away from him and moving *fast*. What was the Air Force doing up-

His visor lit up with the outline of a UN Navy destroyer. Not regular Navy, SOCOM. The *Thomas Paine*. The destroyer had completed its pass and was clawing for altitude, the rumble turning into a roar as the starship's main engines kicked in full emergency thrust.

Jesse staggered to his feet, then jumped, pointing to the retreating starship, pumping a fist. "*Fuck yeah*! That's what I call close space support!"

Jates stared at Dave. "You humans are certifiably insane."

"In a *good* way," Dave nodded. "All right people, the Navy just cleared the road, let's move out before the kitties get their shit together."

CHAPTER FORTY

Back on *Valkyrie's* bridge because I was again commanding and not just observing, I pumped a fist and mouthed a silent prayer for Chen to get her struggling ship back into orbit. The odds were slightly in her favor, as long as nothing vital broke, and the enemy didn't expend any munitions on hitting a target that was retreating. It was a long way to jump altitude, the *Paine's* crew would have to settle for low orbit, check every system for damage, and only then increase speed to climb to jump distance. The destroyer would be able to jump away, the SD network's damping field was tragically offline, due to some jerks being *not* cool. Those same jerks also knocked out the satellites which had generated the disruption field that prevented ships from jumping into orbit. With that field gone, destroyers and frigates could quickly reposition to cover the Thomas Paine, if needed. That was a good thing for us.

You know what the problem is of disabling a disruption field?

Anyone can jump in.

Altitude twenty two thousand meters, speed Mach Fourteen. "Reduce to eighty percent thrust," Chen ordered, with an eye on the 'Q meter' of the display. Q was an engineering term for dynamic pressure, and the strain meter was warning the ship's structure was almost at the design limit. Forward shields were holding, barely, only by shunting power from other shield generators. To continue maximum thrust would collapse the shields and pancake the forward hull into amidships like an accordion. Dial it back for only a moment, she told herself, thinking like a pilot. Thinner air was above them, at thirty thousand meters above the dirt, they could throttle up again.

The threat board was showing orange, no red. Vague hints of threats, nothing certain. Jumping the ship down deep in the troposphere had been a surprise, caught the enemy unprepared. The air defense systems hadn't been ready to shoot at a *starship*, so they hadn't. Twenty four thousand meters, speed dialed back to Mach thirteen. Against the odds, they were going to make it, to reach-

Warnings flashed on the display, alarms blared.

Gamma ray bursts in orbit. A *lot* of them. The IFF system wasted no time in identifying Friend or Foe.

Foe.

The 14th Fleet was back.

The assault carriers were hit first, though the 14th Fleet's commander had to know those ships were nearly empty of dropships and ground-pounders. Battleships with interlocking energy shields protected the vulnerable carriers from weapons fire coming from the planet. Only their own shields defended the Gator Navy ships from attacks coming in from higher orbit. The *Baltic Sea* was struck first, taking maser cannon bolts followed closely by railgun darts fired by the big guns of 14th Fleet battleships. The *Baltic Sea* was gone in a flash, energy released from jump drive capacitors. The *Adriatic Sea* lasted a heart-stopping minute longer, maneuvering wildly to throw off the enemy's aim, to no avail. Shot full of holes, engines offline, the ship cracked in half when hot warhead fragments penetrated a missile magazine.

Two assault carriers gone in the blink of an eye.

The *Flying Dutchman* fared marginally better. As the command and control platform for the assault force, it was protected above by four light cruisers specialized as space defense ships, with stronger shields and additional auto cannons. More than half of the incoming railgun darts were intercepted and shattered, so the impacts were spread out and fragments splattered harmlessly against the shields. The lesser quantity of the sixty two darts were not intercepted, and did slam into the shields. Fourteen punched through weak spots created by darts ahead of them, high speed projectiles that lost a bit of kinetic energy while passing through the shields, still possessed enough speed to tear into the assault carrier's light armor plating. Armor that was designed to protect against space debris and missiles detonating nearby, not from battleship weapons that scored direct hits. The blessing was all fourteen darts plunged into the topside armor and emerged out the bottom without having lost much momentum, and without striking anything vital to the ship's operation. Dozens of crew were killed when multiple darts tore through docking bays top to bottom, creating jagged holes that air shrieked through to escape. A search and rescue dropship was struck and exploded, showering a docking bay with hot shrapnel.

That was just the first salvo of darts. Maser bolts struck the unprotected hull where shields were down, and missiles bored in, twisting and jinking to defensive fire. It was a missile that severed a power conduit and shut down two main engines. That sealed the ship's fate.

"Captain Bonsu," Nagatha's voice was calm as usual. "I believe the ship is, as you would say, going down. Falling into the atmosphere."

Colonel Derek Bonsu had reached the same conclusion, as did everyone who had a view of the main bridge display. The *Dutchman* had not actually been in orbit when the 14th Fleet arrived, Derek had instructed the pilots to use the main engines to essentially hover over Makalva, passing over the landing site but moving too slowly for speed to stop the ship from falling. It was a judgment call, taking a slight risk to the ship to reduce the flight time of dropships coming back up from the surface. The environment on the surface was contested, the battlespace above the atmosphere was not. Task Force Hammer had supreme control of orbit and beyond. Until the 14th Fleet returned, however the hell that happened.

Derek wasted no time with sentimental thoughts. Jabbing a thumb down to activate the ship wide intercom system, he announced as clearly and calmly as he could manage, "This is the captain speaking. All hands, abandon ship. Repeat, all hands, abandon ship. God speed to you," he added., Tapping his phone, he called the ship's CAG, who at the moment had very little air group to command. "Irene, get into a Panther and get out of here, ASAP."

Her reply was muffled. "We have a fire down here, the-"

"Irene, *get off the ship, NOW*. However you can."

A pause, then, "I'll see you dirtside."

He thought that was unlikely. With a catch in his voice, he replied, "See you soon. I love you," and cut the call. To the bridge crew who were all staring at him, he gestured toward the doorway, "Move!"

No one left their stations. The executive officer cleared her throat. "Sir, from here we can coordinate the-"

"Communication is spotty," he gestured to the main display that was showing only orange and red warning lights on a schematic of the ship. "Throughout the ship. What you all need to do is get to escape pods, and pass the word to anyone who didn't hear my order. We-"

The ship rocked again, followed immediately by a harder shock. A secondary explosion, something important had been hit. "Get *out* of here!"

Led by the reluctant XO, the bridge crew began filing out the doorway, walking then beginning to run as the deck tilted. Artificial gravity was fading. The lights flickered, red emergency lights snapped on. He sat, staring at nothing while the ship rocked from impacts, tumbling slowly.

"Colonel Bonsu?" Nagatha's avatar appeared, an effect she rarely manifested in public areas of the ship. "Please do not disappoint me."

"The *Flying Dutchman* survived impossible odds more times than I can count. Now, under my command, I'm losing the ship. I'd say I have disappointed *everyone*."

"No you have not, dear. You know that *I* selected you for this command."

Derek nodded glumly. The Navy had put forth a list of candidates to be captain of the former star carrier, but the ship's AI had stated firmly that she wanted only Derek Bonsu in command. No one in Def Com leadership wished to argue with the Lady Nagatha. "You might have made a mistake there."

"The mistake, if there was one, is entirely the fault of Joseph Bishop. Though I am loath to criticize a man I so admire. Colonel, by disappointment, I meant I hope you are not intending to go down with the ship."

"That is tradition."

"That *was* tradition, and it was always *stupid*. Your military has invested much time, effort, and money into training you for leadership. With the Outsider yet to be defeated, the Navy needs capable, experienced commanders more than ever."

"Yeah, yeah, I hear you," he pulled the lever to release the chair's safety straps. "I wasn't going down with the ship, Irene would kill me if I ever did something so foolish."

"Good," the avatar clapped her hands. "I suggest you move with alacrity."

Alacrity, he thought. Who uses words like that? "General Perkins, is she-"

"Her people are bringing her to an escape pod. Over her objections."

Derek could understand that. The mission was a failure. The Whatsis lost. The ground force wiped out by a nuke. Emily's husband reported missing and out of contact. She had to be in shock, she should not be in command, not that she had any force left to issue orders to. "What about you? Nagatha, there is no escape pod for your core, this ship was built around you."

"A fact I am painfully aware of. What can I say? I had a good run," the hologram flickered. "An experience I will cherish forever. Or, for approximately the next eleven minutes until the ship breaks apart."

Tears stung Derek's eyes, he wiped them away angrily. Reaching out a hand, he felt a tingle from the hologram. "It has been," his voice choked up. "An honor to serve with you."

"I will see you on the other side, Dear. Now, please *go*!"

He half ran, half swam in the fading gravity, ducking through the bridge blast door that was automatically sliding shut.

"Where the fuck did THEY come from?" Reed screeched, trying to rise from her chair and gesturing at the display that showed far too many enemy ships jumping into orbit. The *Baltic Sea* was already an expanding sphere of charged particles, the *Adriatic Sea* and the *Flying Dutchman* were taking hits. Her question had been rhetorical, though addressed mostly at me.

"The Outsider," I muttered, stunned. She stared at me, so I added, "It knew we were coming here. Somehow, it knew."

"No way, Joe," Skippy sniffed, though he was distracted, the ginormous holographic hat not moving when the rest of the avatar did. "Our communications security is air tight."

"Ours is, yes. What about the spiders?"

"They- Ah, um, shmaybe. Shit!"

"The *Dutchman*," Reed zoomed in on that ship. "We can protect-"

"No. We stick to the *plan*," I cut her off. "We stick to the plan, or all of this is for nothing. There are three dropships climbing into orbit, we need to protect them."

Reed took a deep breath, tamping down her anger. "Anything we do to help will only attract attention to them."

"We wait until they reach orbit, that's the *plan*," I insisted.

Her knuckles turned white as she gripped the arm rest. Waiting, doing nothing, was not in her nature. She did it anyway, acknowledging me with a curt nod. We would stick with the plan.

Frey called. "General Bishop? The pilots tell me we have a Maxohlx fleet in orbit now?"

"Uninvited guests. Frey, there is no change. Proceed as planned," the words sounded hollow to my ears.

"Understood," Frey ended the call.

"Sir," Reed pointed to the display, "the plan didn't include squadrons of enemy ships crashing the party. There are four cruisers converging on the STAR force's trajectory."

"I see that. We-"

That's when the plan was Overcome By Events.

The dropship carrying STAR Team Sword had the bad luck, it was just pure rotten luck, of being painted by a narrow active sensor beam from a Maxohlx battleship. That ship's sensors had been aimed at a Hammer Force battleship, the *Barcelona*, and when the *Barcelona* maneuvered wildly to avoid a salvo of railgun darts, the beam raced onward at the speed of light, briefly illuminating the particles of plasma that clung to the Panther's hull. Briefly, the flight path of the Panther only intersected the beam for half a millisecond before the spacecraft moved upward and the beam panned to the south. The damage was done. Maxohlx warships above the hemisphere opposite Makalva were itching to get into the fight, looking for something, anything to shoot at. Their AIs noticed the brief sensor flare, and one cruiser was ordered to investigate the unlikely contact. The first two sensor pulses returned nothing, having been aimed in the wrong direction. The third pulse got a solid return, and within seconds, active sensor beams from three ships had locked onto the soaring Panther, burning through the stealth field.

A maser beam followed the sensor pulses, and the Panther bloomed into a fireball.

"Oh, *shit*," I groaned. Someday I will learn to resist the instinct to get out of my chair when I see something alarming on the main display, but not that day. "Signal the STAR force to throttle back to minimum power to hold altitude."

Someone behind me acknowledged my order.

"Sir," Reed leaned closer and whispered, "they won't reach orbit that way. We can't recover them."

"We can't, but *you* can."

"Sir?"

"Fireball, I need you in the pilot couch."

Her eyes grew wide. We had served together long enough to understand what I meant. "No. no way. This is-"

"Doable."

"This is insane," she hissed. "The impact-"

"Will be survivable. Probably."

"Probably? There are nineteen people aboard each of those Panthers."

"We are only going to recover Team Razor, and we only need the Biscuit." Holy shit. When had I become so callous?

When it was needed for the mission. My job sucks.

"Sir, I, I'm not a pilot."

"You average nine hours a week in the flight simulator, most of that is training to fly this ship. Get in the pilot couch now, that's an order."

"That, I-"

Clearing my throat, I announced, "This is General Bishop, I am assuming command of the ship, effective immediately. Note it in the log. Fireball, do your thing."

She didn't like it. She followed orders, relieving the lead pilot and sliding into the couch.

"Colonel Frey?" I called.

"Sir? This was not in the plan."

"It was not. Tell everyone to strap in *tight*, this will be a rough ride."

She also guessed my intention. "The Biscuit container is fastened to the rear of the cockpit bulkhead," she advised. The strongest part of the Panther's hull. "Aim for that, if you have no other choice."

Reed grimly acknowledged that statement with an emphatic nod of her head.

"What about Team Tiger?" Frey asked.

I bit my lip before responding. "We will have to come back for them."

She knew that was bullshit. She also knew I didn't have any good choices. "Understood. We are all ready here. Sir?"

"Yes?"

"Do it fast, please. I feel we have run out of time."

On Reed's initiative, *Valkyrie* jumped. Not toward the planet, we emerged two lightminutes farther away. The ship had constantly been maneuvering to maintain course and speed to match the course and speed Razor's dropship should have at the planned rendezvous point. Now, the ship had to slow down to match speed with a spacecraft that was below orbital altitude and moving too slowly. Without me needing to say anything that would be useless anyway, Reed fired the boosters so we could change course and slow down right fucking now rather than burning time Team Razor didn't have. Over the roar of the boosters, I shouted, "Weps, when we get to the party, hit those cruisers."

"Check," came the reply, and the boosters cut off.

We jumped again, before I could take a breath to settle my stomach.

Valkyrie emerged in the upper atmosphere, behind the Panther and to the right of the spacecraft's flight path. There was no way the dropship could have flown into an open docking bay as we passed by at three meters per second, and our battlecruiser couldn't fly sideways in the airstream. Instead, a tough nanofiber recovery net extended out from a docking bay, three nets set in series in case the Panther missed the first one, or a net tore apart from the strain.

We snagged it on the first try. The Panther was jostled hard, the net collapsing and drawing tight around it, hollow fibers inflating and sticking together to form an airbag surrounding the entire hull. Some of the air leaked out when fibers touched hot parts of the dropship, others took up the slack.

"Got it," Reed grunted.

"Outstanding," I had to raise my voice over the sizzling of maser cannons and the thumps of railguns, audible proof that we were engaging the enemy cruisers. "Reel it in. Fireball, get us to jump altitude."

Gently since we had a dropship dangling from a tether, Reed advanced the throttles, keeping the Panther on the opposite side from the approaching cruisers. The enemy had to know they were engaging *Valkyrie* and they were not intimidated, they were eager for glory. The ship shuddered, the feeling distinct from the fluttering from the ship boring a hole through thin air.

Have you ever dived to the bottom of a lake, you touch bottom and look up and even though the surface is only ten or twelve feet away, your brain screams oxygen now and you realize those twelve feet look impossibly far away? It was like that for us, jump altitude was a long, *long* way above us and I was beginning to have serious second thoughts about my rash action. My latest rash action.

"Sir! General Bishop," a voice in my ear called, it was a crew chief in the docking bay. "The Panther is stuck, we can't pull it in!"

"What's the problem?"

"I think the engine pods are hung up on something on the hull."

Shit, I cringed. The people in the captive dropship had to be bouncing around like shoes in a dryer. "Is the cabin aligned with the docking bay door?"

"Yes, affirmative."

"Shear off the tail if you have to, but get the forward cabin inside ASAP."

He wasn't surprised, he sounded relieved. "Pull the cabin in, understood." He left the microphone open, even through the armored windows overlooking the docking bay, I heard a horrific screeching, a loud BANG and a series of thumps. "Got it! Cabin is secure! Um looks like, everyone aboard survived."

"Outstanding. Fireball, the package is inside, pedal to the metal."

"Pedal to the metal, aye," a flick of her thumb ignited the boosters again, loud as hell from the shockwaves of sound being transmitted through the air around us. It would have been worse if the soundwaves could have caught us, the hypersonic speed had the sonic boom trailing behind.

"Admiral Allard?" I called.

His response was immediate. "Bishop? What the hell are you-"

"I need all of your ships to keep the enemy away from *Valkyrie* until we can jump. We have the package."

"Package?"

"The Whatsis," I explained, he hadn't heard the terms 'Biscuit' or 'Collector' and there wasn't time to explain.

"*You* have it? How-"

"I will explain later. Can you assist?" On the display, I saw that icons for enemy ships were moving in on intercept courses. They would reach us before Hammer Force could do much of anything. I really hadn't thought my snap decision through to the end game.

"We are- Bishop, my ships are out of position, and we're taking a beating here. If you had given me a heads up about what you were doing, we might have-"

"Bring in your reserves."

"My reserves are fully engaged! The 14th Fleet was supposed to be-" A loud BANG interrupted him.

"Admiral? Admiral Allard?"

"Joe," Skippy said, "his flagship took a hit, it has been a primary target since the three assault carriers were knocked out. Communications are down."

"Shit. We'll have to do this the hard way, then."

Skippy's voice switched to my earpiece, so only I could hear. "We *won't* do this the hard way, we won't do this at all. The numbers don't lie, *Valkyrie* can't reach jump altitude. Before we get there, the ship will take too many hits. I'm sorry, that's the truth of it. We are screwed."

"Not yet, we're not."

"Sir?" Reed asked without turning in her seat.

"Nothing."

"Sir?" Gasquet called for my attention, he was still seated along the back wall, my oversight. "Should we load the Biscuit into a stealthed drone, send it away?"

"OK, good suggestion, the Biscuit won't do us any good if *Valkyrie* can't get away."

"We could launch Skippy in a drone also."

"Um, nuh uh," the beer can shook his head. "I am *not* going for that idea. No way."

"Gasquet, thank you. Skippy, what's the alternative?"

"Have faith, Joe."

"Faith in the awesomeness?"

"That also. I meant, faith that everything will work out all right, with a little help from our friends."

What the hell was he talking about, I clenched my jaw. Everything wasn't going to work out all right, *nothing* had gone right in Operation Olympic. All three assault carriers were out of action. The enemy had stopped shooting at the *Flying Dutchman* only because that ship was breaking apart as it fell into the atmosphere, and I didn't know whether anyone had gotten away from that ship. If they did, space around the planet was a hostile environment for little escape pods. For certain, Nagatha was going down with her ship. Team Sword was gone. The landing force had been vaporized in what was basically a megaton-level nuclear blast. Dave and Jesse, and Shauna? I had sent them into a trap, to maintain the ruse. Nothing was *right* about any of that. "What friends?"

"You know how the signals between paired Elder comm nodes can't be intercepted, but I can sort of detect bleedover from other paired nodes, if they are used in the vicinity?"

"Yeah, so? Hammer Force is using several pairs, they-"

"I'm not talking about comm nodes being used by *humans*."

"Who are-"

"Someone out there is using a pair of Elder comm nodes we gave to them. The-"

That's when the cavalry arrived to save the day.

Thirty four Rindhalu warships emerged from jump, and quickly began engaging their enemy. Hammer Force had been knocked on its heels. *Valkyrie* had suddenly become the target of every ship in the 14th Fleet, to the point where enemy ships on the other side of the planet were racing to jump altitude so they could get into the action.

"General Bishop, this is Psychometric Advisor Jemontoos of the Sixty Forth Gathering," the translator struggled with odd Rindhalu military terms. "How may we best render assistance?"

"How many ships do you have?"

"As you humans would say, what you see is what you get. We did not expect to engage a major enemy force here."

Shit. Thirty four ships would not win a victory that day. Ah, we could still win a victory, if not a battle. *Valkyrie* jumping away with the collector, and Skippy, could win the *war* for us. Regardless of what happened later at Omaha. "Advisor Jemontoos, *Valkyrie* must reach jump distance. Can you provide cover?"

"We can try however, the enemy has greater numbers, and they now understand that your ship is the key to the entire battle."

"Do what you can, please."

What the Sixty Forth Gathering could do was a lot. It just wasn't enough. We were within seven thousand kilometers of the hard line that marked where the planet's gravity well was shallow enough for an outbound jump field to form; and we our approach to that line was agonizingly slow. The shields were taking hits so continuously the shocks felt like a regular vibration rather than individual events. The Rindhalu had moved in to shield our hull with their own ships, and their ships were falling out of line as they took hit after hit.

"Sir!" Reed half turned in the pilot couch. "Boosters are offline. Main engine output is down to seventeen percent. By the time we crawl out to jump distance, it won't matter, we-"

"Skippy, can you do any of your usual magic here, give us an assist?"

"The enemy is projecting damping fields, Joe, the effect is-"

"Yes or no, stop whining about it," I snapped.

"The answer is 'Shmaybe' if-"

The lights flickered. Not the usual blinking of all lights at the same time, this was a wave, of every system going dark and quickly back online, starboard side of the bridge to port. When the wave washed over me, I was dizzy enough to ralph and blood pounded in my skull. As soon as it happened, it was gone.

"Whoa, like, that was gnarly," Bilby gasped.

"What the fuck was *that*?" I asked.

"I don't know," Skippy admitted. "Not anything good for us. Some type of Maxohlx sensor pulse? I will have to investigate to-"

"If it didn't harm the ship, I do not care. Flatten spacetime and get us *out* of here!"

"You can't just-"

"None of us can do anything if the ship is torn apart, can you do it or not?"

"Ugh. I hate this when you- Listen dumdum, I can't guarantee where we will go."

"Anywhere but here is good for me. *Do* it."

"Ugh. You don't understand- You never understand, and that never stops you. Bilby, jump on my signal. I must warn everyone, this will be *bad*. Three, two, one-"

It was as bad as he warned. Worse actually, much worse. The jump itself wasn't bad, the distortion effect no more violent than a typical instantaneous transition from *here* to *there*. The bad part was where we jumped to.

Just above the photosphere of a star. Ohmeharikahn's star. The display showed a solar flare arcing above us, our flight path was taking us under the loop of hellish plasma or whatever flares are made of. "Bilby! Why did you jump us to-"

"Dude like, I didn't do this, I aimed in the *opposite* direction. I don't know what-"

An alarm blared, one that made my blood run cold.

I *knew* that alarm.

It was never supposed to sound.

"Hey!" Skippy shouted. "What did you idiot monkeys do this time?"

"General," Gasquet warned what I already knew. "Skippy's escape pod has been ejected! It wasn't us," he added, "this was an uncommanded action."

"Launch the ready bird," I wasted no time.

"Joe, don't," Skippy sighed. "A dropship would only get scorched and melted out here. Hey! Stop that! The escape pod jets just fired, they are pushing me into the star."

"Reed," I pleaded, out of ideas.

She was struggling to keep *Valkyrie* from falling into the ball of fire below us. "Sir, I, I got nothin'. It will be a miracle for us to get out of here."

"Skippy! Do some, spacetime warp, or-"

"Joe, there is nothing I *can* do. Oh, this was perfectly planned," he groaned. "That funky wave we experienced was not a Maxohlx sensor, I know that now. The Outsider *played* us. It played *me*. It wanted to know which Elder artifact we could use against it, and it wanted to take me out of the game. Now it understands the potentially deadly object is a collector. And I am about to take a very long dirt nap in a star. Ah," he sighed. "This sucks. Joe, I'm sorry."

"Skippy, there has to be a-"

Reed interrupted my worthless conversation. "Sir, it's no good," she lifted her hands off the controls. "We don't have enough juice to avoid getting pulled down into the star. Not even," she anticipated my inappropriate joke, "if we all get out and push. It's just a matter of time now. The engines are overheating and going offline."

"OK, OK, uh," I looked around, out of answers. "Reed, Gasquet, you two handle the ship, I relinquish command, I have to focus on recovering Skippy. The-"

"Joe!" Skippy shouted, though his voice already sounded far away. "There is nothing you or anyone else can do to help me. But I can help *you*."

"How are you-"

"Promise me one thing: your foggy mush of a monkey brain will find a way to beat that asshole Outsider without me."

"We're not doing anything without you, we will get you out of-"

"To everyone, it has been an honor serving with you."

"*Don't-*"

He did.

When we were in the star system where *Valkyrie* almost got trapped in the crushing, frozen atmosphere of the ice giant planet we called Snowcone, Skippy had caused the ship to suddenly stop dead in space, by absorbing the substantial kinetic energy of our battlecruiser's momentum. At Omaha's star, he did the opposite. His own momentum was transferred to the ship. Not just the structure of the ship, that would have turned the crew into a thin layer of goo. Everything aboard the ship received the same boost of momentum. In the blink of an eye, we were racing away from the star at nineteen hundred kilometers per second.

Holy shit.

Reed lifted her hands off the controls, and not just because she was stunned as the rest of us were. "Sir, I think it's best that I not do *anything* right now? Sir?" She prompted me.

Closing my eyes, I shook my head to get my brain working again. "Right, sounds good. Skippy?" I waited for a reply that never came. "Skippy?"

"Dude," Bilby sighed. "He's like, gone."

"*Gone?*"

"It's like Isaac Newton said, you know? Every action has an equal and opposite reaction? When he gave us that momentum boost, it took from his own momentum. He fell right down into that star's gravity well."

"I hate physics."

"Physics can be a bitch," Bilby agreed.

"Do you know where he is?"

"Other than somewhere inside a yellow dwarf star, no."

"Oh," I hid my face behind my hands. "Shit."

"Hey like, I have a bit of good news? The Outsider's malware, that made us jump in the wrong direction, and ejected Skippy's mancave? It was isolated to those two systems. Isolated to backup, subsidiary systems, that only became active when the jump drive coils spun up. That code is *gone*, I purged it with extreme measures."

"If I had waited when Skippy wanted to investigate that pulse, you would have found the malware?"

"No, nah, Dude. You made the right call. There was no time, we had to get out of there. Besides, we wouldn't have been looking for malware, especially not in backup systems that weren't active then. Hey, I have some other good news? The shields are down hard, but I can have the stealth field active in a few minutes."

"Uh, sure. Whatever you think is best."

"I'll handle the ship, Sir," Reed rose from the pilot couch and resumed her place in the command chair.

"Right. I, uh," I slowly glanced around the compartment. Everyone looked away, avoiding my eyes. I had gotten thousands of humans killed. We had the collector, but without Skippy, Operation Olympic was all for *nothing*. "I'll," I waved a hand. "Be in my office."

Reed followed right behind me, I didn't realize that until I went to close the door, and she caught it with a hand. Slipping through the doorway, she let the door close. "Talk to me, Sir."

"Reed, I got nothin'. This wasn't just my greatest fuckup, it was the biggest fuckup *of all time*. I am so proud of myself right now."

"The Outsider planted the collector on Omaha, to lure us there?"

"Huh? No, no way. It waited for us to get the thing, so it would know which type of object we need to defeat it. Now, if there are other collectors it knows about, it will be certain to destroy them. Without Skippy, it doesn't matter anyway."

"It learned we were coming to Omaha, and it withheld that intel from the Maxohlx?"

"Yeah. An alliance of assholes. They deserve each other. It withheld the intel, then intercepted the 14th Fleet on the way to Parchlund. Turned them around, and waited until the crucial moment. My mistake, my *fatal* mistake, was designating *Valkyrie* as the recovery ship for the STAR force. If I had assigned three random cruisers to the recovery job, the Outsider might have still been guessing whether we had acquired what we came here for. Once *Valkyrie* jumped in, all it had to do was follow us. We led it right to the prize!"

"So, this is game over, Sir?"

"What? No, fuck that. The Outsider wants us to give up, so we are not doing that."

She flashed a smile. A sad little smile, but a smile anyway. She had wanted to hear me say we weren't giving up. "The Merry Band of Pirates never give up, Sir."

"That might be a sign of stubborn stupidity but, hell yes."

"What's our next move?"

"Get the ship combat ready again, if that is possible."

"We'll do our best. After that?"

"After that, we pull Skippy from the core of a star."

She cocked her head. "Has anyone ever done that?"

"According to Skippy, no. Certainly not with the technology we have today."

"Then, how do we retrieve him?"

"Right now," I leaned my head back, overcome by a lifetime of weariness. "I have absolutely no idea."

THE END

Printed in Dunstable, United Kingdom